"WE GO IN TOMORROW: H-HOUR IS 0830."

"I think it's going to be a holy terror."

"As bad as Tarawa?"

"Worse."

"Jesus. Bad as the Canal?"

"Worse. The Japs want to hang on. They're losing: before, they were top-dog."

Lying on one of the ammunition cases New-combe listened to the talk: the somber inquiries, curses, coughs, laughter, snatches of song. Above him—far, far above him—the stars sparkled in a soft depthless drop of velvet, limpid and measureless . . .

The Big War

by the bestselling author of
THE LAST CONVERTIBLE

**"POWERFUL,
MOVING,
BEAUTIFUL,
AND TRUE!"**

—*San Francisco Examiner*

Berkley books by Anton Myer

THE BIG WAR
THE INTRUDER
THE LAST CONVERTIBLE
ONCE AN EAGLE

THE BIG WAR

ANTON MYRER

BERKLEY BOOKS, NEW YORK

THE BIG WAR

A Berkley Book / published by arrangement with
the author

PRINTING HISTORY
Meredith Press edition published 1957
Bantam edition / January 1958
Dell edition / September 1965
Berkley edition / June 1981
Second printing / March 1982

ISBN: 0-425-05721-6

A BERKLEY BOOK ® TM 757,375

PRINTED IN THE UNITED STATES OF AMERICA

Dedication: For my Father and Mother
and for Weldon Kees, a casualty

Many brave men lived before Agamemnon: but they are all bound, unknown and unwept, in the long night, for there was no one to sing of them in sacred verse.

—HORACE, *Odes*

PART ONE

Towers

1

THE RAIN CAME in squalls, in slanting silver sheets and bounced on the helmets and ponchos in a million little bursts of light, ran glistening down the folds of the camouflaged fabric and merged with the streams flowing along the two ruts of road. Off to the right at the edge of a field the fuselage of a plane, an old mock-up stump of a body without wings or tail, used in training some long-departed paratroopers, lay like a rotting prefabricated cigar. Beyond it through the pines the rain fell in a cold white streaming on the gray plate of the river; and to Alan Newcombe, dizzy with sleeplessness and exhaustion after three days and nights of field problems in the Carolina swamps, it was as though everything were finally melting away—they were all, pine woods, fuselage, the whole platoon—floating away, dissolving into the curtain of cold, endless rain.

The idea had in fact a certain pleasing, if morbid, inevitability about it. It completed the farce—a fitting sequel to the three days of patternless, confused digging and running and crawling: to walk solemnly out into the gray, fetid water, knee-deep, waist-deep, chest-deep, rifles held at high port—so of course as to keep them dry—finally, implacably, transformed into three columns of helmets bobbing like turtles or, overturned, floating like so many listing coracles, filling with water. Crescendo and curtain. Bye bye, second platoon, bobbing helmets gurgling, foundering: bye bye. Slow dissolve . . .

"God *damn* it, Al—"

He had stepped on a heel in front of him again. He muttered, "Sorry, Jay," to O'Neill's exasperated backward glance. Why couldn't he keep from stepping on O'Neill's heels? Some fatal attraction, no doubt: some strange trajec-

3

tory curving back to Mother's oxfords moving ahead of you
on the swept dirt paths of the Public Gardens. Ah, they have
left you far behind now: have left you lost and wandering—

They had stopped. That was odd: after three days and
nights of interminable, purposeless movement there was no
reason they should have stopped now. Was there? Yes, there
were their huts—the black tar-paper and cardboard
huts—which being only cardboard should not be dry inside
but *were* dry . . . and occasionally even warm enough. But
they, the huts' occupants, stood out here in the rain: as was
fitting. Like rows of sodden, wingless fowl.

Beside him O'Neill snuffled twice; turning his bony face
toward Newcombe he said in a low, conversational tone:

"The good word. The good, warm, dry word for today."

"Straight from Olympos," Newcombe answered him.

"All right," Lieutenant D'Alessandro said. Tall and well-
built, with handsome, delicate features, he advanced a step or
two, pushed his helmet to the back of his head and confronted
the platoon with his hands on his hips. "That was a terrible
problem we secured. A terrible problem. I suppose you know
what a terrible problem that was. You all heard what the
Major said, didn't you?"

Nodding solemnly he paused for emphasis. The platoon
stood silently in the rain and waited.

"Now you men listen to me: I've got a private ambition.
I'm going to run the snappiest crack platoon in the entire
Marine Corps . . . Let's call it a vanity of mine."

Rocking back on the heels of the yellow paratrooper's boots
the affected Lieutenant D'Alessandro nodded again; flashed
all at once a bright, disarming smile.

"Look at all those pearly teeth," O'Neill observed.

"D'Alessandro for the smile of beauty."

"And the boots. Don't you wish you'd got to go to
Quantico, Al? That could be *you*, son: you too could be a
handsome officer."

"All right," Lieutenant D'Alessandro went on, oblivious,
unhearing. "Now it's been pretty wet out for several days, as
you're all probably well aware of by now . . ." He flashed the
bright broad smile again.

"You see? He's hep. He's got his ear to the ground."

"Comfort of the troops solely."

". . . and there will be a weapons inspection tomorrow
morning when we fall out."

There was a murmur of protest from the platoon.

"Knock it off," Sergeant Hamway sang out in a soft nasal twang.

Lieutenant D'Alessandro frowned and bit his lower lip. "Now let's not have any gum-beating about it. I know you're fagged. I'm fagged myself. You're going to be a lot more fagged than this, too: I can promise you that."

"Old salt," O'Neill muttered; his nostril gurgled again thickly. "Old salt from Quan-tee-co, V-A."

"Straight from the equine orifice."

"Now just *what* the pete does that ninny know about—"

"All right, now," Corporal Kantaylis, standing beside them, murmured; and they both fell silent.

"And it isn't too far away either, that day." Lieutenant D'Alessandro threw back his head in an odd little nervous gesture. "So let's all get with it now, and settle down and get on the ball. Shall we? Whether you want to admit it or not, your rifle's your best friend: she's dearer to your heart than any of the little chippies in Kinston, or back home either—and don't you forget it. And when I say clean weapons I mean just that: clean weapons. By formation tomorrow morning . . . Well, I guess that's about all." Sergeant Hamway leaned toward him and whispered something and Lieutenant D'Alessandro straightened and said: "Oh yes. Sergeant Hamway reminds me that there's a training film tonight at eighteen hundred."

A moment longer he passed his eyes up and down the front rank with an expression half-yearning, half-reproving—a nervous, wistful, indecisive gaze; smiled again and splashed off through the mud in his paratrooper's boots.

Sergeant Hamway wiped his face slowly with the palm of his hand and said, "All right: you all heard what the lieutenant said. Now, all of you who are going on furlough tomorrow night they don't want you going up to the company office, they don't want you barging in there with fool questions and pestering them. O'Neill, I hear you already been up there with a lot of fool questions. They don't want you bothering them, they're busy enough as it is. You'll get your papers tomorrow after we secure. All right. Dismiss . . ."

The hut smelled of damp and creosote, like an abandoned garage. Metal fastenings clicked and snapped, cots creaked woodenly, wet clothing dropped in sodden lumps on the floor. Alan Newcombe sat down heavily, drew a cigarette from the pack on the orange crate beside his cot. The hut, after the interminable movement and muddle of the field problem, was all at once invested with an eerie, delightful quality of permanence and stability. Ridiculous: a shanty built of cardboard an angry man could put his fist through—and many had. But it was true, somehow: one's horizons diminished under pressure of circumstances, it seemed, until a shanty *was* a palace in comparison with no shanty at all. Everything was, doubtless, relative . . . On an impulse he leaned forward and peered at himself in the mirror above his pillow: a thin face, unshaven, chapped and reddened, his eyes red-rimmed and squinting meanly with fatigue. He stared at the image in somber fascination, moved his fingers along the line of his jaw. The new face: the new visage of war. My—you look so pale and ineffectual, Mr. Mars.

"Okay, Helthal," Corporal Kantaylis said. "You're up. Let's have some heat in here."

"No, I'm not." Helthal turned with a surly scowl. "I was last."

"No, you weren't." Kantaylis consulted a chart tacked to the wall above his cot. "You're up. Woodruff was last."

"The hell I was," Helthal retorted. "I draw that damn stove detail every five minutes."

"Come on, Helthal," Kantaylis said in a strangely quiet tone. "You know it's your turn. Come on: we're half frozen."

Helthal stared for a few seconds at the far end of the hut; a dull, unfocused expression, his round gray eyes completely depthless. Then he went over and picked up the two stacked buckets beside the stove.

"The voice of command," O'Neill said. "Pip pip and carry on. Wot? Wot ho." Huddled in the lotus position on his cot he gently squeezed the toes of his left foot. "Man, just listen to these doggies bark." He threw back his head and yelped twice. "Say, what you going to do the next five days when you're all alone, Mr. K? You and Freuhof and Hamway and the other old salts? Without all us peons to stoke the fires?"

"Don't you get to go on furlough, Danny?" Connor said.

"Who—him?" Capistron boomed. Towering stark naked at the far end of the hut he slapped his big belly once with satisfaction and disdain. "Hell, no—he just had one. What—is he supposed to get one every couple months just because he was a hero? Rack that guff."

"Well, everybody ought to get one *now* . . ."

"What you ought to get isn't what you get in this league, Chicken. You ought to know that by this time."

"Say, is that right, Danny?" O'Neill queried. "That you had a chance to go on a bond tour and turned it down?"

Lying on his cot with his hands behind his head Kantaylis smiled at him. "Who told you that?"

"Lapata, over in first platoon. No kidding, did you?"

Kantaylis blew cigarette smoke in a long gray plume toward the roof. "Don't believe everything you hear."

"Man, that must be something," O'Neill marveled. "Coast to coast in a private Pullman car, high society, keys to the city, movie stars rubbing up against you every time you turn around—man, that's the routine . . ." Dressed now in dry utilities, barefoot and with a towel draped over his head he went into a crouch in the narrow area between the two rows of cots, his hands cradling an imaginary submachine gun. "I'm gonna bag me Japs by the gross. I'm gonna blast 'em and rip 'em and slash 'em—ta-*ta*! taeta-ta-*ta*!" He swept the bristling wall of jungle ahead of him, sprayed the palm trees clear of snipers. "I'm gonna rack 'em up by the carload, they tangle with *O'Neill*. What I mean. Man, they're gonna detail a couple guys as traffic-clockers just to keep up with me."

"Knock it off, Jay," Connor said crossly.

"What's the matter?"

"That's no way to talk, for Christ sake."

"How do you know I won't be a hero?" O'Neill demanded. "Old Kantaylis did it, there. Seven Navy Crosses and eight How-do-ye-dos. And look at him!" He extended one thin arm dramatically. Several of the squad looked at Kantaylis who was watching him quietly, grinning.

"Hero," Ricarno said, and snorted. "You'll be dead long before you're a hero, Jay. You'll be starched like a shirt."

O'Neill sobered suddenly. "Maybe so. Maybe so. But I doubt it . . . Hell, you can't stop an Irishman on a good day, don't you know that?"

"What did you do up at the company office?" Newcombe asked him. "How'd you come by all this recent notoriety?"

"Oh, that . . ." O'Neill waved his hands, waggled the towel around his head. "Yeah, that was a daisy: I went up and asked Top for fifteen days."

"Go away . . ."

"That's straight. I said to Top I said: 'How about ten days on account.' 'Account?' he says. 'On account of what?' 'Just on account,' I says. 'Here I'm going to be overseas five, maybe ten, fifteen years. How about giving me ten days more along with these five and let me work 'em off—like a loan.

You know—pay-as-you-go plan.' Christ! He hit the roof. He got all red and puffed in the face and his hair stood up like an old porcupine's. He didn't know whether to squat or go blind. I mean. 'You Goddamn madman O'Neill,' he says, 'get the hell out of here before I throw you out. If you weren't a crazy redheaded Irishman to begin with I'd toss you in the brig for the duration. Now get out of here before we both have to turn in to sick bay just to pry my foot out of your ass!' ''

Immersed in a fit of laughter he staggered around in the aisle, bumped into Helthal entering with the two buckets filled with coal: Helthal swore at him and elbowed him out of the way.

"Hey now, Mister Gunga Din," O'Neill cried.

"Ah, shut up," Helthal muttered; kneeling before the little square mouth of the stove he began stuffing wadded-up newspaper into its belly.

"Man, I'm going to really ramble this trip," O'Neill proclaimed; he wrapped the towel around his head turban-fashion and tucked in the loose end. "No more plans and preparations—none of that chivalric crap, doc. No more of that telephonic pleading. Leaning over the counter wheedling for five hours: 'How about *Wednesday* night then, if you're free?' None of that. I'm going right down the line. I'm going to get all the lucky babes and crowd 'em all into one small room about the size of a telephone booth and then I'm going to tell 'em: 'All right, kids, this is it: I haven't got all the time in the world. Lock and load, that's all. Lock and load.' ''

"You talk one hell of a ball game, Mick," Ricarno said from across the hut; scratching his bristling black stubble of beard he grinned darkly at O'Neill. "One *hell* of a ball game."

"I play one too, Babe. You want to see me travel."

"I'll bet you've never gone down for doubles."

"Are you kidding? Man, I'm a ring-tailed tiger all over town. I'm a terror." Floating, double-shuffling past Helthal's sullen, genuflected figure he sang in extravagantly Negroid intonation:

> "Yeah, the gals'll scream and the gang'll shout
> When I turn that whole town inside out,
> I mean Jackson, I want to say—
> I'm coming home to-day!"

"Shipping-out furlough," Newcombe said disdainfully,

looking up from the book he was reading. "Sop to the fodder."

O'Neill eyed him laughing. "You don't want yours?"

"Sop to the cannon fodder: make the victims happy before the big impaling."

"The bard," O'Neill crowed; raising his arm above his head he let it slowly fall, the fingers fluttering. "The bahhhd of Hahhh-vard says we're cannon fodder . . . Al, what makes you so sour, old buddy? So lean and mean?"

Newcombe closed the book over his thumb, peered up into the mild, dancing blue eyes. "It's my ambience: it's just caught up with me."

In wonder O'Neill stared down at him, shook his head. "Al, you're a daisy. You ought to be our lieutenant. Ambience, for cripe sake. You ought to be our hero. Then you could stand out front of us there and use some of that gay old education. Give us the old pooperoo . . . Right— *ambience*!" he shouted, and did a clomping right face. "Left—ambience!"

"Ah shut up, O'Neill," Helthal said. "Why don't you stop shooting your mouth off, for a change." Reaching into the stove with a tire iron he poked the pieces of coal this way and that; and smoke began to billow out into the hut in little black rolling clouds.

"You tend to your stoking there, Gunga. What are you doing—sending up a smoke signal or something? wiring home for more dough?"

"Shut up."

"You're in a great mood today, aren't you? Everybody's in a gay old mood this P.M."

The door swung open violently. Sergeant Hamway's beaked, bony face loomed against the streaming gray light, and a bundle bounced on Ricarno's cot. "Mail," he said gruffly. The door banged shut again.

Ricarno broke the twine and began to deal the letters like cards, intoning over and over the names:

"O'Neill, Woodruff, Helthal, Freuhof, Newcombe, Woodruff, Capistron, Woodruff, Woodruff, Woodruff— God *damn* it, Woodruff!—Helthal, Kantaylis—"

"Funny thing about old Hamway," O'Neill philosophized to the hut. "Just when you've made up your mind that he's a real, five-alarm, going-away three-striper—just when you think he's the motherated flag-waving incarnation of the Mah-reen Coah, for pete sake—then he comes up with something like that. People are weird."

"Better not let *him* hear you," Capistron said. "He wouldn't like that none at all, Hamway wouldn't."

"Ah, he's not so rugged," O'Neill said.

"He's not, ah?" Capistron, his pink moonface bland, eyes narrowed in amusement, towered over O'Neill; emitted a low, rumbling murmur of laughter. "Why, he'd pull you apart like taking the wings off a fly."

"He'd have to catch me first, sport."

"You can run faster than him?"

"If he's chasing me, I can. I *mean* . . . For God's sake, Helthal, open the door or something: we'll all be under in five minutes."

"You don't like it *you* make the Goddamn fire," Helthal retorted sullenly. Coal fumes belched out of the stove in great clouds, began to cover them all with a rain of fine black motes, gritty and pervasive.

"You got the damper down, Helthal," Ricarno said. "Open the damper."

Helthal turned around and confronted the rest of the hut. One hand on his hip he shook the tire iron rhythmically and declared, "Next guy that gives me advice on this fire is going to get this iron: right up the shaft."

"Do you mean it, Helthal?" O'Neill asked him eagerly. "Do you mean it?"

Helthal stared at him dully, mutely, like a dog unable to make up its mind about an approaching stranger; then turned away and began tearing more newspaper into long, fluttering strips.

"Hey, how about a little game?" Ricarno, astride his cot, an unlighted cigar distending his thick lips, riffled the deck of cards twice— *rrrp! rrrp!*—shuffled deftly, cut in quick succession a king, a nine, the ace of diamonds. "How about a little twenty-one, anybody? Ah? I need furlough money. Hey, Chicken: what do you say?"

Connor, lying on the cot next to him with one slender, bony arm over his eyes, shook his head and said mournfully, "You took all my money last week."

Ricarno laughed a raucous laugh; cleared his throat with a rattling liquid sound. "That was *last* week. Always another new day." His hairy fingers fanned, returned, cut and shuffled in swift, even rhythms. "Hey, Woodruff. What do you say?"

"Well, no, Babe," Woodruff drawled in a heavy Arkansas

accent. "See, I got all my mail to read . . ."

"You can read it later. Where's your sporting blood?"

Woodruff went off into a high-pitched cackling. "No, see, the thing is, I just can't do without my mail . . ."

"Say, they're having lovely weather back home," O'Neill remarked. "Lovely fall weather. Aunt Grace thinks it might rain, though: *might* make with a lit-tle pre-cip-ita-tion. Isn't that cozy? Doesn't that just tickle the soles of your tootsies, though?" He stopped all at once and glanced over at Newcombe who was reading, indifferently, the book propped on his chest. "Hey Al, you got a letter there . . ."

"Yeah, I know."

"Well aren't you even going to read it?"

"I guess so. Later."

"But it's from your folks!"

"I know. I can see it all right through the envelope."

"Yeah—but from your *folks* . . ." O'Neill's gaze was puzzled, deeply reproachful.

"Okay," Newcombe said. "Anything to make you happy, Jay." He picked up the letter lying by his foot and let his eyes skim along the closely written lines. Letter from home. Exhortations and abjurations: a mélange of small talk, jocose gaucheries—or gauche jocosities—sifted over a feebly veiled anxiety. *Will let us know if there should be anything you hoping you will get the furlough you mentioned both well as may be expected same old trouble with the flues again Dad has had workmen in has to be expected with these old houses and of course the people you get nowadays are necessarily.* A labored, farcical affair—like everything else at the tail end of 1943 with the world gone rocking away toward chaos and old night, heeled over crazily, foundering in the cold, drifting rain. The fragments we can't even say we've shored against our ruins . . .

Two cots away he saw Kantaylis raise himself with a lurch; propped on one elbow the Corporal hung there staring at the little gray square of letter paper in his hands, not reading it, his deep-set eyes staring darkly from under their brows; his broad, handsome face strangely perplexed and drawn.

"What's the matter, Danny," O'Neill asked him, "—she cutting you in about that terribly nice boy?"

"She's giving him the old Minnesota shift," Newcombe said. "She's telling him about the awfully nice boy from Westover Field. He's so clean-cut in his flying togs. What do you bet?"

Lowering the letter Kantaylis looked at him—a slow, even gaze, while his prematurely seamed and yellowed face darkened until it looked like hammered bronze and the pupils of his eyes became jet-black. Newcombe, startled, lifted a hand in a vague, half-formed propitiation; smiling nervously he turned away and taking another cigarette out of the pack lighted it with care.

"Miss Haviland," Capistron said from the end of the hut in his deep, booming voice. "Miss Buff Haviland." With one eye closed he squinted at the sarong-clad figure posing above Helthal's cot across the hut: half-turned, arms couched behind her flaming hair she thrust toward them violently up-tilted breasts, one swelling thigh; smiled at them all invitingly, daringly—a gleaming, winsome courtesan's smile.

"Little Miss Haviland," Capistron rumbled; his moonface grinned in speculation. "Little Miss Teasie-Bubs. Like all the rest of them. Baby, you need a sticking." His hand lifted the fighting knife out of its scabbard at his waist and he set himself carefully, left leg slightly forward. "I bet she's never been stuck with a seven-inch blade before: I bet that's one sensation she's never, never had." His little round eyes narrowed, his right arm went up and down. The knife struck with a *pock* just to the right of the photo and went halfway through the cardboard wall. Miss Buff Haviland, indifferent to the danger, maintained her lusty, winsome pose.

"Not quite," Capistron announced; stepping across the aisle he retrieved the knife, snapped his blunt fingers against her buttocks. "You juicy little box, you: this time you get it square."

Helthal, his mouth and eyebrows rimmed with coal soot, peered around the stovepipe. "What the hell you up to, Cappie?"

"I'm going to stick your little sex-box, there. I told you I was going to some day."

"The hell you are. Cut it out, now." Holding the tire iron Helthal straightened and came around the stove.

"Just one quickie."

"No. I'm telling you, Cappie, you touch that picture I'm going to clip you with this iron."

"You wouldn't do that, would you?" Capistron boomed. His arm went up and down again. The knife drove into Miss Buff Haviland just above the thigh and went in all the way to the hilt; and Capistron called, "Hey! That's the ticket . . ."

"Goddamn it, Capistron," Helthal shouted. "That did it!"

Capistron, hands on hips, regarded him with sleepy satisfaction. "I told you to take that broad down or I'd stick her some day. You just didn't believe me, that's all."

"Look at that . . ." Helthal pulled out the knife, stood gazing crestfallen at the thin, triangular puncture, put his hand to it as though to smooth over the tear; then with a quick, angry gesture he flung the knife to the floor and stamped on the blade.

Capistron's sleepy blue eyes opened balefully. "What you doing?"

"What you think I'm doing?"

"Give it here."

"The hell I will! You think you can foul up anybody's gear any old time you feel like it you got another think coming . . ."

Capistron took a step forward and Helthal said: "Where you going?"

"I'm going to get my knife, Helthal."

"You cross the foot of my cot you get this," Helthal declared with dull savagery. He brandished the tire iron whose end was soot-blackened and full of menace. "I'm not kidding . . ."

"I'm going to get my knife," Capistron repeated; and his eyes narrowed into slits. For an instant they stood watching each other intently, then Capistron sprang across the aisle and Helthal swung with the iron; and they closed, grappling, panting, flailing at each other.

"All right, *all right*, now!—"

Corporal Kantaylis appeared suddenly between them, wrenched them apart.

"All right, now!" His voice rang out again, metallic and clear. Holding them in a swift, fierce grip he glared from one to the other. "All right, that's all. I won't have any fighting in my hut. You hear me?"

There was a silence. Rain drummed on the tar-paper roof and a cot creaked as someone sat up.

"Keep up your bright swords, for the dew will rust them," Newcombe chanted sonorously. They turned and stared at him; he smiled a thin, scornful smile, and looked away.

"Now, that's all," Kantaylis said in a lower tone. "Let's you two knock it off."

Capistron twisted away from him and demanded: "You going to pull your rank on us?"

"No, I'm not going to pull my rank on you. I'm just telling

you. I'll have no fighting in my squad."

"You talk big enough."

Kantaylis swung around and faced Capistron squarely; his eyes, dark and intense, moved over the big man's face. "I mean it, too."

"You're not so tough, Kantaylis."

"You want to try me? Come on, then."

For a long moment they stood in the center of the narrow aisle, almost toe to toe, Capistron nearly a head taller, Kantaylis broader in the shoulders. A silence that grew and grew, tightened, held the hut's onlookers tensed and motionless, like attendant figures in a frieze. Then Capistron all at once relaxed and gave back a step; and at the same instant O'Neill vaulted up on his cot, helmeted, his rifle in his hands and shouted, "I'll take you on, the whole bunch of you!—just line up to the right . . ."

"Shut up, O'Neill," Kantaylis said; turned back to the two. "What's the matter with you guys? Ah? What the hell are you fighting about—that, for Christ sake! *That!*" He pointed at Miss Haviland's inviting voluptuosity, gave a short, exasperated laugh. "At least find a real one to fight over . . . What the hell—you've been buddies since boot camp, haven't you? You're all beat out and bushed and you let go at each other. Now come on and shake hands and drop it."

Capistron and Helthal stared at each other, mute and uncertain.

"I mean it. Come on."

"Might as well," Freuhof said sourly. He, alone of the entire squad, had not so much as stirred, and now looked up at them with a flat, derisive grin which his hawklike, faintly cadaverous features seemed to accentuate. Like Kantaylis, his face was yellowed with malaria and deeply lined. "Won't be long you'll be getting all of that you want, and then some."

"*Shake*," Capistron ejaculated, "—what should I shake for? Who are you—a boy scout? Frig that noise. I told him he didn't take that broad down I was going to stick her. I told him."

"You've got a mean streak in you a mile wide, Capistron," Kantaylis said softly. "It's going to cost you some day."

The sleepy, amused expression returned to Capistron's round face. "I'll wait."

"Sure you will . . . All right," Kantaylis said, suddenly angry, "go ahead out in the boondocks and roll in the mud. Beat each other's brains out over a pin-up. I don't give a damn." He turned away, turned back again toward Capistron's huge, sullen figure. "But you do no fighting in this hut, no matter what. You hear?" He went up to the stove, where smoke was still fitfully escaping along with bits of wet ash. "Now let's get some heat in here. What gives with this, Helthal?"

"Rain's soaked the bottom."

Kantaylis pulled a bottle of lighter-fluid out of his seabag and went over to the stove again. "All right. Let's try this." He lifted the lid and sprinkled the contents of the bottle over the coals, clapped the lid back on, slid open the front vent and drew a match from his pocket and tossed it in. There was a low *pooff,* a violet-and-azure fan of flame, and then the coals caught and the pipe near the damper began to creak faintly. Kantaylis set the damper down almost tight and stirred carefully the bank of coals; his face glowed orange in the square of light.

"All right now, let's keep that going, Helthal. This place is like an icehouse." Standing beside his cot Kantaylis slipped the letter into a pocket of his utility blouse, picked up his poncho and put it on, slid the liner out of his helmet and clapped it on his head.

"Where you bound, Danny?" O'Neill asked.

"Going to get one of your fifteen-day furloughs." Kantaylis smiled at him and stepped out into the rain.

"Probably going to put us on report," Capistron rumbled from the far end of the hut.

"Ah, for Christ sake," O'Neill said. "You're off your rocker, no kidding. Who has Danny ever put on report? Name somebody."

"There's always a first time."

"Sure there is. There's always a first time for somebody to get some brains, too. He's never run one of us up. Not even after that little caper of yours and Helthal's in Kinston. Remember?"

"You sucking for something, O'Neill?" The thick, ruminative grin flattened Capistron's round face. "What's with you—you hot for that Greek bastard all of a sudden?"

O'Neill laughed, his blue eyes dancing. "I didn't hear you calling him that five minutes ago, Cappie."

"Just keep sucking around for something you'll get it, O'Neill. You sucking for something?"

"Not me," O'Neill said amiably. "I'm happy right where I am, chief."

"Okay."

"Okay." O'Neill rolled over on his cot and contemplated Newcombe again. "Hey, what you got there, Al?"

"A book."

"Ah—funny man. Come on: let's see." He leaned out from his cot, twisting his head. "The Il-i-ad," he announced. "Oh yeah. Homer. Yeah, I knew him well: we used to play ball together with the old Pawtucket Panthers. Is it salted down with sex, Al?"

"Not too heavily."

"Oh, it's a classic, ah? I got you. Hey, what I want to know is, was he wicked with his weapon? Was he, Al?"

"Couldn't say. He was blind."

"Drunk again, eh? Just couldn't let it alone. What a shame . . ." Leaping to his feet suddenly O'Neill went into a tight lindy-hop pattern between their cots; extending his left hand he translated an imaginary partner to the left, to the right, brought her back to him again, his face impassive as an Indian's, while he sang in harsh boogie-woogie rhythm:

"Hey! hey!—was he *wicked* with his *weapon* that's *all* I *want* to know!"

"Crazy Irish madman," Ricarno said. "Hey, come on: anybody! A dime gets you in. Let's go, ah?" Cards fluttered out ahead of him on the green blanket. "Look at that." He dealt again, flipping them off his thumb. "Look at that. Busted. You'd a had me, Chicken, you'd a had me. Look at that."

Connor said resentfully: "That's because I'm not playing with you."

Ricarno grinned his vile and merry grin, gathered in the cards; the cigar, still unlighted, rolled back and forth across his mouth. "You ain't just a-skit-skootin', Chick . . . Look at that. Name of the game."

Alan Newcombe put the book under his pillow and rubbed his eyes. Rain faded, came again in washing waves against the frail roof, and the stove thumped and cracked. Beyond it Capistron, reclining on his cot, folded his hands complacently over his big belly and stared at the ceiling. Helthal, across the aisle, went on smoothing the tear in the pin-up photo with awkward, painstaking little gestures of one hand.

In the deepening dusk the rain had faded to a soft whisper and a dripping spatter below the eaves. From down the row there came a shout, then another, and the rattle-and-clash of mess gear carried running. Silence again, broken only by the

stovepipe's metallic creak. And then some distance away a
trombone—that would be Kinkaid's trombone—began to
play over and over again in a halting, adenoidal, quavering
bray the refrain:

This world's too small by far
Let's travel to a star
It would be heaven—to soar beyond heaven—with
you . . .

Alan Newcombe withdrew an arm from under the blankets
and laid it across his eyes. Just a song at twilight. The twilight
of the absolute, floating, sinking in the dreary rain, sinking
through layers on layers of time; resting at last on the lonely,
brute universality of an army encamped. Caesar's beskirted
legionaries scampering through the rain in hither Gaul,
clashing mess gear, skylarking in the chow line; the Sun
King's fusiliers quarreling, dueling over a Watteau pin-up of
Madame de Maintenon; some strong-greaved Achaian on the
plain before windy Ilium strumming on a battered lyre: *it*
would be heaven—to soar beyond heaven—with you . . .

Credibility has slipped off the rim of the world and borne
you with it. At this moment Mother sits in the front living
room near the window with a copy of *Harper's* and ticks with
her thumbnail the places she intends—vainly—to make note
of later; Hallowell and Meriwether loll indolently in the effete
sanctity of Lowell House and sip at tumblers of gin roseate
with angostura, exchange observations on Rimbaud and Bed-
does and Tristan Corbière, phrases infinitely amusing and
profound; not far away Sue Trumbull, clad in plaid skirt and
shapeless, pale blue sweater, descends with a casual, swaying
gait the stairs to the dining hall, one hand absently curling the
ends of the hair below her right ear . . . At this very moment in
time they are all doing these things—and they are not doing
them because they are moving only in my mind's eye: my
mind's eye, Horatio—and I *will* them not to . . .

The door opened and someone entered quickly, closed it
again behind them with care. Newcombe raised his arm from
his eyes, felt rather than saw it was Kantaylis, bent over rum-
maging in his seabag. In a drowsy voice he said, "Hello,
Danny."

Kantaylis straightened, wheeled around. "Who's that—
Al?"

"Yes."

"I thought everybody'd gone. Aren't you going to chow?" He walked to the end of the hut and snapped on the switch. In the stark, yellowed glow from the naked bulb Newcombe saw he had shaved and combed his hair. "What's the matter—you sick?"

"No. Just beat out."

"Aren't you hungry?"

"No . . . I thought I'd rather just pass away right here."

Kantaylis smiled down at him—the slow, mournful, almost wistful smile; slipped out of his dungaree jacket and trousers. And Newcombe's gaze fell upon the scars: the long tear like a swollen purple crescent traced along the thigh to the hip, the wine-red-and-white gashes and furrows on shoulders and neck and ribs—and, as a focal point for all the others, the puckered crater high on the left breast, gathered into a ruddy, star-shaped configuration. That one had gone all the way through—had emerged in a still-larger, shiny, gathered dent on the shoulder blade which became visible as Kantaylis turned and reached into his seabag again. Newcombe watched them in covert fascination. Look sir, my wounds: had I as many eyes as thou hast wounds, poor, poor dumb mouths and bid them speak . . . what would they say? It was a great fight, Ma: it was rugged out there in the Pacific: it was hell out there but we slapped the Jap, we ripped the Nip, we . . . A constellation of suffering and misery. How could he live with all those wounds? Newcombe, you will never be a hero: not this day . . .

In the complicit silence of the hut he said in a low voice, "Do they still hurt any, Danny?"

"What's that?" Kantaylis, sitting on his cot dressing, turned his head.

"Where you got hit."

"Oh. Yeah. These two." His thumb tapped his thigh, the puckered star on his chest. "It aches. The whole arm gets to aching: it feels as though the blood has been shut off—you know, the way it burns sometimes? . . ." He stared into the red glow from the stove grate musingly. "I've got no complaint, though: doctor told me if it'd been an eighth of an inch lower it would've hit the lung."

"Uh-huh."

So there was death: death had burned through his flesh like a white-hot, terrible wire, had transfixed him deep in a jungle—out on the flaming periphery of death and violence which was still raging, burning . . . and now here he sat calmly, cigarette drooping from his lips, bent over, tying his dress shoes.

Kantaylis straightened, went over and took his greens blouse down from the hanger. The blue shield and Southern Cross of Guadalcanal flashed once as he swung into it: the shoulder patch only, no ribbons over the pocket. Buttoning it he drew it down with care and buckled the belt; reached up for his overcoat.

"Going in to town tonight, Danny?"

"Yeah. Something like that." Kantaylis locked his seabag, picked up the little green sack that held his shaving gear and hefted it a moment, then slipped it into an overcoat pocket.

"What's the score, Danny?"

"I've got a problem." He smiled faintly at the startled, apprehensive expression on Newcombe's face. "Will you do me a favor, Al? Don't let them take my rifle and seabag over to the police shed. I'm going over the hill for a couple of days."

"Over the hill?" Newcombe raised himself on his elbows. "No kidding? How come, Danny? What for?"

"That's *my* problem. Now will you do that for me?" He flipped the key to his seabag on Newcombe's cot. "If I don't make it back by the time you guys do. If you see Hamway alone some time, tell him I'm planning to be back by Monday at the latest. Okay?"

"Sure, Danny . . . but can't you promote a furlough or something? Most of us are getting them."

"Well. I don't rate one."

"I know—but couldn't you get even a seventy-two? Whyn't you go and see—"

"I was up there. Drew a TS slip. Giles said under no circumstances."

All at once grave and concerned, Newcombe sat up and clasped his arms around his knees. "What the hell, Danny— you'll get a summary."

"Yeah: probably."

"You might not even make it. The trains are crawling with MP's north of D.C."

"I know. It's a chance I'll have to take."

"—Can't you work an emergency or something? You'd think they could make some kind of concession . . ."

Staring at the pin-up over Helthal's cot Kantaylis nodded solemnly. "Yeah. You'd think they could, wouldn't you?" He spoke in a soft, musing tone, but his face was suddenly

animate with outrage—a swift, wild, imploring glance that
filled Newcombe with dread. "You'd think they might give a
man a break once in a while. A little time . . . even if it was
only a mistake—" He looked down, his face, in full shadow,
again firm and somber and resigned; pressed the visored
barracks hat firmly on his head. "Well, see you around."

Newcombe said with urgency, "Danny—"

"Yeah?"

"You've absolutely got to go?"

Turned at the door Kantaylis nodded. "No choice."

"You're up for sergeant . . ."

"Yeah, that's right. Well, that's how it goes." His eyes
moved around the hut once, steadily; came to rest on
Newcombe again. "You'll do me that favor, uh?"

"Sure . . ."

"Thanks a million. Good luck, kid."

"Good luck, Danny—"

The door bumped shut. The metal cleats on Kantaylis' heels
clacked briskly away along the duckboards, vanished into air.
Newcombe lay back again and drew the blankets up to his
nose. Over the hill: over the hill to the mill-town on the floss.
Steady old Kantaylis: a hundred thousand years on Guadalcanal and invalided back riddled with steel and malaria and
now on the verge of shipping out again—steady Kantaylis!
Their veteran and mainstay . . .

The letter: there was something in the letter. Those deep-set
eyes, sunken and dark with suffering, measuring me: how
scap'd I killing when I cross'd you so? He put it in his pocket
before he went up to the company office, he put it in his
blouse pocket again just now . . . But what was there in a letter
that could cause a man to toss over the slender authority of a
corporal's stripes, run the deadly gambit of a skull-shaven
brig-rat without hope or privileges—all for a few hours at
home?

The floodlighted nightmare atmosphere of the brig flared
along the wall of his mind, and involuntarily Newcombe
shivered: sagging tents and tangled strands of wire where
shadows drifted by almost like men . . . *That* for home: a
shack in a mill town on the Housatonic: a few frantic hours,
laced with the tear-splotched greetings and farewells, the interminable, maddening table conversations . . . What in the
name of Christ was the matter with him? Couldn't he see what
home was? Couldn't he see it was the most preposterous joke,
like Norman Rockwell drugstore scenes and Mom's apple

pie—all part of an idiotic tableau robbed of intellect or
reason—Jesus, couldn't he see *that*?

No. Obviously he could not. Obviously. Oh judgment thou
art fled to PFC's. And hope is sunk in treason.

Inexplicably angry and fearful and bereft, he sat up and
swung his stockinged feet to the floor, padded over to the
stove and dumped a shovelful of coal into its mouth; stood
listening a moment as Kinkaid's trombone went on in nasal,
wavering persistence, traveling to a star, soaring beyond
heaven with you. Returning to his cot he slipped his rifle out
of the tie-tie slings, spread a piece of rag across his knees and
started to strip the weapon. For a man's best friend is his rifle:
no trifle. The operating rod glided back and forth under his
hand: *ratta-racketa-racketa-racketa*. Two cots away Kantaylis' seabag, rimed with salt and streaked with the mud of
malevolent jungles, sagged against the wall like a headless,
limbless torso. *Racketa-rack*. Another bolt shot home. And
the shaggy-headed beast crouches in the mat of jungle,
waiting: the pupils of his eyes are points of red.

There was the rhythmic clatter of mess gear outside and
then voices, followed by the hollow thump of field shoes
coming along the duckboards. Newcombe bent his head over
the rifle and began lifting the little bridges and cylinders of
metal out of each other, one by one.

2

"ALMOST MISSED YOU," Sam Flannery said; peering through
the frosty windshield he ducked his neck inside his overcoat
collar. "Standing there so close to that building. Darn near
went past you."

"It was out of the wind," Kantaylis said.

"Oh. I get you. What in Tophet possessed you to come by
way of Northampton?"

"It was the only ride I could get. Cars are pretty few and far
between at four in the morning."

"Especially these days. Hitched your way up, eh? Kind of
low on the mazoo?"

"Sure am."

"I get you." Sam Flannery's glasses flashed as he turned his head. "I used to hitch home from Devens the last war. Same thing: no money, had to get home and see Amy while the getting was good." He grinned at Kantaylis; his face froze in sudden surprise and he sneezed. "By *God:* cold as the old Harry this morning. Down around twenty-two, twenty-three. You must have been frozen half to death."

"I was."

"Snappy enough to freeze the plumbing off a brass elephant, if you know what I mean." He chuckled, his eyes darting, birdlike, over the road.

"How's Fred?" Kantaylis asked him.

"He's fine. Got a letter yesterday. He's still out in Colorado. Says he's hoping to get a leave some time after the first of the year."

"Good enough."

The maples were bare, and the birches; only the oaks still clung to clusters of brown, gnarled leaves which trembled in the light breeze. Thick hot air from the car heater swam up into his face, mildly stinging. There was the Corners and Fairchild's Drugs, and someone—Ed Fairchild probably, he couldn't quite see, it looked thin and stooped enough to be Ed— leaned forward over the window display and waved, and he waved back. The road curved uphill now, up and to the right past Detlef's Bakery and the A & P, and the familiar constriction mounted in his chest and throat; there was the sudden open growling roar of the mill, and the long flank of windows of the beater room where a big, bald figure in overalls was walking quickly along the cat walk between Numbers Sixteen and Seventeen beaters.

"Carl Striebel, isn't it?" Sam Flannery said, nodding.

"Yes, that's right."

"He'll be glad to see you. He was telling me they really miss you over there. Haven't found anyone yet who can thread up the way you could."

They were crossing the bridge over the dam, the water below frozen and smooth as polished glass; past the bridge, the road still curving uphill and to the right where the Scarborough Oak stood, rude and massive and indomitable. On both sides the concrete retaining walls were like a stone gateway unfurling. And the houses, neat and white—Burchalls', Macks', Winoskis', Wileys'—flowed in a blur past his eyes.

"Don't go out of your way, Mr. Flannery," he protested

suddenly; put his hand on the door handle. "Just let me off right here at the corner."

"Don't give it a thought, Danny. Don't you give it a thought." Sam Flannery drove to the end of the street and swung in near the drive with a little flourish. "Safe and sound. They know you're coming?"

"No, they don't."

Sam Flannery thrust out his lower lip. "Might have been nice to let 'em know. Give 'em a moment or two. You've been—"

"I know. I didn't have time."

"Sure. I remember: it's always that way. Well: come by and see us, now."

"I'll try," Kantaylis said. "I've only got a seventy-two this time. Thanks again, Mr. Flannery."

"Not at all, son. Good to see you again."

Sam Flannery gave a solemn little salute with one finger to the brim of his hat and pulled away; and Kantaylis turned around in the center of the walk and passed his gloved hand over his eyes.

Home.

The porch was sinking at the east corner: the end he had gone flying off on the scooter when he was six. He had put his fingers to the back of his head and felt the blood; Nick and Stevie had stared down at him with wide, wondering eyes; the front wheel of the scooter had been broken, too. The dogwood tree—the one he'd tried to climb and had fallen out of, skinning his arms—why had he always been falling out of things?—was brown and wizened: maybe it was dying. The whole place needed a coat of paint. But it was all right. It looked all right. The yellow gingerbread trim wabbled and swam before his eyes as he moved up the walk. He put his hand in the mailbox automatically, felt nothing.

The hall and living room were dark. Pale sunlight swept in ahead of him, flung his shadow far down the hall floor, gross and misshapen: a horned, helmeted figure, full of menace, lurching over the threshold, bringing death and doom . . . He scowled, closed the door behind him and moved quickly down the hall and pushed open the swing door into the kitchen.

His mother was on her knees scrubbing the kitchen floor: for the weekend, he thought instinctively. For an instant he watched her, head bowed, her broad back arched, her big arms moving in quick, vigorous rhythms, while a cultivated radio voice coming from the sideboard behind her pleasantly summarized a movie star's impending nuptials with a Moroccan prince. Papers covered what she had already scrubbed: fragments of headline darted up at him—NAZ: SSIAN: RAF: DRIVE: HITS: BOM: BEACHHEAD ON. Planes hung like black, blunt birds, like flights of bolts, dark figures ran crouching under walls, smoke billowed and spewed from flaming towers—the whole world writhed and shuddered in its boiling hell of death and violence, and his mother moved her strong, full arms in tiny rapid circles over the patterned green linoleum floor.

All at once he regretted having come upon her this way without giving her any preparation; troubled, he looked behind him, shifted his weight as if to withdraw. Then he turned again and said in a quiet voice:

"Hello, Ma."

Her face whipped around to his, dark and amazed, almost outraged.

"*Danny!*" she cried. She scrambled to her feet and smelling of BAB-O and hot water hugged him to her, pressed her cheek against his; burst into sobs. "Oh Danny, my darling boy Danny, oh my fine, strong Danny—"

"It's all right," he said gently, patting her. "It's all right, Ma . . ."

Just as abruptly she stopped sobbing, brushed the tears from her face, shook her head smiling, weeping still. "Danny—you shouldn't come on me like that. Just out of nowhere. A *surprise*—! I thought for a minute . . ." She stopped, held him back from her, held in her hand the square, handsome face like her own, the steady dark eyes like hers. "You look so tired, Danny."

"I am," he said. "I just got in off three-day bivouac."

"Oh. Out in the woods all night?"

"That's right. Three nights."

"Oh—so cold . . ." Her face brightened again. "You had breakfast? Look!" She pointed to a glass crock over the stove. "Buckwheat cakes: your favorite!"

"That's swell, Ma."

"How long you home for? Why didn't you let us know, Danny—Nick could have met you at Pittsfield. What train did you get?"

He slipped off his overcoat and blouse and sat down in his father's chair by the window; let the thick, close heat of the kitchen sink into him while his mother moved about quickly, snuffling and smiling, firing questions at him in her deep voice. Staring idly out of the window at the field behind the house his eyes moved over cornstalks like wasted skeletons clothed in rags, an aluminum pail upended, a rake leaning tines-out against a wooden wheelbarrow with one of its sides gone; encountered a saw-tooth, slant-eyed, grinning jack-o-lantern sitting on a post. And all at once his eyes filled with tears.

"How's Pa?" he asked abruptly, turning from the window.

"All right." His mother brought a plate of buckwheat cakes over to him. "The same. He had a cold two weeks ago but he got over it all right."

"He had the pains much?"

She nodded once, her mouth set in a firm line. "They come and go. They're so painful for him: the way he moans! . . . He got out last week. Stella was downtown shopping and I had just stepped over to the Winoskis' for a minute. He was stopping cars on the Post Road and shouting at them. Billy Burchall brought him back. You want milk as well as coffee?"

"If you've got enough. How are the kids?"

"They're fine. Nick got his papers last week."

"Army?"

"That's right." Hand at her hip holding the spatula she hesitated, said, "Stevie says he's going to go in to Pittsfield and enlist." When he didn't answer she went on, looking at him intently from under her brows: "He says he's going to enlist in the marines. Like you did."

"Tell him to keep his shirt on," he said. "They'll get around to him soon enough. There'll be time enough for everybody." He sat back and wiped his mouth with a napkin. "There's going to be time enough for everybody to get into the act."

"You don't think it might be over soon, Danny?" She gestured with the spatula toward the white plastic grill of the radio. "They say now that Italy's surrendered—"

"No, Ma," he said.

"—a man was saying, with all our planes now—"

"No, Ma," he repeated gently. "I don't care how many planes. It isn't going to be over for a long, long time."

She nodded briskly, blinking. "Well: Stevie says *you* enlisted so why can't he?"

"I didn't know any better. I didn't have anybody to tell me the time of day. He does."

"Will you talk to him, Danny?" She came up to him while

he methodically went on eating the buckwheat cakes; put her hand on his black curly hair. "While you're home? Tell him to wait—what you just said now?"

"Sure I will." He set down his fork, pushed the plate back, put his arm around his mother and hugged her to him. "Sure I will, Ma. I don't know what good it'll do but I'll talk to him."

"He'll listen to you, Danny. They all do. They always used to. Look at that time when Nick was going to quit high school and you—"

"This is different, Ma. This isn't kid stuff now. I'm not a big brother now."

"You're not? . . ." She looked down at him uncertainly.

"No. That kind of thing doesn't cut any ice now. This is all different."

"Tell him not to go, Danny," she murmured in a sing-song, pleading voice, "he'll listen to you, they all do, tell him to wait. All I'll have left is little Jimmy—"

"And the girls."

"And the girls. Danny, you going to have to ship out again? They can't send you overseas again, can they? Don't let them, Danny. All that time," she went on, more swiftly, her voice rising, "all that time you were on Guadalcanal and then Australia, and wounded all over, months and months in the hospital, why can't you tell them you can't go any more—"

"Now, Ma . . ." He moved his hand slowly up and down her broad back, patting it softly. "They have to do what they want to do," he said finally. "Everybody has to go his own way and learn for himself. Have his own experiences. They'll have to, too—all of them: Nick and Stevie and little Jimmy. And the girls too. They'll all have to, Ma." He hugged her to him and looked up at her fondly. "They'll be all right, Ma. They'll come out all right. Don't worry now." He released her and stood up. "I want to wash up a little."

"You going over to the mill and see the boys?"

"No. Maybe later." He turned up his starched sleeves with care. "I'm going over to Andrea's."

Her eyebrows arched in surprise. "So soon?" She paused, said: "You'll be back for lunch?"

"Yeah, I guess so. I don't know for sure."

As he was drying his hands at the sink she came up to him. "How long you going to be home, Danny?"

"Not long this time, Ma." He buttoned the blouse and got into his overcoat again; buckled the smooth, gleaming black-leather belt. "Today and tomorrow. Andrea and I are going to get married, Ma." he said.

"Good," she said firmly, and nodded. "Good. You should have got married when you were home in August."

"I know."

"When?"

"I don't know. Today. Soon as we can."

"Oh—" she gazed at him in reproach, "—why didn't you let me know, Danny? I haven't got any food in the house . . ."

"Don't worry about it, Ma."

"I'll get a roast. I'll ask Mr. Dlugasz. What would you like the most for supper?"

"Nightingales' tongues."

"What?"

"Nightingales' tongues," he repeated, and grinned at her. "Guy in my outfit says they're a great delicacy."

"Oh—!" She laughed, threw up one hand; sobered again instantly. "How about her mother? She know about this?"

"No. Not yet."

"What will she say?"

"Something sarcastic, I suppose. I don't know . . . *Don't worry about it*, Ma," he said; he threw her a mock glower from under his brows. "We're going to get married and that's all there is to it. And she'll just have to get used to it, too."

"Good," his mother repeated. "Just today and tomorrow, Danny?"

"That's right."

"You'd think they could have given you longer than that. For getting married."

He smiled at her affectionately and kissed her cheek. "Well. They're not very impressed, Ma. Let's be thankful for little things."

"That's right, Danny." She followed him down the hall. "The boys have the car over in the mill lot."

"It's all right. I'll walk it." He turned and blew her a kiss as he swung open the door. "Be back soon."

"All right."

Stepping into the parlor she waved at his retreating figure, though he did not look back. "My danny," she murmured softly. Holding aside the flowered curtains watching him move away down the street in the tight-fitting overcoat with the scarlet chevrons she was shaken by a sudden, violent, choking sob; and the tears began to stream down her cheeks.

●　　●　　●

She saw from one of the windows the green-uniformed
figure moving up the walk and raced through the dining
room, her heart caught between hope and apprehension, and
flung open the front door. He was standing there quietly on
the stoop—the broad, lined face, the deep-set, steady dark
eyes. She said faintly, *"Danny—"* and clung to him with all
her might, felt the sweet solidity of his arms around her, cried
to herself, Ah, it's Danny, he's here, he's here with me; and
the world assumed some of its wholeness again.

"Hello, honey," he was saying in a soft murmur. "Hello,
honey girl . . ."

"Oh Danny, oh I didn't dare hope it was you." She looked
at him furtively. "I saw you through the window . . . I knew
you'd come, oh thank God you got home—"

"Amen to that," he said.

She was crying now, trying not to, she'd promised herself
she wouldn't, biting her lips and sniffling, looking up at him;
her hand was trembling on his face. "Oh Danny, it's been
awful, just awful. I didn't know what to do, all I could do was
pray and pray you'd come home . . ."

"Sure, honey. Well: it's all right. It's all right now." He
smiled a slow, infinitely sad smile that clutched at her heart,
and said, "Let's go in. You'll catch cold standing out here."

"I don't care, I don't care at all now." She turned, one arm
still around him, and moved inside. He pushed the door shut
with his shoulder and looked at her, drew her to him again.
This time she kissed him, almost fiercely; her arms went
around his neck, one of her hands knocked his cap off his
head. It rolled around them on the floor on its wire rim.

"Never mind it," he murmured; his cheek was harsh and
cold against her own.

"Who is it, Andrea?" her mother called from the floor
above.

"It's Danny!" She broke away from him, turning. "It's
Danny, he's just got home . . ."

"Oh! How nice." Virginia Lenaine came down out of the
light from the head of the stairs: a tall, angular figure
descending with nervous haste, bent-kneed. She was wearing a
heavy, knitted hip-length sweater, unraveled and full of
snags, whose lumpy contours served to accentuate her flat
chest and long, bony arms; her hair was gathered up in a
scarf, tied tightly Aunt-Jemima fashion at the peak of her
forehead.

"Hello, Daniel," she said with bright, arch cordiality,

extending her hand. "Well, aren't you up early in the morning, though? I guess that's the army life, isn't it? How good you were able to get home again so soon."

"I hope I didn't disturb you, Mrs. Lenaine," he said. "I know it's a funny time to be calling."

"Not at all."

"Oh Danny—any time's all right, you know that," Andrea broke in; she threw her mother a quick, angry glance. "Good heavens . . ."

"I don't have very long this time," he went on, "and I wanted to see Andrea so badly."

"Of course you did!" Virginia Lenaine's lean face grimaced in a smile laced with wrinkles; her dilated hazel eyes watched him as he retrieved his hat from under the telephone stand. "Of course you do, it's quite all right. You must excuse us: we're having ourselves a real old-fashioned knock-down-and-drag-out house cleaning. One of the charming, unsung tasks . . ." Still smiling she glanced at Andrea—a look sharp and inexplicable; turned away abruptly. "Well, I'll go upstairs again if you'll pardon me."

"Of course, Mrs. Lenaine," Danny said.

"This is the week for cleaning out the attic *closets*." Her voice, rising up the stairs, laid great stress on the final word. "There are forty years of Berkshire *Eagles* Grandma Abbott stored away up there. Would you believe it? All in order, too. And shoe boxes and tin foil and Lord knows what else. Everyone thought it was so silly but now—you see?" She threw out one thin hand airily; light streamed about her like an aureole. "It's all needed so desperately. Our little bit, you know!" Her voice faded away above the landing, brittle, falsely blithe. "Life has to go on, you see—*everything* can't be stopped . . . come up . . . manage . . . Andrea . . ."

"What?" Andrea called after her. "What did you say, Mother? I can't hear you!"

There was a pause; then the voice came down again—a different tone this time, irritated and long-suffering: "I said *don't* come up unless you *want to*, I can manage . . ."

"All right—" Andrea whirled around to Danny angrily. "Honestly: don't come up unless I want to—with *you* here!"

"What's the matter?"

"Oh, it's all such an *act*. Don't you see? That ridiculous sweater—" She brushed a lock of hair out of her eyes. "She knew it was you all the time—she probably saw you from the attic window. This is one of her Dolly Madison routines: you know—salvaging the nation's treasures: the agonies we must all go through for the Four Freedoms. She's had the whole house upside down for five days now while she pries out every last wad of tin foil Grandma Abbott cached away up there in her dotage. She's even had Dad dragging junk around up there after work nights till he's ready to drop. She's impossible."

"Honey—"

"Or maybe it's the Florence Nightingale act, I don't know: she's got so many of them you can't keep track if you tried . . ."

"Honey, take it easy. You're all wound up."

"Yes. I guess I am. Oh God, it's been awful, Danny: these last two months. Just horrible. The house in an uproar and nasty little digs at you every time she thinks of one: 'Daniel still a corporal, is he?' 'Daniel getting ready to go overseas again?' Sometimes I could strangle her, I swear . . ." She felt suddenly all unstrung; rubbed her face with her hands. "She knows everything, *everything* that's going on—she's got some kind of radar built in—"

"Don't," he said.

"Don't what?"

"Don't hate her."

"I can't help it." She turned and looked at him. "All right. I don't care now you're home."

"You mustn't hate your mother."

"—You don't have to live with her!"

"That's right."

She glanced at him in surprise, and smiled. That was like him: he was always saying something like that, something that meant nothing, really; and yet it did. It was the tone more than the words themselves . . . And oddly enough it was true: the maddening irritation her mother could always provoke in her already seemed vastly diminished, despite her outburst—or perhaps because of it. But it was Danny's doing: his calm presence released her again, as it always did, from anger and confusion. Raising her head she was conscious for the first time that morning of the pale aura of sunlight outside, the reedy, plaintive singsong of a chickadee in the big maple. "You're funny," she said, and put her arm around him. "You're sweet. Oh, Danny . . ."

The living room was long and narrow and savagely overheated; couches and chairs and chiffoniers poised themselves stiffly around its edges like people at a funeral. The floor was waxed, the ash trays were clean, the table surfaces were bare except for one copy of *Life* magazine. There were no newspapers anywhere, no personal effects at all. Andrea halted at the doorway, peered in distastefully.

"Come on in Dad's den," she said. "He won't mind. I can't stand this living room: she's got it looking like a doctor's office. It gives me the creeps. I feel if I sit down I'm soiling the chairs."

He followed her into the den and they sat half-facing each other on the little worn couch. He opened his mouth to say something, closed it again, reached up and passed his hand over her hair, held his fist softly against her cheek; as she watched his eyes deepen with love she felt the sustaining intensity of his presence fill her slowly, thunderously, until it began to throb like distant surf against her heart.

"How are you, honey girl?" he asked gently. "All right?"

At the sound of his voice her lips began to tremble again. She pressed a hand to her head and her eyes filled; looking down she shook her head rapidly several times, then raised it again with a little defiant toss. "Oh, it's all right. Now. I was so worried. Not knowing whether you'd get home or not. I didn't think I could—"

She leaned forward and pressed her forehead against the hollow of his shoulder. Something hard chafed her temple: she looked up, saw it was the eagle-globe-and-anchor of his blouse insignia. "Oh thank God you came, Danny. I was going half crazy . . . Do you know I prayed you'd get home?—night after night. I really prayed."

"So did I," he said.

"Did you? . . . I think it's the first time I ever prayed for something and it came true. The one time I wanted it most."

"Good enough," he said.

He looked so tired. She moved the tips of her fingers around his mouth and chin. So unutterably tired: as though he hadn't had enough sleep in years and years, had lost so much he could never catch up again, all the rest of his life; his face still had that sallow, yellowish hue—his atabrine tan, he'd called it once dryly—and above the edge of his collar, just beyond her fingertips, was the white, gathered triangular point of a scar, like the imprint of a milky quartz arrowhead. His lips were full and mobile, and his eyes—he was still regarding her quietly—were alive with that steady reassurance which had stirred her so, ever since she had fallen in love with him—at fifteen; that had always made her feel she could be more than she'd ever thought possible . . .

"You're beautiful, Andrea," he said simply.

She felt she was going to cry again and looked away.

"It seems so unfair," she said after a time. "So unfair . . ."

He was looking at her the way he had that night at the lake: the steady tender gaze tempered with something troubled and restive—as though he were asking her something he knew could not be answered . . . It was the moonlight, she thought with sudden, poignant memory; the moonlight, lying on the lake like a quicksilver wash, that turned the little licking waves to molten silver, ran among the sickle blades of the reeds, the tips of the fir branches above their heads, and filled the night air with a wild and magic silver light. The tree toads were roaring their high, soft roar, and the reeds rustled with a faint seething—she could see them bobbing against the moonlight—but the wind had made no sound at all, nor the firs; and finally the reeds themselves had stopped rustling and bobbing and she was no longer aware of the fierce, faint chant of the toads, nor the wind among the reeds, nor the dark looming mass of the firs . . .

"Just that once—" She bit her lip. "Just that one time and after all the years we didn't even—"

"I know, honey." He paused, said: "Are you sure? Real sure?"

She nodded rapidly.

"Well: that's how it goes. Don't feel bad about it. It'll be all right now . . . We should have got married then, when I was home."

"Well I wanted to, darling," she said, "it was you—you said we ought to wait, that that wasn't any time to—"

"I know."

"I wanted to terribly, just terribly, you said we—"

"I know that." He sighed slowly, shifted his feet. "Well: I was dead wrong. I—it didn't seem the right thing to do. I didn't think it was fair to you, for one thing . . ."

"But don't you see, Danny, you know you're the only one I care about in the—"

Above their heads there was a metallic crash, like the dropping of a stack of trays, and then the rolling bumping sound of something heavy falling down a flight of stairs, ending with a thump that shook the building.

"She's fallen—" Andrea said. "Oh God." She jumped to her feet and ran into the hallway and called, "Mother?"

There was no answer.

"Mother!"

They heard a faint, strained answering voice.

"Mother, are you all right?"

". . . What?"

"I said, *Are you all right!*"

She raced up the stairs, conscious of Danny close behind her, turned the corner and came on a battered antique commode lying on its end at the foot of the attic stairs. The doors were sprung, one of them hanging loosely, and the bottom was split. At the top of the landing Virginia Lenaine stared down at them; she was holding on to the banister, one hand to her forehead.

"What happened?" Andrea said. "We thought you'd fallen . . ."

"Nothing," her mother said with dogged calm; the scarf had been pulled over to one side of her head and hung down like a dejected rabbit ear. "Nothing at all."

"But *something* must have. How did the—"

"I was simply moving a few things around in order to get at something else, that's all." She looked down at them glassily; her breath came in uneven spurts. "And it got away from me." She pointed at their feet. "Grandma Abbott's cedar commode. It's always been in the way over there. Under foot—I was trying to fit it in the niche, between the—"

"But you ought not to try to move heavy furniture around," Andrea said angrily. "Dad'll be furious. Why didn't you let us know if you were going to—"

"It's all right. I didn't want to disturb you."

"I'd have been glad to move some furniture around for you, Mrs. Lenaine," Danny said.

"Not at all." She extended a hand toward them in formal demurral. "I can manage perfectly well. I wouldn't dream of disturbing you." She moved away with great dignity from the head of the landing. "I know how precious your time is . . ."

"Will you promise not to move any more heavy furniture?" Andrea called after her. "Will you, Mother?" The answer was inaudible and she repeated, "Will you? I can't *hear* you!"

". . . All right . . ."

"Oh, come on," Andrea said crossly. "Let her break her neck if she's so bent on it."

Danny set the commode on its feet and closed the broken

doors. "Don't say that, Andrea."

"Oh for heaven's sake," she burst out at him, "don't you see? This is all to make us feel—oh, I don't know . . ."

"Sure I see."

"Well, then . . ."

Back in the den, seated again on the couch he said, "I'm sorry I let you in for this, honey. We should have got married then, you were right. I figured with Pa the way he is now, and Jimmy and the girls . . ."

"But Danny, we've got to live our *own* lives, you can't—"

"And your mother being so dead set against it too, and the war still on . . . I couldn't see it any other way."

"But that's the trouble, Danny, you always can see only one way to do a thing, you make up your mind and then that's the only—"

"All right," he said, raising his voice a little, "let's not get into a fight about it. Okay?" Smiling he took her in his arms and rocked her back and forth gently. "Honey, you're so upset, you're all tied up in knots—"

"I know I am. And so would you be if you'd been hanging around this house the way I have for the last two months, not knowing what was going to happen . . ."

"Sure, honey. I know. Look: I admit I was wrong. For fifty reasons. A hundred. Let's go on from here, now. A step at a time. We'll get married first thing."

"When, Danny?"

"Soon as we can. I haven't got much time, this time."

"How long have we got?"

"Today and tomorrow."

She felt her face grow long with fear; watching her, the centers of his eyes tightened slightly, as though with pain.

"Well, all right," she said in as resolute a voice as she could manage. "That's it, then."

"That's it."

"Mother will want a wedding, I suppose."

"Well, there's no time for that kind of thing now. She'll just have to get over the notion. I'm going over to the mill and see Bob Westerveldt about a license: he'll know the fastest way to get one."

"Oh yes, a license." It struck her as odd that she hadn't thought of a license before in all this time; the omission worried her, made her obscurely fearful. "Do you think you can get one today?"

"I'm going to try. We'll get one tomorrow for sure. Maybe they'll make an exception with a—"

There was another series of clattering clumps and bumps from overhead.

"Oh God," Andrea exclaimed. "She's horrible. She's impossible."

"How about her, though?" He nodded in the direction of the attic, from where there now came the rumbling, scraping sound of something being dragged along in short intervals. "Hadn't we better go up and tell her now? Get it over with?"

"No." She shook her head decisively. "Come back at noon when Dad's home for lunch. He'll back us up. He's always liked you a lot, Danny."

"I know he has."

"We're going to need all the support we can get. She's going to make one terrific scene of it."

"I suppose so . . . Well, I guess I better get going."

"Danny, where'll we go? What'll we do—for the honeymoon?" She smiled at him wanly, absurdly.

"I'll work out something. Don't worry, now. It'll all come out all right." He embraced her, kissed her forehead and cheek; she shivered for an instant, involuntarily. "What's the matter, Andrea?"

"Nothing. I don't know. I've just got the trembles or something."

"You aren't getting a cold, are you?" he said with solicitude.

"No. It's your being home, I guess. So suddenly. You go ahead, darling; go on over and get the license."

"All right. I'll be back at noon or else I'll call you."

She kissed him briefly, stood in the hall staring at the door after he'd closed it behind him. The tremor passed over her again in a feverish wave, and she gripped the newel post for support. She felt dizzy and faintly nauseous and *strange*—as though the house she'd been born and raised in, with all its appurtenances, had been rendered suddenly alien to her. It's all right, she told herself with great solemnity: it's all right now. He's home now.

"Andrea?" her mother's voice sounded faintly. "Andrea?"

"Yes?" she shouted; and muttered, "My God: we ought to have a set of walkie-talkies."

"Has Daniel left already?"

"Yes, he's left."

"You could have asked him to stay to lunch if you'd wanted to, you know . . ."

"I did, Mother. He's coming back." She tossed back her hair with a quick, characteristic gesture. "One terrific scene," she said, and looked up at the ceiling. "One grand scene of it . . ."

She started up the stairs with a slow, resolute step.

3

THE SIDEWALK WAS of brick, uneven and sloping and smooth as glass; the curb was high—absurdly high for a curb—and the street was paved with cobblestones like the tops of worn, primeval skulls. Some of the panes of glass in the bow windows were blue with age. Above them iron balconies traced a delicate, sedate calligraphy in front of the living room windows of the second floor. The pattern was repeated on the lamppost he passed, whose cap was like a sooty antique casque, and on the foot scraper, also of black iron, sunk in the stone steps. The plate on the front door bore the spencerian legend *Newcombe*, its black paint had been worn away with polishing and time so that only the etched indentation served to reveal it.

The hallway was, as always, dark and quiet. Light filtered in pale shafts from the dining room windows, gleamed darkly on the mahogany table, glinted in the tall, glass-fronted service cabinet. A little marble-topped table near the cloak closet carried in Roman block letters the inscription SICUT PATRIBUS, SIT DEUS NOBIS. He smiled at it indulgently, became conscious of a faint stir in the kitchen. That would be Mrs. Hinshaw. Or Channing. As it ever has been, so it ever shall be, world after world in the still, dusty, mote-laden silence: amen. The world reels onward far below, on dune and headland sinks the fire, dictators come and go, but the Hill, the Hill, the Hill, the Hill—the Hill goes on forever . . .

"Alan?" he heard his mother call. "Is that you, Alan?"

The stairway was sheathed in dark green carpeting; the wall above it was a faded ivory. He mounted without answer, moved his ungloved hand along the polished mahogany, felt musingly its lightly oiled, satin surface. Do I pass my hand over this banister, tread these soft stairs for the last time, or no? Quien sabe? as Ortega Y Gassett once said to Yvonne de Carlo—

"Alan . . ."

She was coming toward him: the long aristocratic face with its fine nose—the nose which had been the sole reason the sculptor Engelbrecht had once begged to do her (he had explained it all most passionately)—the silver, faintly wavy hair; those eyes which bore such weight of approval and disapproval—such weight!—swept toward him, moist with tears . . . She had embraced him and the faint, firm odor of her perfume, not quite musky, not quite austere, floated around him like a nimbus.

"It's so good you could get home. How long do you have?"

"About five days."

"Five days. That's fine. That's wonderful, isn't it?" She turned back toward the room with a slight arching of her neck, an awkward little tremor; said, "Are you cold?"

"No. I'm fine."

"It's been so raw all fall. The northeast wind . . ."

Beyond his mother's slender figure light fell softly from the long windows, rested in a dull shimmer on the wing of the grand piano, the curly-maple secretary, the soft, waxen Rodin nude. Superimpose—say you were to superimpose this décor on the hut, group it insouciantly around the coal stove—or better still, as an exercise in juxtaposition, drop the cots—with their occupants—into *this* interior: Helthal could shake down the ashes in the fireplace grate and Capistron could throw his knife at the Stuart portrait of Great-grandfather Lemuel and O'Neill could bang out boogie-woogie on the old Chickering and holler: "Hey, we're living!" . . .

His mother was speaking: he gave himself a little shake and snatched at the tail of the sentence.

"—thought you might like to go, if you cared to."

"I'm sorry, Mother," he said. "I was thinking of something else."

"It doesn't matter."

"No. Really. I'm sorry. What was it?"

She smiled, said with gauche reiteration, "It was only that Robert Frost is reading his poetry Monday evening over at

Sanders Theater. I thought you might like to hear him, that's all."

"Oh. Yes. Perhaps so. I'll have to see—"

The front door banged shut below; hangers in the hall closet clattered and jangled and then steps thumped rapidly on the stairs and Amory Newcombe hurried into the living room with a triumphant, nervous air and shook hands with his son. His steel-gray hair, cropped short, was repeated in the silver bristle of mustache above his thin lips.

"Hello, son. Thought I'd catch you if I got home about now. Just get in?" Stepping back he assayed Newcombe quickly, brightly; the round, steel-rimmed lenses of his glasses winked once. "Well, how's everything? Freeze to death on the way up?"

"It was cold, all right. We couldn't get seats till we got north of Washington."

"What a shame," Charlotte Newcombe said. "What did you do?"

"We sat on some seabags out on the platform. You know, where they hook the trains onto each other." He sat down in one of the deep chairs and clapped a hand on each arm.

"Don't you want to take the Buick down there, Alan?" his father said. "I should think it'd save you time, you'd avoid all that mess at Wilson and Union Station and no seats and all."

"There's really not much sense in it, Dad. Just for the few times I'd be able to use it. I'd have to leave it out down there, and somebody's liable to cannibalize it or something."

"What's that?"

"Oh—you know: strip it down. Lift a lot of the accessories."

Amory Newcombe was staring at him uncertainly. "But don't they have facilities for safeguarding people's property?"

"Well—they're not very extensive. They don't care too much about private property, you know . . . It's the service."

"Yes, but someone's *car*—I should certainly think they would have made *some* provisions . . ." Mild consternation marking his pale, bony features, Amory Newcombe rose and going over to the fireplace began stirring the smoking embers inside the grate with a poker.

"Have you had anything to eat, Alan?" his mother said. "Mrs. Hinshaw won't have dinner ready till seven. Wouldn't you like some sandwiches and milk, something like that?"

"—I'll tell you what," Newcombe said. "Right now I'd

like a good, stiff shot of Dad's I. W. Harper."

"Fine." His father laughed shortly, glanced at him with a faintly wary expression. "We'll have one together."

"But don't you want something to eat?" Charlotte Newcombe persisted. "You look half-starved."

"I've been creeping on my belly through all the swamps in Carolina for three days and nights while a lot of former hardware store clerks and hod carriers bellowed at me. I've had it." He smiled ingratiatingly at her. "Pure exhaustion, nothing else."

"You do look tired," she said. "In the rain and all?"

"In the rain and *all* . . ." The whiskey was bright and hot and smooth, all at once; he held it in his mouth for a few moments, then let it slip in gentle stages to his innards where it spread like some benign, annealing oil. In the fast-fading sunlight the motes fell slowly, turning over and over like lazily tumbling flakes of snow.

"Here's luck," Amory Newcombe said.

"Over the falls," he responded.

"Over the falls," his father repeated, and smiled his quick, bright smile. "That's one salutation I've missed."

"My bunky always uses it: he's got a million of 'em, to coin a phrase. He's a redheaded Irishman from Pawtucket or thereabouts. A really nice guy, even if he has got the dizziest comic sense I've ever run across."

"Have you found anyone at camp who's convivial?" his mother asked. "Someone you could talk seriously with—someone who's had the kind of background—"

"Not a soul." He shook his head at her solemnly. "No: they all know how to jitterbug and think Buff Haviland is the girl they'd be most happy to be flung up on the shore of a cannibal isle with; and drink beer out of cans. It's great: they think the drama is some kind of rare Greek coin . . . Believe me, we're a long, long way from the new Golden Age."

"That's too bad. I'd hoped so that you could find someone who might be interested in poetry or painting."

". . . Oh, it's not so bad. It's war, you know." He grinned widely, a bit foolishly: the I. W. Harper had fanned out and out until it was lapping against the farthest confines of his body, licking against his toes, his fingertips. Flood tide. He felt lulled, indolent, again secure; slumped down in the deep chair he propped his feet—it was the first time in his life he'd ever done so—on the cocktail table with the legs of Florentine iron. "After all, seen from one point of vantage it's an admirable time for gathering material. The titanic surge of the great epic: look at old Homer, look at Dante, look at Siegfried Sassoon, look at Rupert Brooke. No, don't look at Rupert Brooke. It's just what I need to give my work scope. And depth. Why, I might even—"

"Alan, your shoes!" his mother exclaimed; one hand to her lower lip she was staring in alarm at the soles of his feet. "They're worn through! You've got holes in them: you've got holes in *both* of them!"

"Oh, yes, that's right. I forgot. Sorry." He raised one foot and held it up toward her. "I put cardboard in them, though: several thicknesses. See? They're all right."

"But what happened?" she went on, distressed. "In this weather—you shouldn't wear your shoes that long without—"

"I didn't. These aren't mine. Somebody lifted mine."

"Lifted them?"

"Yeah. We went over to the beach one afternoon for a swim and somebody exchanged with me." To their blank, consternated gaze he added, "Semper Fi, you know."

"What's that?"

"An expression of cynicism in the corps. Translated roughly—very roughly—it means: I rejoice in finding myself for the time being quite adequately accoutered; hence I am not overly burdened by a sense of obligation for *your* personal welfare. Something like that. You know."

"But couldn't you have got another pair?"

Watching his mother's troubled, unsure face he had all he could do for an instant to keep from snickering. "Oh, sure. I didn't have time, actually. I was thinking of it. See, we wear field shoes all the time and I didn't think we were going to get this furlough . . . right at this time," he added hastily, leaning forward; but his mother's face had already gone rigid with apprehension; her glance darted to his father, then out at the stately Bullfinch façades across the square, muted by the lacy filagree of the elms' drooping branches. Alan Newcombe lowered his eyes and lit a cigarette. Well, I suppose I should tell them. Some time. Now as good as any. No, wait till the last day . . . She knows already, though—

"But that's ridiculous, Alan," his father was saying. "You can't go around wearing shoes like that in this weather."

"I seem to be doing it."

"Why, you can't pass inspection in those, can you?"

"Don't stand inspection in dress shoes, Dad. This is just for off the post. You know, like what dear old Aunt Het used to say about handkerdumps: one for show and one for blow." He shrugged. "I'll get some tomorrow. I really will. Don't worry about 'em. I feel fine. Pneumonia'd be just about the best thing that could happen to me right now."

"Alan, don't talk that way," his mother protested.

"It's true: get over there in sick bay and sack in for days, nice clean sheets and a corpsman to hand you chow every once in a while instead of dragging your—uh, dragging through the boondocks all hours of the day and night . . ."

On the mantel lay a tortoise-shell snuffbox which had belonged to his Great-grandfather Silas; the poker in the rack beside the grate had a squat gold eagle perched irately on the handle and had belonged to his Great-great-granduncle Endicott, who had been a Brewster; the pewter plates and cups standing on the top of the secretary had been brought over by his Great-great-great-grandfather Amasa, who had been, incredibly, both a Newcombe *and* a Brewster, in 1637 . . .

"Maneuvers?" his father was inquiring with raised eyebrows.

"Field problems, they call them. It was great: we advanced in a vast circle of withdrawal and backed into the enemy, in order to let him take us in the rear. Element of surprise, you know. Good strategy. Only it didn't work: the enemy were backing into us, too . . ."

"Don't you have good officers?"

Newcombe eyed his father in surprise. "Good officers? Lord God, I don't know. Same as everyone else, I suppose . . . No, I'll take that back: the idiot we've got for platoon leader takes the peach preserve. He's the silliest, most pompous jackass I've ever run across. He thinks he's the Latin Lover or something: direct descendant of Valentino—he's actually been heard to declare he's irresistible to women . . . Old Herron's all right, I guess."

"Who's he?"

"Our colonel. He's a frosty old bear but he's okay, I guess. They say he was terrific on Guadalcanal."

"Have you heard anything about the officer training?" his father asked.

Newcombe looked away, shook his head quickly. Ah. Here we go. Talking too much. Talk too much you talk yourself right into a cul-de-sac.

"Have you got in touch with Major Marrill?"

"No, I haven't."

"You shouldn't let something like that slide, Alan." His father's lips were compressed in poorly concealed annoyance. "He told you he'd—"

"I know. I haven't had time for it."

"Well you must have time after you're off duty, don't you?"

"I honestly don't think there's much chance, Dad. Really. I think what Pearson said was final and I ought to let it go at that."

"You can't know till you've tried every available avenue, Alan. There's no reason at all why you shouldn't be an officer. You could get a waiver on that eye. He told me personally he'd be glad to do whatever he could—"

"I think we ought to drop it, Dad," he said sharply, raising his voice. "Let's drop it."

"Certainly," Amory Newcombe said in a quick, hurt tone. "I was only trying to be helpful, that's all." He rose, his face strained, and walking to the front windows stood looking out, hands behind his back, eyes sightless and blinking; bit at the underedge of his mustache.

Newcombe sipped again at his glass. "Let's leave it in the lap of the gods," he said. "Along with the fate of several hundred million others . . . Leave it up to the old thunder-darter himself," he added in a faint attempt at levity; glanced at his mother. "Things *seem* to be pretty much in the lap of the gods these days. Truth to tell."

Meeting his eyes his mother smiled—a nervous, unhappy curving of her lips; her soft brown eyes passed grieving from father to son, son to father. Watching her he felt all at once oppressed, and aimlessly contrite. Now you've done it, Newcombe: irreparably marred your return to the home front. This is no way to act. For pete sake: for Montezuma's sake: you're a marine, a two-fisted, hard-drinking, steel-chewing, hell-roaring leatherneck of a devil-dog—you ought to stiffen the sinews, summon up the blood, disguise fair nature with hard-favour'd rage, blow wind come wrack, what the hell, do you want to live forever?

Well. A little while longer, anyway. My wants are modest.

At any rate you're pretty high: oddly so . . . He felt with care the muscles of his cheeks.

"That blue car," Amory Newcombe said. He peered down through the curtains in rising irritation, absorbed. "That same damn blue car." Turning he walked quickly to the hall and called, "Channing?"

There was a pause and then footsteps came in soft, measured intervals from the kitchen to the front hall, and a solicitous, faintly mournful voice said: "Yes, sir?"

"Channing, would you find out the name of that idiot who keeps parking right in front of our front door?"

"Yes sir, I'll try. I didn't notice, sir."

"Or get his number and I'll report him to Callahan. Some people have about as much consideration as a hatrack. Has the paper come yet?"

"I believe so, yes sir."

"Never mind, don't trouble to come up. I'll get it." He ran erectly down the stairs.

Newcombe looked moodily at his feet. Across the heavy-napped green wool of his trousers the last pale distillations of sunlight fell in thin columns. He felt warm and indolent and drowsy, almost drugged. In the stillness the motes were like time sifting, drifting, nearly standing still . . .

"We have tickets for Casadesus on Sunday," his mother said. "Perhaps you might like to hear him."

He raised his eyes. "Casadesus?"

"Yes . . ."

She was regarding him steadily again—that sweet, affectionate, unbearable gaze: it stirred him into sullen anger.

"I don't know," he said. "I think there are some things I'd rather do."

"Of course, dear. It was just an idea, if you—"

"I haven't got too much time, you know," he added.

An unnecessary brutality: why had he said that? He saw her eyelids tighten with fear again, and repented, doubly chagrined. "Well—it might be fine, it's true," he went on with false, forced interest. "We heard him two years ago, didn't we?"

"Yes."

"He played that strange thing—that piece with all the furious dissonances. Who was it?—Hindemith? Tansman?"

She frowned faintly, stared off at the diffused mauve-and-amber light of the square. "I can't remember . . ."

They were silent, and again she looked at him, smiling awkwardly—and the weight of expectation in her eyes was so fervent, so intense it shook him. What *was* it she was asking of him? What expectation, in God's name? Expectation of *what*? An affectionate, burdensome demanding of him something he could not give—because he had never, for the life of him, been able to tell what it might be . . . He swallowed his drink and lighted another cigarette, hitching himself around in the chair.

Amory Newcombe came running up the stairs again, entered hurriedly holding the *Traveler* opened before him in both hands, like a ship's prow.

"Well, they've hit the Ruhr again," he declared in terse excitement. He seated himself in the chair near Alan Newcombe. "Two hundred Flying Fortresses. In one raid. What do you think of that?" He reached over and slapped his son's knee. "You old pessimist: always looking on the dark side of things. You wait. They can't stand up under this kind of pounding. They'll holler in no time. *Two hundred* Flying Fortresses! . . . It'll be over by next summer." He looked around brightly. "Want to bet?"

"Sure I'll bet."

"All right: what do you want to bet?"

"Fifty dollars."

His father glanced at him in surprise over the steel rims; thrust out his upper lip. "All right. It's a bet." His eyes ran racing across the span of newspaper, darting from column head to column head, pausing, darting on. "They can't stand this pasting the air force is giving them. Why, their aircraft plants, their factories, their heavy industry—they simply won't be able to stand up under it."

"Wouldn't you?" Newcombe asked him quietly.

"Wouldn't I what?"

"Stand up under it?"

"I tell you they can't, Alan," his father said with impatience, thrusting his neck about inside his collar; his lantern jaw flexed, flexed again quickly. "They haven't even *begun* to feel it. Why, we're sending planes over there in swarms. With Italy out of it now, and Rommel taken care of, and Russia building up her war potential—it won't be long now before they'll *have* to call it quits . . ."

Sitting deep in the chair Newcombe gazed vaguely at the Allenby portrait of his grandfather at the far end of the living room, still half listening to his father's words, feeling the crisp, vigorous, unbounded optimism coursing through them, virile and certain. It was another world from the one he knew—the world of the Allenby portrait was what it was, actually: the world of the simple, impulsive phraseology of

Dewey at Manila Bay, of Teddy speaking from the porch at Sagamore Hill—even some of the earlier, less flamboyant yet more implacable righteousness of Emerson and Alcott. The big picture: the neat, remote, distant outlines of the long view . . . He thought all at once of the morning of June 22nd two years ago down at the Marshfield's house, a Sunday morning, with Iris and Ted playing croquet on the bumpy, sloping lawn below the verandah.

"Alan!" His sister's angular white face, rapt and imploring. "Oh, he's—oh! *Look* what he's done!"

The thick, sodden *pock* and the croquet ball bouncing away over the grass and Iris shouting, "Mean! Mean! Did that just to be *mean*—" beating at Ted's impervious back and arms; turning to Newcombe again, gesturing wildly with the croquet mallet. "Honestly! Aren't you going to help me beat this mean, dirty-playing—"

"Sock him out of the lot," he'd called laughing from the verandah. "Come on—you can do it to him, too . . ."

"Fine brother you are!"

It was then that the screen door had banged and his father had hurried out on the verandah holding the copy of the *Herald* in both hands.

"Well, they've gone in," Amory Newcombe had said. "The Russians are in it."

Turning, Newcombe saw the stark, black, staccato hieroglyphs of the headlines: NAZIS INVADE RUSSIA. *Thousand Mile Front Aflame.* Beyond his father's close-cropped silver hair, beyond the green mat of the marshes the dunes lay in a long series of smooth, tawny mounds and slopes; and through a notch the water of the bay glittered and winked, and slipped sparkling away to the right. *Thousand Mile Front Aflame.* The flames had spread leaping, the dark lodestone had drawn nearer to them in a bound; chaos had taken a quarter turn.

"Well," his father had said with a strange, musing sense of finality, of satisfaction; he bit the underedge of his mustache, his eyes darting about. "The market will go up tomorrow."

He had turned toward his father slowly, in blank amazement. "The market will go up?"

"Well, that's just a surmise." Amory Newcombe had nodded to himself; his eyes pursued the wobbling, curving trajectory of a croquet ball over the sloping lawn, rested briefly on his daughter as she shrieked in mock anguish. "It's just a guess, of course. But I think it's right."

Later, joined in the game, tapping the red-striped ball through the spidery wickets Newcombe had felt burdened with the unhappy sense that he not only understood his father still less than he thought he did, but that he understood the whole world around him much less as well. Much, much less . . . How many people thought of that awesome, cataclysmic moment in terms of the stock market, or pay boosts, or increased consumer buying? The thought was like a raw easterly blowing through the porches of his complacency . . . Some weeks later, still goaded by that moment on the verandah, he had gone to Charlotte Newcombe and asked her what his father's attitude had been during the first war.

"Attitude?" she had said; she had looked at him reflectively. "I don't think he had much of any."

"Didn't have much of any!" he'd burst out. "Well, he must have felt *something* . . ."

"No, I don't think he did. It simply didn't concern him. Iris was a baby then, you see. And he was so involved with his business . . . I don't think he thought about it much at all."

Now, sunk fuzzy and lightheaded in the deep chair, he found himself listening to his father's voice with a kind of frank wonder. The pivotal moments in history. Such at least was history as old Gresham had taught it: the big picture, the portmanteau image, the long view. But in ditches and foxholes men—life-size men—cowered and flinched and quivered, flung themselves upon each other with screams and curses, lay sprawled in a welter of blood and shattered bones and pulp; and in the night wind letters, photographs of their loved ones blew blithely away. Ted was training in Texas now, would be flying with one of those swarms of Fortresses some night soon, staring into a dark shot through with drifting, bursting flashes, tracer streams . . . and would it still be swarms of Fortresses then? Would the market probably go up? Probably.

He looked over at his father's firm, bony, energetic face as though he were appraising him for the first time. Between their two chairs a monstrous chasm yawned away. Good God: his father might as well be wearing a horned helmet and bearskins and he himself a chiton and sandals. What the devil were they sitting in one room for? how had it ever entered their heads to be father and son to each other? Almost against his will he felt himself invaded by the old, familiar, all-pervasive exasperation—felt rather than saw one side of himself leap up from his chair and bend down, ranting at his father, waving

his fingers in his affronted face: Do you think that kind of
talk makes any sense? any sense at all? Look: I've just come
from one of the places where the war's going to go on for ever
and ever, war without end amen, look, I've scrubbed urinals
with a toothbrush, I've walked and run and walked until I
reeled and staggered, I've wriggled under forests of concertina
wire while they fired machine guns inches over my trembling
head for hours and hours . . . do you think for one minute
that kind of talk cuts any ice with me—or anyone else with a
minimum amount of gray matter who happens to know what
the score is? Wise up: pull yourself together and get hep, for
pete's sake! Act your age. Nine. Or ten. Why not? You're
only old once.

But in actuality he said nothing, did nothing; merely sat
there feeling waterlogged, inundated with the overwhelming
sense of lethargy that always claimed him in this house, the
torporific burden of vested time—sat there nevertheless
quivering, almost starting with nervous irritability. Amory
Newcombe had returned to the officers' candidate theme
again—as he might well have known he would—was discoursing on the meits of Major Marrill, a fine marine officer,
how enormously helpful he'd been with Charlie Bulkington's
boy (a pill if there ever was one, whom the very combined
chiefs of staff couldn't have told where to find the can), if
Alan would only look him up now, it was simply a case of getting in touch with him *now* before it got cold, *now* while he
was still in their minds (and clear out of his own), why
probably the whole misunderstanding could be cleared up, he
certainly *should* be an officer, why should the matter of an
eye—

Ah, what a farce it all was—what a delightfully ridiculous
parody!—society and family and officer candidate school and
parental love and the wondrous, tenacious, doddering blindness of humankind! . . . The house is burning.—Really?—
Yes: the house is burning.—Oh: draw the curtain a little, will
you? Thanks so much.—Quite all right. Little more tea?—
Splendid. No sugar. Now: did you say the house—?

He leaped up from the chair, stood with his feet planted
wide apart, one hand gripping the back of his neck. His father
was looking at him in surprise.

"Excuse me, will you?" he said rapidly. "I think I'll go up
and rest for a while. I feel kind of weary." He peered with un-
due ostentation at his watch. "What time is dinner? Seven?"

"Unless you'd rather eat later," his mother said. "If you'd

like to get some sleep. You look as though you—''

"No, it's quite all right. Fine. I'll be down at seven.''

He turned from their mutually troubled gaze and fled from the room—ran against a tall, somber figure in the darkness of the hall and recoiled.

"Oh! Channing. How are you?''

"Why fine, sir.'' The butler's face cracked in a sere, courtly smile. "Good to have you home again.''

Alone in his room on the fourth floor he leaned his elbows against the bowed window casing and gazed at the stately façades across the square. In the soft, pearly dusk lights came on tentatively, like cats emerging; a candelabra descended the stairway of the house opposite with ghostly, rhythmic solemnity, was followed by Mrs. Perkins' white, ghostly face. Above the steep slate escarpment of the roofs the ventilators fluttered in the winter wind, swung their conical prows east, then north, then east again; and beyond them more lights glittered across the broad face of the Charles. He looked down. Below, almost directly below him, Sergeant Callahan passed with portly dignity beneath an iron-capped lamppost, encountered a hurrying, long-skirted, long-cloaked figure, touched two fingers to the visor of his cap. Ivy and brocade and time . . . Newcombe rubbed his hand back and forth over his forehead. The still, soft beat of the past pressed about him, throbbed in his ears . . . grew, changed rhythm, rose steadily into a muttering roar, climbing and straining—and raising his eyes he tracked the winking riding-lights of a heavy plane—what was it, a transport, a bomber?—crossing from East Boston over the salt-shaker towers of Longfellow Bridge, heading southwest. Below its half-distinct, big-bellied form river and city and lights all seemed to tremble, to shiver momentarily—then, less easily, breathe again as the thunderous roar fell away to a throbbing drone, already tenuous and indistinct. Sicut patribus. All changed, changed utterly . . .

He pulled off his tie and unbuttoned his collar; crossed to the bookshelves and ran his eyes indifferently along the spines. Nothing. They understood nothing of him or his estrangement. His mother might as well be a Nereid, whose brilliant profile Hephaistos begged to translate into timeless alabaster. She could not hear him. And his father—!

But they were sitting below now, gazing at each other with

hurt and baffled eyes. Why had he raced off in anger, considering the circumstances? A gratuitous cruelty. Couldn't he realize they must have been waiting for this moment for months, with an apprehension which bordered on terror? What in God's name was the matter with him? He was home on furlough—a *shipping-out* furlough—something he himself had lain trembling on his cot and prayed and prayed for—why didn't it *mean* more? He was home—standing before his beloved bookcase in his room at home . . . why didn't the significance of this fact penetrate to the marrow of his bones, set him quivering with sheer delight?

On an impulse he went over to the little cabinet beside the bureau and opened it: two empty champagne bottles, their resplendent labels covered with scrawled signatures and drolleries; the heel of a bottle of Vermouth; and a fifth of Old Overholt, half full. He carried it with a highball glass to one of the crimson-upholstered chairs he'd had in his college room in Lowell House, and which his father had had before him, and poured out a generous drink. What the hell. Tomorrow he'd go over to Cambridge and look up Hallowell; and the next day drive out to the virginal halls of Wellesley and see Sue. For lack of anything better: for lack of anything.

4

HE SAW THE note the moment he swung the door behind him: propped up against the island of condiments in the center of the kitchen table, written in his aunt's beautiful, looping, Palmer-penmanship hand. He went up to it and leaning forward read it intently, snuffling from time to time, holding a thumb to one nostril.

Dear Jay—
  I am down at the shop, be home at five. Charlie probably around six. There is a coffee cake in the top of the bread tin and some hard boiled eggs in the

*refrigerator if you're hungry. Very very glad to have you
home again, dear. See you soon, love,*

Aunt Grace

*Don't touch the orange cake, it's for the children when
they get home.*

O'Neill set the note down and looked around. The linoleum
on the floor was frayed through around the sink and stove in a
maze of cracks and blisters like the surface of the moon; there
was a steady whine from the refrigerator in the corner, and
across the room the radiator emitted its interminable, calamitous, scraping clatter at ten-second intervals.

"Buck 'n' Bubbles," he snorted and shook his head,
"Bleeding Buck 'n' Bubbles act. If I ever."

He went to the bread tin, lifted the top and took out the cof-
feecake and cut a slice from it, poured himself a glass of milk
and sat down, staring around him absently. The window
above the radiator was soaked in steam and the curtains, a
frayed gray gauze, hung wearily, as though enervated by the
thick damp heat. On the chair across from the one in which he
was sitting a coat of his uncle's hung, black and gaunt and
threadbare. "The black hand," he said aloud, staring at it.
"Old Man Mose." Beyond it he encountered a faded sea-
green housecoat hanging from a hook on the back of the door
into the hall, and his lips puffed in disgust. "Couldn't even
buy her a new one." He wagged his head solemnly, chewing
on the cake. "Hell no: she hasn't worn it ten years yet. Like
cutting off his arm . . ."

Leaning back, he surveyed the room through half-closed
lids. "The old homestead," he proclaimed. "The old 'appy
'omestead. Looks like it's on its last wheeze . . . Well, that's
how it goes. Far be it from me—" Jumping up, wiping his
mouth with the back of his hand he burst all at once into song:
"*How* I love ya, *how* I love ya, mah—deah—ol'—*homestead*," in a metallic quasi-Jolson inflection, slipped into a
soft-shoe routine across the room to the sink where he rinsed
his glass. The left-hand faucet was swaddled in a great fist of
friction tape and copper wiring, like an outrageously swollen
joint, through which water had found its way in a steady running drip; when he turned it on his shirt-sleeve was sprayed by
several minute jets. "Look at that," he muttered. "Just glom
on to that. Well, of course: he can't soil his *hands*. Not the
kind of work *he's* doing."

His face a mixture of indifference and scorn, he went on

shuffling, singing down the dark hall to his old room—
stopped abruptly on the threshold and peered in astonishment
at the litter of trucks, dolls, comic books, tricycle parts, ray-
guns and miniature baby carriages strewn everywhere.

"Well, the punks," he remarked conversationally. "The
punks have taken over. When the rat's away the cats'll jump.
Man, I mean."

Filling his arms with toys he cleared the narrow cot and
threw himself down on it—stopped again, his eyes riveted on
an open comic book at his feet describing the hero's frantic efforts to escape from a horde of clamoring, voluptuous girls
clad in shorts and halters; he picked up the magazine and grew
still more amazed as he read on—learned that the hero did
ultimately get away, though at great peril.

"You simple tool," he said in indulgent contempt, his lips
curling. "You poor, simple tool. Don't know when you got it
made . . ."

He sailed the comic book across the room and looked at his
watch. Two-thirty. Too early. Wait an hour or so: keep it just
a touch on the casual side. "No more of this crazy-cat stuff,"
he said aloud firmly, reminding himself. "No more of that
hysteria. Easy does it." The lean, hard, quietly-embittered-
and-resigned combat marine. That's the ticket . . . and
relaxed, eyes closed, he felt his face settle in an attitude of
heroic, mournful resignation. There was no rush about it at
all. She'd been waiting around for months and months,
everybody gone, sitting on her fanny and palpitating: she
could wait another hour or so.

"And for grope sake, O'Neill, *be cool*," he admonished
himself. "Take it easy. You've got five days. Remember that,
now: *five days*. Be—casual."

An hour of shut-eye would be the routine. He was suddenly
immensely tired—as though the field problem and the interminable, cramping train ride had caught up with him in a
rush. An hour of sleep and then shave and off to battle. Off to
the front. This tickled him immoderately and he chuckled, settled his head on the pillow and closed his eyes again. He was
reminded for no reason at all of a dress Lorraine wore occasionally—an electric-blue dress which described a large,
bright yellow V, like an inverted chevron, at the exact point of
her pelvis. She had worn it that Labor Day night at the big
ballroom at the Totem Pole, with Ziggy Elman and Dorsey
and Buddy Rich high above them jamming away for hours
and hours on "Deep River," building it up steadily while all

the couples looped out and in and out again around them.
Wolfe and Hannon now and then flashing into view, all of
them stomping away to the pounding rhythm which rose and
rose until it was like a crazy fluid pumped into them all;
Lorraine's round face was bright and flushed, her eyes
sparkling, and he could feel the blood throbbing in his head
until everything blurred at the edges and faded out of sight
and nothing existed at all but his grip on her hand and the
fierce driving presence of the rhythm itself, the smash of brass
in riff chorus after chorus pouring over them, bathing them
all . . . In a transport of expectant tension he had led her
outside and they had floated rather than walked through the
warm night over a wooden bridge and under the birches where
the lake glittered in the looping chains of lights from the
pavilion.

—*Oh Jay, oh, yes, Jay darling,* she was murmuring softly,
and he bore her off under the pines and slipped with her to the
mat of pine needles, spongy and firm in the dark. She drew
against him, her full, malleable body against his, she was
moving her hands over him with a marvelous, practiced deft-
ness that amazed him, her breath hot against his cheek, murmuring over and over again his name—

Lying half asleep on the cot he felt invaded by a warm,
dulcet pressure that stirred him, swelled to a somber ache in
his vitals; and for a few moments he lay without moving,
lulled by the voluptuous intensity of the sensation. Then with
a rueful smile he turned on his side and rubbed his nose with
one hand.

Dreamland. None of it had happened that way. Not a whit.
No. Her face had clouded with apprehension, she had thrust
him back protesting.

"No, Jay, honestly, no really, please don't—"

"Ah come on, come on," he had urged, straining, holding
her.

"We *can't,* Jay . . ." Her breasts were heaving and her
voice was rough and unsteady. "You know we can't—"

"Why not?"

"Because we *can't* . . ."

But she was trembling, and he drew her back to him. Lurid
phrases from movies and magazines swooped and dived
through his head and he said, "But I'm crazy about you,
baby, you know that, we need each other, we *do,* this night
was *made*—"

"Oh, Jay—*please*—" and there was an element of

desperation in her voice that made him jubilant, "I just—*can't* . . ."

He slapped his thigh, snorted, threw one arm over his eyes and rolled over on his back on the narrow, squeaking cot, his lips still curved with the rueful smile.

For then, right then when she'd been faltering in his arms, when her lips trembled against his throat and she clung to him, swaying, for support—right then he'd uttered that idiotic remark which had ruined it all: that one cockeyed, japing phrase which had blown the whole ball game wide open.

"I bet your pants are dirty!"

What in the name of pete had made him say that? The appeal of its utter implausibility—or perhaps its plausibility after the hours of violent dancing in the long, hot hall: it had flashed into his head and out again like a ridiculous, gilded balloon and he'd said it before he'd even thought . . . Why did he do things like that? It always cost him. Always. The Celtic madness, Newcombe called it. Old Newk, he thought with a quick little rush of affection; old Newk sitting calmly in a coach seat—nearly at Boston now—jiggling to the *lackata-whunk lackata-whunk* of the train, reading one of those tongue-twisting, high-wire tomes of his: *Beyond The Infernal,* by Percival Pleasuredome. Now and then looking up, gazing with distant, gray-blue eyes at the dead, bleak winter fields. Or maybe he was already home. A mansion on Beacon Hill and living parents who wrote him all the time, sent him a constant stream of socks and sweaters, fruit cakes, chocolate creams—which he shared casually enough with the rest of the squad . . . Well, he was all right. He had that sour-ball blue-blood Boston streak but he was okay. And half the time he was right. *Women are creatures of decorum, Jay. No kidding. Love is real and love is earnest: the illusion will be main-tained—you know what I mean? Or else. You've got to curb that Celtic madness of yours or you'll wind up like John the Baptist.*

Well: things would be different this time. He was a lean, mean, hard-bitten, disillusioned gyrene—right? Right. He was shipping out. This was it and no mistake. Pick up the old receiver and play it suave, almost reluctant.

—*Oh, Jay! Are you home?*

—*Bad-Penny O'Neill, they used to call me.* (Take a two-beat.) *I happen to be featuring a couple of days between trains.*

—Oh! How are you?

—Just fine and dandy. A little weary. (Take a three-beat. Then:) *How about our going hi-de-do somewhere tonight? I'd—I'd kind of like to take a last look around. . .*

That would do it. Hold that and see what she says, play it from there. That was the ticket . . . Oh Lorraine, Lorraine, how have you been able to torment a guy for so many years? Miss, please have some pity: with those dancing eyes, that high, bubbling laugh, those full round breasts—when you spin in the lindy and your skirt swirls to the right, and left and right again, and those swelling, nyloned thighs flash and flash and dazzle me . . .

With a sigh he shifted his position on the cot, eased his shoulders where the pack-straps had chafed them, and sank toward slumber; evoked again the image of Lorraine lying beside him in wild abandon, passionate, disheveled, moaning her love—

He felt crushed by something, heard cries and laughter and felt something thump him in the ribs—sat up with a start to find two little bodies squirming over him, clinging to him, pounding away and shouting.

"The punks!" he cried. "You crazy little punks!" Half awake he clutched at them as they squirmed over him, finally pinioned first one wriggling body then the other under each arm, and pressed them against his sides.

"There. Give up?"

"No!"

"Okay . . . Give up?"

"Yes, yes!" they squealed.

He lifted them so they were each sitting on one of his knees and looked at them with a black scowl he couldn't maintain.

"What do you mean waking me up that way? Out of a sound sleep?"

"He did it," Allie said quickly; she touched the end of her nose with the tip of her tongue.

"No—*she*! she did it," Bobby said. Grinning at each other and then at O'Neill they pointed.

"Got to show some respect for your tired old uncle."

"Hey, will you help us build a boat?" Bobby said.

"Sure."

"How long are you going to be home?" Allie asked.

"Five days, almost."

"Oh, that's a long time!"

"Sure it is."

"Are you AWOL?"

"AWOL! No—of course I'm not AWOL!" He looked at her. "Who said that to you?"

She paused. "Daddy did."

"Oh he did, did he—well you tell Daddy when I'm AWOL from this lash-up he'll know all about it."

"How'll he know?"

"How?" he scowled ferociously at her. "Because I'll be breathing fire and brimstone. I'll be tearing up trees with my bare hands."

"Your *bare hands*!" they cried.

"That's right. I'll be pulling up the sidewalk squares along Harbor Street and stacking 'em like flapjacks. And then I'll take off like a great ruffed bustard."

"Where to?" they shouted.

"Why, straight for Saskatchewan, and Valparaiso. Where do you think? And the tundra."

"And Tierra del Fuego!" Allie said.

"Sure." He pinched her in the side and she squealed. "What do you know about the Terra del Fuego?"

"We had it in geography. It's way down at the tip end of South America and it's ringed all around with fire . . ."

"Wow. How do you get to it, then?"

"I don't know." She giggled merrily. "You *run* through it, I think."

"Oh."

"I don't really remember. It's very cold, though. In spite of the fire . . ." She paused, put her hand demurely to the back of her head and fluffed the edge of her reddish-gold hair. "How do you like my hair this way?"

"Swell. It's really groovy." Her face was sharp and angular and alive, her eyes a bright blue; Bobby had taken after Charlie, God help him, but Allie was slim and bright and Irish, like Aunt Grace. Maybe his mother had looked like Allie when she was eight . . .

He glanced at his watch, slid the kids off his lap and stood up.

"Where you going?" they called.

"I've got to make a phone call. And I don't want any horsing around until I'm through. This is serious."

He dialed the number with exaggerated punctilio, muttering to himself firmly: "All right, O'Neill. Tall in the saddle, now. Cool on the draw." He listened nervously to the idiot-whine of the phone ringing and ringing. Nobody home? Impossible.

Unthinkable. Well: three more, for luck.

At the next ring the line clicked and the heavy voice of an older woman answered.

"Mrs. Tyler? Is Lorraine home? This is Jay O'Neill."

"Oh, Jay! Hello. No, I'm awfully sorry. Lorraine's down in Washington."

"Washington!"

"Yes. She's got a war job down there. She begged and begged us to let her go and do her bit and finally we let her. I know she'll be awfully sorry to miss you. Are you home on leave?"

"Yes, that's right." Holding the phone loosely he gazed, slack and disconsolate, at the wallpaper's unending pattern of roses-in-diamonds; moved the edge of his shoe back and forth in a groove in the floor, hearing Mrs. Tyler's rich, melodious voice—Lorraine's voice half an octave lower—rambling along.

"Well thank you anyway, Mrs. Tyler . . . Yes, fine. Thanks . . . Yes . . . Goodbye."

He banged the phone in the cradle and slapped his knees. "You see?" He gestured toward the frayed and faded housecoat. "This is what comes of babes not answering letters written to them for months by their heroes who are going out to die for them in a matter of hours. D.C.! Of all the stupid dodges: of all the numb routines. She could have done her bit by answering a Goddamn letter once in a dinosaur's age . . ."

He sank into a chair and pondered moodily, examining his fingernails.

"Jay!"

The two heads popped around the corner of the bedroom door and he waved them back. Picking up the phone again he dialed a less familiar number still more slowly, was greeted by another heavy voice. God! Another mother.

"Mrs. Howell? Is Ginny there?"

"No, I'm sorry. Who is this?"

"This is an old friend of hers, Mrs. Howell. Jay O'Neill."

"Oh, yes. You're in the marines, aren't you?"

"Yes, that's right." He grinned through his teeth. "The marines."

"Yes, of course. Reason I asked is Ginny's been gone for a long time now. She joined the Waves, you know."

"Oh. Really? That's a shame."

"What?"

"I mean I was hoping to see her. I'm only home for a few days."

"I see. I guess *you're* surprised! Yes, she joined right after you left."

Mrs. Howell's voice hurried along, vastly amused, and it nettled him. He thanked her curtly and hung up, stood with his shoulders hunched and his hands in his pockets in the middle of the sitting room.

"Lots of mothers." He pursed his lips. "Man, the old mothers are really fighting this war . . . Well, that's how it goes. S—O—L, to quote the bard. Hitting eighteen: what I mean." He walked down the hall to the bedroom to get his blouse.

"Jay," Allie said, "where you going now?"

"Where am I going? I'm going down to Moran's and have a swifty or two."

"Oh." She looked up at him in entreaty. "Will you help us make a boat?"

"Sure. Some time soon. I told you I would."

"Wouldn't you just—you know . . . get us started off?"

He took the long square piece of wood out of her hands. "White pine." He pressed his thumbnail into the grain. "Good piece. Where'd you get it?"

"Over at McKelvy's. It was just lying around."

He looked at Allie again, slipped his knife out of his pocket and sat down on the edge of the bed. "All right. What'll we make?"

"A pirate ship."

"All right. What'll it be?—a lugger, a proa, a felucca, a catamaran?"

They laughed, gazing at him earnestly, repeated: "A pirate ship!"

"All right. We'll make us a catamaran."

As the knife-blade began to raise long slivers from the block of pine his features slowly relaxed into an easy, preoccupied smile.

He flung himself upward and out, uncoiling with a snap, rejoiced as his body hung arched in space—broke the pale green stasis of the pool in a clean *schloop* and soared, waterborne now, held in the cool, pleasant shock of the water; lifted through the translucent green, kicking automatically, and fell into the lazy, lifting rhythm of the crawl, laved in the first moments of unfatigued delight: the most complete

homecoming of all, in this element which was all one and yet
dispersible—he had marveled at it even as a little child,
squeezing it in his hands and crowing—which could act like
concrete or a gauze veil, which he could not live in but which
never failed to sustain him—which bubbled and boiled and
washed against him, enclosed his stretching body in its sliding,
shifting viscosity: the ludicrous, simple, unanalyzable miracle
of water which always made him want to shout with laughter,
with irrepressible exuberance whenever he first entered its
world . . .

Pete Harcourt was standing at the pool's edge watching
him, studying him intently, motioning with both hands;
caught in the flash of vision permitted by the snatch-breath he
looked like a caricature in a badly spliced film—a nearly
naked frog reaching out and down, arms rotating in odd
gyrations, arching his bald round head, waggling it and
calling something. O'Neill was seized with a fit of laughter,
felt bubbles boil past his cheeks, inhaled some water and
coughed; taking the turn open he rocked his head in to the
wall, flopped over and thrust away mightily, shot in perfect
silence through the dreamy water. Pete was calling something
to him again but he paid no attention now, traversed the
length of the pool again, pulling harder, thrashing, gained
speed, hit the turn and came down the lane all-out, the broad
black line below unfurling like a smooth ribbon, slapped the
wall and stopped. His head was pounding wildly. He took
some water in his mouth, bobbed his head backward a few
times and rolled over lazily, wringing his arms and legs,
pushed over to the ladder and climbed out panting; grinned at
Pete's round and earnest face.

"Great shape, aren't I, chief?"

"You're pulling up short, Jay." Crouching from the waist
Pete rotated his heavy, flabby, old swimmer's arms. "You're
recovering too soon."

"I know: I'm all tied up. My wind's all right but I'm all tied
up like a pretzel." Bending loosely from the waist he touched
his toes with his fingertips, finally bounced down and slapped
the floor with the palms of his hands. "Look at that. Haven't
been in the water for eight months, chief. Except the time I
fell off a rope in the obstacle course. Man, I hate those
things."

They walked together on the blue-and-white tiles toward the
office, O'Neill rubbing his face and head with a towel. From
one of the far lanes a stocky figure riding a kick-board called

to him and squirted a plume of water between his teeth, and O'Neill waved back.

"That's Johnny Kresnich," Pete said. "Frank's kid brother."

"Yes: I know him."

"Going to make a good sprinter, I think. Gets off the mark quick as anybody I ever saw. But his turns are bad."

The walls of the little office were covered with snapshots, flash-bulb photos, clippings framed and unframed: silk-suited figures hung extended over slick, still water like luminous oil or crouched, tensed, expectant, their arms back and slightly raised, at the pool's edge. At the end of the wall nearest the door O'Neill, drying his body absently, stopped in front of one of them, beheld himself laughing, his arm around Tim Aherne, drops of water glittering on their bodies, the lights above their heads like rows of moons.

"Hey, wasn't that the night though, chief?" he said, smiling in dreamy recollection. "Hey, I was a five-alarm fire that night, eh? Yeah, we really fooled 'em."

"You sure did. Me included." Pete Harcourt shook his bald head incredulously. "Going out like that. Fifty-five hundred on the way to a quarter mile! You scared me half to death."

"It worked though: didn't it? Didn't it? And that Crankshaft or Crankscrew or whatever his name was fell for it like an old hound-dog."

"Croonquist. Only because he lost his head. You guys were lucky."

"Psychology, chief. We used psychology on him."

"Psychology my foot. He knew what he could do in the quarter."

"Sure he did. But we got so far *ahead* of him, chief. That's what did it: he began to worry in spite of himself. 'Will I have enough left to catch 'em? Am I off my game tonight?' You know: that little old element of doubt. That's what tied up old Crankshaft."

"Croonquist. You guys drove me nuts that night. You and Timmy. Jumping like that in the relay—"

"The hell we did!"

"You left early. Both of you."

"They didn't call it, did they? Johnson had his hand on our feet, didn't he?" Laughing, O'Neill thumped at the side of his head with one hand, danced about on one foot, then the other. "Look, chief: Timmy and I had it figured. We knew we'd have to shave it a little close if we were going to pull the relay out.''

"A little close." Pete swung the white plastic whistle at his neck round and round. "And I wonder why I'm bald as a cue ball at forty-three. You could have blown the whole meet."

"We'd have lost it anyway if we'd played it cozy, chief: you know that. Sometimes you got to take chances to win. You got to gamble . . . Where's Wally?" he asked suddenly.

"Caserta."

"What do you know. And Jack at Benning . . . Say, we'd have had a world-beater this winter, wouldn't we, though?"

Pete Harcourt's bland, full face sobered, began to tighten with excitement; he twirled the whistle faster, his eyes snapping. "Just one more year. If I could have had just one more year. We would have taken them all. Providence Boys' Club and Brown and Worcester: even Springfield. A perfect season . . .''

"That's right. You're right as rain, chief. A perfect season."

. . . And the now empty stands beyond the little glass-enclosed office were alive again, rising up tier on tier of faces, white shirts and the scarlet and lemon splashes of women's dresses; he heard again the cathedral-like stillness on the mark, the bright solemnity and tension, saw the starter leaning forward, heard the terse, quiet words: "On your marks—" and then the always unbelievably loud crash of the gun and up and out and the churned surf of water and the wall, and the roar rising and rising, the flash-caught glimpses of a face and an arm a yard or so away, and Wally at the turn in a warm-up suit leaning down, hands cupped to his mouth screaming *"Eight! Eight!"* and away again; the crowd-roar rising still higher, the face across the corks red with strain now, the eyes closed—and the boiling expenditures of all strength, all efforts in one last furious, gasping burst; and then the pennants of the tape and the faint pattering applause, strange and inconsequential after the roar and Tim's arm around his shoulder and the slow, seething world of the water laving him, buoying him up, washing everything lightly, laughing, full of soft rejoicing release—

Pete Harcourt was saying excitedly, counting on his fat fingers: "—and then I'd have had Wally for the butterfly and Jack could have doubled in the backstroke and you again with Tim in the quarter—"

O'Neill threw down the towel.

"Hey! Where you going?"

"Another swifty," he called over his shoulder, raced along the tiles and up on the mark, took a high, ludicrous jacknife of a dive, rose slowly and began lazily stroking down the still pool.

Along Harbor Street the air was biting, and his sniffle came back. The hair at the base of his neck was still wet, and stung with cold. The old easterly. Below him the wind piled waves against the sea wall, flung them in a surging, rolling crest of water; and he felt the blown spume drift back lightly to his face, salt and fine. Out in the channel three boats pulled at their moorings, yawed and reared and plunged; their tarpaulins flapped and rippled in the bursts of wind.

He stopped and watched one of them, a black-hulled sloop. Going to get me one some day: thirty-foot ketch like the one Wally had, go down the inland waterway and sail all through the Caribbean, all those pirate lairs—Tortugas and the Silver Bank and Flamingo Cay and Miraporvos Island, take a long swim every now and then, catch your own fish as you go, just cruise along . . . Man, that was fun the time we went to Block Island. Blowing a gale, all of us hanging on the rail, heeled way over, just hanging on, soaked to the bone, everybody laughing like crazy; and then we went ashore on that deserted island, little bleached hump of sand and witch grass and piles of lumber washed ashore. And Wally holding up an oar, taking possession. *I hereby christen this place Great Hannon Island . . . and hereby take possession in the name of Queen—Eleanor!* Sitting around the fire later drinking beer and doing imitations, and Wally did that one on Maurice Chevalier and Milly Carens did one on—

Milly Carens!

He stopped suddenly, slapped his thigh and broke into a laugh. Of course. Of course! Any port in a storm. Any storm in a port—conversely, as old Newk would have it. Milly-Dilly Carens. Sitting in the front row at the pool on meet nights, little hands gripping the brass railing, her mouth open, little round headful of curls bouncing around. You could have made out with her any night of the week if you hadn't gone chasing the will-o'-the-wisp through the swamp fire. O'Neill! Do you hear me?—you ninny? All right, lad. Never too late. Hope springs eternal.

He hurried along, turned the corner on to Olivier Street, saw the lowercase sign *holiday music shop* and moved toward it with a jaunty stride, snuffling, thumb plugged against his right nostril; stepped inside and moved toward the counter. She was there: he watched her turn and recognize him with a little silent cry of surprise, saw the over-broad mouth break into a scarlet, over-broad smile.

"Jay! When did you get home?"

"Just yesterday."

"I'll bet you're a happy cat!"

"Off and running." He rested his elbows on the counter and slouched forward over it. "What's with the beat, sugar?"

"It's buzzin', cousin. I mean. Want to buy a record rack? Want to buy a fabulous secondhand portable? Magnavox."

"Sign me up. It's pocket-size, I trust."

"Not yet: we're working on it." She blinked at him in surprise, her short curly hair bouncing about. "Aren't you still at New River?"

"One-night stands only. I'm hitting the trail, podnah."

"Overseas?"

"New location: everything—must—go . . ."

He gazed with what he felt certain was a commanding devil-may-care into her narrow, angular, wedge-shaped little face, her over-small blue eyes—was conscious of a rising sense of disappointment. Now Lorraine—if this were Lorraine, standing here, leaning toward him . . . He became aware of the thump of a rhythm section, the thin, frenetic shriek of a trumpet in the upper register, racing off into nothing.

"Who's that?" he said, tossing his head toward the booths.

"Lunceford. 'Yard Dog Mazurka.' " She brightened all at once. "Have you dug Erskine Hawkins' 'Bear Mash Blues'? It's solid-old-man. What I mean." Throwing her pelvis forward slightly she swayed, squeezed her long-lashed eyes shut and emitted a thin, nasal, crooning hum; paused after a few bars. "Mmmmm: it's way out there . . ."

When she opened her eyes again he leaned forward a bit farther and said, "How about moving out with me tonight? Can you see it?"

Her face gleamed with delighted consternation. "Oh Jay—I couldn't!" she cried.

"Why not? I only got a day or so more, and then I've got to take off like a purple emu. No guff. Across the blue Pacific."

"I can't, Jay. Honestly."

"But why not?"

"Well, I'm engaged now. See?" She extended imperiously a thin, freckled hand; the third finger was adorned with a tiny gold band on which were mounted several pale blue pin-points. "Three months ago."

"Well. Congrats," he replied hollowly. "Who's the lucky victim?"

"Oh, you . . . You don't know him. He's not from this miserable dump, I'll tell you that."

"Can't blame you there. Pawtucket, I suppose?"

"Don't be silly." She paused, said loftily: "He's from Muncie, Indiana."

O'Neill was taken with a violent fit of laughter.

"What's the matter?" Her eyes narrowed accusingly, all lashes. "What's such a riot about that?"

"Nothing, nothing," he protested, coughing, laughing, wagging his head. "It just—it just happened to get me where my craw sticks. Sometimes. Fellow in my platoon from Muncie. Stuff like that. I'm sorry, I really am. I just happened to think of something. No kidding, that's wonderful," he said. "When's the big day?"

"Oh, not for a while yet, I guess. Bill's at Devens."

"I see."

"He doesn't want to get married until he gets his commission."

"Oh." He stared at her in strained gravity, then bent forward over the counter again. "Come on down to Moran's with me for an hour or so. Can't you? Bill wouldn't mind. Why hell, we'd get on fine if we knew each other . . ."

"Well, it's a good thing you don't."

He grinned. "No, just for old times' sake. What do you say?"

She peered wistfully at the street outside. "Well, maybe . . . No, I can't, Jay. I really can't."

"Say, remember that time we went to Block Island—Wally and the whole crowd of us? I was thinking of it just coming over here. Remember when we were doing imitations and singing? around the fire?"

"*Do* I! Solid-old-man. Was that fun." Her forehead contracted into a series of tiny ridges. "Funny: it seems so long ago, doesn't it? It was only summer before last . . ." She brightened again. "Gee, that was a kick, wasn't it?"

"Yeah. We used to have a lot of fun together . . . Come on, sugar," he said softly, leaning still nearer. "What do you say? . . ."

For an instant she gazed at him directly from under her

brows—a look he remembered from high school; emitted a
slow, faint sigh. "Oh, Jay," she said awkwardly. "Why
didn't you let me know a few things?"

"Well, I just got away yesterday: I didn't know—"

"I didn't mean that." She shook her head all at once; the
forest of little blond curls waggled wildly about. "No, I can't,
Jay."

"Come on. Just a few beers and a little dancing. To
celebrate Bill's getting his commission."

"No humor."

"I'm sorry . . . No, but how about it?"

"No, I really can't, Jay. I mean. Please don't crowd me.
Please."

Her narrowed eyes, the tone of her voice were suddenly
suppliant and unsure; and staring at her O'Neill felt curiously
saddened. He straightened, thrust the barracks hat back on
his head.

"Okay," he said lightly. "You're the doctrix. Maybe I'll
give you a ring before I take off, okay?"

"Fine, swell, Jay."

"Let me latch on to that Hawkins, will you?"

"Sure. See you."

"See you."

He slipped into one of the soundproof booths, set the
record on the turntable, ran his thumb deftly under the needle
to clear the tip, and put the top down. The raucous, pulsing
music enveloped him, mounting—stilled all at once: a tenor
saxophone glided into the aperture with cool, syrupy woman-
tones, slipped gelatinously around the blues phrase. Milly was
at the far end of the counter, filing some cards in a box; she
looked up and glanced toward him inquiringly. Raising his
eyebrows he nodded and made the Ballantine-sign with one
hand. The brass came in like a wall of hard sound and he
opened his coat and leaned back, resting his head against the
wall of the booth.

"Muncie, Indiana," he murmured. Bobbing his head to the
rhythm he smiled mournfully; then broke into a high cackling. "Muncie, Indiana! Hand me down my walking cane . . ."

5

THE LAND FELL away from the cabin in steep russet folds, swept plunging down and down, crisscrossed with foundering, mouldering stone walls, leaped a two-rutted card track and swept on until it was brought up sharply by the stand of sugar maples at the edge of the brook. On their right stood October Mountain, granite-shouldered, harsh as flaked flint, spotted here and there with juniper bushes like shaggy, crouching birds; and away to the north between two hills old Greylock loomed, massive and dark. The clouds had come out of Greylock the way they always did, thrusting layer on layer on a curving black funnel that fanned out until it swallowed up the sky. For one brief, final moment while they stood watching the sun burst through—a wild, vacuous, rolling eye; then the lumbering black clouds swallowed it up: a steely, pearled light without wind like a pause, a slow drawing of breath. And in the stillness the snow began to fall.

"It's snowing," Andrea cried, turning to him. In the colored stocking cap and ski clothes she looked like an astonished little girl. "It's really snowing!"

"Yes. Going to be a big one."

"Do you think so—this early? Oh, that'll be wonderful . . ."

Her face was glowing with delight. Kantaylis drew her to him and kissed her softly. Arms wrapped around each other they leaned against the porch railing of the cabin and watched the slowly falling, twisting flakes.

"I told you it would," he murmured in her ear. "Are you sorry?"

"About the snow? Don't be silly."

"We could still go in to Pittsfield if you want."

"Oh, no—this is wonderful." She looked around at the cabin, the long plunge of the hill. "I wouldn't ever have thought of this. How did you happen to?"

"That's easy: it was the first place I thought of. I used to come up here hunting with Ned and Frank Stacey."

"Oh. I bet you'd have liked to go hunting this time, too."

He shook his head, smiling at her. "No more hunting."

"Why?"

"No more." He hugged her to him, turned away. "I've got to get a fire going in there. It's cold as a tomb."

He walked with lithe purpose through the whirling snow

down to the shed. As he opened the door something scurried away near the end wall, and for an instant he paused listening, mouth open, the way he had as a child. Picking up the maul and two wedges and an axe he carried them around behind the shed where the wood was stacked. He rolled one of the oak logs away from the pile, studied both ends for a moment, critically, then turned it a little and put two smaller sticks under each side as chocks to keep it from rocking. Setting a wedge near one end he tapped it firm, then began to drive it in with full, powerful strokes; the iron fell on iron with a rhythmic *tink!—tink!—tink!* sharp and bell-like in the silence. He became conscious of the strange pressure of the wedding ring on his finger, drew off the glove and looked at it, smiled gravely. Through one of the cabin windows he saw Andrea moving about, still wearing the stocking cap with its bright red-and-yellow bands; that reminded him of how cold the cabin was and he picked up the maul again. When the first wedge was in to the head he started the second one, several inches farther along. After a dozen blows there was a groaning crack, then a series of popping sounds like a hurriedly tapped gourd; and all at once the wedge went in all the way with a sharp, ringing sound and the log split apart like a melon, its grain full of dull bronze whorls flecked with white. He stood for a moment looking down at it in satisfaction— then crouched over it all at once and pulling off his glove again passed his fingers along the whorls and ripples of the grain.

The snow fell in silence around him, lay on his hands and thighs in tiny jeweled constellations. In a pine branch above his head a chickadee declaimed its reedy, mock-plaintive melody of two notes, hung suspended, bobbing, pecking, upside-down; and watching it he nodded. Hunched over the split log he felt pervaded by a sense of tremendous serenity. At rest: he was at rest with things again, he was sinking gently, like a pebble dropped down a well, into the still sweet crystal water, was resting on the firm, clean sandy bottom with a few leaves, a dead beetle perhaps, some other white and black pebbles that had been dropped before him . . . He gripped the smooth, undulating wrinkles of the wood and again ran the palm of his hand over it lightly, an exorcising gesture: there was in the touch something of the warm shock of rediscovery at seeing an old friend given up for lost—like seeing Turk Farrell, say. But the image of Turk's thin face, gray-green and gaunt and remote, no longer living humanity, staring up from

the mud-spattered shelterhalf struck him with such clarity he
passed the heel of his hand over his eyes and nose.

". . . Well, Turk," he said in the stillness. *Hey now we got
ourselves into one fine old cool dee sack.* The slow, leanly
amused grin, the long lean muscular jaw like a horse's flexing,
flexing below the dancing hazel eyes. *Slimy end of the ba-ton,
what I mean* . . . Now he was mouldering in the rich black
muck, under this same crust of earth, ten thousand miles from
home: resting, too . . .

When he looked around again the ground was already white
and it was snowing harder—fine, dry flakes that stuck where
they landed, covered his old Bass boots while he stared at
them in quiet wonder. He stood up, shivering a little, stamped
his feet and picked up the maul. He split the halves, then the
quarters again, pulled a length of pine out from the end of
the pile and quartered and split that too, and choking up on
the axe handle began to shear off pieces for kindling. When
he had enough he selected one of the whole oak logs from the
top of the pile, swung it to his shoulder and started up the
slope, putting his feet down crabwise to avoid slipping.

Inside the cabin the air was hollow and cold, like a sea
cavern. Andrea had laid out all the utensils and condiments
and supplies they'd brought on the counter beside the stove:
arranged in a row they looked festive and preparatory.

"Will that burn?" she asked doubtfully, turning. "It's so
big."

"Backlog," he said.

"Dad always splits them up in pieces."

"You've got a furnace at home," he said, smiling. "This is
all we've got. It's going to have to go all night long." He
swung it to the back of the irons, wedging it against the heel of
the chimney. "The draft follows that, keeps it going," he
said, gesturing. "It throws the heat back into the room. You
keep building the fire against that."

"I see. It doesn't look as if it'll ever burn."

"It will, though: it's the only way to keep a fire going all
night."

"Oh lord, Danny—you sound like Grandma Abbott," she
exclaimed; shaking her head at him she laughed, went on in a
quavering falsetto: "There's only *one* way to do a thing and
that's the *right* way! . . ."

He grinned at her. "You wait and see. I'm the best
firebuilder in Berkshire County . . . Well: one of the best."

He built a layer of kindling over some old newspaper,

lighted it, added one of the split pieces when it got going, then another, stood watching it with his hands in his pockets. The fire hissed and crackled, and as the draft caught began to roar with a pulsing rhythm; and the warmth floated out toward their faces like a benign breath.

"Stay inside a while and get warm," she said as he started out.

"I've got to split some more wood," he said. "For the stove, too. Before it all gets snowed under."

"Have a cup of coffee first."

"All right."

She pulled the thermos out of the basket and poured them each a cup; and they stood by the fireplace sipping at it.

"You looked so tired, Danny," she said. She moved her eyes intently over his face. "Don't you get enough sleep at camp?"

"Never," he said. "Never enough sleep." He paused, added with a grin: "Glamis hath murdered sleep."

"What?" She stared at him.

"That's what Newcombe says every morning at reveille. A guy in my squad. It's from *Macbeth*."

"*Macbeth?*—the play *Macbeth*?"

"Yes. I think so. He's a poet. He went to college. He's always quoting all kinds of stuff like that. The day I went over—day I went on furlough he said *Put up your swords or*—put up your swords or something or other. They're all from the classics."

"You mean he goes around reciting Shakespeare all the time?"

"Well, you know: at some moment or other. And then he laughs this kind of dry laugh: damned if I can understand why . . ."

"That's funny. Who else is in your squad?"

He glanced at her, looked up at the split-beam rafters. "Oh, there's Jack Freuhof who was on Bougainville, and a couple of knuckleheads named Capistron and Helthal who are always getting into trouble with themselves and everybody else, and a quiet little kid named Connor who I think is under age, though I'm not sure."

"Under age?"

"Yeah. Fraud status. I'm not sure, though. And there's a rowdy character from Brooklyn named Ricarno who can't think of anything else except cards and women, and a crazy Irish mick named O'Neill who's always doing something screwy: you know, for laughs. He's from Rhode Island. Near Pawtucket. There's a whole lot of 'em. They're all a pretty funny bunch, I guess. Me included."

"You are not."

"Sure I am. We all are. It takes all kinds."

He stopped, watched the leaping flames from the fire glow and fade and glow again on her face. He placed his arms under her elbows and put his cheek against hers. "I love you, Andrea," he said. "I love you with all my heart."

"I love you . . ." she answered; but as she leaned back he saw a shadow pass through her eyes, a flicker of—what? apprehension? distrust?—like the shadow of a hawk slipping up a rock face. It startled him: all at once he felt as if he were seeing her from a great distance, almost unattainable, and the shadow in her eyes had fallen across her whole body in sliding, liquid patterns like the shadows from palm fronds, lianas, giant ferns . . .

"Oh!" she exclaimed suddenly, and gave a little jump.

A spark had shot out of the fire and lay on the bear rug at their feet: an angry eye of fire. Instinctively he reached down and flicked it into the fireplace again, all in one motion.

"Didn't you burn your hand?" she asked.

"Not a chance." He grinned at her. "Didn't have time."

He put another of the split logs on the fire and went down to the shed, felt with pleasure the dry creak of the new-fallen snow under his boots. He worked rapidly and steadily, the way he had afternoons after school, splitting a log and then carrying several pieces up to the cabin to pace himself. A sense of continuity seemed to flow out of his arms through the maul into the wood, into the winter earth; time expanded around him in the whirling snow, fanned forward and backward soundlessly until he was rocked in it, contained in it wholly, it was as though he had lived all his life up here at Ned Irish's cabin behind October Mountain, splitting wood and carrying it up through the dancing, whirling flakes to where Andrea was moving about getting supper ready. A pleasant weariness began to course through his arms and legs, a weariness whose sundered familiarity moved him; the cold stung his nostrils.

He had put the tools away in the shed and was just turning away when he saw the sled; and remembering he smiled. On an impulse he dragged it out, sat on it, pushed his feet against the bars. He felt the four wooden runners, slid them back and forth tentatively in the snow. It was just possible: there was already an inch or so. In the shed, half concealed on the narrow shelf made by the two-by-four cleat and the eave, beside the oilcan and the whetstones he found a cake of beeswax like a wizened, scoriated soapstone, brought it outside and began waxing the runners.

". . . Are you finished splitting wood?"

He looked up in surprise at Andrea's figure on the porch, waved to her.

"Hey: want to go for a slide?"

"What?"

He cupped his hands. "I found a sled. Let's go for a slide."

"Where?"

"*Where?* Right here," he shouted back. "Where do you think?" They were both laughing, leaning forward and shouting at each other through the snow.

"Is there really enough?—to slide?"

"Won't matter." He laughed, pointed on down the hill. "It's so steep it won't matter . . ."

She came down the slope running, slipped and sat down, slid several feet on her thigh; and his face grew long with concern.

"All right?"

"Oh sure. You must think I've become a softy." She jumped up smiling and came up to the sled. "What a wonderful idea! I didn't know there was a sled up here."

"Sure—we used to roar all the way down to the Post Road when there was snow enough." He put the beeswax in his pocket. "All right. Sit on behind me and hold on tight. Put your legs in close alongside mine. That's it. And lean when I tell you to. All right. Here we go—"

They rocked it into motion, started with a lurch, slowed, gained speed again. Junipers flashed by on either side; the air stung their eyes to tears.

"Too—fast!" Andrea's voice shrieked in his ear.

"We've just got *going* . . ."

They sank, rose, dropped with a clean lightness and swept on. A hump of granite loomed in their path like an animal asleep. *"Lean—left!"* he shouted, kicked the bar with his right foot and they swerved past it in a curving spray of snow, careened on down the slope. The slithering hiss of the runners, Andrea's wild laughter filled his being; shouting himself, his eyes blinded with tears he bore to the right, leaning, and they shot through the gap in the stone wall and down across the lower field, rising and sinking on the hummocks like a soaring bird.

"The brook!" Andrea was shouting between fits of laughter; her arms gripped his chest so he could hardly breathe. "The brook! The brook!"

"Frozen solid!" he shouted back.

"You—think—so!" she shrieked, and gripped him still tighter.

At the wide place it was always frozen: that was where they had always crossed. He steered farther left. They soared up over a mound, swooped down and across the flat, unbroken surface of the brook, crabbing on the slick, and up the far bank—struck a thicket and lurched up, tilted, tipped over, spinning, and rolled off and down the bank.

Laughing, Andrea scrambled to her feet. "You crazy—man!" As he got up she threw a snowball at him, made another hastily and threw that one too and hit him on the shoulder while he ducked. "You'!" she called. "You taught me!—how to throw—!"

He ran down the bank as she hit him again in the leg, the loosely packed snowball bursting like sparkling powder, lost his footing on the ice at the brook's edge and went lurching and sliding out into the middle, his arms flailing, until his feet went out from under him and he sat down in frank surprise, still sliding, while Andrea shrieked with laughter and kept pelting him.

"Sitting duck!" she shouted breathlessly, stooping, making more snowballs. "You're a sitting duck!"

It took him nearly a minute to get to his feet. Finally he made it and crept back over the ice and flopped on the sled, dizzy and out of wind.

"Gee, you were funny . . ." Andrea came over and sat beside him, panting, talking in bursts. "You looked—just like one of those contortionists—clowns at the Ice Follies. Honestly. Let's come down again."

"Sure."

"Soon as I get my breath, I mean . . . Look where we came," she said, pointing back.

Looking up the long slope they could see here and there their tracks where they had cut through to the bare, tawny winter ground—faint, swerving tracks like the tails of ferrets—on up through the gap in the stone wall and up to the clump of firs beside the shed; and above that the cabin where

purple smoke twisted away from the massive stones of the
chimney. In a crevice of the stone wall on the far side of the
brook a chipmunk watched them piercingly, askance; darted
away between two round gray boulders. The maples looked
etched against the bowl of the sky.

"I feel all alive again," Andrea said. "Don't you, Danny?"

"Yes," he said.

Her face, close to his, was flushed with excitement. A lock
of hair curled in against her throat, and snow crystals lay in
the corners of her eyes like tiny stars.

"It's lovely, isn't it?" Her breath came against his cheek in
hot little suspirations. "It's just as if—nothing were happening at all anywhere else. No war, no troubles, no anything.
Isn't it?"

"Yes, it is," he said. "That's just what it is."

The fire burned more heavily now, a vibrant roaring, and
the backlog had caught and emitted a steady thick hiss like an
angry reptile. The heat sank into the corners of the cabin—a
benign, invisible vapor that might have been distilled by the
soft glow of the kerosene lamp on the shelf by the stove.
Sprawled before the fire on the bear rug that was Ned Irish's
pride and joy, Kantaylis felt after the wood splitting and the
sliding pleasantly indolent and tired: the sensation of resting
at the bottom of a well persisted, lulled him. Cradling his head
in his arms he watched Andrea moving around the stove. She
had changed into a skirt and sweater, and her arms and face
and hair flashed in the light from the fire as she moved. Her
profile was outlined against the dark wall of the cabin and he
dwelt on it happily—the delicate, slightly turned up nose, the
faintly oriental cast to her eyes, the high forehead and cheekbones, the long, dulcet sweep of her cheek . . . His wife now:
she was his wife. To have and to hold, to love and cherish for
richer for poorer, till—

"Hey, you look awfully busy," he said.

She smiled at him—the quick, volatile smile that always
stirred him so tremendously, in which her face seemed to fill
with light.

"You look just the way you did the first time I saw you:
know that?"

"Oh no," she protested. "I do not."

"The first time I was interested in what you looked like, I
mean."

"When did you first notice me that way, Danny?" She put
down what she was doing and came over and knelt beside

him, her face bright and expectant. "When was that?"

"Oh, it was when I saw you twice in one day: you were sitting in the hammock with Marge Taylor when I was going to work. You were talking together and giggling, and then you said hello very seriously—and then you both burst out laughing again, right after I went by."

"We weren't laughing at you—"

"And then later you came in to see your Pa, and you were all worried and asked Carl Striebel where you could find him. You were all upset. I remember I turned around and looked at you and said hello. And you just nodded at me with that very worried look on your face—and then you smiled. You remember it?"

"Yes. That was when Mother was ill. Or said she was. I think she did it just to torment Dad. Honestly, she's beyond belief."

"That's all right, honey."

"No it isn't all right. Wouldn't even kiss you after the ceremony!"

"Well. Can you blame her?"

"Of course I can! . . . I can get along with her if I have to but I can't ever forgive her for the way she's acted toward you. Ever."

"Don't say that," he said. "Ever's a long time."

"I mean it. You don't know all the—"

"It's all right, honey," he repeated. "It doesn't matter. She wanted you to marry somebody—you know, like Phil Ainsley or Arthur Hale."

"Oh! *That* arrogant—"

"Well, somebody like that. Or George Holbrook."

"George Holbrook was killed. Did you know? In Italy."

"Yes. Nick told me. Truck backed over him. Tough break."

Her eyes flashed up at him. "What? But they said he was killed in action—by enemy action . . ."

"No. Nick said a friend wrote him how it happened."

"But that's what the—the dispatch said," she protested. "His commanding officer wrote Mrs. Holbrook a long letter."

He smiled at her gently. "Well. Maybe that's right. It doesn't much matter."

"What? Of course it does. Doesn't it matter?—how you die?"

"I used to think so. Now I don't so much any more. I think

it matters a hell of a lot more how you live."

"Oh that, of course . . ." And her face became grave and unhappy.

"Your Mama's all right," he said after a moment, watching her.

"You couldn't say that if you knew her the way I do."

"Maybe so. She's just mixed up, that's all. She sees you doing what she did and she's all upset about it."

"What do you mean?"

"Marrying down," he said simply. "She thinks she missed her chance in this world and she's all bitter about it."

"I suppose it's true, in a way. Don't you think so? What other chance has she had?"

"Lots. We've got lots of chance. All the time. We all do."

She turned her head and looked at him steadily. "You're funny, Danny. You really are."

"I guess so."

"You don't look at things the way other people do. It's as though you see everything from a different angle."

"Maybe so. I don't know."

"Yes, you do. Things like the future and jobs and things like that."

"The future," he said. Reaching up he moved his hand lazily through her hair, watched it glint in the light from the fire. "They're all too worked up over the future all the time. They miss all the important things. You know—they're always thinking about success or a raise or social climbing or the next vacation. Or whether their kids'll grow up to be a credit and an honor to them. They don't spend enough time enjoying the present." He stopped playing with her hair and looked at her directly. "Like this moment here with us. The moment right now: it's beautiful."

"Yes, but—"

"But what?" He swept one hand around him. "It has everything we could want, Andrea. Don't you think that?"

She stared at him a moment gravely, shook her head.

"Why? What more do you want?"

"I don't know. It just seems to me there ought to be more to it than that."

Abruptly she said: "You look just the way you did on the float at Lake Pontoosuc. Remember? That's when I fell in love with you: right then. Or began to, anyway. You were lying on the float and I thought you were Phil, that was why I splashed you. And you looked down at me so perplexed—as if you didn't know whether to be mad or laugh or what. Your hair was all matted and curly the way it is right now . . . Know when that was? July 28th, 1937.''

He smiled at her in disbelief. "How can you remember that?''

"I always remember dates, things like that. If something happens that I know is crucial—you know, really important—I say, 'This is July 28th,' or whatever it is. And I never forget it.''

"You're half elephant.''

"Oh, funny. At least I *remember*. You've got it all mixed up: it was two different days, when I was on the swing with Margie and when I went over to the mill.''

"No, it wasn't.''

"Yes it was because I went down to Springfield with Mother the next day. And the day after *that* she was sick.''

"You're mixed up.''

"No, I'm not. That was much later, anyway. I was already in love with you and you never knew it, you were so dumb. I was in love with you years before.''

"How could you expect me to, before that?'' he asked her soberly. "You were so scrawny. Your knees were all knobbly and your face was broken out—''

"That's not so—I didn't have knobbly knees—''

"—and your hair in a pigtail down your back like a Chinaman's—how can you expect a decent, self-respecting man to—''

"Self-respecting!''

"—sure, an upstanding—''

"Oh, you're crazy,'' she cried. "You're just a hopeless, dumb—loony—Greek!''

She pulled the cushion out from under his head and cuffed him with it. He caught at her and she sprang away, hit him again as he got to his feet, then leaped behind the table. For a moment they dodged from side to side, their eyes locked on each other, laughing soundlessly; then he leaped around the table and caught at her sleeve and missed, lunged out again and tripped on one of the trestle legs of the table and sprawled across the rug on his face and lay still.

Her laughter stopped on a gasp.

"Danny—'' she said. She stared at him an instant, then knelt beside him and put her hands to his head. "Danny— what did you—''

He seized her suddenly around the waist with both arms.

For an instant she gaped at him in amazement, then started struggling violently.

"You cheat!" she shouted. "Oh—! You mean, miserable, sneaking—*cheat*!" A moment longer she struggled against him, laughing and panting, while he gently, inexorably over-bore her; then she relaxed and lay back on the old moth-eaten bearskin rug. "You cheat," she repeated softly.

"Am I?"

"Yes." Her face was bright and glowing and alive, her breasts were rising and falling, her fine white nostrils distended; flames danced in her eyes from the light of the fire.

He leaned over and kissed her and she clung to him fiercely; for a moment they pressed against each other, gripping each other's back and shoulders. But when he placed a hand on her thigh she stiffened and twisted away from him and said, "Don't, Danny . . ."

"What's the matter, honey?"

"I don't know." She sat up, fingers to her forehead; and the shadow he had seen before swept across her face. "It doesn't seem right."

"But—" he was immensely bewildered, "—but we're married . . ."

"Yes." She gave a mournful smile. "At least we're legal."

"We're more than that, Andrea. We're married. We're a family, we're together in life . . . Don't you want to?" he asked her softly.

"Yes. I want to terribly . . . That hasn't got anything to do with it." She looked down. "I—we spoiled it all," she declared suddenly; and her face set in a stony, despairing expression that staggered him.

"No, we didn't—"

"Yes we did, *we did*," she insisted almost with desperation. "All for a few crazy moments. All for that!"

"Well, sure it was a mistake. I know that, honey: we should have got married back in August. I know that. I didn't think it was fair to you—"

"Fair to me! But look what happened—"

"I know, I know," he said, raising his voice; he paused again. "Look, honey: we've squared that now . . . I've gone to a good deal of trouble to make that good. Now let's go on from here."

"But it was *wrong*, don't you see? And now we've got to pay for it . . ."

"What do you mean, pay for it? Look, Andrea." He took

her firmly by the shoulders. "Look: we do a lot of wrong things in this world and we get away with them. We do a lot of things right and have to pay for *them,* too. Just as easy. Don't you see it doesn't matter? The thing is to take what you get and make something out of it."

"Yes, but getting married doesn't wipe it out. Society doesn't—"

"Ah—society," he said; and his face darkened. "Society says a lot of things. Society says a white man's better than a Negro. Society says the Abbotts are better than the Kantaylises, society says slobs can be generals—society says it's all right to kill people . . . under certain conditions. Society has a lot of answers. And then changes them around every five minutes to fit something else."

"Yes but what then, Danny?" she said. Her lower lip was quivering. "What is there to hold on to? What *is* there?"

Taking her hands he drew her close to him, still looking at her steadily. "Love between people, and the love of God. The feeling in the heart and soul. I mean it." He held her eyes with his. "That stands fast. That's the only thing they can't twist around and foul up and make into something else. Everything else slithers under your feet like mud."

She stared at him, said: "How do you know that?"

"I don't know: I just know it, that's all. That's the only thing that lasts."

"Oh, I'm so afraid, Danny," she said; and all at once the tears swam in her eyes.

"Afraid of what, honey?"

"Oh—of everything. I'm . . . I'm afraid we'll be punished," she said in a rush like an exhalation of air. "I'm afraid about you and the baby and the war—all I can do is pray and how can I pray if we sleep together just like any—"

"But why?"

"Because that was what made all the mess we're in . . ."

"We're not in a mess," he protested.

"Yes we are, we are—"

"No, we're not, Andrea . . ." In his urgency he shook her, said slowly and firmly— "We love each other and we're married and we're going to have a baby. What's so terrible about that?"

"But you've turned it all around."

"No, I haven't . . ."

"It was wrong, don't you see?—and how can we do wrong and pray for what's right?"

"Andrea—"

"The body made all this trouble—the body!" she cried, and broke down. "So how can I pray to God to spare your body, don't you see?"

"But the body—" he said.

He looked at her with apprehension; she was sobbing now, steadily, her hand to her mouth, and it struck him that she must have wept like this many times during the past year. "But the body," he repeated, wondering, staring at his hand. "But what about eating and hiking through the woods—what about sliding out there just now—that was good, wasn't it?"

"That's not the same . . ."

"Sure it is. Why isn't it? That was your body on the sled going through the snow, that was you laughing and hugging me, wasn't it? How can you separate it? It's all one: here we are, on this earth, and our bodies are what we've got to work with. That's what's got to carry us through. Do you want to do without your body altogether? You weren't meant to do that . . ."

She shook her head, weeping; shook and shook her head. "I don't know, Danny. I don't know. Maybe you're right. Oh, I'm so mixed up . . ." She reached out to him blindly. "Help me, help me, Danny, I'm so mixed up about this and I want to do right . . ."

He took her in his arms and rocked her softly to and fro while the fire hissed and soughed, and the floor and walls and ceiling cracked with the sudden strange heat. The fire threw their shadows against the far wall rippling, and above it the snow came in faint, stinging bursts against the window. Still he rocked her slowly, patting her in strange little rhythms until she stopped weeping and lay huddled against his shoulder in silence, staring at the fire.

"You've got it all fouled up, honey," he said after a time. "I know you have. The body isn't bad or good—the body isn't anything at all. The body's just a tool. Like an axe: you can use it to split wood to keep your family warm or you can lay a man's head open with it. It's what we do with it that's bad or good . . .

"I love you, Andrea," he murmured in the same deep, even, crooning tone. "You know I love you with all my might and main . . ."

He rose then and took her up in his arms gently, so gently that she was scarcely aware she was being lifted, and carried her over to the bed. Lying beside her he began to unbutton her sweater.

"Don't, Danny," she said, but she felt herself it was a protest without conviction.

"Yes," he said softly. "This is right, Andrea. This is right for us. And you know it is, too."

"I don't know . . ."

"Then trust me that I'm right, honey. Believe I'm right."

. . . He was near her; very near and she was trembling, not afraid but taut, rigid, caught up in an agony of remorse and desire. The harsh forms that had tormented her for years whirled repeatedly across her mind—a phantasmagoria of fears and admonitions and threatened vengeances like spidery, darting claws, and at whose vortex stood—she recognized it instantly—her mother's angular, wildly gesticulating image: a constriction that was like a bobbin in her vitals wound tight and knotted in a hundred places, so tightly snarled it was almost painful, it would be painful perhaps or at least distressing but there was no other way, it had to be, it was the only way to escape the fitful, darting grip of the claws, the piercing shapes that wracked her so, she must be *free* . . . and he loved her, her Danny, there was no doubt whatever that he loved her tenderly. In a little spasm she reached out and drew him down to her, felt strangely, ethereally invaded, replenished, replete, the tight burgeoning heightened still further in uncoiling rings, in swiftly seeping waves, rising, foaming with dulcet pressures, higher, fiercer, almost unbearable—and all at once at flood, the bobbin loosed in a spinning, streaming release and she was soaring, freed of the dark constriction of the claws, borne aloft through gold-and-azure skies, through clouds on clouds of flashing lights and at the same time streaming, a vast dispersion over hills and valleys—she was the source, the fount, the copious seat of all delightful, gasping, rocking, plunging, streaming release in life, alive, she was alive, living . . . and then the earth returned, slipped back beneath her, sustaining and she melted into it, lay sprawled in joyous abandon on the huge old bed in the cabin, bearing his weight, his strength, his beauty—her darling, he had done this for her: it was all renewed, made good again, it *was* . . .

"You darling," she whispered in his ear, conscious that she had been speaking for some time without awareness. "You darling boy. You're right.'' She bit tenderly the lobe of his ear, pressed her lips against his eyelids. "We never had each other before,'' she said.

"That's right.''

"We never lay together. This is our first time. This one . . . We were soaring!'' she cried softly, rapturously. "Did you feel it?''

"Yes. Oh yes,'' he said.

"This is our first time,'' she repeated in a firm voice. "Our baby came from this time . . . All right?''

"Sure.''

She stretched her neck. "You're laughing!'' she accused him. "You're making fun!''

"No, I'm not,'' he said. Smiling he passed his lips over her cheek and stirred a little, and a tiny wave of sensation went over her. "That's all right if you want.''

"Yes. That's what I want. I'm serious. Danny?''

"Sure. I said sure.''

"Ohhhhh . . .'' She moved languidly. "I feel all alive. Oh, thank you, darling: thank you . . .''

"Don't say that.''

"I can feel every part of my body. Every bit of it. And yet I feel so relaxed.''

"You've got a lovely body, Andrea,'' he said. "A beautiful body. Don't turn away from it, now.''

"I won't. Oh I won't. Ever again. How could I? . . . We're really one, aren't we?''

"Yes. Am I too heavy on you?''

"No, oh no—don't go away.'' She pressed him to her so hard she groaned with the effort. "Oh, you can't ever go away . . .''

6

"YEP, THINGS HAVE been pretty hectic around here,'' Sue Trumbull said. Drawing furiously on her cigarette she rolled her eyes upward and grimaced. "Considering the fact that there hasn't been a man—a decent, honest-to-God *man,* I mean—around the place in ages." She pushed her coffee cup away and leaned nearer him by the simple expedient of shifting her weight onto her left elbow and murmured, "Ooooh, it's good to see you again, Al. Real yummy. I've missed you something terrible."

"I'll bet you have," Newcombe said.

Her blue eyes widened. "What do you mean?"

"Why didn't you write? You realize you owe me two letters, don't you? Not one but two."

"I know, Al, I know I should have." She rolled her eyes up again. "I knew you'd bring that up, I meant to, you won't believe this but I started four letters to you and tore them up. Honestly. I've got a real block about correspondence."

"I'll say you have."

"No, I mean it, I haven't been able to study or anything. Nobody around here can. Honestly you haven't any idea how perfectly silly it is, everyone's just going through the motions, going to classes, going to movies, going to the libe . . ." Glancing at him again she made a self-deprecatory pout, shrugged her thin shoulders. "I know it's nothing to being in the service but it's so silly. This place is getting to be a loony-bin. No, really. Bobby Nowden went over to Framingham two weeks ago and got absolutely stinking. All by herself. Can you imagine getting stinking in *Framingham?* Peg and Katie Allerton and I had to go over there and sneak her into Katie's house and sober her up. We just got her in the house when Dean Goffre drove by with Mr. Newton. It—was—ghastly . . ."

"It must have been."

"Oh—rib me if you want. We almost got canned. All of us."

Folding his hands below his chin Newcombe watched her, studied with remote interest her thin, angular face, the sharply uptilted nose, the deep, straight, vertical line between her brows; he had, it occurred to him with a humorous little shock, almost forgotten the details of her features.

"I didn't tell you about Jane Conder, did I?" Sue said.

"No. What's her problem?"

"Strictly oedipal. Her father's a brilliant scientist out on the coast. He's one of those men that just gets handsomer with age—you know, silvery white hair and wonderful lines in his face. Like Stettinius. She's completely wrapped up in him: writes every night, has three photos of him on her bureau, almost never goes out on dates—you know. We've all got the problem, I guess, but with her it's terrific: she can't oxydize any of it at all.''

Staring out at the sun glittering on the snow she smiled reflectively; and her eyes widened. "You should have heard the talk Dr. Marriott gave us, honestly I'd have given a mint if you could have been there. Or any man for that matter. It was priceless. It was just to the seniors." Lowering her voice to a deep, sepulchral note she proclaimed: " 'It is a known fact that eighty-five percent of the girls in his college indulge in harmful practices.' Then she stopped and looked over the whole hall: you could have heard a bobby-pin drop. 'And I don't mean just vague daydreaming, either. I mean direct practice.' Isn't that terrific?''

Newcombe smiled thinly. "And who hath measured the ground?''

Sue giggled softly and ducked her head. "Ooooh, you're so suggestive, Mr. N. And so lit'ry. All in one breath. No, but it was really something . . . And she's right, you know, we're all a bunch of screaming neurotics if the truth were known: a whole passel of repressed, anxiety-ridden females. It's impossible to be in a woman's college in 1943 and *not* be a wreck . . .''

"Oh, I don't know. You never struck me as so very repressed.''

Sue made a little throaty murmur of satisfaction again; her eyes rested on his in cool appraisal, unblinking; narrowed as she smiled. "Well, I'm better off than most of them if I do say so. And I've got a lot of junk dredged up and cleared away working with Dr. Sardor: she says I've had less resistance than any girl she's worked with.''

"You're still in analysis with her?''

"You couldn't call it an analysis, strictly: it's mostly a sort of informal, freewheeling conference, you can let yourself run and she makes comments and asks a question now and then. I guess you couldn't call it a formal analysis, though.''

"But does she get right down to the basic issues?''

"You wouldn't be pulling my leg, would you, old bean?'' She paused, turned her spoon over and over in her saucer. "After all, the whole problem is how to live with your own libido. And not go off the deep end.''

"I guess that's right.''

Several girls came in—a montage of reversibles, bootees and red and yellow scarves; their eyes darted to where

Newcombe and Sue were sitting and their voices called languidly, indifferently: "Hi . . ."

"Hi," Sue called back. "Hi, Jar." Pointing to a short, round-faced blonde in a ski costume she said in a low voice, "That's Jarrell Slade—the boy she's engaged to was just KIA."

"Was what?"

"Killed in action. Palermo."

"Oh. That's rough enough." With rising incredulity Newcombe watched Sue; her eyes were fixed on the round-faced girl in greedy intensity. KIA, for Christ sake. KIA . . .

"It was awful when she got the wire. I thought for a second she was going to faint, then the next moment I thought she was going to jump out a window or something. She just—went—wild. We've been, you know, sort of going around with her."

She sighed, picked up her coffee cup and sipped from it, set it down again, a meniscus of bright red lipstick on its rim. Water dripped from the eaves outside, fell in sparkling diamond drops through the sunlight.

"It's been like that all fall. Everyone's either got married and left or they've turned loony or sunk into a deep blue vapor."

"You're in the vapor section?"

"That's me, son. I keep getting fits of depression. I suppose it goes back to that business with the cello, mostly. God. That instrument is *guaranteed* to give any young girl a complex of some kind or other. It's mostly this idiotic seminary atmosphere, though. No kidding, Al, it's disgusting: I want to get out in the world, come to grips with something, anything at all. I really do."

"Why don't you join the WACS?"

"I've been thinking of doing that very thing." She looked out at the tall pseudo-Gothic buildings soaring above the trees across the courtyard. "I may join the WAVES."

"More class?"

She frowned. "No—more spirit. You know. The WACS are so *bedraggled*, Al . . . Hey," she said abruptly, tapping her nails on the formica, "have you heard that new number of Stafford's? with Elman? My God. It's terrific."

"No. What's the name of it?"

" 'You Took My Love.' It—is—terrific, it's a kind of Russian folk melody or something. It gives you the shivers." She trembled briefly in mock reminiscence, her head back, her eyes nearly closed: and Newcombe felt all at once a faint stirring in his loins.

"Say," he said, lowering his voice, "time's winged chariot's hurrying near. How about going in to town? The Terrace Room or something?"

"Yummy."

"Stop saying that idiotic word. Can you get an overnight?"

Her expression became fake-coquettish; she leaned back again, fluttering her lids. "You tempter, you."

"You said it. How about it, Suzy?"

"I don't know." She grew thoughtful. "Maybe I can soft-soap old Chalmers into it. I've used up all my overnights for the term but I can try."

"For pete sake, what did you do that for?"

"Honestly Al, I didn't know you were going to get home, a girl has to go out once in a while, you've no idea how—"

"Okay, okay. Long as you can get out of here. What do you say?"

Peering at her closely he saw her eyes become very wide and clear and scheming; a look he remembered from former times.

"It'll take some doing," she said thoughtfully, "but I'll work it."

At the Terrace Room the tables rose like disembodied samite discs; on the dance floor far below, made soft and dreamy by the muted lights and cigarette haze, couples drifted in sedate somnolence, and from the shoulders and breasts and throats of blue and khaki uniforms metal peridots winked and sparkled. At a nearby table one tier below them a chinless army captain was listening with great seriousness to the chatter of a tall, rawboned girl with blond hair falling over one half of her face; as though aware of Newcombe's gaze the captain turned, regarded Newcombe's unadorned uniform with indifference, glanced back to the girl again.

"Mmmmm," Sue Trumbull said. "I like it here. But mucho mucho. I always have." She sipped her drink idly, looked off toward the slow sway of the dancers. "I feel so funny tonight. I can't get over it: everything's sort of dreamy, you know?"

"Dreamy?" Newcombe said.

"Yes—all fuzzy and far away and long ago. I know it's crazy, it's probably my damned sense of alienation creeping up on me again. I guess most of it stems from the old childhood. Being youngest sibling. You know, Al, I still dream about it? Ralph and Tom and Nancie were just like demigods. Real demigods: way up there in the air, floating away to dances, tennis matches, driving cars . . . it'd give any kid a sense of inferiority." She put her chin in her hand. "I've often wondered if I was a menopause child. It would account for the fits of irritability, the tendency to hypochondria. You know, sometimes at night I can't stop lying there and imagining all kinds of things going wrong with me: I can actually feel them starting to happen inside me, getting worse and worse by the minute. All my organs going out of whack one by one. Pure morbidity, no excuse for it, I know, I know. Displaced affect—I wanted the family to need me, be concerned with me as an adult instead of my being the mewling and puking infant . . ."

Folding his hands on the white tablecloth Newcombe let her voice slip on outside his thoughts, not hearing the words, merely keeping in contact with the modulations of her voice the way a sleeping cat will carry the conversation in a room. He had long ago got used to Sue's stream of self-analysis, the reveries and asides, the sudden speculations, the careless unfurling of terms like a string of gaily colored little flags; formerly he had been intrigued by these sallies, had welcomed them with the clandestine excitement of beholding a spectacle expressly forbidden.

What preoccupied him now was his own indefinable malaise. Sue's bright, inconsequential talk had not affected it at all; and oddly enough drinking—this was either his fourth or fifth—only altered its substance slightly, transformed it into a tight, gaseous element like some dangerous and evanescent explosive. What the devil was it, that it hung around him like the fetid breath of fever, and turned all scenes of former glory and delight into some unsavory, blighted thing? Only the previous afternoon he had gone over to the room in Lowell House he'd shared with Hallowell and Meriwether, had sat in the muted orange light and watched with steadily rising exasperation Hallowell pacing up and down, drink held before him like a ceremonial offering, the sleepy lashless eyes twinkling merrily, enjoying his own wit like some extremely succulent sauce. "Say, how about batting us out some combat poetry, Newcombe? Some villainous villanelles. The rag could probably use 'em if you do. That is, *if* they're flawed and fragmentary. Something impactual. You know—hot off the beachhead." "Swell," he'd answered. "How'd you like a snapshot of me with a flag up my ass?"—and had been

quietly amazed at the heat in his voice. Hallowell had stopped
pacing; his roguish expression had changed to one of wary
displeasure. What in hell had made him say that? Odd: he had
always revered Hallowell so—the intellectual assurance, the
carelessly proffered knowledge, the cold blue flicker of his
wit . . .

Perhaps it was the room itself—that sybarite's retreat with
its wine-colored window seats and monk's cloth curtains, the
white-birch record player with its three ebony dials, the Bosch
reproductions, the rows and rows of slender volumes in blue
and silver boards, the discreetly solemn teakwood cabinet on
whose top sat a gin bottle of translucent glass like a bathroom
window and beside it a bowl of spun aluminum lined with
cork guaranteed to keep ice cubes from melting for eighteen
hours. An impeccable taste he's once admired—and which
now seemed as barbarous, as alien as a native hut in darkest
Oceania or the craters of the moon. Why was that? Something
was grievously out of key: the day, the season the eon most
likely; even, possibly, himself . . . They had gone on to talk of
Bilibin's seminar on Joyce, of Spengler and Pater and the
poetry of Gerard Manley Hopkins, but it had made no difference; the raging exasperation he'd felt had been almost like
something he could heft in his two hands.

An hour later, fuzzy and morose from hunger and too
much gin he had said a brusque, flippant farewell and stalked
up Plympton Street in the wintry dark. It was starting to snow
faintly; a wind had come up, raw and gusty, flung the flakes
in jeweled swirls around him. At Massachusetts Avenue he
stopped and gazed up at the looming monolith of Widener,
where cubicle after cubicle glowed with hooded light: a comb
of learning, a mighty, segmented aquarium where crusta-
ceans, cephalopods, sphyrnidae, gadidae—strange fish
indeed—shirt-sleeved and intent, conned texts in silence.
Veritas, veritas! Ye shall know the truth, and the truth shall
make you—still more hung-over, lonely and despondent than
you are . . .

Three figures came racing toward him from the direction of
the Yard, slipped and skittered on the ice in Massachusetts
Avenue, arms whirling like windmills, hooting at each other;
catching sight of his tall, uniformed figure they peered into
his face abashed—fled on down Plympton Street with wild
cries. Idiot, idiot game. Had he once been one of them?
Staring up at the lights of Widener once more he felt burdened

by the cheerless sense that neither he nor Massachusetts Avenue nor the college nor the country was equal to the impending dark—that it would all shiver, totter, and go down. The wind around him let up briefly and flakes swirled upward, hung turning, gray and gossamer, like the flakes of ashes from the embers of a dying city, topless towers. Flakes of ash, they settled on his sleeve, his gloved hand: he closed his fist on them with a sad, vengeful feeling of finality. Craters of the moon . . .

"—I don't care," Sue was saying in a blithe tone. "You haven't been listening to me for hours and hours but I don't care a hoot or a holler. You look so funny, Al . . ."

"Do I?"

"You certainly do. What's the trouble, son?"

"Oh . . . I guess you'd call it the disparateness of things."

"Yep—it's a funny old world all right . . . This is wonderful, though," she said abruptly. "My God, for the first time in months I feel alive again. It's like old times, isn't it? Don't you like it here?"

"I was just thinking," he heard himself say dispassionately, "how monstrously repulsive it is."

Her face went blank with surprise. *"I'm* sorry, Al. I didn't know you didn't like it here. We could go to the Copley—"

"You think it would be any different there? . . . Look at it. With a little objectivity, I mean. As though it were Samarkand or 1789 or something. It's right out of Tolstoy or Stendhal: a whole society of rank and privilege—rank *with* privilege, you might say, and I suppose somebody has—waltzing away the hours. Choost like alt Fienna."

"Gee, you sound so bitter, Al. Do you really feel that bitter about everything?"

"No. Hell no. I'm just delighted with it all. Just filled with all manner of delight."

"You ought not to be that bitter. No kidding. You'll just develop a whole bundle of terrific hostilities—"

"You rummage around in your own attic, Suzy. My problems are my own . . . Sure, I'm bitter," he went on in a taut, bantering tone. "I've had to clean out latrines with a toothbrush. In a given time. I've had to stand on top of a hot stove and scour it with steel wool, I've had a drill instructor belt me one in the teeth while I was standing in ranks. Among other things. I've really been living, Sue. Yes, sir, this is war . . ."

"Have you heard anything more about OCS?"

"No—I think that might well be called a dead issue. Real dead."

"Gee, that's a shame. Maybe you can get transferred or something."

"Also highly doubtful."

"Have you started your advanced training?"

"Finished it."

"Finished it?"

"Well: this part of it, anyway. The graduate seminars are still to come, we are told. On other shores. San Diego and Pearl Harbor and—quien sabe?—even the enviable isles . . ."

"Oh. Al . . ." She leaned forward, startled, gazing at him earnestly; the straight, thin line again appeared between her brows. "Al, I told myself I wouldn't say it but I can't help it, honest. Does this furlough have a special significance?"

"Well, it depends on how much significance you attach to the word significance."

"Oh, stop it. I'm serious."

Staring at her he nodded without expression.

"I see." She placed her hands flat on the tablecloth on each side of her drink. "Ask a brutal question you get a brutal answer." She looked up again brightly, tossing her head. "Well, let's live tonight then, huh?"

"Right you are."

Still he watched her, chin resting on his hands. She was resolutely observing the dancers, her head on one side, her hair swinging—and he couldn't for the life of him tell what she felt. He had never known: it was as though she were reading lines out of a play—a rather bad, mannered play—lines she remembered perfectly but which had never been her own. But were his either, truth to tell? were any lines their own any more, in November 1943, with the world rotating inexorably toward night, its sunny side—the side on which they were now sitting so comfortably—aglitter with brass and braid and Valentina originals and laughter; the earth still turning, bathed in light . . . how would they fare when it came *their* turn to dip down into the blood-boltered dark?

Pushing aside his empty glass he said, "Let's go somewhere, Suzy. Come on."

She smiled her quick, mischievous smile. "Oh Mr. Newcombe, you're so impetuous."

"You're damned right I am."

"Do you find me—" she paused, leaned back in parody of

the classic enchantress, "—*alluring*?"

"You could put it that way." The physical pressure he had felt earlier at the Well was suddenly stronger; he drew in a lungful of cigarette smoke and held it, in a state of ethereal, half-dizzy suspension.

The intensity of his gaze was so great that it unsettled her: she laughed soundlessly and glanced about. "You *are* ardent, darling . . . Remember that weekend at Iris and Ted's? How crazy that was . . ."

His mind was swiftly flooded with the recalled sensation of the couch in the darkened room, and Sue's body, half-unclothed, pressed against him, panting in the stillness.

"Iris always took her role as duenna very enthusiastically," he said in a dry voice.

"Yes, but pounding on the floor like that! With her shoe!"

"Better than if she'd come downstairs, wasn't it?"

"Oh lord. But I mean what possessed her to do that?"

"I don't know. Sibling jealousy. Castration complex. *You've* got all the signs and symbols, not me." Leaning forward until their eyes were only inches apart he put his hand over hers and began to squeeze it in a slow, rhythmic manner. "Come on, Sue. Let's go somewhere."

She squinted her eyes, smiling back at him—a strangely measuring look; and at the thought that she might not sleep with him he became unsteady with impatience: how could he have been so indifferent to her sexually for so many hours?

"Come on, sweetheart," he repeated in a low voice. "That chariot is even closer."

"What chariot?"

"Time's winged."

"Oh, that one. Yes, it is, isn't it." She looked at him a moment longer, levelly. "Okay. Long as I get back to Katie's before daylight. She's covering for me at the house."

"Suppose you get caught?"

She shrugged. "Then I'm a compromised demoiselle. *Canned*, as the saying goes. Unless you want to marry me. Want to marry me?"

"Sure. Why keep milk."

"Ha. Precious little milk from me, son." Her expression became serious again; he felt her hand move under his. "You're shipping out soon?" she said in a flat, even voice.

He nodded again, his face solemn. "And it's the last," he said. "The very last."

And yet there was—he was aware of it—mingled with the

liquor-distended feverishness of the situation unmistakably
another element—he was on stage too, portraying the
doomed, tight-lipped soldier, soon to ride the tide of battle;
perhaps—who knew?—be swept to the shades . . . Did he
believe that? He'd better Goddamn well believe it, it was
going to happen to him soon enough. Why then was he unable
to conceive of it—how could he prolong this preposterous
drawing-room-drama role with its false, phony stoicism?
Because he felt none of it: none of it at all. His ancient, con-
suming malady . . .

She was taken aback all the same, though, he could see: she
was startled, for all her blandness, her bright sophistication,
was gazing at him unsurely. The drama of it! Jesus. They
must look like the Lunts, twenty years earlier . . .

"Why didn't you tell me, Al? I can take it, you know—I'm
not exactly the shrinking violet type . . . I'm not a clinging
vine type either," she added with a trace of emphasis.

"I know that," he answered. "I didn't mean to tell you at
all." Was that true? Something inside him shrugged indolently. Probably not. "It just came out—"

"I know, but you could let a gal know . . ."

"Sure. I didn't want to spoil things."

She looked at him for a long moment, sucked in her upper
lip. "You're a funny guy, Al," she said finally in a
musing tone. "How did I ever get mixed up with you? You're
a puzzle. You really are."

"At least I'm consistent. I'm a complete and total enigma
to myself, just incidentally."

"Ain't life rich and strange?" She brushed her hair back,
watched again the bandstand where the lights were lower, and
where in a blue spot a girl had begun to sing "The Last Time I
Saw Paris" in a husky, unsteady voice.

"I hate that song," Newcombe said.

"So do I." Sue withdrew her hand and reached for her
purse. "Let's go."

In the car she said, "Better go to the Bradenton. Out Commonwealth."

"What's that for?"

"We're going to see someone there."

"But I don't *want* to see someone. Can't we just get a room
somewhere?"

"Now?—in this town?" She laughed. "You've been away a
long time, son. Don't you know," she queried in a harsh nasal

falsetto, "there's a war on? You could drive all over town tonight and never get one." Settling herself in the seat she said, "Wally can get us a room somewhere. He's done it before."

"I see. Who's Wally?"

"A friend. I would have said something earlier but I didn't know how you felt about things."

Drawn up at a light he leaned over and kissed her below the ear. "What is there to be in doubt about?"

"I mean just things between us. In general."

That startled him; he started to say something, anything, merely to fill up the void, but she went on rapidly:

"It's all right, it doesn't matter, darling. These are troublous times, that's all. Did I tell you about Ginny Sargent? She used to go around with Russ Tunner, you know. He's in the marines, too. At Quantico. They were going to get married when he got a furlough. Then a month ago he was on leave in Washington, on a date with a girl he used to know and they got in a ghastly smashup and the girl was crippled. For life. And she insisted it was his fault, he did it to her, never mind the circumstances, and says he'll have to marry her. Which Russ is going to do like a good and faithful knight-errant."

"Lord. That's bleak enough."

"Isn't it? Isn't it, though? Ginny's just about broken in two over it. She went down to see Russ and then she saw the girl too but she doesn't know what to do. And what can she do? She can't force the girl to give Russ up and she doesn't want to influence Russ—though she tried to hard enough, I guess, when she was down there. A mess, it's just a mess; completely awful . . ."

"That *is* bleak," he repeated.

"Bleak! It's unbearable!" Lights swept across her face. "It's a wonder the poor kid hasn't gone right off her rocker." She cried in sudden anger: "She been in love with him for *three years* . . ."

Driving through the familiar streets, past somber, ghostly statues of bronze and marble, he felt vaguely displeased—as though he were being asked to perform some feat he couldn't cope with, a feat which he sensed to be faintly repugnant, almost frightening. What the devil was she so wrought up for? It was almost as if she were threatening him about something . . . He opened his mouth to make some rather flip remark, or

something sentient and faintly mournful—something to disengage the tension . . . but nothing came: for the moment he
could think of nothing to say.

Before he could she had put her arm through his. "Oh
well," she said in a bright, hard tone, "all God's chillun got
problems, as the man said. This is good enough, park
anywhere along here, and we'll go in and get us a little love
nest . . ."

In the lobby she turned left at the entrance to the cocktail
lounge and walked purposefully down a corridor. A man in a
white bartender's jacket with red-and-gold epaulets stepped
out of the cloakroom as they approached, and said, "Hello
there, Miss Trumbull."

"Hello, George," she called. "How's every little thing?"

"Just fine. Except for all this early snow."

"Wally in?"

"Yes." George lifted his round, expressionless bartender's
eyes to Newcombe. "I believe he is, yes."

"Good," Sue said; she turned casually to Newcombe. "It's
down here."

Following her along the dim, carpeted hall Newcombe
rested his gaze on the sheared beaver coat, the rhythmic bobbing of her oak-blond hair with faint amusement and speculation. She came here often, then: she had built up "contacts" here where she could get favors. Did she give them in
return? Obviously: the road to connections is paved with
reciprocity. She had slept with other men at college and out of
it, too; he knew that, had known it for nearly two years. She
had used up all her overnights for the term. Yet the thought
didn't irritate him at all, and he wondered vaguely why; on
the contrary he felt only amused, even a bit excited by the
idea. Yet it was strange—this bright, metallic assurance that
she, a Boston blue-blood and a Wellesley girl, had so quickly
mastered and made her own; this suave yet resolute way she
strode, coat open, one arm swinging briskly at her side,
toward contacts with the Irish and the Italians, the North End
demimonde. Quite a metamorphosis, truth to tell . . .

At the end of the corridor Sue knocked twice and swung
open the door. Three men were in the room: heavy-set men in
dark pin-stripe suits huddled beneath dense sworls of cigarette
smoke, talking in low, desultory voices. Their eyes lifted in
unison to Sue's face, to Newcombe's, filled with indifference
and dropped again to the desk where lay sheets of paper filled
with figures and lines of very fine type. Only the man sitting

directly behind the desk opened his mouth and said with a heavy, rough familiarity, "Well, hello there . . ."

"Hi, Wally." She went directly up to him. "How's everything? Wally, this is Al. I've told you about him, remember?"

"Glad to meet you," Wally said. He took the cigarette out of his mouth and extended a thick, strong hand.

"How do you do," Newcombe said.

"Wally," Sue said, "I don't want to bother you but can you do me a favor? Just a little one?"

"Anything, Suzy. What's on your mind?"

"Could you fix us up for a room for tonight? Somewhere nice?"

His little bright-blue eyes shot to the desk top, to Newcombe, to Sue again; pursing his thick lips he began to shake his head slowly. "This is a bad time, Suzy. See, with the—"

"Can't you, Wally? Really and truly? This is Al's last leave, he's shipping out the day after tomorrow." She leaned over the desk, her head on one side, said in a complicit, wheedling tone, "Can't you? Just this once, Wally? Please?"

He drew his lips back over his teeth, kicked himself around ninety degrees in the swivel chair and stared without expression at the other two men who had gone on discussing the condition of a building on Fayette Street. Still without looking at Sue he picked up one of the phones, kicked his chair around again and dialed rapidly with the eraser end of a pencil. Phone hooked into the hollow of his neck and shoulder, he spoke inaudibly into it for a moment, waited, spoke again, hung up abruptly and said: "Okay. The Perigord. Tell them I sent you over. Here: you better . . ." He pulled a slip of paper out of a drawer and scribbled something brief and indecipherable on it. "Better take this over. They got a new clerk over there don't know which end is up." He grinned broadly at Newcombe. "Young Dietz used to be over there went into the army."

"Oh thanks, Wally," Sue said. "You're a darling. You really are."

"Don't give it another thought, Suzy. Pleased to have met you, soldier," he said to Newcombe, kicked the chair around again and plunged into the argument with the other two men without preliminary.

At the car again Newcombe said, "You've become quite the woman of the world. Quite the woman of parts."

"Do you think so?" Her thin face was flushed and

animate, her eyes shining; it amazed him.

"Yes indeedy. This is a side to you I haven't seen before."

"There are a lot of sides you haven't seen."

"You've become quite the little old operator. Are you running a black market in tires on the side?"

"Oh, stop it." She smiled tolerantly, said, "A gal has to make out somehow in this rat race."

"I guess that's right . . . You're quite chummy with this Wally character, aren't you?"

"Why, Mr. Newcombe. I believe you're distinctly jealous."

"He thinks I'm a chump, doesn't he? Well, he's right. I am: a grade A, five-star, six-alarm chump and a half."

"No, you're not."

"Sure I am. How'd you meet him, though? I'm intrigued."

"Oh, I ran into him a long while ago. Wally's a swell guy," she pursued. "He's got all kinds of irons in the fire. He can get you a genu-ine star sapphire if you want. Or a gold urinal."

"Gee, thanks."

She laughed gaily. "He really knows everybody. Everybody! He can get two tickets any time to see the Bruins. Right on the boards. Want to see the Bruins? Want a seven-story apartment building on Saint Botolph Street? Want to see the Irish-American Golden Gloves at the Arena, want an interest in a night club in the South End, want to hear the results at Hialeah over a private wire?—what do you *want?*" she almost shouted.

He glanced at her nervously—at the glitter in her eyes under the wan glow of street lights; the taut, white, strained look on her face.

"I want you," he said, "—right this minute."

But she only laughed. "Do you really?"

"For Christ sake—what do you think?"

"I don't know: I really don't. You've got such a funny attitude at times. Nobody ever knows what you're thinking. You're such a sphinx, Al. Honestly."

"I suppose so," he said bleakly. "Sicut patribus."

"What does *that* mean?"

"My eternal and infernal watchers . . . Wait a minute."

He pulled up in front of a drugstore and went in, emerged in a few minutes with a cheap little furlough bag. While she leaned out of the window staring at him, puzzled, he paused, turned and went over to a newspaper stall and bought half a dozen *Travelers*, came back to the car and got in.

"What on earth was all that for?"

"A plan. A deep-dyed careful plan." He began methodically wadding up the newspapers and stuffing them into the blue canvas bag. The headline flopped over in angry reiteration: TARAWA FIGHT AT CLIMAX.

"Why, you—oh, *no!*" she exploded all at once. "Al, you're priceless!"

"So they tell me down at camp."

"Oh my God!" She doubled up with laughter, her hands to her face.

"There." He patted the bulging furlough bag speculatively, hefted it. "There we are. Just to give it that comme il faut touch . . ."

Still shaking with laughter she looked at him wonderingly. "They haven't made a dent on you," she said. "Not a dent. You're still a blue-blood. You're still from Beacon Hill . . ."

He started the engine with a thrust of his body. "How profound you are, Suzy gal. How profound . . ."

Alone in the room, after the farcical preliminaries of registering (he had written *Pvt. & Mrs. J. A. O'Neill* on the registry blank, filled with a barely repressible mirth) and the fussy, superfluous ministrations of a kindly old bellhop with ill-fitting false teeth whom he had for no accountable reason wildly overtipped, they turned and looked at each other for a moment.

"Well," Sue said; she raised her arms, let them fall to her sides in a gauche little gesture. "It isn't much but it's home."

"It takes a heap of living."

He came up to her and took her in his arms and kissed her slowly and urgently; she gave a gusty sigh and the tension grew inside him with a rush until he could feel his thighs quiver.

All at once she broke away and went over and sat in one of the chairs.

"What's the matter?" he asked.

"Just a minute." She sat with her hand over her face for a minute, then raised her head. "I'm sorry, Al. I always feel this way in one of these." She gestured around the room. "It always makes me feel like a whore. I don't like it."

"Nonsense, Suzy," he protested, "that's crazy . . ."

"I don't like feeling like a whore." She kept her head

averted, her hair hanging over her face. "It's all right," she went on, her voice muffled by her hair. "I'll get over it in a minute."

He stood by the window and looked down; his mouth was dry. Snow lay in grayed streaks and patches at the edges of buildings. Cars slithered along like bulbous black fish, swerved and stopped, swung away again. Far off, a neon sign on the Cambridge side of the river said CARTER'S: INKS: CARTER'S: PENS in staccato progression. A moment of pathos. Did she mean this, really feel what she had just said? Ah, they were both playing games, he was, too, they'd played the Jake and Brett game and this was the Frederic and Catherine game and the next one would be Harry and Marie (were they all Hemingway games, for God's sake?)—and what came after that? The Robert Jordan and Maria game, obviously—but she'd have to cut her hair for that. And he'd have to let his grow, and they'd need a sleeping bag—

"It's all right. It's all over now. I'm okay now." She was coming toward him, wantonly provocative: her dress was un-buttoned down the front and the skin beneath was like a fierce bright scar. He seized her and covered her neck and throat with kisses.

"You *are* excited, aren't you?" she said in a silky voice. "Baby's all tensed up . . ." After a time she drew away again, this time more reluctantly, and said, "Let's get undressed, shall we?"

Stumbling around getting out of his trousers he found his loins were shaking; he cursed himself in silence, held his hands against his thighs in anger. Why did he always tremble like this? Why was he always burning with an objectless ferocity that was so far beyond elation it most closely resembled fear? Was it? He was like a victim of some kind of libidinous palsy, his mind as well as his body in torment, wracked with disor-dered images of lust and violence and abandon . . .

"Al, you're all so hot and bothered, honey boy," her voice came through the dark, benignly taunting. "Why can't you take it in stride? like the other boys do?"

Her flesh smote him like burning. He gripped her in his hands, pressed against her with all his might to overcome the taut, palsied trembling. Was it bliss or agony? He could not tell; he could not for the life of him tell.

She was moving beneath him: a strange, slow, dream-like writhing.

"Ah," she said somnolently, matter-of-factly, as though

just awakened from sleep, "the hell with the metaphysical poets."

It was amazing the things she could say, and the times she could say them: absolutely incredible! While he—Well: bestiality was required, was it?—the plunge into the mire, the wallow in unspeakable, obscene delight . . . Jesus, was it *delight?* Anything, anything to wipe that blasé sophistication off the face of her mind—

He tried to be conscious of nothing but their naked bodies, the gelatinous pool of her belly, the firm liquidity of her breasts; strove to sink his mind into the fierce hot union, imminent, effected, the spastic clutch of her fingers on his back and shoulders. But his mind careened rebelliously about in time, alive with crazy, volatile bursts of imagery—an abandoned Negro shack in the boondocks whose outer walls were covered with garish, peeling snatches of billboard advertisements, an ancient moss-covered tree bent earthward like a kneeling, weeping woman, rain dancing on the surface of the river, O'Neill standing on his cot, rifle in hand, laughing his wild Irish cackle . . .

"Oh Alan," Sue was saying thickly in his ear, "oh darling this is wonderful, oh God how I miss you you can't know how desperately I've needed you nights I just lie in bed and quiver all over with wanting you every minute—"

Dizzy with tension he only half heard her voice racing on, faster and faster—it was hideous how she could talk through anything, anything at all!—scarcely heard her in the hoarse, scalding savagery of the instant . . . He was struck with an almost irresistible impulse to laugh, and only with difficulty stifled it. She was still talking.

"Oh Alan darling boy, oh Alan, oh my darling dearest—"

Later, lying on his back beside her, smoking, he listened to her voice—once more flat, dispassionate—without translating it into meaning. He felt light, utterly substanceless; floating in time like a hollow cylinder in a darkened pool. She moved; and now, incredibly—he smiled at the contrast—he felt nothing: nothing at all but a rather sluggish indifference tinged with depression. Post coitum tristis, was it? . . . Idly he wondered what it would be like to be married to Sue: the mixture of Swedish modern and hand-me-downs, Ronson cigarette lighters like pouter pigeons, the dining alcove aggressively gay with its formica boards, the modernistic Russell Wright ware and the heavy silver with its interlaced double-monogram—a pattern repeated ad nauseam on the bedspread and china and towels. She would come up to him in a housecoat (also monogrammed) and mules, looking rumpled and provocative, sipping at her coffee. *Good morning darling, here's your notes, don't forget to drink your orange juice which I squeezed with my own two little hands, I won't be in this afternoon till late, tell Harriet Barstow I'm awfully sorry, will you? it's twenty to nine right now so you better get a move on* . . . Was that what it would be like? The bright directness, the self-analysis, the wanton sexuality—and the steady, brimming, assertive practicality that made one's teeth ache merely to think of it. And what in God's name would they *talk* about? what would they say to each other?

And yet it ought to be spoken of, hadn't it? No: why should it? They knew where they stood, both of them. Sue knew what she was doing. In a world at war many swallows tail. Staring upward, clearheaded and alert, watching the slow fans of light sweep across the ceiling he felt he could see the whole crazy welter of life as never before, in all its pettiness and preciosity and ignorance: a frenzied clash of atoms in the dark . . . The sense of revulsion was staggering in its breadth; for an instant it all but took his breath away.

"What are you thinking?"

He turned; Sue was lying with her arms behind her head, watching him intently.

"Oh, nothing much," he answered. "This and that."

"No, it isn't. That's not what you were thinking. That's all right, your thoughts are your own." She was silent a moment. "This Tarawa business is pretty awful, isn't it, Al?"

"It sounds like a bad one, all right."

There was a longer pause, and then she said quietly: "Are you scared, Al?"

"Scared? No. Not particularly. There's no sense in asking for troubles before you've got them." But even as he said it he wondered if he really felt that. What would it be like? The heat, the glaring sand, the smashed trees and looped scrawls of concertina wire, the log bunkers, the deadly black slits that meant pillboxes—all of that he knew from pictures, training films, the oblique, tart references of Freuhof and Lapata and Kantaylis . . . but what of the rest of it, the parts they didn't talk about and which the training films couldn't register? All at once he thought of Danny sitting on his cot, the swollen blue-red furrow in the thigh, the gathered knot at the shoulder—the scattered welts and trenches all over his body, each one of which had meant pain and more pain, anguish unendurable from which one's lifeblood spouted in greasy streams and consciousness ebbed like tide in a marsh . . .

"You're so *buried*, Al: don't you ever get worried about it? You never let your hair down, the way people do. Ever. You're so Bostonian. I thought the marines would change all that. Or the war or something. But they haven't: you're just as withdrawn."

"That's because I'm a scion," he said. "If you're a scion of an old Boston family you've got to take it seriously."

"See—now you've gone all facetious on me. No, I mean it. You're so *remote*." Her voice was low and sonorous in the silence of the room. "You seem to be sitting outside of everything, I mean it's as though you don't feel things the way everyone else does, you don't look at things the way they do. It's as if everyone's dancing and you go on sitting on the edge of the dance floor, looking on . . ."

"Oh, for pete sake," he said in sudden irritation. "You've got such a tight rationale, Suzy: you think the whole problem is in getting rid of inhibitions. It isn't that simple."

"I didn't mean that," she said, raising herself on one elbow. "You—you don't seem to be living in the moment as it's happening . . . Do you? really?"

"Christ, I don't know," he retorted angrily. "As much as the next man, I daresay. What in hell is there in the moment to get so bloody excited about?"

She was silent and he said, "Oh, I didn't mean it that way, Sue. I mean taking existence as a whole—what's trying currently to palm itself off as existence, anyway. The whole stupid game of blindman's buff. When *everybody's* wearing a handkerchief over his eyes it begins to lose its purpose."

"But you can't feel that way, Al, if you—"

"Who says I can't. I'm doing it, sugar . . ."

"Oh, this war," she said with a little moan; and to his amazement he saw her eyes glitter wetly. "This damned old war . . ."

He looked around the room wearily. This was over, too—had passed like a series of images on a shadow screen; they lay like two shells now: spent, fleshly shells that barely grazed each other. Still, she had read him far more astutely than he would ever have given her credit for: an uncomfortably proximate appraisal . . . Now they would take their farewell: he would drive her swiftly out along the stately, bestatued colonnade of Commonwealth Avenue, past the dull, oily glitter of the Charles and over Watertown Bridge to

the Turnpike. She would murmur snatches of melody from a
recent musical and the tires would hiss on the slush in the low
places, with the snow ghostly white around them. At Katie
Allerton's house they would kiss in silence, and then she
would get out with alacrity and walk up the path to the door
with that brisk, long-legged stride, her beaver coat open—she
always walked with her coat open—her head erect, her oaken
hair bouncing on her angular, slightly hunched shoulders; and
he would sit behind the wheel and watch until she slipped
through the hall door and the nightlight in the vestibule
winked out. It was the way it had always been. But the areas
of predictability were getting scarcer now, it seemed . . .

"It's like living at the end of an old tunnel," Sue said in a
somber voice. "One of those mammoth caves with no way out
of them."

"More or less. More or less . . ." Roaming around the
room his eyes encountered near the door the little blue canvas
furlough bag stuffed to bursting with copies of the *Traveler*;
and slowly, thinly he smiled.

7

"WELL, IF IT isn't the admiral himself," Charlie Tarrasch
said. He looked up from the table in delighted surprise, wide-
eyed; smiled a false, ingratiating smile. "Home from the
wars! Haven't seen you around for supper the last couple of
days."

"No that's right, you haven't," O'Neill answered. Sliding
into his old chair at the round oak table he winked at Aunt
Grace standing by the stove, regarded his uncle for a moment.
The old contest. The old contest of skill and science. With that
lovable, huggable Mr. T. Aloud he said: "My public, you
know. Testimonial banquets and that sort of guff."

"Sure. Down at Cookie's, I suppose. Moran's Bar and
Grille."

O'Neill eyed him calmly. "I put in an appearance."

"Sure you did. Nothing wrong with that." Charlie

Tarrasch glanced up from his soup in deeply feigned astonishment. "What's the matter, admiral? Aren't you going to wear your uniform to the table? your full-dress horse-blanket, there?"

"Say, you're in a gay-time mood tonight, aren't you, Charlie? A real old play-time mood . . ."

Aunt Grace was shaking her heard at him rapidly, her lips compressed. O'Neill picked up his napkin and said: "No, just mufti tonight, sport."

"I see." Bending forward Charlie Tarrasch devoured his soup, sucking it up into his mouth with fierce little hissing sounds.

"Really fine, Grace," O'Neill said; he raised his spoon toward her and bent forward from the waist. "Captain's compliments and pip-pip. You're still the tops."

"Why thank you, sir!" She turned from the array of pots and pans with a flash of delight that magically transformed her gaunt, white face into a younger, handsomer woman's. "It's not so special." She brushed back a lock of reddish-gold hair with one hand; and remembering her face bending down to him, tucking him in bed ten years ago O'Neill felt the old deep, dull anger. Can't give her a decent word. Not one. God, it would kill him.

"I mean it," he protested. "Your hand has never lost its skill. Isn't that right, Charlie?"

Across the table Charlie Tarrasch uttered a short, mirthless laugh, went on spooning his soup rhythmically, hunched over, supporting himself on his bared elbows. Finished at last, he thrust the plate away from him with his forearm.

"Well now, admiral . . ." He inspected O'Neill with great interest, turning his swarthy face and lean, undershot jaw from side to side. "You're looking a little undernourished. They been treating you badly down there?"

"Why, it's been a picnic, Charlie. A picnic. We've got an old-style country club going down there."

"Is that right?"

"Oh sure. Night clubs, cabaret girls—you missed out on something good, Charlie. Free booze, even."

"Oh. Well, that makes all the difference, doesn't it? Of course I wouldn't miss the booze as much as you, admiral."

"No. I guess that's right . . . You might miss some of the other things, though."

"Can't we have a little pleasant talk?" Aunt Grace said; her voice was thin with apprehension. "The one time Jay's

home with us in month's? Can't we? Eat your suppers and
let's have a pleasant evening, can't we?''

Charlie Tarrasch looked away, cleared his mouth of food
for several seconds with his tongue; his eyes roamed darkly
around the kitchen—alighted on O'Neill in sudden malevolent
joy.

''Well—since it's all such a picnic down there, admiral,
what, may I ask, is the occasion for this furlough?''

O'Neill buttered a slice of bread with great care. ''I'm in
pretty good down there, Charlie,'' he remarked airily. ''What
I say goes. As a matter of fact I was guffing around with the
CO the other evening at a dance. I said to him, 'Harry'—
we're all pretty informal down there, Semper Fi and all that,
you know—I said, 'Harry, I'm a deserving Democrat, I did
you a good turn out on the golf course last week when I fixed
that bad lie for you, how about a little change of—''

''They're sending you overseas, aren't they?'' Charlie
Tarrasch demanded in a sharp, nasal voice. ''That's why they
gave you the furlough. Isn't it?''

Of course. The Tarrasch touch. His aunt's hand had
stopped in the act of lifting a saucepan.

''I wouldn't say that exactly,'' O'Neill parried.

''You wouldn't. And what kind of new word have they got
for it?''

Is it true, Jay?'' Grace was watching him directly now; a
strained, anxious gaze. ''Are you?''

''*Sure* he is.'' Charlie Tarrasch turned to her with disgust.
''Of course he is. Look at his Goddamn address down there.
Thirty-ninth Replacement Battalion. Replacement—they're
replacing the ones that already got bumped off.''

''Charlie, please don't talk like that, please don't . . .''

''Getting sent overseas and you're still a buck private. You
chump.''

''Give me a little time, Charlie,'' O'Neill said evenly.
''Look how long it took you to rise up to walking around inside sewers.''

''There's nothing wrong with being a sewage inspector. It
happens to be a lot more important job than most people
think.''

''Who said it wasn't, sport? Only you're not exactly a
dollar-a-year man, you know.''

''I make more than fifty of them a month, I can tell you
that much.''

''Please stop it, both of you,'' Grace said to them tearfully.

"Do you have to bicker and fight the one time Jay's home?"

"You chump," Charlie Tarrasch repeated; chewing methodically on a piece of veal he rotated his head from side to
side, watching O'Neill with sour satisfaction. "Going to be a
hero. *Volunteered* for it! Going to be one of the Halls-of-
Montezuma boys. My God. That's the trouble with you
O'Neills: you're all alike. Go off half-cocked, full of big talk,
big ideas, going to set the world on fire . . ." He cupped his
hairy hands together over his plate. "Last war I waited till
they drafted me. I looked around up at Devens till I'd sized up
the place. Saw just the job I wanted, best job on the post:
headquarters company. *They* were sending everybody *else*
overseas. See? I got myself fixed up there. Wound up a
sergeant and never went east of Boston."

"That's pretty smart all right, Charlie."

"You bet your life it was smart. I'm here: I'm not in
Flanders with the rest of the chumps. None of that flag-
waving big talk for me. I knew just what I was doing."

"Say, that must have been hard, though, wasn't it?"
O'Neill asked in docile interest. "To size the place up, and all
like that?"

"No. Not very." His uncle glanced at him with a touch of
uncertainty, rubbed a hand across his thick, pliant nose. "I
found out who were the right people to know and I got to
know them. The army's just like anything else: you get to
know the ropes, you get ahead. I got to talking with one of the
company clerks down at the latrine after chow, he was a corporal, and then one afternoon I asked him if there was
anything I could do for him. You know. Following week they
made me a battalion runner and then I got in as a clerk. It
wasn't hard. Nothing you can't do if you apply yourself."

"I guess that's right, Charlie. But tell me something, will
you?"

"Sure." His uncle's eyes rolled up and away.

"When you went to chow, how could you taste what you
ate after all the brown-nosing?"

"Jay!" his aunt cried.

Charlie Tarrasch reared back; his face went dark with
anger. "Pretty wise, aren't you?" he burst out, stammering.
"Pretty—you think you're pretty clever—"

"Just a natural step to municipal sewage, wasn't it,
Charlie? Wasn't it, now?"

"I suppose you don't do what you're told. I suppose you
don't take orders, wise guy!"

"Sure I do. But that's a lot different from getting on that old mainsuction line . . ."

"Please," Grace begged them. She put a hand on her husband's arm; tears were hanging in her eyes. "*Please* let's have no more of this—"

"All right, smart guy. You go ahead and be independent. Be a Montezuma hero. You go ahead." Charlie Tarrasch's face had become mottled and splotched with dark patches; picking up a table knife he pointed it at O'Neill, bobbed the point up and down between thumb and forefinger. "You know what's going to happen to you, Mr. Smart Guy? You're going to wind up in a pine box."

"Charlie!—"

"Ha! You'll be lucky you even *get* a pine box. Sure. There're dying like flies on some poor, pitiful excuse for an island right now. What's the name of it? Tarawa. Yeah. That's you, Mr. Hero."

"Charlie!" Grace repeated; she clutched at both their arms, her lined face tense with entreaty. "Charlie, don't talk like that!"

"It's the truth. The plain, unvarnished truth. Shipping out a buck private. They'll stick you in the first wave—"

"I wouldn't say that."

"No, of course you wouldn't. You're an admiral, aren't you? A real-five-star strategist. You five-star chump." He transferred his false, angry, contemptuous grin to his wife, then back to O'Neill. "You O'Neills are all alike. Big, high-flying talk twenty-four hours a day—"

"Charlie *please* listen to me—"

"—and what do you do, any of you? Not a Goddamn thing. You couldn't find your way out of a paper bag—"

"Well you haven't done so brilliantly," O'Neill retorted hotly, "for all your cozy-dog sucking around . . ."

"—hopeless, shiftless, footloose no-goods. Booze and dreams—"

"Better than sewers and—"

"—you're just the same as your old man—"

"*Never mind my old man!*"

O'Neill came to his feet with a lurch; there was a clatter of china and coffee slopped in the saucers, ran across the red-and-white checkered tablecloth. "You shut your mouth about my old man!" Standing astride his chair he leaned over the table toward Charlie Tarrasch's amazed white face. "I'll tell you something, laughing boy: I'll cut you in on some hot skinnay. I'm coming back from this clambake . . . I'm going to make you a little wager.'' Slowly he extended his hand; he could feel the blood beating in his face. Across the table his uncle seemed to ripple as though behind a pane of bad glass. "I'll bet you five hundred dollars I come back."

". . . Where'd you get that kind of money," Charlie Tarrasch said in faint disdain.

"Never mind, I'll get it."

"Not much of a price to put on yourself, is it?"

"It's enough. Come on!"

Charlie Tarrasch hesitated, blinking, staring at O'Neill's outstretched hand.

"Stop it, both of you!" Grace broke in on them; she was weeping now, her voice hoarse and wild and oddly shifting key. "Stop it! Oh, this is terrible . . . Jay! If your father could hear you—"

"Well he can't," O'Neill said curtly. The sight of her thin, imploring face cut him, but his head was still pounding; the anger clutched him—a decade of mounting outrage and frustration all at once too fierce to contain. Looking at his uncle again he said hotly: "What do you want—me to give you odds? You want egg in your beer? Come on, big-time operator: put up or shut up."

Charlie Tarrasch's eyes darted over to Grace, back to O'Neill.

". . . No," he said with deep distaste. "No, I won't shake on that. I won't bet on that."

"You'd like to though, wouldn't you? Sure you would. You'd just love to see me six feet deep, wouldn't you? And by Jesus you'd say it was booze, too: if it was a tank fell on me. Wouldn't you? *You're* the hero, all right . . . I'll give you something, Charlie: for your files. You're a mean little man. You hate your own guts because you're so mean, so you take it out on Aunt Grace and the kids—and by Christ it makes you feel all the meaner. You're a mean little man and you're yellow clear through . . ."

Charlie Tarrasch rose out of his chair, rage and amazement sweeping in a still darker flush over his sallow cheeks. "Why, you scrawny little shanty Irish rat," he shouted, "I ought to thrash you good—I ought to pin your ears back for you . . ."

"You want to try it, Charlie? You want to?" O'Neill shook off his aunt's pleading hands, his eyes on the older man. "You got your work cut out, mister. This isn't Rogers Park now; or Christmas of '39, either. I'm warning you."

"You're warning *me*—!"

"Yes. Times have changed. You've pushed me around long enough."

He glared mesmerically at the round black little eyes, quivering, bathed in his anger. All right. Over the falls. Now. Let it come: now let it. Oh the son of a bitch! Clean the slate. If he moves one hand. One finger.

"—fight!" Grace was crying at them. "All you do is fight, fight, fight—both of you! Don't you care about anything else on earth? Doesn't being together for an evening mean anything to you at all? . . ."

"No?" O'Neill asked softly, staring across the table; then, still more softly, "No. I thought not."

"Get out," Charlie Tarrasch said. He had coughed up a ball of phlegm in his raging and struggled to swallow it, wagging his head about. "Get out of my house, you—you filthy rum-soaked dirty little Irish mick!"

"Charlie—no! You can't!" Grace cried at him. "Drive him from our *home*—!"

"Who says I can't!"

"How can you talk this way to my brother's boy—he's going overseas to risk his life and you—"

"Sure he is—and he wouldn't have to if he had any brains . . ."

"I haven't got your kind of brains, Charlie."

"You bet you haven't—"

"Mine are right here." O'Neill tapped himself over the heart with his fist. "Yours are in your belly."

"Get out of my house!"

"Sure. I'll get out," O'Neill said relaxing a little. "And you can call me anything fine you feel like—the way you've been doing for years. But one more word about my old man and you get one square in the teeth."

"I'll say what I want . . ."

"Then go ahead!" O'Neill screamed, and came forward a step around the table. "Come on, let's hear it!"

Charlie Tarrasch backed up a pace. "You're an ungrateful little pup—"

"What for?—for you helping yourself to my wages at the A&P before I hardly got my own hands on them, and then holding up to me what a drag I was on your royal household?—No. We're quits, mister. Clean slate. I don't owe you anything but trouble. I'm making out an allotment for Aunt Grace—and so help me God if you touch one penny of it, Charlie—*one scrimey penny* of it!—I'll come back with a bayonet and gut you like a haddock. And that's my word to you."

"*Get out*," Charlie Tarrasch whispered hoarsely. "Get out of my house before I call the police!"

"Sure. With the greatest of ease." O'Neill paused, turned toward Aunt Grace. She was leaning against the sink, weeping soundlessly, hands clenched at her sides; and his heart wrung him. The ball game. Why did it always make trouble? when you fought for your rights, for anything? Why did the wrong person always get hurt? Ah Jesus: all the years of lousy abuse she'd had to take off him, all the *years*—

"I'm sorry, Grace," he said; he put out a hand—a brief, ineffectual gesture. "I didn't mean to get going. I'm sorry. There's just so much . . ."

She said nothing, merely looked down, weeping steadily; rocked her head from side to side.

At the entrance to the hall he stopped and leaned back into the kitchen. "I'm considering that a bet just the same, mister. I want that five hundred on the line when I come back."

In the little room he stood motionless, on tiptoe, between the cots; bent forward. Bobby was breathing deeply and thickly, almost snoring. He could hear no sound of breathing from Allie's cot and bent over still farther—saw all at once that her eyes were open and staring up at him.

"Allie," he whispered.

She didn't answer him and he knelt down and whispered again, "Allie . . ."

There was a violent little movement in the cot and all at once he felt her arms around his neck—her cheek, smeared with tears, pressed against his; and still tense and trembling from the quarrel he felt the tears rush into his own eyes.

"Jay, come back, please come back, please," she sobbed quietly, "I'll wait for you outside the house—I'll wait for you by the school—"

"Wait for me?" he murmured.

"I'll meet you outside the school. I don't care what Daddy says. Up at the playground, Jay . . ."

"All right," he said. He felt as though he were strangling; a sob shook him so he nearly choked. "Goodbye, sweetheart. Say goodbye to Bobby for me. I've got to go now."

"All right." As he rose she held on to him with her arms crooked around his neck until she was standing on the bed.

"Remember, Jay?—the playground, over where the swings are: by the elm tree . . . ?"

He drew away, disengaged her arm; stood in the middle of the room, silent and shaking with grief, and put his hand over his eyes.

8

IN THE DULL orange light shadows swung here and there like pendant knives, like saw-edged fronds, bobbed against his eyes alive with a jocose and evil menace. They were only shadows, he told himself resolutely, they were only shadows moving but his weariness was too great, there was no certainty: time leaped open in sudden, boundless gaps and closed again over the knife-shaped fronds, which made with the fitful orange light a slowly turning, malign tangle of serpent skins, swelling, growing more luminous, more darkly patterned and offensive . . . until all at once they materialized in a horde of olive-dark, grinning oriental faces—and with a curse that was almost a shriek he fired, fired again and again, felt the jerk of the '03 against his cheek. The olive-dark faces were all around him now; they hovered behind the writhing mat of jungle, vanishing and reappearing while he stared at them in soundless terror—his '03 was gone, it had been plucked away somehow by the swinging shafts of sulphurous darkness, and he dove for cover knowing that what was imminent would be too terrible to be endured. He had one glimpse of Turk Farrell's face frozen in anguish, mouth distended in calling *Danny, Danny*—a soundless, despairing cry—and then the writhing serpents had fallen on him like lanyards, an animate rope netting that pinioned him, bound him tighter and tighter until he couldn't move. There was a blinding flash, then a series of thunderclaps, each louder than the one before it, and he saw the little black-and-white cylinder lying by his head. *Jap grenade*, his mind said, How long had it been there he couldn't tell, but it was death for them all now and finally, it lay there neat and small and scored with its shiny serration. *I am death*, it said without saying; *I am death and I am as you can see marvelously near*. Glaring at it he tried to move and could not, tugged and wrenched at the serpent netting while the sweat poured down his throat in streams and the seconds ticked away with terrible indolence. As the flame-bursts swept in upon him he succeeded at last in tearing one hand free, snatched at the grenade in a paroxysm of fear and as he flung it from him felt the explosion sear him with a million needle points of agony. He looked at his right hand and saw it was gone—nothing remained at the end of his forearm but a dull ivory knob like a poker handle, blunt and stained: a horrible sight. His right *hand!* And with a great effort he wrenched himself up and away. There above him were the chipped, rough oak rafters, the wall, the fireplace, the bearskin rug; one of the logs had burned in two and rolled out on the stone hearth where it was sputtering and flaming. He stared at it in a trance, blinking owlishly. His face and chest were soaked in sweat.

His right hand had gone numb. He worked the fingers clumsily, urgently, until feeling came back into it; then turned and glanced at Andrea. She was sound asleep. Her arm thrown back above her head exposed one of her breasts, which lay like a smooth milky marble pear, whiter than the white of her body. Half-turned, the blanket lying diagonally across her hip and breasts, she looked in the fading firelight like an antique statue, the work of some legendary and masterful sculptor, half-excavated in the bed of an ancient river. Her face was completely at peace, the eyelids still, the lips closed, relaxed in the faint trace of a smile. Raised on his elbow, still dazed and sweating from the nightmare, he marveled at the complete serenity that held her. *Andrea*. He mouthed her name in silence. Andrea my darling wife. He knew beyond any doubt it was the most beautiful moment in his whole life.

He leaned forward impulsively to kiss her, feared to waken her and stopped; eased himself away from her with care. She stirred faintly but didn't waken. Swinging his feet to the floor he slipped out of bed and walked over to the porch window.

It had stopped snowing. The sky was clear and the stars hung in the expanse of night like polished, pendant jewels. Far below him lay the pond—a flat white lozenge from whose sides the firs rose in two shaggy masses. he looked up again, watched above the high, harsh shoulder of October Mountain the stars gleam with greater and greater intensity; radiant, snow-sharpened, they assumed a luminous brilliance he had never felt before—expanded in the cold, clear silence into waves on waves of new stars, winking and glowing in their majestic order. The silence grew around him while he stood watching, swelled to a deep hum. A shooting star curved out of nowhere, soared off to the right, faded like a spent rocket; and the vast order hung suspended, controlled as before. Put up your swords, they said, bobbing, winking in the humming silence; put up your swords . . .

He became aware that he was shivering violently, naked in the open window; turned and padded across the cold boards to the stone hearth and stood there. The backlog was still burning as he knew it would—a bar of molten bronze along whose face ran tongues of flickering green and blue flame. Leaning forward he put his hands against the stone mantel; the heat struck him in a slow, fierce wave, made him shiver still more.

What had Newcombe said? Put up your swords or—what? What was the rest of it? Something in the phrase had struck him, touched him deeply—even in the heat of the moment, almost at hammer-and-tongs with Capistron. Strange: the way he had lain there on his cot with that thin, distant smile—as though he were amused at something no one else could fathom—and yet not really amused by it at all. College boy. How would he do when they went ashore? Probably all right. He was too nervous though, too unsteady: he'd have to watch him at night especially, along with little Connor. Connor was too young, Helthal too stupid. Ricarno was steady, so was Capistron probably, for all his mean streak and boozing, so was Woodruff; O'Neill was crazy as a bedbug but he'd be all right in the clutch, and so would Healey and Dancoe.

He shifted his feet, stared down at the embers. Damn fool: you won't even have the squad. Maybe you won't even make it back to ship out with the battalion. Jack Fruehof'll get the squad. He'll do all right. Well. He'll do as well as he can: go as far as he can go . . . Ah, they didn't know what they were getting into, any of them, except Jack; jitterbugging around the stove, running out into the boondocks behind the huts ducking working parties, throwing knives at pin-up girls, squabbling, grab-assing around. They didn't have the faintest, dizziest idea—and it was probably a good thing, too; in some ways it was. If they knew: if they really knew for *sure*, any of them, what was waiting for them . . .

All at once, poised before the fire he was inundated with fear: a dread so great it shook him to the heels and he stood there trembling, clenching his teeth. A cold, impassive fear that he would never survive this war, he would never survive the next operation. The Canal was the worst he could imagine; now they were saying this Tarawa was still worse. It sounded bad enough. How in Christ's sweet name could it be *worse?* But that was what they were saying.

He shifted his weight again, felt the full, even heat of the fire against his loins; let his gaze travel slowly around the room. Here all about him was home, the fond, familiar textures of granite and oak and the bark of birches; this roughhewn, dilapidated cabin perched on the hillside was his only home, the only one he was ever to have, where behind him Andrea—his wife Andrea—lay like a classical image, half-human, half-divine, in the bed against the far wall and held already in the still safety of her womb their child . . . and it was all slipping from him with the dry, nervous, overrapid ticking of his watch; it was melting away, the stone beneath his feet had turned to water, shimmering and insubstantial in the light of the flames, it was all slipping away behind him while he walked, burdened with war gear, toward death—

Leaning forward he bowed his head, gripped the rough stone of the mantel until the flesh of his palms was on the point of tearing; breathed slowly and deeply, his eyes squeezed tight. Oh, what a joy it would be to slip his pack, drop his rifle, fling his helmet a thousand thousand miles away, turn his back on that quaking, crashing perimeter of fire: oh Jesus what delight! To never gaze on another buckle or strap or bullet again—to sit here on this porch, say, and watch the long summer evenings drift toward fall, the haze heavy in the valley like wood smoke above the dull shimmer of the goldenrod and the sumac bristling its wine-red spears; the blue shadows sliding down the slopes and the crickets singing in a soft frenzy, and the first stars gleaming through the depthless arch of the sky . . . To slough off for good and for ever the interminable lonely waiting, waiting, waiting around, the shaking fear and tearful exhaustion—and the leaping nightmare shapes which even now reached after him and clutched at the edges of his mind asleep . . .

Durrell had gone over the hill for good. Minnesota? Somewhere up there. And never returned. *I can go places they'll never find me, I know boondocks back home they can't even walk to, let alone drive a car. This here's my tour:*

I've had it. No more for me. you wait and see. Wild, harsh face, eyes cold and blue as a northeast sky, *You wait and see.* Guys were doing it, plenty of them. For good and all . . . Why not, for Christ sake? Why the bloody hell not? Put up your bright swords—

He sighed and gripped the stone; staring in morose despair at the flames all he could see for the moment was O'Neill—that crazy Goddamn Irishman O'Neill—standing on his cot rifle in hand, his face wild with foolish delight . . .

She awoke gently, as though emerging from several slowly turning cones of silence, and saw him standing naked in front of the fire, his body glowing like a bronze nimbus. For a few moments she let her eyes dwell with fond indolence on his head and shoulders, the narrow waist, the small buttocks and slim, hard thighs. Slowly she stirred in the close warmth of the bed, keenly aware of her belly and breasts and hips; moved languorously, rejoicing in their sudden, miraculous nascence. To her very fingertips her flesh felt tingling and alive. This was what she had been afraid of: this! *We don't mention that, Andrea. We don't talk about that. We never talk about such things.* Her mother's face, tight-lipped and forbidding, a maze of lines. Had it always been that wrinkled and reproving? The body was evil, the body was treacherous and foul, and there was vengeance and retribution repaid tenfold for wrongdoing: the weight of inference had been clear enough . . . Now, stirring rapturously in the old bed, gazing at Danny's straight, beautiful form framed by the hearth glow, she exulted. It was not so: there *was* no wrongdoing where there was love; there could not be. That much she knew now beyond question . . .

Then she heard him sigh, and saw his head sink forward on his chest. He twisted from the hips—an awkward movement like a bound man trying to avoid a blow—and she saw in the ruddy light from the fire the long, curving groove on his thigh, and then the gathered pucker of the wound below the left shoulder; and her heart contracted suddenly. He was going overseas again: there was no doubt about it. They were training and he was going out again, to another horrible island filled with Japanese and death and disease and horrors. They were going to start again—the months and months of not knowing anything, then the terse, wrinkled V-mail scrawls, the paper streaked and splotched with mud, in which the exhaustion and despondency breathed through the laconic sentences. *Not much I can tell you, honey. We're in a dif-*

*ferent place from where we were last time I wrote. I'm okay,
darling, and feel fine. I miss you.* And then suppose no letter
came? A letter had always—even after unbearably long intervals—finally come . . .

"Danny," she called softly.

He raised his head and turned toward her; and now all she
could see were scars pitting and slashing him.

"Danny—come over . . ." She reached out her hands to
him. He came toward her in his lithe, easy stride and slipped
under the covers, slid his arm beneath her head.

"Oh . . . you're warm," she said.

"Yes. I've been standing there a while."

"Why didn't you wake me?"

"I almost did."

"Why didn't you?"

"Well. You looked so beautiful lying there like that, so
peaceful, I couldn't."

"You sweet. You darling boy . . ."

Her hand, moving across his hips, encountered the slick,
broad furrow; she withdrew her hand, placed it there again.
For a time they lay silent, staring at the ceiling. A tongue of
flame at the heel of the fireplace guttered in a series of quick
little suspirations, like a voice.

"Danny," she said.

"Yes?"

"Is it true you had a chance to go on a war bond tour
around the country?"

He turned his head. "Who told you that?"

"Your sister: Stella. Did you, Danny? Please tell me." He
was silent and she repeated: "Please tell me, Danny . . ."

"Yes," he said, after a pause. "Yeah, I did."

"And you turned it down."

"That's right."

"Wouldn't it have meant you wouldn't have to go overseas
again?"

"Maybe so. Probably. Yes, I guess so."

"Why didn't you do it?"

He moved his legs about under the covers, rubbed his chin
with his free hand. "I don't know. It's hard to say, honey . . .
It just wasn't the right thing to do."

"But a lot of them did—there was that sergeant you
knew—"

"I know. Maybe it was all right for them. But it wasn't for
me, that's all. I couldn't do it, Andrea . . ."

She was silent a moment, watching the light quicken and fade along the rafters. "Is there always only one way, Danny?" she said. "Always only one way to do everything?"

"That's right," he said.

"But that's crazy, Danny—how can you look at everything that way? There are a hundred ways to do anything, anything that comes up, there isn't just one, clear-cut—"

"For me there is," he answered. "All I know is I couldn't."

"But you've *gone* overseas once, Danny, you've done more than most boys will ever do for your country."

"Maybe so, I don't know."

"But do you *want* to go overseas—?"

"Want to! Jesus. What do you think?"

"But why, then?"

"Because—I don't know. Because it wouldn't be honest . . . If I got up on a box at a defense plant and made a big gung-ho speech I'd be standing for a Goddamn hero, don't you see?"

"But you are a hero, you *were* a hero, the citation said so—"

"Frig the citation."

"Danny, please don't use words like that—"

"I'm sorry: I forgot. There's no such things as heroes, Andrea. You find yourself in a bad deal you do your best to get out of it."

"But you did more than—"

"I did what everybody else would do—or try to, anyway. And I was lucky. Turk did more than any of us—and he's dead. There's no such thing as heroes at all: not the way *they* mean, with their citations and medals and all that crap . . ." He broke off, reached for a cigarette and lit it. "I couldn't go around giving a lot of war workers a big line of jive about get-in-there-and-pitch and gung-ho and all that . . . Don't you see, I don't want to stand for the *war*—" His chest rose and fell rapidly; the cigarette bobbed between his lips. "It's wrong, Andrea, it's all wrong: it's wrong to kill people, it's wrong to order people around, treat them like animals, make them do a whole lot of degrading things—it's wrong, that's all . . ."

"But you're going to ship out again," she said quietly.

"Yes. I am." He looked at her, looked away again. "But it's all wrong. I don't see any way out of it, I don't see we've got any choice now except go all the way, kill as many of them as we can—but it's all wrong, just as wrong as when Jesus said it was. Or the Ten Commandments either. And anything that makes a big, glorified deal out of killing is rotten through and through: anything at all. It's a foul, dirty, cruddy business— you haven't got any idea . . ." His face was all at once so hard and stern it frightened her. "And it's only right we're doing it in a lousy, cruddy jungle, too. Perfectly fitting and proper . . ."

"Oh," she said softly. "That's why you won't wear your ribbons, then."

"That's right. I'll wear the uniform because they say you have to, but I won't wear that other crap . . .I just did what I had to do to stay alive, that's all. You ask any guy that's been on the line if there's heroes. He'll laugh like a bastard, he'll tell you just what I'm telling you: you do all you can and hang on and pray to God it won't get too bad and you won't be able to stand up under it. And even then you need luck. Plenty . . ."

She felt as though she had had a glimpse of a dark and alien world, immense with menace; she was conscious of her heart pounding thunderously, filling the silence.

"I see," she said in a whisper.

"That's the whole thing in life: take each thing as it comes and try to meet it as well as you can. And hope for your share of the breaks. Try to do as right as you can—as the stupid Goddamn world will let you . . . Tell the kid that, too. Be sure and tell him—"

He stopped abruptly; his cigarette described a long, slow parabola to his lips; paused, flaring, then returned to his side.

"Oh Danny," she burst out. "Don't say that . . ." Against her will she felt the tears welling up into her eyes. "Oh Danny, don't say that, don't say it that way . . ."

She reached out and clasped him, drew him against her with all her might. "Hold on to me," she breathed, struggling to keep from sobbing. "Hold on to me tight. Tight as you can. Please, please . . ."

9

"Well, we fooled 'em good," Amory Newcombe said. "Caught 'em without a leg to stand on. We got Texas and they got the coast."

Standing, bent forward slightly, arms extended at the elbows in a manner oddly reminiscent of certain concert pianists, he carved the roast with rapid expert strokes. The studs on his dress shirt winked and flashed in the candlelight. Alan Newcombe, sitting far down one side of the gleaming white table, straightened in his chair self-consciously, caught on his mother's face the look he knew all too well—that faint, pleasant smile that sent forth a gray weariness in little shuddering waves; it filled him momentarily with its somber vapor.

"Yes, sir," his father went on, carving rapidly and neatly, transferring the slabs of beef to the plates where Channing took them with imperturbable calm and bore them to the other places. "They outsmarted themselves. First they offered to trade town-for-town in Kentucky and Tennessee. No, we said No, we didn't think that was quite right; and we countered with dividing up the coast. No mention of Texas yet. By anybody. We knew they'd balk at splitting California and they did. Russell began to rub his jaw back and forth and scrape his shoes together, and finally he couldn't contain himself any more and said, 'Amory, you're just not equipped to develop California.' 'Want to bet?' I said. 'We've got a whole sales promotion organization all ready to roll out there, I've had Harry Danning and three other men working on it for two years.' 'Why, it's been an organic part of our plans for years now, Amory,' he said, and tried to look shocked. 'You must know that.' That's the way the Chicago crowd have always been, you know: no one's ever thought of anything before they have. 'Oh, is that *so*?' I said, exhibiting great surprise. 'Well, that *is* news, Russell. I thought you'd given it up after Tilburn went out there.' That nettled him—he's never got over the way Tilburn made a flop of the whole setup out there three years ago, the New York crowd have been needling him about that something terrible—and he said, 'Why, we've been planning it ever since Ohio.' 'Florida's gone ahead of Ohio,' I said, quick as a wink. And I had him there. 'Look, Russell,' I said before he had a chance to think of something else, 'we're not getting anywhere like this. I'll tell you what: you take

California then, since you've got your heart set on it, and we'll take Texas, and we'll work out Kentucky and Tennessee town-by-town.' And we had them off-balance: we were being awfully nice about Kentucky and Tennessee after all the spade work we'd done down there already, and they couldn't object and start a furor after all the ranting and raving about the coast. So we got Texas without another murmur.''

Glancing brightly at his wife and son he sat down, replaced the white linen napkin on his lap with a quick little flourish, and said: "What do you think of that?"

"That's fine, Dad," Newcombe said. "Fine." He watched absently his father's intent, bony face, the beady eyes behind the steel-rim spectacles. Tarawa was secured today with five thousand casualties. The Second Marines waded in through the lagoon for a thousand yards. Waded in breast-high water while the Japs cut them down like flies, and lay in their thousands rocking softly in the green water, helmets bobbing: slow disolve . . .

"That's splendid, Amory," Charlotte Newcombe was saying. She looked at the far wall with a preoccupied, faintly troubled air. She still had not touched her plate. She never seemed to eat, somehow—she always gave one the impression that she was too all-contained, too beautiful and ephemeral to need food, to be soiled with the eating of it, the sordid ingurgitation; Newcombe was always surprised—had always been since he was little—to look at her plate after a time and discover it was empty.

"I rather thought," she said, "we might hear from Iris today."

"She still at New Haven?" Amory Newcombe asked, bending quickly toward his fork.

"Yes." Charlotte Newcombe's eyes swung to her son's. "She wants to go down and live at the camp with Ted."

"She was down there for a while, wasn't she?"

"Yes. She feels she'll have a better time of it now that Ted's an—now that things are different there with him," she finished rapidly; and went on as rapidly to cover the slip which both she and her son acknowledged once and covertly—noticed too that Amory Newcombe had caught it for all that and glanced at them with the sure, alert brightness of the idea recognized and marshaled—then had rejected it, thought better of it now, perhaps.

Newcombe wiped his mouth with his napkin; the glazed linen felt ceremonial and strange against his lips. Well: his father would bring it up later, with the coffee and apple pie and cheese; or perhaps tomorrow night before he left—part of a final buck-up speech at parting . . .

He sat back, feigning participation in the table conversation, and turned his wineglass slowly by the stem. Croisset '28: the bottle, a dull, dusty green, stood on the serving sideboard behind his father's head. Burgundy and beef: they had spent points—all the red points they had no doubt for months and months—for this dinner. No sacrifice too great, nothing too extravagant for the boys, for Jack and Jill and GI Joe . . .

His father had said something evidently witty and he joined hollowly in the laughter, studied the firm, sere, faintly hawklike features of the man who had sired him—watched Amory Newcombe rub the lobe of one ear and look down, his jowls settling in slender folds above his collar; and Newcombe felt all at once the sluggish stirrings of affection. Well: they had walked the beach at Marshfield, had played catch and punted a lopsided, heavy football back and forth on frosty, darkling afternoons, they had driven home down the Mohawk Trail together in the ice storm of '35 with the windshield wipers stuck and on both sides the abandoned cars like rows of black boulders in the drifts . . . But things rose between them now. Too many things reared like new-born mountain ranges, harsh and impassable, between what had been and what might have been: the tight green uniform he was wearing, the black cigar rolling across Ricarno's lips above the fluttering cards, Capistron's sleepy, malicious, moon-faced grin, the frozen jerk of the M-1 against his cheek and its chafing drag against his shoulder, the chafe of the helmet liner across his forehead; and now here, his father's impeccable dress jacket, the long table gleaming with its stiff white cloth and its candles and silver, the market going up, clouds of planes, the effete somnolence which this old house seemed to distill like some rare fermentation—in which, sitting in resentful acquiescence, one felt that one might never move again, that one was slipping backward through the millennia, in benign torpor reversing Darwin: animal, vegetable, mineral—what? Too much to traverse; it was too much and too alien and too preposterous, all of it . . .

His father alone seemed unaffected, went on cutting up the slab of roast beef into squares and triangles, forked it, fused it with mashed potato, masticated and swallowed it—all the while discoursing brightly, forcefully about the SEC and overrides and ten-percent loads and something called blue-sky. What in the name of hell was blue-sky? . . . Texas for California: fair enough—probably cheap at half the price. Both should be overjoyed. A simple enough transaction when entered in the proper spirit. I'll give you Greece if you'll give me Ireland. Feed me a Turk and I'll slip you a tiger; okay?—Ah, but what about Czechoslovakia, Poland and fair France, what about Wake and Guam and the Philippines? The case is altered. Who'll give back Tarawa now? . . .

The phone rang and he said, "I'll get it," leaped to his feet in a little quiver of nervous relief and went out into the hall; was surprised to see Channing, receiver in hand, nod to him.

"It's for you, Mr. Alan." A straight, thin personage, correct, imperturbable, with his clipped gray mustache and silver hair Channing stood holding the telephone like an embassy official in a British spy film, waiting for the attaché to receive the coded message which would spell safety or doom.

Newcombe took the receiver and said, "Hello?"

There was a crackling and several clicks like stones struck under water; then a voice called: *"Al?"*

"Yes?"

"Newk? This is Jay. Jay O'Neill."

"Oh—Jay!" Newcombe felt all at once elated, like a child given an unexpected present. "How's the boy?"

"Never better. Hitting eighteen. Who was that?—your old man?"

"No. That was Channing."

"Channing? . . . You mean you got a *butler*, Al? Jesus." There was a pause at the other end of the line. "What you got up there, a mausoleum or something?"

"That's just about it. Where are you?"

"Pawtucket. I'm glad I caught you in. Look, Al, things are kind of rough down here. I'm fed to the teeth. I'm taking off like a singed penguin."

"Right now?"

"Yeah. I got to . . . You remember Lorraine, gal I told you about?—well, she's down in D.C."

"No kidding."

"Yeah. Isn't that a swifty? Luck of the Irish. Yeah, she's down there with a couple of other babes. War job. So I'm going down tonight. Tell you what: I'll meet you in Union Station day after tomorrow. Okay?" Newcombe didn't answer and he said anxiously: "Al: you still there?"

"Yes. Wait a minute." Newcombe stood for a second or

two thinking, listening to O'Neill telling him urgently to shake it up for pete sake if he had anything to say, things like this cost money. Through the partly open door he could see his father, bent forward, lifting forkful after forkful of food to his mouth.

"Jay," he said quickly, lowering his voice.

"Yeah? What's the scoop?"

"I'm going down with you tonight. See you at Providence, same time. Okay?"

"Why sure, Al . . . Things are like that with you too, uh?"

"More or less."

"Jesus, that's too bad, Al: I thought with *you* . . ." O'Neill's voice sounded strangely wistful. "You're sure, now? I don't want to hurry you into—"

"Don't worry about it. Same time, same station. I'll save a seat for you. First three cars. All right?"

"Swell. If you're sure, now . . ."

"Right. Gung ho."

"Pip pip."

Newcombe hung up, stood for a moment listening to the voices of his parents. His mother's was clear and even: smooth, round globes of sound. Only the words were indistinct. Well: a day the more, a day the less.

"Who was it, Alan?" his father asked him.

"It was my outfit," Newcombe said steadily, coming into the room. "A sergeant in my outfit. I've got to go back a day early."

"Back to camp?"

"Yes." He glanced at Channing, who was regarding him with an expressionless austerity. "I've got to leave tonight instead of tomorrow."

"Oh," his mother said. There was a swift, slight contraction of her brows and her eyes narrowed, as though with sharp pain; then her face was again as calm, as handsome as before. "Is there a particular reason for your returning early, Alan?"

"Yes," he said. "There is, Mother. We're shipping out very soon." He pushed a scrap of roast beef unhappily across his plate. Brutal enough indeed: why didn't you cut the chain to the chandelier and drop it in the center of the table? Well—now as well as later: later as now. Now, past and soon are wound around each other . . . and all slip strangling through the soundless night. I must be cruel to be—cruel. Wrong way: I should have waited. I might have written. My forte. Avoid the bright, firm barbarity of human speech.

"*Orders?*" his father was saying. "Well, that seems like a highly inefficient way of doing things, I must say. Suppose you'd been out? Suppose you'd been out of town somewhere?"

"They'd have kept calling, I suppose. That's the service, Dad."

"I know, but you'd think when they gave a fellow a furlough—"

"It's all right, Amory," his mother said with a strange, soft urgency. "It's all right. Let's not spend these last—this brief time discussing the army and its ways . . ." She paused, looked again at Newcombe with the strained, troubled smile. "Well, in that case we'd better have our dessert, hadn't we?" Reaching forward she picked up a little glass bell in the shape of a swan and tinkled it; and Channing's deliberate, deferential tread approached them from the butler's pantry.

His mother's room was dark; he set down the furlough bag and leaned in around the door, saw—or thought he saw—her figure reclining on the recamier divan near the window; then she moved and he saw the beautiful, attenuated profile, the fine nose, the high clear brow.

"Mother," he said softly.

She looked around as though she had been caught at some dishonest action, and her face contracted again. Holding her housecoat firmly at the throat she swung her feet to the floor.

He came over to the divan and sat beside her. "I ought to be going now," he said.

"Yes. It must be time for your—"

She broke off, compressed her lips and nodded rapidly; then with an intensity that astonished him she turned and clasped him to her, released him as suddenly and began to weep.

"Oh, Alan . . ." she said. "Oh Alan . . ." And to his amazement she broke down completely, bowed over, sobbing into the crook of her arm.

He sat beside her in the dim light, chewing at the inside of his cheek; silent and disturbed beside her bent, anguished form. He had never, even when he was little, seen his mother cry before: it should have moved him mightily, it should have swept him too into a torrent of anguish—shouldn't it? . . . But all he felt was a thick, heavy constriction in his throat which was like burning, so that he had to breathe through his mouth.

"You'd think . . ." his mother said; her voice was rasping and low. "You'd think they'd give . . . a person a little time. After all the . . . just a little time together—" And as though the thought had released some additional reservoir of grief she rocked forward still further and gave way to tearing, strangled sobs.

Her words, barely intelligible through her weeping, puzzled him; he sat pondering them, scowling, repeating them over and over—until all at once he realized they were in substance the same words that Danny Kantaylis had uttered just before he'd gone over the hill.

"Mother," he murmured; he put his arm around her helplessly. "It's all right. Don't . . . don't feel upset, now. Please . . ."

What was the matter with him that he couldn't feel this!—any of this intangible force that wracked his mother? But he could not. Well, he could *understand* it, that is to say; but the simple, adamantine fact was that he—the real Alan Newcombe, that is—stood outside this, somehow—stood outside even his corporeal counterpart, his buttoned and belted double, and looked on in faintly troubled, faintly mournful detachment . . . Sue was right, doubtless: he was a cold fish, a Hahhhvahd esthete, a Nash-Kelvinator personality without the capacity to feel, to immerse himself emotionally in the swelling vibrance of the moment, as others did . . . was that true? Doubtless. Doubtless it was true. A wretched interdiction.

He hadn't always felt that way, though, had he? What of the night his father had taken him at the age of eight to see Jack and Ted Endicott play polo against some army officers' team? He could recall his immediate sensations then, peering down at the long, floodlit field, the slim helmeted figures leaning out and down along the ponies' gleaming flanks, the slender mallets sweeping down and up like curving wands and the *pock* of the ball; the furious galloping and the high, fierce cries. Even the referee's horn with its ludicrous little honk had been part of the bright, complex, breath-caught newness of it . . . Or did he only recall it with such poignance now?—did he only think he felt that way at the time?

No. It had been there, then. It was later that this lesion of empathy had seeped into him, transformed him into a gaunt, cold spirit that watched the present moment with a faintly amused or faintly mournful smile.

And yet in the room at the Perigord, in bed with Sue, he

had trembled like a man with fever; and later she had said—

Ah, but they were too transitory, too ephemeral to put one's faith in—such moments. They moved in oscillating waves of mirth and anger and despair, without permanence or dignity: they did not deserve one's firm allegiance. They deserved to be met with a healthy skepticism, didn't they?—provided of course it *was* a healthy skepticism and not the trappings of a remote, congealed evasion . . .

It was hard to say. It was hard to say what he felt at all. He had from one point of view mishandled everything—had angered or irritated or wounded everybody during the past three days.

But at least he would be honest. If he could.

His mother had stopped crying; he had passed her his handkerchief and she was blowing into it and wiping her eyes. Outside, the luminous taper of a searchlight shot up through the square of window, swept eastward, crossed with another: thin cold blue rays like the fingers of the soul.

He stood up and said, "Goodbye, Mother," and bent and kissed her. Raised toward him in the half-dark her handsome face looked wrinkled and old, as though laid under a curse. Grief made us old, then. Was that why his face had almost no lines, no furrows? Neither grief nor happiness had grazed him . . .

"Goodbye, Mother," he said again softly.

She made no reply, and he knew it was because she feared if she spoke one word she would break down again; her lips moved, she seized his hand in a fierce little grip with both of hers and then released it. And he turned and went out.

His father hurried out of his study as he came down the stairs and said: "All set?"

"Yes." They stood looking at each other awkwardly for a moment. Newcombe said quickly, "Don't bother to come down with me. I'll pick up a cab on Charles Street."

"Oh. All right. Did you see Mother?"

"Yes."

"Oh here, I meant to give you this." His father pressed a tightly folded wad of bills into his hand.

"I won't need it, Dad."

"Well . . . just for anything that might come up."

"All right. Thanks. I am kind of low on dough right now."

"I thought you might be."

There was a pause. Newcombe buttoned his overcoat and cinched the wide black belt around his waist. Now: now he will say it. Oh, for the life of an officer. Admonition and exhortation. Through the bars to leaves and stars. No reason why you shouldn't, what with your, simply a question of, thing is to get in touch—

But Amory Newcombe only put out his hand to him. They shook hands solemnly, and then his father embraced him once—a short, awkward gesture, and stepped back. And Newcombe was amazed to see that his eyes were filled with tears.

"Take care of yourself," he said.

"I will."

When he reached the far corner of the square he stopped and looked back. His father was standing in one of the dining room windows, staring after him. Newcombe waved his free arm. His father looked startled—raised a hand and waved back; then rubbed his nose rapidly and disappeared.

10

THE AIR OUTSIDE Union Station was clear and bracing; silver-edged clouds moved majestically, like the clouds in Gilbert Stuart paintings, through a sky of the deepest, purest blue, hung over the glittering Potomac in billowing white scrolls. Captains with briefcases manacled to their wrists sprang adroitly out of cabs, glanced around them alertly, keenly, like field dogs on point, checked their watches—sprang into other cabs. Eminent naval officers glided by in limousines, gold-braided hat bills bobbing like the beaks of gaily colored birds, their eyes vacant with thought, with responsibility. The red neon signs at the circle flashed WALK: DON'T WALK: WALK—flipped and flopped again, and the cabs and olive-drab service cars swooped away in a series of guttural roars: armored horses breaking from the post. Things were getting done here in Washington, brightly, purposefully: things were going forward. The very air was charged with it, gleamed and quivered with the knowledge. Office girls in twos and threes threw back their heads and laughed extravagantly, gesturing at each other with little gloved hands, and through them moved intense, catlike men in pin-stripe suits and club ties, bearing the slimmest of tan leather folders, pregnant with decision.

"Hey, it sure is good to know," O'Neill remarked conversationally.

"What's that?" Newcombe murmured. They had just come out of the bar in Union Station and the light dazzled them, made them glance around at everything unsurely.

"They've got it all wrapped up, son: it's in the old satchel, you know what I mean? That's the trouble with being stuck down in the boondocks. You get all out of touch with the hot poop."

An army colonel debouched from a car near them, turned and bade farewell to a still more mighty personage in its deep rear seat, listened intently for a moment, nodded emphatically, smiled a salutation and left on the run.

"Man, just look at that Mr. Brass chop-chop," O'Neill marveled. "Doesn't it give you that old gung-ho feeling, though?"

"Downright inspiriting."

Up in the Northwest section of the city the pace was slower but still purposeful, still sedate. Embassies presented venerable coats of arms and lofty, wrought-iron gates, and silken flags; and from French windows eminent figures—ambassadors obviously—peered out at them with unrestrained hauteur as they passed. And everywhere were baby carriages, pushed by nurses, governesses, maids—from whose hooded turrets infant faces scowled and crowed and mooned. One carriage bore down on them with a neat little Union Jack painted on its side.

"Wot ho," O'Neill said, bending down. "There's Mr. Churchill now. Say a few words, Mr. C."

The governess, who was sturdy and stout and wearing a blue-and-red guardsman's cape, glared at them coldly; the baby, a strikingly accurate replica of Britain's indomitable chief, gazed up vacantly, made no reply.

"Wot ho," O'Neill repeated jovially. "Right-o and pip pip." He waggled his fingers and pouted at the baby, who suddenly threw back its head and gave a silent little chuckle. "Eh? Bip? wot?" The baby laughed and shook its head; the governess glared even harder.

"I like kids," O'Neill said, waving to the departing carriage. "They knock me out, no kidding . . ."

The air remained charged at the Four Hundred Club. Gleaming red leather alcoves half-surrounded tables too small for anything but glasses. A waitress in complete harem attire—vest, headdress and pantaloons of transparent gauze—approached them, oblivious of their intense scrutiny, set down their drinks and turned away.

"Thank you," they said in unison.

They watched her depart, dwelt with sybaritic indolence on the firm, flat area at the small of her back, the slim white thighs that scarcely grazed each other.

"Oh daddy," O'Neill murmured. "Don't you wish you had twenty of those."

"King Solomon had a thousand."

"Poor King Solomon."

"Poor devil. He had it."

"Didn't he, though?" O'Neill stood up abruptly. "I'm going to call 'em again. While we're on the subject."

"Attaboy. Unswerving purpose is the price of deviltry."

An afternoon of the war. Alan Newcombe leaned back against the slick red leatherette, eased his trousers belt beneath his blouse. Outside admirals and PFC's brushed elbows, saluted woodenly, passed on. Crossroads of the world of Ares. Across the high-ceilinged room an American flag was stretched tautly against the wall, and below it a tiny triangular pennant with four blue stars. Sons of the Four Hundred Club, off to the wars. Highball me, son, I'm mashed in a gin-sling: I'm jiggered, sir. Noble Four Hundred. The whiskey was warm and dense inside him: now and then it stirred, like a great sleeping beast. Another waitress in filmy, transparent pantaloons passed him, bearing a tray of drinks; and following her undulant course he felt his loins give a faint, slow throb. *Ah, the hell with the metaphysical poets. My baby's shaking so.* Two nights ago—or was it three?—he had lain with Sue in a room at the Perigord, spent and surfeited; had listened to the low whine of tires on the avenue, someone saying a noisy, prolonged farewell to an old friend. And here he sat now, tracking a pair of gauze-veiled thighs, and felt his body tighten, stir with desire. *And into ashes all my lust.*

"Couldn't raise 'em." O'Neill was back again; close-cropped red hair, black belt looped fourragère-style through a shoulder strap, smiling happily: the young marine, slim and wild and debonair. "Not a soul. Hope they aren't otherwise engaged. What I mean."

Three soldiers came in, enlisted men with ribbons, the third man swinging behind them on crutches—suddenly revealed as without a leg. They watched covertly as the trio sat down several booths away.

"Dismasted," O'Neill observed in a low voice.

"How it goes."

But their nonchalance was forced; they drank for a time in silence.

"Funny thing about Danny, isn't it?" Newcombe said. "Taking off like that. I can't figure it."

"Yeah. He had his reasons, though."

"You think so?"

"You can bet your last buck on it."

"I wonder if he'll make it back in time to ship out with us."

"Probably. If he has a little luck. That's all you need. Once he gets down here he'll be okay."

"Till he turns himself in."

"Oh. Well. That."

They paused, finished their drinks and ordered again.

"Who'll get the squad?" Newcombe asked. "Jack Freuhof, won't he?"

O'Neill shook his head solemnly. "He's taken a bust. Cappie'll get it."

"Oh Christ."

"He's not so bad."

"He's a son of a bitch."

"He's not so bad, Al."

"He's a bully and a boor. He and Helthal—what a pair . . . He's got a mean streak a mile wide, just as Danny said."

"He's got a mean streak, all right."

"You bet your life."

O'Neill had taken a toothpick out of his shirt pocket and was working it around in his mouth with methodical preoccupation, a habit which annoyed Newcombe intensely. Newcombe watched him with rising irritation for a few seconds, then said: "He's got it in for me."

"No, he hasn't."

"Yes he has. I know he has. He thinks I'm chicken."

"What—because of that time with the landing nets?"

Newcombe nodded, smiled sourly. "He thinks I'm a yellow-bellied esthete."

"Look, Al, you ought not to chew around on that. Everybody has something that gets them down. *I* can't stand the bloody obstacle course, that damned rope . . . Hell, he's probably forgotten all about it."

"No, he hasn't."

"Don't worry about it. Don't antagonize him, that's all."

Newcombe uttered a short laugh. "Don't worry about *that!* Danny's the only one in the squad that can handle him."

They were silent again for a time, drinking, gazing about them. Sunlight all at once flooded the room: long, swimming shafts that turned the glasses in their hands into prisms, the walls into panels of dulled gold; the waitresses were suddenly invested with an airy flamboyance that was enchanting. Across the room the one-legged soldier, who was not drinking—his glass stood full in front of him—was listening to his two companions and cleaning his nails with a long silver file.

"Say, Al: they say it still hurts if you lose a leg or an arm. You think you've still got it and it hurts like a tiger. Is that right?"

"Beats me. Safe in a ditch he bides, with twenty trenchèd gashes on his head."

"Who's that?"

"Old friend of the family. Don't mind me. I'm getting loop-o."

"You're a crazy bastard, Al, no guff. You open your mouth sometimes and Mr. Nostradamus himself wouldn't know what's going to come out."

"I'm a caution. Danny told me his still hurt."

"No kidding. Jesus. *All* of 'em?"

"The one in the hip. And the one where the bullet went through him."

"Oh. Seems funny, doesn't it?—a bullet going right through your body?"

"Yes. It sure does."

Held fast in the sunlight they looked at each other directly—a long, baffled glance; reached for their drinks almost in unison.

"Getting late as a gate," O'Neill said. "And not a solitary iron in the old conflagration. I'm going to try 'em again."

"Fire at will."

"Stand by for a ram." He stood up, stalked away with extraordinarily martial bearing toward the phone booth in the rear.

November 24th, 1943. Four-twenty in the afternoon. Eastern War Time. Alan Newcombe stared in absorption at the tips of his fingers. He—his uniformed Doppelgänger, that is—was undoubtedly high, quite high indeed: that telltale, fuzzy, aqueous sense of things had caught him up rather neatly. Caught his Doppel, of course: not him himself. The light streamed around him solidly, a bubbling gold effluvium in which he swam; against the light his fingers lost the penumbra of their substance, faded off in pleasing translucency, with only the columnar shadows of bone to fix the too too solid flesh, recall mortality. Rattle his bones, over the stones, he's only a Doppel nobody owns.

Yet it was odd: something nevertheless reposed at this vortex of alcohol and uniforms and dreamy-dreamy muzak (they were playing "Whispering" now—an oldie, as Jay would say); something which eluded analysis. What was it?—what lay at the heart of this frenetic, patternless quadrille and said succinctly all that could be said about it? all that would ever need to be said? . . . For the merest flicker of an instant, staring out at the shimmering golden aura of the street, Newcombe felt grazed by something—a benediction curious and elemental, as though he were on the point of some soul-shattering discovery which would transform his very life, throw existence into meaning: a revelation in a burst of light . . .

Then in the next moment he distrusted the epiphany—or near-epiphany or false-epiphany or whatever it was—and his thoughts settled in fuzzy resignation, like an owl caught in the sun. He was high, of course: and when had an abiding vision ever visited on a drunk? or even on a semi-drunk? Lord, I am not worthy: but speak the word only. For I, Lord, am one of the miserable ten percent that never seems to get it . . .

O'Neill was back again, amazingly—almost surreptitiously: grinning like the proverbial canary. The one that swallowed the cat, that was to say. And why not? All was further blessed in this bust of implausible whorls . . .

"Got 'em," O'Neill was saying. "They just got in. Dying to see us. How's that? Let's just have one for the road and then take off like a pair of red whooping cranes."

"Splendid. Like a pair of sacred ibises from the lower Nile, you mean to say?"

"Right, sport. What's an ibis?"

"A lady ibid. No, that's obsolete. I tell you what: it's a metaphysical heron."

"For Christ sake. Who'd have thought of that?"

"Who indeed?"

"Not this chicken." O'Neill raised a new glass and intoned solemnly: "Hey, we're living." He leaned forward in a pantomime of conspiratorial elegance, his eyes wide. "I'll make a confession to you, old-timer: this gal Lorraine is the light of my life. I was—frankly—*crushed* when I found out she was down here."

"Natürlich."

"Right. Wait'll you meet her, sport. She's a dazzler. She's a bit on the solid side—a touch of what old avoirdupoise—but Jackson, it's *where* she's got it that makes all the difference . . ."

"Vive la différence. To par a phrase."

"Check. And now is the time. Over the falls." O'Neill stood up, cap under his arm. "Are you with me or against me, sport?"

"To the hilt. Do you want to live forever?"

"Just through tonight."

"Leonidas."

"Garibaldi."

Outside the air, though softer, was also somehow brighter, marvelously taut and winelike, tingling like knife-points. They swung along in stride, skimming over countless minute and lowly rectangles of concrete.

"Man, I am feeling *no* Angst," Newcombe declared with spirit. "Man, I am feeling neither Sturm *nor* Drang."

"Sing 'em, baby, sing 'em. Hey Newk, have you ever thought about what you looked like as you were strolling along like this?"

"Sure. I let Doppel take care of all that."

"What? No. I mean the way it hits you at times like this. You know—if you had some kind of a third eye that was stuck up above your head—"

"You'd be a submarine."

This struck them both as immensely funny and they went off into a fit of laughter, pounding each other on back and shoulders; spied at the same time an army captain of serious mien approaching them, carrying a bulging briefcase in his right hand.

"Highball," said O'Neill. "Snow job routine 3A. Roger?"

"Grudger over and under."

In step again, monumentally martial, they swung toward the captain, came abreast of him; their arms rose smartly, they sang out as one:

"Good evening, sir!"

The captain glanced at them apprehensively, shifted the briefcase and threw up his arm in a floppy, awkward gesture as they passed by.

"Did we snow him," O'Neill said. "Armchair doggie."

"Oh he's a fireball. Right out of Fort Bel-vwah."

"Whahr?"

"Bel-vwahhhhr . . ."

"Oh. Say, you know we really carried that off."

"We got poise."

"We got military bearing."

"To say nothing whatever of looks and brains."

"You know what *I* think? *I* think we're the two handsomest men in the Marine Corps."

"Right. And if General Wittaker were here right now I'd stomp right up to him and snap-to and give him the old royal how-de-do."

"Sure you would."

"I would. I'd say: 'Hel-lo Chief, what's to this beef? What's all this I hear about you being a chicken-crud wedge-ass? Eh? What's to this yarn about you being a fubar character from the word advance?' "

"Know what I'd say: 'Witt, old poop, glad to have you aboard. As for me, I'm going to be an outboard.' "

"Not bad . . . Say, sergeant—I meant to tell you, you got a bump to sergeant last night but it hasn't come through yet—where do these siren maidens hang out, anyhow? Where we bound?"

"Beats me."

"What?"

"*I* don't know. You started off like one of Carlson's raiders I thought you knew where it was."

"But *you* called them . . ."

"Sure. And I told you the address and you took off like a green flamingo."

"Pink."

"Green."

"Blah . . ."

They stood in the cool afternoon light at the edge of a circle into which fed six streets; studied them earnestly but without success.

"Coffee," Newcombe said suddenly. "Jay, old campaigner, I don't know about you. But I for one am going to need a quintessential cup of Java."

"Aw, Al—what do you want to take the edge off for?"

"Better take off than fall off. Just one fast cup. Do you want me to slide down the bobo and disgrace you sempiternally—not to say armpiternally—with your lady-love?"

Circumnavigating the circle with caution they found a cafeteria, where the air was thick and dim and swiftly moving, like the insides of turbines. Crockery clashed and clattered around them, voices relayed the calls of other voices in and out of echo-chambers; mops thrust at their feet from across the room.

"You know, I feel sort of on the crest of something, old buddy," O'Neill said; he waved an arm about airily, blew at his coffee, rippling its surface. "No guff. I feel as if I'm on the crest of a great adventure."

"Good for you. I feel as if I'm on the crest of a great collapse."

"Aw come on, buddy-ro. Buck up. Don't go chicken on me, now."

"Not on your life." The coffee stung Newcombe's lips and tongue, ran in short, fiery streaks down his throat and made him gasp for air; but his head felt suddenly clearer, more substantial.

"She's sort of my ideal, Al," O'Neill was saying; tilted against the wall, his head back, he squinted askance at the white porcelain mug. "But I never had any luck. You know, you've got to have a little. One night we were down at Brill's Cove—that's a beach near where we live where you can build fires, cook supper, go swimming at night, stuff like that. We'd just been in swimming and we were lying on the blanket together, getting all steamed up—you know—and she was panting and squirming around like crazy and I thought this was it for sure—and whammo! All of a sudden eighty-gatus searchlights started waving up and down the beach and over us and everything else. I got up and the road was plugged with cop-cars." O'Neill put his tongue over his upper lip for emphasis, and wagged his head. "Some character had knocked over a hamburger heaven in town and they took off after him and radioed ahead and he got on to the Tiverton Bridge and saw them waiting for him at the other end so he stopped the car and jumped off the damn thing. And they were combing both sides for him."

"Amazing."

"Can you imagine?—the one and only night I was down at the Cove alone with her."

"You were pinned and wriggling," Newcombe declared. "You were gaffed."

"I was."

"Sure. You can't fight those things. Your mahat-mavantaras were in the ninth ascendant."

"That right."

"Absolutely. Out goes y—o—*u* . . ."

An odd thing had happened: passing strange. For emphasis Newcombe had thrust, capriciously, his right forefinger through the smooth round handle of the coffee mug. It had gone all the way through to the third knuckle and now it was caught. In surprise he gripped the cup in his other hand and pulled, but nothing happened; he twisted and turned it, slopped coffee over his hand.

O'Neill was staring at him blankly. "What the hell's the matter?"

"Cup," he said tersely. "Can't get it off."

"Aw, come on, Al . . ."

"I'm not kidding. I can't *get it off.*"

"How'd you happen to do that?"

"I was trying it on for size. I don't know, for pete sake."

"Lick it," O'Neill offered sagely. "Put a little spit on it."

In rising vexation Newcombe tried in turn spittle, coffee, drying the finger, relaxing, rotating the cup. All without success.

"Old Al," O'Neill said; he was leaning forward, chin in his hands, watching in absorbed fascination. "It looks mighty permanent, doesn't it? *Migh-ty* permanent. Well, old buddy. Of course you could always take up panhandling."

"Very funny."

"Probably be the first panhandler on active service in the history of the corps . . . You could cut the finger off, Al: exempt you from combat duty. Stateside survey. Draw recruiting duty in Muncie, Indiana."

"No kidding, Jay, I can't get the damn thing off."

"Here. Let's see."

"Take it easy, now."

O'Neill took hold of cup and finger and for a few moments they wrestled mutely, with grave faces. A cab driver in a blue leather jacket was grinning at them from a nearby table, and Newcombe glared at him savagely.

"Nope." O'Neill dropped his hands. "Looks attached, sport. Permanently attached. Well, it'll make it real easy in the chow line."

"Cut it out, Jay. I'm in a jam." Newcombe felt gingerly the end of his finger, which was swollen now and faintly blue, like the fingers of old professors. "What the hell am I going to do?"

"Want to try to break it?"

"What with?"

"On the table. Go ahead: just give it a good smart wallop."

"No—I'm liable to cut hell out of my finger."

"That's true, too." O'Neill looked at his watch, sprang up.

"Where you going?"

"Come on, Al. We've got to get going. We're late already. I tell you what: wear it out."

"What?"

"Just wear it out. We'll get a hammer or something at Lorraine's and break it off."

"*I* can't go like *this!* . . ."

"Sure you can." O'Neill's face broke into a violent grimace of delight. "You ain't got no choice, son: we break it here we're liable to get locked up for creating a nuisance . . . Besides, you'll be a man of distinction."

"God, you're a card."

"That's why they always give me a fast shuffle. Put it in your pocket."

Newcombe surreptitiously tried this maneuver. "Won't go."

"Well, we've got to take off. Come on: we can't stay here all day."

As they approached the desk the cashier—a thin girl with birdlike eyes—glanced sharply at them, then at the cup.

"Miss, I can't get this off my finger," Newcombe said.

The girl's eyes darted nervously from the cup to their faces. "What?"

"He can't get it off: it's stuck," O'Neill explained.

The girl stared at them a few seconds with pent-up anger, then burst out. "Now look here, you marines, you think you can come in here and pull anything you want to—"

"Look Miss, I'll pay for it—"

"—think you can get away with anything, you ought to be ashamed of yourselves, going around—"

"How much is it?" Newcombe demanded, raising his voice. "A dime? Fifteen cents? Here." He slammed a quarter down on the counter with his unengaged hand. "If you think I'm any happier about this than you are—"

Confronted by Newcombe's angry face the girl suddenly went into shrieks of gasping, rising laughter.

"It's *true!*" she cried. "Oh! It's true! You're—oh you—!"

• • •

They finally found the apartment in a sedate block off DuPont Circle and rang and climbed the stairs with care. The door swung back violently, revealing a heavy, voluptuous girl with a round, pretty face and gleaming oval eyes. Swaying, recoiling on slender legs she cried:

"Jay! This is wonderful!"

There was a funny little vestibule, like a closet without doors, which opened on a room crammed with all kinds of furniture, and another girl came toward them.

"—and this is Helen," Lorraine said. "Helen, Jay and—"

"And Al."

"Hello," Newcombe said, and smiled; he had the impression of a soft white face and a high, clear brow with hair in little dark waves on each side of her forehead; and a shy, earnest, almost haunting gaze. For an instant, still vaguely hilarious and receptive from the drinks and the errant walk from the Four Hundred Club, he was imbued with the sense that she was about to say to him something quite valuable—that they were both, laughing and talking in the cramped little hallway, on the very verge of discovering something of unmistakable importance: some mutual revelation which could actually swallow up all their previous lives. Then Helen gave a little toss of her head and stepped back into the light; and Newcombe saw she had a faint cast in one eye.

The sight of it shocked him nearly sober; he was conscious of having started to avert his face. Then in the very next instant he caught himself up in chagrin and followed the others into the welter of sofas and couches which littered the living room.

"We're a little cramped for space," Lorraine was saying to O'Neill. "This town is plugged. Absolutely. Boy, I've never seen anything like it. We've moved twice already. You should have latched on to the place we had before this: wowie!" She stopped, pointed in amazement as Newcombe brought his right hand from behind him. "What's that?"

"We have a problem," O'Neill declared; for the first time since the incident he went off into his high, cackling laugh. "Got a hammer or something heavy?"

"Why?"

"It won't come off."

"Crazy! But how did it happen?"

"I was expounding something and I stuck my finger into

the handle for emphasis—and there it was . . ." All at once Newcombe felt immensely pleased with the idiocy of the situation, his duncelike role. "I've been wearing it around all day and people keep putting quarters in it."

"No!"

"And all I really want is a little old-fashioned sympathy."

Lorraine touched the trapped member lightly. "It's all blue and puffy. Does it hurt?"

"Can't feel a thing."

"It's gone all numb, then."

"*He's* numb, if you want to know." O'Neill came out of the kitchen with a hammer and a breadboard shaped like a catalpa leaf. "This won't hurt a bit. As they say. Put it right here."

"Be careful—"

Newcombe turned: Helen was standing behind him and a little to one side, leaning forward in shy apprehension, fingers to her chin.

"Well, thanks," he said. "I'm glad somebody is showing some solicitude around here. After all, it's only my finger."

"Well . . ." She made a little gesture of confusion and laughed. "Have you tried hot water and soap?"

"We've tried everything but lye and sulphuric acid," O'Neill broke in. "Let's resort to violence. What the hell, Newk, do you want to live forever?"

"Not this partridge."

"Okay, then: stand by. One, two, *three*—"

Both handle and cup shattered with a flat crack; splinters of bright porcelain flew around the room and everyone burst out laughing. They all went into the kitchen then and milled around, making drinks and spreading cheese on crackers and returned to the welter of cots, couches and bureaus and slouched around, tapping their feet to the dance band music from the radio.

O'Neill tilted his glass toward Lorraine. "You look dazzling, sugar. Simply dazzling. You're a knockout drop: what I mean."

"Thank you, sir." She smiled at him merrily and crossed her legs. "You're looking very fine yourself."

"It was horrible. Going all the way up there and you weren't even home. How about that . . ."

"Gee, I know, Jay—"

"Why didn't you *write?*"

"I know I know, I'm so sorry, Jay—I meant to, I started a

letter a dozen times, didn't I, Helen? And then I never finished it."

"E for effort . . . Only reason I went home," he pursued mournfully.

"Oh, go on, Jay."

"I mean it. There's nothing to do at home except fool around with the punks and fight with my stupid uncle: you know that." He glowered, shot his eyes to the ceiling. "Oh my God that uncle . . ."

"He *has* got a terrible uncle," Lorraine explained to Newcombe. "Terrible. The kind that would pull the wings off a fly."

"And the arms off little kids."

"That's horrible!" Shrieking with laughter Lorraine flung herself back on the couch. "Would he *actually?*"

"Sure he would. Charlie is the original Gila monster: he ought to hire out to a Hall of Horrors or something. No kidding, he really feeds on people's troubles: wolfs 'em down like roast beef. Rare."

"Oh, he's not that bad, is he?" Newcombe said.

"He's not, eh?" O'Neill looked across the room at him in amused defiance. "Know what he did last night? Wanted to make a bet with me I'd get starched. That I wouldn't come back from the current Donnybrook."

"Oh, *no!*" Helen exclaimed in such vehemence that they all turned. "He didn't really say *that* . . ."

"I guff you no times. He's a pearl. Then he threw me out of his ancestral hall: tail over teakettle. For good."

"That's pretty bad, all right," Newcombe conceded.

"Pretty bad!" Helen turned toward him in consternation. "I think that's terrible. To say something like that to your own flesh and blood . . ."

"You find that particularly heinous, do you?"

She looked up at him—the quick, shy glance. ". . . . I don't know what you said," she admitted simply. She paused. "He should have given him his blessing."

"Even if he hates him?"

"He should anyway: he should give him his blessing." Seeing his smile she added, "I guess you think that's kind of silly. Sentimental."

"Not especially."

She looked down, smoothing her skirt, and he noticed that she had a beautiful profile: classically beautiful, with arching brows and and a straight, delicate nose. It occurred to him

that she had seated herself so that the cast eye was on the side
away from him—then he caught himself up again irritably.

"Where are you from?" he asked.

"Falmouth."

"Oh—then we're all Cape Codders. Practically. We've got
a summer place at Marshfield."

They talked for a time of hikes and picnics and sailing parties; and behind their reminiscence lay dunes and witch grass
and the wine-dark blur of cranberry bogs and the tawny sweep
of heather; the smoky languor of summer afternoons, the
baleful, boiling fury of the southeast gales. They had sailed
the Bay and tramped the awesome sweep of outside beach
near Nauset; they had dug for clams at low tide and caught
flounders with a hand-line and fallen asleep in the pinched,
proud stern of a dory, rocked to sleep with the water slapping
against the hull . . . They had all these and other things in
common, a fact which had somehow—it struck him with a
sudden little rush of surprise—become extremely important,
more important than breeding or education or sophisticated
repartee or literary allusion or any of the old touchstones he
had always required; more important by far . . .

He set down his glass distrustfully. "I'm talking too
much."

"Oh, no," she protested with a concern that pleased him,
"it's important . . ."

"How do you mean?"

"I don't know." She looked at him directly for an instant,
and he had a sense of something quietly imminent between
them; then as though she had said too much, or had said
something indiscreet, she looked down again. And there was a
little silence.

". . . Oh, you didn't!" Lorraine was saying to O'Neill.
"And on your furlough, too." She was ensconced on one of
the other couches with her legs tucked up under her and her
arms lying along the edge of the pillow behind her head, a
pose lusty and alluring; and O'Neill, by slumping over farther
and farther on the cushions and twisting himself half around
until he looked like a contorted warrior in a bas relief, had
succeeded in bringing his face quite close to hers.

"Honestly, he should have been a mermaid or something,"
she called to Newcombe and Helen, tossing her silky, page-
boy hair about; her vitality seemed to charge the room like an
intangible, bubbling liquid. "He's a terrific swimmer, you
know: he's got metals and everything."

O'Neill regarded her steadily through half-closed lids. "Did you like to see me swim, baby?"

"*Did* I! Say, you know those suits they wear are fabulous. I swear, they're the sexiest things a man can wear. They're pure silk. Skin tight!"

"That why you used to come to the meets, Lorraine?"

"Oh Jay! Honestly."

"Hey, baby, you're a real knockout drop. Know that?"

"Really?" She turned toward him with an air of amused provocation.

"What I mean." His hand knocked over his glass: it was empty of liquor but two ice cubes slid out on the orange-and-purple rug. His dreamy gaze still fixed on Lorraine he fumblingly recovered them with one hand and pushed them back into the glass without setting it upright. "Cross my heart and spit in the ocean. Can't tell you what it means, baby . . ."

The door to the apartment flew open, banged shut again and a girl with high cheekbones and olive skin swept into the room, shrugging out of her coat as she came.

"Ri-ri!" Lorraine cried. "How's everything?"

"Going it deadly." With a sweep of bold dark eyes she appraised Newcombe and O'Neill, said: "Hi. I'm Rita."

"How do you do." Newcombe arose and nodded.

Rita stopped in the act of opening the closet door and stared at him, then at the nearly empty drink in his hand, and cried: "Will wonders never cease!" In a matter-of-fact voice she went on, "I've got to meet him at the Statler and I'm a half hour late already. God, will he be in a roar." She moved diagonally across the room through the couches and chairs, shedding waist and skirt, and clad in bra and panties began rifling a bureau drawer while Newcombe and O'Neill gazed at her openmouthed.

"Are you going down tonight?" Lorraine asked her.

"Yep. Tonight's the night. My—*big*—weekend . . ."

"He's wonderful," Lorraine interpolated while Rita, her dark, muscular body bent over, tossed undergarments right and left. "A lieutenant in the navy. Full lieutenant. He's wild about her."

Rita crossed once more to the closet, to the bureau again, swung around with her arms full of white lingerie. "Don't mind me," she said to the room. "I'll be out of here in a jiffy." The bathroom door pounded shut and both taps roared in the basin.

"They're going out to a place in Virginia," Lorraine said,

"where it's just like an old southern plantation. Silver service and colored waiters and carriages and everything. You know, just the way it all used to be. Isn't that fabulous, though?"

"It's fabulous, all right."

Newcombe and O'Neill fastened on each other a short, quizzical stare; burst all at once into roars of laughter.

"What's funny?" Lorraine said.

They wagged their heads at her. "If you don't know we'll never tell you! . . ."

"Oh . . ." Helen smiled, pursed her lips. "Well: that's Rita's way. She's kind of—bold."

"Bold!" O'Neill shouted. Lying on his stomach on the sofa, half submerged, he kicked his heels wildly. "Bold, she says! the gal's a breakaway bear-cat . . ."

"She is," Lorraine cried, "she's terrific." She turned to them both directly, her eyes dilated, her scarlet mouth opened wide, poised to preface a stunning announcement. "She was coming home alone real late from a date one night and a cab driver tried to abduct her."

"No kidding!"

"Absolutely. I hope I drop dead right here if it isn't. All of a sudden she noticed they weren't going the way they should be so she leaned forward and said, 'This isn't the way to Connecticut Avenue,' and the driver looked around and said, 'Just take it easy, baby, and everything will be all right.' A real gangster type, too. And Ri-ri wasn't scared at all. She thought fast a few seconds what she could do and when they came to a circle with a lot of lights and stores she pulled off one of her heels and said, 'If you don't stop I'm going to smash every pane of glass in this cab.' And he pulled over and she jumped out and went right into a bar." Lorraine paused, her eyes flashing at them. "Isn't that fabulous?"

"Rough and rugged," O'Neill said. "Fate worse than death." But he was visibly impressed.

"And that wasn't all, either," Lorraine went on proudly. "He parked right outside and then he came in and sat down right next to her. Can you imagine? And she had to get the bartender to call a cop and get her another cab." She shivered with delight. "Isn't that horrible, though?"

"By God, that's what we need, Al," O'Neill proclaimed. "Spirit of initiative. Fast thinking in the clutch. Sign that little girl up: give her three stripes and a rocker and we'll let her lead us into action. Wow."

The object of this tale of heroism burst out of the bathroom and began to rummage through the closet again; attired now in bra and panties of a dazzling white, and with silver spiked heels, she looked to Newcombe as though she were wearing some wild, abbreviated Amazon armor, donned for further triumphs.

"Lorraine's been telling us about the big abduction caper," he said.

"Oh, that!" She laughed shortly.

"It's really pretty impressive."

Rita did a swift, bizarre imitation of a curtsy in her heels. "Well, thank you, sir."

"How'd you happen to think of using your shoe like that?"

"I don't know." Her brow clouded momentarily; she scratched her opposite armpit. "It just came to me. In a flash . . . Ooooh, he was a mean one," she declared, and rolled her eyes. "He had a big white scar right at the corner of his mouth." Pondering she put on one blouse, discarded it for another, stepped into a skirt of violent green hue laced with yellow spangles. "I figured that was the fastest way to attract attention: break glass. Take a party—somebody knocks over a glass or a lamp and everything stops for a couple of seconds. You know."

"Weren't you scared at all, though?"

"Nah—I didn't have time to be. I was later, though. Huh, Lorraine?"

"Yes, she got back here and started shaking like a leaf."

"Never a dull moment in little old D.C." Rita snatched up a purse with a huge yellow shoulder strap, and grabbed up her coat. "Ta ta, kids. Have fun. Nice meeting you."

"Not at all." As she left the room Newcombe started to get to his feet again, restrained himself too late; and O'Neill guffawed.

"That's our college man, you know," he chortled. "Cap-and-gown and carry one. He's our intellectual type: gives the platoon class. When we wriggle through them good old south'n boondocks we can say to each other: It ain't so bad—we got our college man to keep us warm."

"I thought you were," Helen said. "I thought you were educated: the way you were talking . . . I'm going to college after the war's over."

"It's the bunk," Newcombe said flatly.

"What is?"

"Education. Complete mess of drivel. There's no relevance. It's all pickings and leavings, pickings and leavings

. . .'' The phrase mysteriously pleased him, and he repeated it still again.

"I don't understand you," she said.

"Oh, it's all phony—slugs of stuffy dust all dried-up and dead, all bound round with the parchments of calculation and timidity. Empty cisterns and exhausted wells"

"That's because you've had it."

"What?"

"Education. That's why you can say that. But for someone who hasn't it's different." She paused, said, "I had a scholarship at the Conservatory and I had to turn it down."

"No kidding." He looked at her. "Music?"

She nodded. "Piano. We needed the money, my mother was sick then, so I took a secretarial course and came down here."

"But you shouldn't have let the piano go—"

"Well: I had to. I'm going to go back to it after the war's over."

"You should. You definitely should . . .''

Fuzzy from drinking and short-tempered with hunger he yet felt oddly soothed by this girl's manner: akin to the fiber of her thought. Why was that? Even as he rebelled against the shy, unsophisticated bent of her mind he found himself attracted; she seemed to be resting on something he could not quite define—some tender simplicity that made her at once vulnerable and entrancing. As they talked he was carried back to the naive enthusiasm he had felt when he'd first gone up to Harvard—the sensation of being on the threshold of vast, hoary truths and wonders, an obsessed yet marvelously disinterested pursuit; to the moments when late at night the fire-laden, glowing lines had started up in his mind unbidden, had shimmered and shaken like phosphorescent serpents' scales until he had leaped out of bed and written them down in the dark, shivering, had scrawled them wildly in notebooks, on pads and envelopes, repeating them over and over aloud, tense with their throbbing, incantatory insistence . . . I had talent, he thought with a quiet wonder; a little. I had the power to evoke a mood, to fashion a difficult thought freshly—and occasionally a little more than that, too . . .

He looked at the girl again, really looked at her as he talked. She was watching him frankly now, her lips parted in a faint, scarcely discernible smile, unconscious of the obtrusion of her eye—as he himself was. How was that? Amazing! How the devil could that be when all his life long it had been the one physical disfigurement capable of driving him nearly frantic?—when for years he had lain in bed gripped with stark and icy terror at the thought that this terrible defeature would be written on his own face?—

The light was draining from the sky; a pale, shell-like suffusion that lay on her cheeks and brow—and that kept reminding him, or trying to remind him, of some nexus of attitudes, some time of his life, some moment . . .

Then all at once, striving for it and failing, he had it: the summer he had stayed with his Aunt Meg at Whitefield, the summer his mother had been ill; coming back from Ollie Greene's in the early morning, walking barefoot with the two-quart agate milk can along the packed dirt of the rut, with the song sparrow's call a reedy, buoyant melody following him; the edges of things firm and defined—all of life a huge, multifaceted stone of the purest crystal, revolving slowly, offering dazzling new faces for exploration day after day . . .

"I'm sorry," he said aloud; he smiled foolishly. "I lost the thread of what I was saying . . ."

"Professor Gresham's modern European history course," she said.

"No. Was I?"

"Yes. You were talking about how knowing history makes you able to—you know, see things in perspective."

He laughed out loud. "My God: how did I ever get on to that. Don't believe a word of it, it's all baloney."

"You sounded as though you meant it," she pursued doubtfully.

"Self-hypnosis pure and simple. I couldn't have meant a word of it in my right mind."

"You *are* funny," she said.

"Am I?"

She nodded, and they looked at each other again; this time it was Newcombe who looked down at his hands.

". . . Baby," O'Neill was saying in dreamy urgency. He had one arm around Lorraine and was drawing her toward him. "Baby, you know I'm just crazy about you. And always have been . . . Tell me—why don't you fall off the shelf?"

"Jay! That's terrible." She leaped back. "Honestly, you never used to say things like that. That's—that's terrific . . ."

"I'm a rough, tough gyrene: stripped down to elementals. I'm a hell-for-leatherneck and tonight's my last night to howl. The very last."

She blinked at him. "Really, Jay?"

He nodded with portentous inference, thrust out his lower lip. "Shipping out in three days. Seventy-two hours."

"Oh." She twisted around and adjusted her skirt. "Gee. That's a shame, Jay."

"So come on and relax."

"Not if you're going to talk like that."

"Okay . . . Let me ask you something else, then."

"All right. What?"

"When you going to go over the falls?"

She jumped up. "Honestly, you're terrible! You've changed . . ."

"I'm not so bad."

"You're terrible . . . Who wants to eat?" she called.

"Aw, there's time enough for that, baby. You can *always* eat."

"No, I mean it. I'm hungry." She smoothed her skirt with exaggerated care, straightened and passed her hands under her hair, looked at everyone radiantly and cried:

"Whew! I'm dizzy. Who wants to eat? Let's go."

Somewhere there was a restaurant where they ate steaks and pizza and drank red wine by the light of candles which had dripped all over the ash trays; somewhere too there was a cocktail lounge where everything was green and the tables were too small and too near together and waiters in tuxedos scowled at them and elbowed them and kneed them in the back; and somewhere else was a vast dance floor polished like horn, over which many-colored discs of light played in lazy, looping spangles and couples swept along with the discs flamboyantly, magically, turning gold and blue and scarlet as though tapped with wands. Newcombe was dancing among the spangles, and Helen floated in his arms with a lithe force that stirred him—and he thought for a time of long-ago dances, former partners drifting with him: dismissed them all blithely. The beat changed tempo then, quickened, throbbing and insistent, pounding in his ear like syncopated surf; he felt all at once fierce and devil-may-care. The girl in his arms started to spin away from him, stopped with a puzzled expression and said:

"Don't you want to lindy?"

"I can't dance the lindy," he said.

"Oh: or stomp."

"I can't do that, either. I wish I could: I really do."

Around them the couples swung apart, spun together again

in short, centripetal loops and dartings; and at the far end of the hall the brass team rose with gleaming horns and mutes like silver derbies held in their left hands, dusted the horns' bells once-up once-down and up-and-down and the trumpets *wah-boo-wahhhhed* in unison, martially, like ancient clarions storming in exultation some barbaric citadel, blowing down its walls. And watching them Newcombe was consumed with longing.

"I wonder if I could learn it," he said.

"I was going to offer." She glanced at him shyly. "I was afraid you might mind."

"Why?"

"Well—right here on the floor."

"Don't worry about that. Right now I could walk around on my hands and knees without a tremor. Let's try it."

"All right: hold me like this." She placed his hand in the small of her back. "Now just step it out. Just the opposite of what I do. It's not hard." She began to pace out the basic step and he watched her feet intently, following.

The number was over then, but the next one was in the same tempo; and he followed her again, not watching now, feeling his feet obey the step—and suddenly he felt he had it.

"You've got it now," she said at nearly the same instant. "Now you pass me out under your arm to the left, then under again to the right, then I come back in, the way we are now. You see? It's just a sort of a pattern. You just do the same step. All right . . . *now*," she said.

He spun her away with the heel of his hand, sent her out to the left, to the right, her skirt swirling like a matador's cape; she came in beside him again—and their steps were in unison: it was amazing! He laughed out loud, saw her smile the quick, shy smile at him in return. He shot her out again, not so successfully, then a third time without flaw; looked around him in elation. The music pounded to a crescendo of crashing brass and thundering cymbals, swept out in plangent waves; all around them couples in rapt obedience spun in and out, held in the fabric of the rhythm, wedded to it: an indissoluble stomp benign tyranny—and he too, through the agency of this sweet, silent girl, was a whirling component, fused in its benevolent empire . . .

O'Neill and Lorraine swept into the scan of his vision—Lorraine spinning and swirling so fast her full thighs gleamed like bronze under gauze, O'Neill going almost to his knees in a series of gliding semi-splits from which he recovered instantly, bobbing erect. Catching sight of Newcombe he threw back his head with a shout.

"Hey, you're looking pretty sharp there, sport. Ho-*ho!* Mighty sharp indeed."

"I catch on."

"Wait'll I tell the officer candidates about this. You'll never make the old war college, there . . ."

"Are you an officer candidate?" Helen asked.

Newcombe shook his head, grinning; for the first time since he could remember the thought of it didn't anger him. "I was working on it for a while but it didn't pan."

"Oh."

"They needed me in the ranks. More valuable there. Leadership at grass-roots level. You know."

They smiled at each other and swirled apart again. Near them an army sergeant and a girl in orange dropped back, back, back with little skidding shuffles—finally swept toward each other in a lurching, swaying, arm-extended parody of a strut. When they came together the girl in orange gave a little cry and they swept away.

"What on earth is that?" Newcombe said.

"The boogie."

"Wow! Let's do that. Okay?"

Smiling she shook her head.

"Why not?"

"I just don't want to, that's all."

"But why not? It looks like real fun. What's the matter?"

She looked up at him with an odd little hesitancy, her eyes crinkled up at the corners. "It's—because it's vulgar."

He stared in surprise. "But all dancing is. Didn't you know that? It's all simply a prelude to sex, always has been. Look at primitive societies—it's perfectly accepted as such."

She laughed in embarrassment. "Well . . ."

"*They're* doing it." He pointed with his left hand.

"That's up to them." Compressing her lips she smiled again. "I just don't want to, that's all. Put it that way."

"Your slightest wish, madame . . ."

Back in the cocktail lounge things were livelier still. Uniforms of many hues flowed by their eyes, couples leaned backward laughing or were crouched in grave discussion. Chair backs bumped against each other, drinks spilled, apologies were exchanged and toasts extended; girls' voices shrieked and shrilled in the dim saffron-and-indigo cocktail-lounge glow.

"This is fun," Lorraine cried; she squirmed happily in her seat, her green eyes dancing. "This is the most fun we've had since we got down here. Isn't it, Helen?"

"Oh, yes . . ."

"Except for all those majors and fliers and jg boys," O'Neill offered.

"That's not so, Jay, we don't go out at all hardly. If you're going to start that—"

"Okay, okay . . ." He grinned at her provocative pout, raised his hands above his head. "Don't shoot: I'll come quietly. But tell me something."

"What?"

"When you going to fall off the shelf?"

"Jay! You promised you wouldn't say that again."

"Oh: that's right. I'm just a slave to my baser passions. You know?"

"I certainly do."

"Hey, but baby," he leaned forward, his head waggling on his fist, "hey baby, remember when we used to go dancing at Norumbega?"

"Do I! Wasn't that wonderful, though? Did you ever go there, Helen?"

Helen shook her head.

"Gee, you missed it: what a place to dance. *Two* floors, and banks and banks of couches with lamps and end-tables. It was just like a sort of—like a sort of an indoor stadium. Say, remember the night Bob Wolfe ran out of the gas on the turnpike and it began to rain . . . ?"

"Yeah, and I found the paint can in the trunk and we tossed to see who'd walk it—"

Listening to their voices carried along on the vibrant antiphony of reminiscence Newcombe felt all at once irritated and out of sorts.

"Say—remember those nights on Capri?" He bent toward Helen in a maudlin parody of O'Neill. "Ah, but wasn't it great *schussing* down the funicular from Gstaad and aquatilting off the Cap d'Antibes? And the cormorants! Jesus, the golden *cormorants* . . ."

Her face, very close to his, assumed a shade of gravity. "Don't make fun of them," she said.

"I'm not making fun of them."

"Yes, you are . . ."

"No I'm not—I'm merely protesting against the whole idiotic, farcical pavane—"

". . . I don't know what you mean." She paused, murmured: "It's good."

"What's good?"

"It's good to have memories."

"Dirty baggage."

"What? *No* . . ." She appeared genuinely shocked, and it amused him. "I wish—" she said, and stopped.

"You wish what?"

"I wish we had some."

"Do you?"

She nodded simply. "They're—well, you know, they're the things you have together. Experiences."

"Not this duckling." And grandly he intoned:

> *"Yea, from the table of my memory*
> *I'll wipe away all trivial fond records,*
> *All saws of books, all forms, all pressures past—"*

He stopped, stared at his glass.

"Go on," she said eagerly.

"Nope. That's all. All for tonight."

"Whoever said that must have hated life something terrible."

"I wouldn't say that. He had a stern injunction. It isn't every evening you run into your father's ghost . . . or maybe it is at that."

"Yes, but to wipe all your memories away—that's like cutting yourself off from people forever . . ."

He was silent and she said, "That must be wonderful, knowing poetry by heart."

"Yeah. Swell."

"I used to read poetry once in a while: you know, *The Ancient Mariner* and *Ozymandias*—that's a beautiful poem, don't you think? where it says that about the sculptor . . ."

Her expression was one of unsure, almost joyful wonder—she hadn't read his sarcasm at all, he saw suddenly: it gave him for the thread of an instant a fierce, lusty sense of power. Then in the very next he felt fatherly and protective toward her. She was so vulnerable!—so sweet and vulnerable . . .

"You're amazingly naïve," he said. "You wouldn't even see the slings and arrows, would you? Perhaps they'd pass right through you like magic and leave you unscathed . . ."

Borne on the dense, reeling uncertainty of the liquor he felt this was somehow enormously profound . . . yet too abstract, too remote for her to grasp. "You'll just get mowed down if you go around like that, you know. They'll slice you to pieces."

"I suppose so," she said; and the simple acquiescence in her voice frightened him.

"Well, *do* something about it!" He pounded the table once. "Draw on a carapace of hammered bronze, arm thyself at all points—all of them!—cap-à-pie in hauberks and heaumes . . ." A vision of page on page of ancient armor swept before his eyes, illustrations in a compendious Webster he was poring over with the most intense scrutiny as a little boy of six: gorgets, morions and tasses . . . He raised his eyes, encountered with surprise a ceiling where buxom cherubs and angels floated, dimly visible through the smoke. Didn't she see where a tactic like that would lead, for God's sake? Oh yes, the lyric cry in sylvan meadows—

Someone was pulling at his sleeve. Jay—old buddy Jay, affable hawk with crest gules, was leaning toward him—the girls had left them somehow—through the winking, eddying lights; was talking to him earnestly. Odd: so much earnest effort all for naught. He listened with aroused disinterest, like a music student at the Conservatory, to O'Neill's voice as it wove its way through the babble and clamor of other voices, glasses, trays—mingled and veered away again like the piano in a quintet. What the hell did they all think they were talking about? Now and then he caught phrases—interesting but disjointed spheres of sound:

". . . last chance I'll ever have to make out . . . marry before they're ten . . . really—happy—routine . . . all *over* D.C. . . ."

"D.C.," he concurred aloud, solemnly. "Danse 'Cabre: Doctor of Claws: Da Crossroads of the world at war. We're right in the center, buddy—do you realize that?" he demanded. O'Neill's thin white face—extraordinarily white, extraordinarily serious—was nodding in assent. "Right—in—this—room . . ." Before his eyes the moment promised hours—was it only hours?—ago was taking shape, assuming substance and grandeur, was swelling into something limitless, something tremendously profound. "The nerve center of the whole bloody bleeding war, expansion of the western world. The command post. We're making *history,* boy! Look at that . . ." Above him a general passed—a *general?* yes, unmistakably a general—with a cropped bullethead like Sibelius, and a little semicircular shoulder-patch that said CZECHOSLOVAKIA. "There's the general of the Czech-oslovakian army," he said casually, gesturing. "For ex-ample . . ."

"Where?" O'Neill demanded.

"Right there."

"By Jesus it is. I'll say hello to him. I'll greet him."

"No, Jay—"

Newcombe rose to his feet in alarm. O'Neill was already gone. With dull, awakening panic he forced his way through the crowd, the sifting cirrostrata of cigarette smoke, came all at once upon O'Neill in animated conversation with the general, who had one short-fingered paw clamped on O'Neill's shoulder. Slidling up nervously he murmured: *"Jay—"*

"Al!" O'Neill turned with jovial welcome, as though he had not see Newcombe in years. "Want you to meet General Milosladj. General, this is my old buddy, Al Newcombe . . ."

"Na zdravi," the general said; beaming he put out his free hand, turned again to O'Neill and rattled off something in an immensely foreign tongue. To Newcombe's amazement O'Neill replied curtly in what was—was it actually?—the same language; and the general burst into a prolonged roar of laughter, his face turning a deeper and deeper red as though he were being pleasurably strangled.

"Come," he proclaimed, gasping with laughter. "You must come to my table and have a drink. Hey?"

"Well no, General," Newcombe said, "thanks very much but we—"

"Come. Hey? Come." The general propelled them one with each hand through the crowd, talking all the while volubly in Czech to O'Neill, who nodded meaningfully and now and then replied.

It was a large round table, red-lacquered and filled with glasses, bottles, ash trays, women's purses. Above it faces and uniforms of all denominations confronted them: a British colonel, impeccable and aloof as an osprey; two lieutenants chatting in French; a dapper little man in an utterly unrecognizable uniform involving a silken blouse with lapels that curved like scimitars; an RAF pilot with the top button of his tunic unbuttoned and tightly curled ash-blond hair; an American army major with a flat round face. Women sat here and there between them, crying shrilly and recoiling; their bare arms moved like serpents under water, like tendrils of pale white seaweed—they seemed to Newcombe's befuddled gaze more real than the bodies which animated them, more real by far . . .

. . . He had a gold-tipped cigarette in his hands: he had just sipped at a drink that tasted like attar of roses mingled with molasses and wood smoke. He found himself talking rapidly to the colonel—talking a trifle ingratiatingly, perhaps, but after all the beggar *was* a colonel—about the English tongue. But how the devil had he got off on that?

"—its remarkable suppleness, its durability of eloquence sustained through centuries of conflicting customs, violently opposed attitudes. What a proud heritage really, Colonel, don't you think?"

The colonel turned toward him the lean, white osprey's face with depthless sapphire eyes not quite in focus; smiled a distant smile and said in clipped, pleasant accents:

"Very sorry, old man. Can't follow a word you're saying."

"—No, but I mean its dazzling contiguity of metaphor, its prodigious flexibility: just think of them—*strike flat the thick rotundity of the world or dropt from the zenith like a falling star* or *thou Eye among the blind—*"

"Awfully sorry. Afraid I don't read very much. Brother's the literary one." The colonel gave a single explosive bark of laughter, exposing rows and rows of even amber teeth. "Little beggar's out in Burma. Digging chiggers out of his bloody bum." He started violently, turned to the girl beside him and exclaimed: "Oh! I beg your pardon . . ."

The girl—a straw-haired creature with jet-black eyebrows and bony shoulders—cried, "That's okay, Dad—I can't hear anything anyone's saying anyway!" Leaning across the colonel she said to Newcombe: "I saw you dancing in there. In the hall. Wasn't it you? You looked cute!"

The girls.

Newcombe lurched to his feet, jostled the colonel's elbow, spilled liquor over the colonel's sleeve. Bending over with extravagant solicitude he said, "Heartily sorry, Colonel: heartily. Disgraceful of me."

The colonel visited on him the genial, distant, unfocused stare; murmured, "Not a bit of it, old man."

Newcombe moved away around the table and plucked at the shoulder of O'Neill, who gazed up at him in vague, expansive benevolence.

"Old buddy-ro," he chortled. "Old bushwhacker. What's up? Name it and it's yours. Tonight I got the world in a—"

"The girls, Jay—"

"Yeah: aren't they lush? Just goes to show what you can do when you're one of the high muckie-mucks—"

"No, no—Lorraine and Helen. Where are they?"

"Jesus. Lorraine." O'Neill's eyes went blank for an instant; then he rose.

"What is it?" the general boomed. "You have a problem?"

"No no no, it's fine, General. Everything's fine. We've got to be moving along. Thanks for the cheer."

"Really? No—stay a while. Hey?"

"No—we can't. We—we've lost our women . . ."

The general burst into a rolling, booming laugh, placed a paw on the bare shoulder of the dark-haired sullen-faced girl beside him. "They've lost their women!" he roared.

"Yeah," the girl said crossly. "I heard."

"Lost their women!" the general shouted again; tears rolled down his red cheeks. His booming phrase pursued them through the chaos of the lounge. ". . . their *women* . . ."

The crowd was even greater now in the foyer; it was as though hordes of people had been sent in on some wild, implausible treasure hunt—they milled around aimlessly, tense with an expectancy which was almost apprehension.

"Dance hall," O'Neill said.

They fought their way through the press into the vast ballroom, where the sound hit them like a rolling wave of concussion, half stupefied them; they split up and drifted in and out among the dancers, dodging, peering about. A girl snapped backward into Newcombe, came down on his instep with a spike heel.

"Ouch, Jesus!" he cried.

She threw him a swift, furious glance. "—hell do you think *you're* doing?" she demanded and swept away, left him confronted with her partner, a swarthy, scowling boatswain's mate. Newcombe hopped about on one foot, muttering, then moved away; creeping none too certainly on the smooth, dully luminous floor, dodging the snapping, whirling couples, he felt dizzy and disoriented—as though his own personal gyroscope had been set awry. "All men are dancers," he mumbled; and gazed around him, wildly disconsolate. What the devil was the matter with them?—how could they have *forgotten the girls?* Who—least of all the girls themselves—would ever believe anything so outrageous? The entire evening had undergone a dark metamorphosis, sinister and bewitched, had turned into an exhausting, fruitless pursuit without meaning. How could they have been so totally idiotic as to—! All men are dancers . . .

He gained the edge of the floor with a sense of enormous relief, pursued his course around the long room, peering at faces which turned toward him with interest, irritation, amusement or dismay. O'Neill was waiting for him by one of the entrances, leaning back against the wall, hands in his pockets.

"What do you think?"

"Beats me. Maybe they're in the can."

"They couldn't be in there all *this* time. They've taken off."

"Where?"

"Gone home."

"Maybe so . . ."

They wandered through the lobby again, oppressed by the crowd, the hour, the sense of their dereliction; descended in despondency to the men's room and stood side by side at the urinals.

"My luck," O'Neill said. "My lovely Irish luck. Hundred to five . . . Al, we got to find 'em," he said doggedly, and pulled at Newcombe's blouse.

"Damn it. Watch what you're doing."

"That's all right . . . I got a confession to make to you, old buddy-ro. A real true confession." He leaned closer, holding on to Newcombe's sleeve. "I have—never—shot the moon with Lorraine. Never. One time—one time was one thing, another time another. You know? I just *got* to deliver tonight. Just got to. It's vital. It's Capistrano: know what I mean?"

"You mean it's mandragora."

"It's cuspidora. Know?" Leaning back he regarded Newcombe askance. In the harsh green light of the men's room his face looked white and extremely pale; an unlighted cigarette was sticking straight out of his mouth like a woodpecker's beak, and the pupils of his eyes were huge.

"You're kind of slozzo, aren't you, Jay?"

"What? Not this duckling. Not this fantail. Not this coot."

"Coot's the word, all right."

"No sir-ree. What's giving you that ridiculous notion? Eh? Answer your old sidekick."

"Your fly's open, for one thing."

"What?—the hell it is."

"Okay, it isn't: it's just my subjective idealism cropping out."

"Well, what do you know." O'Neill peered at his trousers

front in vague surprise, rectified the deficiency. "All the better to conquer with. Do you follow?" All at once his face fell,
his expression turned sullen. "Of all the cheap and lousy
tricks: taking off on us like that."

"Anything for the boys."

"You said it: probably shacked up with a couple of hotrock
pilots at this very instant."

"You think so?"

"Sure I do. Jesus Christ, you can't trust anybody any more
. . . Come on, let's get out of here. Let's go up there and kick
in the door on 'em. Surprise 'em in the sack. Probably picked
up a couple of chair-borne commandos from the Pentagon.
Five pips up. War effort, you know . . ."

In a rising rage they went out into the downstairs foyer. The
crowd had thinned out a good deal, but groups of men in
uniform or couples still passed up and down the long, curving
stairway.

"He cut me," Newcombe said crossly.

"Who did?"

"That colonel. That lousy limey colonel cut me."

"He did! What did you take it for?" O'Neill demanded; he
seized Newcombe by the shoulder and half turned him
around, his eyes blazing. "What did you take it off them for?
We're winning the Goddamn war for them, aren't we? Frig
'em! Nobody gives the corps a bad time. *Nobody*," he announced savagely.

"Winning the war all by your lonesome, gyrene?" a voice
called.

They looked up, saw near the head of the stairs a group of
paratroopers grinning down at them.

"Rough and tough," O'Neill snarled. "Pa-ra-troopers."
He drawled the word out between his teeth. "I heard that,
funny man . . ."

"Did you now?" another one of them called. "Hey, he
must be a hero . . ."

"Rough and tough as Christ almighty, ain't ya?" O'Neill
shouted. Whirling he raced up the stairs and flung into the
knot of men, swinging wildly with both hands. One of the
paratroopers staggered back against the railing, nearly went
over; there was a violent upheaval in the clump of khaki—and
all of a sudden O'Neill came tumbling back down the stairs
head over heels, crashed into Newcombe as he was starting up
and drove him to his knees.

"Jay." He shook O'Neill's head, slapped his cheeks; O'Neill gave no response. Newcombe looked up. A dozen faces surrounded him: hard, hostile faces, watching him coldly.

"You got something to say, marine?" one of them—it was impossible to say which one—said dryly. "You got something to say like your buddy, there?"

"No," Newcombe said; he shook his head. "I haven't got anything to say."

"Okay. That's better."

Then, staring up at the ring of faces the raging flamed out in a thick, boiling puff, dispelled the fear. "Why don't you get your battalion?" he demanded. "Sure, I'll shut up—but if there were two or three of you it'd be something else, I can cut you in on *that* scoop . . ."

"All right. We'll wait for you outside."

"Can that, Maxwell," another one said. "We're not looking for any trouble, marine. Just don't get any funny ideas, that's all."

They moved back up the stairs, stomping in their high boots. O'Neill was stirring, moving his arms feebly and mumbling. Newcombe got to his feet and half-dragged, half-carried O'Neill back into the men's room, propped him over one of the washbowls and turning on both taps full force splashed his face repeatedly.

"Jay," he said. "Come on, Jay . . ."

O'Neill's eyes opened—all whites; the pupils shot into view, danced around like blue marbles in a child's maze game.

"What's up?" he said truculently.

"We're back in the can. You all right?"

"Sure I am . . . Where were *you*, buddy?"

"I wasn't anywhere. I didn't know you were going to take off after the whole paratrooper army."

"Ah, you're such an intellectual, buddy-ro. You're such an awful intellectual type . . . You can't let that kind of thing go *by*—" He put his hand to the side of his head as though afraid it would shatter on contact. "Oh. I really stopped one."

"You sure did. You took the stairs in one. You sure you're okay?"

"Absolutely. Never better." O'Neill was moving around the lavatory in little circles, his whole body oddly inclined to the right; now and then he put his hand to the wall for support. "Feel great. Let's go."

He turned from the wall, lost his balance and sat down hard on the tile floor, his face blank with surprise. Newcombe hauled him to his feet again.

"Come on, Jay. MP's spot us we're in trouble. Hear me?"

O'Neill nodded, said: "Right." He was trying to talk without moving his jaw. "I'll be okay. In a minute. Funny thing: can't seem to stand up straight."

"Come on, now." Newcombe put his arm under him and steered him toward the door. "What you need is some fresh air."

They emerged from the men's room for the second time—and walked right into the girls.

"Where did you go?" Lorraine cried hotly, hands on her hips. "We've been looking all over for you, waiting and waiting around—we even went outside and looked and you never—"

"Jay got clipped," Newcombe said. "Some paratroopers jumped us."

"You mean you've been in a *fight*?"

"Yes. Give me a hand with him, will you?"

"Oh, Jay—you're not still getting in fights—"

O'Neill shook his head at her solemnly. "Never better."

Newcombe turned to Helen and said, "Hello, there."

"Hello."

She smiled gravely, watching him, and he was again struck by the sense of something tender and unexplained and imminent in their encounter. He realized all at once he was tremendously delighted at seeing her again.

"I'm sorry," he said. "I really am. We—got all confused."

"We didn't know where you'd gone," she said. "We waited around everywhere we could think of. We thought finally you'd—"

"Skipped out on you?"

She smiled and nodded. "It looked that way."

"Well, don't you worry about *that*." At this she looked at him swiftly—a dark, searching glance: and he dropped his eyes. He was surprised at the intensity with which he'd said that. "A gyrene never fails to come through," he added facetiously. "Don't you know that?"

"We were about ready to go home," Lorraine was saying angrily to O'Neill, who was leaning on her arm. "Honestly! Of all the crazy things to do—"

"Now, baby," O'Neill said in plaintive entreaty. "We didn't know *what* the score was. We thought you'd taken off and left us—"

"Left *you*—! I like that—we came back and you weren't—"

"Now, baby: case of the honor of the corps. You wouldn't want us to let down the honor of the corps, would you?"

"I don't care what it was. You weren't at the table when we came back. You weren't anywhere in the room . . ."

"Jack, we weren't no-where," O'Neill sang with quick irrelevance. "That's what you mean, baby-doll: *Jack, we ain't no-where—"*

"Oh, you're never serious. Honestly, Jay—you never *realize* things . . ."

"You never re-alize," he sang, *"what's in your baby's eyes, till the moonlight's set the world all-aglow . . ."*

The night, cold and bright with stars, revived them. O'Neill straightened his cap, gave a tug to his blouse and took Lorraine's arm.

"Swell!" he pronounced, inhaling. "Just *breathe* that mountain air . . . Sorry to trouble you all. Where to? What I need is a short swifty."

"No you don't," Lorraine said. "You've had enough."

"Enough!"

"Yes, you have. We all have."

"Maybe so, maybe so," he said lightly. "I don't care—I've found my baby! Yes sir-ree." He bent over and kissed her on the neck and she giggled in protest. "Hey, old Newk," he went on happily; walking along with elaborate punctilio, bent so far backward he appeared in danger of toppling over with every stride, he turned back to Newcombe and Helen. "Hey, Mr. Blue-blood: isn't this great, though?—strolling along old D.C. with all the bounce in the world? You know—there's something you can't quite pin down: a moment like this, here. Know what I mean? Something sort of—I don't know . . . sort of—"

All at once his legs buckled and he went to his knees on the sidewalk, almost dragging down with him Lorraine, who gave a surprised cry.

"Jay," Newcombe said. He pulled him erect again, held O'Neill's thin, swaying form in his arms, looked around apprehensively. And his heart gave a little leap of fright.

Two marine MP's were crossing the avenue at an angle about a block away from them, coming their way; looking back watching for traffic they hadn't seen them yet.

"Jay," he said. "You've got to stand up. Come on, now—"

"Can't make it," O'Neill breathed thickly; his eyes opened and closed with eerie deliberation. "Al buddy. Funny just can't do—"

U S MAIL. Newcombe stared at the big dark green box not ten feet away. U S MAIL. Holding O'Neill erect by main strength he bore him over and backed him up against it. The thought of stuffing him in the package-drop shot through his mind and he had an hysterical urge to laugh.

"What are you going to do?" Lorraine said.

"Now talk it up," he muttered. The sweat was sliding down his sides; he could hear his voice tremble. "Hold him up on that side, Lorraine. Close up more. All right. Let's just talk it up, now. Come on. Anything—"

The girls' voices burst into chatter so voluble it startled him; his whole body was quaking with his heartbeats. O'Neill's head hung forward like the head of a nearly decapitated doll.

Newcombe said fiercely: "Jay. We're in a jam. MP's. Stand by! . . . Goddamnit, boy—*stand-at-attention* when I tell you!"

The harsh, omnivorous, never-to-be-forgotten intonation of the Parris Island drill instructor. O'Neill's head went up, his eyes rolled without focus; his lips clamped together rigidly. Again Newcombe had an overwhelming deisre to roar with laughter.

The MP's had reached the curb, came toward them down the broad pavement in their slow, deliberate tread, half-saunter, half-strut, their eyes glittering under their cap bills—moved past like shadows of death and destruction and everlasting retribution for all earthly sins; stalked away down the avenue and melted into the lights.

"All right," Newcombe said. "I'm going to get us a cab. Hang on to him, now. And for God's sake don't let him go anywhere. I'll be back as soon as I can with a cab." He hurried off, away from the MP's, staring wild-eyed into the darkness, swallowing, trying vainly to coax saliva into his mouth.

When the orange-hued cab swooped over in response to his whistle he was almost sick with relief.

11

"PRISONERS—*halt!*"

The files came to a one-two stomp standstill, flung their arms grotesquely above shoulder level, fingertips on elbows, and stood fast. With their shaved skulls, clothed in odd-lot utilities adorned with the huge block P on back and thighs, holding the rigid, preposterous attitude in the cold streaming rain they looked like mechanical imitations of men: subhuman and absurd.

The MP sergeant, dressed in greens overcoat and barracks hat, walked the length of the column and surveyed them candidly.

"Sugrue!"

"Sir!"

"Five laps. Take off!"

One of the prisoners broke ranks and began to run clumsily along the ten-foot-wide aisle between the tents and the barbed wire, slipped and fell sprawling in the slick mud and got up again.

"You want to lie down, boy?" the sergeant called to him in a soft southern accent.

"No, sir."

"You want some sack-time, that it?"

"No *sir!*"

"That'll cost you two more. Hear?"

"Yes, sir!"

"Now move out!"

For a time the sergeant watched the rain-soaked figure running around beside the wire. He had a round, cherubic face with little pale blue eyes; his expression as he watched Sugrue was pleasantly attentive, almost indulgent. When Sugrue slipped and fell again he murmured something more in a low voice and the two MP's standing near him laughed and hitched at their pistol belts.

Standing in the front rank Kantaylis pressed his forearms against each other, clamped his thighs together tightly. Over the past two days and nights weariness and cold had seeped into him like a filling cistern; and now, at the end of another day of hard labor in the rain, his arms and legs ached as though they'd been pounded with a ball bat and a hot, tight flashing had started behind his eyes. *Chill,* he thought, and his heart filled with dread; I'm getting a chill. Even while he swallowed and swallowed again, breathing slowly, the trembling began—the deep, involuntary trembling that was only the prelude to what would come later. For a few tenuous moments he fought to recall the fanlike caress of the heat from the fire against his legs and loins, the warm pressure of Andrea's body against his own, the stirring, savory warmth of her flesh: then the cold rain and a fierce, tremulous shudder caught him in its malign grip and shook him, shook him again in an ominous silence.

The sergeant was standing in front of him.

Tense with foreboding Kantaylis kept his eyes severely front, above the level of the sergeant's cap; but in the scan of his gaze he could see the soft round face take on a strange, bemused, almost rapt expression.

"Shaking all over," the sergeant said in a soft drawl. "Just the funniest thing in Tent City. Just shaking all over with laughing."

The tremor grew worse; he felt as though he were standing immersed in a tank through which ice-water was coursing—or as though the ice-water were inside him and his bones were the conduits. His teeth clicked against each other and he clamped his jaws together; sweat was streaming through his brows into his eyes, almost blinding him. A swift arc of pain traversed his stomach in a spasm and he grunted with the effort to hold himself rigid. The bug. The atabrine pills were in his seabag, in the police shed; wrapped in a sock. Far, far away now: it might as well be a million miles. In a wooden matchbox inside a sock. Carrington had given them to him in return for—what? Something. The bland, cherubic face wabbled and wavered before him. The dizziness would come later if it were a bad one, and the nausea and more sweating; and the nightmares. Of all the times—

"Stand-at-attention!"

The sudden fierce bark, pregnant with threat, froze him motionless; but the shudder began again immediately, his jaw was working loose like a piece of an engine, the bones of his trunk and hips jarred and clattered and pumped their icy fluid up and down, up and down. In a tight: he was in a tight now, and no mistake. A rotten lousy break. The sweat all at once turned cold on his forehead and neck.

"*Boy* you got to learn here. Snap-to! . . . Stand at attention when I talk to you or you'll be one sorry little brig-rat. Hear?"

"Yes, sir."

"That's right. That's better, now." The sergeant went on watching Kantaylis in mildly pleased preoccupation, gloved hands on his hips; the steam issued in bursts from his small, pursed lips.

"Well now, the hero," he remarked, musing, nodding faintly, his little round blue eyes narrowed at the corners. "Well, now. Was it worth it, hero? Couple minutes' rutting? Ah? *Stand at attention!* Was it worth it? You tell me."

Kantaylis stood stiffly silent.

"Tell me!"

Kantaylis slowly lowered his gaze until it came to rest on the baby blue eyes.

"Sure it was worth it," he said.

The sergeant's brows rose, his round face clouded with petulant surprise, still abstracted and musing. "That right, now?" he said with drawling, rising intonation. "It was. It was all worth it . . ."

And with astonishing agility he swept down and out of the flat rectangle of vision made by Kantaylis' raised forearms.

The blow, full in the groin, turned him sick and hollow all at once; he folded in two, went to his knees, holding on to his genitals with his cupped hands. Something very hard struck him on the side of the head: again. He was lying on his side, his face pressed against the mud. He was staring at two brilliantly polished garrison shoes whose toes were speckled with tiny bright bubbles of rain. One of them vanished while he stared at it, and a broad belt of pain swelled out from his stomach like a flash of monstrously inflammable liquid ignited. With an effort he looked up; his vision blurred and darkened, he was filled with contempt and savage rage, and fought it down. The sergeant was looking down at him: the little pouter pigeon's lips were moving but he couldn't understand the words, he could only hear them.

"—shoot your mouth off in *this* lash-up you've got trouble. Now when I want an answer I want an answer, and otherwise button your mouth. Now get up!"

He started to struggle blindly to his feet, had got to his knees when something lashed down over his head again—a bolt of merciless light—and drove him to the mud.

". . . going to be good?" the sergeant's voice continued, soft and inquiring and unperturbed. "Decided to be a good little brig-rat now and keep your nose clean? Ah?"

"Take it easy, Ransome," another voice said, a bit deferentially. "He'll straighten up."

"You ain't just a rock-knocking he will."

"He's got the bug: that's why he's shaking like that. He was on the Canal."

"You think I don't know about it?" Ransome inquired in a soft, forbidding tone. There was no reply and he went on: "I know all about him. A big-ass hero. Thinks he's king spit. Thinks he pisses Coca-Cola, he can sass old Wittaker himself. Sure. I know him. A hero . . ." He straightened and whirled on the rest of the prisoners, all at once choleric and violent. "You people—you think you can calk off and get out from under by going over the hump," he shouted at them, walking up and down in front of them rapidly. "Getting drunk, getting yourselves some of that juicy Kinston poon-tang, picking up a dose. Don't you, now? Well, we don't give a hoot in a gale whether you're dead or alive or how long you're in here either just so long as you remember what you are: *brig-rats!*—and crud-eating brig-rats besides. You think you're going to shag ass out of this detail. Well, you got another thought. You're shipping out under guard in four days' time, the lot of you. They're going to stick your sorry asses in the first wave on Tokyo and I hope you get blown all to hell! . . ."

The areas of pain had spread thickly, like oil on gauze, until their perimeters had joined in one quaking mass. Kantaylis retched, vomited up a thick ball of something and spat it out weakly. He was shaking now from head to foot, but his mind was clear. Lying in the cold mud listening to Ransome's furious harangue he felt for an instant a tremendous relief, almost elation: they were going to ship out with the battalion. Maybe when he'd done his time Jack Freuhof could ask for him, get him back with the squad. He was going to ship out with them . . .

The ruddy, cherubic face, once more placid and absorbed, was bending over him again.

"Well now, hero: you had time to think it over yet? Or do you want to go round one more time? Ah?"

Kantaylis looked at him warily. I could get you: get you right from here, you low creeping son-of-a-bitch. You gutless stateside garrison commando. If you just bend down a little more: just a little farther—

"Let me cut you in, hero: the only decorations you're going to get in this place are going to be lumps on your sorry Dago hide. And if you don't snap-to you're going to get plenty. You're going to be the most decorated man in the whole wide Marine Corps. And I crap you not. Hear?"

Holding on to himself Kantaylis watched the bland, wide blue eyes. Take it, he told himself savagely. What matters is joining the squad: you know that. Let it go.

"Well, how about it, hero? You still don't care whether school keeps or not?"

The squad. Joining the squad. All that matters. Take it!—

"Was it worth it, big-ass hero? . . . *Answer me*, you frigging brig-rat!"

". . . No," he said tonelessly. "No, sir."

The red, round face beamed in surprise, the little mouth opened in a perfect O. "Now that's more like it. That's the ticket. Now we'll get along a lot better. A whole lot. Just so long as you keep a couple things in the front of your stupid Dago head . . . You seem to have got the idea you're somebody pretty special. Ah? Maybe you've forgotten just where you are," his voice drawled its ominous, soft cadence. "In the brig at Tent City. Yeah." Ransome bobbed his head at him; a slow, bemused nodding. "That's right. You ain't a corporal any more, you ain't a yard bird any more, you ain't a rifleman, you ain't anything any more at all. You're just as low as you can crawl in this world: a low—scummy— ignorant—brig-rat. You've bought it. You got a long, long way to go just to see the light of day. Hear?"

Crouched in the rain, still peering down in amused absorption he reached out and took hold of the lobe of Kantaylis' ear between finger and thumb and pulled it back and forth.

"You catch on, Dago," he said softly. "You just need a little time to get indoctrinated, that's all. Don't you?"

Kantaylis licked his lips; the rain stung the back of his head, which quaked hollowly.

"Yes sir," he said.

In the twilight the wind swept through the ragged, floorless tents like the edge of death; chill and silent. Figures rolled tightly from head to foot in the green blankets flung themselves from side to side or lay staring up at the dark torn canvas, their bodies straight and perfectly immobile: corpses prepared for sea burial.

"Well, he's a mean one," the huge Negro on the back cot declared in a deep, mournful voice. "A mean hard man, that Ransome. Mean and evil. Kind put his own mother in a sweatbox and stand there hold up a can of water right in front of her all day long."

"Well I'm telling you *I'm* going to get that bastard," a

squat Italian boy named Kinsella said darkly from the other side of the tent. "Where I come from guys like that don't last long."

"Where's that, man?"

"Kerry Corner."

"Never heard of it myself."

"You would if you lived near there. Wait'll we get overseas I'm going to get him if I don't ever do anything else."

The big Negro laughed at this; a slow, dolorous exclamation that rang like a gently struck iron gong. "You think he going to ship out with you, boy?" he asked; the whites of his eyes rolled in mock amazement. "He ain't going ship out from *no* place."

"Sure he is."

"Shhhh . . ." The Negro hissed in amused demurral. "He permanent personnel. He going to be here beating up on brigrats when you'se in Af-*ghan*-istan. Come four days you won't never see him again your natural life."

"Then I'll get him afterward," Kinsella muttered. "I'm going to cut the son-of-a-bitch's heart out for what he done to me, Mungo."

"Maybe so. If you still *warm*, that is . . ."

"Well, I ain't warm now."

"You bet you ain't . . ." Mungo's head rolled to the other side of his cot languidly. "How you making it, boy?"

"Okay," Kantaylis answered. "Can't complain."

"No: you cain't do that . . . Whyn't you turn in to sick bay, though—get that tended to? He cain't keep you from going to sick call, you work it right."

"It's no problem."

"You mess with that kind of grope, it don't get coagulated you liable come down with gan-*grene*. Man, then you'se in *real* trouble. Real trouble."

"I'll take the chance," Kantaylis said. "Right now I've got a lot more to worry about than a cut in the back of my head."

"What got into you made you talk like that to the man? give him that back lip?"

"I don't know," Kantaylis said.

"Didn't you know they was going lower the boom, you mess with them?"

"Yeah. I knew it."

Mungo sighed through his nose—a thick, lengthy snort of resignation; the whites of his eyes glittered. "You got to be good nigger round this place. I *mean*. Yessir, Mister Ransome, anything you say, Mister Ransome, gimme a spoon to eat it with, Mister Ransome. Sure. Don't make no difference what color your skin happen to be, either . . . You'se *lucky*, man: plenty lucky. Boy in here last week give Ransome some back talk they carabonged him over the head so many times he looked like a turkey caught his head in a lawn mower. We ain't even *seen* that boy no more, none of us. Mmm— *mmmmh*. He wishing and praying he back in *here* by now . . ."

The floodlights came on all at once: a violent, comfortless blare that struck cut-planes of light and shadow through the tent-flaps, filled the interior with cavernous gloom. Kantaylis pulled the blanket up over his face and closed his eyes. The chill, miraculously, had passed but he was shaking with cold, and his belly and head and groin crawled with burgeoning pain: if he could only vomit for five solid minutes, empty himself out down there somehow, he'd be all right. Or if he could lie suspended in some warm, gelatinous substance—like one of the size tubs at the mill—bobbing and turning in the thick amber fluid distilled from the hides of water buffalos, lying dreamily, laved in warmth, with far away the low growling of the beaters and the blue-white diffusion of light over the screen and beyond everything the high, wire-borne whine of the Jordan like one piercing note endlessly held on a gigantic violin . . .

"What we got tomorrow?" a thin man from Maine asked.

"What you think?" Mungo boomed. "We got culverts again. Culverts and culverts and more culverts. Man, we going to dig culverts all over the area so the officers won't get their shoes unshined. For four more days, anyway . . ."

"Is that true, Mungo? They going to put us in the first wave?"

"You don't think they going make jokes with a brig-rat now, do you? Sure they are."

"What difference does it make?" the man from Maine said. "We'd have been in it anyway."

"No. Probably the fourth or fifth."

There was silence. Near the guard hut, behind them, somebody laughed and spat; a jeep roared away, its tires hissing in the mud, spraying water, and turned on to the highway toward the main gate where its engine faded to a soft moan.

Kinsella said: "You see that about Tarawa?"

"Yeah."

"They say they had to wade in from a mile out. The whole Second Marines got wiped out."

"That right?"

"To a man."

"Jesus."

"Somebody fouled up the detail, that's for sure."

"What you think, Kantaylis?"

Kantaylis opened his eyes. "I don't know. It sounds like a foul-up all right. There always is one."

"There is?"

"Hell, yes. Nobody knows what's really going on anyway, half the time . . ."

He closed his eyes again, held his genitals lightly in his two hands. Their talk went on outside him, touched with doubt and apprehension, punctuated with the darkly incantatory word: Tarawa. Ta-*rah*-waaa . . . Wading through waist-deep water from a mile out, through the humming, whistling cones of menace, the thin white leaping geysers. Two thousand yards . . . Was that how they were going to be from here on—one blood-soaked island after another stretching off into the measureless sea? He seemed to see them—an infinitely long, infinitely complicated series of atolls and palm-fringed islands curving away gradually to the northwest, toward that looming, shrouded heartland of snow-capped volcanoes and torii like massive, exotic grape arbors and a stocky, flat-faced, stubborn people who would never, never, never give in: each island ringed with a curtain of fire into which ten thousand tiny helmeted figures waded and leaped and fell sprawling, arms extended . . .

"Hey, Kantaylis."

"Yeah?"

"Hey, you think they'll shove us in Scouts-and-Snipers?"

"No," he said. "No, I don't think so."

He couldn't sleep. Perhaps if he could dream while waking: if he curled up tightly on this hard canvas cot and dwelt on the sheer delight of the cabin, Andrea's face inclining toward him, her hair shimmering, her eyes full of soft deeps, her lower lip uncommonly red in the light from the fire . . .

But somehow all he could think of was the hollow, heart-sick moment of departure, and his father.

The bus came down the long stretch from Windsor, looming like a great yellow juggernaut against the snow, swept down on them with the ruthlessness of time racing.

"Well," he said. "Here we go again."

Beside him Andrea was gazing hypnotically at the approaching bus; when she turned to him again her face had gone thin with fear and her lips parted, bloodless and trembling.

"It's all right," he murmured. "it's all right, honey girl."

His mother was pulling at his sleeve, saying "Danny—" in an urgent, undefined tone. "Danny—"

"Goodbye, Ma," he said. He kissed her, hugged her to him. They were all around him now, touching him, embracing him—Stella and Nick and Masha and Mr. Lenaine and little Jimmy—they were all saying something to him but he heard nothing: it was as though he were immersed in a mist of emotion so strong it was like a transparent hood; he couldn't cut his way out of it and the faces swung in toward him and swung away again in a dreamy, strangely painful haze. Only his father stood apart, distant and composed, and watched them all with that dull, sightless gaze—as if he were forever listening to some absorbing, disturbing not-quite-intelligible voice in the waste caverns of his brain.

"Goodbye, boy," Mr. Lenaine was saying, holding his hand. "Come back, now: come back to us—"

He was embracing Andrea. She started to say something, stopped, shook her head, shook it again quickly, her teeth pressed into her lower lip in a clean white line. So white and even: it was amazing! Our baby will have teeth like that, flashed through his head. Our baby will . . . There were things he should have said, he should be saying now: what were they? Her fingers gripped his neck.

"Goodbye, honey," he said. "All my love . . ." He released her and mounted the bus.

"Daniel! Wait!"

It was his father. Kantaylis turned on the step, saw them all in suddenly better focus, standing in a clump by the wall under the huge Scarborough Oak which, blasted and snow-laden, shook its shriveled brown leaves above their heads: a tight little knot from which his father had detached himself and was coming forward, his pale, lined face terribly alive, his eyes wide with horror. Along the edge of his hat brim the livid scar curved off into his white hair. He threw open his arms.

"No!" he cried hoarsely. "No, no—*Daniel!* Come back—!"

The anguish in that final cry shook them all; they began to tremble like the oak leaves above them. Kantaylis remained

rooted on the top step of the bus, hands gripping the door
guards, staring down in bewilderment, unable to move; his
bowels clutched and contracted. His father was approaching
him unsurely, almost blindly, his arms extended; tears began
to trickle down his seamed face. He pointed to the driver in
sudden, fierce accusation, shouted, "No! Stop him. *Stop
him!*" and kept waggling his head in a slow frenzy of grief.

Mr. Lenaine and Nick had hold of his father now, were
talking to him in low, soothing voices. The old man said
nothing, gazed up at Kantaylis imploringly, gesticulated
again. They were all crying now, set off by his father's
astonishing outburst: his mother was crying, Stella and Masha
were crying, little Jimmy was sobbing violently; Andrea was
silent, her mouth firm, but tears were streaming down her
cheeks. The sight wrung him. So many tears, he thought,
heavily, so many tears; the world was bathed in the tears of
weeping women and children and old men—and all for
nothing, it was all wrong, everyone could be living in quiet
simplicity, couldn't they all?—a calm, fruitful living out of
their lives—

"All set?"

He turned, startled, encountered the driver's inquiring face.

"Sure," he said thickly. "Didn't mean to hold you up.
My—"

"That's okay," the driver said.

The door clashed closed: they were moving away, the walls
were furling closed like gates behind him, all of them were
waving now, straining toward him and waving, reaching out
as if they were still holding on to some invisible but indissoluble skein that bound him to them—they could no longer see
him but they were still waving . . . all but his father, who had
removed his hat and stood, small and grief-stricken, looking
off across the valley toward Mount Greylock, his hair a fluttering silvery crest against the black rock of the wall.

"Hey, Kantaylis—"

He started. "What?" he said.

"Kantaylis, you think they'll cut our brig-time if they shove
us in the first wave?"

"*I* don't know," he said irritably. "How in Christ's name
should I know? I've never been in here before . . ."

"The guys at Mare Island, I hear they gave them a choice
just the other day: do your time or put in for combat."

"That's a fine choice, now," Mungo said, and laughed his

rumbling laugh. "Now isn't that a mighty fine choice?"

"What the hell, it's a chance against a sure thing," the Maine man said.

"First wave'll be a sure thing, too, way they doing things now."

"That bastard Wittaker," Kinsella said savagely; he flung himself on his other side on his cot. "That bloody butcher B. P. Wittaker. Burial Party Wittaker. He'll butcher the whole outfit in one operation. *He* doesn't give a good God-damn: he's got his sack and his officers' clubs and his broads . . ."

"Ah, hell," Kantaylis said wearily. "He's nothing."

"What do you mean he's nothing?"

"He's just a cog. Like you or me."

"He's a hell of a lot bigger one."

"Sure: but he's still a piece of the machinery. Hell, if *he* was all there was . . ."

Andrea's face, white and still and tear-streaked by the wall, hovered against his mind; he could see her with such clarity he could hardly believe it. Perhaps that was because it was the final moment. "I can't help it," she had said as they were driving down from the cabin; her face had been tense and drawn in the gray light, with deep circles under her eyes. "I'll try not to but I can't help it: I'll be afraid all the time, I know I will. I can't make it stop. I couldn't before." Turning toward him she had given him a brief, forlorn smile.

His groin quaked with a series of twinges that made him gasp, duck his head into his shoulders, grunting, breathing thickly through his nose. Ah, what did they think they were trying to accomplish, anyway? Wasn't it possible, when you were sending a lot of poor sods out to reasonably certain death or worse—sure, there were several things worse than getting killed, he knew three or four of them—wasn't it possible in view of all that to give them all a final, few hours at home—a last chance for a lot of them to be with their wives or girls or families? Or was that asking just too Goddamned much?

Yes: it obviously was. Still, they'd find their stateside brigs a lot emptier and morale a lot higher if they did something like that. But perhaps they *wanted* the brigs fuller and morale lower—no doubt they wanted everyone just about as miserable and bewildered and defiant as possible. He remembered little Gannon on the ship going up to the Canal snarling, "I don't give a crud, I'm so Goddamned mad at the whole lousy lash-up I don't give a crudding Goddamn about anything at all," and Gunny Scopene grinning at him and saying, "That's just the way they want you, fella, that's *just* how they want you to feel"; and Gannon glaring back at him, blinking, his mouth open, speechless with exasperation. Well, if that was what they wanted that was what they were getting . . .

Anger flooded him, warmed him subtly inside the thin wool blankets, coursed through his body until he quivered with rage and clenched his hands. But who the living hell did they really think they were fooling, anyway? What did they think held men together, kept them going through a succession of interminable, hopeless agonies, kept them from flaking out or cracking up under shelling when they were wounded and shaking with dysentery and the bug and a thousand and one other private miseries?—brig-time and brutality? A big rat's ass. What kind of a system was it when they handed you medals for killing and stuck you in a barbed-wire cage for trying to heal? Maybe it was better to care with all your heart than be so crazed with frustration and abuse you didn't care about anything, not even what you did with your own life—as little Gannon had done . . . All right, if it had to be got over with then let's get it over with, kill or be killed, dog-eat-dog, wade in through a thousand lagoons from a mile out, creep through a thousand malarial boondocks till the rotten business was finally over. But wasn't there any chance—just a faint, sniveling, sneaking chance—of doing that and treating the waders and creepers with a little dignity, a little human self-respect, for the love of Christ?

Probably not. Probably that was just the bind: you gave up the one when you decided on the other. You didn't have it both ways in this world; or in any other, either. And there you were . . .

"I'd give about fifty bucks for a skag right now," Kinsella said. "I ain't kidding: fifty bucks."

"Which you ain't got either," Mungo boomed softly. "Which you won't never have time they get through docking your pay."

"Hey, gimme butts on it, Kinsella," another voice said.

"On what?"

"On that fifty-dollar skag you ain't got."

"Funny man . . . *Jesus*, I could use a drag."

"Don't go around on it, boy, only makes it worse. Just take it a day at a time."

"Ah, blow it out, Mungo."

"Suit yourself . . ."

Kantaylis wound the blankets tighter around his hips. The anger had gone; had utterly faded, leaving him lying in the stockade in Tent City feeling colder and emptier than before. His head throbbed and he held one hand over his groin and pressed his legs gently together. The cold sank into his bones. Four days, he told himself doggedly. You've got to hang on for four days, any way you can. Just keep turning over. Then we'll see.

"Well, it's a big long war, as the man says," Mungo intoned. His voice quivered in the cold, still air. "Long, long war. Going to last a motherated ten years long . . ."

Through the tent-flap in the glare of the floodlights streamers of rag and grass-stalk fluttered on the crazily tangled strands of wire.

12

"LISTEN TO THAT little kitty-cat yowl," Lorraine said. Crouched down, her dress billowing around her full flanks, she mouthed softly babycat talk, stroked the animal's scrawny yellow back, scratched it between the ears while it arched its neck and mewed. "Oh he sweety, yes he a cutey-kitty-cat yowler for sure . . ."

"What's his name?" Newcombe asked.

Lorraine poured some milk into a saucer. "We call him MacArthur. Ooh he sweety: yes. Because he's always talking in little sentences."

"I—will—return," O'Neill intoned hollowly from the bed in the far corner of the room.

"And because he's a big, strong, spit-and-polish kitty . . ." Lorraine turned toward Newcombe and Helen with a quick little indulgent grin, picked up her cup of coffee again and sipped at it. "God, that's good. You can just *feel* it work on you."

"Can't feel thing at all," O'Neill muttered from the bed.

"You drink some too, Jay," she commanded. "Come on, now. It's right there beside you."

"Don't want coffee . . . How bout just little Bourbon water—"

"No!"

"—slake my thirst. Know? Keep party rolling long . . ."

"Party—what party?" Lorraine came over to where Newcombe and Helen were sitting. "He's terrible, isn't he?" She giggled, turned serious again and went on in a heavy sickroom whisper: "He never used to be like this. Leaving us like that and then getting into a fight, he never used to get into fights, honestly. Oh, once in a while, you know; but he always had the sunniest way about him. And how he loves kids! Wowie: you know he started swimming classes for little kids one summer down at the beach, he's wonderful with them, he can get them to get over their fear and everything." Her eyes widened. "Did you know he saved a woman's life?"

"No. Did he?"

She nodded. "In the surf. At Panoag. A rich woman from New York. She was going down for the third time and Jay rescued her, and do you know what? Her bathing suit got torn somehow, way up one side, and when he got her back to shore she began to scream he'd torn her suit while she was out in the water. That he was—you know. Imagine! And Jay wasn't even angry at that. He just threw back his head and laughed, you know, that way he has, and said, 'If you'd drowned you'd have blamed it on a dogfish!' "

"She would have, too," O'Neill's voice came sonorously from the end of the room. "Wanted a cheap thrill or something. Should have let her deep-six herself . . ." Sprawled on the tousled bedspread, arms outstretched, a wet towel wound crazily around his head, he murmured, "Lorraine . . ."

She went over and sat down beside him. "How do you feel, Jay?"

"Lorraine." His hands moved unsurely along her full, soft arms to her shoulders. "Lorraine, baby . . ." His voice faded and gathered strength and faded again, like a voice over short wave. "Baby . . . when gonna . . . fall a shelf . . . ?"

She giggled and stroked his hair. "You *are* cute, Jay," she said. "You really are. But you drank *so* much: didn't you?" And she bent forward over him until her hair hung all about his face in silky chestnut waves.

Newcombe stretched his legs, let his head loll back against the cushions. The day seemed to embrace years upon years—a divinely hammered shield of Achilles displaying in a flash the whole riotous, dizzying sweep of human experience. For time had altered its nature—time was moving so swiftly it had usurped both past and future: the future was fast disappearing, the past hung on with but a feeble tenacity—the rush of the present swallowed up everything, confronted them with veils through which they could not see: vows and libations and the clash of armies on alien shores. Ah love, let us be true to one another! for the world, which seems to lie before us like a land of dreams—

He turned to the girl.

"You're pretty swell, do you know that?"

She smiled and he said, "No, I'm serious. I wish we'd met five years ago. Or even three. I do . . ."

She turned and looked at him directly—a silent, enigmatic glance that charmed him. He realized with a little shock that he was no longer conscious of the cast in her eye; that he hadn't been for hours. Well: why should he be? It was after all scarcely noticeable, looked at objectively. The problem was of course that he'd never been able to look at it objectively. It was the deep childhood dread which had always caused him to magnify it out of all proportion, avert his face in a little spasm of terror; was that it?

Lulled in an eddying inebriation he stared solemnly, shutting first one eye and then the other, at the strange, semirecumbent pose of Lorraine and O'Neill embracing. With one—Rodin: Rodin with a snootful. With the other—Lipschitz perhaps: a fuzzy cubist composition of arms and heads abstracted. Yet it was still Jay and Lorraine . . . The eye: the light of the body, the window of the soul, the orb of anguish. Bureaus, lamps, bouquet-papered walls went foggy and sharp by turns. All alike in the dark: all cats (including MacArthur) look alike.

But if thine eye be single—

"Do you mean that?" she said.

"Mean what?"

"What you just said."

"Sure I do," he replied airily. "Of course I do. I never say anything I don't mean. Or mean anything I don't say. Conversely."

She tossed her head—a strange little gesture—started to speak and was silent.

"No, no, go ahead," he prompted, waving one hand. "En avant . . ."

"You're making fun again."

"No—well, only partly. Everybody makes fun one way or another. Form of protest against the slings and arrows. Old Jay was protesting when he lit into that multitude of paratroopers—"

"Oh. I thought you said they attacked *you*."

"What? Well—same thing: we fought back *of course* but the odds were great. The odds were terrible, I can't begin to convey . . ."

She smiled secretively and looked down; then said anxiously, "Do you think he'll be all right?"

"Sure he will. Don't worry about old Jay. Why, you can't kill an Irishman with a fire axe. And a *redheaded* Irishman!"

"Do you think he hurt his head?"

He laughed. "Not on your life. In my opinion he's just plain cockeyed."

Her head whipped away as though he'd struck her.

"—Oh, I'm sorry," he said; he put his hand on her arm. "No, really. I mean it. I am . . ."

She shook her head rapidly, went on looking down at her lap.

"I am. Really," he went on. "I just said it without thinking. I didn't realize there was a—" Her silence troubled him deeply. "Good Lord, it's hardly noticeable. I mean it. It's all my own . . . As a matter of fact I was going to tell you—just a few minutes ago: that's the reason I didn't make OCS—I'm practically blind in my right eye. A doctor once told me he didn't know why it hadn't turned in."

He paused, and she looked at him. "Is that true?" she asked.

"Absolutely. Jay'll tell you. I can't see a thing out of this one. Shadows mostly. I was only lucky. So you see? . . . Ah, it's all the shoddiest chance anyway." He thought all at once of the hut, and Danny standing by the rickety door; and a mood of sullen fatality swept over him. "Like dice in a cornpopper. What a farce: what a hilarious fiasco. We stagger along our separate gossamer rope-ladders over the Dread Abyss, in the dead of dark night, teetering from side to side, fingers clenched on the wobbling balance-pole of our concerns—fears on one end and desires on the other, they never balance anyhow—and listen for the crackling that means the swift, inevitable snapping of the strands . . ."

The ceiling, reflected by a rococo, long-obsolete light fix-
ture in the shape of pansy petals, kept sliding and starting,
wheeled with eerie slowness above his head, flapping its petals
like gross yellow wings. God, what a speech. Couldn't he say
anything—anything at all—without wallowing in a hash of
maudlin rhetoric six feet deep? Doubtful. Highly. Why
couldn't he say what he *meant*, for God's sake? She was perplexed of course, the little line between her brows had
deepened, made her face look lovelier, more classically struc-
tured and symmetrical somehow . . .

"Do you really think that?" she asked.

"Sure I do. Minus some of the meringue. Don't you?"

"No . . . We're not helpless, we're not like that—you make
it sound as though we're just tossed around like chips . . ."

"Well, aren't we? Look at the two of us sitting here, in this
alien city; camped on an impermanent sofa in a rented room:
you've got a war job that might be over in a flash—and I'm
wearing a uniform . . ."

"But we can *do* things," she said urgently, "we decide what
to do—you know, what course to take, whether we do right or
wrong . . ."

"But why do we see choices as right or wrong?—what lies
behind our choices? A fantastic welter of personal fears,
social taboos, hereditary attitudes, racial memory, God
knows what-all else—don't you see there can't be any such
thing as clear choice? Even when we *think* we're exercising
free choice we're feeling the fine, firm hand of destiny
steering us along the aisle . . . don't you see?"

"I don't know," she pondered; then said firmly, "No, I
don't think so. You can change your life, any minute, overnight—anyone can."

Ah, the sweet defenseless child; she actually believed we
were not at the mercy of circumstances! How odd it must be
to feel this, in late November 1943, with our own oblate
spheroid, at any rate, whirling in the red broth of violence . . .
He smiled thinly, still gazing at the revolving petals. For I,
beneath a rougher sea, was whelmed neath sulphur gulphs
than he. And who will wind the clock when I am gone?

Gran-pa-pa.

He rose to his feet in what was principally a stagger,
excused himself with rigid formality and went into the
bathroom—stood in pleased, fuzzy volupté among the
feminine scents and textures, passed his eyes hazily over
phials, lotions, camisoles and stays. Another world: there was

something oddly pleasing about it, something which excited
him, held him bemused . . .

Returning to the living room he found Lorraine standing
above the bed and glaring down at O'Neill, who was lying perfectly still, his mouth open, his head bent sharply like a
hanged man's.

"Asleep," she said in angry wonder. "He's fallen asleep. I
can't wake him up."

"He's out, then," Newcombe answered. "I was afraid he
was going to go under."

"Well if that—" Her green oval eyes snapping, she looked
down at O'Neill again; stood with arms akimbo, one leg rocking beneath her skirt, torn between resentment and affection:
a lusty, baffled Calypso. "Well, *I'm* going to get some sleep,"
she declared. "I'm bushed." She wheeled around and went
into the bathroom.

"Yes, I guess we all should," Helen said. She stood up; as
she went to pass him Newcombe reached out and took her in
his arms and kissed her slowly. For a few seconds she tried
tentatively to draw away, then came to him again with a full
acquiescence.

"You're sweet," he murmured. "You're sweet . . ."

She made no reply: her eloquence was in the still intensity
of her embrace. She was telling him something—was she?
Something he'd never learned, never encountered before;
holding her he had an intimation—a swift, sweet glimpse of
reservoirs of emotion in this girl that no wit or badinage or
casual love-making could ever call forth.

The door to the bathroom opened and she broke away; her
breath was quick and uneven. They stood looking at each
other silently.

"Don't mind me," Lorraine said in a flat, tart voice; she
had changed into an orange housecoat with aquamarine birds,
and looked even more sultry and voluptuous. She threw a last
irate glance at O'Neill's motionless form, then started to pull
a mattress off one of the other couches.

"What's the matter, Lo?" Helen asked her.

"Nothing's the matter. I'm going to bed down in the
kitchen, that's all."

"But—you can't sleep in *there* . . ."

"Sure I can. Why not?" She dragged the mattress, bedding
and all, through the doorway into the kitchen.

"Lorraine, please . . . don't be angry," Helen said.

"Who's *angry*?" Lorraine demanded, raising her voice. "Don't be silly."

"But it—look, it doesn't matter, we can—"

Helen followed her into the bathroom; the door closed behind them, and Newcombe heard distantly the pattern of their voices—Helen's filled with conciliatory entreaty, Lorraine's a series of short, declamatory outbursts.

The whole room was shifting now, tilting and shifting, and sloping implacably down toward the left. "Long day," he murmured vaguely. "End of a long, long day . . . *Newcombe*," he hissed. *"Snap—to . . ."* Fighting the incipient vertigo he moved over to O'Neill's inert corpus, drew off his shoes, shirt and trousers, and stripping back the covers rolled him in. O'Neill's body moved ludicrously: a marionette without strings or costume. "Old bag o' bones," Newcombe said. "Ol' bag-o'-bones buddy. Fallen out of line of duty. They are slaves who fear to speak—for the fallen and the weak. N'est-ce pas, Mac? N'est-ce *pas*. And I Tiresias have foresuffered all . . ." The thick, ringing preposterousness of it!—And this girl. This strange, steady, silent girl who held within the still goblet of her mind some impenetrable amplitude—whose earnest gaze reminded him of someone, of something luminous and majestic . . . Did it? Rot. Rot and rhetoric. And yet she *did*, somehow . . .

Very methodically he creased O'Neill's trousers and hung them over the back of a chair; stood there in bland perplexity, swaying, battling the dizziness and disequilibrium which always assailed him when he'd drunk too much. Musing, rocking on his heels, hands in his pockets, he waited for the inevitable nausea and with it the sour disdain; but it failed to appear. On the contrary he continued to feel light, emptied of ferocity and bile—and oddly expectant. Ah, there was no accounting for human reactions in a world at war—

The room swooped into blackness around him: he swayed, clutched at an end-table to keep himself from going over—whirled around to see by the dim light from under the kitchen door a figure slipping into one of the beds. Rooted in fascination he called softly, "Helen?"

There was no answer. He undressed rapidly, the blood washing against his temples, stood naked in the center of the room in frantic indecision—then as the light under the kitchen door went out he sprang to the bed in two long strides and climbed in, tensed for the ensuing struggle.

To his vast surprise, she said nothing, did nothing. She was wearing pajamas and was lying on her side, quite still. Then as he moved his hand gently over her hair she gave a little gasping sigh and pressed her head into the hollow of his shoulder.

. . . And the trembling was gone. The wretched fusion of fear and savagery that always dogged him had vanished with inexplicable caprice, like fog shredding away before the westerly back home: as though it had never been. What had done it? Perhaps his very audacity had taken his own nature by surprise. He felt all at once intensely joyful, almost reckless.

"Just a minute," she breathed. He drew back, became aware of her kicking and squirming, realized dimly she was trying to get out of her pajamas. Lying there intensely conscious of the intimate novelty of her presence, he heard Lorraine stirring in the kitchen; and at almost the same moment across the room O'Neill began to snore—a long, rattling ingurgitation like a shovel dragged over pebbles. And a saturnine laughter bubbled up in him: the absurdly late hour in this strange, overstuffed room, O'Neill snoring, fallen at the very threshold of victory, Lorraine reclining in pique on the kitchen floor, this invisible figure beside him struggling to kick her way out of her pajama bottoms—it was all too ludicrous, too absurd to be contained—how could any poor soul greet this moment with anything resembling gravity? He burst out laughing, wagging his head from side to side.

The blow snapped his head back, set the side of his face burning. Before he could think of anything to do or say she had slapped him again. He lay inert, amazed beyond reaction, his hand up to his face to ward off still another blow. She had sat up, her body quivering violently.

"You don't laugh," she said with soft vehemence, "you don't laugh at a—at a moment like this. You don't. Or if you do you—can go and laugh somewhere else, do you hear?"

"I *am* sorry," he said, "I am, I mean it, it was stupid—"

"You don't laugh like that," she repeated; and her voice rang in the silence. "You may have gone to college and all that but I know better than that, that's a mean way to act—how can you act like that if you respect anybody?"

Before he could reply she went on: "That's cruel at a moment like this, you couldn't do it if you loved somebody . . . I've never gone to bed with anybody before, I'm not the kind of girl who just sleeps around, no matter what you think. I only—I only did because—"

She was silent. He was aware that she was shivering all over. He put his arm around her bare shoulder; placing his face against hers he was startled to feel tears on her cheek.

"Please forgive me, Helen," he said. "It wasn't that I—I didn't think you—"

"It's the truth," she declared. ". . . I only did because I think I love you."

He was filled with amazement. The words hovered about them in the darkness like large round globes of sound.

"—Oh, Helen," he chided her gently, with rising consternation, "Helen, we've only known each other a few hours. How can you possibly—"

Violently she shook her head. "I loved you the minute I saw you. I knew I did." She was silent again and he knew she was scanning sightlessly his face. "I don't care," she said after a pause. "I know you don't love me. It's all right, I don't care . . ."

It was one of the few times in his life he didn't have a solitary thing to say: he couldn't even summon up anything. He felt, quite simply, very guilty and absurd.

"You're right," he said.

"You don't respect people, you don't listen to them when they're talking, you don't even listen to what *you're* saying half the time. You don't feel for people enough . . ."

Footfalls padded along the hall outside, descended the stairs in a discreet rhythm, and from another room a dance-band trumpet, muted through the walls, pursued a tremulous falsetto wail. Lying motionless, listening, Newcombe frowned. Here it was again: and from this shy child. The hand that mocked them and the heart that fed . . .

"You're right, Helen," he repeated in a low, contrite tone. "It was wrong to laugh like that."

She said nothing for a time; she had stopped shivering. Finally she said, "I didn't mean to slap you like that."

"That's all right. I'm glad you did. It was a—"

Something landed, light and soundless and without warning, on his thighs. He exclaimed, *"Jesus!"* and started violently; and the something vanished.

"MacArthur," Helen said.

"What?"

"The cat. He sleeps with us sometimes."

"Oh—the *cat* . . ." He felt a tremendous urge to laugh again—sheerly from nervousness this time; suppressed it until he became all at once aware that she was giggling.

"You're laughing," he charged.

She nodded. "That's different." Her teeth gleamed faintly.

"Yes," he admitted. "It is."

And he reached out to her and drew her to him.

He was released somehow: time slowed in its dread urgency, drifted toward a languid serenity that shimmered like an afternoon long ago on the dunes at Marshfield, with the sea like a huge cobalt plate and the sky held in slowly unfurling transparencies of azure . . . He was freed of something—he was freed of *indifference:* the realization was like the most enchanting, unhoped-for miracle, a supernal dispensation bestowed on him long after he had given up hope. All the clashing, discordant shapes were gone; for the first time in his life he made love, moving with a sure, tender restraint, a quiet generosity of spirit that amazed him. What had happened? Her quick, murmured breathing evoked a transport of delight that heightened, fanned out in its still, fine radiance until he was borne outside of time, outside of all self-concern, lulled in a resonant, throbbing ecstasy . . .

"You're sweet," he cried softly, caressing her cheeks, her eyelids. "You're a fine, sweet girl . . ."

He said no more than that: he couldn't. But lying beside her in the darkness he felt strangely, deeply chastened.

"Who do you like most?" he asked.

She turned toward him with her quick, shy glance. "Oh, Bach—and Mozart. And Haydn: I don't know Haydn very well."

"I like moderns," he said. "All the dissonances, the screeching and cracking and thumping. Bloch and Hindemith and Bartók. Our modern world coming all apart at the seams. There's a place in one of Bartók's that sounds like a dozen madmen let loose in one of those huge hotel kitchens, running wild among all the rows of pots and pans. It's really like the end of the world, in a way . . . Don't you like them?"

Smiling she shook her head. "I don't know . . . They don't make an order the same way: a simple, ordered form."

"Well, it's a more complex kind of order."

"It isn't that, though. With Mozart there's such a simple, sweet little melody, and it's woven so beautifully . . ."

"Their world wasn't flying all apart on them."

"I suppose not. They must have had their troubles too, though." She added wistfully, "There's such a feeling of *purpose* under it: as though they knew something so absolutely

they didn't have to shout about it, they could just let it happen
. . . Do you know what I mean?''

"Yes," he said. "I know. There's a saraband of Bach's I've
always loved. A very stately piece: mournful and proud and
very exalted, all at the same time . . .''

They were walking along the mall beyond the Lincoln
Memorial; beside them the water of the basin looked like
fretted glass in the afternoon light—a silvery overcast that
hurt the eyes. Newcombe put his hand to his face, massaged
slowly his brows and eyelids. Oddly enough he didn't feel
hung-over at all—only an intense lightheadedness, as though
he were floating through some new, dreamy, aqueous world.
The park, the bare black branches of the cherry trees—the
Japanese cherry trees—were as gossamer, as unreal as an
oriental print.

"Is your head still aching?''

"No. Hardly at all." Opening his eyes he saw her studying
him with earnest solicitude; and he smiled at her lightly. The
memory of the night was still strong—a strangely tender
passage. They had slept for eons, it seemed—slept with arms
and legs intertwined, their bodies pressed against each other;
each time they stirred and wakened it was to a renewal of
delight. Watching the sky turn gray beyond the windows
Newcombe had lain quietly, half afraid to move, pervaded by
a deep and abiding sense of languor, of being in some
alchemical way involved with all the world, and completely at
peace.

Walking now through the chill, damp winter air he found
himself hesitant even to think about it, as though its serene
fragility might shatter under too direct a scrutiny.

"Dancing last night," he said. "That was fun, wasn't it?''

"Yes, it was. I love to dance.''

"So do I. *Now*, that is . . . I never thought I'd see the day
I'd say that." Moving beside her in the still, austere majesty
of the Memorial he suddenly intoned:

> *"Grau, theurer Freund, ist alle Theorie—*
> *und grün des Lebens goldner Baum."*

"What does that mean?" she asked simply.

"It means philosophy is for the birds. And the only thing
that matters—the only thing that matters is life's golden
tree.''

"That's beautiful," she said. "Life's golden tree.''

"Yes. I'm beginning to see what the old boy was driving at."

Her face, turned toward him, was animate with joy; he took her hand in his and they walked along, their shoes scraping on the gravel path.

"All right, let's watch that holding hands," O'Neill's voice called hollowly from fifty yards behind them. "We don't allow expressions of affection around the Memorial grounds."

Newcombe turned. "It's just a gesture, sir . . ."

"Oh. Very good." Gaunt, his face green-hued and pinched under the high-peaked barracks hat, O'Neill clung to Lorraine's robust voluptuosity, raised one hand in feeble, pontifical approval. "As you were and carry on."

"Jay, you're horrible," Lorraine said. "They can hold hands if they want."

"Sure they can. Do you see me stopping them? Do you see me stopping *anybody* this afternoon? Not this gannet." He was putting his feet down with obsequious care, as though he were carrying something intensely breakable on top of his head. "As you were, you people," he called again—put his hand to the side of his face and groaned and said, "Too loud. Way too loud."

Newcombe and Helen strolled on for a time in silence; a breeze soughed in their faces—a damp, cold breeze that sent cat's-paws skittering over the surface of the basin. They both shivered in unison, turned toward each other.

"What are you thinking?" he asked.

"Nothing."

"Sure you were. Everybody's always thinking something. Tell me."

"I was thinking how fast time is going again."

He stared at her in wonder. "You felt it, too . . ."

She nodded, watching him: a steady, even gaze that seemed to gather all her feeling into a beam of tremendous intensity, and then present it with shy restraint: that look which reminded him so of someone, someone seen not long ago, of—Danny Kantaylis . . . The realization made him start inwardly, turned him all at once taut and flippant in spite of himself.

"Time?" he said blithely. "Oh, we have all speeds. All sizes. In what particular shade was madame interested?"

Her lips curled but her gaze was still thoughtful. "That sundial," she murmured, frowning, staring ahead.

"What's that?"

"I don't know: some sundial I read about in school. In Italy, I think. And it says *It's later than you think*."

"Oh, that one. Yes, that's the standard model, all right."

". . . I wasn't thinking that at all," she said then with a trace of vexation.

"You weren't?"

"Well yes I was—but not just that."

"What, then?"

She shook her head. "You won't—you'll make fun of me."

Disarmed, he squeezed her hand and stopped. "No, I won't. I promise. Tell me."

"—I was thinking how much I'll miss you."

"Will you? Really?"

She nodded rapidly, smiling; then all at once her face broke into a strange little grimace and her eyes filled with tears.

He felt suddenly confounded, sore at heart. There she stood with all her heart and soul offered up to him, lying open before him, defenseless and terrible in the purity of its bestowal—and what did he feel in response, he who short hours ago had taken so freely and so well? Couldn't he—for the love of God couldn't he feel things with the anguish and intensity of others?

He looked away wildly toward the black, shriveled branches of the trees across the water; in the afternoon chill his mouth had gone dry as chaff. He cleared his throat, cleared it again. Well, he felt something: he did feel something—he felt more than he ever had before in his life. But honesty: honesty if nothing else. The arch bal-masque business such as he played with Sue would not do here—not a flicker of it. Would he miss *her*—really and tremendously? Any other kind of answer would be most dishonorable in the face of that piercing, utterly committed gaze . . .

He closed his eyes slowly, opened them again. Die arme Gretchen. Die arme Gretchen at Lincoln Memorial. The world will little note nor long remember. Gray, dear friend, is every theory . . . And the slow disquieting sense of inadequacy pressed at his heart again, pressed slowly and blindly, like a little animal trying to thrust open a door.

"Hey, old buddy-ro!"

Standing on a bench a hundred yards away O'Neill was waving to him, waggling one arm in tight little circles and pointing to his head: a feeble pantomime of the platoon leader's "assemble-here-to-me" signal. "Four-thirty . . ."

"All right."

They walked slowly back toward the bench. Helen had withdrawn her hand from his and was blowing her nose hard.

"The world will little note nor long remember," Newcombe said with irritation. "Remember *what?* . . . I used to know the whole thing by heart."

Time was racing again: the clock tower in the center of Union Station glared like a four-faced Janus god, the four minute-hands leaped ahead with martellato definition, snipped like shears; men in uniform swarmed through the swing doors and swept on through the hall, darted to magazine counters, lunch counters, lavatories, rejoined anxious, pale-faced girls—swept on again toward the trains: a tense, purposeful exodus to mountains, jungles, desert sands.

"Don't you want anything to read?" Lorraine asked. The four of them were standing on the platform in a tight little group behind one of the stanchions while the crowd streamed by them on both sides.

"*Read?*" O'Neill cried; bending over he slapped his knee in minstrel parody, laughed in silence, openmouthed. "You're joshing, of course. I'm sleeping all the way."

"What about Al?"

"Don't worry about him, he's got his poetry to keep him warm. He's always got a—you know, some old Homer or Plato or something kicking around. Light reading." His face had regained some color with the meal they'd just eaten, but he still looked pale and infirm.

"You'll never get a seat," Helen said; she was watching the procession of figures moving along the aisle inside the train. "Don't you want to get on now?"

Newcombe shook his head. "We've got the rest of the night to ride on trains. There are never any anyway." A soldier carrying a gigantic olive-drab barracks bag bumped him, apologized curtly and lumbered on again.

"What do you do?"

"About what?"

"Where do you sit?"

"On the floor. In the aisles."

"Oh."

She turned one foot slowly, watching it, started to say something and checked herself.

"What?" he said.

"Nothing."

He could hardly hear her in the roar and hiss of hurrying feet, the calls, the grinding clatter of hand-trucks and wagons.

"Hey, we're not going to go through all that again, are we?" he chided.

She gave a laugh, as though catching her breath, then bit her lower lip with her teeth; a muscle at the corner of her mouth quivered.

"Well," O'Neill said restively; his eyes darted to the train and back again. "We'd better get going. Now *write* me, baby . . ."

"I will, I promise."

"You'd better. After this last disgraceful showing—"

"I promise, Jay . . ."

Steam burst from behind them in a fierce white plume, melted away in the gusts of raw wind. Newcombe gave a shiver which was almost a spasm, opened his arms. Helen came toward him; they kissed quickly, then seized each other with all their might. Then he stepped back and picked up his bag.

"God bless you," she called.

He smiled in surprise. "Do you think He should? I doubt it," he called back; but he felt somehow deeply moved. Lord, I am not worthy: but speak the word only—

A trainman's voice reached them—the old, hoarse, lonely call in rising inflection: cry of sundering. Newcombe stepped on the hollow iron and turned.

"I'll write," he shouted. "I write great letters. You'll never—"

There was a ferocious hiss under their feet and a lurch; steam enveloped them in a dense cloud, vanished, burst around them again. The train was moving: moving away slowly, gathering speed, the girls were walking with it, waving, walking faster now, nearly running. A machinist's mate flung himself onto the steps and heaved by them, red-faced and panting. The girls were gone. There was only the curving web of rails and a strip of sky, more leaden now, above rows and rows of emptied, ghostly cars. Two shafts of iron like the skeleton prow of a ship swept by, were gone. Lord I am not worthy: but speak—

They went in and stood at the water cooler. The water trickled out tepid and vile but they both drank and filled their cups again.

"One thing that's free, anyway," O'Neill said; he put two aspirin tablets in his mouth and swallowed them. "Well: we had ourselves quite a ball, didn't we?"

Newcombe nodded mutely. For a moment he was incapable of speaking. He felt almost physically wounded—as though a terribly vital part of him had just been cut out: a hollow, bereft pain. But for all that it gladdened his heart.

"I'm stony-broko," O'Neill said. "What I mean. We must have shot a hatful of your dough last night, Al."

"Don't worry about it."

"No, I'll square with you at pay-call. How come you were so flush coming back?"

"Bummed some from the old gentleman . . . Jay, what were you speaking with that general?"

"Who's that?"

"The general . . . There *was* a general, wasn't there?"

"Oh. Yeah. The big guy."

They looked at each other musingly, swaying with the jolting rhythm of the train.

"Czech," O'Neill said. "I remember."

"How the hell do you know Czech?"

"My rotten no-good uncle." O'Neill tilted his paper cup toward Newcombe. "Here's to prohibition."

"Parnassus."

"Balaklava."

They threw the paper cups in the slot, stood looking down the aisle of the car where servicemen sat on the seats, on seat arms, on the floor, rocking and swaying like bodies in a trance; looked at each other again.

"Well, old boondocker," O'Neill said. "I guess you know that's the end of the carnival."

"Yep."

"From here on it's over the falls."

"To quote the bard."

"To quote the bard."

Out in the vestibule between the cars they found an empty space and sat facing each other, leaning wearily against the dull green metal doors; stared at each other for a few moments with a gaze to which neither of them could possibly have given expression, and closed their eyes.

PART TWO

Traverse

1

TO MY RIGHT are forked slats and a rusty, fretted, flaking plate of steel: three cots and the ship's side. It rolls upward—a sluggish upsurge against the hot, white sky—reaches a point and dips ponderously down, revealing a swath of oily, gray-blue heaving sea. Lifts away again, and falls. The motion of an utterly weary, utterly resigned old man in a rocker on some twilight porch. Directly above my head is a crazy-quilt pattern of pieced-together ponchos and shelter-halves lashed to pieces of dunnage, torn and flapping and faded, through which sunlight falls in an eerie, dappled pattern: circles and slits of light slide in a rhythmic looping movement over cots, naked bodies, weapons to the ship's roll. Heat presses like a blunt hand, turns every gesture, every contact of flesh with flesh into something infinitely repugnant. There is almost no breeze but all around us the waves—the ship's side has descended again—pursue their unhurried course toward the west—sea, sun, the skittering schools of flying fish like silver chaff, the long line of rolling and dipping LST's strung out behind us: I sometimes have the feeling we aren't using engines at all, that we are borne along by some timeless, implacable force—as though there were an immense lodestone far out there drawing us all—battered, rusty filings that we are—to its malignant bosom . . .

Helen darling, I've meant to start this letter to you for days—it's weeks by now—and even now of course I'm not really writing it, not setting it down on paper, that is. There's precious little sense in crystallizing one's indulgences: the clandestine ones are always the sweetest. And of course I'm reasonably certain this epistle, if made manifest, would never get by the noble, porcelain gaze of Lieutenant D'Alessandro, who sees the corps and all its trappings as some kind of hybrid Appalachian Mountain Club and Arthurian Round Table (as

perhaps beheld from the glittering camaraderie of the
officers' club—now the cozy intimacy of the wardroom or
wherever the hell they *are*, back aft there—it does indeed
appear), and who would never countenance such unmilitary
bearing as this. So instead of a V-letter this is in a sense a
T-letter—a telepathic tomtom with teleological overtones: a
series of impulses thrown across the ether, psyche-to-
psyche . . .

Well: I am lying naked except for my skivvy drawers on a
field cot perched, a trifle precariously, on some drums of
eighty-octane gas pretty well forward on the starboard side of
an LST; a crazy, wildly listing LST embarked—unbelievably—on its third operation (even the high brass feel
they're only good for *one*) . . . and we are, as the quaint
phrase so quaintly goes, somewhere in the Pacific. I suppose
the ship's captain knows where we are, but it's a cinch no one
else does: we've been punting along like this (Jay, who's been
banging ears with some of the ship's company, says it's six
knots an hour, no more and no less) for some weeks now.

If I roll my head to the left—one does eventually have to
roll one's head to the left—I encounter a perfect sea of cots,
lined up side by side with just enough room at the ends to sidle
through: it looks like those newsreel shots you sometimes see
of public buildings in a disaster area, with half-clothed figures
wandering around or reading or talking or playing cards.
Eight of us are ensconced up here on the gasoline drums
though, and inexplicably it's made us a kind of aristocracy (as
Jay puts it, "Exclusive, you know?") which leads me to
desultory pondering over the association of heights with
wealth and social pre-eminence, such as Russian Hill, Murray
Hill, Sugar Hill, Shaker Heights, and so on. (Even—
alas!—dear, stately old Beacon Hill. I was almost forgetting
. . . Can it all be simply a matter of looking down on one's
neighbors?)

We also derive a certain excitement from our eyrie.
Ricarno, who comes from Brooklyn, says (as only he can say
it) we get tagged by a torpedo we'll get blown a mile in the air
with all this high-powered giz under our butts; but Kantaylis,
who ought to know if anyone does, smiles that quiet, mournful smile of his and says with all the ammunition they got
packed away in the tail of this baby it won't make a particle of
difference *where* we're sitting: let's all just pray we don't stop
one. To which I add a fervent amen . . . An entirely inaudible
one, however: we're lean-and-mean gyrenes as you must

know by now, Robert Sherrod says so, and I'm bent on looking just as ferocious and devil-may-dog as anybody else. If not more so. (As a matter of fact I *do* look pretty rugged—I caught a glimpse of myself quite by accident in one of the crypto-mirrors down in the head: a heavy tan and a week's growth and no showers could make even Percy Bysshe look pretty tough.)

Just below my left shoulder, down on the deck at the edge of the drums, little Connor is reading *Batman Comics* for the second time. I know it's for the second time at least because I saw him finish this fabulous epic about an hour ago and shove it under a towel filled with dirty socks and underwear which serves—a touch redolently, it must be confessed—as a pillow. Now, once more awake, he has been drawn back to its charms and is poring over it with an intensity which is almost painful. As I gaze down at the little colored mosaics of underworld figures and balloons of dialogue and the Batman—a muscular, blue-shrouded personage—sweeping down on them from the cornices of skyscrapers I am reminded dimly of Balder and the sea god Proteus and the legend of the Fisher King—but not for long. What absorbs my gaze is Connor's little round face, beardless and bright; the wide, intent blue eyes with their long curving lashes. Is he underage? Very likely. Danny Kantaylis thinks he's in on fraud status and they've never caught up with him; which does happen. It's odd—his face affects me so strangely: it sets in motion a long, maudlin train of thought all tangled up with boyhood and Houseman and Keats and beauty and violence and early death and the fragile things of this world . . .

Poor Chicken: does he have any idea what we're headed for? I certainly don't. Danny does, that's for sure—and Jack Freuhof and Corporal Klumanski and Steve Lundren and a couple of others . . . I can see Danny's back from where I'm lying: you know, the one I mentioned in the letter I *really* wrote you from Pearl—that maze of anguish. They're playing pinochle on Ricarno's cot—he and Lundren against Klumanski and Ricarno: an interminable ritual with a certain—if highly wearisome—rhythm. For quite some time they go along in monosyllables and dead silence: stripped to the waist, crop-headed, burly, glistening with sweat, combat knives at their hips—Ricarno even has a red bandanna handkerchief bound around his forehead to keep the perspiration out of his eyes—they are a ferocious four-some. Teach's buccaneers sat around like this, I suppose, playing skin-the-cat or gut-the-

Carib or whatever their variation was; idling away the hours until the maintop sent down its wild, wavering cry . . .

Then all at once the game explodes in shouts and imprecations. "Why, you lucky bastard!" "Cozy-dog!" "You lousy no-good sandbagger, you!" They pound each other on shoulders and thighs—blows which would fell a good-sized calf—and roar with laughter. Steve Lundren glowers darkly at Ricarno and booms: "Fifteen hearts! *Fifteen!*" and Ricarno, grinning broadly (I warned you this epistle would never, never get by), raises his sweaty arm in gesture infinitely expressive and obscene and replies: "Up the shaft, chief." And Lundren scowls like Ahasuerus.

Which is just what he reminds you of: some all-powerful Old Testament monarch, massive and inscrutable, who broods and broods and cons dark thoughts beyond the reach of common men. Yesterday at weapons inspection—we have weapons inspection every day (your rifle's your best friend, the only one you've got, she won't cheat on you like your broad back home, she'll save your hide if you treat her right)—Lundren was not overpleased with the condition of my piece. "Now, you want to start with a clean weapon," he rumbled down at me from his practically legendary height of six feet six (I can dimly understand what they mean about statuary larger than life size). "You won't wind up with one but you better damn well start off that way . . ." "But I cleaned it this morning, Steve," I protested, "I did, no kidding." "You can't clean it enough out here, Newcombe. All this corroded salt air." Corroded it is, chief: corroded it is. His face is like an oriental wood weathered and carved in deep, blunt passages: the lips puffed and thick, the nose smashed flat and crushed at the bridge into a recess between the swollen cheeks. "You get ashore you'll wish to God Almighty you'd cleaned it a thousand times more. You wait and see." *You wait.* That's what the old men say, the veterans: *Just wait and see.* And we greenhorns fall silent before this admonition which brooks no retort. No retort at all. Riddle-me riddle-me randy-ro, the fields have crosses row on row. His little black eyes burn down at me portentously, like coals. "You get through cleaning it you start in cleaning it all over again one time, hear?"

"Right, chief," I said. And I did. For nobody BUT NOBODY (to coin an immortal phrase)—disobeys Steve Lundren, our platoon sergeant, lord-and-master and high castellan; an old regular who hails from darkest Georgia and is both a Jehovah Tabernacler and an ex-prize fighter who once had the mighty King Levinsky on the floor (you can see we've become all in all quite a cosmopolitan outfit) and who has turned out to be a Bible scholar extraordinaire—that is to say he resounds with sonorous Old Testament admonitions, fearfully fantastic and apt: you feel as though you're dousing your mess gear alongside of Jeremiah. One of the first days out—they were already playing pinochle, on the cot next to mine—Kantaylis overbid and Klu and Derekman set them; and Steve shoved the deck to Derekman and rubbed his eyes and said: "Well, the Book says, He becometh poor, that dealeth with a slack hand." "What book's that?" Derekman queried blandly. And Lundren's face became majestic as a teakwood idol. "The Bible," he intoned, like the voice of Jahveh out of the whirlwind. "The Book of God, boy. Ain't you ever read the Bible?" "Oh sure," said Derekman quickly, "sure—only I never happened to hear anybody quote it like that, right off the handle." "Every man ought to know it," Lundren declared, looking around in fearsome solemnity, fists on his thighs. "Every man ought to know it by heart: so's he can call upon it in the day of wrath and desolation of spirit . . ." And I felt a faint, fine shiver ripple up and down my spine. "Well, there isn't much call for it where I come from," Derekman said. "Where's that, boy?" "New York. Queens." "I knew it," Lundren proclaimed, and his battered lips puffed out in somber resignation at the iniquities and abominations of the cities of the plain. "I knew it. Deal the cards . . ."

Half an hour has passed. Glancing at my watch I am stunned: only half an *hour*! Perhaps it's the motion of the Trades and our own meandering, lackadaisical course westward—perhaps, after the creeping troop-train movement across the country and the months of reassignment and delays at San Diego and then at Pearl, the interminable sitting around and waiting, time has overtaken us at last and we are caught in it: floating bound in its own momentumless vortex. (A neat little problem for Einstein, that one.)

Time *is* just about to catch up with us again, nonetheless: in twenty minutes Jay and I must rouse ourselves, don belts and helmet liners and ascend the ladder to the boat deck and the Number Three starboard forty-millimeter gun and sit, with nothing but a fiber shell between our brains and the baleful white flaming ingot of the sun, and with the sweat pouring off us in streams stare vigorously out into a blinding gray-white haze which ripples and wabbles . . . for four still more interminable hours. Four on and eight off for the duration of the voyage. Danny and Harry Derekman (who had done duty on Midway) sit in the pointer's and trainer's seats and Jay and I, as first and second loaders, on the rim of the gun tub, where the iron cuts unpleasantly across the center of our buttocks, numbing the lower portions with time. Just why we must all assume this asinine corvée—a responsibility of ship's company, if *anyone* is to suffer it—no one seems to know very clearly. But there we sit like lobsters in a shallow iron pot: and bake and broil away . . .

Below our drums and a few cots farther aft Woodruff, that old Arkansas Traveler, is, of all amazing things, writing a letter home: hunched over a pad, his hand moving the pencil stub in slow crabbed loops and jerks (he holds it between his first two fingers and maneuvers it by spastic contractions of his fist). Every few minutes a large gout of sweat drops from his brow or the tip of his nose and splashes on the paper—PX stationery adorned with the eagle-globe-and-anchor of our illustrious corps and with some further legend below it—"Victory, Home and Mother" I think, I can't quite make it out from here—and Woodruff then pulls a very dirty green skivvy shirt from under his pad and brushes the drop of sweat away with dogged persistence. And the slow, tortured formation of words begins again . . .

What is he saying? What in Christ's sweet name can he find in this piteous cosmos of squalor and infinite monotony to write home about, communicate to that antediluvian swamp world of his where sex is something called *poon-tang* and a domicile something called a *wicki-up* and "here, sir" sounds like a bizarre cross between a grunt and a sneeze . . . ? *Dear Ma I hope everything is fine with you and Pa and the price of feed hasn't gone too high and you got a good price for the young hogs. Speaking of young hogs I'm feeling a lot like one right now: we're penned into an area the size of two tennis courts, about eight hundred-odd of us, and it's real fun. The heat is stifling and the refuse and clutter are indescribable and the food is monotonous beyond description—soggy C-rations and a powdered lemonade that smells like sheep's urine and tastes even better—the officers play poker for big stakes and drink Old Fitzgerald in the fan-cooled officers' country, we've been drifting at six knots an hour for weeks now across a fetid, stinking ocean heading for what Christ-all horror we can't imagine but I just wanted you to know everything is fine and I feel just great and the heat and the inspections and the gun watches and the squabbles and petty thievery and fist-fights and salt-water showers all are fine . . .*

Still, he's committing it to paper, which is more than I can say: perhaps there's something significant in that. And there *is* something dogged, something mute and calm and indomitable in this laborious creation of a missive which cannot under any circumstances be mailed for weeks, and which will be censored out of all recognition when and if it *is* . . . A lesson for me there, is there?

For this is an odyssey full of lessons, full of marvels————

2

O'NEILL, WHO WAS leaning unlawfully against one of the fire-guards, turned to the other three in the gun tub, pointed below and said: "Colonel." And a moment later Colonel Herron ascended the ladder beside them—floppy-brimmed army fatigue hat, full florid face with quick blue eyes; the heavy, belly-less body and faded, wrinkled dungarees. At the boat deck he nodded pleasantly and said, "Good evening,"—then, "Kantaylis . . ."

"Good evening, Colonel," the four said, almost as one. Their eyes followed him impassively as he moved with slow, sure purpose along the boat deck, disappeared into a door and reappeared with a collapsible canvas chair. Choosing a place against the wall of the radio shack where the davit-slung LCVP cast a bent oblong of shadow he sat down, tilted the chair against the gray iron, pushed the hat down over his eyes, hooked his thumbs in his belt and rested motionless, his elbows crooked loosely over the chair arms.

O'Neill grinned and tossed his head toward the Colonel. "Crafty old gaffer, ain't he?"

"Slob," Derekman muttered. "Looks like a slob to me."

"You're wrong, Harry," Kantaylis said quietly. "Don't you worry about old Herron. He knows the score all right. He's been to the place."

"Where's that?"

"The Tenaru."

Derekman turned and started at Colonel Herron's heavy, pink body lying in repose. "Ah, they're all alike. Brass."

"No, they're not. You know better than that, Harry. He's the best you'll ever get . . . Old Herron knows the score all right," Kantaylis repeated softly.

"Well I hope to Christ somebody does around here. *I* don't."

"You aren't supposed to, Jackson," O'Neill said. "You're supposed to be young and strong and ignorant."

"You can say that one more time," Derekman retorted morosely; he had his helmet liner pushed forward over his eyes, which gave him a truculent, slightly tipsy aspect. "Jesus, they can't ever tell you anything, can't ever cut a man in on what's going on. It'd break their little brass humps."

"Beat-'em beat-'em beat-'em," O'Neill called nasally.

"Sure I'll beat 'em."

"Sing them blues . . ." O'Neill threw back his head and sang: "I got those can't complete 'em, hard to cheat 'em, I just *got* to beat 'em *blues*—" gave up with a yawn which was part groan and sat down again.

Kantaylis shifted his position in the pointer's seat, passed his shirt-sleeve across his face: it came away dark and wet. The handles of the mechanism in front of him were like little burning cylinders. Sweat ran down his sides, his legs, bathed his loins; and tiny, feathered objects began their erratic course over his body, chafing and prickling. Down below on the fantail a dropped mess gear clattered on the deck and someone guffawed. Two hours to go. More than two. From far astern an albatross came soaring up on them in a series of spidery tacks and glides, hovered above the stern three-inch gun, craning its professorial head about; dropped away again in a long, lazy, soaring fall.

"That gooney bird's a long way from home." Squinting upward O'Neill watched it oscillating in the haze above the LST behind them. "Yes sir, a long old way from home . . ."

"They say they can fly, two, three thousand miles at a crack and never feel it," Derekman said. "There were thousands of them on Midway. They do the damnedest things: when they're making love they stand beak-to-beak and put their heads way up in the air, straight up, and bob up and down and coo at each other for hours. Craziest cooing moan you ever heard.

They used to scare hell out of us walking beach post at night: sound just like somebody creeping up on you. One time I thought the whole Nip fleet was going to jump me. When I found out it was a bunch of damn goonies I was so mad I almost blew their heads off, the lot of them . . ."

"Ah wretch! said they, the bird to slay, that made the wind to blow," Newcombe declaimed.

A complete silence greeted this fragment of culture. Newcombe fidgeted uncomfortably on the rim of the gun tub, shifting from haunch to haunch. "Jesus, that's hot . . . Coleridge," he continued blithely. "The mariner shoots an albatross. Old nautical superstition was if you shot one you were in for big trouble."

"Now you are anyway," Derekman remarked.

"No, they felt you were eternally damned; something like that."

"Well, that's what I am right now." Derekman watched the smoky, luminous curtain of horizon with a grin of dour satisfaction; a matchstick played back and forth between his teeth. "Excommunicatus-gatus. Down the chute."

"You a Catholic, Harry?" O'Neill asked.

"I was. Can't see it any more."

"You know something?" O'Neill offered after a pause. "Religion is for punks and old folks. When you're a punk you need it because you don't know any better and it straightens you up. And when you're old you need it for comfort before you check out. But in between it's no good."

"It's all a crock," Derekman said with finality. "Far as I'm concerned. See this?" Twisting in his seat he pointed to the left side of his face where his jaw hung lower on that side, the bone thick and swollen. "I was out barreling along with my brother Jack four years ago—you know, wheeling around the way kids do, and he hit a guardrail on the Jamaica Parkway. I went through the windshield and smashed my jaw all to hell and he got the wheel in his chest. For about six weeks he hung on and hung on and then he finally died. And all that time I prayed for him: prayed like crazy. And he died anyway. So what good is religion in a deal like that? Not a damn bit of good. That's what my old man used to say back in '33 and '34: 'It ain't getting me a job, is it?' And my mother'd stand there over him and say, 'It would if you'd pray some,' and my old man'd yell back, 'Oh yeah sure,' and then laugh at her. Laugh would tear your heart out. Christ, I had enough of that. No more of that for me . . ."

"You mean you don't believe in God any more?" New-combe asked him.

"You're a brickin'-A right I don't." Derekman extended his two square hands, clenched the fists quickly, hefting them like weights. "I believe in these two hooks right here. That's what I got my dough on."

"Well: it's believing in it that counts," O'Neill said. "You either believe in it or you don't."

"Well I *don't*," said Derekman, and crossed his arms.

They fell silent again, and watched the sea. Below them the water under the fantail seethed and washed. Kantaylis mopped his face again with his sleeve and glanced at Derekman: the heavy, broad, wedge-shaped chin, the narrowed gray eyes confronting the horizon haze. Tough little customer. Midway and Eniwetok. Warehouseman, semi-pro ball. Turned from religion. No atheists in foxholes. Who said that, some preacher? Some frozen-faced ninny like Dr. Kindlbinder back home . . . He thought of Andrea, saw her kneeling beside him by the fire, her face contorted with remorse and grief, shaking her head—still beautiful for all that; the firelight had made glinting patterns in her golden hair. *How can I pray for you when we have sinned?* Was that what she had said? *If we sleep together just like any. The body made all this trouble—the body!* . . . That was her mother talking: the maze of etched lines around the stern mouth, the fierce, bright glance: uncomprehending, unforgiving. Right down to the wire. *I don't see why of all times you had to decide now, I don't see why you can't wait till all this business is over—what kind of a future is there in it for her? Can't you look at it from her point of view?* Waving her hand toward Andrea and Andrea saying, *But Mother, I* want *to marry Danny*, and Mr. Lenaine saying in that tired, gentle voice, *Now Virginia, I don't think we should interpose our own wills here, if they want to get married I think we ought to let them* . . . His voice drowned out in the flood of her incontrovertible logic. *Realize at a moment like this it seems terribly important but I think it's only fair that you look at it from a longer view, what life is there for her wandering around all day from room to room wondering what on earth is happening to you, it's not right to ask a girl to go through that, if you were going to be home it might be different but as it is.* Her eyes, dilated like globes, darting around the room, lighting on everything, never stopping . . . And there had been nothing to say. Funny:

there was so little you could say to people at times. Convinced she was right beyond all question, her judgment was the final, unalterable one, she knew everything there was to be known: her voice hammering on through the protests and interjections—Mr. Lenaine's, his own, Andrea's—until all at once Mr. Lenaine was standing in the middle of the room, his face thin and white and alive. *Virginia! Leave—them—alone! Let them get married. Leave them alone!* And Andrea's face across the room as fearful and despairing as he'd ever seen it. And then her mother had turned and run upstairs . . . What was there in their religion that made for all the fear and guiltiness and want of compassion—the inexorable either-or, Newcombe had once called it . . . ?

Barely turning his head he glanced backward: Newcombe was staring up blankly at the sky, his face drawn and bony in the heat. But his mind was working—an unceasing reverie. Well: he might as well get in all the reverieing he could while the getting was good. If . . . if I had his education, Kantaylis thought, surprised at the sudden intensity of the desire. If I could I'd study this business, read up on it, read all there is to be read about it. How did it all get started? Inexorable either-or . . . He remembered Andrea as a little girl: he saw her swinging at the playground, skating, skipping rope. She had worn pigtails then, two of them in long bright braids that flailed and flounced around and made her toss her head in vexation; he remembered her asking another little girl one afternoon to pass them through each other in a loose kind of knot so they'd be out of her way. In the little classroom, on the other side of the room near the window—two grades behind him—standing thin and tall and awkward, answering Mrs. Sanderson. *The Battle of Bunker Hill was fought on June seventeenth.* Sunlight fell on her too-short green dress, her slender arm, turned her hair to a mass of fine gold wire; a shoulder blade protruded like a small inverted triangle.

—And why did we lose the battle, Andrea?

—We lost the battle for lack of powder.

For lack of powder. The red-coated files reforming for the third time, coming on again through the sunlight, the drifting, milk-white smoke; the tall metal shakos flashing, bayonets a spidery blue wavering line. Tapping the powder horn against the touchhole—looking up to the right, to left, encountering everywhere the same astonished realization, the wide-eyed fear; turning back again hypnotically to the oncoming wall of scarlet, the flickering steel . . . He knew how they felt now. It

had seemed dreamy, long-ago—the childhood images of
history and heroism: romantic and far away and unreal. Now
he knew . . .

Strange how clearly he remembered all that!—from some
ten-years-gone moment of a spring afternoon with all the
windows opened wide and outside the maples green and
drooping and the thick, drowsy humming of insects in the tall
grass: a delicious somnolence. Even Mrs. Sanderson had
glanced once or twice furtively through her bright steel pince-
nez toward the long slope of South Mountain. For lack of
powder. She had been bright and laughing, then: Andrea.
Filled with a soft skipping delight. And yet there had been this
other thing, all unknown to him, that had tortured her; or
perhaps it had been only the night by the lake, and the baby
. . . No: it went deeper than that.

Motionless, bathed in the eddying heat, he wondered if she
had really accepted what he'd said to her that night at the
cabin: if she felt it inside her as good, as right—or whether she
would slip back into that dark world of guilt and penance and
hell-fire of her mother's. Hell-fire . . . He knew what hell-fire
was. But no God had made it: that was man's specialty, hell-
fire. They were sliding and rolling toward it now, with every
wave . . . What was the matter with them? What in Jesus'
sweet name was wrong with the idea of a God who saw us as
we were—filled with aspirations and failings, loving the spirit
and the joys of this world, too—who loved us and *forgave* us
our sins once in a while? Forgive us our trespasses as we
forgive those. The prayer said it, didn't it? Then why didn't
Kindlbinder and the other one, the narrow, flinty one—
Jarreyl, that was his name—why didn't they teach that instead
of giving everyone a weekly dunking in the hopeless sinning of
mankind, in which the body was made out to be some kind of
black and evil power, waiting for the chance to drag the
unsuspecting soul down to scalding perdition . . .

One of the escorting sub-chasers swung alongside them,
rolling in the swell. Several sailors in blue fatigues were standing around on deck, talking, and above the cabin a signalman
was balanced gracefully on the railing speaking in semaphore
to the bridge of the LST, using his hands for flags. A lieutenant jg leaned out of the wheelhouse door, his face bright and
unshaven. Over the PA system on the miniature bridge the
moan of a dance band welled out of the wireless crackling,
and a tenor voice sang in extravagant quasi-Negroid intonation:

*"Ah'm gonna sit right down an' write mahself a lettah—
An' make bee-lieve it came from you . . ."*

"Old Johnny Mercer," O'Neill crowed. "That takes you back, doesn't it though? We used to go up and catch him at the Totem Pole, used to dance off both our shoes . . . You ever go up there, Danny?"

Kantaylis shook his head. "We used to go down to Lake Compounce. That's a big dance pavilion in Connecticut. I can't dance, though. I never could."

"Old Al here's a dancing fool," O'Neill proclaimed. "He's a tiger on the floor. What I mean. At the Pontchartrain ballroom in D.C. he took off like a blue cormorant. Really tore the place apart. They had to call in the Shore Patrol."

"And the paratroopers," Newcombe added.

"Yeah: the paratroopers. For a color guard . . . The old Pontchartrain. What a ball park. Hey, remember when we lost the girls, Al? and found 'em again?"

"Yes."

"Boy, was Lorraine glad to see this pintail heave into view."

"She seemed pretty sore, as I recall."

"Don't kid yourself. That was just a cover. Right at that minute she was the happiest gal in town." O'Neill sighed, dropped his hands in his lap, stared wistfully out to sea. "Man, I'd give about two months' pay for that evening over again. Make it three months' pay . . ."

Grinning at him Newcombe said: "Just as it was?"

"Just as it was."

"You're an impossible sentimentalist . . . You know something? So would I."

"It must have been one hell of an evening," Derekman remarked dourly. "Must have been out of this world. I bet you never even went down for doubles."

"Oh-*ho!*" O'Neill cried, "don't you just think so, sport!" He glanced at Newcombe, who was silent, and said, "Well: we went down, anyway."

"I thought so," Derekman said.

Kantaylis stretched and yawned, slumped back in the seat again. Heat rose from the steel plates in tremulous little vapors. He could feel his cheeks and eyelids puff and tighten in the glare: points and chains of black darted up and down before his eyes: *Our baby came from this time,* she had said. *We never lay together before. We were soaring!* Her face had been flushed and bright in the dancing light from the fire; a lock of curl hung over her forehead. *Did you feel it? This is our first time . . .* Now she sat by an open window and held their son to a swollen, blue-veined breast and he clutched at it with one tiny hand and suckled, gurgling noisily: their son. *Oh Danny, I'm so happy. It was very easy after all my worrying, Dr. Stammers told Dad it was one of the easiest births he'd ever handled. Stevie weighed 8 lbs. 6 ounces at birth. A big boy and he looks like you already, can you imagine? except that he hasn't got any hair or eyebrows or eyelashes. Dreadful! Oh I'm so unbelievably happy, I never knew I could be so happy as this without you here, I don't even mind Mother half the time. All I need—all all of us need now is for you to come home safe to us, to me, darling, oh do be careful Danny, please, now you've got all the more reason to.* She held his son by an open window swarming with summer and the hum of insects . . . and with every sliding, silver-tufted wave he drifted farther from her, mile by mile, sliding half a world away—

Steps rang briskly on the ladder; Lieutenant D'Alessandro leaped on to the boat deck and called, "Good evening, men!"

The four watched him without reply. He was wearing his pistol and had in one hand a large white cloth and a wire bore cleaner. He was sporting the thin dark mustache he'd grown since they'd left Iroquois Point, which added to the sculptured handsomeness of his features.

· "Our hero," O'Neill murmured. "Our bloody bloomin' PX 'ero. Where's his silver bells?"

"In his head," said Derekman. "Instead of the marbles."

Lieutenant D'Alessandro strode along the boat deck in his paratrooper's boots, glancing about him brightly. When he encountered the Colonel's semirecumbent form he gave a little gesture of surprise and delight.

"Well, Colonel!" he cried. He looked down at the heavy body, the top of the wrinkled army fatigue hat with a little quiver of attentive eagerness. "Well: good afternoon, sir."

The Colonel did not stir.

Lieutenant D'Alessandro turned away absently, absorbed. After a moment he drew his pistol out of its polished leather holster, ejected the magazine and ran back the receiver, peering with interest into the chamber. Satisfied, he took up a stance, the pistol held high above his head, and brought it slowly down, aiming at some distant spot out on the water. The hammer fell with a dry little click. Pleased with the weapon's performance he aimed about him several times more, at the forward forty-millimeters and their crews, at the ship's number lettered on the LCVP slung overhead, at the far horizon.

"Jungle Jim," O'Neill said. "Our own beloved Jungle Jim. On safari."

"Good for the hammer too," Derekman observed. "Jesus: what kind of jackass have we drawn?"

"*Grade A*," Kantaylis said with such sudden vehemence they all turned and stared at him. "Grade A jackass. With bells . . ."

"Quite a weapon, isn't it, Colonel?" D'Alessandro queried; weary of aiming for a time, he began to pull the little wire cleaner back and forth through the bore. "They're the darnedest things to keep spotless though, aren't they?" And again turned toward the Colonel's motionless form, his face animate with the bright, engaging smile.

"Ah, that smile," Newcombe said. "The smile of multifarious rare delight, that mirrors back the laughter of the sea . . ."

"It was that screen test," O'Neill declared. "That God—damn—screen test."

"No, it wasn't: it was the personality-improvement course or whatever it was he ran back in dear old Kenosha. That's what gave him the assurance double sure: the Cult of the Big Smile . . ."

"What screen test?" Derekman demanded.

"Didn't you know? He had a screen test in Hollywood."

"Oh, *no*—"

"Oh, yes. Tyrone D'Alessandro or some Goddamn thing. Took himself a seventy-two while we were in Dago and went up there. Anything for the troops, you know. They told him his smile was his greatest asset."

"Greatest jackasset, you mean."

"Ah, that smile," Newcombe marveled. "Eternal smiles his emptiness betray, as shallow streams—"

"Oh shut up, Al."

"*Zum Befehl.*"

"I suppose there are a dozen ways to clean them thoroughly, once you come right down to it," Lieutenant D'Alessandro's voice floated back to them, crisply conversational. "And I've been wondering what's really the best way. With all this salt air and salt water and all. Hardly ideal conditions . . ." He laughed pleasantly in the sun, his rows of

perfect teeth flashing against his handsome, tanned skin.
"When one's been in service as long as you have, sir, with a
record like yours, he gets to know the *feel* of things, wouldn't
you say?"

Colonel Herron stirred ever so slightly.

"And of course I want to keep it in the best possible condition I can," D'Alessandro continued. "I remember what
Major Mowbray said the other day about the ravages of mud
and water." He laughed again, now and then aiming the
pistol at some near object as thought came to him. "And I
wondered if you couldn't give me some really sound advice
about it, you know?" He paused a moment, expectantly,
peering at the Colonel's still form; then leaned forward in his
most engaging manner and raising his voice said: "Tell me,
Colonel—what *is* the best way to keep the bore clean?"

Colonel Herron sat up suddenly and pushed back the
floppy fatigue hat. Underneath it his face was a heavy brick
red. He looked without interest or expression at the tall, handsome figure above him.

"Lieutenant," he said in a loud, clear voice that rang along
the boat deck like a watch bell, "the best advice about the
maintenance of a forty-five caliber automatic pistol was given
me many, many years ago by an old gunnery sergeant who
once said to me: 'Lieutenant, the best way for you to keep
your pistol clean is to keep your Goddamned filthy hands off
it.' "

There was an indefinable jolt among the four sitting in the
gun tub: as though some strange mechanism had run a flash
of current through them. Their eyes met in a running stop and
held, pregnant with amazement—darted back to D'Alessandro's face, which looked pale and popeyed and vacant.

"Uh—yes, sir," he stammered. The pistol, its blued steel
gleaming, dangled from his hand. "Yes, I guess that's right,
sir."

But he was talking to the air again; the Colonel was lying
remote and peaceful as before, hat over his eyes. Backing
away Lieutenant D'Alessandro headed for the ladder with
long strides, his face white and strained, and descended.

The group in the gun tub went into paroxysms; thumped
each other on the back and roared with laughter, wiped their
eyes. Crews from other guns called to them and the laughter
spread, rippled around the fantail, then up forward: a taut,
gleaming hilarity that rose and rose until above and astern of
them the albatross, gliding up on flashing, flaunting wings,

seemed also to acknowledge the incident; wagging its beaked, balding old man's head in bitter mirth.

3

————————IN A WAY I've become fascinated with this idea of a T-letter to you, darling: lying here with a book in my hands for cover (much like the coruscating adventure tale—*Ivanhoe* or *Treasure Island*—behind the arithmetic book back in grammar school) I can spin this yarn off the cuff, so to speak; in complete privacy. And in a place where for over a month there has been no privacy whatsoever, where Jay's foot bumps my cot each time he rises from his own, where thirty of us talk and toss and dream in an area the size of a small dining room, where ten of us sit at stool like cattle in their stanchions any time of day (or night either)—privacy has begun to assume the elements of magic.

I doubt if you could conceive of the kind of degradation that surrounds us: our nakedness, our acute vulnerability. For there is something pathetic about men living together for so long without the dignity of respite or seclusion. The longing for it becomes a nameless, fugitive thing: you keep seeking the casual talk of comradeship, the desultory exchange of reminiscences no one cares about very much—and at the same time you hug to yourself the need for solitude, for clutching your thoughts secretly under your cloak as though they were a bag of rhinestones and gazing now and then at their meager magnificence; for reaffirming in a sense your identity . . . And so you come upon someone suddenly at an odd hour of the night huddled by the rail or sitting in cross-legged contemplation like Buddha in one of the crannies way up forward, or in the little coffin-shaped niche under the three-inch gun: you recoil for an instant, then murmur *Hiya* or *What you say*, and the figure, indistinct, scarcely fleshed in the darkness, murmurs *Tchusay* in reply; and for a time you stand there, you and he, almost rubbing shoulders—pervaded, both of you, with a curious mixture of resentment and kinship.

Held in this strange polarity you watch the moon swing low along the water, a faultless silver orb washed with orange, and the sea slips away beyond you westering, in trembling points and swales of silver light, and seethes beneath your feet. You offer a chance remark about the sea, the moonlight; but he hardly responds, nor do you care if he does: you are both content to stand in silent proximity, graced by the warm, wet night wind . . .

Well, that is our nobler side, I fear: for the rest we are a scummy crew. Gazing over the deck I am reminded of some coy poem of Masefield's about a ship sailed by monkeys and something about "and not a pair of hand-me-downs to breech 'em tight or loose." We've all run out of razor blades and towels and soap and cigarettes—we ran out of them weeks ago—and the ship's stores has now refused to sell us anything except cigarettes, and these on a rationed basis.

And so we stand by the crosswalk where ship's stores are located, waylaying swabbies, shy and aggressive at once, proffering the four bits, the dollar bill: "Hey, any chance for some butts, mate?" "Why should you guys get 'em? We ain't got enough for ourselves." "Ah come on, don't be a wedge-ass, will you?" "We ain't got enough for ourselves, why should you guys get 'em all?" "One-way, ah? Okay." *One-way, one-way* . . . And the veiled insults, the recriminations: "Say, you characters get fresh water showers all the time, ah?" "Sure we do." "What a hardship." "Why shouldn't we, fella? This is our regular duty. You guys are just in transit." "A hardship. Christ, if you went without anything for a day you'd die." "Don't tell me your troubles, gyrene: you got a chaplain of your own on board." Which is true too, of course.

Harry Derekman, who has a dark and brooding side to his nature, declares it's all planned—the shutting off of fresh water in the heads, the petering out of clothes and PX supplies, the steady deterioration of food into a tepid, swimming ooze that resembles nothing so much as dog food soaked in doughnut fat. It is all, he maintains, a crafty system of deprivation and denial, tempered to the moment when we hit the beach and vent the pent-up fury of our pyramided frustrations on a luckless enemy. Jay scoffs at this, taunts him: "What do you mean—they send out directives from D.C. to cut down on fresh water in the heads of a couple of moth-eaten LST's staggering around in the middle of the Pacific Ocean? My God, they don't even know we're *here* . . ."

"Well, maybe not that, but it's planned all right"; and Harry goes on to cite the fact that no leaves were given to half the outfit at San Diego before shipping out, turns for further backing to Danny Kantaylis and says, "How about it—isn't that right? It's all a plan—they want to get you so damn disgusted you won't care." "But why, for pete sake?" Jay asks him. "Isn't that right, Danny?" Harry presses. And Danny smiles that faint tired smile and says: "You may have something there . . ."

Near me Corporal Schulman is playing chess with Capistron. My set: everybody shunned it like the plague when I first broke it out. *Hey, get that. Hey, how intel-lec-tual we're getting this trip. Pahss me my lorgnette, won't you?* (I will leave it to you to imagine the more robust allusions.) But we've been out over a month now (my God—a *month!*) and the comic books and terror tales have all been digested and redigested and regurgitated, and finally Connor and Jay broke down one day after I'd been playing with Schulman and asked me to teach them the moves. And lo and behold it has become a craze, with people waiting their turn and a sort of unofficial tournament under way. My God—that boredom should drive men to intellectual pursuits and pastimes! Heretical thought. Yet so it does indeed seem: Jay is even now dipping into my *Iliad* with mixed emotions ("Yeah, it's not bad, but I don't know, Al—do they really expect you to swallow that King Kong routine?") and Harry is plowing fitfully through *Lord Jim*. Can it be the boredom will reach such heights they'll even (dread conjecture!) essay Yeats and Eliot and Hopkins, or even Shakespeare? Ecad, sir: who knows what properly enforced ennui on the national level might not achieve in the name of culture.

Of course it has achieved other less felicitous results as well—this merciless monotony. The mounting hostility between us and ship's company finally boiled over at noon chow today. The usual pleasantries and asides at the weather door which is the head of the chow line (we gun crews line up from forward, the sailors from aft): "Why don't you let us sail the damn ship for you? We might as well be doing that too, along with everything else." "What is it, a hardship for you?" "Then you wouldn't even have *to* get out of your lousy sacks." "We'll fix you up with a TS slip." Gunner's mate Glaviano, swarthy and massive at the head of the line, grinning at us through half-closed lids. "Beat 'em, ya bellhop heroes. Beat 'em till they bleed." On his bare right arm a

naked girl holding a snake in an intriguing manner wriggles
and writhes as he flexes the bicep: the gesture itself an insult.
"Ya lousy purple-heart bellhops . . ." And then all at once
Steve Lundren's voice, low and rumbling and full of menace:
"That's enough of that purple heart talk, Glaviano."
Glaviano's heavy eyebrows rise. "You don't like it?" "No:
you shut your mouth with that talk." And Glaviano, his eyes
wide and baleful, "You don't like it, buster, you can stick it
right—"

I never saw the blow, though I was watching: I don't think
anybody did. There was a sharp *thwack* and then after it—
distinctly after it—the crash of Lundren's mess gear dropped
from his right hand. Glaviano came off the bulkhead in a half
crouch with his legs braced under him, his face wild with fury
and Lundren's right arm swung forward again—we all saw it
this time—with the deliberate, poised precision of a great
beam: an awesome thing: the sound was like a cleaver breaking through bone and Glaviano's body bounced against the
bulkhead again. This time he came off it with his eyes rolling
above the whites, his knees buckling, falling as he moved; and
a murmur went up from all of us, a faint "Ohhhhh—" that
sighed in the blazing sunlight like a muted choir . . .

And Lundren afterward, his battered face strangely tense
and youthful and alive. "Well, the Book says, Smite a scorner
and the simple will beware . . ." Turned suddenly loquacious,
telling us about his boyhood in the Georgia backwoods, his
running away at the age of twelve to join a circus ("Driving
stakes, roustabout, cleaning cages, stuff like that, I was
always big as a horse ever since I was a little bitty kid, I told
'em I was seventeen"), talking of his years in the ring,
moments recalled from half a hundred battles under the
garish lights and smoke-spun air and the fierce blood-calls of
the crowd. "Shucks, I didn't know how to fight then, I was
just a big kid, I didn't know how to protect myself at all. But I
always knew how to hit. And I caught him just once with my
right and he went down with the funniest look on his face I
ever hope to see. And he couldn't get up. You know what? I'd
busted his ankle . . ." He laughs exultantly and slaps his
thigh, his eyes bright and blinking; opens and closes his huge
right hand. The fingers are long and supple but the knuckles
have been driven back into each other at the joints. His right
ear is like melted cheese which has run down into the center
leaving a tubular indentation through the puffed and bubbled

flesh. "Yeah: once I catch 'em with this one they're speared good and dead."

He gazes off at the sliding undulations of sea rolling west; gazes with somber majesty, mighty even in decline. And listening to him I can feel a fever run through us all: a touch of fever. It's a little like coming up the channel at Pearl Harbor past the newly resurrected hull of the old *Oklahoma*, when the yelling started way up forward and swept aft toward us in a wild, rising roar at the American legend made manifest before our eyes—the comeback, the battered fighter getting up off the floor for the ultimate triumph. But this is edged with something else. It is keener, more cutting: the tang of blood is in it now . . .

The word came over the ship's radio yesterday of the Normandy beach-head. (I came in last in the pool over D-Day, I guessed July 14th—Bastille Day and all that, how utterly ridiculous to think the mil't'ry would take such sociohistorical factors into consideration.) The overcultured, authoritative, pleasantly conversational voice: *preceded by a tremendous naval bombardment from the mightiest armada ever assembled in all history, the initial landings were completely effective and the over-all success of the operation is assured*. And we all know what *that* means: or are beginning to have a pretty damned good idea. The President has also asked the nation to pray for victory . . . I am flooded with a wondrous technicolor vision of every man, woman and child bowed before kitchen sideboard, Bendix washer, desk, press drill and flush toilet; brows wrinkled, faces screwed tight in prayer. (Allll read-y—prayer-call: *pray!* Hep, two, three . . .) Still, Franklin D. *has* asked the nation to mumble a few vague orisons . . . And who holds the lamp aloft for *us?* one is tempted to ask. Who will accomplish the sacred hecatomb, light the fire under the tripod, prepare the offerings and avert the wrath of Phoibos Apollo (or is it the gray-eyed goddess we should fear, the upholder of chastity, sobriety, the inviolable hearth?)—who will free us of this dead hand that sends us drifting endlessly over the vast sea? Unlike the heroes of antiquity, it seems we are to have our odyssey *before* our iliad . . .

Below and aft of my cot, blunted fingers hold a combat knife along the back of the blade, guide a small black nub of stone that licks at the steel in infinite concentric circles: loop loop loop loop. An interminable movement of which I am constantly yet scarcely aware—like the recurrent shadow of an unpleasant dream. Helthal. Peering down at the stone's circular passage with gimlet surveillance: scraggle-bearded and sullen and absorbed. Expecting nothing, desiring nothing, occupied with nothing at all but the barely perceptible motion of a piece of black stone on a knife blade already sharp past comparison. He pauses, presses his horned thumb against the blade's edge, studies it for a time; then as the result of some dull inspiration holds the knife loosely between thumb and forefinger at the very end of the haft and lets the curved edge glide along the canvas where it is pulled taut over the cot frame—watches with no expression of either satisfaction or surprise as the tough fabric leaps apart like silk, revealing the white wood. And watching him, I feel as though my backbone were being slowly traversed by a snake's cold scales . . .

What is it? What is missing—or so alien—in Helthal that sets him apart from the rest of us as though he were painted blue? What soured, mirthless, benighted hovel in the West Virginia hills has put its mark of resolute thoughtlessness on those gross features? Unawakened clay—that is the phrase that hangs in the corner of your mind as you watch the slack, full mouth, the round gray absolutely depthless eyes: the face of darkness. Flat on his belly in the pit's much mire, like Caliban—you catch yourself, foolishly, in a fantastic impulse to touch that face, further define that nose, the brows, the thick, prognathous chin, mold it in your fingers—to ruin it utterly perhaps but at least give it expression, breathe into it some of the trappings of intellect or passion—

You hold your hand, though: you hold your hand. There is something fearful about Helthal, about his deadened absorptions: you are reminded continually of the tireless running of rats in tunneled cages, the stamp of a monstrous hoof, a mole thrusting with slow, blind persistence through the black earth. What is going on below that low, scowling brow? What the hammer? what the chain? In what furnace was *thy* brain, Helthal? What, you wonder—my God! what can he be thinking! And for an instant of chill terror you think blindly: He will undo us all, he will destroy us all somehow with his face of darkness . . .

Capistron has just moved a bishop with great decision. Bluff: a disastrous pass, I can tell from here . . . Capistron is the only man in the platoon who can elicit a response from Helthal. With a joke or a curse or a slap on the shoulder or the offer of a cigarette he can reach him, draw replies in monosyllables. Bound by their absorbing interest in liquor and whores and comic books and the monstrously salacious typewritten stories they treasure dearly, they form an entity: Capistron is the blustering convex side of Helthal's dulled, morose concavity. Together they comprise everything I hate and fear: brutality rampant and couchant. To see them together is to conjure up a series of horripilating visions out of Hesse or Ortega, of a swarming race of brutes everywhere triumphant in a world ravished of tenderness and beauty and reflection: a nightmare image that makes me shudder. Will they be all that will survive this demoniac Armageddon? Capistron's eyes, small and troubled, rise from the board: I avert mine swiftly. I have no desire to cross swords with Capistron . . . But at least he hates and desires volubly, he curses and roars and gets monstrously, outrageously, stupid-staggering drunk whenever possible—even sometimes when not—at least you can make contact with him, take hold of him, if you care. Or dare. Whereas with Helthal—

Schulman has captured the bishop. Capistron stares down at the board in bewilderment, lower lip thrust out, fists planted on his thighs. "What's that? How do you get to take that?" Schulman sighs, crooks a hirsute hand over the stem of his unlit pipe. Balding, with an oddly foreshortened face and black, beady, kindly eyes he looks like a Russian terrorist of the last century: a Bakuninite perhaps, pockets bulging with homemade bombs, waiting with stoic impassivity for the moment of the uprising. He sighs again, recites in a bored, patient voice: "One straight and one diagonal: that's the way the knight moves." "What? That'd be there, then: or there." "No. One over and one *diagonal*." Capistron looks up at Schulman with narrowed, accusing eyes. "Are you trying to con me?" "Of course not. That's the knight's move. Ask somebody, then," And Schulman draws on the unlighted pipe with genial imperturbability. "Okay, okay. I thought it was one up and one to the side . . ." And Capistron, down three pieces now, hunches forward over the board, hand cupped in fat hand: a worried, baffled bear.

The Normandy assault has just provoked a snarling argument on the far cot among Carrington, the corpsman attached to us, and Derekman and Sergeant Fellows, who joined us at Pearl along with some of the others and who has been given command of our squad largely because he's a sergeant, I suppose—no one seems to know much about his

service history. He is what my mother would call an un-
wholesome young man: small blue eyes much too close
together for comfort and a widow's peak and a small
mustache; he also has a slim, disdainful smile which discloses
more teeth than should be there and which reminds me of
some kind of animal, I can't recall just which one. Their
voices reach me in snatches. Fellows is holding forth about the
Wall Street bastards who he says are having us slaughtered
like flies to suit their interests; he's done a lot of
reading—though he's had no college (he maintains a particularly obnoxious attitude toward me, calls me *collegeboy*
continually and gives me every crud-detail he possibly
can)—and will develop at the drop of a hat a labyrinthine
argument involving big interests, trusts, I. G. Farben and
Standard Oil and Lever Brothers till your head it simply
swirls. (Maybe he's right for all I know: I never paid much attention to this cartels-dynasty-of-death business—I suppose I
should have . . . it would at least be good to know if you *were*
going to die for the purpose of extending the acreage of a
Lever Brothers plantation.) Derekman, who has taken a
violent dislike to Fellows and is spoiling for a fight (deterred
only by the stripes but thank God for that) retorts in a surly
tone that we are fighting to save the free world, we're fighting
for the four freedoms. "Which four freedoms are those?"
Fellows replies, and his mouth turns down at the corners even
as he smiles. "Freedom to get butchered for the DuPont-
DuNemours Corporation? Freedom to keep the Negro in his
place? Freedom to use the lockout against striking miners?
Which one do you mean?" And turns his back on Derekman's
stammering rage. One sour old apple, Jay calls him; which is
just about the size of it.

The doldrums: we're in the doldrums, wherever *they* are:
drifting through an eternity of blinding heat. Where the devil
are we headed? Perhaps we're going to sail right off the edge
of the world, as Da Gama's men believed: at least it would be
a dramatic change. The old men shake their heads and mutter
about its being a fubar operation, a colossal snafu, a foul-up
beyond comparison—and the scuttlebutt is that it has twice
been called off and twice reinstated, due to the Jap navy,
about whose whereabouts no one knows. Tempers crackle,
fists fly, and the curses and imprecations roll in one long,
unremitting volley from stem to stern and back again. There is
only the casual talk among the veterans to remind us of the

savagery awaiting us: the veil through which we neophytes cannot see . . .

Nearby, the pinochle game—now played with the remnants of four decks—drags on and on, played with less rowdy jollity than formerly. Jay is cleaning his rifle for the zillionth time and moaning a song which seems to be made up of the one line, *"Good morning, blues: blues, how do you do?"* Even Jay—dear old buddy Jay—can get on one's nerves occasionally. Woodruff is asleep again, his mouth a long oval, his tongue lying in one corner of it like something infinitely distasteful; beads of sweat have collected on his back and slipped down to the hollow above his buttocks where they had stained his dungaree trousers an inverted crescent of deep green.

And on the niche cot below and behind me, on the very rim of my consciousness, the little black nub of a whetstone caresses in interminable loops the graylight steel _____

4

"WE DIDN'T KNOW what we were getting into. We didn't have any idea at all." Lying on his cot with his hands folded behind his head, Kantaylis gazed vacantly up at the torn and sagging ponchos above them; his voice was sonorous, subdued with reminiscence. "We piled out of the LCVP's and flopped there, and nothing happened. Not a thing. After a while somebody got up—I think it was Krantz—and then Sorelli started wisecracking. It was so quiet you could hear him clear as a bell a hundred feet away. Then the rest of us got up and we started walking in through the boondocks. Just walking along as if it was a hike at Pendleton. So quiet it gave you the creeps."

"No Japs at all?" Derekman said.

"Not a one. We came out of the boondocks into an open stretch of ground and we spread out a little more and started across it. Several guys were talking in low voices. And that was when we saw the Jap. He was running right along the edge of the trees on the far side of the clearing, going like a jackrabbit. Everybody stopped and stared at him for a second, and then Krantz let out a yell and we all started yelling at him and firing: it was just like cops-and-robbers—everybody hollering and waving his rifle and running hell-bent after that one little Nip . . .''

"Didn't anybody hit him?" Ricarno demanded.

"Hell, no. Nobody came within a mile of him. We went barreling along after him like a football squad all steamed up for the big game, whooping and yelling and having a fine time. And that was when Sorelli got it. He was about ten feet ahead of me. He grabbed his neck with one hand—sort of slapped at it as if a hornet had stung him—and turned around as if he was going to ask me something; and then his rifle fell out of his hand and he dropped. And then two more guys got cut down and we heard the machine guns. And that put an end to all the big-game crap. There wasn't any more rebel-yelling or rifle-waving after that. Everybody hit the deck and stayed there . . .''

Beyond the edge of the ponchos the evening sky was a long slash of lemon, shot through with dove-gray streaks of cloud. On the far rim of the horizon thunderheads had built up in a boiling black mass, like a row of distant towers. Propped on his elbows O'Neill watched the other figures on their cots, motionless, attentive; rising and falling with the ship's side.

"What did you use for cover, Danny?" Connor asked.

"Anything," Kantaylis said. "Any old thing at all. And there wasn't much of anything, either."

"There'll be lots of shell holes, Chicken," Klumanski said, and grinned. With his massive, hairless body and close-cropped head he reminded O'Neill of some good-natured Mongol chieftain. "If the damn navy don't get any of the pillboxes they at least make for plenty of cover. They saved our wagon on Engebi."

"Now, I don't want you people bunching up in them," Lundren's voice rumbled in admonition from the edge of the drums. "You get ten or a dozen of you in one and everybody's buddies and it's cozy as all get-out and then they drop one on you and you're all in a big sling. I don't want you bunching up in them, now. There's going to be plenty of holes to go round."

"Ain't they going to knock out those little old pillboxes?" Woodruff inquired. "The navy?"

"Well. They'll get some of 'em. They won't get half enough, though. The Nips'll have 'em tied in thicker than fleas on a dog's tail. Covering each other. You want to look sharp and keep on looking, now. I almost went to the Lord on Engebi 'cause I didn't keep my eyes peeled. We were moving along pretty good the second day and I waved Foy and Ellison up and got all set to take off again—and all of a sudden I spotted one of them—smallest one you ever saw. You'll miss 'em sure as all get-out you don't look sharp. Little black slits. They're about two feet long, most of 'em, and built right down to the ground . . . That slowed me up plenty, I'm telling you."

"Can you get them with grenades?" Capistron asked him.

"Sometimes you can, sometimes you can't. You won't get the concrete babies: they've recessed the slit with a kind of pocket so's it'll trap a burst. But you can get the coconut-log bunkers with grenades, I don't care what they say, because Foy and I got two of them. But you got to work your way in real close . . ."

There was a silence, dominated by the slithering rush of water along the ship's side. The sky had turned a deep, flaming orange; glowing on their undersides like melting iron the rain clouds piled up on themselves in ponderous majesty, rushing upward through the twilight. A weird sky; watching it O'Neill frowned. It seemed a part of the admonitory talk itself, woven with it somehow: uncanny, vaguely menacing and comfortless.

"Now, what we're going to do at night is, we secure at dusk and then anything that moves is a Nip," Lundren went on in slow finality. "Anything at all. I don't want any of this stupid wandering around in the dark to water the horse or anything else. Two guys got starched on Pari 'cause they were going around on some fool errand, being sociable or something, borrow a poncho. You haven't got a poncho crawl under a corner of your buddy's and if he hasn't got one then both of you sit there and shiver your tails off. It's a hell of a lot better than getting starched. And you men on watch memorize the password: say it over about a hundred times and then try to forget it and say it around a hundred more. We don't want any foul-ups on the passwords. There's going to be enough groping and sweating around as it is without some goof-off getting blasted all for nothing." He paused. "Now, the passwords are all going to have a lot of l's in 'em, and God have mercy on any poor son of a bitch that doesn't pronounce 'em right. You men on watch, you challenge somebody and he says 'Rorripop,' something like that, you blast him good and we'll find out about it later . . .''

There was a still longer silence. Far aft on the bridge a bell struck seven times: *ting ting: ting ting: ting ting: ting* . . . a ghostly tintinnabulation. Through one of the rents in the poncho above his head O'Neill could see a bold, solitary, glistening star hanging all by itself; soon to be overswept by the onrushing black clouds. Sweat was sliding down beneath his arms but his hands were cold, and he chafed them absently. This was one of those creepy times: no doubt about it. Here they sat in a group, getting the word, huddled on a rusty old tub rolling west toward the islands. The calf of one leg pressed against the butt of his rifle slung under his cot. Soon he'd be carrying it in his two hands, running and diving, crawling like crazy in and out of shell holes . . . And what was it like at the other end of the line? where a bunch of Nips were sitting in some pillbox, sweltering too, bitching about the chow or some worthless crud of an officer, wondering where and when they were going to come ashore, what was going to happen?—just the way they themselves were now. And yet in the not too distant future they'd all be trying to blow each others' brains out. Succeeding, too. A creepy sensation . . .

"The big thing is, don't leave your foxholes and take off," Kantaylis was saying, his voice full of urgency. "No matter what they throw at you: banzais, tanks, bathtubs—don't shag ass. You're *sure* to stop one then—and you've lost everything. Dig in and hang on and you'll make out. They threw everything they had at us on the Tenaru and we never cracked. They shouted at us, told us we were surrounded, the country had written us off—rang bells and blew horns and cranked up sirens and everything else. And we hung on and hung on and they never broke through."

"How'd you get hit, Danny?" Carrington asked him.

"Stopping a banzai. Their biggest one. I got this first." He tapped his shoulder with his thumb. "They got across the river finally and started coming up the bank and they had us pinned down all the time with mortars. I looked up and there was this Jap coming at me like a train. I saw him just the second he saw me. I got this and he got all he's ever going to get. I put a couple more rounds into him to make sure and got three others right behind him, and then I began to feel sick. I thought I'd take it easy for a while till it went away. . ."

He paused; Freuhof's cot creaked and O'Neill saw him turn

over on his side facing away from them, out to sea.

"There wasn't any time for that, though. They kept coming and kept coming. Jesus! there were a million of 'em. We stayed right with the gun, though: right down to the wire. They got Gannon and then Turk and then Krantz and Brugger. By then I was so mad I didn't care *what* I felt like, I didn't even remember I'd been hit, I don't think. They were in so close they were throwing grenades by then, and they got two in our hole and I threw them back. Then I got clipped in the neck here and just then they broke, what was left of them. Shagged ass. And one of the last ones rushed me with a grenade in each hand. I was all out of ammunition by then, I was down to two clips in one of the '03's and Turk's old horse pistol. I remember I saw him let them both go at me at the same time just as I cut him down with Turk's revolver—and that was the ticket. That rang down the curtain for a while . . ."

O'Neill turned his head, encountered Newcombe's expressionless stare. Their eyes held on each other—a long, mesmeric glance as though they had become somehow mysteriously entangled—broke away to the rust and gold evening sky. Old Newk, O'Neill thought. Jeez, I don't know. What do you suppose we've let ourselves in for? . . . O'Neill, you poor shanty-Irish madman, he said silently. You've never been this far away from home; man, you've never been this aching far away . . .

"Next thing I knew I was lying on a trail and nobody was anywhere around. Not a soul. And maybe you don't think *that* isn't lonely! It must have taken me half an hour to get to the CP. I'd walk a way and then crap out for a while. Then I'd try it again. I'd be there yet if that communications sergeant hadn't come by. He'd stopped one in the hand and he was walking along as fast as he could, holding on to his hand and talking a blue streak. He wasn't stopping for *anybody*." Kantaylis stirred, chuckled softly. "I remember I thought, Jesus, if he passes me up I'm a cooked pigeon. He looked down at me as he went by—just a quick glance—and I gave him the most pitiful look there is, I'm telling you. Boy, the pitiful hound-dog look I gave him. So he stopped and gave me a hand or I'd be down there right now with Turk and Gannon and the rest of the platoon. As it was I keeled over half a dozen times more. I was about ready to come all apart by then . . ."

O'Neill put his hand across his eyes, felt rather than saw a series of wild, discordant images race across his mind like sheets of lightning: two little children splashing in shallow water, gamboling and shrieking, the water in curving silver sheets around them; a figure in a billowing white dress swooping over his head, riding a swing, swooping down and far away, down and far away again; a one-armed man washing windows somewhere long ago, his sweating face lifted, singing "Mother Machree" in a sweet, throbbing tenor; and more remote still, another face bending down to him, a being mysterious and strangely lovely to whom he wildly clung, the voice too an unremembered, enchanting murmur, soothing him . . . He shivered. Something inside him was trembling and his mouth had gone completely dry. Glancing around him covertly in the gold-poured dusk he was filled with amazement at the composure of the other faces: they seemed casually, genially interested, unperturbed; even Newk and Chicken. Jesus!—didn't they feel this—*any* of it?

What the hell, he told himself resolutely, and looked around at Klumanski and Derekman and Terrabella. If they could do it so can I: I'm no better and no worse than they are . . . But he still felt disoriented and oppressed.

"Well, I finally got back, what with the sergeant with the shot-up hand and some other guy I never did know who he was. And then came the damnedest thing ever happened to me: I was lying there hanging on to myself and waiting for them to get to me and all of a sudden this guy bends over me and says, 'Protestant or Catholic, son?' Get that, will you? Protestant or Catholic. Christ, I blew my roof at him. 'Why you stupid bastard.' I said to him. 'You stupid, *stupid* son of a bitch. Go peddle your papers,' I said. I remember him looking surprised as all hell, and then I crapped out for good . . . I'll never forget that. I don't know who or what he was but I sure gave him a bad time . . ."

Kantaylis snorted, drew up one of his legs and scratched at it absently. For a time there was quiet; the thunderheads had swept up in a boiling dark pall, grayed silver on their faces, their edges blowing off into the ochre translucence of the sky like smoke sifted through gauze.

"Going to rain again," Lundren said. "Going to come down in buckets and soak all our gear."

. . . It was odd: when you thought about all the ships resting on the bottom of the ocean right this minute, all the men who ever went out on troop transports since the beginning of time, in Egyptian triremes and Roman galleys and caravels and galleons and frigates and God knew what else, junks and sampans—if you thought enough about it, let your mind swing round and round on it enough, it was almost as though, sitting here listening to Danny's voice, you had been all through this once before, this very moment some time long ago—or else you were crazy as a bedbug or something . . . Newcombe was looking at him again, a funny, slow, sympathetic look; but he dropped his eyes nonetheless. For Al didn't understand this either, for all his book-learning. He had spoken of it one night when they'd been standing alone on the fantail and Newcombe had only grinned that wry grin and murmured something about the human condition. But that didn't get at it . . . Maybe there wasn't anything to get *at*—yet why was it so disturbing, so that you often felt if you thought about it another ten seconds you would fall right out into space, be whirled away headlong with the blood rushing to your head—? Like the pitch-black night he had made that crazy bet with Wolfe and had rowed, very drunk, out to the twenty-foot tower in the Cove and climbed to the top of it. Below him there had been not a ripple or a gleam: for an instant, shivering and shaking, he was visited by the wild thought that nothing lay down there at all—no water, no land below it, nothing but black, substanceless void through which he would endlessly plummet, screaming and forlorn . . . He had dived, though: his pride had compelled him, his nerve had pulled him through it. He recalled again the swift rush of air, the ghastly sensation of falling through boundless naked space toward he knew not what. The water had struck him like an electric shock, almost stunned him. By the time he had surfaced he was stone sober and frightened and nearly sick. Treading water feebly in the aqueous inky dark he felt somehow as though he'd been saved from something cosmically dreadful; he vowed he would never do a thing like that again for all the money in all the world . . .

"Say, Danny," he said aloud, leaning forward.

"Yeah?"

"Did it—what did it feel like, when you got hit?"

"I don't know . . ." Kantaylis shrugged indolently. "That grenade—it was like getting hit across the back with a ball bat. A whole pile of them. It's hard to say: it didn't hurt at all at first. The way you think it's going to, I mean. I don't know . . . it was sort of like a sink drain," he said suddenly. "You know—when you used to look down into it when you were a kid, and the water's whirling around and going down

into it, and it's black all the way down? Everything clear and
fine and then all of a sudden you're part of the sink drain
itself and everything's all bright and whirling, you can hardly
see at times. And then it began to hurt like a bastard. Man, it
really hurt like crazy by then . . ."

He sat up on his elbows and stared for a moment out to sea;
looked around at the reclining figures.

"Well: if you get hit you get hit, that's all. It's just good
luck or bad luck. It isn't important."

"It *isn't?*" Ricarno said incredulously, and scratched his
hairy chest. "It's going to be Goddamn important to me.
What the hell's more important?"

"Staying awake at night," Kantaylis answered levelly.
"Staying awake, not letting your buddies down. That's really
important, the most important thing in some ways. Isn't that
right, Steve?"

They all looked at Lundren who solemnly nodded.

"Any way you can think of," Kantaylis went on in his soft,
urgent voice. "Any way at all. Count numbers, write letters,
do sums, count the ages of friends, everybody you owe money
to, all the stupid things you did you wish you could do over
again—anything. I mean it. And when your mind won't work
any longer keep one foot in the air or pinch your ear or your
tail or anything else. *Keep awake.* And keep moving your eyes
around: don't fix on one place or you'll drop off or start
seeing things for sure. And listen and listen and listen some
more. And when you've run through everything you can
remember and think of and make up then just pray like hell to
stay awake anyhow. And that's the hardest thing of all . . ."

The clouds were almost abeam of them now. The sea lost its
pulsing red glitter, turned slate, then onyx; rain advanced over
it in fretted patterns, faded, came on again in dense, steaming
sworls, and the air became quickly cold. The sun broke
through a ridge of cloud for one final moment—a wild red
pomegranate spilling blood through the heavens—then was
swallowed up in a leaden night sky.

5

—————WITH A WORD—the logos—everything has changed. We know where we're going now—at least we think we do; a concrete place with many Japanese awaiting; and everything has become very purposeful and vigorous and grimly cheerful again—there's the same kind of suppressed excitement and camaraderie we had when we came aboard that evening at Iroquois Point. It's extraordinary: it has transformed everyone. Last night I came off watch and went skipping down the ladder in the dark. A man was standing under the ladder talking with someone and my boondocker came right down on his hand. Hard. And I thought: Oh my, here we go. "Sorry, Mac," I said as quickly and carelessly as I could manage (even though of course you're never sorry for anything you do in the Marine Corps, BOY don't ever let me hear you say that word again don't you know you're *never* sorry for anything *stand* at attention yes sir no sir) and got set for the imminent wrath and destruction. "That's okay, mate," he said (he was a Fox Company demolitions man, a monster, weighs two hundred easily, I recognized him with dim horror), and he wrung the injured hand and slapped me full on the back with the other—a blow that almost gave me consumption. "Don't give it a thought. Should've heard you coming . . ." A parlous change withal: three days ago I would have been in sick bay—or committed to sea burial—for such an indiscretion.

Faneráhan. The name possesses an exotic liquidity, an incantatory ring; you can feel it roll off your tongue in sheer delight. It unleashes a thousand flamboyant images: of still streams winding through viridescent jungle where from the tops of lordly palm trees float down the eerie, raucous cries of monkeys and macaws; the ornate prow (there must be an ornate prow) slips through still water where the foliage throws over it the sliding pattern of a dark lace shawl—emerges into a lagoon bathed in a rose-and-copper sunset; pulpy gold fruits hang like voluminous pendants from broad-leaved fronds, and flamingos, egrets, birds of paradise rise from the still water, soundlessly flapping, dripping chains of orange fire . . .

Faneráhan: it means "break in the reef" in Chamorro. And it has leaped from oblivion to become the most important isle of our young lives: already it has dwarfed Pawtucket, Queens,

Chicago's South Side, Boston, Fletcher's Landing; has nearly swept them out of existence. Some of us, it seems, will never leave it—though somehow that seems impossible: gazing around us at these immensely familiar faces (almost none of us has lived intimately or at any length with a woman), glancing at each others' little absorptions and foibles, we seem to each other indestructible. No: we will go on and on—like a ball team, a college class, from defeats and victories; an indissoluble fraternity. Or so it seems—

Oh yes, and we've been having calisthenics and running-in-place in relays in the little open space around the twenty-millimeters until our heads are ready to explode in the heat; and they've broken out the maps and the charts and Major Mowbray, our battalion exec, a fearfully prim and bilious little man with the picturesque (though unofficial) sobriquet of Dry Bones, has waxed most eloquent about the big picture. It's all going to be marvelously easy, it seems. Assorted battlewagons are going to bombard the place for five solid days and nights and heavy bombers are going to pound all the strong points, and TBF's and Corsairs are going to work over the Beach Line from Nénetan to Pajaña until there won't be a live Jap left above ground. We are to go ashore on Green Beach between the mouth of the Atainu River and Ngaián Point (the rock there juts out over the water like the head of a camel, a dramatic landmark—it will be on our left) and drive inland past a Catholic mission and advance to the little village of Machanao, on the crest of a series of low, rolling hills, and secure for the night. By that time tanks and artillery will be ashore and will be pulverizing the enemy, who will be pinned in the flat, S-shaped valley formed by the Atainu and Kaláhe Rivers. Major Mowbray used a pointer with an ivory tip and it all sounded tremendously martial and deadly and synchronized with a chesslike perfection, and we were getting pretty steamed up ourselves until big Klumanski rumbled, "Sure, just the way they did at Betio," and the old men turned to each other with brief interjections and snorts and head shakings and the dark invocation of names like Tulagi and Betio and Engebi: names which make us neophytes glance at each other and grin—and then look away and swallow and lick our lips again . . .

And Ricarno said, "Gee, all we got to do is just stroll ashore and make time with the broads, ah, Major?" And Major Mowbray, who reminds me everlastingly of the little man always put in charge of personal loans, frowned in bilious displeasure at the laughter and said, "Now, you people want to take this operational material seriously. It's damned important and you better pay attention and commit it to memory, you're going to be quizzed on all this data before we go ashore . . ." And Jay, you and Lorraine will be happy to hear, won undying fame in the battalion by calling out from the oil drums: "You mean they might not allow us to go in with the third wave if we don't pass, Major?" And even old Dry Bones had to laugh at that one.

But we're cleaning our weapons with greater assiduity now, and sharpening our knives and bayonets to a fearful edge (I am in mortal terror of taking my own arm off accidentally) and going over our packs and gear with care. There's less bitching and skylarking both . . . And there is an aspect of *strangeness* that hangs over us all, an element almost tangible. Jay expressed it the other night: "You know, it's like I've been through this whole cockeyed routine before, and so has everyone else. The whole bunch of us. And I'm remembering it from some other time. Isn't that a bear-cat, though?" "That's your mahatmavantaras working overtime," I said; but I was only being facetious and evasive: because I felt it, too—this eerie, evanescent mutation of things—the way you used to believe the young squire was changed by the stroke of knighthood, or the prince by the tapping of the angel's wand. Everything is as it was: Derekman soured with dark conjecture, Jay ebullient and cocky, Woodruff full of musing whimsicality, Danny still the quiet, sad, affecting soul—and yet we are all bathed in a strange light, *altered* in some way . . .

Faneráhan: the natives are Chamorrans, American Nationals fiercely loyal to us, who will welcome us as liberators, we are told. They speak a tongue rapid and drawling, soft and explosive at once: the fusion of two etymological strains—the crooning ripple of Polynesia and the harsh bark of the Indonesian mainland, overlaid with elements of Igorot and Spanish. *MAIla fan didiDIi NENkano*, it ripples; *ManGUI i MAagas?* A tongue which has no written version— we are far, far away from the hard, bright architecture of the classics. We lie on our sacks and study the phrases in the JICPOA booklets, memorize vocabulary and the liquid, running place names: Nénetan, Pajaña, Kaláhe, Tálanai . . . That is, Chicken and Jay and I do. Ricarno laughs at us. "What you guys all worked up over that stuff for? Listen: there's one language they all understand. Know what I mean?" Grinning at us he emits a piercing whistle

through his teeth, raises his arm in the perennial obscenity:
with Ricarno all references to the fair sex are invariably
accompanied by this gesture—a sort of code bordello. "That
one right there. Don't be a bunch of marrones." "Damn it,
Ricarno, is tail all you ever think about?" This from
Terrabella, another of the veterans who joined us at Pearl. He
is short and squat, with the tough, impish face of a
Neapolitan street urchin; he also has a fiancée in Ashtabula,
Ohio, to whom he is almost morbidly faithful. "No kidding:
can't you think of anything else once in a while?"

For a time Ricarno reflects, running the peeling, unsmoked
cigar—his last, I believe—back and forth along his thick lips.
"No. No, I think about chow, I think about sack drill, I think
about playing handball with the guys—sometimes . . ."
Speculatively he watches Terrabella; his eyes narrow and the
lynxlike grin slips over his face again. "Terry, you don't mean
to tell me a real, luscious, dusky broad comes right up to you
and gives you that nice, slow roll—that easy grind—it
wouldn't enter your mind? Ah?" "No, it wouldn't," Terry
says hotly; we are all watching him and this obvious untruth
nettles him a bit. "Well sure, I'd *think* of it—what do you
think?" he concedes. "But I wouldn't *do* anything about it."
"You wouldn't." "No, I wouldn't. What the hell, Babe—
they're prisoners, they've been starved and tortured and
beaten and every other damn thing, probably: what's the
matter with you?" "Well: everybody to his taste." Ricarno
peers up at the frayed and flapping ponchos riddled with
holes; circles of light slide over his oily black hair like golden
coins. "Some can take it and some can leave it alone.
Personally—personally I always take it whenever I can get it
. . . You know what I mean?"

So we roll on, through the stifling heat. For no good reason
I glance up at the sun, glance away again: quaking white
spheres drift against the hollow black of my lids, turn red and
green and blue by turns: fade slowly away. All in a hot and
copper sky. "I don't hardly know," Woodruff muses in his
soft, crooning drawl. "I don't hardly think I'll ever see it this
hot . . ." "You're seeing it this hot *now*," Derekman snaps.
"Jesus, why don't you learn the English language,
Woodruff?" and Woodruff gives him a look of grieved,
round-eyed reproach. "That was what I said, Harry. I said I
didn't hardly think I'd ever—" "Ah, never mind. Never mind
. . ." And Derekman looks down in disgust, goes on cleaning
his BAR.

"Chicken," Klumanski says in heavy, genial speculation. "Chicken, how'd you ever happen to get mixed up in this clambake? How'd you happen to go down and enlist?" And little Connor, who seems literally half his size, looks up at him defiantly and says: "My Dad, My Dad was at Belleau Wood with the Fifth Brigade. They won the fourragère." And his boyish, fragile face glows all at once with pride, ardent and touching. "That was in the Great War . . ." "You mean the World War, Chick." "No, the *Great* War." "Well: maybe that was the great one. This is just the big one," Klumanski says somberly; he gazes out at the expanse of lazily sliding sea. "Big as I'll ever want to see, anyway. The biggest and the last." "Ah, there'll be bigger ones," Feuhof remarks from his cot with soft scorn. "There always are." "No there won't, Jack." And Klu stubbornly shakes his head. "Another one like this it'll be the name of the game. Hell, there won't even be any playing field left." "Maybe so." Freuhof sighs once, rubs the side of his face with his arm; and the lines around his mouth sink into bitterness. "Well—they start any more after this one *I* don't want to be around . . ."

We are north and west of Truk now: mighty Truk, where sit (rumor has it) forty thousand of the Emperor's picked troops. (The strategy, according to old Dry Bones, "appears to be to bypass it." Thank you, Major, thank you. Not at all . . .) Easing along now, inside the jaws of Dai Nippon and her Greater East Asia Co-Prosperity Sphere; wallowing along over the course Ferdinand Magellan took four centuries ago (and at about the same speed, I daresay) across the Western Ocean. Magellan put in at Faneráhan, too; but in a far friendlier manner than we shall . . .

Last night at dusk Jay and I were leaving the little niche under the stern three-inch—out of bounds but a favorite perch of ours—when I saw the albatross was gone: the albatross that had followed us for weeks, a tireless, spider-winged wraith trailing us like some benign spirit of—what? I stared and stared. "Come on, Al. Let's sack in." "It's gone," I said. "What's gone?" "The albatross." I kept squinting into the misty twilight; I felt somehow bereft out of all proportion. "It isn't following us any more." "Hell no," Jay scoffed. "You don't think he's got the poor sense to follow after where us sad bastards are going, do you? . . . Goonies may be dumb, but not that dumb. Come on." He pulled at my sleeve. "Stare like that you'll get cataracts." "And the good south wind still blew behind, but no sweet bird did follow," I intoned. "Old Al," Jay said, and laughed softly. "Our wandering bard: a line for every occasion."

An intended compliment, but it isn't true: I fear there are many occasions in the offing for which I shall have no figures of allusion_____

6

"I'M GOING TO square away that Fellows," Derekman said in a low, angry voice; his helmet liner bobbed twice against the night. "Wait'll we get ashore. Down for doubles, boy. There won't be any Goddamn stripes then."

"When we get ashore Fellows is going to have troubles of his own," Kantaylis answered. "Don't worry about him."

"What do you mean, don't worry about him?"

"Just what I said: he's going to be having his own troubles. He won't even be *thinking* about you . . ."

"Well, I'll be thinking about *him*," Derekman rejoined. "Plenty."

"Don't worry about him."

"Latest scoop is the place is loaded," O'Neill said. "Skinnay is they've had it all wrong for months—there's *twenty* thousand Japs on that rock instead of ten."

"Who'd you get that from, Nimitz?"

"No. Halsey."

"Oh: fine."

"—Yeah, but twenty—thousand—Japs!" O'Neill cried incredulously.

No one spoke for several minutes. Around them the dark was taut and hard: it felt to Newcombe as though they were crouched inside of a huge, inverted bowl lined with black silk. The gun tub seemed to give off a faintly luminous glow which made it possible to see nearer forms with some difficulty; beyond the fireguards sea and sky and the rest of the convoy—augmented tenfold now—fell away in darkness, fused in the impenetrable black shell. Most of the gun crews had given up the watch and were sitting, quite unlawfully, on the ammunition racks circling the Number Three gun where Kantaylis was pointer.

"What do you think, Klu?" Capistron asked. "You think it's going to be rough?"

"Beats me . . . It isn't going to be any frigging picnic."

"What do you think, Babe?"

"Easy money." Ricarno cracked his knuckles in a series of rippling pops. "We got the whole U.S. Navy out here, for Christ sake: they'll peel the top off that rock like taking the skin off an orange."

"You think so?"

"Sure I do."

"They didn't peel the skin off any oranges at Betio," Freuhof said in a derisive tone.

"Betio—how come you always bring up Betio? Betio was a foul-up. They won't make the same mistakes twice."

"They never do: they make different ones."

"Ah, they'll pound the place to jelly. You wait: secure the butts in five days, with bells. Be shacked up with some delectable gook quail in seven."

Someone snorted, and there was a short silence again.

"What you think, Danny?"

Kantaylis stirred, cleared his throat. "I think it's going to be a holy terror."

"You do?"

"I think it's going to be a bear-cat."

"As bad as Tarawa?"

"Worse."

"Jesus. Bad as the Canal?"

"Worse—in some ways . . ."

"Je-*sus*," Capistron repeated. "No comfort talking to you . . . How come you think that?"

"How come? The Nips want to hang on to it, that's how come. They're losing, now: before, they were top-dog. They've got two airstrips on it, and a good harbor. They want to keep it."

"Christ, what a pessimist," Ricarno said; he laughed thickly. "For pete sake, Danny, don't start turning into a lousy sour-ball like Fellows. We'll make out all right."

"Sure we will . . . Cappie didn't ask me that, though: he asked me if I thought it was going to be rough."

"That's the way to figure it," Derekman remarked somberly; again his liner bobbed up and down like a turtle on a wire. "Look for the worst and you'll never be disappointed: that's the way . . ."

Lying—also unlawfully—at full length on one of the ammunition cases behind the gun tub Newcombe listened to the mélange of talk: the sober inquiries, curses, coughs, laughter, snatches of song. Above him—far, far above him—the stars sparkled in a soft, depthless drop of velvet, limpid and measureless; they expanded in quiet radiance as he watched them, glowing and flashing, blended with the dull vibration of the ship, throbbed in unison with it: a swarming, humming universe that descended around him, swallowed him up momentarily, left him bodiless and amazed. *Sundered aspiration of the night's long spaces*, the phrase came to him. Was that eloquent? was it meaningful? He had written no poetry since they'd left San Diego months ago. It was the first line that had come to him for a long time and he dwelt on it idly, turning it this way and that . . . No. No, it didn't say quite what it should. Sundered *from* aspiration, it should be: sundered from aspiration in the night's long spaces—cut adrift from all the fury and squalor, the paltry designs and puny ragings of a baffled, misguided humanity that never knew what it really wanted: or knew and kept forgetting . . .

Basking in an indolent reverie, his head cradled in his hands, he no longer heard the voices around him; he was conscious of a sudden, swift progression of half-formed images, light as gossamer, which swooped through his mind like a vision. There was a meadow that sloped toward the sea where a shepherd sat upon a rock playing on a flute—a simple, reedy melody hanging in the still air as pure as truth itself; around him sheep grazed peacefully on lowlands that stretched away to where at the horizon mountains rose up like smoky spires: but the wind blew, brought dust in whirling, shifting clouds and the shepherd was obscured; cities rose from the plain, cities decked with crenellated towers, and through their streets wagons rumbled incessantly, bearing ivory and spices and gold in oval ingots to the doors of mansions where figures in silk and ermine smacked fat lips and struck the table, roaring in mirth: the cities swelled again, burgeoning with factories and forts, prisons and palaces and squares where powerful personages read ticker-tapes in satisfaction and bewilderment, reached with starched white cuffs for phones or argued incessantly across highly polished tables—rose at length, red-faced and choleric, and withdrew: more phones rang, phones by tens of thousands, whistles shrieked and thundered, staff officers hurried down marble steps with tight triumph on their faces. War. A loudspeaker boomed and crackled: men came running to the village square, formed ranks and marched away to a thunderous brass-band cheering din—charged with Napoleonic grandeur down cloud-darkened slopes, a scarlet-and-silver cavalry in full-throated cry—vanished in a torrent that churned its way through awesome gorges, swept out at last into the plains below and merged, gently and innocuously, with the sea, whose million light-points imaged the lordly fulmination of the stars . . . and on the cliff meadow by the sea the shepherd sat in the moss-rimed ruins of the towers and played his flute—a song of boundless innocence that abjured all fury, all desire, and laughed at time; a girl danced to the melody, leaped in delight among the grazing sheep, the sun dazzling on her face; raising a lovely arm she beckoned to the shepherd and danced away through the still, deserted ruins . . .

Then it had vanished. Behind him Ricarno laughed hoarsely, cried an oath. He blinked his eyes. Asleep: had he been asleep or awake? He was lying motionless on the hard steel cover of the chest; his hands underneath his head were bloodless and tingling. He chafed them against each other, flexed the numb fingers, felt sensation return in slow, spastic waves. He discovered he was shivering; all at once he was acutely aware of his body as a very frail and imperfect organism cast adrift on a sea of monstrous estrangement, of menace . . . How good it would be to touch some familiar things, he thought with an ardent, impossible desire: run the palm of his hand down the chalky white dustiness of a white birch, thrust his feet into warm wet sand and feel it slip around his ankles with the wave's ebb, glide once more along the spangled floor with Helen and watch her smile of still, shy delight . . . *Put your hand here*, she had said. *Hold me like this. It's just a sort of pattern.* The hall aflame with sparkling showers of light, throbbing with tom-tom rhythms. *You're fine*, she'd said; *it's as though you'd been dancing it for years—*

They were singing in the gun tub. An attempt at harmony: O'Neill's voice soared into the tenor part with surprising clarity, lost itself, faltered and vanished; reappeared, poised against Kantaylis and Derekman, who were carrying the melody, and Klumanski's sonorous, off-key bass.

> *"Never can tell 'bout that baby named Nell,*
> *She's on a conveyor-belt right outa hell,*
> *She reclined on the sofa—*
> *Turned the lights down low—*
> *Then she clipped me with a bottle*
> *And stole all—my—dough!—*
> *Never know 'bout that baby named Nell . . ."*

"No, no, no," O'Neill protested, "Harry, you go *up* on 'dough' and I go down: we cross over and hold it, *then* switch back."

"What difference does it make? We sang it, didn't we?"

"But that's what makes it so fine, you ninny: what's the sense in *singing* it if you don't do it right?"

"Why don't you *do* right?" Terrabella said: and they laughed and started singing again.

> *"You had plenny money nineteen forty-two,*
> *Now you're in a foxhole wond'rin' what-to-do,*
> *Why don't you live right—*
> *Like the other Nips do!*
> *Shag outa here and—snag me an ice-cold brew . . ."*

Listening, humming along with the lugubrious melody, Newcombe found himself smiling in the dark: a fond, indulgent smile. It was hard to say: none of those indistinct forms over there in the gun tub had his rearing, his concerns or inclinations, not one of them would have held his interest for five minutes on the outside . . . and yet now they affected him: their breezy vulgarity, their illogicality, their squabbles and mawkish sentimentality moved him deeply. What was it?— the exigencies and dislocations of a world at war? No, it was more than that—these inarticulate ragamuffins were somehow bound up with his emotions, indissolubly welded to his heart with bands of steel . . .

That was Helen: that was what her sweet, sure generosity of spirit had done for him; the still certainty of her commitment. *I'll never love anyone but you: I know it.* Her voice in the dark, breathed against his ear, complicit and stirring. *But how do you know?—I just do.—You're crazy.—I suppose so.* Her face at the Lincoln Memorial, and later on the platform by the stanchion: white and defenseless and trembling, the tears hanging in her eyes like little silver jewels. *I don't care. I loved you from the first moment I saw you.* Some deep, instinctual certainty that soared over all the privet-hedges of doubt and analysis, cleared them at a bound and knew its object in a burst of clarity; and now she floated here above him in the dark, so vivid, so *present* he could scarcely believe it! . . . He raised his arms with a soft cry; let them fall again.

This was what love was, then—this sense of anguish, of spiritual amputation away from the beloved: this wild, hot desire to look out on the sweep of experience with one eye, feel it with the beating of one pulse: triumph and despondency both. If thine eye be single . . . Love: self-gratification or self-abasement—these were the counterfeit coins we were forever circulating in our odious Gresham's Law of human relationships; but only the heart knew how to give without stint . . . He loved her, then: he loved her. The admission was like a throb of the most radiant delight, the deepest dread.

> *"You had plenny money nineteen forty-three,*
> *Now you're a sniper sittin' in-a-tree,*
> *Why don't you live right—"*

He brought his hand down on the ammunition cover with a slap that set his palm tingling. By God, it ought to be for a purpose, this snatching up of millions of men, stripping them of their dignity and dreams and blowing them with capricious impersonality to the weary ends of the earth—wafting them on an odyssey at whose termination lay death for some and boundless misery for the rest: it had better be for a purpose. But what purpose, indeed? The market would doubtless go up or down, educators would continue to extol with a meretricious bonhomie the American legend of success and boundless progress, Iowa farmers would no doubt go on feeling all foreigners were inferior, queer, a bit sinister . . .

And yet there they were, see them all, the legionaries of this careless, flamboyant empire, looking idiotic and subhumanized enough in their chamber-pot helmet liners—singing and staring out at a perfectly atrean sea and sky, out of which the most horrific destruction could descend on them at any minute without a trace of warning . . . This really—this had really better not happen again, he felt for the first time with a rising sense of anger; this had damned well better not happen again. The eminent heads of state had better devise some other method for settling international misunderstandings,

some other way to resolve the issues raised by their blocs and
ententes and spheres of influence and national destinies—

The singing had stopped abruptly: someone gave a muffled
exclamation. There was a pause, then rapid talk and O'Neill's
voice broke out loudly and impatiently: "I saw it—I know I
saw it. Keep looking . . ."

Newcombe got up and approached the gun tub. Kantaylis
was saying, "You're right: it's Faneráhan."

"Where?"

"Right about there." Kantaylis extended an arm. "They've
started the bombardment."

"I don't see anything," Ricarno said.

"You will in a minute."

In silence they stared away into the dark. For a time there
was nothing; O'Neill scraped the toe of his shoe back and
forth against the metal rim of the tub. Then, incredibly far
off, like a glimpse of habitation on another planet, came the
diamond-cold, unblinking light of a flare hanging in the
night. Below it tiny red splotches leaped and flickered, merry
as fireflies in a summer garden; and around the flickers of red
a squat blacker-than-black mass assumed outline—humped in
the center, low and flat on one side. Faneráhan: a smooth,
irregular lump of black iron floating on the night horizon.

Then the flare snuffed out and darkness swooped in again
and confounded everything; there was a murmur from the
group around the gun tub strangely reminiscent to Newcombe
of watchers on a Fourth of July evening when the rocket,
after the hissing roar of its ascent, the careening, swerving,
fire-laden course, drops its candles in a rainbow burst and
falls in darkness.

"Ahhhhh . . ."

"Well, that's the number," O'Neill said. Turning he struck
Newcombe lightly on the shoulder. "That's the baby."

"Yes," Newcombe said; his mouth felt dry and filled with a
bitter, foreign taste of tarnish.

Still they stared, straining to hear sounds which never
reached them; watching as flare after flare hung in cold blue
dalliance and the pinprick flashes of exploding shells darted
here and there on the squat black hump of land. All of the aft
gun crews had come over now, and talk rose in nervous bursts
of exclamation.

"Ooh, look at that one. That one there . . ."

"Yeah."

"Imagine what those Nips are getting. Just imagine!"

"Dry your eyes."

"Yeah, but I mean put yourself in their place."

"Not this chicken. You think I'm crazy?"

Something below and to the right of a flare flickered, like signal lights—a yellow-bright twin flash—and someone said: "What was that?"

"That's *their* guns," Kantaylis said.

The group was silent at this; sobered they glanced at each other, shifted their feet.

"They got big naval guns, you think, Danny?"

"Sure they have. They say they brought some over from Cavite and Singapore: six- and eight-inch."

"Jesus," someone murmured. "I hope they get all of those babies by day after tomorrow."

"How many Japs you think are on the rock, Danny?"

"Beats me. How the hell should I know?" Slumped in the pointer's seat Kantaylis stared doggedly at Faneráhan; his face, only just discernible to Newcombe, looked utterly weary and disconsolate. "Probably a hundred crawling million of 'em . . ."

The group fell silent then, for a long time; stared in pale fascination at a new flare descending: a solitary, malignant gem swimming on a sea of darkness.

7

————THERE'S STILL ANOTHER advantage to writing a ghostly, interminable T-letter such as this, darling: you can spin it out effortlessly in the dark while you cradle your head in your arms and observe, through the rents in the tatterdemalion ponchos, that star-glistered sky—which never looked so brilliant and all-encompassing and near . . .

For all has changed, changed utterly. The ammunition has been handed out, checked and rechecked, everybody has gone over his pack and gear and weapons for the last time, they've dug up some clean dungarees and socks from somewhere (had them all along, you see) and handed them out, we've showered in fresh water and shaved and eaten a really sumptuous meal—they've kept *that* hidden away too, for lo, these many moons: ham steak and potatoes and green beans. And of course there were, as you might well imagine, the customary sardonic asides about fattening the sheep for the slaughter, about famous last meals, the little green door; what—no cognac, no cigarette? All the farrago of plaintive, bathetic epithet with which we leanly arm ourselves. Morlecki, the mess sergeant, grins at us as we file past—a harsh, false, mess sergeant's grin: "Come on, come get your purple-heart food, boys." "You not eating any, Morlecki? You staying with ship's company?" Jay taunts him loudly; and in the nervous laughter Morlecki's face tightens around the grin.

For none of us is immune. The nervousness is ubiquitous and deep—you can feel it as you wind your way forward through the cots: a tangible element you can almost squeeze in your hand. Everyone keeps yawning and yawning: I am, at this very moment—a yawn so mighty it makes my jaws crack; and then I swallow . . . and yawn again. And none of us is that sleepy. *No-body*, as Jay says. Off to our left—turning my head I can see it framed in the long meniscus of night sea and sky between the ponchos and the ship's side—lies Faneráhan. They are still shelling her: pinpricks of red wink and die against her indistinct flank like wildly festering sores . . . and then there is the *bump: bump bump* like a train in a faraway roundhouse. Faneráhan: the black lodestone that has drawn us toward her iron bosom for ten thousand watery miles. We can't help gazing at her. Woodruff and several others have been standing up in the bow for hours, mute, absorbed. Now and then at some particularly huge explosion a little tremor goes through them; they turn and murmur to each other and shift their feet as though its concussion, ephemeral yet menacing, had just reached them. Faneráhan: land of a once free people, our goal and our destiny; we are already bound to each other by a web of powerful cords . . .

We go in tomorrow: H-hour is 0830. I suppose I should be writing a real, honest-to-God, flesh-and-blood, pencil-on-paper letter to you (and my parents, too) at this wondrously dramatic instant, this eleventh hour of the soldier. I suppose I ought to be chock-full of crunchy wisdom, just bursting with epigrams (Christ, I almost said epitaphs) and ringing profundities, should be able to sum up and define human experience from muzzle to butt plate, catch it all up in its tragic sweep, its depravity and grandeur: Santayana from the trenches, you might say. Profound Thoughts Before Battle. Think of Brutus in his tent at Sardis, Coriolanus at the gates of Rome, a little touch of Harry in the night! . . . I am emptied of profundity, if I ever had any—and so, I think, were they . . . Shades of Leonidas! All I can think of are idiotic, disparate minutiae: who won the last pinochle game (why should *that* obsess me?), whether I ought to put another pair of socks in my pack (your feet, they say your feet), where my face-net is (inside my helmet liner, where it ought to be?)—and above all the state of my bowels, which rumble and churn like Father Tiber.

And what can I add to what I wrote you—really wrote you—from Pearl? Moments grave with portent don't insure profound visions—nor abiding ones either, it seems. With my mind in this state of distracted irrelevance I'd only burden you further with apprehension. (Or so it strikes me. Jay, who's borrowed my pen, and Harry and a few others are down in the crew's messroom writing letters furiously: Lorraine will no doubt be bombarded with all manner of jocosity and jive-jargon and Bunyanesque—Paul, not John—extravagance and braggadocio.)

They are shelling again. *Crump ump ump ump* it goes, and then the cold, sea-deep light of a flare. A ship moves past us in the dark, churning a ghostly, gray-blue phosphorescent wake: a destroyer going in close to that battered, red-hot ingot of an island where ten thousand (possibly more, possibly many more) Japanese huddle and cringe and wait in rage for us to come in and close with them—

I ought to go to sleep.

Impossible. Hardly anyone can: all around me I can see eyes glitter as bodies turn and toss, get up and grope off through the cots toward the head. My turn will come again soon. Am I scared? Not very, really, I think. But nervous: triggery as a cat on a steep slate roof. Things keep sliding off the ends of my fingers before I can grasp them. (Still, I'm not as bad as Jack Freuhof, who dropped his full mess gear this evening: bent down, gazing at the spattered ham and beans, he looked somehow very grave and shaken in spite of the good-natured kidding. And he's one of the old men, too; one of the veterans.)

I had a bad moment this evening, though; at sunset. I was standing out on the fantail staring at the sun's broad, golden wake across the water (we're going east now, incredibly) and thinking of nothing in particular . . . and all at once I became aware that it had hold of me: I was filled with a fear like the chill breath of an immense cave. It had nothing to do with the hot, dry, panicky feeling you often have, or the other one—the black dread of an imminent and tangible menace. This was like nothing I'd ever felt before: a sort of cold, arching, high-vaulted intimation of doom; and a sense of indescribable loneliness, as though I'd been abandoned on some Antarctic ice pack. Cold ice walls rising all around, and the cave breath whispered: *The sea here, the wind here cares for nothing, for nothing at all—least of all you: you have been deperson- alized—do you know what that means?—atomized in the im- measurable merciless length and breadth of this void which is your destruction. There is nothing to care for you or rescue you here at the aqueous end of a world replete with violence and death: and death and death and death*, it said, quaking through its spanless arched dome, a nameless terror; I felt as if I were sinking through fathoms on fathoms of viscous dark- ness, bereft and lost beyond recall—

. . . I found I was gripping the rail like a dying man: I was sweating and dizzy and I could hardly see, I thought my knees were going to give way. I felt utterly drained of fortitude. All I could think was: Jesus, if you feel like this now, what kind of shape are you going to be in *tomorrow*, you miserable son of a bitch? "Pull yourself together," I told myself fiercely: "snap—to, you pitiful, gutless GFO!" . . . But even the savage drill-field admonition made no difference; I couldn't shake it, could hardly think of anything at all while the sun dipped out of sight—ah Christ the sun!—and the sky turned to pearl, to dreamy rose and coral hues. I know it sounds ab- surd—standing at the rail of a boat crammed to the gunwales with men and machines—but I honestly felt as though I were alone on a wide, wide sea, and going down for the third and final time; that there was no one to succor me.

I looked around, half-dazed and despairing, wondering what I was going to do to free myself from this hellish sen- sation of doom and boundless dread—and looked right into the eyes of Danny Kantaylis not fifteen feet away. He was sit- ting on an ammunition case with his feet drawn up and his hands clasping his knees; and on his face was a sad, direct, tremendously sympatico smile. It was the *strangest* look!—as though he had traversed those very mountains of cold green ice and seen that I was foundering, and offered me the solace of his gaze. I stared at him in a trance, unable to speak . . .

Then in a second it was gone: he gave me a quick, expressionless wink, slipped off the ammunition case and came up to where I was standing. "How's it go?" he said.

I started to say something and couldn't: my mouth was dry as old leather and I swallowed and swallowed. "Not bad," I said finally; then a second later, "Not so good." "Take it easy." He spat over the rail, looked down at the swirl of water through his clasped hands. "Take it easy," he repeated. Then added softly, "You'll do all right."

He stared off into the coral haze of dusk, the slow, seething roll and drop of the waves moving west: broad nose, black hair cropped close, the full, generous mouth; and the steady, acceptant vigor in his eyes that seems to take the measure of the world in all its fearfulness and horror and caprice and continue undismayed. Watching him I steadied as if by magic; took a deep breath and exhaled—took another . . . All at once it was borne in on me incontrovertibly that all our fortunes were bound up in his: as long as he stands we will triumph; if he falls we will all perish. (Preposterous, you would say—but I felt it with such utter certainty I did not think of questioning it; and now, lying here in the moist, tense dark, I still don't.) Right then and there I vowed I'd stick with him, I'd make Jay stick with him too, we'd back him up, cover him, follow him through no matter what legions of nameless and insuperable terrors by day or by night. Gripping the cold metal rail I vowed as I have never vowed before to do this . . .

The deep, arching dread is gone now. Perhaps it won't come back: perhaps such glimpses of doom are immensely rare, like visitations of the devil. I hope to God they are. Right now I feel emptied, whirling, nervous, unbearably alert. I ought to get some sleep. I can't though: I keep turning my head, gazing around me at the undefined faces. Ricarno's profile is a vague blob against the horizon glow; he's talking in a low voice to Terrabella. Klumanski has just told them to shut up or go down to the head. They are silent for a time, and then Ricarno's voice begins again, a softly conspiratorial monotone . . . The extraordinary *changes* they undergo, these faces: standing for inspection, weighted down with war gear they look baleful, heavy with menace, a horde of brutish demigods out of Norse mythology; and at another moment, standing at church services on the fantail the evening light moves over their unhelmeted faces like a caress, the wind ruffles their hair, their dungaree jackets: they look like altar boys, like novitiates washed clean of violence, of mortality

. . . and at such times I find myself filled with a strange, vague exaltation—and the deepest darkest sadness I've ever felt in all my life. Bound: I feel bound to them all, for better or worse, as though by a laying on of hands: something I was never capable of until that splendorous day and night I spent with you. You awoke this in me, darling, broke the harsh crust around my heart; you thrust me into the stream, and if I drown I will still have been immersed in it, one with it . . .

But I won't drown. Oh darling, I long for you tonight: terribly. It's at times like this—in the hot dark, lying naked and sweating on your pad, feeling the ship heave in ponderous undulance beneath you, heaving and falling, to heave again—it's at such times that your loins stir, your brain whirls with fevered images of lust, a delirium of inexhaustible sexual frenzy that nearly swamps the consciousness—

Ah, but it's more than that, far more: it is a need to embrace the image, give form to the vision. That is our pathos: we are sculptors without marble, we cannot make manifest the resurgent clamor of our longing. The lips and breasts and trembling thighs that we caressed are only the avenues to a nobler union—but without them we are puny and absurd: it is *that* which causes us to toss and murmur in inarticulate anguish through the night watches, to pace the cubicles of deck and gaze darkly at the star-dogged moon . . .

For we find only what we give: all roads bend back upon their own beginnings. I held your swelling, pulsing breast in my hand, molded it to my desire—and now I see that that desire was to love you and be loved by you in turn . . .

Jay has just come back from the messroom: says he wants to make sure I've got his Aunt Grace's address. I assure him I've committed it to memory but I tell him I'll put it in my wallet anyway. "Swell," he says. "I've got yours written down: okay?" "Sure. Swell." Staring at his thin, gangling form in the dark, his bony, homely-handsome Irish face I can feel rather than see, I am flooded with emotion: *Old buddy*, I almost cry out, *Jay old buddy we'll stick together come hell or high water, we'll never falter, nothing's going to happen to you, or me either; why, do you know?—I'd lay down my life for you, I mean it* . . . and my eyes—would you believe it?—fill at once with tears . . .

But I say none of it. I put out my hand in the almost-dark and clap him on the shoulder roughly: try to put all my affection and nervousness and concern and trust into the pressure of my hand. It is, I feel, a gesture laden with as much emotion as any man has ever felt for any other. "Goodnight, Jay," I say. "Take it easy." "Goodnight. Hasta luego." "Défense d'uriner." "High colonic." "—Will you guys for Christ sake knock it *off?*" big Klu says in a thunderous, exasperated tone. "Before I klonk your simple heads together." "Right you are, Jackson," Jay says with sudden, false obsequiousness. "Truly sorry to disturb you: truly." "Shut up." "I really am. Even though I know you're never sorry for anything in the Marine Corps. Never."

Klumanski growls ominously. Jay's cot creaks, creaks again. His face, suddenly between me and the sky, is wild and very large. He turns toward me and murmurs: "Take it easy, Al." "Écrasez l'infame." "Roger. Accept no guff from the higher cuff."

The ship lifts and falls against the night. Above us a million stars of the southern galaxy hang timeless and eternal—

PART THREE

Temples

1

"MAN, IT LOOKS big enough, don't it?"

"It's not so big."

"What do you mean, it's not so big? Look at it stretching away, there. Look at those mountains."

"Yeah, well, it's only an island . . ."

They were all up in the bows: jammed shoulder to shoulder, two and three deep, staring and pointing. Dead ahead of them lay Faneráhan. In the rapid, rushing pearl light of dawn it looked solemn and vague and immense; a gray-green pall hung low over the beach, a mantle of dust and smoke through which yellow flashes came and went like mirrors crazily tilted. Beyond it the land rose in soft velvet folds, obscured here and there by more smoke, gave way to a harsh line of mountains capped in the center by one, gaunt and omnivorous.

"Mount Matenla," Kantaylis said; he tossed his head in indication.

"What a monster!" Ricarno whistled. "Jesus, we going to have to go up *that?*"

"That ain't a mountain," Woodruff drawled. "Why, we got hills back home make that look like a chigger bite on a bear's butt."

"Do tell, Woodruff."

"I wouldn't snow you one time, buddy-ro."

There was a deep, thunderous boom, and to their left a battleship lobbed three shells in a graceful parabola: fiery red ovals that dove into the band of smoke, and they heard the thump of the hit. Then suddenly it was lighter and to the north end of the island a vast, boiling cloud like an apparition rose and rose.

"Je-zuss. It isn't going to rain, is it?"

"Oh Lord. *Rain* . . ."

At that moment the sun cleared the southern shoulder of

243

Mount Matenla, slipped over the water in swiftly flowing points of light: a gay tableau, innocent and shimmering. The scores of slate-gray warships seemed to be resting on a bed of quicksilver.

"Where we going in?" Terrabella asked Freuhof. "Where we going in?"

"Beats me." Freuhof glanced at him irritably. "How the hell should I know? You can't even see the damn beach . . ."

It was true: the beach was totally obscured. The rolling crash and billow of the barrage deepened, swelled in intensity, swept against their eardrums like a palpable substance. LCVP's were already skittering in lazy looping patterns around the two transports near them: little brute bugs on the glittering plate of water.

"Man, I wish they'd pop-to," O'Neill said. "When the hell we going to get the show on the road?"

Klumanski turned around. "Hold your urine, Jack. You'll get there soon enough."

"Well. It's all the hanging around."

"Take it easy. You'll get all of that beach you'll ever want."

Newcombe, silent, peered in at the land. The sun lay high over Mount Matenla now, and the island all at once assumed focus: a dense green mat of jungle, with a saffron belt of higher ground behind it. Sword grass, that was: slashed your hands in raw, painful welts if you took hold of it. Waved gently in the breeze, false grain: but care must be used in prehending. *Below it the land is broken up in ravines and swiftly flowing streams, with here and there small banana plantations and stands of ifil, dog-dog and banyan trees. The areas along the shore consist of a mixture of sand and decomposed coral, known as cascao. In many places the jungle will be virtually impenetrable. The rivers will be swollen with the seasonal rains* . . . The bombardment grew in volume, a rolling cascade of cracks and booms and the smoke, dirty-yellow and roiling, welled upward like a noisome exhalation, blotted out the hills behind Pajaña and Fofogáda; and he swung his gaze off to the south where the land ended in the shaggy green mass of Nénetan Peninsula, where the airstrip was.

"There's your lovely Pacific isle, Al," O'Neill offered conversationally. "Palm trees, dusky maidens, moonlight playing over the old lagoon . . ."

"That isn't moonlight playing over *that* lagoon," Derekman said.

"Not right now." Newcombe felt himself smile, he didn't know why. He said, with exaggerated sonorousness: "Ay, many flowering islands lie in the waters of wide Agony . . ."

"Our poet." O'Neill wagged his head, jabbed Newcombe under the arm. "Yeah: poet laureate of the Second Platoon. Bard of the boondocks."

". . . NOW HEAR THIS," the PA system voice behind them chanted thickly. "NOW HEAR THIS: MARINE PER-SONNEL FALL IN ON THE BOAT DECK IN FULL COM-BAT GEAR . . ."

Lieutenant D'Alessandro was standing before them, resplendent and tall. He wore no leggings and had his trouser cuffs tucked into his paratrooper's boots. His pistol holster shone dully in the sunlight; the muzzle end was tied around his thigh with a rawhide thong.

"Just like a real old hang-town draw-fighter," Woodruff marveled softly, and cackled out loud. "Hot diggerty damn. Where's his chaps 'n' spurs?"

"All right now," Lieutenant D'Alessandro was saying. "I suppose you all realize that this is it. The big moment. The goal we've been sweating and straining for since New River." He paused, thrust out his lower lip and ran his eyes over the men before him. "Now I want to see you all pull together, stick with each other in the pinches. But don't bunch up and draw mortar fire. And above all: *move out*. This is the day that's going to separate the men from the boys."

"Platitude alley," Newcombe murmured. "Every thought a D'Alessandro creation."

"Oh, he's the inventive type. Just can't help himself."

"Now I've told you you're going to be the best hell-for-leather platoon in the whole Marine Corps. Bar nobody and nothing. I know it's going to be rough in there and a lot of people are going to get hurt. But let's not go making a liar and a pop-off character out of me now. Okay?" Rocking back on his heels he surveyed them all again, flashed the quick, dis-arming smile. Hardly anyone stirred. Klumanski turned and grinned meaningfully at Freuhof, who stared back at him without expression.

"The ideal marine," Newcombe murmured. "You've got to admit it: handsome, reckless, debonair . . ."

O'Neill pushed his helmet down over his eyes and jutted his jaw out: a violent leatherneck caricature. "Sure-fire. How can we miss—with a hero like this? . . . Hey, that's poetry, Al."

"Splen-diferous."

The bombardment thumped and roared and crackled behind them. From Nénetan, beyond the fringe of jungle, a column of rich black smoke boiled up like a vile and merry genie.

"Dump," Klumanski said. "Scratch one." And there was a murmuring and craning of heads.

Newcombe shifted his shoulders inside his pack suspenders uncomfortably, hitched at his belt. The weight of his gear seemed all at once insupportable, a mad joke without point. His head ached dully and sweat streaked his body under his blouse. Lieutenant D'Alessandro's voice went on and on, brightly conversational and admonitory, cautioning them against bunching up in holes and drawing fire, against booby-traps on Japanese dead and equipment, about half-buried mine detonators in shell holes and communications trenches. Two fighter planes with the clipped wings and heavy bodies of flies swept over head and droned in toward the land.

"Jungle Jim," O'Neill said, and stirred. "Isn't he going ashore with his combat knife between his teeth?"

"No," Derekman muttered sourly. "His finger up his ass."

"I got you."

"NOW HEAR THIS: NOW HEAR THIS," the stentorian voice above them thundered. "MARINES MAN YOUR DEBARKATION STATIONS . . ."

The air in the tank deck was foul and damp; figures bumped into other figures, pushed past each other in steady, inexorable motion. Voices echoed through the dark cavern like children hooting in a culvert.

"Capistron!"

"Ho!"

"Connor . . . Connor!"

"Here."

"Answer up, damn it, and knock off all that talk. Derek-man!"

"Yo . . ."

Newcombe sat down on a case of mortar ammunition; the straps of his suspenders felt all wrong: why the devil was that? The night before they had seemed perfect. Now they squeezed air up and out of his lungs, pinched him in the neck. He stood up and hitched nervously at them.

"Get off my toes."

Ricarno was frowning at him. He lifted the offending foot

and said in explanation: "Pack feels wrong . . . Jay," he turned to O'Neill, "see if something's caught back there, will you?"

O'Neill, similarly attired and looking similarly uncomfortable, prodded and pulled at him while he stared ahead dumbly. He shivered once, a spasm, then felt his head swell with heat. A thin substanceless pressure thrust against the arch of his ribs. He inhaled slowly once, twice; again. Derekman's tough, sharp-chinned profile coiled out of rings on rings in a screen beyond his gaze: a faint twinge of vertigo that made him blink and raise his head.

"Terrabella!"

"Ho!"

"Woodruff! . . . Goddamnit—*Woodruff!*"

Amtrack motors started like explosions, roared to a clattering, howling crescendo; a choking blue vapor rose around them.

"Where in hell is Woodruff!" Fellows was glaring at them, his face sweaty and agitated; he waved a crumpled roster sheet in his fist.

"In the head," someone shouted.

Ricarno laughed his raucous laugh. "He fell through. Twelve to five. Dizzy bastard been down there all morning long . . ."

"He better get his ass in gear," O'Neill said. "This choo-choo ain't gonna wait for no-body. No-body at all."

Staring absently at Fellows' narrow, angry face Newcombe was struck all at once with the conviction that he'd left something up on deck: something terribly important. He ran his fingers with automatic rapidity over his belt: pouch medical and jungle, combat knife, canteen, poncho, bayonet, canteen, entrenching shovel. His lips moved as he felt the objects. Still vaguely dissatisfied he looked up, saw Klumanski grinning at him.

"How you feel, Newk?"

"Okay."

"Ready to go?"

"Never better." He grinned back glassily at Klumanski, but his lips were dry. Around them men were still dropping through the hatches like clumsy birds, like lost and over-burdened souls falling through trap doors into hell, their cries drowned in the roar of the amtrack engines: all silent and all damned. What the devil *had* he left topside? For an instant he almost gave in to the wild, compelling desire to go up on deck again, fight his way through the hurrying procession; suppressed it with annoyance. His bowels stirred with a sudden loose pressure, filled him with apprehension: subsided. Well here we go round the bullberry briar, bullberry briar, bullberry briar: here we go round the bullberry briar, but not, but not for thorning.

"Woody boy!"

They turned at Ricarno's shout and saw Woodruff, bulky and misshapen in all his gear, moving along the gunwale of the amtrack behind them with his sinking, bent-kneed farmer's stride. He paused uncertainly, grinning, called: "Got room for one more down there?"

"Oh yes! Any number can play . . ."

"Where you been, lad?"

"Come right on down here with us chickens."

"Ya-hoo!"

Woodruff jumped down among them, losing his helmet which rolled clanking under their feet.

"Where you been?" Lundren thundered at him through the clamor.

"Well, see, Steve, I got all my gear on—and then I had to go. So then I had to shuck out of it all and go down there to the head, and then I couldn't hardly find me a hole. And then after that I had to—"

"I know—get into your gear all over again," Derekman said sourly; but he was grinning. "Let me guess."

"Well, that's about the size of it, Harry . . ."

Ahead of them the bow doors opened: reflected sunlight burst in upon them, flooded the damp hot cavern with light and air. Someone in a nearby tank kept yelling, "Yahoo! *Yahooooo!*" through the din.

"Through these portals," Ricarno was saying, pointing a finger dead ahead, "through these portals pass the saddest sacks in the whole frigging world . . ."

"And about time," O'Neill said tersely. "Let's go. *Let's go*—"

"Take it easy," Klumanski said. "Won't be long you'll be wishing you were back in here."

". . . It's cold down here."

"Well, we'll fix you up on that in no time. Just no time."

"Belly of the great saurian," Newcombe blurted suddenly.

"What?"

"Jonah. I feel like Jonah."

"Well, I feel all hollow," Derekman said. "Christ, I'm hungry."

"*Hungry!*" Newcombe stared at him, incredulous.

"Yeah. I feel half starved."

The roar of the motors became overpowering: gas fumes swept back over them, stung their nostrils, made their eyes smart and water. Through the bow doors light bombarded them, flashed from the waves like coiling serpents' scales. Newcombe averted his eyes, leaned against the cool metal side of the tank; there seemed to be no stomach, no viscera inside him at all—merely a hot void that pressed up into his chest, his throat: a thin hot gas. He breathed deeply several times, was seized with a fit of coughing from the amtrack fumes.

"—matter, Al?" O'Neill was peering at him with concern.

"Nothing," he said. O'Neill couldn't hear him but he shook his head, still coughing, grinned wanly back. "Feel great." Things, people kept bumping him, almost spinning him around; his gear was in everyone else's way and his own. He glanced at his watch, was amazed to see it said seven fifty-five. Later than you think. She said a sundial. In sunny Italy. Which Claus of Innsbruck cast in bronze for me. Paint must never hope to reproduce the faint half-flush that dies—

O'Neill had tapped him on the shoulder, was pointing forward: sunlight glittered in his eyes. Looking ahead Newcombe saw an amtrack rock up the ramp like an evil gleaming beetle and drop to the water with a great splash, rolling and pitching, slide away, water-borne, its treads ejecting curving paddle-wheel arcs of spray, out of their area of vision.

"All right, let's pull the plug," O'Neill was shouting. "For Christ sake—let's—go!"

The roar of the motors rose to a bellow; they were moving forward with a shuddering, pitching, staggering motion that clattered like a score of anvils. Newcombe gripped the gun-wale with his free hand, felt O'Neill seize him around the waist as they shuddered up the ramp, hung for a vast instant motionless and plunged down: Newcombe felt his feet go out from under him, water cans and ammunition cases bumped against his shins, spray soaked them in a raining white shower. Then they were in bright sunlight, bobbing slowly, rolling in the sea; drops of spray clung to their helmet covers and blouses like scattered amythestine bubbles, strings of pearls.

They heard shouting, looked up and saw heads, blue work

shirts lining the rail above the bow doors, waving to them and cheering; Glaviano too was leaning far out, grinning down at them, had his hands clasped above his head in the prize-fighter's pantomime of victory and salutation. They stared back, smiling uncertainly, felt the amtrack wallow and fall away in the sea.

"Good luck, you guys," a voice carried down to them with surprising clarity. "Good luck, now . . ."

"Ah, fungoo and your fresh water showers," Ricarno yelled. Grinning he squinted upward, spat over the side.

The rolling cacophony of the barrage all at once receded, and clinging to the gunwales they peered toward the island. Sunlight burst off the water, turned their faces all bright and glowing under the helmets; they looked to Newcombe like children masquerading in their fathers' castoff war gear, playing at war.

"Well, old buddy," O'Neill was saying. "Old campaigner. Here we go."

"Over the falls," Newcombe answered. He was grinning foolishly and knew it; his voice sounded thin and tremulous.

"Hey, that's my line."

"I know. But it's so apt."

"You know—I was going to write to Lorraine—I was going to tell her—"

"I thought you did."

O'Neill shook his head. "Didn't sound right. I don't know . . . I couldn't put it the way I wanted to. What I wanted to tell her—" He stopped and shrugged. "What the hell: I'll bring her a samurai sword."

The amtrack's motors roared again, deafeningly. The command LCVP raced past them, its bow high, slewing over the waves. Newcombe caught a swift, sudden glimpse of Captain Frey and Lieutenant Prengle shouting at each other, their helmeted heads pressed close and bumping; then the amtrack lurched ahead and Lundren, towering dark and majestic at the bow, called:

"All right get down, you people!"

Newcombe crouched down on a water can, ran his hand around his belt again, hitched at his pack suspenders. He felt perpetually out of breath, on the verge of a colossal dizziness that threatened to upend him. He looked around him aimlessly, encountered nearby Terrabella absorbed in pressing a huge pimple on his chin. For a few seconds he watched, repelled he knew not why, but infinitely repelled—turned away in irritation. Behind him Derekman, clutching his BAR to his breast, yawned, yawned again: a round black hole in his white face that distended in brutish absurdity; closed like an anemone surprised.

What did Jay want to tell Lorraine?—that he'd found out he loved her too? that words were inadequate to reproduce the faint half-flush—? Possible: anything was possible. Fine, great, never better, they'd all have a double wedding in the Lincoln Memorial, be each other's best men (and why not) with Hallowell officiating in cap-and-gown-and-carry-one and Suzy for maid of dishonor and a doggy paratrooper color-guard beneath whose arching sabers the four of them would soar away to a fifteen-second honeymoon at Norumbega Park, there was still time, lock and load and *for broad sake* no scrunching up in the sex-holes—

"God *damn* it," O'Neill said and struck his thigh; his face, close to Newcombe's, was importunate and wild. "Where the hell are we? How far out are we?"

Newcombe on an impulse raised his head—saw no beach: saw nothing but a broad swatch of gray-green water and rolling, sifting ochre bands of smoke through which black and white jets leaped like eerie plumes. No palms, no bunkers, no lagoon—

"Keep your Goddamn head down," a coxswain shouted at him.

He ducked down again, disconcerted. No palms, no mangoes, no glittering sand. This was a foreign country: this was a foreign land they were entering—an interminable wait through customs, interminable—where the outward shores be leaky valves and all the old—

The old what?

He felt all at once a great need to say something to Jay, old bunky buddy Jay, something he'd wanted to make sure to tell him. He tapped him briskly on the shoulder.

"What?" O'Neill shouted.

He opened his mouth—shrugged helplessly: he couldn't for the life of him remember what it had been. Forgotten. Completely. He grinned—a foolish, fatuous grin; but O'Neill had already looked away again.

Norumbega, was it? What? No. At Norumbega they all dance, they dance the night away. Across the square light fades on blued panes, a footfall echoes ghostly, paces out

sicut patribus toward the Longfellow salt-shaker towers of old
Nokomis by the shining big sea water. Enough of that. But
what?

Above the amtrack's gunwale a tall white plume soared
geyserlike; another, still taller, like a sea-borne emanation—
swept over them like blown spume and the vehicle dipped and
yawed away, roared on. Hot off the beachhead. Newcombe
started to wipe his face, found he couldn't, discovered he was
gripping his rifle in both hands with all his might. Releasing
his hold on the upper hand guard he wiped the spray from his
brow and cheeks.

Across from him on the port side Freuhof, his face sallow,
his mouth a tight, straight line, lipless, stared rigidly at the
bow of the tank; swallowed, swallowed again thickly. He's
seasick, Newcombe thought—then in the next instant: No.
He's scared: he's scared to death. He looked away as though
from something found unclean, glanced back again involuntarily and saw Kantaylis lean forward and say
something to Freuhof who listened without turning, nodded
twice stonily; Kantaylis' face, bending near, was slick with
sweat and marked with the same violent rigidity. But for
Danny to look like that—what the devil was it? . . . The
thought upset him deeply for a moment and he stared down at
his feet.

I'd have loved you anywhere. Knew from the first minute I
saw you. Ah love, let us be.

No. But what?

Salt air, feet in the sand at Nount's Head, surf pulling water
through the toes, fiddler crabs clicking in and out of holes in
the mudbanks beside the runs. No more. No more. Jesus. Interminable! Remember to keep going, press in, get off the
beach, for God's sake keep your *mind*—

Another geyser rose up on their left, towering, as they slid
by. Something clanged against the bow and at the same instant Lundren turned and faced them, his massive arms
protruding from the too-short, faded sleeves of his blouse and
shouted: "Lock and load! Lock and load!"

Newcombe pulled a clip out of his belt. Savage teeth, well
aligned. His rifle looked strange to him: curiously proximate
and bright. Why was that? Never had it possessed so many
corners, so many facets of gleaming metal—an amazing,
faintly oily, gleaming complexity that nearly dazzled him.
This was better, though: movement was better, any movement

at all. He rubbed vigorously at the bolt with his sleeve, looking about. Now remember—

There was a shock: they rocked violently, lifted, began to shudder forward in a vibrating, beetling crawl. *The reef*. They were on the reef. He saw Klumanski's mouth, now strangely far away, form the words.

"*Stand—by!*" Lundren roared.

The grinding shudder increased—a lurching, dipping palsy that jarred their bones. Then all at once they struck something with an impact that sent them sprawling into each other, clutching at one another wild-eyed and cursing. They were stopped dead.

A coxswain was shouting something frantically. He could not hear. There was a swift rattling crash and a rectangle of air and light and water leaped into view, blazing in the sun: he ran toward it without thought. Someone was screaming over and over: "Wire! Watch for *wire—!*"

He was splashing through water to his thighs, his knees, his thighs again. His foot encountered nothing—*Jesus!*—he went down and down, water bubbled boiling past his face and eyes, he thrust his rifle high and clawed the water with his left, reeling panicky in a weighty, insupportable maelstrom. Something was jerking him up again: sunlight swept into view, hands were pulling him up, his feet were stamping gratefully against solid ground. Someone was shouting something in his ear, a face he didn't recognize. Pothole. He'd stepped in a pothole: his rifle was still dry. Water knee-deep, now ankle-deep, went clumsy weary dragging. Move out move out drive in get off the beach get off the beach come *on*. Ahead of him boiled a yellow-gray vapor without coherence: figures floated past on either side, faded back again—all were floating in a slowly dreaming whirl where time stood still and drunken, musing, bound in a maudlin roar of all sound ever anywhere devised, a roar so vast, so compounded it was soundless, indecipherable. A figure whirled upward near him, sank away in the shallow water, whirling still, helmetless and bright.

Land. He was on land. Something flung against him, hit his helmet with a clang like a wash-boiler struck. To his right a yellow-black plume rose towering, full of menace. Get your ass off the beach move out move out. He tripped on something, almost went sprawling. Jesus. He was hardly lifting his feet. What was the *matter* with him? He was weary, so tired he could hardly run, his legs hung like leaden mealsacks waterlogged, without spring. Impossible. He'd only—

Something struck his ankle again. Wire. God *damn* the filthy stuff! He dragged his foot over the snarled strand of barbed wire with a puny, tottering hop, staggered on in a dry-mouthed, gasping agony of windless exhaustion, fell forward into a shallow hole. All done. All done in. Hardly got. Even got going. Get up you yellow sick son of a bitch *get up* you think *they*—

He drove himself to his knees, gasping, flung himself reeling to his feet and ran on weaving, rubbery legs toward lazy curving trunks of coco palms, his head down, doubled over and running to keep from falling; felt something whip against his trouserleg, stumbled and fell forward, rose to his knees once more in a whirling red foam and slid head first into another hole and lay there. Never. Never so tired in all. He was retching, swallowing, retching again. His head crashed in reddish-black pulsing explosions that made the earth leap and dart before his eyes. A figure plunged down beside him, crashed into his shoulder: a blow he scarcely felt. A face he'd never seen before. He stared at it in solemn apathy. And the thumping crashing roar swept in on his mind like some cosmic sound-effects machine turned up beyond tolerance, the dials broken, abandoned, run amok; shuddering the world apart with noise.

Another second he stared at the foreign, stern face near his: then without a word he rose and staggered forward again in a jerky, shuffling caricature of running he knew to be ludicrous, abysmal, folly beyond all—

The air turned black, violent with dust: something flung him outward and back, sent him whirling away from himself and the boiling roar was beyond belief. His feet had lost substance: he was tumbling backward down an incline—was it?—filled with bumps and shocks; was still. Lying still. None of him belonged to him. At all.

"Newcombe!"

He opened his eyes with fearful care. Klumanski was glaring at him. No: someone who looked like Klu—was masquerading in Klu's full, heavy face and narrow mongoloid eyes: a clever deception but was it actually worth it right now? altering self to someone else? Odd: to be so *altered*. Klu—or Klu's cunning impersonator—was gripping him by the shoulder.

"Newk! You hit?"

His head was ringing with such intensity he could hardly see: he shook it dumbly. Klu's concern was so pronounced it startled him. Comical, in a sense. But comedy—

Someone else fell on top of him, fell as though from a great height; knocked the wind out of him and rolled away. He looked back, saw a figure on hands and knees, teddybear figure with head hanging, doubled up and slowly writhing. The air sang gaily *soo: soo, soo*—a plaintive, murderous song, and puffs of dust spurted along the edge of the hole.

"You all right?" Newcombe called to the crouching figure. "All right?"

There was a thin, towering, descending shriek and he cringed in a spasm—felt nothing; the earth jarred against his hands. He looked up in amazement, nearly gleeful.

"Over there." Klumanski was looking at him without expression. "When they whistle they're not on you. What you got to watch for is when they hiss soft. It's when they hiss—"

He threw himself flat, and Newcombe crouched instinctively. There was a high, trembling sigh, like the inhalation of a colossal, baleful breath, and the earth rocked and heaved. The sky, the staggered universe turned black, then red with flame, then brightly shot with wires and sparks. And a steam shovel greater than a warehouse dropped a forest of rails on a steel griddle vast as Cape Cod Bay.

"See what I mean?" Klumanski was grinning at him. Yes: unbelievably: grinning. "It's when they do that soft whistle. Like that one. See?"

"Yeah." His voice had vanished, had been replaced by a cracked and wheezing falsetto: some old man's. He was quivering: noticeably. And covered with sand. His rifle was fouled with it—he could hardly see the bolt. Jesus. He cursed and cursed in fear, pawed at it with his hand, his sleeve.

The other man—a round-faced boy with blond hair—had turned over and was sitting up at the other side of the shell hole and looking at him strangely: a fearful, cautious look.

"You all right?" Newcombe shouted.

The boy shook his head. With infinite trepidation he removed his two hands from the base of his throat, disclosed a ragged hole from which blood welled in pulsing spurts—cupped his hands quickly over it again as if ashamed.

"Jesus," Newcombe said. "Jesus. Klu!" He clutched at Klumanski who was crouched at the forward edge of the hole and peering ahead, his rifle thrust out ahead of him. "Klu!"

"What?"

"He's hit! He's bleeding like crazy . . ."

"What you want me do? Give him a beer?"

The soft descending whisper came again. The air turned dark and thick and terrible and burst into flame: a thousand evil things whined in fury overhead, whined and circled above them with leisurely menace; subsided. Newcombe stared again at the round-faced boy whose eyes were on his, mute and wide with beseeching. No idea. He was still out of breath, his body tense with cringing; his mind, swept off its feet, kept splitting apart into sections that reeled and swayed like phantoms, crackled apart in showers of sparks. No idea anything like this and who would. *Who would.*

He crawled in a sudden burst of energy to the rear edge of the crater and peered out, shouted "Corpsman!" at the top of his lungs, roared *"Corpsman!"* until his voice broke, disintegrated into an ineffectual croaking. There was no corpsman anywhere. Figures jerked up, jerked down like badly manipulated marionettes, ran bent double with shuffling, faltering strides, dropped out of sight again.

"Newcombe!"

Klumanski was motioning toward him, his flat mongol face irate. "Come on! When I give you the word, come on ahead. They want us up there."

Want us? He moved up beside Klumanski, peered ahead—for the first time became aware of coconut palms, sand piled in mounds, the fire-blackened corner of a blasted pillbox. *Pillbox.*

He called, "Where's the rest of the guys?"

Klumanski tossed his head. "Up ahead. Some of them. Over there. What can you do when they got—"

The dread sigh came and Newcombe clenched the earth to him with his body: the earth nevertheless swept up at him, fell away, jolting and tipping. A hundred freight cars were scattered by some malicious and puissant hand down a chute broader than the Worcester Turnpike.

His nose was bleeding: one nostril. He'd bumped it on the operating rod. Sweat stung his eyes, crawled on his cheeks and neck. He wiped his face with his sleeve. His mouth and eyes were full of grit. But he was all right, apparently: he still—

Klumanski was shouting into his face:

"When I flag you up, come *on* now!"

He was gone all at once, bent low and lumbering, a shambling gait, bearlike and absurd. Couldn't he run faster than that?—could anyone? Sand spurted—a chrome puff—to

Klumanski's left and he threw himself flat, spread-eagled, rocking forward on to his rifle; ran on again, dropped out of sight. Newcombe fastened his gaze on the heaving, jarring terrain in front of him. The ferocity of the light struck him for the first time—a savage glare that hurt the eyes, pressed them to slits. Below it the sand glittered like yellowed salt under the gentle arabesque of the palm trunks. The corner of the blasted pillbox looked like a shattered cube of ivory. For God's sake, where was everybody? The crown of a palm disintegrated while he watched it, drifted upward in slowly whirling shreds of fronds. Ay, many flowering—

A hand rose from somewhere—Klumanski's hand—inscribed a slow, looping motion. He brought his legs up under him. The high, whistling crash came, disgorged a mountainside of iron filings, jarred the earth atilt again. He leaped up and ran, faster now, a sprint that faltered with fearful brevity, warbled and failed him. A harp-note thrummed by his head: a brief and ominous threnody. He fell sprawling, short of the crater, struggled to his knees in a dumb agony of urgency, failed to make it, rolled, cradling his rifle, wriggled and writhed, conscious of barking his shins and elbows on bits of stone, down into the hole. Lay there in dulled exhaustion.

Five men: he recognized no one . . . saw one of them was Klumanski, another Ricarno, another Jay—Jay!—but Jay so changed he could not believe his eyes. His face stiff and narrow with strain, masklike: a mask of Jay O'Neill badly done. Faces without depth. All were transformed, he himself no longer looked like Newcombe. No longer was Newcombe at all. Probably. All, staring at the Gorgon face were changed, changed utterly. And why not? No mirror for a shield—

He gazed at them in pale apathy, gasping; his heart quaked in painful thick spasms.

No one had spoken: they had looked when he tumbled in on them, then turned back to the front edge of the hole. Water. He had to have a drink of water. To survive. He pulled at the flaps of the canteen cover on his right hip: they were fouled with sand. He snatched at them in a frenzy of need, tore them open at last, unscrewed the top and put the metal cylinder to his lips. He could not swallow. Then he could: cool sweet slaking ichor, more precious than . . . He marveled at it, drank again—felt all at once deathly ill and nauseous. He gagged several times but nothing came. The near *thrmmm* close beside his head rang in his brain without cessation. Only then did it dawn on him what it implied.

His breath had returned; or some of it. The earth had changed again from pulsing red to a bright saffron glare. He replaced the canteen, tested the operating rod of his rifle. It wouldn't move. Frightened he yanked at it for several seconds, grunting with the effort, finally kicked it open with the heel of his shoe and brushed the bolt free of sand, got it working again; then moved up beside O'Neill, shaken by the failure of his rifle to function, the malignant harp-thrum of that bullet that had only just missed him.

"Jay," he said. The nausea had vanished but he was trembling badly.

O'Neill turned toward him in silence the flat, alien face.

"Cold," Newcombe said.

O'Neill nodded, staring: sweat was streaming down the sides of his face at his helmet strap in white blotches.

"Cold," Newcombe repeated; his lips formed the word sluggishly. "Cold as a—" But he could think of no metaphor; left the phrase hanging, inane, forlorn. O'Neill was looking ahead with increasing agitation, and he eased himself gingerly to the rim of the crater and peered out.

There was a huge white sugar-loaf of concrete with a long black slit on its near face. Two figures were crouched close against the aperture, signaling to each other, stark against the white glare of the concrete: a stiff, macabre pantomime. While he watched in increasing astonishment, stunned by the immediacy of the tableau—there was only a brief strip of intervening ground before the hillock of sand where they were crouched—the figure on the right leaned his rifle against the side of the pillbox, a gesture leisurely, almost careless, rested on one knee, clenched something in one hand and reached up and out: the grenade hung in the air for what seemed whole hours, a furry black oval—dropped all at once behind the emplacement. Another and another. Then the two figures conversed again in their bizarre semaphore. And above their heads—fearfully close above them—the black slit flashed once, went *wink-wink-wink-wink* and the sand in front of Newcombe kicked up in a darting, snake-writhing pattern. He cringed. When it stopped and he looked up again the figure on the right had bowed his head, as if intolerably weary, and pressed a hand to his temple. Something in the gesture seemed familiar and disturbing; Newcombe turned to O'Neill who was shouting, "Pour it to them! Pour it to the bastards!"

"Where's Danny?" he said.

"There, there . . ." O'Neill pointed excitedly. *"That's* him! That's Danny—"

That was Danny, then: up there frail and defenseless on that slope of sand—crouching, throwing, crouching again; a convulsive saraband against the cascao. A helmet bobbed up out of the rush matting of jungle growth on the far side, then another, moving with incredible, fearsome slowness, like divers approaching a sunken hull. One of them had two bulking cylinders strapped to his back. Flame-thrower team: Diebenkorn and the other—the Texan, what was his—

Someone was pounding his elbow. Klu. Shouting in his ear against the thunderous, boiling clamor, something he couldn't hear—which he realized all at once had something to do with his going up there on that naked murderous height of glaring sand where Danny was. He stared at Klumanski in sheer amazement, speechless—was compelled to look back where he saw the man with the cylinders come up to the left of and directly beneath the slit. The gun was firing again: *wink-wink-wink-wink*, and someone nearby cried out and rolled, hands to his face, into the bottom of the shell hole. Still staring forward Newcombe saw a figure leap up high behind a bunker beyond and to the left of the pillbox: a squat figure in a shining conical hat. Then another—a quick darting recoil. Jap. He knew in a flood of certainty and consternation. Japs throwing grenades. Beside him Jay was shouting, "Did you see them? Did you?"

He nodded. There was an explosion near and below Kantaylis, who threw himself flat for an instant: rose again, resurrected, unharmed.

"All right now! *Drop* the bastards!"

"He can't see them, Danny can't see—"

One of the figures jumped again: squat jack-in-the-box with arched arm. Newcombe fired, felt for the first time the recalled slam of the recoil, the faintly numbing jerk against his cheek, heard the other rifles around him: a quick, crashing roar.

The Jap was gone: popped down out of sight. Missed. They had all missed. The black-and-white cylinder tumbled down below the slit of the pillbox, exploded in a dry puff of dust. Danny lay flat again: did not rise.

"—Danny!"

He was shouting, his mouth was shouting, and for a time he was unaware of it. Jay was staring at him, perplexed. "Danny!" he cried. "He can't see the bastards! Can't—see!"

There was a spewed billow choking black-and-orange flame like a wild, evil tongue, and the pillbox turned soot-black. And the machine gun stopped.

He was running. Up and running chained in tight, boundless apprehension. Prone figures and debris floated by like vague unpleasant dreams. How or when he'd got to his feet he had no idea. The pillbox, blackened and cracked around the slit, loomed nearer like a wall of surf; beside it Danny was getting slowly to his knees again, pulling the pin on another grenade, moving with the dreamy deliberation of a somnambulist. He was all right then, ah, thank God for that, thank God—

Something droned by his head. He plowed up the soft sand, sobbing for wind, threw himself down. A machine gun opened up, deafeningly, chillingly loud: a bright, metallic slapping. He was invaded by the lunatic image of a Jap machine gun with its conical flash-hider pressed like a megaphone against his skull—a vision that made him gasp and press himself desperately in the tiny fissure between the sand and the concrete. Danny—a remote, strained, older brother of Danny—was watching him curiously. He tried to shout but windless, gasping, could not—wagged his head, his eyes, in wild admonition—saw all at once the grenade: a shiny black-and-porcelain cylinder, a ridiculous oversize spark plug—tumbling toward them down the slope; rolling and tumbling it passed right between their crouching bodies, rolled on out of sight. He stared at Danny stupefied.

The wind went into his lungs then. "Behind you—bunker—*grenades*," he shouted. His voice amazed him: a shrill old woman in hysteria.

Danny nodded quickly. His face looked almost oriental in its absence of expression or feature; as though the edges of chin and nose and lips had been shorn away. He was motioning to him, talking to him.

"Up there. Take it easy."

He crawled, a momentous labor, up the mound beside the burned-out pillbox, reached the edge of the rise and slowly raised his head. Dirt kicked in darting patterns in front of him, sand stung his face. He pressed his forehead against the cascao. There was a noise like a madman beating a rush mat in a frenzy: unbearably near, unbearably loud.

Then it stopped. Newcombe raised his head, saw the wild khaki figures leap again and throw. Kantaylis threw at the same instant, a quick snap throw, lobbed it over the top of the bunker. The Jap, gone again, leaped up almost at once and the grenade—their own now, a serrated oval green melon, their own grenade—hung in the air for hours and hours, slowly turning, passed overhead with indolent enormity, struck rolling and exploded at the base of the concrete: a short, heavy roar. Fragments whined around him: something slapped against the sole of his shoe. He felt out of breath, deafened and faintly dizzy: his hands were shaking uncontrollably now.

"*Grenade,*" Kantaylis was shouting. "Give me—"

He groped for one on his suspenders, couldn't disengage it, fumbled with it absurdly, dropped it in front of him on the sand in an agony of trembling. Kantaylis' extended hand snatched it deftly up. Newcombe gazed with deepening alarm as Kantaylis pulled the pin and held it while he counted, hefting it in rhythm, *one—two—three,* and lobbed it high out of sight. There was a deep crash behind the bunker, then a succession of dull, muffled booms.

A figure was wandering toward them, huge in the blinding light: walking slowly, hands hanging at his sides, twisting and lurching, his head thrown back. Sunlight flashed on the buttons of his tunic. All at once he spun around and fell sprawling; rose quickly and continued his wavering, lurching progress toward them, mouth distended in a soundless scream; and again went down. Newcombe stared at him in dazed wonder—raised his rifle and fired. Nothing happened. The bolt was caked with sand: he pawed at it feverishly, pounded the operating rod into working again.

Below him to the left the billow of flame shot out toward the bunker like an oil refinery on fire, belching black smoke—ceased abruptly and heat swept back into his face like the breath from a furnace. The lazy sibilant floated near, and the earth dissolved in jarring detonation without end. When he uncoiled and raised his head again his whole body ached as though he'd been beaten.

Someone plunged down beside him. Jay. Old Jay peering up under his helmet rim in cartoon popeyed surprise. Old buddy. Comfort seeped into him; he felt for an instant almost elated.

"Well, old-timer," he said. "How you doing?"

"Not bad. They almost had me with that last one: hung up between second and third. What's up?"

"Beats me. They're working on that bunker, there. Danny just got—" "*Ahhhhhhh—*"

The cry reached them through the cacophony of roaring crackling hissing. A cry of sheer pain: thin and boundlessly forlorn. Newcombe looked over the edge, saw a man rolling down the incline in front of the pillbox like a log, armless; rolling and rolling. At the same instant something bright spurted down the back of the man with the flamethrower, like mercury poured from a pitcher; smoke belched—and all at once flames spread across his back and legs: crisp, bright, dancing little flames. Writhing the man slipped out of the cylinders, shrugged out of his jacket, beat wildly at his trousers—began to scream in high, yelping animal cries, leaped up in a terrible dervish dance and fell writhing and screaming, *"Ah-ah-ah—ahhhhhhh,"* still beating at his legs; his cries appalling and clear through the incessant roar of small-arms fire.

"Jesus," Newcombe muttered. "Oh my—Jesus . . ." Someone was yelling at him: but he couldn't turn his head, gazed with mounting horror at the soot-blackened, smoking, writhing figure. A hand struck him on the neck, and with a stab of pure physical pain he wrenched his eyes away. Danny was glaring at him fiercely.

"—covering fire! Give me covering fire on that bunker now! And hang in there!"

He leaped away down the sand. Newcombe thrust his rifle up ahead of him, raised his head and lined up the bunker at six o'clock, fired at the malignant black rectangle which winked back angrily, and something ripped into the cascao by his hand; raging he fought back the panic, refused to cringe down, was conscious of Jay firing along with him now, squeezing off round after round.

All at once the bunker went silent.

"Got 'em!" Jay was screaming. "Got the bastards! Now pour it on!"

Newcombe pulled another clip out of his belt, inserted it and went on firing. The air went dark with sound: earth heaved under them, a quaking subterranean boom, and gray-white smoke belched from the slit in the bunker. More smoke billowed from its rear and suddenly there were figures scurrying crablike and wild, with arms extended. Then they were gone.

"Did you see 'em?" O'Neill was shouting. "Did you see 'em run?"

Smoke was still pouring from the embrasures. They yelled at each other, pounded each other on the arm in fierce delight.

"Hey! What'd we do?"

"Hit a magazine! Something . . . Blew it to hell-and-gone! Sons of bitches—"

A dark hilarity possessed them: they fired at the smoking slits, at distant clumps of bush, into a trench behind the emplacement. Fired and fired in a raging gleeful frenzy while around them the coco palms lashed and flailed and the earth threw back a thousand savage points of light. And turning they waved wildly to the helmets in shell holes behind them, and called: "Come up! Come up, you guys! . . ."

Kantaylis came around the corner of the pillbox, his face gaunt and green, half-carrying, half-dragging the flame-thrower man.

"We got it—got it, Danny! You see them take off?"

"*Give me a hand,*" Kantaylis said.

Newcombe jumped down the slope, took hold of the man's other arm and they lifted him up behind the concrete wall of the pillbox, propped him against it with rough haste. It was Diebenkorn, his stolid face fire-blackened and transformed by pain into a hideous minstrel effigy; his helmet was gone and his head rolled back and forth in a slow, agonized rhythm, his tongue lolling in his mouth, moaning. His eyes opened and shut strangely: a mechanical dilatation. He kept reaching toward his legs, made little feeble parodies of slapping at them with raw, burned hands. Newcombe, following his gestures, looked at the still-smoking legs where trousers, leggings, flesh were all scorched and charred in an indistinguishable mass.

"Oh my God," he said faintly. "Oh—my—God . . ." All the savage hilarity went out of him. He felt sick and puny and exposed: at the mercy of a universe filled with boundless ferocity. "What are we going to do with him?"

"Do?" Kantaylis, astonishingly haggard and worn, an unlit cigarette in his mouth, rubbed his blackened hands on his trousers. "*Nothing* we can do. Wait till Carry or Dee or somebody gets his ass up here . . ." He turned and faced the beach and waving his arm cried angrily, "Come on! Come on, you people! Let's go! What are you waiting for, a brass band? Let's go!—and Goddamnit let's have a *corpsman*—"

The shelling had let up, moved off to the left like a demonic giant striding away, released the rolling roar of rifle and carbine fire. Diebenkorn was making a series of sobbing blubbering animal sounds: indecipherable, abhuman. His eyes rolling upward left only whites, swept here and there, driven by the ubiquitous, monstrous pain.

"Poor bastard," Newcombe murmured; stared at him dully. The stench of burned flesh assailed him, turned him pale and giddy.

"—going to lose his legs?" O'Neill was saying.

Newcombe shook his head, bent forward. Diebenkorn was looking at him now; was trying, with prodigious blind exertion, to say something to him. He bent nearer. Diebenkorn, gazing at him imploringly, kept pointing to his rifle, reiterated the thick, sobbing, animal grunts. He was—he was asking him to shoot him.

Newcombe looked away, beset with a thick, boundless horror that froze the air in his lungs. Awful. Beyond all—beyond all imaginings. War, sure: war, of course. But this. This was—

He began to retch, steadily, rhythmically—had a brief, preposterous vision of a gently sloping green meadow bordered by willows through which a stream of clear, still water softly flowed. Still retching, wagging his head, he tore at his canteen and drank greedily, realized he was spilling it over his cheeks and chin, precious cool water you Goddamn stupid fool where do you think you'll get any more around here *knock that off!*

He put his head down between his knees and shut his eyes. The retching stopped. He leaned back against the concrete; his fingers were jerking like spindles pulled with wires. He felt exhausted, apathetic, without energy or will. With arduous care he avoided looking at Diebenkorn, glanced over at O'Neill who was sitting in much the same way, slumped over his rifle, his knees drawn up. Above them Danny was crouched at the top of the mound, waving his arm and shouting.

If I get through this. If I get through this I—

But he couldn't finish the thought: stared numbly at the cloth-covered turtleback helmets bobbing nearer in the hot light.

2

"MAN, HE CAME out of there like equipoise leaving the barrier." Ricarno wiped his mouth, thrust the canteen back in its cover behind his hip. "And all of a sudden the ammo on his belt started going off. Christ! He looked like a string of ladyfingers on legs . . . You see him, Danny?"

"No," Kantaylis said.

"He was heading straight for Terry, coming like a roman candle on wheels, not one of us hit him. And Terry's eyes got bigger and bigger till he looked like a frog with a helmet on—" He laughed boisterously, and pointed at Terrabella. "Just like a frog! I'm telling you, you looked some funny, boy . . ."

Terrabella, his street urchin's face drawn and sweating, glowered back at him. "You'd have looked pretty frigging funny yourself," he retorted sullenly.

"Where was that, Babe?" O'Neill asked.

"Where was that—*I* don't know: Thirty-fourth and Lexington—how the hell am I going to know *where?* I don't know where I am *now.* Back there . . ." Ricarno tilted his head back, in the general direction of the beach.

They were lying in cover created by two shell holes and a section of communications trench, on a slight rise just below the remains of a church so battered that only two walls and an undercut piece of bell tower remained. The shelling had let up again for a time and small-arms fire crackled like twigs in a hot blaze over toward Maidinilla. Kantaylis, leaning back against the wall of the trench, chewed apathetically at a piece of tropical chocolate, let his hand drop to his lap again. His head ached monstrously and his eyes, for no apparent reason, kept going out of focus, darkening and blurring unless he forced them to fix on some object. His neck had started to stiffen. He put his hand to the compress, felt it gingerly, hunched his head into his shoulder. Right in the same place: the very spot. Jesus. Well: lucky enough. If it doesn't get infected. Pain—familiar, recalled—sank back into him like cold through stone. He shifted his position to favor it a little, ran his eye over the group around him. Almost everybody accounted for. Got ashore with hardly any casualties. Luck of a green outfit . . .

Even as he idly counted the recumbent figures Woodruff and Derekman loomed up at the edge of the crater and slid down the side, and Woodruff called: "Anybody home?"

"Where you been, rebel?" Capistron said.

"Well, see, I got all fouled up on the de-tail, and got turned around kitty-corner. Then I ran into Harry and we came over this way." His face brightened all at once. "We just been where there's a Nip radio and a God—damn old kimono with a dragon!"

"Do tell."

"Plain unvarnished truth . . ."

"You seen Jack Freuhof?" Kantaylis asked him.

Woodruff scratched his forehead and frowned. "Well, no, I haven't, Danny, come to think of it. Not that I recall. Not since we were in the amtrack, that is to say . . ."

Kantaylis bit at a nail, burdened with an increasing sense of concern. No one had seen him, all day long. Well: maybe he'd picked up a dreamer and gone back to the beach. Something in the leg or the arm, fat flesh wound . . .

Woodruff was staring at him wide-eyed. "You hit there, Danny?"

He nodded. Several of the others had turned and were looking at him anxiously. "Grenade fragment," he said briefly. "Just broke the skin."

"Where'd you get that?"

"This morning. Hitting some pillboxes."

"You'd ought to shag ass down to the beach," Woodruff said.

"It's all right."

"You get it infected you're liable to be in a whorehouse of a fix, now."

"Carry put some sulfa on it. Be all right."

The sky beyond the church had a vague, orange, unearthly color he found oppressive. Why in hell did his eyes keep fogging up like this? as though they were all tired out: just too tired to keep looking at anything . . . Well: they'd been lucky. The rest would keep dribbling in for an hour. Absently he ran his eyes over the squad again. Newcombe was lying on his back, his face green and slack with exhaustion, his eyes closed; the lids trembled and twitched. He looked all done, as though he wouldn't be able to get off the ground. Maybe not, though. He'd been fine at the pillbox; what had ever made him come up like that, with everybody pinned down? You never knew, that was the plain fact of the matter. The last man in the platoon he'd have said would have come up at a time like that was Newcombe. Beside him O'Neill, digging at a tin of eggs with his combat knife, caught his eye and winked once, went on eating. Ricarno was reciting a dirty limerick to Capistron, who was lying back with his hands cupped over his big belly like an alderman. Helthal, sitting hunched forward, studied a spot in space not fifteen inches from his eyes with a cold, dead absorption; puffed absently at a bent cigarette . . . Well: they were all right so far, anyway. God knew what would happen tonight, of course: tonight the Nips would throw everything and the kitchen sink at them, for sure. The works. Well, they were steadier than he'd thought they'd be, so far. Of course Chicken hadn't shown up yet, or Jack or—

He caught himself up with a snort of irritation. The hell with it: it's not your squad. Let it go . . . The problem was Fellows'—Fellows who was still arguing about something with Lundren in the adjoining crater: a high, tense tone of voice—too high, too tense . . . Well. Take it easy: lie back and relax, before Frey or somebody came by and they had to crank it all up again. No doubt about it, this was going to be a bad one all the way. One of the worst. He would have to look sharper, too: that bunker, snuggled in behind there—why hadn't he spotted that when he came up? He'd been lucky, they all had: bull lucky. The way that grenade had rolled down between him and Newcombe . . . The memory of it tumbling down the length of his body caused his stomach to quiver, depressed him intensely. Let it go, he admonished himself. Relax and collapse, as O'Neill says. And wait for the word . . .

Behind him in the adjacent shell hole Fellows, whose voice had risen still higher, was saying querulously:

"—*I* don't know, Steve, how should *I* know where he's got to . . ."

"You mean you haven't seen him all *day?*"

"Not once. Good Christ, I've had my hands full enough—"

"Well, for pete sake." Lundren rose and stepped through the trench and called: "Any of you people seen D'Alessandro?"

Grins, murmurs, head-shakings greeted him.

"Yeah," Woodruff said. "I saw him. I think I did. He got hit. Way back this morning some time."

"He did?"

"The hell he did," Ricarno said with scorn. "I saw him. Back this morning. Taking off for the beach like he had a hurry call to the head."

"That's right," Woodruff agreed docilely.

"Hell, he wasn't hit."

"What was he doing, then?"

"What you want—me to guess your weight or something? Maybe he forgot his eyebrow pencil. Maybe he was on the chop-chop for Mowbray. How am I supposed to know . . ."

Lundren stared at Ricarno for a moment; turned back to Fellows and said, "Well, we can't begin to set up a line along here if he doesn't show up. I haven't seen Frey since I ran into him with old Herron two hours ago."

"A line!" Fellows said with terse incredulity. "A line—!"

"Sure. A line." Lundren regarded him calmly. "What do you think?"

There was a silence. Kantaylis, his hands behind his head, had a swift dart of premonition. Here it comes. I knew it. Goddamn. Here we go.

"Danny . . ."

I knew it. Oh I knew it! He turned his head; Lundren's sad, battered, dark face was watching him. "Yeah?" he said.

"You think you can find him, Danny? or his Goddamn map case or something? Find out the score?"

Kantaylis sat up and fastened his cartridge belt. Of all the slimy details: of all the stupid, slimy . . . What was the sense in it? Just what? He was filled with a hot surge of exasperation, beat it down. Measuring Fellows' drawn and harassed face he wondered how much to chance in talk. Finally he said: "It may be pretty tough to catch up with him, Steve."

"I know . . ." Lundren, gazing at him mournfully, gave an almost imperceptible little shrug. "Well: do what you can, will you? We got to have the dope: we can't function till we do. Frey said we were supposed to tie in way above this but I don't know, way things are going."

"Jesus, a *line*—" Fellows burst out again, and stopped.

Kantaylis pushed a foot back and forth in the sand; got up and buckled his helmet strap. His reluctance to leave was an almost physical constriction. "Give it a try," he said. "I'll give it a try."

The tanks were ashore: standing great-bellied and stolid they rocked along a few feet, paused at the edge of shell holes like fat men hopelessly drunk at a busy intersection. Kneeling in a crater with two corpsmen and a silent, terrified weapons man with both legs shattered at the knees, Kantaylis watched the tanks with increasing apprehension and thought: Now we'll really start taking it again. Even as he stared at them the familiar, high whine came arching down and the beach leaped in protest: a column of angry smoke fifteen yards to the right of the nearest. Inscrutable, bewildered, the tanks remained motionless: sitting ducks in full armor.

His wind regained, he got up and ran in a crouched shuffle to another hole, another, working his way down toward the water. Coming back like this depressed him deeply; he was unable to shake off the conviction that now, with his back to them, he would be hit—a spot no larger than a quarter between his shoulder blades, at the base of his neck: the place burned with portent, distinct from the throbbing area a few inches to the left where the grenade fragment had struck him. This was the moment they were waiting for, the snipers: right now. Why not? Strange faces stared at the blood on his sleeves and collar and looked away and said nothing; or they grinned unnaturally and said, "How's it go up there?"

He thrust out his lower lip for answer, or shook his head. His mouth was dry. All his teeth ached in one mighty pulsation, and his hip and thigh hurt so he could hardly run. He saw no one he recognized; pausing he watched the amtracks still unloading beyond the barrier of concrete blocks and wire, men still coming in through the lagoon, their faces stern and white and blank, devoid of individuality. Poor bastards, he thought, gazing at the clean dungarees, the well-oiled gleaming rifles, the unspotted helmet covers. Poor bastards: they haven't got the faintest idea.

A tall, thin boy clutched his arm and said: "Do you know where Second Platoon is?"

"What company?"

"George. Or the CP. Do you know?"

The boy's eyes were wide with worry and confusion. Kantaylis patted him once on the shoulder and said, "Take it easy, fella. You'll find them."

"I can't find anybody in my outfit. Anybody at all. They told me to go over that way and then someone said they were over *there* . . . They said the CP—" All at once he noticed the blood caked on Kantaylis' collar and said in frank alarm, "You been wounded?"

Kantaylis shook his head, smiled faintly. "Take it easy, now. You'll run on to them. Just keep asking people, there's plenty of time yet before dark. And keep your head down."

He moved off again, kept working his way to the left, away from the tanks. Crow bait: suicide to hang around them. He

squatted behind a smashed ammo cart and peered here and
there at the swarming morass of men and equipment. Never
find him in this. Not in a million years. He was either right on
the beach, at the very edge of the water, or he had gone back
on an amtrack with some wounded. He might have faked a
wound. He could have . . .

Something moved behind his shoulder. He spun around,
saw the cannibal crab lurch out from under an abandoned
pack, claws up and flaring. He struck at it with his rifle butt,
smashed it into a feebly groping mass; looked away in anger
and revulsion. Filthy Goddamn things, give a man the creeps.
One of them the less. He took off again, walking frankly now,
limping, darting his eyes into hole after hole—encountered an
unending montage of bending and reclining figures, shattered
bits of palm trees, rifles, smashed water cans, burst or half-
buried ammunition cases, dead bodies, swarms of flies. A
man sitting near a frantically busy corpsman held to his
mouth and nose a sopping red dressing like a scarlet sponge;
watched him with bright, unblinking eyes. Poor bastard:
square in the face. Hell. Here was hell all right. Complete with
sound effects and technicolor. Mrs. Lenaine should latch on
to this, he thought grimly. She'd high-tail it back to her own
in a flash. If the devil can do any worse than this I hope to
God I never see it. Never. He raised his eyes—saw beyond the
reef the ships riding gently on the blue water, serene and firm,
all hard bright gleaming corners and angles: a million bloody
miles away . . .

He rose to his feet again—heard the high malignant whisper
and instinctually let himself tumble back into the hole. The
earth shivered and shuddered in a dark spasm: lumps of
things struck him, spattered against him in a dreamy, ringing
mist. He was out of wind again, all out of wind. He had fallen
in the snow, lost his footing on the ice and snow and she was
pelting him with snowballs, laughing and shrieking at his
plight. Her eyes were dancing like snow crystals, her stocking
cap with its fuzzy red pompon flailed around her head. *You!*
she cried. *You taught me how to throw!* . . . Now she sat by an
open window, rocking and crooning, fed their baby from her
breasts and looked out at the summer haze like golden dust
across the valley . . .

Starting to get up again he froze; gazed in sudden cold fear
at the gray face below him, the faintly hooked nose and high
cheekbones. Jack Freuhof. At the edge of the temple a neat
black oval hole like the product of a make-up kit. He resisted

the impulse to turn the head. So small a hole. So *small*—

"Ah," he said. "Jack."

The face held no expression: Freuhof looked neither bitter nor frightened nor at peace. He looked like nothing at all but what he was, now. Huge green flies clustered at his mouth and swarmed at the back of his head and Kantaylis flicked his hand at them, but only a few rose, weaving, then settled down immediately.

"Jack," he repeated dully; still gazed down, transfixed. Hardly got ashore. Such a *tiny* hole! Staring in confused sorrow at this graying, swelling, fly-ridden corpus that had been Jack Freuhof, the man he had swapped stories and laughed and gone on liberty with and who had, like himself, survived a hellish, previous ordeal and wounds, the futility of this struggle, with its ruinous expenditures, chilled him. All the bitter despondency he'd felt on returning to the beach increased with a rush; he was inundated with a sense of calamitous foreboding—of a final, culminating disaster at the core of which lay the certainty that he too would die trying to avert it, that he would die in vain . . . He stared at the immaculate sanctity of the warships lying beyond the reef with a wild, hopeless longing; cursed them between his teeth.

He pulled Freuhof's poncho from his belt and covered his head and chest with it; patted his leg once—a brief, ineffectual gesture—got to his feet again and broke into a heavy, staggering run toward the far end of the beach, away from the tanks, who were coming under increasingly heavy fire. He looked at his watch. Four-fifteen. Jesus. I'll give it ten minutes more, he told himself: ten and no longer. Beside him in the still, shallow water bodies rocked faintly, bloated ragdoll sacking: a weary undulance—as if, tired, pressed beyond endurance, they had lain down to sleep, to be rocked to sleep . . .

Moving slowly at the water's edge through the welter of men and gear he saw all at once what he was looking for. Where the beach ended, in a promontory of rock that loomed black and fierce, the white planes of concrete built into its face pocked with black holes and rents, there lay an overturned boat, some kind of Jap landing craft from its lines: shattered and twisted by gunfire. The top of a helmet protruded from a shell hole near the stern. From the pitch of the head he knew it was the object of his labored, preposterous search. He plodded toward it panting, favoring his left leg; when he came around the corner of the boat, whose bow was adorned with two enormous, vacant black-and-orange eyes, he knelt on one knee and said in a low, even voice: "Lieutenant."

Lieutenant D'Alessandro turned his head and regarded him through narrowed lids; looked away. He was sitting awkwardly with his back against the blackened, twisted metal hull, his legs sticking out straight. His pack and carbine and map case were gone. Great moons of sweat lay under his armpits and across the front of his blouse, which was stained with vomit; sand had caked to it in fine, sugary layers.

Kantaylis said again, "Lieutenant: Steve sent me back to find out where you were."

Lieutenant D'Alessandro started to say something, checked it with an indecipherable grunt. The shelling moved back toward them, deadly and methodical, searching out the position of the tanks; every time one of them exploded D'Alessandro flinched and his hands clapped together once, then fell away. His face looked strangely thin and sunken, as though he'd lost a tremendous amount of weight in the intervening hours.

"How about it, Lieutenant?" Kantaylis said.

"—I'm staying here on the beach," D'Alessandro brought out suddenly, looking at him. "Right here. Not leaving it. I'm waiting for orders."

"What?"

"Colonel Herron instructed me to wait here for orders." He gestured toward a cruiser lying just beyond the point. "He's checking on the situation with General Wittaker."

"Herron?" Kantaylis said slowly; he moved his thumb over his shoulder. "Herron's up *there*, Lieutenant. Up on the line . . ."

"Are you arguing with me—?"

"I saw him up there. A little while ago." He leaned forward, said a bit more firmly: "How about it?"

"I said I'm not leaving this beach."

"But Lieutenant—"

"*Did* you hear what I said?" D'Alessandro cried in a quick, violent voice. "I'm not stepping off this beach . . . I've been up there," he went on, his eyes rolling and white. "I've been up there . . . You can tell them—" he started wildly; stopped, cleared his throat. "You can tell Sergeant Lundren Lieutenant D'Alessandro is indisposed. I've been sick. Good and sick."

Kantaylis watched him without expression.

"Well, what are you hanging around for?" D'Alessandro

shouted. "Take off! That's an order . . . Go ahead up there and get your stupid ass blown off, all kinds of horrible . . . go ahead," he pointed at Kantaylis' neck and shoulder, "get blown all full of holes again and be a big-ass hero, do you think I give a rotten—"

"I'm no hero, Lieutenant."

D'Alessandro made a violently disdainful gesture with one hand, looked away again.

"I'm no hero," Kantaylis repreated. "No more than anyone else. We're just trying to get the Goddamn filthy stinking business over with, that's all. We're all sick and scared and—"

A shell crashed monstrously near them, sent fragments whining through the air like plucked strings. Lieutenant D'Alessandro said, "*Jesus*—" in a high, hysterical tone; relaxed his clutched hands again. "—Don't you talk to me like that, Kantaylis," he shouted, "you went over the hill yourself, it's entered in your service record—"

Kantaylis nodded quietly. "That's right. But not when my buddies were getting cut up."

"You watch your tongue, Kantaylis, I'll have you up for insubordination in a combat zone, disrespectful conduct, bring charges—I'll see you get a general court for—"

"There aren't any court-martials here, Lieutenant." Kantaylis shook his head, watching him. "No charges, no brig time here. None of that . . ."

"I'll go to Mowbray—"

"You think you can even *find* Mowbray? It's taken me an hour and a half to find *you* . . ."

There was another *wheeeeet* above their heads, like a giant file drawn rapidly along the edge of the glass plate of the sky. Kantaylis hugged the earth with all his might, felt something hit him in the arm. A piece of palm tree: he gasped with relief. His head was filled with a burning, humming set of shadows laced with colored wires.

"—never talked about *that* sort of thing," D'Alessandro was shrieking above the roar, pointing to a leg that had appeared with hideous alacrity from nowhere at all: a leg like his own, like anyone's still shod and bloodless. "Not at all!—simply no preparation for this, never once—

"We'll all be killed," he said, and stared at Kantaylis with hollow outrage; his hands were clamped behind his neck, and his head was shuddering minutely. "Do you realize that?—all blown to pieces, arms and legs and nobody *cares*—!"

"Maybe."

Kantaylis watched carefully the rigid olive face, the eyes wide with fear and petulant despair and thought, The hell with him: take off. No hope with him. Let the pitiful sad son of a bitch goof off. He's lost the Goddamn map case anyway: ditched it when he shagged ass. What the hell are you hanging around here for, shooting the breeze with him? He's liable to blow his roof anyway. Like Laffler that night on the Ridge. He just might blast me with his darling pistol if I don't watch it. Well: at least Laffler had some reason for blowing his top . . .

No. He won't blast me or anybody else.

Lieutenant D'Alessandro, now hugging his knees, had begun to babble wildly, his voice rising through the detonations—a racing dialogue of boundless panic in which both parties were filled with horror-stricken protestation at the things, the terrible things that were permitted to transpire all around them—

Kantaylis leaned down, his face very close to D'Alessandro's, and said roughly: "Come on. Get your ass in gear. Nothing any worse can happen to you than is happening to you right now."

The lieutenant's face went long with horror. "What? Don't be ridiculous, there's a thousand—"

"Oh no, there isn't. You'd rather die. I mean it: lose your legs and arms and eyes than live the way you'll live after today—"

"I can't. I tell you there's—"

"—they'll curse you: your mother and father will curse you. Your own kids will curse you for the man who ran out on his own. When nothing else mattered. Nothing else in the whole world."

A white plume rose loftily in the sea just beyond the reef, subsided in a great frothing fountain. D'Alessandro stared; his eyes shifted back and forth along the beach. His mouth was working, as though he were rolling on his tongue some nauseous medicine he was mortally afraid to swallow. He waved a hand about him helplessly.

"I didn't ask for *this*—"

"You're in it, Lieutenant. You're *here*—with people looking to you."

"But I—can't." His eyes rolled up imploring. "I know I can't . . . you don't realize, I saw a man's chin—"

"How do you know? . . . *Jesus Christ*," Kantaylis cried,

angry at last, filled with fury and disgust—recalling suddenly Jack Freuhof's graying, hawklike face. "Jesus Christ, you don't even know! You haven't even had it yet so you don't know how bad it can be—and still you won't! You worthless son of a bitch . . ."

He rose to one knee again, peered back along the beach where black geysers were spurting magically around the motionless tanks. The hell with it. Let him rot in hell for the rest of time, the chicken-livered ninny. Get back to the squad before dark. If you can ever find them again . . .

"Wait. Kantaylis. Wait—"

He looked back at D'Alessandro as though he were dead. "What do you want?"

". . . All right." D'Alessandro's face was pale and twitching. "All right. I'll go up with you . . . But what good will it do?—what can anyone do against that—that—" His hand described a jerky wave to the accompaniment of a distant shriek and detonation.

"Enough, Lieutenant. Enough. Even just the two of us: a beat-up old retread and a hot-shot Hollywood cowboy. Even we can make a difference." Shaking with wrath he reached down and seized D'Alessandro by the collar and said fiercely: "Come on, now: call on the guts you haven't got! For a change . . ."

The lieutenant stared up at him for a moment as though trying to draw courage from his angry gaze. "All right," he said with an effort. "All right. Let's go." He paused, put a hand on Kantaylis' arm. "You won't tell them? any of them?"

Kantaylis looked at him mutely, shook his head.

"All right. Let's go." His mouth kept going tight and slack by turns. A shell burst high on the face of the cliff behind them and he ducked his head, raised it again.

"Where's your gear?" Kantaylis asked him.

"I don't know." He motioned vaguely. "Over there, I think . . ."

"Never mind. Let's go."

The shelling near them had slackened for a time. They moved forward in short runs. Going back again Kantaylis felt better, but the heavy, disconsolate dread still hung poised behind his mind like a claw ready to clench: a cold expectancy that made him hunch his shoulders and hug the ground. Beside him Lieutenant D'Alessandro's face was tensed and alien with fear, and he wondered, Is this any good?—lashing

him into it like this? Maybe it's worse than letting him cork
off on the beach—maybe he'll only foul us up worse and
Steve'll come down on me . . . Well: you've got to play them
as you see them. Maybe he'll buck up in the clutch. Eschelman
was the worst eight-ball in the whole First Division and he
came through fine: Morris too. You never know. Look at
Newcombe . . .

He tried to move faster, resisted with all his might the desire
to lie down in some hole and sip at his canteen. Ayee, he was
tired: a mountainous exhaustion that had caught up with him
all at once and pressed him earthward, dragged at his feet. He
had to get back up there, as soon as possible. They'd be trying
to set up a line now, somewhere near the church: if they could.
The Nips would be staging a banzai tonight for sure, try to cut
them in two.

An enemy machine gun opened up on their right and he
plunged into the nearest hole head foremost, sliding on his
forearms: It was occupied by two marines, both dead, already
swelling in their clothes. D'Alessandro was staring intensely,
his mouth working, at the nearest one, who had an enormous
hole high in the center of his back.

"Better take his belt and rifle, Lieutenant," Kantaylis said.

"His?" D'Alessandro asked. "His?" He seemed oddly
dulled, hard of hearing.

"Sure—his. *He's* not going to be needing them . . ."

D'Alessandro was silent, staring at the contorted, battered
body. Just when Kantaylis was on the point of kicking him he
lurched forward and disengaged the man's cartridge belt from
the suspenders, buckled it on above his own web belt, took up
the rifle and stripped the bolt back deftly. It worked fairly
well. D'Alessandro ran the operating rod back and forth
several times, clicked on the safety and nodded. When he
looked at Kantaylis again his face was firmer, his eyes more
steady; and Kantaylis felt an immense relief. Should have
thought of that long ago: get a weapon in his hands. They say
he shot expert at the range. Maybe he'll be all right . . .

With a casual assurance he knew to be absurd, ridiculous,
as impossible as the sun and moon and all the stars in heaven
he said, "What the hell, Lieutenant. Maybe we'll make out,
after all: the bunch of us. Maybe we'll drive the sons of
bitches into the sea and come through it without a scratch."

"Sure," D'Alessandro said.

"And hoist a beer in San Francisco some one of these days

in—commemoration. With the whole lousy mess behind us . . . All set?''

The lieutenant nodded.

Kantaylis hunched himself forward and took off again, moving a little more to the left up the rising ground toward the white, scarred wall of the church.

3

NIGHT WAS A swarming pressure of lights and silhouettes and shadows. Ahead of Newcombe, as he swung his gaze from left to right over a hundred-and-twenty-degree arc, were two crouched figures, a tall man with an unwound burnoose, a turkey gobbler, two twisted stove-lids, another stealthy crawling figure. A flare burst high above him and the shadowed apparitions morphosed subtly, cleverly, into two shrubs, a blasted coconut palm, a maguey plant, some corrugated iron shards. The flare descended—a solemn, swaying incandescence, and shells *chuff-chuff-chuffed* overhead in glowing flights of four, crashed into the jungle beyond; and the shadows around things crept under cover to wait . . . Then the flare went out and the crouching figures, the man with the burnoose returned, advanced a step. They advanced a step with the death of every flare.

He was fixing again: fixing on one thing—that configuration to the left of the ruffled turkey gobbler. Keep turning your head: make yourself turn your head rhythmically, sweep back through the flash-scarred dark to where Danny's helmet protrudes from the hole slightly ahead and to the right. Old Danny. Our rock of ages. On this rock we will found us our battle line: oh rock of our far-flung battle line, beneath whose awful—

Keep turning your Goddamn head.

Mosquitoes floated against his face in a high, whining drone, stung him savagely before he could wave them away; lighted on his wrists and hands in spiderlike finesse and bit him still more. He had tried wearing his head-net but with it he'd been able to see nothing at all; and the sensation of meshed enclosure had driven him almost crazy. The air, hot and damp and heavy, bore them along on its soft, invisible combers, was filled with their malignant humming. At the end of his traverse was Derekman's helmet, turning too: thousands of cloth-covered helmets slowly turning in the dark, eyes beneath them straining against the night like watchers on a hostile shore. Watchman, what of the night? Ah, what indeed?

His legs were aching from the strained crouch he maintained at the edge of the hole; his shoulder pained hollowly from some time when he'd gone sprawling, crashed into something. He shifted the alarm cord Kantaylis had rigged up for them to his left hand and chafed the shoulder gently.

Another flare, brighter this time, and the hissing, locomotive-run-amok passage of shells. An eerie, sunless light: like Xanadu, where Alph the sacred river ran through caverns measureless to man. Hades might be like this, perhaps: the jewel-lit crepuscular illumination of Hades. *Might* be—!

Damn: it was falling behind them, behind their lines; swinging in its pretty silk parachute it swayed lower, in evil, tantalizing dalliance. *They* were silhouettes now. Jesus. Was he in a Jap's sights—helmet, shoulders, quaking heart—?

Don't think of that.

He had hunched his shoulders instinctively, as if to draw them up under his helmet like a turtle. Eyes were fastened on him from the dark. El miedo tiene muchos ojos: fear has many eyes. Courage only one.

And the dark a thousand more.

The flare snuffed out, darkness rolled back around him in a kindly wave; and he felt his shoulders and neck relax again. All are equal in the dark. In the grave. All cats look alike in the dark. When had he thought that? Ah, the night with her: that entrancing, achingly brief night with her . . . He felt the lightly burning shock of her hand against his face with awesome vividness. *You don't do that,* she had said. *You don't do a thing like that.* If she could see where he was now, what he was doing, what—good God—he had done that day, what would she think? Huddled in the hot darkness he had the eerie sense that in some way she *could* see him, was observing him that very instant with an expression of mingled anger and reproach. *You don't do that,* she still seemed to be saying, shaking her head, her eyes glittering with tears. *You don't—*

Something struck the back of his hand: he jumped in fright,

felt another tap on his shoulder, his knee. Rain. Huge drops coming in rapid succession they thickened, driving down, swelled in an instant to a roaring torrent. Cursing he thrust his rifle between his knees, wrenched at his poncho, pulled it out of his belt and removing his helmet put it on over his head. His shoulders and thighs were already soaked through. The rain lashed down in seething waves. Under another flare it turned to darting silver spikes that bounced on helmets, points of wood and metal.

Beside him O'Neill was stirring; Newcombe heard him mutter something in an angry monotone, then the crackling of his poncho as he broke it out.

"My watch?"

"No: you've got half an hour yet."

"Everything okay?"

"Swell. Perfectly swell."

He heard O'Neill settle himself again; his shoes pushed against Newcombe's thigh, a contact which he welcomed. The rain fell in torrents, began to trickle in icy ribbons down his neck and up the backs of his legs. All at once he was chilled; his teeth began to chatter and his hands shook monstrously. He rubbed his hands and feet, got out his brush and worked at his rifle under the poncho sightlessly, watching ahead. Far to the right the wall of the church, a ghostly gleaming silhouette in the glow of another flare, rose like an emaciated suppliant with one arm raised toward the heavens: devout or mocking, it was hard to say . . .

Time had stopped, it seemed: time too was exhausted after such a day as this; had given up, succumbed to the inertia of the void and could progress no more than they. His legs and body ached with the wet cold, shrank from it in nervous little spasms: his head started to vibrate. He went on brushing at sand he couldn't see. Here on his second watch the day's exhaustion caught up with him and seeped into the marrow of his bones, blended with the wet chill; water streamed in a steady, blinding curtain through the cloth of his helmet cover. Oh, that there would never be a day such as this day had been; never again. His mind, foggy and sharp by turns, started and slowed: geysers black and awful rose on either side, the figure came toward him with its wavering, stumbling walk, Diebenkorn again gazed moaning up at him in immense, horrible supplication . . .

He shut his eyes, opened them again, blinking rapidly. It was that nobody knew. Nobody knew, or they would never have suffered this kind of thing to rend the body, blacken the soul, reduce the spirit to a gibbering caricature that begged, that begged for death—

The man with the burnoose had moved. Jesus. His heart leaped softly. He'd almost gone off, he'd damn near nodded off and he never would have seen it. Advancing stealthily, on mincing feet, through the downpour. Of course: waited for the rain. He thrust his rifle out ahead of him, felt feverishly for the grenades sitting in the sand by his right knee; picked up the alarm cord lying across his thighs and hefted it. Be sure, now: make sure. His temples were pounding against his helmet liner; with each pound there was a little flash of light across his field of vision.

Yes: it had moved. Get ready. He raised the rifle to his shoulder, pushed off the safety catch. Why hadn't Danny spotted him? or Harry? What was the matter with them? He forced himself with a great effort of will to look away to the right, then slowly back again. Yes: it had moved, had thickened. A Nip was using it for cover. Jesus—he was close enough to grenade them all to hell and gone. All right. Watch him till he moves, watch nothing else now. Then blast him.

Light exploded from above like a violent, heavenly dispensation, streaming points of rain—revealed the same blasted, shattered palm trunk. It was alone, unaccompanied: the same as before. He almost cried out in sheer relief.

Derekman's head dipped down near him. He glanced at his watch again. Two five. It was after two! Actually after. He put his hand on O'Neill's calf and pressed gently, murmured: "Jay . . ."

O'Neill started violently, kicked out at him. "What's the matter?"

"Time to take over. Two o'clock."

"Oh . . . okay."

The rain let up a little, fell in soft, sibilant streams around them. O'Neill moved up beside him, said, "Jesus: this is a daisy, isn't it?"

"Yeah. Great."

"Been quiet?"

"Yes. Some firing way over on the left. BAR, some grenades . . . Here's the cord. Look sharp now, Jay: it's hard as hell to see in this."

"You wouldn't snow me now, would you?"

He smiled faintly, patted O'Neill on the shoulder, moved back and lay down—became aware of water several inches deep around him. He pushed along in it, felt his shoes slither in the thinning mud. His rifle: he'd got mud smeared all over the butt. Mud was suddenly everywhere: it stuck to his fingers, smeared everything around him; his poncho was picking it up in folds and ridges. But his rifle—

He pulled the front of his skivvy shirt out of his trousers and rubbed the bolt clean with the tail of it; checked the safety again, drew the rifle in between his legs and lay on his side, head cradled in his helmet . . . He awoke in a flash of wild dread: something struck him on the hip and he lurched to a sitting position. A rifle went off close beside him, then another, then a BAR in a rolling crash. A voice was screaming something over and over. He rushed to the edge of the hole just as O'Neill fired again. The blast almost deafened him; his hands were shaking so he could hardly hold the weapon and his heart, swollen to prodigious size, was choking him unbearably.

"—lllaaaaa!" someone screamed. *"Louelllaaaaa! . . ."*

There was another burst of firing and Kantaylis' voice shouted: "Hold your fire! Hold your fire!"

"Password, he's giving the password," O'Neill called.

"Could be a Jap," Ricarno answered him. "Look out."

"Could be . . ."

"All right," Kantaylis was saying, his voice clear and metallic in the clamor. "Who are you, chum?"

"Patrol. C Company," the voice called faintly.

"All right. Come on. Slowly. Your hands over your head. Come ahead—"

"Watch it, Danny—" Klumanski said.

The figure got to his knees with incredible slowness, rose and tottered forward in a strange, drunken lurch, waved one hand and fell again. Kantaylis was out of his foxhole running, knelt above him; and Newcombe saw him fling one of the fallen man's arms over his shoulder and stagger back toward them. Several others left their holes; scuffling in the murky dark they got him into the hole Derekman and Klumanski shared.

"Where's CP?" the man panted. He was holding one arm against his chest; blood lay in broad black streaks across his shoulders and back, cast one side of his face in a slick shadow. "CP—"

"Down the line," Kantaylis said. "Pass the word down for Carry . . . Where you from?"

"C Company CP—"

"C Company—you're way off base. We weren't even alerted for you. C Company's down—"

"Get hold of Herron. For—Christ—*sake*—"

"It's Moore," Ricarno said suddenly. "Ain't you Moore?"

"Yeah. Staging. For a heller . . ." He swayed forward, would have fallen if Klumanski had not held him; the air wheezed in and out of his throat in a whining singsong. "Right away quick . . ."

"Where's the rest of your patrol?" said Lundren, who had just come up.

"Got 'em all. All. But me." He gripped his arm tighter and tighter; his head waggled loosely, his eyes open and staring. "Get me CP, will you? They're staging—"

"He'll never make it," Kantaylis said. "Pass the word for Herron."

Flares burst in profusion above them—four, five, six—their canisters fell whistling into the dark around their holes: light burgeoned—a fierce yellow illumination that disclosed helmets, heads, white smears of faces looped with shadow. His rifle was working smoothly; Newcombe put a clip on the edge of the foxhole near his right hand and opened all the flaps on his belt. In the crazy, fabricated daylight of the flares he felt calmer, but he was soaked through and shivering and the wild panic of half an hour before when the firing had wakened him still persisted: he could hardly draw air into his lungs. Steady down, you craven chicken, he told himself savagely. Be worth the trip, for once at least. For once in your life.

Slowly he turned his head and looked at O'Neill and said: "All set?"

O'Neill, fixing his bayonet with great care, looked back, nodded curtly. "Ready as I'll ever be . . ."

Detonations leaped in a row of orange blooms along the hill beyond the jungle, raced in and out in mad neon patterns; and above their heads the air became alive with sibilant, droning menace.

Newcombe pressed his elbows against his sides in an effort to steady himself, reduce his shivering. Somewhere near him a serene, dispassionate voice was saying over and over again, "Keep your fire low, boys, remember to fire low, now—" He looked around in amazement, saw Colonel Herron walking along high above him with badgerlike, sure-footed determination, carrying a carbine; with his free hand he made slow, flat sweeping motions as he spoke. ". . . keep your fire low, now . . ."

"For God sake, Herron, get your ass down!" Klumanski bellowed at him—a roar of anger and concern. The colonel nodded to him, gave him a benign, almost indulgent smile—kept moving along in his fantastic, leisurely stroll while invisible objects of incalculable malevolence whined and hummed and crackled around him, searching him out; his voice still floating intermittently, a calm, paternal admonition, through the flash-shot bedlam:

"—come up and meet them when they . . . cover each other, boys . . . see every man—"

Then his voice was gone, swallowed up as he moved off to the right, into chaos and uproar. More flares burst in wild incandescence, turned the night into an eerie subterranean afternoon. Ahead of them the tops of palms lashed and flailed like mops brandished by madmen.

Danny was shouting something to him: he couldn't hear, leaned forward, perplexed. Danny, his face dead white and full of dark hollows, called something again—all at once raised his fist and shook it in fierce exhortation. He nodded dumbly. There was a brief lull and Lundren's voice thundered:

"*Stand by*, you people!"

From the jungle beyond them came an unrecognizable sound which resolved itself into a high, wild cry, like a chant but thinner, more disembodied: "*Aaaaaaiiiii . . .*" An unbroken wail filled with savagery and despair, it rose and fell away, rose again to a fevered pitch and held it. Newcombe found he had his rifle in both hands and was shaking it as though to clear it of dust. Jay had grabbed him by the arm.

"Newk—"

"Yeah?" he said.

O'Neill still clutched him fiercely, a grip that pinched his arm with a pain he welcomed.

"Stay with it."

"Right," he said. "Right." He ground his teeth on each other, gritted them: lights glowed and shrank before his eyes. Beside him O'Neill, gazing ahead intently, crossed himself; raising his right hand he swiftly followed suit, though he had never done that before in his life.

There was a crackling in the jungle like herds of elephants trampling all the gathered twigs in the world—and then suddenly there they were in the clearing: lumps of ghostly dancing

figures who swelled monstrously without advancing, changed
aspect in an agony of trance to flapping birds, to goats, to
antlike crabs with helmets glinting; came on in bands, in
spidery striations, and everywhere was the wild, ghostly
scream: ". . . . *aaaaaiiiii*—" neither animal nor human: lost
limbo scream . . .

Low: fire low and squeeze 'em off.

The gun kicked him, kick, kick, kick: he pressed in toward
the recoil with his shoulder, a fierce affection: brass bubbles
flipped past his eye's scan, curving out of sight. Another clip.
Quick. Jay was shouting something. They were puppet
figures—jerking along on arms and legs, jerking stiltlike,
idiotic in blobs and patches, in hordes; swelling in clarity.
Holes: they had square holes in their faces: their mouths were
open, they were screaming, uttering that fierce, despairing cry
that floated above the pounding, cacophonic roar. *Banzai*,
they were shrilling: *banzaiiiii* . . .

Low. Fire low and steady. He clawed another clip out of his
belt by feel, with marvelous agility, and jammed it home. His
nose was stinging. Rags and snatches of bodies they grew with
dreamy alchemy, making crazy, graceless motions: they held
curving strips of ribbon that flashed blue-white, dazzled him;
flashed and flashed.

All at once they were nearer—broke asunder, split into
screaming, arm-waving men, the enemy, full of hate and
death: one of them leaped high in the air and fell, clawing
arms and legs in space: another doubled over and slid out of
sight, another tripped, rose laughing—*laughing?*—tripped
again and fell. He himself was yelling now, a hoarse, unin-
telligible yell, he knew by the unremitting ache in his throat,
Jay was yelling, all of them were. Filled with rage he rose out
of the hole, rose to meet a figure sweeping toward him—a
broad olive face convulsed with screaming, shiny conical
helmet polished or lacquered, something strange, with the
little star aglow; bubbles of sweat ringed the mouth and
cheeks. The figure burst against him in a mad dance, and the
great blue sword in his hand gleamed as if on fire . . . And
everything slowed. In a floating lurch, like dreamy soundless
surf he crouched, feinted to the right, lunged in. He had
missed. No: the blade had gone in to the haft with fearful
ease: between the buttons. He could hardly believe his eyes.
How easy it is to kill with the bayonet, a thought flashed, they
never told us that, if they knew why didn't they—Bound in the
dreamy lethargy he wrenched back and plunged again, con-

scious of the blue sword raised higher and higher, and of a hand that danced in space, clawed at his nose and chin. There was a clangor on his helmet like the clatter of a thousand forges, an awful shocking weight: lightning streamers swarmed before his vision, turned it ruddy, black, again fitfully bright, through which the sword rose again, wavering now and slow. The face had vanished: reappeared a mask of boundless consternation. In a transport of fury he swung the butt with all his might at the hated face to smash it senseless, sightless, out of sight—

Something was wrong. He was floating in a dreamy, hazy surf. The Jap was above him: no, below him—foul, foreign smell that enraged him beyond measure. The face was staring with wild terror into his eyes. He shouted but no sound came. A carbuncle thrust out beside the nostril, distressing, red and inflamed against the smooth, sweating olive skin . . .

There was a thunderclap which seemed to originate in the base of his skull: his sight darkened, narrowed to a blue-gray band of light through which he endlessly whirled. Something hit him full in the chest. Down. He was on the ground on his back. Get up *get up*. He got to one knee with drunken deliberation, stood swaying in the midst of an epicene nausea where figures pirouetted and danced in silly convolutions. Odd: how no one—

Rifle: his rifle was gone. He saw a space where there was nothing—absolutely nothing!—filled an instant later with two forms locked and swaying. He drew his knife with a movement which was almost a paroxysm. They both were gone. Another thunderclap of unspeakable intimacy spoke behind his eyes. Smoke enveloped him: smoke and whirling dust. He was on hands and knees again: retching in a hollow, moaning gloom. Up. He had to get up!

All his joints were broken: or petrified. He rose on wobbling, watery legs; a man swept in front of him, a face turned—a wild tight face, flat helmet. Jap. He struck at it, clutched, drove the knife in, fell sprawling on the squat, writhing body: leaped up again, saw Danny—unmistakably Danny—rise up too, attached to a figure which soared over backward, arms flung wide; a soaring scarecrow. Someone roared a word in his face: he saw Harry standing calmly, as if on the range, firing offhand, the empty shells in a rising curving glinting stream of carnival delight. But he could not see the end of Harry's rifle. Odd. Someone was rolling near him: rolling back and forth like a dog bathing in dust. He saw a rifle lying near him, snatched it up—stared in owlish bewilderment into the mad moonlight of the flares. He was conscious of a series of whip-crack-booms of fearful magnitude immediately in front of him—black, boiling whorls which caught at him, swept him backward. What was wrong? Men leaped and fell in their dusty vortex, tight tunics and flat helmets. Japs. They were running. Running away. He raised the rifle, an instinctual, almost casual gesture, fired again and again into the splashed tin-foil shapes of light. Ahead the figures whirled into oblivion, swept away through rifts and floating scars of smoke. Scampered and danced in the black boiling rifts. Had vanished utterly.

All over.

It was all over. A stillness as though a crystal bell had been clapped over them all; then lifted—and cries and screams more horrible filled its place.

Jay. He could see no one, now. A man was doubled over, holding both hands to his head: a bubbling moaning. Marine. He cried, "Corpsman!" without thought; peered into strips of light and darkness that cut his eyes like knives.

It was over. The slow surf-lurch of nightmare was over. Fancy . . . He turned around, enclosed in a bewildered exhaustion beyond anything he'd ever felt. As though his body had been shocked into a quivering, paralyzed mass of flesh, a stupor from which it would never recover.

"—Al!"

He turned again, staring dumbly through the hurting, luminous strips. Jay—old Jay . . . Jesus!—was staring at him: a face frantically white and drawn.

"Al! You make out?"

"Sure," he panted. "Sure, sure . . ." Blood was welling up in his mouth from somewhere; he was choking from it. He coughed up a thick gout of blood and spat it out in revulsion.

Now time was racing again, absurdly. Ridiculous: after all the hideous dreamy timelessness, time now raced away. Things happened but he couldn't keep up with them, couldn't take part in them somehow, move in *their* time. He was cognizant only of a dulled cone dead ahead where Ricarno stood above a groping prostrate figure and fired down once, again, the muzzle kicking, spurting fire: the cone swung in eerie trajectory, far too slowly, to where Carrington was kneeling over someone, extending like a fluttering ribbon rolls of yellowed gauze; farther on Lieutenant Prengle was saying, "Don't talk: don't try to talk, Mario . . ." and Lieutenant

D'Alessandro, pale as death itself, looked up at him with glittering eyes, his lips moving steadily, and from a smooth, lazy crescent in his throat blood streamed in a curtain, like a silken scarf—

He was still holding a rifle, not his own. His right hand was sticky against the stock; he looked at it curiously, the sticky noisome jam that darkened his palm . . . It was as though he had lost his hearing, his voice, his human density—had lost contact somehow with the world of movement where time had unfairly speeded up again. Too bad: at a time when—

Lundren was thundering at them: Lundren, towering before them, wrapping a green skivvy shirt tightly around his left forearm. His voice bombarded Newcombe like a spirit, a stern, ghostly admonition:

"All right now, stand fast, you people! Get into line and stand fast. Take cover, all of you. They may try it again, now . . ."

"Oh . . ." He turned and gazed away beyond the groaning and cursing and the cries—gazed at the dark, depthless mat of jungle: it was as remote, as soundless as the far shore of hell. The appalling implication of what Lundren had just said penetrated to the deepest deeps of his heart and wrung it. *"Oh,"* he said, and squeezed his eyes shut.

"Newcombe! Get your ass into the hole!"

Lundren's voice again: he was moving already, without thought. Jay was speaking to him, something that also pricked his consciousness with swift force. Bayonet: there was no bayonet on the end of the rifle he held. His own. He wanted his own rifle and this was not his. He stepped out in front of the foxhole and got his own. It was lying beside the man he had killed, now a twisted carcass without dignity or grace. The face, bent sidewise, regarded him: smooth and oriental and stamped with horror and despair. The carbuncle glinted at the edge of one of the nostrils; the mouth, like the eyes, was still open, still soundless. Staring down, Newcombe knew with the most implacable certainty that this face would never leave him all the rest of his life; that he would never lie in some sunlit field in thoughtless, happy reverie again.

To his right Derekman and Woodruff and Dever the corpsman were huddled over the massive, inert body of Klumanski, who held his groin in both hands and kept iterating in thick, hissing pants: "Got me from the ground. Son of a bitch—stuck me from the ground . . ."

Newcombe stepped down into the hole, laid his rifle across

his knees and gripped his head in both hands. Calls, cries, explosions clanged about in his head with discordant reverberation, rang on and on in his brain, obviously in an effort to tell him something, establish definition, impart some truth—was that it?—but failing somehow. Purposeless, anyway. Yet he ought to—he ought to . . .

Off to the left, toward Pajaña, firing rose to a ragged, rattling crescendo and shells moaned and thumped in glowing arcs.

"Broke through," Kantaylis was saying. "Down there. C Company."

"That barrage came in the nick," O'Neill said. "They'd have gone through us, too."

"You ain't kidding one time."

—time.

—time.

"Barrage?" Newcombe said dully. "Barrage?"

"Hell, yes—barrage. What do you think that was, the Fourth of July? . . . Saved our ass."

"It's a wonder they didn't blow our heads off though, the bunch of us: cutting it that fine . . ."

—fine . . .

—fine . . .

Newcombe shut his eyes, opened them again: ahead of him bodies lay in strewn lumps, no longer human; no longer anything at all. Scant minutes ago they had been filled with fury, with wild, preposterous hopes and fears; now they were mere vulgar lumps, already one with the blasted palm, the maguey plant, the tattered iron shards . . . Strange the—the metamorphoses implicit in—

"You sure dropped that bastard." Ricarno, standing upright in his foxhole, was grinning at him. "Jumping him like that. Bastard would have had me. What happened to your rifle?"

—your rifle?

—your rifle?

He watched Ricarno's heavy, wide-mouthed face with puzzled interest. Odd: he looked no different, not a whit. He might have been crossing a street, sitting at a—

Ricarno, staring back at him, scowled and said: "He all right?"

"Sure," O'Neill said. "Take it easy, Al. Relax and take it easy, old-timer."

He looked out at the dark, now flareless and full of deeps;

then held his right hand to his face, rubbed the thumb against the glutinous substance lacing the fingers No: this my hand will rather. This my hand—

He put his head down suddenly and retched, brought up nothing; rubbed and rubbed his hand against his trousers. A flare burst, hung in the night sky: a dazed and solitary candle.

4

IN THE QUICK gray dawn light faces leaped into being like negatives rapidly developed: etched negatives of faces dirty and worn and dazed. And with the dawn the voices—hushed, brief, sepulchral.

"... Awful the way Klu got it."

"Yeah. How bad off is he?"

"Dee says he'll lose 'em."

"Oh God."

"D'Alessandro really got it, though."

"No!"

"Sure: where were you? Had his head cut damn near off."

"Jesus."

"Steve said he turned tiger: got four of them hand-to-hand before they got him. One of them was a major."

"He may crock off, though. He lost enough blood to float a boat. Jesus: what a pool of blood under him! I'd never thought there was that much blood in anybody . . ."

"Cuts no ice with me. If he's a son of a bitch to me living he's a son of a bitch to me dead."

"Don't call him that, Harry. He saved my cotton-picking ass."

"He did?"

"I *mean*. I was trying to clear a stoppage and I looked up and there were three of them coming at me in a lump. God! That bayonet looked big." Woodruff uttered a low, whinny-ing laugh. "Old D'Alessandro was dropping flare shells in the mortar and he saw 'em coming, and damn if he didn't out with that crazy old pistol of his and let go: *blam! blam-blam!* Right from the hip. And dropped the lot of 'em. Cool as you please. Then he turned around and dropped another flare in the tube.''

"No!"

"I swear. Just like old Wyatt Earp. Boy, I never thought I'd be beholden to that man for *anything* . . .''

"I saw him. Just before they took off. He was all tangled up with about five of them; his whole throat was laid open. He looked up and saw me and said, 'Terrabella: get on the flares.' Just like he was asking me to get him a beer. He could hardly talk, even.''

"What do you know. And after yesterday—''

"Well. It just goes to show you never know, now do you? Man'll be a worthless no-account, and then all of a sudden he'll take hold.''

"What the hell did you do, Danny—paint his tail with turpentine or something?''

Kantaylis smiled faintly. "D'Alessandro's all right. He just forgot where he was for a while, that's all.''

"Man, I *still* don't know where I'm at.''

"Frey's going to put him up for a Silver Star.''

"No kidding. Where'd you hear that?''

"Steve told me.''

"—we got off lucky. They really took it over in C Company. They took it all night. Nips overran them twice. Sixty-five percent casualties, Top said.''

"Jesus.''

O'Neill, crouched at the edge of the parapet to the foxhole he shared with Newcombe, listened vacantly to the voices, ate the caked, gelid tinful of eggs without haste or appetite, spooning it out on his knifeblade. In all his life he had never felt as bad as this: never. His insides churned with a thick griping pressure and his head ached savagely—as though something were caught in the front of his mind, pressing, straining to break its way out into the still morning air. No one had slept since the banzai; they had all kept the watch, waiting with fear and dread for the second attack that never came. Now, in the swiftly growing heat, he felt sick and dizzy with sleeplessness and tension: so tired he wondered if he could go another day like yesterday if he had to. Jesus, he muttered; yesterday . . . He stared at Newcombe who was lying on his back at the other end of the hole, motionless, his feet drawn up. His eyes had a glazed, futile look that disturbed O'Neill; since the banzai he hadn't spoken more than ten words.

"Al," he said, "Have some eggs?"

Newcombe threw an anguished glance at the proffered tin, shook his head.

"You ought to eat something, old bushwhacker: keep your strength up and all that poop."

"I had a piece of chocalate."

"That's no kind of chow for a growing lad. How do you expect to have those strong, white teeth and straight, white bones?"

Newcombe looked down without interest; studied his right hand, where he chafed the fingers against the thumb.

"—A captain," Ricarno said, above them. "At least." He was standing in front of their foxhole, peering down at one of the Japanese Newcombe had killed the night before. "Never thought you'd wind up starched like this, did you, you slope-head son of a bitch?" he said levelly; he spurned the body with his foot, reached down and picked up the sword. "Hey, this is yours, Newcombe. Man, what a toadstabber: lucky he didn't goose you with this number, ah?" Raising his arm he swept it through the air: it made a low, sibilant hum. "Listen to that . . ."

Newcombe was staring up at him; a dulled and listless gaze.

"What the hell—don't you want it?"

Newcombe made a swift, violent grimace, looked away.

"For Christ sake." Ricarno turned to O'Neill; in the gray light, mud-spattered and with a bristling black growth of beard, he looked surly and tough. "What's the matter with *him?*"

"Leave him alone," O'Neill said. "Leave him alone, Babe. I'll take it. Give us here."

He ran his thumb along the smooth, blued steel, followed the delicately chased vines and scrollwork. In the hilt were gold rosettes and two stones that looked like emeralds. It was heavier than he'd thought it would be, but with good heft. It felt strange sitting in a foxhole in the summer of 1944, holding a sword in your hand: it felt—more powerful, somehow: as though you ought to be a chieftain, leader of a band of wanderers, traversing the seven seas . . .

In a low voice he said: "Don't you really want it, Al?"

Newcombe looked at him as if from a tremendous distance away, said, "No, I don't want the filthy thing. Take it if you want it . . ."

O'Neill went over to the dead man, disengaged the scabbard from the black leather belt, sheathed the sword and lashed it to his pack so that the hilt came just at the level of his left shoulder. For Lorraine, he thought; he had a swift, implausible image of himself, dressed once more in greens, sitting in one of the couches at the apartment in D.C., showing her the bizarre, curving, square-tipped blade. Or the punks: it would mean more to them . . . Then, hefting it again, he wondered about the extra weight it would mean. Over the field figures moved slowly, bending, rising again; called to each other, displayed swords, hara-kari knives, little silken battle flags.

"Hey, O'Neill!"

Capistron was standing astride a dead body with a sword in each hand, brandishing them both and grinning. He waved back vaguely. Not ten feet from where he sat a slim, khaki-clad figure lay on its face with arms outstretched, like a mariner spread-eagled in the rigging during a gale: one of the two men he had killed at close quarters. The eyes had gone wide with surprise: sheer surprise: he had put a hand to his face as if he'd been trying to remember something; then he'd dropped like a stone. Maybe a wife like Lorraine, two kids like the punks in some rice paddy outside of Tokyo . . . For an instant he felt a deep, hollow regret; thrust the thought down harshly. What the hell: he took the same chance as I did. That's how it goes . . . He had another impulse—to go through the man's gear; abandoned the thought and went back to their foxhole and sat down again. Apathy sat inside him like a jailer; the pressure at the front of his head redoubled, made him wince with pain.

". . . stand by . . . stand by . . . stand by . . ." the voices said, moving nearer and nearer along the line in the dawn quiet; a hissed murmur. "Stand by to move out; pass the word down . . ." Clearly audible now, even before Derekman had turned and said it to him, and he had turned to relay it to Woodruff: there was no need to say it but he did, without thought. Then all at once the import of the phrase sank through the weary indifference of his mind, assumed meaning—and he groaned and looked around him wildly.

"Move out, for Christ sake—! Move out *where?*"

Sunlight flooded them gradually, poured depth into the surrounding jungle, the slowly moving figures. Over to the right the church wall, which had lost its bell tower during the night shelling, looked still more naked and forlorn in the sun.

O'Neill folded his poncho and fitted it over the back of his belt, slipped into his pack suspenders. Near him Ricarno, holding a fluttering silk battle flag up before him, said with gusto: "And it's another *beau*tiful day in Chicago! . . ."

Looking up again O'Neill saw for the first time Mount Matenla, its sides covered with sword grass: a gaunt, harsh mountain like a hungry animal tensed to spring. Looming high in the swift, distilling light with little shreds of orange cloud near its summit it seemed an incarnation of the nauseous churning in his guts, the tight pressure in his head, the sleepless exhaustion and the terrors of the previous night and day.

"You monster," he said with implacable hatred. "You Goddamned filthy humpbacked monster."

"Thomas Hardy should have lived under that mountain."

He turned and saw Newcombe, his pack on, gazing upward too. Oddly enough he looked a lot better. The little movement of preparation seemed to have helped him; his face had more color, more substance.

"Who's he?" O'Neill said. "A mountain goat?"

"Man who wrote about doom . . ."

"Only person be interested in that mountain would be a razorback," Woodruff said. Squinting, chewing methodically on something hard he regarded Matenla in sleepy, bemused appraisal. "A mean old razorback hog."

"Or Procrustes. God, he'd have loved it."

"All right, you people," Lundren called to them. "All right, let's move out."

"Let's move out, now . . ."

O'Neill buckled his belt, picked up his rifle and stood up. Lieutenant Prengle, who had just been in a murmured conference with Captain Frey, came up to them; short, heavy-muscled, his broad face was at once placid and intent. Mud was caked in welts to his hips and shoulders.

"All right, now," he said in a flat, emotionless voice. "Keep the line. The guide is right. Let's go, now . . ."

They were moving forward toward the jungle: moving with infinite care and reluctance past the bushes of the night before, the blasted palm trees, the shattered heaps of bodies. O'Neill hardly saw them; they slipped below his gaze as remote as fish resting on the bottom of the sea. He was conscious only of the harsh curtain of jungle drawing slowly, ominously nearer, of Newcombe on his right and Derekman on his left. The heat grew with a rush. He discovered that his

stomach had already tightened in spastic bands, and his legs
were quivering.

They entered the jungle as effortlessly as diving into a
bottomless pool. "Keep contact," voices whispered in the
green opacity and gloom. "The guide is right . . . right . . .
right . . ." The trees—ifil, banyan, some kind of stunted,
bristling palm—thickened, the ground vegetation became
heavier: around them liana vines hung swollen and menacing;
the roots of the banyans arched in tubular ribbed clusters, like
the legs of giant spiders; canteens slapped hollowly against
buttocks, leaves and the fronds of giant ferns swept back with
him, slithering sounds. It was so quiet! Only the desultory
bump of artillery far off to the right, near Nénetan,
disturbed the stillness. Ahead of them Prengle raised a hand
and they froze, sweating, peering into the impenetrable green
mat which was still dripping from the night's rain. O'Neill
swung his head to the left, encountered Kantaylis, who
winked once. He winked back palely.

They moved forward again. The jungle thinned to a semi-
clearing laced with banana trees and palms and long stretches
of sandy soil; and the sun again burned down, hot and furious. This is where they'll be, he thought with foreboding.
Now: right now. Lieutenant Prengle, Terrabella ahead of him
were moving with tense, jerky movements, almost like
cripples, and he thought, I don't like this at all. It's better in
the boondocks: then nobody can see anybody and you've got
half a chance. This way its murder, and you're a clay pigeon.
Up for grabs. And the ominous tension increased, made the
blood pound in his temples and throat. Ahead the land rose
sharply to a ridge which curved around on both flanks like a
horseshoe, or the undershot jaw of a barracuda: the image,
though it distressed him, was inescapable. This is where, he
said again with a dread that sought to become anger. Jesus
Christ: three for a nickel. Three—

A rifle roared, another—and machine guns opened up in a
long, brutal burst that shattered the hot silence, smashed it to
roaring fragments. Terrabella whirled around in a hop-skip
fall-away dance, figures plunged forward in dreamy crashing
haste. He found himself with no sense of transition in a little
declivity near a banyan's roots, crouched flat and clinging,
while the machine gun shuddered in long runs, searching
about in the brush: *slap-slap-slap. Slap-slap-slap-slap-slap-
slap-slap.* Slippered feet running on metal floors, running him
down where they could see and he could not. He pressed with

all his strength against the shallow concavity of earth, held it to him with his fingers: if he held on to it firmly enough he wouldn't float away, float high into the blue air where *they* were searching, running him down . . . And the shivering came again, a dry-mouthed tremor that fused with the cold and apprehension of the night and squeezed his belly like a remorseless, spastic fist. Jesus, he said: oh—my—Jesus. For grabs. Voices were screaming, "Corpsman! Corpsman!" and someone rushed by him toward the rear, tripping and stumbling and crashing through the roots and vines. "Goddamn-fool-hit-the-deck!" he shouted—was not sure a second later he had shouted anything at all. And just ahead and to the left, so terribly near, so terribly far away Terrabella was lying in no cover at all, one leg doubled under him crazily, his head turned to the side, crying *"Corpsman!"* his tough, narrow face distorted in a wail of immeasurable terror. Terry: Jesus. He looked directly ahead of him, could see nothing at all. His rifle was fouled with sand. Newcombe, who had been only scant feet away moments ago, was nowhere to be seen. He raised his head a few inches—saw earth spurt from beside his left eye; pressed flat again and held his breath. Bad. Very bad. "If you could only *see* the bastards," he cried softly. If you could only *see* them . . . The sense of impending catastrophe closed around him like a sentence handed down by some omnipotent and terrible magistrate, one from whom there was no appeal whatever, and he knew it was only going to get worse: worse and worse, no matter what they did, until they all lay like Terry, bleeding and writhing without cover, screaming for a corpsman who would never come.

"—air support! Can you give us air support. Yes: at K8. K8. We can't move the way it is *now* . . ." Captain Frey, lying on his side with the field phone wedged between his head and shoulder, stared upward at the crackling sky in popeyed outrage, his lips working. "—can't—! Well Goddamnit you people better give us something before they start dropping mortars . . . I don't give a damn *what* you think, we're getting cut to pieces!—why can't they . . . All right. All right. Can you give us a tank. Anything! We *can't move—*"

A V-shaped geyser of earth and bits of vegetation rose up immediately to the right, followed by a coughing roar and the high, nasal whine of fragments, and Lundren shouted: "Move out, some of you people! Spread out!"

No one moved. O'Neill clasped his hands under his rifle,

pressed his helmet against the cascao. They were lying—too many of them—in a shallow, debris-laden ditch behind a felled coconut palm; every now and then one of the machine guns ahead of them would fire and pieces of bark would chip away from the top edge of the log and everyone would cringe still lower. Connor's face, inches away from his own, stared wide-eyed at him: misery and fear and bewilderment compounded; the muscles around his mouth jerked and ticked as if pinched by invisible little fingers. It suddenly struck O'Neill that Connor was on the verge of cracking up; he gripped him hard behind the elbow—a swift, automatic gesture. Connor's face remained as white and striken as before. O'Neill looked away quickly: Kantaylis, on the other side of him, was cleaning his BAR with meticulous care—a deliberate calm so great he could only stare at him openmouthed. Something crashed behind and ahead of them at once like hot, malign surf, and he glared up at the umbrella-vaults of the palm fronds and cried raging, "Where *are* the bastards? where in the name of God are they?" Since the moment, hours before, when they had first been pinned down he had felt frustrated, debilitated slowly by the might and craft and invisibility of the enemy, until it seemed as though the very coco palms and strips of corrugated iron, the tussocks of maguey were themselves armed and animate, enemies too, firing down on them and laughing . . .

"Spread out, spread out, you people!" Lundren roared at them. "That's mortar fire! You want to get us all killed?"

"No—cover, Steve!" someone at the far end of the log yelled back. "Can't see any cover! . . ."

"Then shit some!"

"I'm doing that *now,*" O'Neill muttered. Kantaylis—could he possibly have heard him?—turned and smiled at him: a quiet smile that made him angry. Someone at the far end of the log got up and scuttled away. No one else moved.

"What the hell we going to do?" O'Neill said tightly. "Wait here all day till they start working us over with mortars—knock the bunch of us off?"

"Take it easy," Kantaylis said. "Frey'll get us something. Hang in there. We'll get out of this."

Shells came over with their runaway-train chuffing and burst in the jungle screen on the face of the horseshoe beyond; the crowns of palms lashed and swirled overhead like eelgrass in a riptide, and things rained down on them. A machine gun up ahead opened up with its dry, slithering *slap-slap-slap* and bullets ripped into the log, droned by like notes plucked on a satanic viol; and O'Neill pressed his face against the dusty powder again.

Two ants were struggling with another one that was hurt: he watched them, not three inches from his eye, as they suddenly became huge, man-sized—and he was watching them from a great height. Helping the one that's hurt, he said, forming the words with his lips, studying the frantic struggle under a chip of bark as big as a house. Help the poor bastard, he told them urgently; his forefinger, a wrinkled ridge of hill, twitched toward them. Give him a hand—

The chaotic roar increased: a Revere Beach madhouse filled with surprises, mirrors, blasts of air—but aimed at their destruction. He could feel his senses diminish in the din: words, sounds, images, thoughts all lost their meaning, their importance. There was no sense in thinking at all because—there was no sense in it. But Christ!—nothing was worse than lying here in this filthy ditch, unable to move forward or back while they dropped everything terrible in all the world square on your head . . . He felt a violent urge to leap to his feet and race away through the brush screaming and howling, brandishing his rifle, anything to *find* the sons of bitches, behold them face to face—an impulse instantaneously supplanted by a shudder at the suicidal folly of such a desire. Hang on, he told himself with tremulous urgency, sweating; hang in there, we'll get out of this, old Danny'll get us out—was dismayed to see that Kantaylis' face had gone gray and tight with strain. He reached back for one of his canteens.

There was an ear-splitting crash—a double discharge he couldn't place—another: a section of the root bole of the tree beside them flew into pieces and the air turned black and flaming and terrible and burdensome as jelly. Dazed and shaking, O'Neill looked back and saw the tank looming behind them—a dark, angular monolith, the dread barrel of the gun with its bulbous flash-hider depressed toward them like a prehistoric snout leaning down to devour them all. The barrel flamed again and earth and trees and fragments swept around their heads. Someone screamed and clutched his face and flopped backward, arching.

"Why the *crazy*—" Kantaylis was shouting, "the *crazy*—"

With the monstrous knowledge that the tank, one of their *own* tanks, was firing at them, depressing that terrible snout stupidly, methodically to blow them all to bits while they lay there helpless and vulnerable, O'Neill felt the last of his nerve slip away: he cringed deeper into the faint concavity of earth and sand, clawing frantically with his hands, clutched something, saw it was a foot—a Jap's foot with some of the wraparound puttee still on it, shoeless and scabrous and utterly hideous—plucked it to one side and squeezed himself against the foul-smelling muck in a paroxysm, his eyes shut tight, while the pounding doublecrash came again and again. He heard distantly someone cry out in agony and then Kantaylis' voice in a high-pitched scream:

"Get out of here!—Get that frigging heap out of here!"

I don't care, he told himself numbly: *don't care about anything ever any more.* He seemed to be drowning in some gelatinous substance which had been evilly substituted for water and through which he sank endlessly, his lungs squeezed flat and with no air, no way to breathe—

A hand seized him by the shoulder: Kantaylis was leaning close to him, his face white with rage.

"Jay. We got to get over there. Come on. Come on—"

He gazed back through waves of nausea and fear; shook his head. "No. Can't—"

"Got to. *Jay! Come on . . .*" Kantaylis' eyes bored into his with infinite ardor and ferocity and supplication. He stared up in amazement. There was nothing: in all this unspeakable stupid crashing horror there was nothing so important as that gaze. It took hold of him tangibly, held him like the hand of God.

"Okay," he said between dry, unfeeling lips.

"Okay. Come *on*, them!—"

He was gone: the infinitely supplicating eyes—Danny's eyes—were gone. Vanished from the earth. O'Neill cringed in the face of an enormous detonation that seemed to erupt from between his knees: his sight slid into shadows, fluttered in an eerie galaxy of darks and lights, returned in faintly coiling rings. His hands were shaking like taut wires. Danny. He raised his head dizzily, saw Kantaylis reappear in a low, crouching run toward the tank. In the open: all in the open. A geyser-line of spurting dust danced along the cascao ahead of him, skipped behind him adroitly, and he went down. Oh Jesus. Danny—

The gap was immeasurable, terrible. Like diving through a mile of night into a lake of boiling sulphur. No chance. But Danny— He clenched his teeth, sucked in a lungful of air as though he were leaving the mark, and flung himself out of the hole, went weaving and lurching in awful, dreamy plunges through an air like scalding water toward the looming silhouette of the tank till he could go no farther, flung down sprawling into a hole in thick, gasping pain—caught sight of Danny crouched at the rear of the tank, close to the treads. He gathered his legs under him and leaped up again, dashed over to him and again dove, skidding forward on his elbows. The gun roared above their heads in stunning concussion.

"You all right, Danny?" he shouted. "You got 'em?"

"—*broken!*" Kantaylis was holding a piece of dangling wire in one hand. The phone was gone: the door to the box was smashed away and hung like a disheveled metal ear.

"Oh my God . . ."

For an instant they huddled there against the tank, staring at each other. The gun crashed again, monstrously: *BA-PAM*—was echoed by faint, faraway cries like those of bathers on a windy day. All at once Kantaylis' face tightened with a desperate, almost unbearable ferocity. He jumped to his feet. In sheer amazement O'Neill watched him leap up on the bogie wheels, the treads, climb in quick, jerky motions to the turret and stand, huge against the bright, smoke-sifting sky, driving the butt of his BAR against the iron dome: a wild and terrible tableau. The hatch, incredibly, opened at once: began again to close. Kantaylis had thrust the barrel of his BAR into the spidertrap aperture, was shouting: "—our guys! . . . firing at . . . *knock that—*"

Two figures were running toward them from the left. O'Neill wrenched his eyes away from Danny's fearful silhouette, glanced at the oncoming men absently. His heart nearly stopped. Japs. They were Japs, big men both of them, burdened with what he knew must be demolitions, running heavily. He fired from the hip, threw his rifle to his cheek and fired again. The foremost figure whirled around and fell as if thrown; the second raised both hands to his head. O'Neill squeezed the trigger: the rifle misfired. He raced forward, saw the Jap strike both fists to his helmet—a ridiculous child's gesture: the two grenades rose into the air, flashing in the sunlight, trailing orange sparks, swept overhead. The Jap, a huge, catlike man, danced to his left, his right: drew with fearful suddenness a black pistol from a holster. O'Neill lunged in: the man danced to the left again, his face bearded and sweating and terribly close, the teeth bared; only one eye was open. There was a sickening instant that swelled to an utterly unendurable eternity as O'Neill realized he'd missed with the bayonet, was falling forward, off-balance: instinctually he drove the butt around high with his right hand, felt it hit solidly. And at the same time the Nambu went off with an explosion so near it deafened him.

The man was lying on the ground, already rolling away. He himself was on one knee. He pounced on the Jap, seized the sweating throat in one hand and struck again and again in a gasping paroxysm of fury at the heavy-bearded face, the solitary rolling eye. He felt an excruciating pain in his groin—a swift, pervasive lesion of his resources, and thought, Kneed me, bastard kneed me. Falling away he snatched out his knife and drove it into the Jap's throat. The man screamed once, sharply, flung his arms back against the ground.

. . . He was dizzy and sick and weak as water. He started to get up, sank to his knees, toppled over on his side: forced himself doggedly to his hands and knees. Everything swirled and dipped in a vertiginous rhythm he couldn't figure out. Whirlaround. The Whirlaround at Norumbega, with the world outside a racing trail of blue and orange sparks . . . *Move out*. He snatched up the pistol and thrust it into his belt, picked up his rifle, pounded the operating rod free; pressed his hand against his groin. The Jap lay on his face shivering, his fingers opening and closing in slow, feeble rhythms. He looked up, saw—unbelievably—Kantaylis standing with the barrel of his BAR still stuck under the hatch, talking with violent absorption. The gun had swung away from the ditch, was facing uncertainly skyward. All that time . . . ah God—had Danny been up there all those hours and hours? Tank, Danny, the fallen finger-clenching Jap swirled and trembled—swept up, then down in dizzy looping configurations: an interminable hellish drunk from which he could never regain sobriety. He went to his knees again.

"Danny!" he shouted. "Danny!" Something struck the side of the tank with a clang, moaned off into space. *"Dannaaaaay!* Come down—!" He crawled in under the brute iron lee of the tank and fell against the tread, leaned his head against it drunkenly, sobbing with exhaustion.

5

DUSK HAD COME with a rush and driving rain, and they dug in silent urgency; lifted the thick muck on their little shovels and dumped it out ahead of their holes. After a time shovels became too clogged with mud to wield and they banged them against the splintered stumps of palms or scraped them with their knives. The talk was short and monosyllabic and intense.

"You hear about old Herron, Danny?"

"No. What happened?"

"Sniper got him in the elbow. Smashed the bone all to hell-and-gone."

"Ah, Christ."

"He won't let them evacuate him, though. Jesus, this mud! . . . Top says he told him: 'You tend to your troubles and I'll tend to mine. I'm not going down till they have to carry me.' "

"Rugged enough, uh, Danny?"

"Well. He'll have to go down . . ."

Across from Newcombe O'Neill straightened, hunched his bare shoulders and dropped them; sweat was pouring down his chest and back in streams. They both paused in their digging, looked at each other—a mute, expressionless, dogged gaze—breathing through their mouths.

"Think it's deep enough?"

"No."

"I don't either. This lousy *mud*—"

It was everywhere, a part of the racing twilight; adherent and obscene it clung to their hands, their arms and legs, accumulated layer on layer until it dried and caked and cracked and chipped off in little clods, and slimed over again freshly. Its weight was everywhere, too—part of the accumulated frustration that sapped spirit and flesh. Far over on the right beyond a patch of jungle the single wall of the church rose, white and battered and infinitely forlorn.

Someone piled into him with a crash and Newcombe whirled around and shouted: "Watch what you're doing!"—saw it was Derekman and subsided.

"Safe enough," Derekman said, and grinned without smiling. "What's the scoop?"

"Beats me. Pull back again, I suppose."

"Oh, *no*—"

"What the hell else?"

Behind them in the bottom of the shell hole Carrington was bandaging the arm of a replacement named Torrance who had joined them only that morning, talking to him in a quiet, unhurried voice.

"Haven't got a thing to worry about. It's good and clean. Just hold that real tight."

"Should I take off now?" Torrance said shakily.

"No . . . I wouldn't take off now. May be better in a little while." Carrington turned to Marchand, who was holding an unbleached dressing to the side of his face. "Now let's have a look, Jack."

Helthal, sitting with his hands around his knees, said: "Let's pull back. What the hell."

"Not till we get the word from somebody," Capistron answered him; with his bayonet he chipped at the rim of mud around the soles of his shoes. "Stick around . . ."

Ahead of them the Horseshoe reared up like a shaggy wall, unsleeping and impassable: a ring of fire they could neither surmount nor evade, which lashed out at them each day with capricious impartiality and scorched them one by one . . . Newcombe looked back; huddled where he was on the leading edge of the crater he could see a strip of the beach at Nénetan—a fanned slice of glittering green-and-amber water beyond the reef where amtracks and ducks crept blackly. That little way. Three days and only that little way: *three days—!* He was swept with a sense of futility so great he felt like weeping, beating his hands in a frenzy against the cascao. How much of this did they think a man could take? an infinite amount—?

He glared wildly at Derekman; but Derekman was peering ahead and muttering through his teeth. "Over a barrel. Over a lousy, crudding barrel. We're never going to do it this way. Frontal deal. When the hell are they going to wise up?"

Shells sizzled overhead from the seventy-five battery at Nénetan, crashed in booming patterns high up on the face of the Horseshoe. Fellows came running from the front and slid into the hole, out of wind and gasping, and said, "Have you seen—Frey or Lundren?"

They shook their heads.

"We're pulling back. As we can. I sent. O'Neill for more smoke. We've got to have. More smoke." He looked at each of them: his face was gaunt and his eyes leaped nervously about. Directly overhead there was a burst like a quick, light clap of thunder, and a whorl of black smoke bloomed against the chaste azure of the sky.

"Time fire," Fellows said in agitation; licked his lips. "Jesus. We got to get out of here. They start in with that . . . We're pulling back," he shouted at them. "Now." Another thunderclap, nearer, and invisible bits of steel whizzed around them with falsetto moans. "Newcombe—you go on ahead with Torrance. We'll follow you—"

"Shut up a minute," Derekman said.

"What?"

Derekman held up his hand. Tensed, listening, they heard ahead of them and to their right a strange cry.

"What the hell is that?" Capistron said.

"Somebody in trouble." Derekman straightened, raised his head.

"Derekman," Fellows shouted at him, "don't stick your head—"

"Shut up."

"Buddyyyyy! . . ." The cry was high, rose to breaking point and fell away: an absurd, forlorn wail in the incessant roll and crash of gunfire. "Aw . . . *buddyyyyy!*"

"Jesus," Newcombe murmured. "Jesus. That's some poor bastard over there."

"Let's go over and get him," Derekman said. "What do you say, Al?"

"You're crazy," Fellows shouted. "Buddy, hell! It's a Nip routine, I'm telling you. Suck you out there and —"

"Shut up!"

"Buddy . . ." The voice came again, ghostly in its invisibility; it seemed everywhere around them, still more desolate and lost. "It's me . . . Maury . . . help a *buddyyyyy—*"

"It's Schulman," Derekman said with certainty. "Maury Schulman. I know it's Schulman, I can tell."

"Don't be a Goddamn fool, Derekman. You want to stop one in the head? That's just what they're waiting for!"

Derekman turned to Fellows with a hard little grin. "What do you care?"

"What?—I'm responsible for this squad, that's why—I'm damned if I can see you wandering around out there looking for somebody you don't even know if he's there . . ."

"Yeah, he's right," Capistron said, "we're in bad enough shape as it is."

Derekman paused and looked at them slowly. "So that's

how it is, ah? That's how it is." A small white spot appeared at the corner of each nostril; he spat angrily in front of him. "Semper Fi. Let him rot out there. Leave him for the Nips to cut up tonight. Is that it?"

"You get hit going over there and then who'll get you?" Helthal asked him in a dully curious tone.

Derekman's eyes narrowed to slits. "Not you, that's for sure. You lousy one-way son of a bitch—" He turned to Newcombe. Come on, Al. Let's get him."

"—You stay here!—both of you!" Fellows shouted hoarsely. "That's an order!"

Derekman looked at him with cold, immense hatred. "You shove it, Fellows. That's an order back. Come on, Al."

"All right."

"You're crazy, both of you, I tell you we've already got—"

Fellows' voice, threatening and hysterical, faded as they left the hole and ran to another, then another. The machine gun that had got Terrance and Marchand was silent. They lay panting, heard the wild, wavering cry again.

"More to the left," Derekman said. "What do you think?"

Newcombe nodded mutely. His gear felt impossibly heavy and cumbersome, his helmet far too prominent; his heart was slamming against the pressure of his suspenders like a pump gone crazy.

"Lousy son of a bitch. Leave his own mother to rot," Derekman said tightly.

Newcombe stared at him: it was only after a few seconds that he realized Derekman was referring to Fellows.

They ran in short, tandem dashes; again heard the cry, now violently loud and piercing—came all at once on the hole where Corporal Schulman—it was he—was lying doubled up, holding onto his legs. One foot was blown away at the instep, shoe and all: a blood-soaked pulp laced with chips of bone and tendon like little white wires. His broad, heavy-browed face was bathed in sweat and trembling; all his genial composure was gone.

"Harry, buddy," he cried in a pitiful, quavering croak. "I don't know what . . . Help me, Harry: give me a hand—"

"Right you are, Maury. Take it easy, now."

They secured a poncho to his and Newcombe's rifle, working quickly while Schulman gazed up at them, moaning feebly. Silence sank around them like smoke. Rain clouds loomed up behind Matenla in a gray, seething wall, swept over the sun.

"Rain," Derekman muttered. "All we need. Bastard." He was talking steadily to himself, the broken lump of his jaw white and hard. "Semper Fi, boy. Hope *he's* lying out here some one of these days: scream his chicken-livered guts out for all I care . . ."

Schulman broke out again in a series of sobbing moans. "Ah, Harry . . . what happened, Harry?" he cried. "What *happened* to me!"

"You stepped on something, Maury," Derekman answered tersely; and Newcombe saw that he was as harassed and fearful as he was himself. "You're in bad shape. Hang on, now . . ."

"Don't leave me, Harry . . . don't leave me here—"

"We'll get you back, Maury: I swear it. Just hang on, now." He looked up at Newcombe, his face slick with sweat. "Set?"

"Set."

They lifted Schulman on to the improvised stretcher. He gave a great gasping shriek and started sobbing wildly, "Ah, let me go, let me go—"

"All right, Maury, it's all right," Derekman cried. "Hang on, now—"

"Ah let me, I can't, ah I *can't* go with—"

"Hang on now, Goddamn it! Come on. We'll get you back there soon as we can . . ."

Rain started in fine patterns, hissing on the dead palm branches, the torn pieces of poncho. They lifted him; he shrieked, *"Ah God—!"* and his hands fell to the ground, dragging in the mud; his face rolled to the side.

Newcombe said, "Harry—"

"Passed out. Make it easier. Come *on*, for Christ sake—"

They lifted him again, slipping in the mud, bent low and staggered back to another hole and knelt in it, gasping, looking at each other apathetically. The machine gun was still silent. Toying with us, Newcombe thought: filthy sadist bastards!—what they want, play with us . . . They took off again in a panting, staggering crouch, Schulman's round head rolling and flailing against his chest, the shattered foot bloodying the strained poncho; a monstrous growing burden. This is what they've been waiting for. All this time. A fat bead on the base of your skull . . . He saw a horrid, bearded, oily oriental face grinning, squeezing in a leisurely caress the trigger, and felt his shoulder blades tighten in a spasm. A hole just under the helmet rim, a hole no bigger than an ink blot:

but in front, his face—Jesus. He could not fight the image
away.

On the next rush he slipped, felt a terrific surge of pain in
his left shoulder; went to his elbows and knees. Derekman was
looking back at him, his face wrinkled with urgency. "Come
on, Al, *let's go*—"

No cover. He forced himself up, lifted the rifles, groaning,
his head crooked in toward his collarbone with the pain, and
they made the shell hole. The machine gun opened up then in
a long, racketing burst and rifles crashed back in answering
fire.

"Asleep at the switch, you slope-head bastards," Derekman panted; he snarled at them between his teeth and spat in
their direction. "Had your chance, you motheraters . . ."

"I can't pick him up again," Newcombe said. "I pulled
something. I can hardly lift my arm."

"Jesus, they're right over *there*, Al . . ."

"I know. Yell for somebody. Carry or somebody. Yell for
'em. I can't do it."

"Okay." Derekman called, "Carry!"

"Yeah?"

"Come over!" He raised his hand. "Can you see me?"

"Yes."

"We got Maury. He's in rough shape. Come over!"

"Okay. In a minute . . ."

Newcombe sat huddled up holding his arm close to him: the
pain—a hot bright depthless pain—had taken the last ounce
of strength he owned, left him nauseous and shuddering.
Never should have tried it, he told himself. Never should have
got into this.

The rain came down in sweeping white streams, muted the
roar of the barrage.

There was no clean line of demarcation between sleep and
waking any more. Things kept crumbling into each other,
breaking in at the edges distressingly. The days, the nights extended in a viscous interminability in which the connection
between admonition and consequence kept faltering: the lines
had been shorted, somehow. You must put halezone in your
canteen because—because . . . because then you won't get
dysentery. (But you have dysentery anyway.) You must watch
to the rear as well as forward because—because . . .because
Japs had infiltrated the night before. (But that was the night
before.) The Japs had infiltrated because . . . because . . . The

lines sputtered and shorted, labored on.

"Al: Al!"

A hand would clutch his leg and he would heave himself clawing up through layers of drugged exhaustion, his eyelids puffed and burning with a thousand mosquito bites, and gaze stupidly at the ghostly, dimensionless blob that was O'Neill, listen—barely comprehending—to the insistent whisper:

"Al. Time to take over . . . You awake?"

"Yes. Yeah: I'm awake."

His mind and his body couldn't seem to work together. They were like two stray dogs in a lightless alley, watching each other with savage distrust: on the verge of flying at each other's throats. His body had already buckled his belt, checked his grenades and picked up his rifle: his mind however had no intention of doing any of these things—stood apart with a sullen, evil smile.

". . . Oh." His bowels clutched at him, released momentarily, gripped him again: a quick, hot, violent pain that made him gasp and bend double. That was why his mind had smiled so evilly: it knew his body couldn't do it, either—

"What's the matter, Al?"

"I got the runs again. I've got to take off. Take it for a couple minutes more, will you? just a couple?"

"Sure. Got 'em real bad?"

"Worse yet."

He pulled the cord—three slow, distinct pulls—crawled out of their foxhole and crept into the brush toward the rear, realized he would never make it to the one-two-three trench at the foot of the little gully and crouched under a banyan tree among some shrubs. Something brushed his neck and he startled, flicked whatever it was away irritably. His entrails griped and griped inside him—let go with a fierce burning spasm that made him groan; sweat broke out on his chest and back and his legs trembled so badly he had to support himself with his hands. His shoulder throbbed as though it had been transfixed by a cold bar of iron.

"Oh God," he groaned softly. "Oh, my God . . ." He was conscious of voices murmuring tensely nearby, then of nothing but the pain: his very innards were streaming out of him, all his organs in a boundless, convulsive debilitation until he would collapse in the dark. Bad: it was bad to be this weak. He'd have to try to bum some more paregoric from Carry in the morning, anything to stop this hot, sickly—

There was a sudden burst of firing so close beside him his

heart stopped. Tracers sprayed in the shower of orange wires above him, smashed into the palm trees, the banyan, sang over his head.

"Lillian!" he screamed into the firing. "Lil-ee-an! . . . I'm taking a crap!" he shouted wildly. "I'm Newcombe taking a crap! Newcombe!—Lil-ee-an! . . ."

The firing stopped all at once. He was lying flat, naked against the cold earth, his trousers around his ankles. "Trigger-happy bastards," he muttered, almost sobbing; his teeth were chattering uncontrollably inside his head. "Blast their own mothers . . ."

He crept stumbling on hands and knees through the brush—realized he had lost his orientation completely. Jesus. Vines and leaves brushed his face like wet, filthy hands. In a panic he lurched to his feet and stood sweating and trembling, peering wildly about.

"—He pulled the cord," O'Neill was shouting in a voice savage with anxiety. "But you didn't know that, did you?—because you didn't have a hold of it, no—because you were crapped out again, you no-good goof-off son of a bitch! . . . By the Jesus, Hethal, if you—Al!" he called. "Al! You all right?"

"Yeah," Newcombe gasped. He was shaking so his legs would hardly move; orange-glowing tracers whizzed before his eyes—a cosmos run amok and crashing. "Yeah, I'm fine . . . You stupid bastards," he yelled suddenly at the dark. "You stupid, stupid bastards!—"

It was a cold, damp substance that tasted sourly of eggs. It wasn't, of course: any more than anything else was anything else. That was the game—a macabre game in which nothing bore any relation to anything previously experienced, despite the odious pretensions of appearance. Newcombe dug at it apathetically with his knife, forced it down mouthful by mouthful while the light around them quickened in still, swift measures—revealed the face of O'Neill hunched beside him, eating too: a gaunt and alien mask, bearded, filthy beyond belief, with eyes that darted like bits of mirror. Jay had winked at him, but the wink bore no more relation to Jay—the Jay he had drunk and sparred and reminisced with—than anything else. Changed: they had been changed utterly, by some force as swift and malevolent as Circe's wand: a race of numbed, exhausted beasts in holes, wolfing mechanically the tasteless contents of green metal tins. His fingers, extended before him, were caked with mud except for the nails, which stared back at him obscenely, like vacant, fleshy eyes—

He shut his hand and looked away. There was something, he thought with weary urgency, almost with distress, *something* I—

But it had vanished before he could recall what it had been: he knew he could never recall it. What difference did it make? But if they had to go up there again, up into that Horseshoe—

He shut the thought out of his mind with all his might, went on eating, scraping the edges of the tin. His shoulder ached to the bone, and his bowels kept dragging at him, bending him double. Faces, figures around him stooped and straightened, stood up or reclined, raised food to their mouths in maudlin, inane repetition: contemptible and disgusting. But when he closed his eyes worse terrors came, vomited forth on charred and bubbling legs, flung high bleeding bony stumps of limbs, faces swept with agony and a hand clawed wildly at his nose, his eyes—

He found himself gazing in hungry fixation at Woodruff's placid visage, watched doggedly while Woodruff grinned at him, sagely opined, "Well now, I don't believe I ever ate a meal tasted so downright nourishing in all my cottonpicking life . . ."

The talk bore no relation, either: to itself or anything else. But it was something to snatch at, cling to as a point of anchorage in the warm, still air.

"That stew is good, you know? Considering it's cold. Mighty good, son."

"Considering it's cold and canned and made out of road apples."

"—half shot, I suppose . . ."

"Imagine! Talking *out loud*. Wouldn't have seen them at all if one of them hadn't said something."

"Probably half-shot on saki."

"I wouldn't mind being half-shot right about now."

"Hell, I'd settle for a cup of hot coffee. I mean."

"Did you hear?—they sent old Herron down yesterday."

"Oh Christ. That's all we need."

"—got Tico. You know, Garcia. Nip jumped him with a knife: got him in the back and Tico choked him to death. With his bare hands. They had to pull him off him."

"Jesus. Last night?"

"That's right. Just before Danny and I got those three."

"What the hell were they doing cutting across in *front* of our lines if they broke through?"

"Beats me. They're just as fouled up as we are, I guess."

"I hear we go back in reserve today."

Several heads turned.

"Where'd you hear that?"

"Larue. Said he got it from Morlecki."

"*That* makes it authentic!"

"Straight skinnay—"

"Well, we Goddamned well *ought* to be in reserve . . ."

"What you ought to be isn't what you get in this outfit, Jack."

"What do you think, Danny?" Ricarno asked in an anxious tone.

Kantaylis bit his lower lip. "Steve said to stand by to move out."

"Move out—! Move out where?"

"Beats. Horseshoe again, I suppose."

"But we've had five *days*—"

Newcombe wiped the blade of his knife on his trouserleg, shoved it back in its sheath. A blank shell was revolving with painful slowness inside his head: so still, so clear it presaged something imminent and dreadful which he could not avoid. It would burst out of the front of his mind on some subsequent revolution, spring forth full-armed and baleful, like Athene, and cut him down. It tossed things forth without sequation, idly. The better the day the worse the deed, it tossed, with crafty irrelevance. Hell in all its storming legions could not . . . could not what? The gaudy, blabbing and remorseful day is crept into. Crept into. Though hell should bar the way. And fire purge all things new . . .

"How you doing, Al?"

Old Jay: a poor old man, as full of grief as age . . . The lines from nose to mouth were incised with eyebrow pencil: a garish theatrical touch that amused him faintly. But only for a moment.

Lundren was coming toward them, massive and bulking in his gear, accompanied by Captain Frey; coming like doom itself, their faces set and stony, lips compressed. Watching them draw near, hearing the conversation falter and die, his heart fell away. He knew if he didn't look down and brush at his rifle he would start to weep.

"Give me back!" Connor cried. Helmetless, without pack

or weapon he swayed before them in the sinking twilight, shaking his head in a slow, dazed, ineffectual protest. The entire left side of his face twitched rhythmically; tears streaked the mud on his cheeks, where there was still no beard, only a faint silvery down. "Ah, give it back—"

"It's all right, Chicken," Kantaylis, who was holding him, said gently. "It's okay. Hang on, now . . ."

"Our own patrol!" Fellows shouted at him. "Our own people! You crazy, *crazy* son of a bitch—!" He whirled around, said between his teeth, "Just get him out of here. Get him out of here. He's crazy . . ."

"Give me my rifle!" Connor screamed.

"Rifle, hell! You won't ever *see* a rifle again . . . What the Christ were you trying to do—get us all killed?"

"Take it easy, Fellows," Lundren said. "No one got hurt."

"No, a Goddamn miracle—"

"All right." Lundren studied Connor for a moment. "Well," he said mournfully. "He'll have to go down. Harry, you or Jay go down with him, will you? I don't want him wandering around by himself. Tell them I said it's okay."

Connor's head went up. "Ah, you can't!" he cried. *"Don't* make me . . . I'm as good—I'm just as good . . ."

He subsided all at once in short gasping moans, still obstinately shaking his head. Shells swept overhead with a tearing shuttling sound and crashed in jungle off to their right, and the twilight deepened.

"It's all right, Chicken," Kantaylis repeated in the low, crooning tone. "It's all over, now. Let's go."

"—No!" Connor violently shook off Kantaylis' grip but stood there without moving; disconsolate, weeping, imploring them all. "Ah, don't send me . . . Just because I—you think I can't—"

"All right, Chick," Derekman said; he came up and took him by the arm as Kantaylis had. "Take it easy, now. You need a rest, Chick."

"I'm just as good—"

"Sure you are."

Connor looked at them, bewildered; his face kept jerking and twitching grotesquely in the falling light. He dropped his head and moaned: "Ah you *can't*—you guys . . . I kept going, I did every . . . You guys think—"

"We don't think anything, Chick. Let's go, now."

"Yes you do, you do! You think I—"

They moved off down the trail, Derekman on one side of

him, holding him loosely. At the edge of the perimeter Connor turned around, his face thin and wild, his mouth drawn down with grief.

"No!" he screamed, sobbing, wagging his head. "Ah no . . . You *can't*—send me down!—"

The figure lay on its back. The hands were blown away, the guts spilled in bloodied pearly chains around the feet: a gaping hole through which bits of rib protruded like carved ivory splinters.

"Blew himself up," Capistron said. "When Harry hit him in the legs."

Standing in a little ring they looked down at the dead Japanese sprawled not twenty feet behind their holes.

"Thank God you spotted him, Harry. He'd have had the whole lot of us."

"Name of the game . . ."

"Jesus," Woodruff said softly. "I couldn't do that. Jesus."

"You think that took guts?" O'Neill said.

"Sure I do . . ."

"The hell it did. He just couldn't stand the gaff. They do it every time they get in a squeeze."

"Maybe it's part of their religion," Newcombe said.

"Maybe so. It's one hell of a religion, then. Life isn't as cheap as all that . . ."

"What the hell, Jay," Derekman said. "He was gone, anyway. We'd have got him: he probably knew it."

"Okay—but he knew where *we* were by then, too. Why didn't he give you that grenade? What's so rugged about blowing your own guts out when you know you're going to go anyway? why not at least take two or three with you on the way down?" O'Neill prodded one of the dead man's feet with his gently. "Son of a bitch took the easy way out—"

Newcombe, silent, gazed at the shattered mass of flesh already swarming with flies. Why play the Roman fool? A point: a point in fact. Play the chance against the adverse sure thing. Ah, but death was everywhere, hovered silently around them. Sacrifice and violence in one fierce embrace. Dulce et decorum. Happy those, who with a glowing faith . . . Jesus. Wretched, wretched. It was not sweet to die: it wasn't sweet at all. And fitting—! To come to this—a maggot-ridden substance consigned to putrefaction, breeding pestilence in season, out of season . . . Nausea rose in his gorge again; he turned away slowly. No: they can never sell us on this as human destiny. Never again. No matter what they do. There is a world elsewhere . . .

"I don't rightly know," Woodruff was drawling gravely. "I just wouldn't have the guts to do that. I know I wouldn't . . ."

"Nothing I can do for him," Carrington said. Kneeling over Sergeant Hansen's still-quivering body he shrugged, flipped his thumbs outward from the wrists: an umpire's gesture.

"Hansen too, for God's sake." Fellows gazed feverishly at where the cropped blond hair ended in a jagged crater oozing blood and brains. "Hansen too . . ." More shells fell behind them in the strip of jungle and in the open ground ahead: desultory, aimless, wandering death. At each shellburst Fellows' eyelids twitched and his head jerked in a little spasm. Newcombe, crouched in the same hole watching him, found himself becoming steadily more afraid and looked away.

"Ah, my God." Fellows waved an arm distractedly. It'll be all of us next, that's what. They don't care if they kill us *all* off, one by one. They don't care . . ." His voice broke off on a high, rasping note, was drowned in a thunderous detonation that made them all cringe. "Leave us here till there isn't a single . . . Newcombe!" He whirled around. "Where are O'Neill and Woodruff and the others?"

Newcombe shook his head uncertainly. The sight of Fellows' slack, dead-white face—the haunted eyes, the voice borne on an ascending hysteria—filled him with personal dread.

"I don't know," he muttered.

"Goddamn it, I *told* you to keep contact with them!—at all cost. I *told* you this morning when we took off—"

"Take it easy, Fellows." Lundren, sitting calmly at the very bottom of the crater, his left forearm made still more huge by a sleeve of tightly wound gauze, spoke in deep, sonorous tones. "He did the best he could. You can't keep contact with all this going on . . ."

"I don't care, I give him a job to do he corks off on it—" Fellows broke off himself, glanced away; his eyes fell on Hansen again. "For God sake, cover his head, *cover his head!*" he shouted at Newcombe. ". . . They don't care, they're perfectly willing to leave us here till there isn't one of us left, not one!—"

"Take it easy, Fellows." Lundren's face, seamed and pounded and now glazed with exhaustion, was like a tribal death mask from some remote people; his little eyes were hardly visible. His great shoulders drooped wearily. He paused, said in a low, mournful voice, "The Book says, To everything there is a season, and a time to every purpose under the heaven. A time to—"

"Tells you everything—that book, doesn't it?" Fellows said with sudden shrill violence. "Does it tell you who's going to get it next?—does it tell you *that?*"

"The Book says, A thousand shall fall at thy side, and ten thousand at thy right hand; but it shall not come nigh thee."

"Ah—so you're the lucky one are you, ah? the elect—!"

"Take it easy, Fellows." Lundren still watched him calmly, mournfully. "You know better than that . . . It's not for us to quarrel with the word of Jehovah . . ."

"For Christ sake!" Fellows screamed over a shellburst. "Fuck your book, Lundren!—you hear me? I said *fuck* your b—"

Lundren moved with a swiftness that amazed them. There was a flat slap as he struck Fellows' carbine out of his hand. Seizing the sergeant by the collar Lundren swept him up close to him so that their heads were not three inches apart.

"You close your mouth, Fellows! Don't get me going." His little eyes were hard as onyx stones, with glinting lights at their centers. "I don't want to get angry at you, Fellows." He held him another moment in a grip of iron, shaking him slowly back and forth; then relaxed his hold and set him back on his feet. "Now don't say that again to me. You get hold of yourself, now. We've got a long hard way to go yet . . . If you've gone and turned from the Word of God that's your business. But don't you curse the Book to me again. Ever! Understand?"

He released Fellows and the fierce little lights in his eyes fell away. "Bruce," he said to a thin, gangling man in the hole with them. "Soon as this lets up a little take off over to the left of that smashed-up tank and see if you can run onto somebody that knows something."

"All right, Steve." Bruce licked his lips, moved up the forward slope of the hole and waited. The sound of automatic rifle fire drifted down, dry and dusty, from the hills around them.

There was the open place without a tree or a bush and then

the slope, slimy with mud and the passage of all those who had gone before. Newcombe crouched panting on one knee between the two water cans, his hands resting on their tubular grips. His shoulder burned so savagely he could hardly think of anything else. Ahead of him Ricarno scuttled into the open ground, laden with box of grenades, passed the very spot where the sniper had hit Caylor the day before and proceeded up the rise in a violent, slithering, slipping pantomime which should have been funny, *would* have been funny long ago—something right out of Harold Lloyd. He failed to laugh, however: remained on one knee, panting, watched Ricarno finally gain the crest and slump exhausted behind a little hummock covered with dead and blasted vegetation and the burned-out chassis of a Japanese officer's car.

Now. Come on. And don't let up, don't let up—

He lurched to his feet, felt the agonizing pain race up his forearm and across his shoulder and back like the lash of a whip, ran across the open space, eyes rigidly in front of him, and staggered up the rise; felt his feet go out from under him as though swept away by a malicious hand. He was on his knees in the ooze, still gripping the cans, was sliding helplessly, ludicrously down to the bottom. Ah God. A lone shell arched over with a shrill whistling drone. He let go of the cans, got to his feet, picked up the cans again and worked his way upward in an ungainly, crablike walk, a paroxysm of effort, sobbing the air into his lungs—slipped and went to one knee again but this time checked his descent with hands and feet; felt the warm wet streaming inside his trouserlegs, and was swept with raging mortification and helplessness. So weak! Bastard, bastard, bastard . . . The shrill whistling came again—a fresh variation—resolved itself in a bomb-crash in the jungle to his right. From behind the hummock of land Ricarno watched him anxiously, swept his arms up in a quick, exhortative gesture. So Goddamn *weak*—

He heaved himself up again, clawing for his footing, drove stumbling up the rest of the slope now frankly dragging the unendurable weight of the water cans and collapsed beside Ricarno, utterly spent, racked with nausea and quaking debility. Red rings burst and uncoiled against his eyelids. He knew he could not get up for a full minute on any condition whatever. He *had* a minute, though, he knew, with almost tearful exultation: or nearly a minute anyway, until Bruce followed them up the slope with the case of chow. Ricarno was saying something to him but he was only half conscious of the words. God help me, he thought: I'll get this water back up there and that's all I can do. All I can ever do again. No matter what they say . . .

Bruce arrived beside them, gasping, panting words. Ricarno left again. After another minute Newcombe hauled himself to his feet. Cover now: they had thick shaggy blessed cover the rest of the way. Along a path which forked, curved up to the right past shelterhalves, holes, torn ponchos, empty faces turning, regarding them with an indifference so great it was almost hostility, to the little clearing where the wrecked tank stood, their landmark: an oval clearing littered with crushed water cans and splintered boxes, on one of which a figure sat with his head in his hands, and a long furrow torn in his helmet through which the fabric of the liner showed; staring, dazed and sightless, at the ground between his feet.

Ah, the road to hell is beset with the evils that call themselves reality, that interpose their foul presences between man and the serene vision: lie heaped layer on layer, vicious and implacable, conjoint with all manner of suffering and despair . . .

They were moving downhill in driving rain: stumbling and slipping stiff-jointed through a landscape of horror and debris. The earth swept up and down beneath his feet in lurching, uncertain waves, mocked his sickness and exhaustion, toyed with him in his debility. For nothing could ever be the same again: ever. The sun no bigger than the moon had crashed in darkness, trees hung inverted underwater, houses, vehicles, human beings drifted by in a dolorous trance that never closed their eyes—screaming soundlessly, all of them, in a dark nausea of solitary cells without appurtenances of hope or love. All were doomed, all guilty and forsaken . . .

They had stopped: they were huddled under a piece of corrugated metal on which the rain beat with a high metallic roar, covered the world with dense silvery streaks. But it was not real, either: it was all fraud and charlatanry, dancing about him in a gibbering masquerade, trying to induce him to believe. How could it fob itself off as reality? The revolving shell was turning again, like a cement mixer, spewed forth Klumanski rolling in anguish, rolling and writhing, Diebenkorn crying in thick, fuzzy moans, the cratered horror of Hansen's head—a sickening montage of smashed bones and spilled viscera and steel baited with blued guts, screams and blood-red frothing rage and clammy fear . . . What *stupidity!* It could not be: he would not let it, that was all.

None of it existed, all were the passes of subjective imagination screaming—idiocy and lies, all of it, lies and idiocy this vault to brag of and there was no need to accept any of it, needed only to be willed out of existence, *willed away*—

. . . Someone was talking to them: insistently. A clean white face, clean-shaven, with an uncovered helmet and a clean map-carrying case. The mouth adorned with a neat black mustache in a slight droop. Bright black darting eyes. Talking and talking: a voice brightly conversational and absurd.

Newcombe was surprised to find he was holding a cigarette in his hand: a clean white smooth round cylinder that said spencerian *Chesterfield*. The fingers that held it looked like slimy shaking claws. O'Neill had one, too: they all had them. The man with the clean white face was passing them out.

"What's going on up there?" he was saying. "You've just come down from the Horsehoe, haven't you? Been pretty rough up there, hasn't it?"

His mustache moved up and down when he talked: an eerie black bandage. Newcombe stared at him with dulled uncertainty . . . A correspondent. That was what he was. The white cellophaned pack of cigarettes he had passed around had disappeared. He was holding a pad in his hand now; was asking them what the situation was up there, what were the principal areas of resistance.

"Principal areas!" O'Neill said. "What do you mean, *principal areas?* The whole frigging place . . ."

The correspondent laughed easily, his white teeth a pleasant, even line; his mustache wavered and drooped in the rain. Clever weasel face. Newcombe felt a prodigious, burgeoning hatred for him.

"The press, the press, we must respect the freedom of the press," he chanted all at once.

The correspondent turned his head toward him and said, *"What?"*

"Oh, yes the press we must impress, we can't suppress and cause distress without finesse, we must undress and then confess—caress the blessèd, blessèd, press—"

The correspondent was scowling now: looking at him narrowly. "Now, look, I just wanted to ask you men a few questions . . ."

A tired, patient, long-suffering voice: the voice of parent, governess, mentor, patron. The voice of universal au-dessus. Newcombe stared hatefully at him, said: "Teacher spank."

The correspondent turned to the others. "What's the matter with *him?*"

"There isn't a Goddamned thing wrong with him," O'Neill said. He leaned forward, his eyebrows raised. "You want to know what's really going on up there, mister?"

"Of course. That's why I—"

"Then hike your ass up there and find out!"

The correspondent looked at him in amazement.

"Go ahead," O'Neill shouted at him. "You want to find out, go ahead—"

"Take it easy, Jay," Kantaylis said with a note of warning.

"—spend a few days up there, nothing to it, all we been doing is lie around on our dead asses . . ."

"Don't take that attitude, Marine," the correspondent said. "I'm just out here to get the story, that's all . . ." He offered with soft conciliation: "Wouldn't you like your name in the papers back home?"

"Oh Jesus, yes—that's all I need," O'Neill burst out savagely. "My name—listen, you simple tool, I've been busting my hump for seven days to keep my name *out* of the Goddamned papers—"

"But your folks back home want to know what's going on, don't you—"

"Don't hand me that! I know what the folks back home want to know. Shove off!"

"Now just a minute, Marine—"

"I said *shove off!*" O'Neill leaped to his feet with amazing agility, pulled the Nambu pistol out of his belt. "You think that kind of talk cuts any ice with us? Get out of the road—!"

"Jay!" Kantaylis said sharply. "Put it away."

O'Neill lowered the pistol, but shouted: "I mean it: take off! Go get someone else to do your dirty work for you! . . ."

The correspondent splashed off through the mud and rain, looked back at them once wildly, disbelieving; hurried on again. Vanished around a turn in the trail. O'Neill was still standing with the pistol, glaring after him and raging on about big-deal stateside bloodsuckers; the tasseled hilt of the samurai sword stuck out behind his neck like a mad, phallic totem. A ludicrous scene, perhaps—but it didn't matter, it had not happened either, it drifted along with the trees and bloated corpses underwater, outside reality . . .

Someone had tapped him on the arm. They were moving again, walking in the rain and muck and dying light. The world was dying, the light of the world; the road to hell was an interminable march through fetid, malignant jungle that leaned and leaned, and thrust him down—

He had fallen, was sliding foolish and mealsack-limp in the ooze; felt it sluice against his face and neck. Someone was helping him up again. Woodruff: gazing at him in round-eyed consternation and mouthing soothing drawling southern sounds. Insufferable idiot swamp rat! He flung Woodruff's hand off, glared at him in a transport of rage and turned away, filled with shame and nameless anguish. He was on the verge of weeping, shut his eyes—beheld in an instant the ever-attendant host of leering, screaming hobgoblins with the honeycomb eyes of flies dancing before him. Horrors. I have supped with horrors . . . but they are not real, any of them: the only reality is . . .

The only reality is—

But he could not say. It was sadly, monstrously true: he could not tell what the only reality was. After all the courses, the lectures and term papers and texts, all the earnest and devoted inquiry in the still, humming small hours of the night he could not answer this. Perhaps he had been studying the wrong things, then: the peripheries, the outward shows—the effects, in short: not the actual verities . . . perhaps these earnest labors had borne the same relationship to the truth of things that his pseudo-sophisticated, pseudo-affectionate, pseudo-mature liaison with Sue possessed in contrast to what he and Helen had between them—

Ah Helen. Ah Helen if you—

Perhaps he would never know: doubtless that was one of the penalties of bestiality—you were made to move out on the high road to hell without sufficient equipment to combat the leering hobgoblins, the demons charged with driving you down and down till all the rings in hell had been traversed and scoured . . .

There was a clearing: a chow line rigged under tarps where figures bent and straightened, reached out and ladled and poured. "Bakery," Jay was saying. "Fresh bread." And at the same moment the thick, sweet, hot odor reached him.

"Bread?" he murmured.

"Yeah." O'Neill was looking at him: Jay, old buddy Jay, thin as a scarecrow, with eyes bright and fevered behind the mask of mud and dust, the mad orange stubble of beard. Vincent self-portrait, with helmet. But of course all *he'd* lost was an ear: and his sanity.

But fresh bread—

He had a canteen cup full of steaming coffee: rain was falling into it, cratered it with huge drops. And half a loaf of bread, hot and spongy in his hand. He slipped it under his blouse, felt its soft warmth against his skin.

They were under a corner of a tarp, several of them, leaning back against some crates. It was raining again and getting darker, but it didn't matter. The coffee burned his lips, descended in a warm, expanding column to his stomach; and the starved clutching of his belly dulled and slowed. He tore off a piece of the bread and put it in his mouth, chewed it marveling. Fresh bread. A warm, sweet redolence: he had never tasted anything so good in all his life. He become conscious of voices around him, gestures and intonations, the lettering on the crates. GUBA, they said in neat black stenciling: GUBA 93. A hugely comical dictum. His senses returned, expanded in one slow, ardent throb of recalled sensation: an afternoon long, long ago, sitting on the porch railing of the house at Marshfield, swinging his bare feet, eating one by one a succession of chocolate cookies and listening to the faint, magical tinkling of the Chinese wind-bells that, turning slowly in the sunlight, cast their shifting spectral patterns along the porch floor; a pure, fugitive serenity that had held him enraptured, almost afraid to move . . . He sank his teeth into the dough, felt it pressing soft and delightful against his gums; chewed it slowly, in felicity. It was so unbelievably good—and *real:* it was so *real*—

He paused, his mouth open. This was reality, too. This also, of course, was reality . . .

He frowned in sudden bewilderment, closed his eyes. The hot cooked bread seeped into his consciousness with a gentle reassurance that lulled him. But then—but then if all that other was not real, neither was this . . . Yet here it was, soothing and restorative and infinitely good. Balm in Gilead. And if this was reality, then so was *that*—! wasn't it? Ah God, wasn't it?

Tears stung his eyelids; he felt them run down his cheeks, slip suddenly salt into the corners of his mouth. The rain thundered on the tarp. Jay, old fidus Achates of a sempiternity of hours—Jay crouched beside him was reality, too: was he to deny him at cockcrow, after the Armageddon they had endured together? Ah Jay, he thought with weary maudlin affection, in the name of all we've both endured, the succor and comfort we've given each other, I would die rather than deny you, gladly die . . .

No. Accept it all: accept it all, both terrors and delights. What other conclusion was there? what other honorable course?

Yet the bread. This bread. In his perplexity and exhaustion the tears still streamed down his cheeks; his throat swelled. Little comfort in the grave. For those of us who ain't so brave, there's little comfort . . . He thought of Helen with a pang of sheer longing that was greater than ever: she swam before his eyes invested with a sad, concerned gravity, a love that never wavered, obscured though she was by the thousand flitting hobgoblin horrors that spilled out of the churning shell of his mind, danced and screamed and confounded his spirit, left it reeling, without peace. What was truth? what was reality—when the mere lees, the mere lees is left this vault to brag of lighted fools to dusty death?

He couldn't accept them: couldn't, couldn't accept them as reality. To do that was a betrayal of—a betrayal of . . . Bewildered and numb he went on eating the soft, hot bread, sipped at the tart coffee.

"Take it easy, Al." Jay was gazing at him with mournful, gray concern, his eyes haggard and wide. "Take it easy, old-timer . . ."

Old Jay: you and I, we've traversed the horrors of this earth, the bottom rings of hell; and here we sit—

He shook his head, went on weeping soundlessly; watched the rain sweep in silvery sheets over the ragged, blasted wall of jungle.

6

IN THE LATE afternoon stillness the Poplar leaves swung slowly on their stems, in quick dull flashes of silver. The sea was a metallic blue beyond the dunes. Down in the garden a cicada started its harsh, rattling whir, carried it to a clamorous, almost unbearable crescendo—fell away in silence. And the sound of the sea once more returned. Sitting motionless in one of the rockers on the long verandah Charlotte Newcombe gazed at the sea, the distant dunes and thought: He's on Faneráhan. He's on that island. Right now.

I can't seem to think of anything else but that.

Clouds lay low along the horizon, coming in bulbous silver rolls like silken sails. There would be a breeze later, perhaps rain. One of the croquet wickets was still planted in the lawn at the far end near the wall; Amory and Iris had missed it last night in the dusk. It looked foolish and yet somehow oddly menacing: a kind of spidery trap, a signal. Tom Morison had caught his foot in one three years ago and gone sprawling, had pulled all sorts of tendons in his leg. Everyone had laughed at first. Odd: how at certain moments the ludicrous and the tragic fused, how one's sense of perspective—

Iris was coming down the stairs: clump-*clump:* clump-*clump:* clump-*clump.* Two at a time, turned sidewise, she had always descended stairs that way, her hands held up before her; ever since she was little. Strange how people never relinquished certain mannerisms, certain habits . . . She heard her moving about in the front hall, then her voice:

"Mother?"

"Out here," she answered.

Iris came out on the verandah. "You mean there wasn't any mail at *all?*"

"No. An ad and several duns."

Iris made no reply, went up to the railing and stared out at the bay. The cicada wound up again—an idiotic atonal siren, still louder this time, died away in a harsh suspiration. Like a death rattle, Charlotte Newcombe thought; like a mechanical imitation of a death rattle.

"Oh, that animal!" Iris exclaimed; she slapped the porch railing with her hand. "Honestly, isn't there *any* way to get rid of them?"

"I've never known any."

"They're just manic. They ought to be wiped out . . . *Listen* to that!" In the low heels and short skirt and with her hair long, nearly to her shoulders, she looked very much the way she had when she'd gone off to school: as though no college or marriage or war had ever intervened at all. Watching her Charlotte Newcombe thought, Time is strange: time is nothing we think it is, somehow. Nor parenthood or love or anguish. All are disguised and we see only the bland, sub-stanceless masks we choose to see.

Still frowning at the bay Iris said: "Oh, why don't they *write,* Mother? What's the *matter* with them?"

Charlotte Newcombe looked up calmly, rearranged her

hands on her lap. "Well, I imagine there just hasn't been the opportunity for writing."

"But there must be! They're not marching or having inspections or flying planes every *minute* of the time. I know that much. They sit around in PX's and clubs and things, you see pictures of them sitting around and relaxing . . . I know Alan never used to write at all—months and months and then a long tome full of all kinds of wild literary allusions you couldn't even follow half the time, he despises short notes, I know. But Ted used to write every day before we were married. Every other day, at the *least* . . ."

Charlotte Newcombe regarded her daughter, passed her eyes over the clear, sharp profile, the dark hair, the bright, scintillant, nervous gaze; and thought, She doesn't feel anything, really. Not really. It hasn't touched her. Her worry is superficial: it's not deep in her vitals. Perhaps that's youth; or the difference between lovers and parents—

She said aloud, "I imagine they're very tired and very busy and they just can't settle their thoughts."

"But just a few lines to let a person know . . ."

"Perhaps it's impossible, Iris. If they've been on ships for a long time—"

"But they must stop *somewhere* . . ." Iris peered into the hedge a moment, scowling, chewing on her lower lip; turned all at once and said, "Let's go over to the beach."

"No, I don't think I will," Charlotte Newcombe said. "You go on if you want to."

"Oh come on, Mother: it'd do us good, get us out of the house—"

"No," she repeated, a bit sharply. "Why don't you go in to the store? Didn't you say you had errands?"—regretted instantly the tone of exacerbation. There was no need for that, she ought not to lash out at the girl, heaven knew she had troubles enough of her own . . . Am I getting to be an old woman? she wondered: a crochety old woman with lace cuffs and a gold-headed cane, like Grandma Brewster? It's only that today—

Iris had fallen silent. After a moment she said, "I'm sorry, Mother. I didn't mean to upset you."

"You didn't, dear. You didn't. It's all right. I'm tired today, I guess. It's just today . . . I want to be by myself a little, that's all."

"Sure." Iris bent over and kissed her lightly on the forehead, then the cheek: an ancient ritual that touched her strangely. "I'll go on in, then . I've got to get some shampoo and a couple of other things. My hair's full of salt. Driving me perfectly crazy. Nail polish remover." She extended a row of fingertips on which the nail polish had chipped and flaked away in scabrous vermilion patterns. "Look at that. A sight . . . Well, who cares. Do you need anything?"

"Yes. We're out of Kleenex. I don't know why."

Charlotte Newcombe listened remotely, vacuously, to Iris walking away down the gravel drive: the quick, martellato stride, like Amory's. Kleenex, she thought: Kleenex. We don't have any idea what they're going through: no idea at all.

A bell struck softly in the distance: ceased. Three o'clock. Amory would be home soon. There were so many things to do . . . But now, she knew with a clarity informed by dread, now was no time for any of it. If she could sit here for a time, quietly, in the shade and watch the sea, the silver clouds unfurling, and come to some firm, meaningful conclusions about things . . .

She could not. She simply could not. The newspaper this noon had shattered it: her ability to think in a serene, ordered progression of ideas, proceed from step to step . . . But why this sudden cold despair?—she knew he was on that island, had known for days: why this hollow aching dread that held her bound so? It was the picture, she thought, protesting, querulous, the picture—

The picture was impactual, yet indistinct. The caption beneath it read: FANERAHAN BEACHHEAD: *As our forces move inland on enemy positions*. Charlotte Newcombe stared at it quietly, holding the folded paper in two hands; peered closer. There seemed to be a strip of clearing—or what could pass for clearing—where shattered coconut palms stood like blasted scarecrows. In the right foreground were some vehicles, boats like tanks, or tanklike boats—and a welter of crushed boxes and cans and what looked like old rumpled pieces of fabric. And debris and more debris in such profusion it assaulted the sight. And through and over this preposterous jumble—she could see them now, as though a glass had been brought slowly into focus—figures, helmeted and slovenly and dejected, crawled like some species of baffled and ineffectual insect, struggling toward something they could never hope to find; as though, gazing at this awesome, insuperable morass their very spirits failed them.

It was beyond any doubt the most overwhelming confusion she had ever seen in her whole life. Still staring at it with a

fascination she knew was morbid, an apprehension of boundless measure began to seep into all four corners of her mind.
Lost. They were all lost, all overwhelmed by chaos and fury.
Fury and chaos. *Hard-bitten marine veterans have called this
the hottest beachhead of the entire Pacific war, including
Tarawa and Saipan.* At this moment—at this very instant
Alan—was what? doing what? Had he crawled up that hummock, climbed through that shattered, riotous waste, those
rag-doll blotches of fabric? . . . Dead bodies. Those were
men's dead bodies—

She closed the paper on her thumb. The most dark and
direful thoughts she had ever known came in flapping legions,
assaulted her like a troop of cavalry crashing through a glass
shop-front. She felt dizzy, unprotected, inundated with a
sense of desolation so great she felt as if her soul were
foundering. The war: yes, the war, men were dying, of course,
men ran here and there giving orders and went out to die—but
this was not war, this was the end of clarity, the end of the
world, in which nothing, no single thing was sacrosanct or
safe—

Ah dear God.

Not Alan.

She almost leaped to her feet, walked rapidly, blindly,
along the verandah and down to the garden, tried to fix her
mind on the feathery patterns of witch grass and bayberry, the
still blue swath of ocean. Somehow—ah, dear God—not
Alan, in the midst of that uncaring chaos. He would be alone
and unharmed, untouched, would return pale and gaunt and
silent, hurt inwardly perhaps but not. *Ah God,* not—

But the picture behind her on the porch gave her no solace:
there again were the blasted trees, the incomprehensible welter
of the wrecked and shattered equipment strewn in a blinding
light—

I—see—light, he had said: as a baby, nearly the first thing
he had said. A slow, deliberate infant crow, his eyes round
with amazement and delight, little clenched hands extended.
I—see—light . . .

Tears blinded her: she stumbled into one of the bobbing
forsythia branches, thrust it aside in wild petulance. I must
not give way to this, she declared, and clenched her teeth. I
must not. He—there is no reason to suppose anything terrible
has happened to him, that he's in danger: perhaps they're
resting, the time is different, the time is very different there,
perhaps they're asleep . . .

Oh God, if only I hadn't seen that picture.

She was at the end of the hedge: through the gap in it she had a different vista of the sea, calm and unruffled and glittering, the dunes in a sweeping progression of tawny slopes under the hot, white sky.

He must come, she thought, staring hollowly before her. He must come home to me alive: he is my life, my hope, he must, *he must*—thought all at once of Martha Townsend, her boy killed in Italy, and Mrs. Healey's son a flier missing in the South Pacific; and was flooded with a hot sense of shame, the hopeless, inexplicable inequity of things. And in truth—she blinked rapidly, stared unseeing at the luxuriant, immaculately tended stretch of flower bed below the verandah—why should she excape when Martha and Mrs. Healey hadn't, when a thousand thousand weeping mothers hadn't, when many parts of the world, many places, looked as desolate, as monstrously cataclysmic as the scene in that photo?—why should she be exempted?

From out in the bay there came a succession of dull, sonorous booms. Depth bombs. There were four, then five more: like measured tolling bells, like muffled claps of doom. She was trembling; standing in the hot white sunlight near the sedate, silvered artemesia bushes her fear and desolation of spirit were so deep they seemed measureless. Her thoughts scattered like a flock of birds, deserted her. We must pray, she thought blindly. We must all pray. At this hour. Please, God, she murmured half aloud, please, if You see that he returns safely home I—I'll do anything to—to praise Your name . . . and wrung her hands in her awareness of the emptiness, the foolish inconsequence of her vow; yet still in her anguish repeated soundlessly, Please God, I pray You to spare him, save him, he is a good boy, a fine boy—checked herself again at the wretched implications of the entreaty, thought again of Mrs. Healey, Martha Townsend. Ah, just save him because I pray to You—knowing that too was empty, ridiculous beyond measure . . .

The cicada started, then: the slow, sizzling monody swelling outrageously until she felt it would burst her eardrums, shatter her very sanity in a thousand whirling shards: a tense prophecy, descending at last, infinitely dry and threatening.

Do something. I must do something, anything. As hard as possible. Busy my hands.

She hurried back along the path toward the gardening shed, her head thrown back, breathing deeply; brought her features to their former composure. But the cicada began once more, and she knew that something which had been eminently secure within her would never be so again.

Amory came in rapidly and kissed her on the brow, walked over to the porch railing, walked back to the other rocker and stood near it, slapped an evening edition of the *Traveler* against his leg; regarded brightly in turn garden, poplars, dunes and sea.

"*Boy*, it was hot today," he said. "*Boy*, it was hot. Fry an egg on the corner of State and Congress. Where's Iris?"

Charlotte Newcombe stirred herself; she hadn't moved out of the chair for over an hour. "Why, isn't she back? She went to do some errands."

"Any word today?"

"No."

"Oh." He nodded, opened the paper; closed it again. "I've got to go down to New York next week. We've decided to take on Armistead. I'll have to go over most of it with him myself."

"What a shame, Amory," she said. "In this heat."

"Can't be helped. He's the best man in the country. Bar nobody. At least that's my opinion. Things are moving so fast right now we've got to keep abreast of them, develop along with them . . ."

She nodded. She felt tired, and faintly dizzy; as if she were coming down with a fever. Amory's voice swept along, talking of Armistead, singing his praises. "He's fed to death with that Bonham crowd down in New York. That's why he's free to deal now. It's a marvelous break: we won't have a chance like this in years."

The locust had stopped for the day. In the marsh across the road a redwing perched on one of the cat-o'-nine-tails sang his strange, softly harsh evening song: cong-*cree* . . . cong-*cree* . . . He had loved them: he used to lean out of the car when they drove past the marsh and point them out, tiny black sentinels bobbing, turn and cry. "The redwings! the redwings!" his face flushed with triumph. When they'd found the dead blackbird that Labor Day weekend long ago he'd insisted on keeping it, had insisted on taking it himself to the old taxidermist on Stuart Street. "Can you fix him so his head is up? so his mouth is open, the way it is when he's singing? Can you fix him that way?" The taxidermist had sent the bird back mounted and enclosed in a glass dome, but he'd taken it out immediately and kept it on his desk; in the evening doing his

homework he would lean forward in the conical shaft of light
and stroke the feathered head once or twice, lightly . . .

Amory had opened the paper again: the headline leaped at
her FANERÁHAN BATTLE MOUNTS and at the black-
and-white splotch of photo she snapped her head away and
closed her eyes. No more chaos: no more tableaux of impotence and confusion in a blinding light—

"What is it, Charlotte?"

She shook her head, holding back her weeping. His chair
creaked as he left it and came toward her.

"Now don't you worry, Mother."

The dear, solicitous, awkward phrases of their life together,
everybody's life together. He was good: he was loving: a good
husband and father. Anyone would say it. But he didn't
know, he didn't seem to realize this—what this really *meant*,
somehow—

She patted his hand and nodded. Dread froze her silent.

"Don't you worry, now." His voice running on,
monotonal in the late afternoon stillness, vaguely soothing.
"Why, they've broken through and the Japs are in retreat at
all points, I was just reading here they say it'll be all over in a
few days at the most. You're all tired out from this dratted
hot spell we've been having. Don't you worry, now . . ."

She withdrew her hand after a moment, wiped her eyes
quickly with a handkerchief and stood up. "That's right," she
said. "I'm sorry, dear. To give way like this. I was just
thinking and I . . .

"Oh Amory," she said, and looked at him fearfully. "I
don't think we have any idea of what they're going through. I
really don't."

"I suppose not." He bit on his mustache with his lower lip.
"Well, don't you worry about him, Charlotte: he can take
care of himself. I've had Matsen start on the bookcases."

The juxtaposition of these two ideas was too much for her;
she looked at him in frank bewilderment. "Bookcases?"

"Yes: the built-in shelves we talked about. With the sliding
glass doors." His expression was pleased and intent. "For his
study. He'll want those when he comes back. And the desk—I
talked to Staunton at Morse's; he says they've got one of
those desks with a typewriter-well that tips up."

"Oh," she said. "Yes."

"I talked it over with Matsen, about the possibility of con-
verting the whole fourth floor into one room. You remember,

the idea of making it a sort of combination bedroom and study. He could even have a roommate over occasionally if he felt like it. When he comes back it'll give him a place to entertain . . ."

A breeze stirred, warm and gusty, in the garden, set the rhododendrons to swaying. I should say something, she thought; I ought to say something . . . She became conscious of a change around her, the disappearance of light—glanced up and saw the clouds, overhead now, tumbling in swift silence. Massed shadows swept over the moor, the lawn, engulfed them in a rush of wind. The newspaper lying in Amory's chair flopped to and fro, skittered a few feet along the porch like a dead sea-bird.

"Oh," she said: a faint, anguished groan that made him stop and glance at her, his eyes startled and apprehensive behind his glasses.

"Do you feel all right, Charlotte?"

The fond, shy, awkward glance. Dear, dear, fond man: dear blind man! The *semblance* of things, she thought with rising anguish; we've been deceived by the semblance of things—

"What is it, Charlotte?"

"—But what if he *doesn't* come back?" she cried.

His eyes widened; his mouth dropped open. He looked infinitely ludicrous all at once: a baffled child. Ah the dear man! He—

"What if he doesn't come home?" she repeated unsteadily, the sense of inadequacy and dread swelling inside her like a malignant yeast. *"That's* what we've got to face," she cried. "It's *that!* . . . It does no good to—"

She couldn't go any further, compressed her lips and shook her head wordlessly from side to side. Standing on the wide verandah they gazed at each other in still, painful amazement while ever-darker shadows glided over the lawn and leaves tossed and blew rolling around them.

Then Amory Newcombe threw out his arm. "But he can't!" he cried. "He's got to come back! Why, if he doesn't there's no—there's no *sense* to it! . . ."

She looked away at the poplars swaying, the leaves whirling like glittering coins against the dark sky; looked again at her husband's face slack with consternation. We aren't equipped, she thought heavily, and the tears burst into her eyes; universal education and central heating and all these miracle drugs, but they don't do us any good, they don't help us any. We're not equipped to face the consequences of our actions, somehow . . .

And there he stood facing her on their beloved porch, talking of built-in shelves and typing wells when in the midst of a furnace-bright chaos half a world away Alan—

But now he had turned; was standing at the railing—exactly where Iris had earlier; the exact spot, how odd—his hand to his mouth. He was distraught: pale and shaken. She had done it. Had she the right? And what good had it done? There was enough misery now spread over plains, over continents. It was only that he seemed to be so—calmly unprepared . . .

She went over to him and took his hand; absently he put his arms around her.

"I'm sorry, dear," she said. "I shouldn't have said that, I guess. I don't know. I shouldn't have given in to it . . ."

He said nothing, smiled affectionately, his eyes glistening; patted her shoulder.

"Amory," she said, "can we go back to town early?"

He looked at her, startled. "Why yes, if you want, dear. Of course we can. It's awfully hot—"

"I know: I know it's early. I want to. I think we ought to go back early."

"All right," he said. "We'll go up tomorrow if you'd like."

In the darkly silver light the air suddenly turned cool. The wind descended in fiercer gusts, lashed the poplars and elms; and the first rain began to fall in huge, spattering drops on the porch floor at their feet.

7

THERE WAS NO end to it: no end at all. The hours, the days, the nights all ran together, merged in a limitless marsh of odious, terror-laden repetition through which they waded: tearing the waxen brown wrappers off K-ration boxes, wiping mud or sand or dust fitfully out of weapons, racing tense with fear from shell hole to shell hole or tramping in apprehension through a dense jungle whose creepers snagged forever on helmets and bayonets and arms and feet. No end to the business. A tortuous, confused procession toward no discernible object, obeying a strategy which for them extended no farther than the next mound, the next creek, the next bristling patch of jungle. Aching sick, worn to the bone they groped their way forward until whatever was in front of them fired on them. Then they plunged to earth and crept along in painful, dry-mouthed fear and flushed out the enemy; and groped their way forward again. If there *was* a grand strategy, some master plan with whose majestic orbits they were in accord, they knew nothing of it. Their world had constricted to tufts and hummocks and vines and each others' gaunt, increasingly harassed faces: to private miseries and a multiplicity of desperate little ignorances and confusions.

. . . There was a little valley where trees like gnarled willows swept their foliage low to the stream, brushed the tops of woven sacks filled with wet and rotting rice, heaps of empty saki bottles and little square boxes adorned with delicate rice-grain writing; there were ranchos smashed to chaos, their thatched roofs tumbled in on weapons chests serving as hastily contrived operating tables, where dead Japanese lay on blood-soaked blankets with swarms of huge green flies clustered on their mouths and eyes; and worst of all was a high cliff-face like a curving bastion pocked with caves that rained down on them a murderous fire without warning and where Lieutenant Prengle, caught in the open and shot through both knees, waved them all off and dragged himself with the slow, terrible persistence of a crushed beetle back to where O'Neill and Newcombe lay, stared at them with a dull, musing expression and said, "Sons of bitches are going to blast us all yet"—and passed out.

After endless confusion and delay they got air support and the Corsairs came howling in overhead and with banks of rockets shrouded the cliff in billows of smoke and flame—pulled out in a series of shuddering shrieks and swept away like celestial war birds, omnipotent and invulnerable. And there the caves still stood, their hollow black eye-sockets peering down full of menace, and spat down hellfire as before. And to Newcombe, cringing supine in a mat of tangled, fetid vines and vegetation, the sense of impotence and frustration was like a physical grip on his chest and throat.

They cleaned out the caves that day and the next, with the

help of flamethrowers and dynamite: grenaded and blasted them empty, one by one—found themselves at one point grouped around a stocky, uniformed figure with silky black hair drawn tightly back on each side of the head. Turning the body over they saw it was a woman.

"What is she, a native?"

"No. Geisha. There were some on Eniwetok, too. They're the worst of all: they never give up."

"What are they doing here?"

"Sack in with the troops."

"I'll be go to hell. What—one to a squad?"

"Beats me."

"Say now," Capistron said, "that makes it almost worth it."

Kantaylis looked at him slowly. "Nothing makes it worth winding up like this."

Newcombe, watching too, turned away. The idea of this corpse being the corpse of a woman, grenaded, her woman's entrails spilled in the harsh light of day, the soft fullness of her body faintly visible under the tight, quilted jacket, became a peculiar tribulation. It unnerved him subtly. Their one day in reserve had afforded them no rest, no recuperative solace: they had slept fitfully if at all in the unremitting shriek and crash of high explosive probing for their vitals. With a mounting despondency he realized that he was already more desperately depleted now, this second time back on the line, than he had been that rainy afternoon they had been relieved; everything seemed to cut deeper, last longer, sink into some hitherto unknown region of increased poignancy and enigma. It was almost more than he could bear.

"But a woman . . ." he murmured.

"What the hell!" Derekman retorted in a hard, flat voice. "A Nip all the same. She'd have starched you just as fast as a man."

"I guess so . . ."

It was a betrayal: a betrayal of some kind . . . Was that it? He had fallen prey to a mountainous, stunned confusion that rode his mind's shoulders, bore him down. A deep betrayal. Something opened hollowly in his soul, something cold and pitiless; he closed his eyes.

There was another day, then: gray with rain and the promise of more. They moved on, along higher ground where the stream, bubbling over stones like onyx skulls, swung sharply left and formed a narrow meadow between two hills that rose to left and right, high and forbidding. There was, oddly, no resistance: none at all. In uneasy wonder they pushed along where the riverbanks widened—sparse jungle, as though some natives had heroically cleared the area of all but trees and the jungle were only now beginning to reassume its hegemony. Still there was nothing; they proceeded even more cautiously, tense with foreboding, in a silence that turned their own stealthy progress into a riot of snapping and crackling verdure. They watched one another anxiously, peered ahead and on both sides, feeling the excessive silence like a weight on their shoulders, sweating, straining to see . . .

The point up ahead checked, threw up his rifle—and the ravine erupted in a crashing crescendo of machine gun and mortar fire that swept them flat like giant hands. Voices cried, "Cover! Cover!" and bullets spattered on the fronds, a rain of sniper fire. *Trap*, Newcombe found himself crying silently in a wild, hot fright: trap, trap, we've walked right—

Someone leaped up running, calling something to them: he couldn't hear—saw it was Steve Lundren pointing back and to their right, waving the huge bandaged arm, roaring. All at once he was gone: was on his knees, still upright and waving his carbine, thundering: "Back, back—pull out, you people—" Through his open dungaree blouse holes spurted in his massive chest like hose punctures. Still again he rose, staggering and swaying—a mighty, indomitable apparition with bared arms like beams, waving them in a frenzied pantomime and crying hoarsely, "Pull *out*, you people—" then sprawled forward, streaming, spouting blood, rolled over and over down the little slope and lay still.

Lundren. *Lundren*. Newcombe looked around fearfully—encountered Fellows huddled behind a tree trunk, kneeling, his mouth open, wringing and wringing his hands. Lost, he thought, in a mortal terror that was a culmination of the fears of the past ten days; we're lost now. Something smashed into a clump of maguey beside him, showered him with bits of rubbish that stung his face and arms. Fire rolled down the slopes on both sides of them and the cries of the wounded rose in a prolonged, monstrous moan. Our Father, he muttered in desperation, unaware of the words, unaware that he was even trying to pray. Our Father who art in heaven hallowed be Thy kingdom come in earth as is. In earth. Thy will be done. Our Father. Fellows was wringing his hands and staring at him imploringly. He started to get up, found he could not move his hand; stupidly he looked upward through the layers of sea-green jungle growth that shrieked and flashed, said *death, death, death* with every brutal exhalation. He clenched his hands. Gazing again at Lundren's great battered face frozen in a terrible snarl, the massive body ripped and blasted into death, he felt his guts turn moist and cold—realized in a spasm of despair that it was the Horseshoe all over again, only worse, because they were fewer and wearier and more vulnerable: that the final, irreparable disaster had struck them all. He buried his head in his arms and lay there shivering, unable to move.

"Well, what are we going to do?" The voice was Derekman's: a morose, exasperated tone in rising inflection. "Climb up on the top of that Goddamn mountain and stick a flag up our ass and wave like hell, or what?"

Newcombe opened his eyes. Everything danced in unpredictable ways, as though fronds and leaves and helmeted heads were all vibrating on taut little coil springs; a sickly sensation. From somewhere behind them came the sudden, rippling pop of automatic-rifle fire and he glanced around furtively. No: it was far away. It couldn't hurt them. But how had they got here?—this handful of them, clustered in a knot in scrub jungle on an alien slope, staring at each other in bewildered apathy?

The automatic rifle popped again, was answered by a machine gun, unquestionably Jap, in a long, flat burst: the BAR failed to answer. That meant . . . that undoubtedly meant that the man firing that BAR, crouched behind it—

The ragged, toy-pistol rattling of small-arms fire rose to a faraway crescendo, punctuated now by the *bump bump bump* of artillery firing with a desperate rapidity.

"They're still going," Kantaylis said.

"Hell, yes—probably gone all the way to the frigging beach by now," Derekman muttered savagely. "Filthy slope-head sons of bitches . . ."

"Maybe not," Bruce offered. "Maybe they'll pull back now the seventy-fives have opened up."

"No," Kantaylis answered. "They'll send everybody in. Big gung-ho banzai, try to exploit it. Pour in everything they've got. That's the way they always do it."

The air was hot and moist and foul; water dripped in sodden reiteration from the leaves of plantains and banana trees. For a time no one said anything. Fear hung over them, stifled their talk; their eyes roamed, nervous and mistrustful, over the wet, hostile terrain. Newcombe drew up his knees, held his left arm close against his body. Heavy flies hovered in mid-air, gathered on the bloated, spreadeagled body of a dead Japanese in clots that became black, writhing swarms. The shoulder hurt like grating bone: if he held it to him gently it was better. A little better . . .

"Filthy bastard mountain," O'Neill said between his teeth.

He opened his eyes again. They had been closed, without any perceptible transition. It was as though he had been asleep—but not really asleep: floating instead over some unpleasant borderland filled with squeals and groans and eerie flashes. He would never have believed one could be this tired—so drunk with sheer exhaustion and despondency it became a prodigious effort simply to lift one's head or raise a hand. And yet sleep was out of the question . . . There it lay, however, above them and to their left—the great, gaunt distortion of a humpbacked boar, bristling with fine golden hairs: hairs that slashed your hands in painful welts. They would never leave it; they would never be out from under its hateful shadow.

"How you doing, Newk?"

Woodruff was grinning at him again: that stolid, stupid, gap-toothed grin. Dirt lay under his blond stubble of beard like grayed measles.

"Just fine," he heard his lips say. "Just great . . ."

"You don't look a-tall like one of America's fighting marines, old buddy-ro."

"Not very much," he muttered. "Not so you'd notice." He felt all at once a most terrible hatred for Woodruff; he dropped his eyes. Dog-ged, plug-ged Arkansas mule: couldn't kill him with a fire axe. How could he keep that Goddamn grin on his face—*how could he!*—when everything had gone down? . . . Ah, it was an infection, the obscenely bristling jowl of Mount Matenla had spread to Woodruff's face, infected it somehow: that was why he was grinning like that. Disgusting. And what was the sense in it, anyhow?

"All right, you're the big hero," Derekman was saying with cold, implacable anger. "Come on, give the orders, Fellows, give the great commands, you're the big-ass hero sergeant . . ."

"How you feeling, Babe?" O'Neill said.

"Not so good." Ricarno's face was yellow and drawn; his lips, which he held together tightly, were quivering, and his head was gripped by a tight little tremor, as though he were mortally cold. When he opened his mouth his teeth chattered. "Not—so good at all—"

It was going to rain: black thunderheads were beating up behind Matenla, piling up like a tower. Rain on top of everything else. The draining nausea in his vitals was worse, advancing in fearful lurches; his legs were without substance, without muscles or tendons or bones, were merely a fibrous collection of pain that swelled and ebbed and swelled again. The ball of his right foot was split like a ripe persimmon, oozing pain. Rain would pelt down in silver sheets and drench them all, set the palm trees to flailing and crashing but it would make no difference: they were cut off now, a handful of them; desolate and lost.

"What you want to do," Woodruff was saying to him in genial, drawling explanation, "is get hold of some beeswax and creosote and mix it up into a poultice. Plug you up in no time. Fella back home—"

"Why don't you shut your face, Woodruff."

Woodruff was blinking at him, blue eyes wide and round and aggrieved. His own had suddenly filled with tears, and he looked away again. *End of the line*, a thought said to him: end of the line. Well, he protested with maudlin fervor, I hung on as long as I could—I went as far as I could go . . . But he knew even as he said it that it didn't matter. It had all run out. The count had run out and nothing would ever be the same: ever. One glance at that filthy boar-humped monster of a mountain or your own trembling hands would tell you that . . .

"Well come on, Fellows," Derekman said again. "Take the Goddamn initiative. You're the rank around here. Go ahead and pull it, you've been eager-beaver enough before . . . What do we do now?"

Fellows raised his eyes, looked around at them vacantly; his face was pallid with fear and exhaustion. He looked down again. "I don't know," he muttered. "I don't know what to do . . ."

"No—you want your rank backed up when it gives you trouble, don't you?"

"Leave it alone, Harry," O'Neill said wearily. "For Christ sake, leave it alone . . ."

"I don't care . . . I don't care about it—" Bending forward Fellows shook his head and wrung his hands convulsively, his mouth working.

"You aren't worth a good Goddamn, Fellows!"

"Take it easy, Harry," Kantaylis said quietly. "Relax, now."

Rain came in odd, spattering patterns. No one moved: they were too weary to pull on their ponchos, too weary to do anything. Ricarno rolled over on hands and knees and began to retch in violent, rhythmic convulsions, ejected a yellow bile in lumps. The rest watched him apathetically. Heaving he looked up at them, waved one hand feebly, embarrassed.

"Christ oh Christ I'm sick," he panted. "I *never* been this sick . . ." He lay back shivering and shaking; the breath sang in and out between his teeth in short, staccato hisses.

Carrington went over to him and said, "Here you go, Babe. You better take a couple of these."

"Can't swallow," Ricarno said, staring at the pills, which were oval and the size of horse-beans.

"What—with that big mouth? Sure you can. Come on come on, get 'em down."

"What's the matter with him?" Kantaylis said.

"Dengué." Carrington shrugged. "Start of the big epidemic. Dengué, dengué, who's got the dengué . . ."

Newcombe closed his eyes again; exhaustion settled inside him with a soundless, bottomless crash, as if all the properties of his being had been dumped down some cosmic incinerator chute and the lid been banged shut. The lid had clanged shut on all of them, they were floating painfully, whirling—this pitiful handful of them that were left—through the angry dark toward slowly tumbling breakers of sleep, sweet angel sleep, sinking in eternal repose, never no more to wander, free of terror, washed clean of the hob-goblin goat-cat forms that screeched and gamboled in the tempest of the mind—

A machine gun far away opened up—the Jap gun—ran off its metallic clatter, and now behind them there was the crackle and thud of mortar and rifle fire.

"Listen to that!" Derekman burst out savagely. "You aren't worth a crock, Fellows!"

"Ah, lay off me," Fellows cried. "Lay off! I don't care—"

"No, you bet you don't—just like with Maury—"

"—we'll never get out of this, never get out alive—"

"You gutless Semper Fi son of a bitch . . ."

"Take it easy, Harry," Kantaylis said. "Relax. That isn't getting us anywhere."

"Leave a poor bastard out in the boondocks for the—"

"*I said shut up!*"

Derekman fell silent. Kantaylis looked at him a moment, lowered his voice again, went on. "Let's knock off the feuding. We're in a jam, we've got to get out of it. Let's get the show on the road." He turned to the sergeant. "What do you say, Fellows? Let's get moving, ah?"

"What you asking him for?" Derekman demanded hotly. "He doesn't know whether to spit or go blind . . ."

"How about it, Fellows?" Kantaylis repeated. "Don't you think we ought to shove off out of here?"

"But—we're cut off! We *can't* . . ."

"Sure we are. So what? There's ten of us and nobody's been hit and we've got plenty of ammunition . . . You think nobody's ever been cut off before? We'll get out of it. We've just got to be careful, that's all. Play it right." He paused, repeated in a low, steady voice: "We'll get out of it, all right. I mean it. You wait and see."

Fellows stared at his feet, his head dropped forward on his chest. Finally he looked at Kantaylis and said: "Take over, Danny? Will you?"

Kantaylis nodded.

"It was your squad anyway."

Kantaylis nodded again; got to his feet. "All right. Let's go. Let's get the show on the road." He looked down at O'Neill. "We'll get out of this, Jay. You wait and see. Let's get going."

"Sure, only where to, Danny?" Woodruff said.

Kantaylis raised an arm and pointed. "Right up through there."

"Up that Goddamn mountain?" Derekman cried incredulously.

"Not all the way. See where it curves over that shoulder? the clear ground? . . . Right on the other side of that hill is the Atainu."

"No—"

"Want to bet? We go down through that heavy cover and make the lines tonight." He paused. "That's the only way to do it."

"I say follow the creek here downhill," Woodruff said.

"And walk right into them. In force. That's where they'll all be, staging. It'll be like jumping right into the frying pan. Listen." He held up his hand. Firing popped and spattered away directly behind them; the artillery, which had stopped for a time, was again firing furiously. "No. The best bet in a deal like this is to be where they aren't looking for you. And that's right up there. It's the only way.''

"Hell of a gamble," O'Neill said.

"Sure it is. But it's a good one. Hell, we can't do anything till we can *see*. And at least we'll be on the high ground looking down *their* throats for a change . . . Come on," he repeated, walking back and forth through them. "Let's move out. Let's hit it. We hang around here much longer we'll all be as bad off as Ricarno. What do you say? Better to do *anything* than nothing. I mean it. Let's go, now . . .''

It was true: anything was better than this. They got heavily to their feet. Kantaylis went over to Ricarno and crouched beside him.

"Can you make it, Babe? If you don't have any gear to carry?''

"Got to," Ricarno said; he grinned mirthlessly. Gripping Kantaylis' shoulder he got up, stood on rubbery legs in front of them, his face unbelievably drawn and white under the broad flange of the helmet rim. "Yeah. I'll make it all right.''

"That's the ticket. Woodruff, you and Bruce swap off on Babe's rifle and pack, he can't carry them himself. Newcombe and Bilkota, stick with him and give him a hand if he needs it.'' Moving past Newcombe he winked at him, patted him once on the shoulder. "Stay with it, Al. Only the good die young.'' At the head of the file he turned and watched them all a moment, appraisingly. Newcombe studied him: his face, though worn and lined and yellow as parchment, was nonetheless stamped with the same rocklike fortitude and assurance. It was amazing! After all this—

"All set now, you guys? Okay: let's go. Harry, you and I alternate taking the point. We stay in column of files until we hit that clearing up there, then we go to extended.'' A moment longer he looked at them all. "We'll make it back all right. Just hang in there . . . All right, let's move out . . .''

They were walking again, drifting through jungle, passing the word back as before; along the edge of the stream and up a slope, across a clearing and around the brow of the hill, into jungle again. The sun came out, burst forth like a blazing god and hurled bolts of light around them, and the massed verdure flashed and gleamed, dripped scattered diamonds. Some of the numbing dread slipped from Newcombe's mind. It was possible, then: they could throw off this dead hand of paralysis and defeat. He felt strangely inspirited, almost buoyant. They were moving again, full of resolve, and Danny was at the head of the file. As it should be. They'd get out of

this: Danny, their talisman and mainstay, was at the point . . .
Each of you is a leader, a phrase came to him; and slipping
under the branches and vines he found himself repeating it
like a mystic incantation, in a rhythm of three strides. Each—
of you—is a leader. For a moment he wondered as to its
source—then all at once remembered, nodding. The old
Greek, he thought happily, foolishly, shaking his head. The
old Greek NCO himself. Mister X. It was a prayer, a war
cry—a still, small affirmation in the face of disaster. Out of
all the horror and ignorance and exhaustion, whatever was to
come, he had salvaged this much: this one thing he could hold
pure as an emerald in the palm of his hand.

"Each—of you—is a leader . . ."

"What?" O'Neill had turned around, was staring at him in
perplexity. "What's that?"

"Proverb," he replied. "Very old, profound Greek
proverb." O'Neill had turned away again irritably but he
smiled a secretive, musing smile, watched as he passed it a
lizard lying on a plantain leaf like a slender, glittering green-
and-gold jewel. "Not in very general usage nowadays though,
that proverb," he added. "Not what you'd call widely
known . . ."

There was light ahead; through the dense mantle of shadow
they could descry dimly a clearing. Which meant relief: which
meant danger. Still, it was light. It reached out to them as they
plodded forward, like the sun's rays to the diver ascending
slowly, arduously, from a dark ten fathoms. Light!

Kantaylis had paused; moved on again cautiously. His
helmet rose and fell against the pattern of the leaves. At the
edge of the clearing they clustered in a group, saw before them
a long, grass-covered field that sloped upward until it was
finally bounded by a canebrake. Three dilapidated ranchos
stood in a clump halfway up the slope under some banana
trees. A gentle sunlit scene that touched Newcombe all at
once, made his throat ache with an indefinable longing. This
was what it had been like, then: the way it had been before
they or the Japanese had come . . .

"Might be a native up there," Derekman said. "Find out
where the hell we are. Let me go up, Danny. Cover me."

Kantaylis shook his head. "We've got to play it safe." He
pointed briefly. "Up that way and come down behind it
through the boondocks is better."

They were speaking in low voices, scarcely audible to each

other; the breeze from the clearing blew in their faces, moist and cool.

"All that way? There's nobody up there—"

"I'm not so sure." Kantaylis turned to the others "I say we go around and come down in back of them. How about it?"

Several of the squad nodded in agreement.

"I still say—" Derekman began, and stopped.

A man was standing in front of the nearest of the ranchos. Bareheaded, in wrap-around leggings and unbuttoned tunic, he stood calmly, oblivious of their presence, hands to his groin; and a bright stream arched in front of him, sparkling in the sun. Staring vacantly, straddle-legged, he broke into song—a tune full of dissonances and astonishing variations, and with no discernible melody. The squad froze into immobility, hardly breathing, gaped in stupefaction as he finished relieving himself and buttoned his trousers. Still singing, his head thrown back, he stretched, arched backward, gazed about him idly—and saw them; and his face stiffened in immense surprise.

Kantaylis and Derekman fired at almost the same instant. The Japanese started instinctively toward his left, caught himself up and darted back in the direction of the rancho; all at once leaped up and fell, still running, and thrust his face along the ground, his legs churning feebly under him. There was a shout then, a series of cries, and suddenly the hill was alive with little crop-headed figures running wildly, half-dressed, out of the ranchos and up the slope. Everyone was firing now, offhand, standing in a tight group, rifles and BAR's in a solid, coughing roar. Two more Japanese fell and the rest fled, screaming and chattering, into the protection of the canebrake. And there was silence again.

"Ever see such a crazy sight in all your cotton-picking life?" Woodruff said.

"No." Derekman shook his head. "Can't say I ever did."

"And you were planning on sashaying up there cold turkey."

"Never mind."

They ran up the open field now, frontally, in ones and twos, waved each other forward, and checked the ranchos. They all were empty, littered with Japanese weapons and equipment and stacks of tinned food. Blankets were laid out on the floors and two field cots of a wire mesh. The deep ether-and-wine stench of saki was everywhere.

"Sacked in," Derekman said. "Sacked in cute as can be."

They were huddled around the cans of crabmeat and beef and the boxes of cigarettes, stuffing them into their blouse pockets and packs.

"High on the hog," Woodruff proclaimed. "Just living high on the hog."

"Not bad duty, Woody: sack-time, lots of hooch . . . Look at that." Derekman flipped over a ragged magazine filled with photographs of nude girls. "Tokyo Spicy Detective. All the comforts of home."

"Royal chow-down . . ."

"Hey," O'Neill called to them from outside. "Hey, you guys: look!"

They hurried to the back of the ranchos and followed his outstretched arm, saw at the crest of the hill behind them a stockade of massive posts laced with barbed wire. Pressed against it were figures in bright rags of clothes waving, calling down to them in strange, indecipherable cries.

"It's the Chamorrans," Kantaylis said.

"Yeah, the Chamorrans . . ."

They started up the hill in a body, walking more and more rapidly, following O'Neill, who had broken into a run. The cries drifted down to them through the warm, still air, rose in volume.

"—senDAlun ameriKAno SIha, *ameriKAno*!"

"AtuNGO HIta hau!"

"MAIla fan didiDIi NENkano, por faVOR . . ."

"—TOdos maLANGo HIta—"

"AmeriKAnon, Atso ameriKAnon!"

O'Neill waved to them, ran up the slope in a frenzy. "The Chamorrans!" he shouted, turning, brandishing his rifle. "The Chamorrans, you guys! Come on . . ."

They were singing behind the wire; quavering, faint, a few voices rose on the wind, ebbed and swelled—were joined by more voices in a wordless singsong child's litany, preposterous and stirring:

> "—Ah gunry dis ah thee
> Swee lan ah liberdee
> Ah thee ai sing . . ."

At the gates O'Neill stopped in grinning, amiable confusion, wrestled with the bolt, saw it was padlocked fast over a double bar and struck at it vainly with his rifle butt; turned again to the rest of the approaching squad, his rifle, held in both hands, hanging across his hips.

"Like animals," Kantaylis said with a groan. Newcombe was startled to see his face was dark with anger. "Stuck in a cage like animals—"

"Christ, Danny," O'Neill called. The clamor and singing beat about them like surf. "What we going to do?"

"Do?" Kantaylis cried. "*Do?* Why, smash the filthy son-of-a-bitching thing to pieces, that's what to do! . . ." And he drove the butt of his BAR against the gates: three, four furious blows, and a strand of barbed wire snapped and jounced away singing in the air. The bar, a massive ifilwood plank, held. His chest heaving, Kantaylis looked around him, put down his BAR and picked up a heavy oval stone in his two hands, took up a stance and shouted, "Stand back, you people!" With a face like sudden night he ran against the gates and threw with all his might at the bar. It shattered in a rending crash of splintered wood and the gates burst in.

They were engulfed in a swarm of mankind; felt the clutching fingers of children on their trouserlegs, stared down at the drawn, huge-eyed faces, the voices chattering in the explosive tongue, through which words of English filtered like strange petals: *NENkano hau, por faVOR, NENkano, food aSIi tsu HAnom, water, maKAno ESte, por faVOR;* looked up from the children and encountered the men and women—the drawn, bearded faces and the running sores and bruises and sharply etched rib-cages, the tattered rags of clothing, the weeping and hysterical laughter . . . and the accumulated weariness and tension of the past ten days swept over them in a wave, swelled in them like a tremendous wineskin and burst in copious release. In urgency, in distress they pulled the tins of meat out of their pockets, shrugged out of their packs and gave their remaining rations, their ponchos and cigarettes and extra clothing, gave away everything they possessed in anguished, rapturous frenzy of bestowal.

"MAIla fan, MAIla fan! . . ."

A little boy was tugging at his shoulder; kneeling in front of his pack Newcombe handed him a tropical chocolate bar. The boy took it, thanked him, hesitated, fingering the wrapper. Newcombe pulled off the wrapper, broke the bar in half and offered it again, nodding: "It's good—eat it! ESte MAUlek maKAno . . ." The child's eyes widened. He bit down on it, bobbed his head; broke all at once into a smile of furtive, complicit delight.

". . . Ah! si TSUus maAsi," they were crying, *thank you,*

thank you, their eyes dark with deliverance, with joy. "Thank you okayyyy!" they cried softly, and raised their hands to their foreheads; the tears streamed down their dark cheeks. "DANkulo, DANkulo TSUus . . ."

Newcombe put his hand on the boy's head, looked into the deep-set, trusting eyes. This is what it is all about, he thought with sudden, prodigious simplicity; his eyelids had begun to smart. All of it—in this one dirty, wasted, fearful, ecstatic face of a half-naked child. He does not know me nor I him, we cannot speak the same tongue, he has lived his short life ten thousand miles from mine: but he is a part of me all the same. One momentous, indissoluble entity we are, and he needs my succor—*and it is just as much my need to succor him.* This is the vindication of our destiny—not the high-heaped verbiage of ideologies and waspish reasonings, the chill mask of thought, but simply in the comforting of man where he is in misery. For we are all in misery, in darkness, nightwalkers all of us, toiling toward the light, the light—

It was a vision of a sort: a vision too tremendous, too painful to contain. In his turmoil and exhaustion he felt the tears spring into his eyes: he was weeping for love—he, Alan Newcombe, who had never wept for love nor memory, who could never feel . . .

He stood up, awkwardly, dazed with wonder; bombarded by the shouts, the cries, the pressure of humanity. Near him Kantaylis was crouched on his thighs, tearing open a ration box for two little girls, his expression infinitely stern; and tears were running down his cheeks. O'Neill was talking to him, his emptied pack hanging limply in one hand, the dirt streaked on his gaunt, orange-bearded face.

"Jesus, Al," he said in a thick, strangling voice, "—what you going to do? What you going to do?"

Newcombe shook his head. Through a rippling film he saw an old woman with skin like burned mahogany sitting on the ground bent over weeping in silence, her head bowed, her hands clasped over a crucifix, rocking back and forth, praying and shedding tears. The sword of the Lord and of Gideon. Oh that Lundren could have seen this moment! . . . Lord, we are not worthy: but speak the word only. Lord, behold Thy servant Kantaylis with the hard hands and the terrible stigmata: behold Thy servant Derekman with the cold blue eyes and the dark fury and Thy servant O'Neill with the careless mien and Fellows the disdainful and Ricarno the foul-tongued and Woodruff the benighted and all the rest: yes and behold Thy servant Newcombe with the learning of the ages and the wisdom of a fool . . .

He put his hand gently on the old woman's shoulder. "It's all right," he said with a trembling certainty such as he had never known. "It's all right. You'll be all right now."

Slowly she raised her head: an infinitely sad and supplicating gaze.

"We were afraid," he said. "Afraid you were all dead. HIta maAnao—TOdos naTAOtao MAtai hu hau . . ."

She shook her head; the tears continued to course down the deep, wrinkled folds of her face. "NANGa hu HIta CUANtos mes . . . CUANtos ninGAIan . . ." We have waited for you many months, many forevers—

Ah mother, he wanted to say, we can't know what you've endured but we rejoice at your triumph: for it sustains us too . . . A fine moment: a moment of great affirmation and nothing can ever make it any the less, ever. Nothing man or the devil can do can take this away from us: for this is what we can be. Ah—for we are all lost and all found, all fallen and all saved, homunculi and demigods as well; and there is no security in this world—none at all in heaps of weapons and war gear or splendid isolation or boundless wealth or knowledge—no security except what is in love and selfless succor and generosity of spirit. That is the only rock immutable, and anything else is a dance of shadows painted on a gaudy screen . . .

This is too great to contain, he felt with trembling exaltation: it is too momentous a thing to hold. We will burst, all of us, with its magnificence, overflow with it and burst out upon the dry plains and the hard people and fill them with it, too; and the calves of their lips shall be opened, and their hard necks shall be bowed: our vision shall be their vision, and our joy their joy—

When, an hour later, crouched at the edge of the Ngaián-Pajaña road surrounded by a little horde of chattering Chamorrans, they saw the amtrack heave in sight they greeted it calmly enough: they would by now have hardly been amazed to see Poseidon swoop by in a chariot drawn by brazen-hoofed horses. Haltingly they stepped forward, then stopped and stared.

The vehicle seemed to be sprouting men: they were perched on the gunwales or leaning over them, singing and shouting in a steady, unremitting pandemonium. Someone shouted at the

driver and the amtrack clattered to a stop, flailing mud from
its treads; and one of its inmates called airily: "Hey, what-
tayasay, mates! Whazzaword, whazzaword? . . ."

"No word," they said.

"No—*word*!" The amtrack's occupants went off into gales
of laughter, pounded each other on chest and shoulder. "Hey,
what are you guys—the Sal-a-vation Army?"

"Something like that . . ."

"Fraternizing, eh? Thaaaat's the ticket—goin' native!
Gonna settle down and raise anopha-lees. Gonna raise—"

"Roly," a hoarse voice bellowed. "Hey Roly, give the poor
sods a bleeding drink, for creep sake. They look plumb
tuckered."

There was a little flurry of activity inside the amtrack and a
man with a black spade beard leaned down, extended a
long green bottle toward them. "Something for the road,
chums . . ."

"Hey, can you give us a lift?" Kantaylis called.

"Why—sure thing! Why in thunder didn't you say so! Glad
to have you aboard. Only let's go, let's go!"

They helped the Chamorrans over the gunwales, climbed
aboard themselves—and gaped in amazement. One end had
packs piled in fabulous disorder. At the other a great pyre of
saki bottles bristled, a farouche hoard. Water washed to and
fro in the bottom and more bottles and broken glass rolled
and slithered about in it, and clanked against the sides.

"Yessir, lads: the old guard fries but never surrenders. You
got me?"

A tall man was smiling at Newcombe merrily. He wore no
helmet and his hair grew long down his neck and hung over
his forehead in loose blond waves; he had his rifle slung over
one shoulder and the sleeves of his blouse were rolled to the
biceps.

"Yessir, folks: to the victims belong the coils." He in-
dicated the saki bottles with a grandiloquent sweep of his arm.
"England expects every man to get his booty."

"Where you guys been?" O'Neill asked him.

"Where? . . . All over, brother. All—over . . . Front's
broken up."

"No! Where?"

"All around the Atainu."

They gaped at him. "You mean the ravine?"

"I believe it has been recently christened Death Valley. In
honor of those last full measures of devotion. Yessir, another

such victory and we are unstrung. Do you follow?"

"But what happened?"

"Quien sabe, lads?" The blond man paused, declaimed with elaborate articulation: "With their inscrutable oriental wisdom the emperor's minions inscruted themselves over the hump: a strategic withdrawal to unprepared positions. Shagged ass. Yessir, folks, we have met the enemy and they are theirs. Exclusively." He gave a quick, engaging smile, reached down and picked up a bottle and smashed its neck off on the metal gunwale of the amtrack all in the same motion. "Glad to see you've been disporting yourselves with the native populace. This must be a peace of victors, not of the vanquished. Don't fire till you see how they're hanging, now will you . . ."

Genteelly he offered the bottle to Newcombe. "Go ahead. There's quite a sufficiency, I'd say. We just ran into the biggest cache of the stuff you ever saw—dug right into the side of a cliff. Officers' club, I presume. Yessir, we've made war to the end—to the end of the *end* of the end . . . Go ahead," he said to Newcombe who, bottle in hand, still hesitated. "And may I remind you, sir, there are others waiting—"

The amtrack started with a wild shuddering jolt that sent them piling into each other, clutching at one another and the gunwales for support. Newcombe fell into the tall man, who held him upright and swaying, laughed a boisterous rolling laugh.

"Eternal vigilance, by God!" he roared. "Eternal vigilance is the price of—*puberty*!"

On an impulse Newcombe drank, the smoky alcohol-and-ether flavor rolling on his tongue—felt a swift, ferocious burning in his throat, his vitals. He gasped, coughed, gasped again. "God *damn*" he declared, watery-eyed and breathing deeply; handed the bottle to O'Neill.

Across from him in a clinging, weaving knot were four men trying harmony on "Sweet Genevieve." In the bellowing, shuddering, jarring stagger that characterized the amtrack's progress the quartet would lose cohesion, and one of its members would fall down into the welter of broken glass and packs and entrenching tools adrift in the water; then the others would haul the errant to his feet and the chorus would discordantly begin again. Up front two men were engaged in argument with the driver who was shouting back at them and manipulating the maze of gears and gadgets before him with

disdainful aplomb. In the rear of the vehicle a man wearing
what looked like a Japanese naval officer's dress cap was
perched precariously, brandishing a bottle in each hand and
singing to himself.

"Well, here's to the Maine and I'm sorry for Spain," the
blond man was saying. Head tilted back he drank, the chords
in his throat rippling. "Know not what course others may
shake but as for me—give me Old Currycomb: guaranteed to
peel the fixtures off a brass plumber. Yessir—like Patrick
Henry, or Henry Patrick, I regret that I have but one life to
give—Chee-rist, I wish I had nine like a Goddamn cat I'd have
a chance of getting out of this biological necessity . . ."

"Say, what outfit are you guys?" O'Neill asked him.

The blond man's face sobered: the brows drew down over
his extremely blue eyes—a stare all at once rather forbidding.
"Raiders," he intoned proudly, and his lower lip curled.
"The noblest aggregation that ever wore the green."

"Raiders?" Newcombe said. "But I thought they were—"

"Never mind what you thought!" The tall man's face went
dark with sudden anger. "Never mind where your maun-
dering suppositions so evilly lead you . . . Ah, *you* don't
know," he taunted them, "you're like all the rest: herd-
men—stumbling, skull-shaven boots, a-*reap*-hartch!—a-*reap*-
hartch!—yes sir, no sir, grovel in the gravel all day long—"

"For creep sake, Cowen," the man with the spade beard
said to him amiably. "Take it easy. We're all in this
together."

"All in this together," Cowen mimicked, pursing his lips.
"Isn't that cute: all a bunch of bilious Rotarians rotoring.
Let's all sing the Stein Song, for Christ sake: let's all sing like
the birdies sing—"

"Well, knock off the sermon, anyhow. It's all over . . ."

"The hell it's over! Not to me it isn't!" Cowen glared up at
the tops of palms as they flailed and wavered by overhead.
"Filthy, conniving brass in D.C.!—they couldn't stand it,
no—because then look what it was doing to their pretty little
system of ignorance and oppression: in short *you*—my docile,
feeble-minded friends . . . Surveyed out like a sick dog!" he
roared. "I'm telling you, if you could *once* have sat and
heard—"

There was a series of terrific clanging shocks against the
gunwale beside them; involuntarily they dropped flat. The
man perched on the stern shouted, "Tally-ho! Tally-ho!" and
tumbled forward to the deck, sliding half the length of the

vehicle through the water and broken bottles, laughing crazily. On both sides bullets spanked against the sides—a fierce, racketing clamor like hailstones driven by an insane wind. Cowen had already unslung his rifle and he and another of the raiders began methodically snap-shooting over the gunwale. Up forward one of the advisers gave the driver another drink, and the quartet, now sitting in the water with their arms around each other's shoulders like children at the shore, persisted in their labored harmony:

> *"But still—the hand—of mem'ry weaves*
> *The golden dreeeeeams—of long ago-o-o-o-o . . ."*

Newcombe reached out and tugged at the jacket of the bearded raider and said, "What's the scoop?"

"Beats me. I suppose Dolf's trying a short cut again. He don't know *where* the hell he is. Probably going smack spang through a Jap bivouac." He uttered a short, genial laugh, his teeth small and white against the beard. "He can't drive an amtrack any better than my great-aunt Melissa. We just swiped the damn thing this morning . . . Dolf there," he nodded toward the driver, who was roaring in heated argument with the other two, "he's always getting some fool notion like this. Just 'cause he got thrown out of amphib school at Duneddin. You know how it is."

"Yeah, sure." Newcombe nodded, crouched still lower among bottles, ration boxes, filthy ponchos, exchanged a brief, expressionless glance with O'Neill. A bullet whanged against the iron right beside his head. "Sure. I know how it is."

"The finest man that ever walked this fouled-up globe," Cowen declared, and drank; wiped his lips and repeated: "The finest."

"That's blasphemy," a voice said.

"All right, it's blasphemy. You think I give a fat rat's ass? You ought to know me better than that, Barnwell." Cowen paused, peered with proud ferocity at the faces around him. "The noblest man I ever hope to run across. I swear it."

"Brass," Derekman said dourly.

Cowen threw back his head and roared with laughter; his wide blue eyes flashed in the light. "Brass! That's all you know, you simple sod. *Brass*—he hated it as much as you do . . ."

The room was large and nearly bare. One wall had been blown away and shelterhalves and ponchos had been hung across it as well as the windows. In the center of the floor a battered Coleman lantern emitted a steady hiss—like a kettle at boil, but flatter, more remote; in its cold, blue-white glow the faces were struck full of eerie lights and hollows, like symbolic stage faces or a bal masque. When anyone moved shadows leaped high along the walls.

Lying in one corner, his head resting on his helmet, only half listening to Cowen or the voices beside him, Kantaylis let his eyes roam indolently around the room. The bed had been smashed, the mattress lay a sodden, disheveled mass on the floor where several of the Chamorrans who were still with them were sitting or lying asleep. A table of ifil wood, darkened by smoke and time to a satin, ebony hue, remained, and so did a three-legged stool. Above the table hung a configuration of bamboo strips tied together in a strange design, and below that a fan, crushed and spread out against the wall like a smashed moth. A man and a woman had lived in this room, had clasped and sundered on that bed, borne and reared children, had lived their own faltering, intimate, fragile lives where now a score of strangers—conquerors and conquered—lay in weariness and filth and in their bewilderment drank far too much saki. He thought of a horde of foreign soldiery slouched around the walls of Ned Irish's cabin and was filled with sadness and disgust at the image; rubbed his hand across his eyes . . . Perhaps she was feeding Stevie right now: or rocking him, perhaps—was sitting on the bed in her room upstairs, rocking and humming some nursery song and watching him, her neck arched proudly, the line of her nose and brow a clean straight silhouette in the lamps' glow; and outside the maple softly brushed its leaves against the screen and the Striebels' dog barked and barked at nothing at all—

"Now you take a night like tonight," Woodruff was saying, "what we used to do was go square-dancing over at Pensimers' barn. You get likkered up, a little, and then you start to dance and you sweat—God!—you do the Cotton Eye Joe for hours and hours whooping and hollering, you're wringing wet and dizzy and laughing like all get-out . . . Ever go square-dancing, Carry?"

"No," Carrington said. "Couldn't see it. We used to go ice-skating at the lake. Build a big bonfire on the island and skate round and round and just when you're almost frozen to death, just about to lose all your fingers and toes you go over and toast hamburgers on rolls. Man, there's nothing like it . . ."

"—walk among each other with dignity!" Cowen shouted. He was standing now, swaying back and forth, his hair hanging in his eyes, haranguing the Chamorrans, nearly all of whom were asleep. "*That's* what he believed: that it is for some to lead and others to follow, but that everyone should know what is to be done, and the reason for it, and the price to be paid—and have a say in the doing, too. Yes, and he'd be here with us yet if that creeping, conniving, brown-nosing wad of braid in D.C. hadn't pulled the plug on him! . . ."

"Listen to that Cowen," Woodruff said. "He is really wound up, now, ain't he?"

"Way out there," Carrington concurred. "Who the hell's he ranting and raving about?"

"Carlson," Kantaylis said.

"Say, was he all the fireball they say, Danny?"

"He was pretty fine, all right."

"You ever see him?"

"Yes. Once." He recalled the lean, rocklike face and heavy brows, the tough, spare frame. Old Yankee with a new idea. Yeah, they'd had to get rid of him, all right . . .

In another corner the quartet, now increased to six, gently waved bottles to and fro and sang:

> "*A good gook is hard to snag,*
> *You can always get a mean old bag . . .*
> *Just when you think you've copped a nice big feel*
> *You'll find she's giving you—a double deal!*
> *Man, then you'll howl, you'll growl,*
> *You'll even holler foul—*"

"Hey now, have another pull at the jug, old Danny-buddy."

"No, I'm fine," Kantaylis said. "I've had it. Stuff tastes like lighterfluid gone sour." All at once he had a memory of cider: the sweet, tart tang—so vivid it amazed him. "You ever drink cider, Woody?" he said. "Sweet cider?"

"Cider? Why, sure. My Uncle Hardin used to make it every fall."

"Did he use Russet apples?"

"No. Can't say as he did."

"Russets are the best. You can't beat them. I remember

once Ned and I were working up an old apple tree on his place that had split open in a storm. We had a gallon jug of Russet cider down in the brook, good and cold. It was one of those real hot days in September, you know how they get. And we'd finish a cut and then take a drink. Man, I never tasted anything so good! I can still remember it. We kept on, a cut and a drink, another cut and another drink—and we drank so much of it we both got deathly sick and just lay there on the grass and looked at each other: we were afraid to move! . . ."

"Two-man crosscut?" Woodruff said.

"Yes."

"We used to cut sycamore. Ever cut any?"

"Yes, once. Tough enough."

"Ain't it, though? Make an old man out of you."

"Do you know that kerosene-and-water trick?"

"No. What's that?"

"You take a wine bottle with a screw-top and puncture the cap four or five times with a nail, and fill the bottle with half kerosene, half water. And then before you start a cut you sprinkle it along the teeth. It's great: cuts the pitch or the sap, keeps it from binding . . ."

He stopped, put his hand to his forehead: the sweat was standing on it in little bubbles. Why was he running on like this? like a garrulous old man? Listening it struck him that everyone who wasn't asleep was talking, pouring out a stream of memories, arguments, dreams . . . It was because of this moring: they *had* to talk, all of them—it was as necessary as gasping for air when you broke water after a dive. It was—proving you were still alive, in a way . . . which was probably why he now felt with such aching clarity the crouched lunge and recoil over the high, dusty whine of the saw and Ned across from him lunging too in rhythm, the sawdust spurting in thin yellow tongues at his left boot toe; the sun hot on his bare back and the early fall breeze rippling the pines and aspens, curving the tall grass, brushing it like a hand passed lightly over a fox pelt . . . She would sit there on the stone wall with Stevie and watch them, would bring them cider in a jug and a long loaf and a salami and they'd all sit in the shade and look off toward old Greylock rising up out of the soft, smoky light—

"You know what I loved the best?" Derekman was saying. "I've just been thinking of it: Sunday morning. What a kick! Get up around ten-thirty or so and eat breakfast, and then take your cup of coffee into the sun porch and crap out with the papers. Take the sports section and go through it with a fine-tooth comb: read the write-ups on the Saturday games, check the box scores—Christ, I miss that most of all, I think . . . What'd you like to do most, Danny? just everyday living?''

"I don't know . . ." His thoughts wandered aimlessly around, encountered a pastiche of recalled images, fastened on one. "Coming off work when I had the graveyard shift. Get off about ten of seven—you always relieve the man on the tour before you a little early, you know, it's a sort of a courtesy—and go across the dam and up the street, it's real cold and snappy, the sun isn't up yet, and the frost is all over the ground; and come in and Ma would have buckwheat cakes—ever eat them?''

"No," Derekman said.

"Why, sure," Woodruff said. "My Ma used to keep some working in an old blue crock in the back of the pantry.''

"That's right. And Ma'd make about six of them, good and big, with maple syrup and lots of butter, and two cups of coffee. You feel all tired and a little fuzzy and a good six, seven hours of sleep to look forward to. And just then the sun would come up over October Mountain and everything would turn all gold outside . . .''

He paused, put his hand across his eyes again, and fell silent. It wasn't what he was thinking about at all. Funny: it was this other image, long buried and forgotten and yet so clear . . . Derekman was talking again, telling something about a paper stand but he shut it out deliberately, dwelt in the burnished memory.

. . . It stood in the far corner of the long living room. A strange gleaming black three-legged bird with its great wing lifted: a terrible and marvelous instrument. He had heard it: he knew. He approached it with slow deference, never taking his eyes from it, slipped onto the bench and contemplated the dazzling patterned rows. After a long, still moment he poised a forefinger, brought it down: a column of sound rolled off in space. A round, delightful tone. Another, down to the left: a deeper, more somber note that rolled farther still. Another. Pressed together they were richer, like bells. Some were more right than others, played together. Some were purer alone: pure and still, bowling off into the valley with magical ease. He had never felt anything like this before—the shivery, ringing delight of the bell-tones . . . He whirled around: Mrs. Spencer was standing in the doorway with her hat and coat

on, watching him—a strange, intent look. Frightened, he
didn't know what to say, slipped off the bench and stood
beside it, his hands at his sides. With a sudden movement she
turned and was gone. She would tell Mama and then there
would be trouble. He *knew* he shouldn't have done it! Mama
would be angry at him for this. He knew better: he'd been told
not to go into any other part of the Spencers' house except the
kitchen and basement, even when they were out. Had she gone
to tell Mama? But she hadn't looked angry; only funny and
troubled . . . He went to the door, paused, heard his mother
moving about in Mr. Spencer's bedroom now, cleaning;
turned again and contemplated the great black piano, fancied
he still heard the round globes of pure sound flowing off
across the valley, carrying with them the miraculous, eerie
beauty that had set him quivering with delight . . .

"—don't believe it, do you? Of all the stupid—! Does every
last mother's son of you have to be thrown in a hole and
sprayed with penite before you learn what it's all about? To
get out from under: that's what. Get out from under this
whole lousy, depraved, degrading, filthy, lying swinishness!
All wrapped up, right there . . ." Cowen paused, sweating,
glared at the wall beyond him. "Right—*there!*" he roared,
and hurled the bottle in his hand at the wall with all his might.
It shattered like a grenade exploding and men plunged to left
and right from the shower of glass, tumbling over each other
and cursing.

"Don't mind old Cowen, will you."

Kantaylis turned his head. A squat, bearded man, one of
the raiders, was smiling at him apologetically; he tossed his
head to where two men now had hold of Cowen and were
pacifying him steadily and systematically in low, soothing
voices. "He don't mean half of what he says. It's only when
he gets tanked up he goes loco. He's just like the rest of us
most of the time . . ."

Kantaylis nodded vaguely, closed his eyes. The most
tremendous exhaustion settled over him: a vast tidal wave that
slipped him down through this floor on which he lay, down
and down into some snug subterranean vault buried in the
earth's core—a still, inaccessible pocket where he could rest
for years and years unmoving, forget all about Captain Frey
and going up on the line again and his responsibility for these
nine men . . . To be clear of this, completely free, even for a
day: oh Christ!

●   ●   ●

> *"You had plenny money nineteen forty-five,*
> *Now you're the only gyrene left alive,*
> *Why don't you do right—*
> *Like the other Nips do? . . . "*

The lugubrious, moaning, nonsensical refrain slipped along parallel with his thoughts, kept tangling with them . . . Maybe the plug had been pulled, somehow. The front had broken up: maybe the Japs had lost more men and equipment in the counterattacks of the last ten days than anybody had thought, maybe they'd run out of gas and folded up. Hadn't they done something like that once before? Bougainville, Vella Lavella, somewhere? Maybe they'd run all the way to the sea before they turned; maybe they'd blow themselves up by the thousands and it'd all be over in a couple of days.

Maybe the moon was made of fine green cheese.

Well: the hell with it. He was here, however briefly, in peace and safety: corked out. And the rest of them were worked out, too. When tomorrow came they'd sweat out tomorrow . . .

He folded his hands on his chest. The bedlam of talk and singing, now more subdued, the hiss of the Coleman lulled him oddly. There seemed all at once something very important about the scene around him, something profound he couldn't grasp but which he knew was *right* in its essence: Woodruff and Derekman beside him swapping endless alien reminiscences, Ricarno and O'Neill in the corner talking to one of the Chamorran girls, Cowen raging at the departed glory of Carlson and the raiders, Newcombe hunched over that little mud-smeared notebook of his, writing furiously, half blindly, his face tight with effort; the expanded quartet singing on and on in dreamy tautology—all seemed to dispose itself in a pattern of meaning he would give a great deal to decipher. It was like the piano tones struck in clusters: a thing you could understand if you only had the key, the training, the mastery over it . . . I'm going to learn to play piano when I get back, he thought—knowing even as he said it the monstrous, hollow impossibility of the resolve but, dizzy with sleeplessness and saki, lulling himself with the idea nonetheless, elaborating on it, seeing himself playing at a piano, not the concert grand up at the Spencers' but the upright at the Striebels', say—moving his fingers with light, sure dexterity, hearing the harmonies flow rapturously around him, held in an indefinable ecstasy, playing

on and on, improvising, inventing . . . and in a slow,
tumbling succession of billows sleep came toward him
with a blessed surge.

*Helen darling—I don't know where to begin. Time,
place, memory—all the dimensions we used to know and
honor have been swept away beneath us and we are left
floundering. After the past ten days—ten days? it seems
like a decade or more, the way one looks back on events
in grammar school—and especially after this past one
(which is still going on, more or less) I guess I just don't
understand much about the world or its inhabitants,
about life—God help me, I've been trying to cling on to it
so desperately I haven't had time to ponder much about
it. All I know is that I must write to you tonight, my
dearest. Weary unto death itself and full of aches and
pains and half-crocked on vile saki (not a habitual practice, believe me) I've got to speak to you, fragmented and
fuzzy and non-sequitur-laden as it will undoubtedly be:
really write you, this time. (Never mind what that means.
Someday I'll tell you: right now it's too complex and
unimportant.)*

*I am alive. To begin with. Still alive, thank God, and
so is Jay and so is Danny. But we have lost nearly half the
squad and over half the platoon, that we know of—and
we don't know what's happened since this morning. I feel
like a boozy, woozy, battered Tiresias—a thousand years
old and condemned to witness all manner of human folly
and depravity since the beginning of time: to sit by
Thebes below the wall, and walk among the lowest of the
dead . . . For I never thought I could be killed, I can see
that now; never really believed it could happen to me, I
mean: not a scion of the Boston Newcombes, of Beacon
Hill and Harvard College—not me personally. Oh no. A
light wound, perhaps—something trifling and colorful
and not too painful, a sling and a bit of braid and much
noble stoicism—but nothing more. Now I know differently: I know that I can be—any time, any place. Like
a rat in a sewer. In the awful colloquy the gods hold
above our heads there is no longer any place for ro-
mance.*

*It's that nobody knows: that's what is at the core of it.
And no one who hasn't confronted this Gorgon's face
can conceive of its hideousness. Oh yes, war, we think: of*

course, toujours la guerre, a time of suffering and sacrifice, of heroism and pro patria mori: we cluck and shake our heads—and turn the page . . . We have been seduced by the ermine and the crimson sashes, the boots and mustachios and spurs aglitter on parqueted floors, by cuirasseurs sweeping down sunlit vales in plumed, cloak-waving charge toward sparkling little brass cannon where the old purple-and-gold standard flutters gaily. Errol Flynn, in brief: Errol Flynn. The dashing, resplendent hero we have been led to ape—the hero that never did exist. We have been bewitched, all of us, by the seductive abstractions that have nothing whatever to do with a man, a friend—even as you or I—holding up to you his shattered stump of a leg and sobbing piteously his anguish and bewilderment

No. I can't begin to describe it to you, any of it. Sweet Christ—how describe the steady disintegration of humanity in one's own heart and soul, the noisome parade of fear and ignorance and pain and worry, the pure oppressive worry, and the sights that shriek to heaven itself—the great salt wastes of terror and remorse and rage until all that remains of us is blinking, doddering brute? You cannot imagine it and thank God for that too, for spirits not seared black with anguish

Which is partly why I am writing this scrawled jeremiad to you, my dearest: so that in a future day you can help me. So that if I am ever, God help me, in danger of forgetting this, of sentimentalizing or assuaging it, of slipping back into an idiot's litany of folly, you can present these fouled and wrinkled pages and say, Remember: stanch this lesion of your resolve . . . *And not just rhetoric, either: not the globes of silver sound mouthed by those personages mindful of their careers or else caught up in the fraudulent abstraction, who cry, "It must never happen again," Thursday evening and roar, "We will not countenance, we cannot in all honor permit," on Friday morn—*

Inevitable, they say: a time when war is inevitable. It is as inevitable as pimping or thievery or conceit, and no more . . . a monstrous debauch without levity or release: without atonement. What can be atoned? Where is the victory? Is there victory in Lundren's riddled body or little Connor's shaking, palsied spirit—or in the vagaries of my own reeling mind? Victory—we have already lost:

*by our violence we have made the next resort to violence
all the more proximate, all the more terrible. Fuit Ilium.
Ah, we could all be near the angels, a little less than
angels, I know that now, beyond all doubt—and we have
forfeited it: we have thrown it all away. . .*

No. No more rhetoric: but a revulsion which we must
carry in our vitals like a glowing, white-hot, agonizing
coal—which will never heal into romanticism or indifference. And care and care and care. With passion.
Care desperately, indefatigably for our lives, our souls,
our individual dignity. For there will be no victory: the
only triumph is within—over our own murderous folly,
our criminal misprisions. Sitting surrounded by wreckage
and misery and loss I know this: more ultimately is
destroyed than can ever be attained. *That is what we must
dedicate ourselves to saying, hour upon hour, on waking,
on sleeping, with all the fervor of the zealous acolyte:*

More ultimately is destroyed than can ever be attained.

I know that much as truth. The rest is bewilderment:
weariness and despondency and saki in unequal parts.
The air glows and fades, my fingers proceed with slow,
detached prehension around the pencil stub I've
treasured for days like the jewel richer than all my tribe.
All around me they sit—these personages I didn't know
existed two years ago, and who have become dear to me
as life itself. Drinking, singing, reminiscing or asleep they
are coming back into life like sea anemones cautiously
unfolding, are snatching at remembered adventures and
delights—the burden and proof of their communality,
their imperilled existence. We have been a long way from
home. We need reminding that we have homes we once
left long ago

And more: we have salvaged a bright, brief moment
this afternoon in the hills above Maidinilla. A moment of
sweet and selfless glory in a marathon of savagery.
Perhaps all is not lost while we are capable of something
like that. Perhaps we're not lost yet, perhaps someone
will bear a sumptuous, prodigal gift before the altar fires
and Athene won't avert those cold gray eyes—even if to
leave one only to return to tell thee, leave (as Woodruff
moans the melancholy refrain) one singer to mourn,
leave oh leave one singer to mourn . . .

Oh my darling: I am a long, long way from home

•   •   •

."They torture you up there?" Ricarno asked. "In the stockade? The Japs torture you? beat you up?"

"Nnnnh—" The girl shook her head slowly, uncertain, her eyes dark and intent. O'Neill lowered the bottle from his mouth and looked at her. Her face was gaunt, olive, with a series of deep curves underneath her eyes; the yellowed gauze of a bandage was taped to the side of her neck just below her ear. Sitting in the midst of the chattering, gesticulating figures, her silence marked her: she might have been standing alone on the end of a pier.

"They make you shack up with them?"

"For Christ sake, Babe, knock it off," O'Neill said in disgust. "Don't you know better than to ask her something like that?"

Ricarno turned in effrontery. "What's the matter?"

"You were up there and they came for you some night, what would you have done? let them bayonet you for fun? Don't be a slob all your life . . ."

"Ah, fungoo. What do they know?"

"More than you, maybe . . . Why don't you lie down and pass out, Babe? You look terrible. You look as though you won't last the night."

"You jerks," Ricarno replied; shivering he lay back and closed his eyes.

O'Neill turned to the girl again and said: "HAtsa naANmo?"

"Ah—Felicia Lamargas . . ."

She smiled faintly, lowered her eyes. In the eerie blued light of the Coleman her face looked softer, fuller than it had that afternoon; and he saw that before the war, before the Japs and the invasion and the stockade, she had been beautiful. He felt quietly impelled to sit there, gazing at her and essaying a succession of friendly, foolish smiles.

"I'm Jay O'Neill," he said, putting his thumb to his breast bone.

"Oney?" She glanced up at him—a quick, shy eagerness that moved him.

"That's right. Where do you live? MANgi HAgo GUma?"

"GUma TSUlang." Her eyes flashed sadly, her lips pouted and burst in a little explosion. "DANkulo bakuDANG! FaMIlia GAUhu PUnu-un, TAta, NAna, GUma TSUlang, TOdo TSUlang . . ."

"Oh," he said. "I'm sorry. Well, that makes us even: I haven't got any home, either. Or parents. That gives us something in common. GUAhu maLINGan GUma.''

"Ah, HUNgan . . .''

She nodded, her face sad and surprised—a swift sense of commiseration—and he went on in a sudden little rush: "My folks are dead, too. My no-good uncle kicked me out last time I was home on furlough: we had a real beef. Number eight-hundred-and-eighty-gatus. Can you beat it?—yeah, told me never to darken his door again. Which I won't, don't worry—except to collect on a little wager we have . . . Otherwise I'm a sort of citizen of the world, you know? Loose as a goose. I'll have to start all over again, same as you will. It's not so bad, though—no deadwood to have to clear away, anyway . . .''

He took another drink from the bottle. Her eyes were on him, mute, alert, attentive—almost beseeching in their bright intensity. Did she understand this? any of it? Ah, what the hell did it matter, anyway? They were sympatico, as Newk would put it . . . He glanced around, saw Newcombe leaning against the wall, his head hanging, notebook in his crossed hands, asleep; turned back to the girl. They clicked—he knew it and so did she: they knew how it went. Somehow or other, ten thousand miles apart, GUma and tenement, east and west, Pacific and Atlantic, they struck some faint, indefinable response from each other. Amazing . . .

Relaxed by the hot, harsh liquor, suddenly very deeply pleased, he smiled at her gently and said, "This must have been a beautiful island before the war, Felicia; wasn't it? I couldn't live away from the sea, you know?—I don't have to be right *on* it but I've got to be near enough to know it's right there, close around, where I can walk to it at least. Stick me in one of those desert towns like Albuquerque or Santa Fe I'd go crazy: why, you feel like you're sitting in the bottom of a sink as big as the earth and no way to get out. Trapped. No rain, no water anywhere around—no sea . . . It's just knowing it's there, near you, coming in and out with that lazy, even rhythm, washing the land clean. People don't love the sea there's something wrong with them, you ever notice that? They're a little goofy, all dried-up and cold or something. Look at the kids at the shore—the way they yip and yell and race the waves, go curving in close and run back squealing . . . You know what I mean?''

She didn't—or maybe she did: it was hard to say. She *seemed* to, somehow: she shook her head but her eyes were dark and shining, with little dancing points of golden light at the centers. *She got eyes way down deep shine like Klondike gold*, the old blues phrase swept back to him; and he hummed it for a moment, smiling.

"Do you swim much?" he asked, moving his hands and arms in a quick, deft pantomine. "Swim a lot here, beyond the reef? SanHIjong i MAmaAit?"

"HUNgan!" She nodded, pointed to her left. "HIhut Paraisso." She ran off a light, rippling run of Chamorro he couldn't follow; couldn't catch a word of it. Well, that was all right—he'd been guffing away in English. What a soft, bright way of talking it was! A dazzler. Marveling he shook his head.

"PAra MAnu hau ensiGUIdas?" he said, gesturing. "Where you going to live now?"

She shrugged, pouted her full red lips. "Nnnnh—Tálanai, i nuEbo SENGsong . . . Cilifairs."

"Oh—the new Village." He nodded; he had heard of a village Civil Affairs was planning to build below Nénetan to replace Ngaián and Maidinilla and the ghostly battered white skeletons of Pajaña where they now sat and drank, mindful only now and then of the dull, dim rumblings of war. All destroyed: a sad thing, all the homes blown up and smashed, all the places people had sunk their hopes in . . . He was struck with a sudden twinge of panic that he would lose contact with her in this ceaseless wash of homelessness and violence, that she would vanish behind the dark, feathered fringe of jungle beyond Nénetan Peninsula, the amorphous scores of newly erected ranchos and still, dark faces and brilliant scarfs and chininas and he would never see her again—or worse yet, that he would pass right by her and not recognize her at all . . . He peered at her closely. She dropped her eyes, embarrassed; and he stopped his wild, avid scrutiny.

"PAra MAnu hau PAagu?" she asked him softly.

"Tomorrow?" He looked away at the cracked walls, the battered dangling fan, the recumbent figures shaggy with gear and dirt and exhaustion. Newcombe's face, helmetless and sunk in sleep, looked ghastly white in the fading glare of the lantern—looked drained of life, a head-lolling corpse propped up against a shattered wall—

He whirled away in angry agitation. "Beats the living hell out of me," he said flatly. "Back up on the line, I suppose." Where else? Where the bloody hell else?

"Ah—"

She understood that, all right. You'd get *that* word in any language, Hottentot or Hungarian: no problem there. She had thrust out her lower lip. Her eyes were so large and sad it startled him.

"Don't you worry about that, sugar-doll," he offered in light, bantering rejoinder. "I'll be around for quite a while. Quite—a—while . . . Don't fret your little head about shanty-Irish Jay O'Neill. I'm a five-alarm fire when I'm cranked up: I'm a bear-cat . . ."

Dominated by his tone, his grimacing extravagance, she smiled; but her eyes were still wide and grave and apprehensive. GUma TSUlang: home go-blooey. It was true—they were in the same boat: they were both cut adrift and floating. It was a bond between them—a bond as palpable and absurd as if a cord had been tied to their wrists . . .

Impulsively he reached out and took her hand.

"I'll see you, Felicia," he said. "I'll get down to Tálanai and see you. Next time we're relieved. Cross my heart and spit in the ocean. Okay?"

Still she stared back at him timidly, said something rapidly in Chamorro.

"What?" he said. "TihuTUNGo, baby . . ."

All at once she drew her hand away and he frowned, disconcerted; saw she was fussing with something at the back of her neck. With a swift, graceful movement she lifted her arms over her head, reached forward and looped them over his. And looking down he saw the medal on the little gold chain.

"Oh—" he said in consternation, "don't do that—don't part with *that* . . ."

She was nodding at him rapidly; she put her hand on his arm. "HAgo MAgof naGUERra, LAala-a, MAIla tiPUnuus na GUERra . . ."

She pressed the medal to his throat and smiled at him: a wan and feeble smile whose deep resilience moved him strangely; awed him.

"All right," he said. He took her hands in his, gazed at her fondly, in wonder: a wild, fierce moment in which their common afflictions were fused, explicit, everything between them was laid bare and understood and made good . . . Then he was again conscious of the Coleman's hissing, fevered light, the clink of bottles, the descending monotone of voices around them. He felt sustained as he had never been before.

"Good for you," he said. "Si TSUus maAsi, baby. That's all right . . ."

8

THE THICKET MOVED: A slight, stealthy tremor. Was still again. Derekman, crouched behind a tree cradling his BAR, looked at Kantaylis inquiringly. The thicket rustled again. Woodruff, on the other side, raised a grenade in his two hands; Kantaylis shook his head. The silence descended around them—a silence so dense, so thick with heat and pestilence and menace it screamed in their ears. Kneeling behind a tangle of roots and vines, his heart beating in huge, painful thumps, Newcombe glared at the brush ahead and thought frantically, *Come out*—why don't they come out of there, get it for God's sake *over* with—

Kantaylis all at once picked up a swollen piece of root and threw it—a lazy, end-over-end parabola that struck the thicket with a crash. There was a swift crackling sound and a little wild pig scampered into the open and crossed the trail, squealing—a bristling black and gray form; vanished into the jungle in smothered grunts and snuffles.

Everyone relaxed and looked around at everyone else.

"Should have let me blast him, Danny," Woodruff said, and chuckled. "Have us a little roast pig chow-down . . ."

They started forward again. The trail wound to the right, to the left like the trail of a great, slimy serpent. Harassed and fearful, they followed the ridged scales; far away in the jungle something screamed—some animal or bird: a single, high, raucous cry. Then the silence, humming like wires, returned.

Newcombe hunched his shoulders painfully against the pull of the pack and harness. It had never possessed such sheer *weight*; it burned his back like a monstrous bedsore. His canteens thudded heavily against his buttocks, dragged at his hips. He kept stumbling on roots and low-looping vines, on nothing visible; it was as though his feet were in a secretive, malicious revolt against his will. An increasingly successful revolt. The shoulder—oddly—was better, but his foot, which Carrington had painted the night before with purple and orange liquids and carefully bandaged, stabbed at him with raw, excruciating pain at every step and forced him into a heaving parody of walking. But what was particularly unbearable was that his senses, while frighteningly numbed in their response to any external cause, possessed a razor-sharp acuteness to the dozen spheres of pain that racked him. Why should that be? Wasn't there any kind of—any kind of compensatory—

The replacement Carney stepped on his heel; he whirled around, hissed, "God *damn* you!—watch it!" whirled back again, trembling and enraged—the image of Carney's baffled face struck like a medallion on his vision. Stupid. Why blow off like that? Things were bad enough as it was: bad enough and stupid enough and exhausting enough for everybody in the world. Any number could play. Hooray . . . But fourteen days of it: *fourteen days* of creeping and crawling and cringing from one hostile ravine to another while their numbers dwindled from thirteen to seven . . . Danny and Jay and Harry and himself; and Capistron and Helthal and Woodruff. All the rest were replacements now. What were they to do?—stagger on and on from jungle to grass to jungle again until finally they were all cut down, every last man of them? What did they want? what did they *want*? Fevered, jigsaw images whipped back and forth before his vision: the edges of ideas, places, people broke and broke and tumbled in kaleidoscopically toward a center which consisted of nothing more than a dulled, stoic ferocity, a snarling resolve to hang on, hating and raging, and endure everything—to spite the senseless tyranny that could impose such anguish . . . His back and chest were streaming sweat.

Time and space had played them tricks again. The past fourteen days had swollen to monstrous proportions, usurping all the previous decades in their mountainous unreality, their boundless suffering. Space on the other hand had contracted: the minute squares on the map at the CP—K7, K8, K9—the streams and hills and sword-grass ravines surrounding Mount Matenla were all their world now—mocked the rest of the island, the vast, watery leagues of the Pacific they'd traversed, all the homeland hemisphere sprawling away behind them, far behind . . .

There were, nonetheless, spheres unaffected by this parade of confusion and horrors. Remember that, he told himself fiercely, panting, grunting with the scorching pain in the ball of his foot. Remember that: a world elsewhere, no matter what this cosmic misery declared—a world as rare as Camelot or Xanadu, where children skipped and called on grassy riverbanks, in sunny, open fields, and old men sat in dreamy contemplation . . . *She* was free of this, thank God: at this moment she was seated demurely, efficiently at her desk, typing something in octuplicate. Or was it later, was she strolling along Pennsylvania Avenue in the soft dusk, or lying on her bed, shoes kicked off, hands behind her head, gazing with untroubled serenity at the car lights slipping across the walls? . . . Had she ever gone back to the Lincoln Memorial, walked again beside the slate-gray water? Ah, the world will little note nor long remember what we had there, only she and I the love we bear each other—

They had stopped: the bodies around him again informed with tension. Near him Helthal scowled ahead dully. He was wearing two bandoliers crossed over his chest; the thin metal hilt of a Japanese knife protruded from under the bandoliers near his right collarbone. Sullen, absorbed, he looked the very incarnation of war—of unthinking, indiscriminate destruction. Newcombe studied him with a gaze contemptuous and fearful, looked away.

It was all right: without moving, the figures around him relaxed. It was all right, then. Kantaylis motioned them up and they came forward doggedly, in a dragging, bent-kneed slouch that in another day, long departed, would have been vaguely comical. It was a cache. Japanese food lay strewn hastily in piles—packs, a rifle, several bottles of the inevitable saki: a thick, pulpy stench in the swarming noon air.

"What do you know?" Capistron said. He pushed his helmet back on his head, bent down and picked up one of the bottles and broke its neck off on the butt plate of his rifle. "Just what the doctor ordered."

"Not now," Kantaylis said.

Capistron turned, affronted, the bottle to his lips: a big-gutted, filthy dancing bear. "What'd you say?"

"I said not now," Kantaylis repeated in a hard, flat voice. He seemed to have shrunk during the past fortnight, to have shriveled away in the heat and tramping and ceaseless combat; his blouse hung loosely on his square frame. "You carry it along with you if you're fool enough to. But I don't want anybody half-shot on our hands. Things are rough enough as it is."

"What you mean, half-shot?" Capistron stared at him slowly: a look of sleepy, half-aroused cunning. His lips parted in a thick smile. "You talk like you was a frigging colonel, Kantaylis."

"I mean it, Capistron. You going to put that bottle away?"

Still Capistron paused, peering at Kantaylis askance, as though measuring him, the bottle near his mouth. "Now listen, buster—"

With a quick, violent motion Kantaylis lunged out and struck the bottle out of Capistron's hand. "Now knock off that crap!" he hissed. "Don't mess with me!" His face was tight with strain and anger. Capistron, stunned by the speed of the action, gazed back at him stupidly. "What's the matter with you?—you think you're back in Kinston on liberty? You make me sick . . ." He glared at Capistron a moment longer in hot disgust, then turned away.

"All right," he said. "We're taking extended order. This is the end of the boondocks for a while. There's a hump and then a little valley and then the ridge. The draw runs right up to the top of the ridge. Hamway says there are caves along the far side. Woody, I want you up with me: how many sticks of dynamite you got left?"

"Five, Danny."

"All right. We'll shoot the rest of it on the caves if we have to. Harry, you take the point for a while, will you? All right, let's go . . ."

They stared at him mutely, without moving. Capistron, subdued and glowering, squatted beside the stack of bottles and thrust two of them into his blouse pockets; the rest of the squad watched him with neither satisfaction nor disapproval. Something more deeply afflicting chafed at them; but what it could be they were too weary, too worn and sick now to care. They stood around dazed and bewildered, blinking owlishly in the sun.

"Well, come on," Kantaylis said, raising his voice angrily. His face looked to Newcombe gaunt and wrathful—as though the preceding days had stripped away, scalpel-like, layer on layer of the calm, indomitable assurance and left only exasperation and a naked, prideful fury. The white gauze of a new compress stuck up inside his collar, made the skin of his jaw appear all the more mottled and yellow. "Are you coming or aren't you? What's the *matter* with you people? . . . Now let's go! Let's move out—"

They arranged themselves raggedly in a line of skirmishers and began toiling their way up the rising round. The altercation between Kantaylis and Capistron, rebellion and wild irascibility, had shaken them; they eased their way through the rippling yellow sea of sword grass, flicking at one another glances of furtive distrust. The sun swept out of sight behind a rolling barrage of clouds, and far away on the left flank Corps Artillery commenced to bump sonorously. To Newcombe the day seemed dark and blighted. He thought of the mournful admonition of the old men: *Each time back on the line is worse; each time they send you back up is ten times worse than the time before.* A desperate truism . . . The bastards—how many times did they think men could take this, how many weeks and miles of it until they were all reduced to slobbering, shaking idiots or mangled corpses? Fury and despair struggled inside him for supremacy: his thoughts moved in tight, querulous circles, like a knobbed cane shaken by an hysterical old crone. Back somewhere in Nataífan or Pearl Harbor or Washington they were pins on a map, the slovenly, dejected, wobbling line of them—one pin, or the part of a pin, vermilion possibly, or Paris blue: forming part of a strategy grand and lofty and unquestionably ir-refutable where admirals and brigadiers, immaculate in starched suntans, smiled frostily at each other and bit down on pipes and moved the pins again. By God, if *you* were the pins for just one day, he thought raging, hobbling along, if for only twenty-four hours *you* were the pawns on the board ringed round with knights, rooks, bishops of awesome powers—change places and handy-dandy, which is justice, which is the thief? What, art mad? A man may see how this world goes with no eyes . . . But how many gyrenes can stand on the head of a pin?

Ahead of them the land rose in gentle undulations, led up to a crest where the soft breeze ruffled the grass in little sickled curvings, white against the boiling clouds. They slowed, came on more cautiously, raised their heads above the crest—saw in the clearing at the edge of the jungle three figures, one sitting with legs extended, the other two crouched over him: a sudden, stark tableau.

One of the figures turned and cried out, and Derekman fired. The Japanese raising his rifle dropped it carelessly and toppled over to one side. The other two rose then, in slow un-certainty, their hands raised above their shoulders as though fastened by invisible manacles to the air behind them.

"All right," Kantaylis called. Raising his hand he beckoned them forward. "Come on, then. Keep your hands good and high. Come on . . ."

The Japs hesitated a moment more, debated something rapidly in an undertone; then came toward the squad in stiff, awkward strides, like sleepwalkers, or like cripples learning to walk again. And for one fantastic instant it seemed to Newcombe, watching Kantalyis with his arm raised, beckon-ing, the hesitantly oncoming Japanese, as though it were all a chance encounter in some strange and legendary country; that they would draw near and exchange civilities, inquire of each other in shy, halting tones about each others' native lands . . .

There was a roar right beside his ear that almost deafened him. The Japanese jerked like figures in a silent film, and ran for the jungle. The roar went on, a rolling crepitation, and the bareheaded Jap staggered and fell, lurched to his feet in leisurely, puzzled strides and fell again. The other man reached the fringe of jungle and disappeared.

Newcombe turned his head. Helthal was watching, with a dulled, expressionless stare, the place where the second Jap had vanished. A dirty gray ribbon of smoke unwound slowly from the end of his rifle barrel.

They moved down the slope with care, came on the soldier Derekman had hit, who was dead, and then on the second, who was not. An incredibly young face, round and beardless, faintly handsome. The folds of flesh on his upper eyelids quivered. Blood lay in a thick, swelling pool behind his neck and under his back.

Kantaylis bent over him, felt him for grenades. "Water?" he said softly. "You want *water*?" He raised an imaginary cup to his lips.

The Japanese stared up at him with an expression thoughtful, almost musing; then with a quick, feeble effort he pursed his lips and spat upward—a spray of bright blood that fell back on his own cheeks and brow. And his eyes set in a look of the most intense hatred Newcombe had ever seen.

"Don't waste the water, Danny," Carrington said. "He'll crock off in five minutes. He's all through. He's got two in the lungs."

Kantaylis appeared not to have heard him. Watching the dying man he slowly shook his head: an expression of desperate regret. He drew a little box of Japanese cigarettes from his pocket and said with quiet entreaty: "Smoke?"

The Japanese made no reply, stared up with infinite scorn and hatred; coughed up a glistening scarlet bubble and rolled over on his side, bent double and quivering. Lay still.

Kantaylis put the pack of cigarettes back in his pocket, ran his fingers along the edge of his face; then rose to his feet and looked at Helthal, who was standing nearby.

"Helthal," he said thickly. "Helthal . . . didn't you hear me tell them to come on ahead?—didn't you—"

"I told you I ain't taking no prisoners," Helthal said,

squinting at him. "You can be a Nip-lover if you want, I ain't taking no prisoners."

"For Christ sake, Helthal," O'Neill muttered.

Kantaylis came up to Helthal and stopped. Blinking heavily, sweating and fatigued, he seemed for a moment not to have comprehended what Helthal had said. Then slowly his face darkened until it looked like fire-hammered bronze.

". . . You're wise, ain't ya," he said, his voice shaking. "Oh, you're tough. Jesus!—you're so tough . . ."

"I tell you I ain't taking—"

"*I tell you shut up!*" Kantaylis said with such violence that Helthal gave back a step. "All right, you're fine, you filled him full of holes, you're happy, ain't ya? And the other one. Where's he? He's gone now, isn't he? Right over there . . ." He swung his arm in a short, fierce arc toward the looming mass of jungle; he was breathing thickly and his eyes were black with anger. "He'll get him a rifle now, and grenades. He'll try for us again, too. Sure he will. Oh, you're tough, all right. You stupid son of a bitch, you had your way you'd kill 'em all, wouldn't you?—them and us and everyone else. Oh you're wise! Real tough. A rugged combat gyrene, bandoliers and a toadstabber. Kill everything, ah? Kill every frigging thing on earth would make you feel better! You—"

Wild with rage he took a step toward Helthal who blanched, gave way again; brought his rifle up before him as though to ward Kantaylis off.

"All right, you're so bloodthirsty, you're so gung-ho—go ahead, go in there after him. Go ahead! We'll wait for you. He's just in there waiting . . . Go ahead," he cried, his eyes filling suddenly, "you fire-eating son of a bitch! *Go ahead! . . .*"

Helthal lowered the rifle. Slouched to one side, a thumb hooked in one of the crossed bandoliers, he peered down at his feet.

"Look here, Kantaylis," Capistron interposed, "look, you got no call—"

"You keep your ass out of this!" Kantaylis said savagely. ". . . No, not so rugged now, are you," he went on, his eyes still riveted on Helthal. "No—that's something else, isn't it? He'll find his outfit now and get grenades and an automatic weapon. And he'll go through hell to try for you again . . . Well I hope he gets you, you stupid, blood-drinking, yellow son of a bitch! I hope he starches you good and proper. You're a sweetheart, you are. You're the kind—"

His voice broke and he looked away wildly, struck his hand on his thigh. When he wheeled around again his face was gaunt and fierce and importunate. "You're all gone, the bunch of you!" he shouted at them. "You're all gone to hell! You don't even know what you *are* . . ."

A moment longer he stared at them all, as if he couldn't believe what he saw before him. Then his lips came together tightly and his face set in the grimmest resolve. "All right, let's go. Let's get the show on the Goddamn road. Woodruff, I want you to stick close with me. When we get to the ridge I want everybody down . . . All right," he repeated in a hoarse, tired voice. "Let's go."

They moved on, skirted the strip of jungle, passed onto higher ground. Darkness swooped down around them; clouds hung overhead in a churning shroud, and the wind fell away. To Newcombe's clogged and fretful mind it was as though some terrible forfeit had to be paid, some retribution monstrous beyond belief which would require them all. With a throb of sad wonder he fought to recall the afternoon at the stockade, remembered painfully the clutching, grubby little hands, the chirruping voices, the singing, the imploring eyes, the tears . . . When had it been—only four days ago? A horrendous, debilitating gulf lay between these two afternoons: an insurpassable abyss. For they had all fallen from grace, fallen tumbling through waves of pain and sleepless terrors and killing to their separate hells of dereliction. And Helthal—

He turned in a spasm of revulsion toward Helthal, encountered instead Woodruff's patient, foolish, happy grin. He glowered back fiercely. Jesus: if Woodruff grinned at him like that agin, just once more, he'd clout the simple son of a bitch in the side of the head with his rifle butt—push that gap-toothed grin out the other side of his silly Arkansas face. What a—good Christ, what a *ninny*!—

He plodded along, subsided in querulous mutterings. On their left, below them and far away, was the sea: a vast and slowly heaving pewter plate shot through eerie lights. The darkness bore down on them like a weight, clogged their lungs, dragged at their hips and knees. The dense flank of jungle on their right seemed to quiver like the pelt of an animal deeply enraged. For another instant Newcombe strove to recapture the afternoon at the stockade; but his memory, fitful and benumbed, yawed away like a tillerless vessel, flapped about among torn and bloody fragments—shattered bone, throats dissolved in blood, eyes that bored up into his own gorged with more hatred than one would have thought possible on this earth . . . We've forfeited it already, he thought in dogged despair; we've thrown it all away in our fury and blindness, who are but weasels fighting in a hole—

You could do just so much.

It was the one fearful, incontrovertible fact of life that Kantaylis had come upon, had found to be true without exception. You tried to do well, do all that was asked of you and maybe at certain times a little bit more. Then finally you ran out of gas—and one man's meat was another's poison, one succumbed one way, another another—and went down, after hanging on as sturdily as you could. That was life: accept your responsibilities, try to harm as few people as possible, and hope for the best . . . and meet your destiny as cleanly as possible, anyway.

Now they were all done—look at them: played out, stumbling along like old men, or like crazily aged children— haunted, hollow, fear-ridden caricatures of the men he'd trained with, played pinochle and drunk beer with . . . He glanced back to his right, his left, measured the haggard, stoic faces. An unnamed exigency lay heavy on him: a sense of terrible urgency and dread. No good was going to come out of this. They never should have been sent up again this soon without more of a rest. And the idea of using them to probe with was insane: some fresh outfit could hike it in half the time—if there were any fresh outfits left, of course . . .

But what the devil was the matter with them?—did they all have to turn into monsters, into raving, blood-drinking butchers and rummies and dope-offs and everything else? Ah, they weren't worth it, they were all gone to hell: he'd turn himself in to the aid station in the morning—might even get ticketed for evacuation. His neck was infected, probably: it felt like it, that incessant itching burning. Well: see how things went tomorrow . . . But the rotten scheme of things that could do this, though—

He shook his head quickly, violently, as though to shake off a pestilential insect. No more of that. Excessive morbidity, Newcombe called it. Supped with horrors, he'd mumbled one night, tossing about, hissing the words. Well: they'd supped all right. Jesus yes. A roaring bellyful and then some . . . And now they were coming apart: slowly but surely going to pieces like granite under a hammer, each in his own way. He'd have to watch them now: all except Harry. And maybe O'Neill and Madden. And of course Carry. Thank God for Carry. Ah, a good corpsman was the ticket, the pearl of great price, the sun and moon and all—

Automatically he froze: at the same instant his hand went up. Ahead of him, high up ahead in the brush at the top of the ridge he thought he heard a cry. He waited, BAR hanging at his hip, while his stomach knotted and clutched him with the old instinctive dread—heard all at once the faint, frenzied chant of voices: Japanese voices unmistakably. A treble singsong babble, wind-borne and terrifying.

He swept his hand down, plunged into the grass and crawled steadily toward a tiny hummock up ahead. On their left was the shallow draw that led to the top of the ridge. Woodruff was moving up toward him, so were Derekman and Newcombe. His neck burned like fire at every gyration of his body; the saw teeth of the grass laced his hands and wrists with dozens of minute, painful streaks. The shouting was suddenly louder: "*O-ho, o-ho, o-ho—*" an hysterical incantation, followed by a welter of shouts and cries.

He reached the hummock, worked his way up on it with meticulous care, keeping the BAR well up in front of him. Raising his head he saw a great hulking shape in the thickets lurch and stop, lurch ahead again. He squeezed his eyes shut and opened them, strained and strained to see. There was a flatulent bellow of motors and all at once the object burst into view: a Japanese tank, rocking drunkenly over the uneven ground, crashing about in the thickets. Hanging on the front of the turret a wild, white, sepulchral object bounced and rolled: a skull, a horse's skull—

A tank

For a few seconds the sight of it deprived him of all thought. It was too unexpected, too terrible; they were all far too tired and worn and vulnerable to cope with anything like this. A tank, he thought with stupid fearfulness, oh my God, a tank. The horrific memory of their own tank firing down on them the morning of the second day swept over him. Away, he felt with vague, enormous dread; they must get away from this barren slope of grass and scrub brush where all manner of disaster and mutilation prowled. There was still time, they must get away, off to the right, away from the draw—

Then, still staring and trembling, he saw what it was all about. It was a banzai: a good old banzai. They'd salvaged or stolen or found some Goddamn tank and got liquored up and now they were going to follow it straight down the draw in a roaring horde, would curve left across that flat above the Kaláhe between C and B Companies and tear the front all to hell; or worse yet they would go left down the Atainu and crash into B's bivouac area and lay about them, butchering and butchering until someone got on the phone and they rushed up tanks or thirty-sevens. But by then it would be too late for a lot of people. A lot of them . . .

But to drag a tank way in hell-and-gone up here—!

Well, it was too bad. Too Goddammed bad. The stupid— suicidal—bastards . . .

He was filled with mounting, choking rage; then with the saddest, weariest, most forlorn resignation he had ever felt.

"Jesus," Derekman was saying, pulling at his trouserleg, "Jesus, Danny, let's shag ass—"

"Can't," he said tightly. "We got to get it."

They gazed at him, speechless.

"They're going to come down the draw. Right here. It's a banzai. They come down the Atainu they'll go through B Company bivouac and rip them to pieces before they even know what hit them. Be a massacre. We got to stop it. Got no choice."

They still stared at him with wild incredulity. Newcombe put his hand to the side of his face: a faint, faltering gesture that disturbed him.

"Jesus," Derekman said nervously, "Jesus, Danny, we can't stop a *tank*—"

"Got to. No choice." He turned from one of them to the other. Newcombe looked as though he were going to crack up. Even Derekman was shaky enough—

"Woody," he said slowly, "how many sticks did you say you got left?"

Woodruff was watching him, round-eyed and sweating. "Five, Danny."

"Give us here." He peered up at the indistinct hulking silhouette of the tank, the pulsating yells; handed his BAR to O'Neill and took the hard, dirty cylinders in both hands.

"All right," he said. He felt dizzy and aching and out of breath. They were gazing at him openmouthed, frankly fearful. "All right: when it starts down give it all the grenades you've got left. Shoot the works. Try to lay 'em on that exhaust pipe lying behind the turret, under the treads. Then open up on it. Never mind the rest of them, just stop that tank. I'm going down by that bush there—see it?—and when they turn to give it to you I'm going to get in as close as I can. For God's sake when you see me, hold your fire . . ."

"Ah, Danny—"

"What's the matter?"

Newcombe was reaching toward him, his face distorted with anguish. "Danny, don't try it, let it go—"

For an instant, confronted by their white, entreating faces and Newcombe's hand, he wavered; then—"Goddamn it, we got to," he said fiercely. "It's the only way. Now, come on. Pass the word."

"Danny wait a minute, why can't we—"

"Shut up!" He whirled away in the grass. "No time! Make it good, now. Pass the frigging word! . . ."

He crawled down through the grass, passing the word himself, encountered consternation and protest and fear as thick as jelly. When he reached the heavy hummock near the draw he turned around, facing uphill.

It was still there. It had crabbed over to the left, backing and filling uncertainly; was stopped again, its motors clattering. Tearing his eyes from its conical, faceted body he found a piece of cord in one of his pockets and tied the sticks of dynamite into a bundle: rough, faintly dusty paper sacks like fingers. Dusty death. He felt unarmed and fragile without his BAR; it was practically the first time he hadn't had it on or about him in days. Fourteen days. Blades of grass, the helmets of the squad strung out along the edge of the draw started and jumped before his eyes. His mouth was so dry he could hardly open his lips. He reached for his canteen, thought better of it, decided to anyway, drew out the full one on his left hip and drank—four, five slow swallows; held the last mouthful, sluiced it around slowly, cool trickling water. A swift, inexpressible sensation. Screwing the top back on the canteen, replacing it by feel he thought, Maybe they won't come down: maybe something's wrong with it or they're too drunk or tired out or something. Maybe they'll go over the ridge to Fofogáda . . . If they only would take off. Oh Jesus! If that one thing could happen. Oh God, if that could just happen and take us off the hook, just this once . . .

Darkness increased, swelled downward until it seemed as though it would press the earth beneath its weight; the sword grass turned silver against the boiling black clouds. Rain, then: rain, for God's sake—maybe they'll give it up and take off. Let it come down in sheets. He was trembling now, sweating in streams; his neck and shoulders prickled and bur-

ned unbearably. Maybe they'd get it with grenades. Harry and
Woodruff were good with them, maybe they'd blow a tread
off the Goddamn crazy tin-lizzie monster. That car Fred had,
wobbling all over the road, loose steering knuckle and wobbly
wheels, scare you half to death to see it wavering and wobbling down the Post Road at fifteen miles an hour, and Tom
Healey glaring and swearing and laughing at it all at the same
time *I swear I'm going to impound that vehicle before it runs
onto somebody's front porch and kills the cat.* Or the Stanley
Steamer old Miss Scarborough had with the lever for a
steering wheel, sitting up like a tintype photo stiff as a
ramrod, that time she came across the bridge by the mill yard
with Andrea and—

Ah.

He passed his fist down the side of his face; the knuckles
were slick with sweat. Water was dripping from his chin, his
brows, and his teeth were chattering. He was invaded with a
swift, riotous cavalcade of moments. Of Andrea laughing or
curious or intent against a shifting composite of woods,
snowbanks, porch screens, the blue glitter of Lake Pontoosuc;
was wrung with a sense of stark deprivation that made him
gasp. None of that, he told himself ruthlessly. None of that
crap. *Put it away!* He thrust them out of his mind with wild
urgency, studied the outlines of the tank's turret; became
aware that the screaming singsong incantation had ceased.

Now, he thought. Now they'll come. In a minute now—

It lurched forward, the tank, with an alacrity that alarmed
him, started down through the brush like a crazy aggregation
of metal pots and pans, a ridiculous mock-up of mechanized
war—rocked once dangerously and came on, straight down
the draw, its gun pointing skyward; the horse's skull bounced
and banged against the turret. And running silhouettes began
to appear behind the ridge.

They were throwing. He saw the first grenade curve over
and bounce against the turret, fall to the ground; there was an
explosion against the tread and another almost at the same
instant in the air behind the turret; then a succession of
crashing bursts. Still the tank came on, rocking and lurching,
its gun swinging around now, the machine gun above and
behind it slewed around sharply to the left, firing in quick,
shuttling runs.

Jesus, he said in anguish, it's not stopping. Oh Jesus they
aren't going to—

All right, then. All right—

Now.

He broke from cover, ran down toward it in long leaping
strides, slipping and sliding, carrying the bundle low against
his thigh, caught as a flickering background in the scan of his
vision the oncoming, lumpy, hurtling figures, saw the machine gun swing wildly around toward him, the barrel glinting like silver against the swooping black sky beyond—was
aware, in the leaping, absurd image of himself descending
alone and unarmed through the dark boiling air toward the
tank, that this was the last, the final culminating sacrifice; the
last and utmost and most awful he could ever hope to do.

It was upon him, clattering alongside him moving with fearsome, unpredictable swiftness—a gray metallic uproar of vast
dimensions. Something droned through the air beside his
head. He flung himself forward, gazed with fierce intensity at
the terribly bright, terribly clear machicolation of the
flickering, undulating, screeching treads; hurled the dusty
gray bundle against it with all his might.

—He was asleep. In a sleepy land from whose profound
somnolence neither he nor anyone else could ever fully
awaken. Drugged with opium and ether both, his sight
frosted, his limbs languid with drowsy stillness like newfallen
snow . . . But something was wrong: the tank: something had
gone wrong, had snatched at him in fury—he was bumping
and sliding, something was dragging him by the foot,
dragging him head-hanging through stones and red dust, his
body bumped and battered like a flail, through a corridor of
explosive chaos that defied comprehension. And through it
now with the speed of light pain slid screeching down a wire
and burst with a crash in his innermost vitals—an unbelievably thin, penetrating, hotly all-consuming blade; and
ran him through.

Then all sank into darkness.

Lying flat at the edge of the draw and firing at the tank with
the screaming handful of Japanese floating dreamily by—
there were, incredibly, only a handful, coming in twos and
threes, the shattered remains of a platoon like themselves, he
saw in a curious flash of insight, like themselves—Newcombe
saw the dark scuttling figure, the stunning flash of the explosion, the eddies of black smoke boiling upward. The tank had
stopped; started again crawling in a half circle, beetling
around its broken tread, tipped, canted crazily and toppled
over rolling and crashing down the slope in a series of fan-

tastic detonations and burst into hot, roaring flames like a kerosene blaze, rocking and quaking with each crash as its ammunition exploded. The Japs, dismayed, were running off toward the strip of jungle, diving for cover. Someone near him was uttering sharp cries: Carney, holding his elbow, his eyes rolling.

Everything was over: everything was still.

Danny

He raised his head—saw a crumpled configuration far down the draw: like laundry, a crushed bundle of ragged olive-drab laundry. It stirred feebly, was still again.

Ah, the bastards. Ah, the bastards—

He was on his feet, filled with a terrible fury, was running down into the draw. Someone behind him was shouting, "No, Al, *no*—" There was a quick, shrill whistle in the air beside him. The bastards, the bastards! A figure rose before him, leveled a rifle: he did not care. Not for any filthy thing in the world. The rifle muzzle puffed fire and white smoke. He fired from the hip, fired again and again. With a shriek the figure sank away: he ran into it, struck the sinking head aside with his rifle, ran on in a raging paroxysm and dropped down beside the torn and shattered flesh, the pearl-gray ooze of entrails, the crushed leg like a wasted bloodied stocking.

"Danny—!"

Kantalyis opened his eyes, dazed and sightless; closed them again. One hand moved, twitching—then clenched tight.

Newcombe whirled around. No one was coming. They were all crouched at the edge of the draw.

"Well come on!" he shouted. "Give me a hand . . ."

They stared at him, still and stricken; waved him back. A bullet chirped overhead. Behind him the wrecked tank continued to crackle and roar.

"Come on!" he screamed at them. "Get your asses over here! Are you *dead*—?"

They came, then: Jay and Carrington first, Derekman and Woodruff; running low, bent double, their mouths gaped wide with breathing. Tumbled down beside him and stared.

"Don't touch him," Carrington said in a quick, harsh tone. "Can't you see his guts are hanging all over his legs?"

"What are you going to do—leave him here, for Christ sake?"

"Course not." Carrington's hands moved rapidly in and out of his dressings case. "Going to have to tie him up plenty, though . . ."

They crouched around him, uncertain and silent. The rest of the squad came over in twos and threes. All the firing had stopped. The tank, lying on its back in the bottom of the little ravine, had stopped exploding but was still furiously burning.

"What do you think, Carry?" O'Neill said.

"He's in a bad way. Hell of a bad way."

The face was gray as dirty water; a gob of mucus fouled the upper lip. Newcombe couldn't bear to see it there, wiped it away with his thumb. Ah God help us, he thought blindly. Ah God help us. Now we're alone. Alone and helpless now.

"Rig a stretcher," Carrington was saying in his calm, matter-of-fact voice. "And chop-chop. Going to be a long carry."

"He's dead, ain't he?"

They looked up. Helthal was squinting down at them. Bristling with cartridges, knives, black whiskers: bristling man of war.

"No," Carrington said, "no, he's got a chance . . ."

"What the hell you all worked up over? So he got his, that's all."

Newcombe got to his feet; the aching, wild fury that he felt seemed scarcely a part of him—it was more like some demonic hand lifting him above the earth. Black little chains of serpents danced up and down before his eyes. He held his rifle in his two hands and shook it slowly back and forth.

"Helthal," he said in even measures, his voice shaking, "Helthal, if you say one word against Kantaylis again—*one simple word!*—I'm going to blow your head off with this rifle. And I don't care what they do to me. I swear to God Himself if you say one single word—"

"Now listen, Newcombe—"

"Say it!" he screamed in a frenzy. "*Say it!*"

Helthal's face had gone dead white and long; he was backing away, one hand held up before him. He had never seen a face so full of fear. Odd. Something was impeding him: someone's hand. He lowered the rifle. Someone had hold of his arms, was talking to him steadily: but he could hardly hear.

"Don't Al, don't," Jay was begging him; tears lay in his eyes. "Please don't. Please don't, now. We got to get him down. We got to get him back down—"

They were starting one of the Eastman runs and all the beaters and the Number Three machine were covered with white gauze like the looping skeins of tent caterpillars: the lights bathed them in a high brilliance. The beaters roared their low growling roar and Carl Striebel called to him: "Okay, Danny, thread her up! . . ." He moved forward with alacrity, lifted the soft, pliant edge of the paper from the suction pumps to the couch rolls, passed it through the first press, the second, wove it over and under the steam driers, dancing past the slowly turning gleaming wheels on wheels, tearing again and again to get a clean leading edge, the paper slipping along with him, following him obediently like a great blinding-white serpent, assuming form and substance under the heat and pressure, steaming, flowing in and out of the size tubs and through the Barber driers and the stack calendars and over the finish roll: and panting, sweating lightly he stood staring up at the glazed white mesmeric flow, hands on his hips, as he had done a thousand times before . . .

But something was wrong: Carl Striebel was shouting at him, redfaced and angry, waving his arms; he turned in bewilderment, realized that he had made some fatal, irreparable blunder—heard a thunderous *clank!* like all the forges on earth dropped, saw with looming horror the stack calendars buckling and tumbling like giant spindles gone mad, bursting and tumbling about him: pain shrieked through his belly like rods of fire, he was pinned, his legs were crushed—

In a frenzy of despair he wrenched free, found to his amazement he could stand, that he was racing through the sudden nightmare horror of the beater room, past the reddog cylinder of the Jordan, the stuff chests, the pulper, hounded by men's hoarse cries—why was he *running!*—still racing out of the back door and across the dam and up the path in the cool dark where stars wheeled in capering galaxies against his eyes. He had fallen. Where was he? On the Post Road—the Post Road!—was up again and fleeing from the blaring lights and bedlam of the mill on up the hill past the concrete gates unfurling, past Prentices', to the left at the fork, past the Lovelock Farm, up and up the narrow high-crowned road to where it forked again, had bent to the left unerringly, running in the dirt rut now, hard-packed frosty ground through thickly falling snow, slipping and sliding in the white, seething silence under the pines—saw at last far above him the clearing and the cabin: and his heart almost burst with relief. Home: miraculously he'd made it home. Standing at the edge of the brook in the winter stillness, overcome with boundless joy he saw the fawn. With a cry of recognition he went toward

it—saw it turn, afraid, sidle on awkward, stiltlike legs. He
threw away his BAR, his knife, his belt and grenades, his
helmet; came toward it with open arms, fell on his knees and
clasped with tender longing the smooth slender furry throat:
felt tears stream down his cheeks. He was forgiven: finally
and totally forgiven . . .

—But the fire had no forgiveness: it was gaining, coming on
in swirling black towers, all of the meadow and Paunce Hill
were aflame, and he was tired now, so weary he could hardly
move. He faltered, went to his knees, then hands and knees,
writhing at last over the harsh, snow-covered stubble—felt the
long tongues of orange flame lance out at him, sear his thighs
in a scalding excoriation that made him shriek. And looking
up at the cabin, smoke-wreathed now and in shadow, he knew
beyond a doubt that he was never going to make it, it was too
terribly, unattainably far away. He had let them down and
they were weeping, all of them standing at the wall by the
Scarborough Oak, they were all weeping, Andrea was
weeping, his mother, Stella, Maria, Mr. Lenaine—all were
dressed in somber black and weeping, wringing their hands,
singing a strange, wild lament; all except his father who stood
with his head swathed in bandages, gaunt and ghostly and
mad in the white stillness. Exhausted, on fire, his very vitals
on fire, he turned toward him pleading, but his father
remained obdurate, inflexible, shook his bandaged white head
and slowly raised one arm. Following its indication he looked
behind him, found he was staring into the deep, rectangular
trench of his own grave—

He was surrounded by a dazzling globe: bobbing in a globe
of pain so intense and bright he could not descry its origin.
And swinging, rocking suspended between heaven and hell—a
precarious perch: Mrs. Lenaine was below him, ranged beside
the devil—or *a* devil, anyway—laughing wildly, vengefully at
him, in anticipation—for he had sinned unpardonably against
her daughter and all the world should know it now at
last—crying for vengeance. But she had no *power,* only the
desire to see him cast below: an important point. The decision
lay somewhere else: it had been postponed—had it?—which
was why he was jolting and rocking in this hellish, fire-laden
suspension. If he could cut the tent-layers of webbing that
shrouded him, struggle up through the flashing, painful
darkness and appeal, appeal to someone—great Jesus, if
someone would only intercede for him, if he could only put
his fate in someone *else's* hands—

Rain stung his face. Rain unmistakably, lashing down: remotely comforting in the bright globe of pain. With the greatest effort he had ever made he opened his eyes. Newcombe and O'Neill: gasping and panting, their faces constricted with prodigious exertion. They were carrying him, helping carry him slung suspended between heaven and earth. But they could not intercede for him. Down: they were going down, sliding and slithering in the mud, the rain. After all these years. All these years beyond years. Three times and out.

They had paused a moment, were resting. The rain drove streaming against their faces. Newcombe was gazing at him: a look so fond, so fervent, so wildly desperate he could have laughed. He could have laughed if—

"—get you down, Danny . . ." The words floated toward him in taut, agonized exhalations. "—get you down—last thing we do. I *swear*—"

Going down. His mind's eye, unfettered by the pain, careened away, went winding fancifully down that slope beside the draw along the hogback to the rancho, through jungle to the flat beside the Atainu, along the stream past the banana plantation and Death Valley to the Horseshoe, the church, the humped sand hillock above the beach, the water's edge, the reef. All that way. All that murderous way to go. They must be half dead: half dead with carrying—

They were talking back and forth in the rain; calling to each other in gasps and shouts but he couldn't make out what they were saying, couldn't quite catch the drift of it. His foot was cold, unbelievably cold for this climate and pain quaked and churned through his being like a river in flood. He was distantly aware that he was groaning aloud. Rain lashed his face softly. His helmet was gone. Funny: first time he'd been without his helmet since D-Day in the morning. A naked, cold sensation: why didn't they give him his helmet? The least they could do for a—the least they—

Great pain came in a light, sick, wire-borne screech again, more terrible than he would have believed could exist: a blunt dark bolt of sheer agony that transfixed him, rent him apart. *Hang on,* he shouted to himself through its roar: *hang—on!* But he was too weary now, much too weary for it and it was too much—ah! too much by far. No more. His mind, his very being were swept off into the vast whirling sink-drain—but now instead of down he was caught up, borne up and away— what solace!—through the streaming clouds, the thunderheads, the calls and gasps and haggard faces and the pain to where hung fields on fields of bobbing stars, lambent and glowing and perpetually serene . . .

They carried him down, the four of them—Newcombe and O'Neill and Derekman and Woodruff—carried him with laborious, tender care, exhorting each other hoarsely, until they staggered and reeled and bumped against each other, until they had to kneel on one knee, singing with exhaustion. Then they went on again. When they finally reached the company bivouac area and saw the weapons carrier pulling out they screamed at it and waved their hands for it to stop.

At the field hospital they eased him off the ridged metal of the truck bed and bore him into the deep green hospital tent and set him down. A corpsman with a long, thoughtful face gave him a cursory glance and whistled and said: "Bad one, eh?"

"Yes," they said. "Real bad."

A doctor—a man with a fat body and hairy, vigorous forearms—came out of the confusion and bent over him, started to cut away the gauze binding Carrington had made fast, looked at him again, felt his pulse, pried back one eyelid, straightened and said:

"Why, he's dead."

"No," Newcombe said doggedly, through a haze of exhaustion, "no, he's not—"

The doctor turned and stared at him, his bushy black eyebrows raised; pried up one of Kantaylis' eyelids again and said with terse, barely controlled exasperation, "I said he's dead. Are you going to argue with me?"

"—But he looked at me," Newcombe burst out. "He spoke to me!"

The doctor regarded Newcombe a moment, his eyes bright with sudden suspicion. Then he rubbed the side of his face with his wrist and said, "I don't care what he did. He's dead and that's all there is to it. Now damn it, take him over to Graves Registration. You can't leave him here, we haven't got room enough here for people as it is. You should have known better than to bring him in here in the first place."

"But I tell you he—"

"That's enough!" the doctor said sharply. He turned away, melted into the alien pattern of supine forms and blood and gauze. They stared at each other mutely, forlornly. Then raised Kantaylis' body and went out.

Across the road at Graves Registration they cut off his dog-tags and filled out a slip on him. A red-haired corporal went methodically through his pockets. The watch: the dark leather wallet, its surface cracked and blackened and green with damp rot, which contained a five-dollar bill and snapshot of a middle-aged couple with their arms around each other, surrounded by children of all heights and ages, smiling into harsh sunlight, and another one of a slim blonde girl standing with her hands placed between the trunks of two birches, her head back, laughing: the wedding ring on his finger and a pocket knife and a chip of closegrained wood the size of a half-dollar, worn and faintly oily. The corporal slipped them one by one into a little green sack and tied the neck of it tightly.

"You're sure it'll get to her all right?" Newcombe said. "His wife?"

The red-haired corporal looked up at him askance, squinting against the coil of smoke from his cigarette. "Sure it'll get to her. What the hell do you think—we hawk 'em?"

"No," Newcombe muttered. "I—just wanted to make sure. He . . . he was a very wonderful guy."

"Sure, sure," the corporal said. "They're all wonderful guys. They're all swell."

It started to rain again, beating in roaring waves against the high roof of the tent, pouring down with a greasy spattering sound beyond the flap. They turned their backs on the corporal and squatted on the ground near the entrance, stared out at the rain in dazed fascination; as though it might hold some answer for them, some solace.

"I just don't know," Woodruff said, and sighed. "I just don't think I'll ever see it rain like this here."

"You're seeing it *now*, for God's sake," Derekman snapped crossly.

They fell silent again, waiting for it to let up a little. On the earth near them Kantaylis lay stiffly, head lolled to the right. Shivering, gripping his left shoulder, Newcombe gazed at him dumbly. A face strangely wizened: gray and shrunken and old. Not Danny at all. The blued lids, not entirely lowered, revealed crescents of white. Those are pearls that were his eyes. Those are. No victory. Danny, he thought; *Danny.* That that dirty, torn, desiccating clod of earth should be—

Grief choked him all at once. No dignity in death, he thought with raging hot despair, looked away. There was no dignity in death, death was a grinning monster who wiped

away grace and all gentility. The dead tree gives no shelter . . .
But it was not all: *this was not all!* Why should this be the
ultimate landfall?—for the man who had endured all manner
of hell-fire, who had led them—callow, trembling neophytes,
sustained them all through fourteen terrible days and nights
and endowed them with what constancy, what scant nobility
of purpose they—

His eyes filled. He looked down, gripped his hands between
his knees and his shoulders shook.

Jay's hand was on his shoulder: old Jay, old friend who
sticketh closer than a brother.

"Take it easy, Al."

That the finest of the, the noblest . . . Where was there any
comfort? It is the stars, the stars above us, govern our conditions. These are gracious drops. Then I, and you, and all of
us fell down: lost, all of us, desolate and naked before the
fraudulent machinations of the principalities and powers. Ah
God, let this not be the end, here in a rain-soaked rotting tent,
for a man who lived nobly—

"Take it easy, Al . . ."

Blindly he raised his head.

"—I saw him look at me," he cried out in anguish. "I saw
him! He spoke to me!"

9

HE HADN'T SEEN the bicycle turn in from Laurel Avenue; he
only became aware of it gliding toward them along the street,
the boy's thin silhouette slipping between the trunks of the
maples, feet rising and falling languidly, without haste—as
though it had been there always, as in an unpleasant, recurrent dream, floating toward them. And watching its approach
through the screened windows Sidney Lenaine was conscious
of a slow, stealthy disquietude.

The bicycle wavered, stopped all at once in front of the
house. The boy swung off the seat with surprising awk-
wardness, leaned the vehicle against one of the trees and

turned, visored cap tilted over one ear, peering up at the door. Sidney Lenaine lowered the paper, staring, still burdened by the oppressive apparition, transfixed by it. The boy hesitated, scratching his head—started at last up the walk, and at the same instant Andrea said, "Why, that's Jerry Harris," put down her knitting and got up and went out of the screen door, her face alert and tense.

"Wait—" he started, "let me—" But she had gone. Standing now, the Berkshire *Eagle* hanging from his left hand, frankly alarmed, he watched her descend the porch steps and go down the walk and say: "Hello, Jerry . . ."

The boy stopped, startled, came close to her and put a hand on her arm, said something inaudible and low; then, still talking, backed away to where the bicycle leaned against the tree, swung onto it and stroked away, faster and faster down the street, melted into the dusk. Andrea, the yellow sheet of paper waving in one hand, looked back once toward the house—a wild, imploring glance; dropped her head on her breast, hands hanging at her sides. And Sidney Lenaine, rooted in front of his chair, thought stupidly, numbly, *death and disaster, death and disaster;* closed his eyes.

"Sidney," Virginia was calling from the kitchen. "Sidney . . ."

He opened his eyes again. The room was the same, utterly the same: the pillared, paneled highboy of a radio (silent now, mercifully silent, it was the one time of the day when it was and thank God for that), the portrait of Grandpa Abbott on the wall above it—hard, inflexible mouth, fierce brows and mutton-chop jowls: a good likeness. On the adjacent wall his own painting of Greylock, done long ago, a fanciful depiction of an Indian, bow in hand, standing in the reeds at the edge of Lake Pontoosuc gazing up at the summit of the mountain all aflame (he had loved to use reds and yellows) in the dying sunlight. Below it the couch covered with flamboyant pattern of poinsettias and egrets, and next to that the bookcase filled with ancient, solemn, undisturbed tomes: his father's pride and joy. The chairs, over-stiff or overstuffed. None of it had changed. Why not? Why for God's sake not? Their lives had: their lives had just undergone a terrible enough transformation—

Fearful, indecisive, he looked out again. Andrea was still standing where the Harris boy had handed her the telegram, motionless in the cool twilight. Ah, there was no sorrow so strong as the quick, wild sorrow of early loss—there was nothing with which to temper it: none of the acquiescences of age or disappointment. In a distended instant he thought of wet, gray little villages in France, the mud and endless rain, the cryptic grunt of artillery growing greater like the muttering of approaching giants; and the letter: *know this will be a terrible blow to you Sidney but writing like this you just can't break things gently you'd hear sooner or later anyhow and I'd rather it was from us it's been awful here the whole town is closed down now it seems at times as if everyone will catch it sooner or later thank God you hadn't got married at least.* Lowering the letter finally, looking at it askance, only half comprehending, sick with misery. And there welled up before him the image of a slim, pale face and overlarge eyes, a certain proud, innocent carriage of the head; a voice he could only with difficulty recall . . .

Virginia was still talking to him from the kitchen: calling in a brisk, half-audible tone. A habit of hers he detested, but which he'd suffered to continue, like so many other things. Something about the hose, taping the hose near the joints with friction tape.

He sighed, thrust up his glasses and rubbed his eyes. Then, as though suddenly wakened he cried to himself: *Go on, go out there, for God's sake go out and comfort her!*—dropped the paper on the floor and went out on the porch and down the walk, amazed and angered at so vast a dereliction. He paused and called softly, "Andy?"

She was standing exactly as she had been before, her back to the house, bent forward, arms stiffly at her sides: a slender figure carved from stone. Then she looked at him, only her head turning; a mute, agonized look that made his belly turn over.

"Andy," he said again, still more softly; came toward her across the grass, the first fallen maple leaves. Trembling faintly she looked away again—then came running against him with such force it staggered him.

"Oh," she gasped. "Oh—" And all at once she broke down; sobbed and sobbed, her forehead against his chest.

"Oh honey. All right, honey-girl," he said; his own eyes were hot with tears. "It's all right—" knowing the total inadequacy now of words, speaking gently, a soft crooning tone he hadn't used with her since he had walked the floor with her as a baby, or comforted her as a little girl. "Ah, Andy honey-girl . . ."

He stared at the telegram she held crumpled in her hand.

Couldn't they—for God's sake couldn't they devise some gentler, less brutal way than this?—why didn't they simply fire a flaming rocket in your front window, hissing and glowing, illumined with the phosphorescent words HE'S DEAD and be done with it? . . . Well: what difference did it make, death always came in stealthy strides, wind-borne, on bicycles, in seven-league boots, and pounded on the door. "Ah, honey-girl. Let it go. Let it go, now. Ah, honey . . ."

Clinging to him she went on sobbing steadily, hopelessly, catching her breath in rapid gasps; stopped after a little and looked up at him.

"Why," she said, her voice hoarse and low. "Why *Danny? Why?* After all he—"

She was still gazing up into his face, seeking; she was looking to him for an answer. He felt decades older in a bound: an old, old man, bowed and bent and crossed with questions too baffling, too enormous ever to resolve. The cool evening air bit into him tartly and he shivered.

"I don't know," he said, and shook his head . . . As long as we feel killing solves something, he thought with a fierce little wave of vexation; as long as we seek the release of killing and glorify it and the ones we get to do it for us—checked the angry flow impatiently. She could not bear that. Why should she? There was no solace in that thought. Not now or ever . . . What could he say? Weary and defeated, he remembered all at once an old woman sitting at the base of a wall in a destroyed village near Montfaucon: an old, wrinkled face, a heavy lump of a body that seemed to be actually dissolving in the steady gray rain, already a part of the earth; sitting immobile near the ruins of her home, unable to leave, unable to stay. The buildings shelled to rubble, the livestock driven off, sons killed or away, her husband dead, she had watched the column pass without the faintest gleam of hope; without interest or concern. *Poor old woman,* he had thought then, with the bright largesse of healthy youth; *poor old thing.* And hard on that, *Those bastard Germans, bastard bastard Germans*—a quick, focused anger that warmed him faintly in the soaking rain; well, they would put an end to this, once and for all . . . Now, twenty-six years later, he knew differently; he understood some of what she had felt.

"I don't know," he said aloud. He was shivering now, severely—a hollow trembling he sought to put down. "Sometimes—I think there are those who die for others: and

those who live for themselves . . ." Was there any sense in
that, any truth? did he believe it? It sounded so over-
simplified, so callow. But it might comfort her a little: could
it? Doubtful: what words could have comforted him when
Lorna had died of influenza? The blanket on his cot had had a
crease just below the border. After all these years that was
what he remembered: a staggered wrinkle like a lightning bolt
on the brown cloth . . .

"You're cold," she said. She had stopped sobbing, was
blowing her nose. "You'll get cold out here."

He patted her shoulder softly, stroked her hair; thought of
old George Kantaylis, half-destroyed and mad. Would he
know—would it penetrate to the heart of that wounded brain
that his eldest, his most beloved son had fallen, lay a torn,
defiled mass of flesh half a world away? Yes: he would know,
in that disordered, circuitous path his intuitions took—as
though the blow from the burst beater belt had liberated him
strangely, and in forfeiting the capacity for that ordered,
sequential thought that passed for intelligence he had gained
an awareness of a higher order—he would know, as he knew
now that a war had come, another, fiercer war than theirs,
one that dragged on from year to dreary year, and to which
his sons, all but one, had gone . . . I was spared, he thought. I
was spared that, at least.

"Yes," Andrea said. They were walking back now, up the
porch steps; his arm was around her, holding her. "Yes,
maybe that's it, Dad. The whole thing."

Her voice was flat, bitter, forlorn. What did I say? he
wondered; he had completely forgotten. Still supporting her
he thrust open the screen door, saw Virginia standing in the
archway to the dining room, blinking at them in astonishment.

"What is it?" she said. "What's the matter? You didn't answer and I—"

He threw her a quick, beseeching glance; saw her eyes dart
from Andrea's face to the telegram and back again.

"—Is it Daniel?" she whispered.

"Yes," he said. "It's Danny."

"Oh Andrea," she said, "oh my dear . . ." She came forward then and took her in her arms.

"It's all right," Andrea said weakly. Motionless she suffered herself to be embraced, then dropped on to the couch,
bent forward over her knees. "I'll be all right in a minute. In a
minute or two."

He sat on the arm of the couch beside her. She looked so white it frightened him: as though her lifeblood were a vapor escaping from her minute by minute. He realized with a start how thin she'd become since the baby. He put his arm around her again, stroked her forehead and hair with an automatic gesture.

"Oh dear," Virginia was saying nervously. "Oh dear, oh dear . . ."

With swift apprehension he looked up, saw his wife begin to rub her hands one with the other, a furtive abrasion; saw the tight, shuddering tremor start in her head and neck, the mouth vanish, lips swallowed up in a pursed line above the pointed chin, the eyes darting in a feverish dance from object to object: a mask faintly insane, scarcely human. Watching the old, familiar performance of fright and tortured remorse he had seen so often at any one of a dozen crises over the past two years (and before that, God knew, years before that, there was the time they'd skidded on the ice in '37 coming back from the Daytons' and sideswiped the telegraph pole: instead of being thankful no one was hurt, none of the three of them, miraculously, wonderfully, not even a cut or a bruise despite the awful grinding smash of it—in place of the dizzy gratitude he and Andrea had felt there had come this raving outburst of grief and hysteria over the car, the car, the terrible accident, the shock of it and—what else?—some damn thing else, for God's sake, some weird unpursuable inverted glorification of the whole incident as *deserved*—and her own reaction to it, *her reaction*—!)—watching the same old ritual begin he thought with a groan: God's punishment for all our horrible sins. Jesus. And then: No—not this time. No. Andy couldn't bear it.

"Yes," he said aloud, looking directly up at Virginia. "This is a hard time now. For Andy. We've all—we must all stick close and help her. Help her through this all we can."

She turned away, moved over to one of the south windows where she stood wringing her hands still more wildly, and said: "Oh, what did we do to deserve this? What have we *done?*"

"Nothing," he said. He pressed Andrea's head to him. "We've done nothing to deserve this but be living in the middle of a world war . . . Is there coffee made?" he asked. Anything, anything to keep her from cranking up on God's Avenging Wrath, the dies irae, jealous lightning-dealing Jehovah stalking through the world . . .

Andrea sat up quickly, said, "That's Stevie," and ran out of the room and up the stairs. And though he had been aware of nothing when she spoke he heard now the faint, fretful chuckling sound of a baby just awake.

Still sitting on the arm of the couch he put his hand over the lower part of his face. Danny, now dead, lived in Stevie. Did he? Feet moved quickly above his head, crossed to the dresser, to the crib; to the dresser again. Widowed and orphaned in a blow they clung together, one feeding, the other fed . . . How strange life must be, viewed from some cold, timeless, astral point-of-vantage: the passage of this race of forked bipeds who thrust upward from brutishness, developed speech, articulate thought, ideals, surrounded themselves with myriad mechanical devices and boasted of them—legends they themselves knew were false—who devoted millions of man-hours to perfecting the most ingenious instruments for slaying their own kind . . . and never for all the erratic and dazzling achievements in art or philosophy lost their popeyed reverence for the general, the panoplied, smoking man of war who surveyed the field moaning with the agonies of the dying and said calmly: "Another victory like that and we are done for . . ." Well: we were done for, all right—

"What will she do? What will she *do*, Sidney?"

He looked up. Virginia had turned toward him, white-faced and gaunt. He could hardly believe it: again, as so often before, he was held in stupefied amazement at the memory of the slender, pretty, painfully shy girl he had married twenty years ago, confounded now by the harsh, grimacing visage, the darting eyes. Odd: he had mistaken the shyness for a natural reticence, an inherent softness, something . . . had he? No. No, that was not true, it had been there: it had been there certainly until the baby died, the little boy. That awful, interminable, hopeless spring. Andy had been four: and very hushed and bewildered. *Daddy, what's wrong? What's happened, Daddy?* Now again she was asking him what had happened; was looking to him for comfort, for some definition to existence he could not give. The derangement of loss: was that it? Well, he'd felt it too, God knew—a hollow, cold tingling that pressed against his consciousness like an amputated limb; he still could not think of the chill afternoon and the lowering of that preposterously tiny coffin without a numbed throb of deprivation . . .

But for Virginia it had taken the form of a steady, almost mortal lesion—something from which she could never either

quite recover or die. It had been—the baby's death—some
form of retribution, an act of terrible vengeance for something in their lives, some monstrous and unpardonable trans-
gression. But what was it, then? What did she think it was? he
would ask her, sitting at her bedside, holding her hand in his.
"I don't know, I don't know," she would murmur, shaking
her head back and forth and soundlessly weeping. Baffled and
apprehensive he would leave her at last and go into Andy's
room and read the child to sleep.

Nevertheless, they were guilty as charged; and therefore
must atone. Picnics, parties, celebrations, vacation trips—any
occasion for levity or mirth or indolence, were suspect; even
their life together. They were bathed in sin; and these were
vicious things. With an arid, stony resignation she gradually
withdrew from them all . . . and in their place had come the
fevered religiosity, the tense, overbright, electrical nervousness after Kindlbinder's sermons, the rolling, darting eyes
("Wasn't it superb, Sidney? wasn't it *fine?*"), alternating
with moments of this hand-wringing self-deprecation and
despair—

"Do?" he echoed. "Go on living, I guess. Like the rest of
us."

She shot him another glance, restive, violent, her eyes all
whites. "Yes but I mean with a baby. And no father, no one
to provide for her, fend for her—"

"We're here, Virginia."

She made a quick, unhappy gesture, clenched her hands
together again. "What can she do? Ruined, ruined . . . I knew
it," she said.

Her mouth was set again: the indented, lipless line he hated
and feared. *I knew it knew it all the time they had no business
whatever getting married with him*

"Oh, I knew it would happen. They had no *business* getting
married, God knows I tried to reason with them but no,
they—"

He was not surprised at the audible echo of his conjecture;
he had long ago ceased to be. Arms folded across her breasts,
staring bleakly out of the window she was going on and on,
about their foolishness, their heedless folly and the of course
consequent and inevitable retribution. He let the phrases slip
along the edge of his mind, thinking with a steadily rising
despair: At a time like this. Sweet Christ, at a time like this,
with her own child, her own and only child sitting upstairs
wild with grief and she—

He took the pack of cigarettes out of his shirt pocket and methodically selected one, knowing she would speak to him, knowing before she said it she would say:

"Sidney, do you have to smoke in here?"

"Yes," he said, tapping it against his thumbnail. "I have to."

"It does seem that you could refrain from smoking in the one room where I've asked you—"

"Yes, I have to," he repeated. He lighted it and smoked steadily, disconsolately (this filthy habit of his she had long deplored), puffed great clouds of smoke around him; watched the soft August day sink into darkness. The street light at the corner came on, cast its febrile glow. Virginia had returned to the ill-starred-marriage theme again; her voice, risen a note, was harsher and more clamorous . . . It was strange: one grew up full of dreams and visions, became beguiled by them, married and settled down; settled down to marriage and a job which were not at all what one had fondly dreamed. How full of ironies life was: how dense and swarming with mysteries! For people were good, basically: friendly and well-meaning and steady, basically; amenable to reason . . . And then things happened, events transpired to turn them into fierce, bright patriots packing their sons off to death and horror, collecting old newspapers, rubber, tin foil—great Jesus, *tin foil!*—calling to each other witless slogans in place of decent Christian greetings. Events transformed them into iron statues of righteous vindictiveness such as the one he was now unhappily regarding. The derangement of loss . . .

Virginia, he wanted to say deeply, powerfully, unanswerably, going to her and taking her in his arms, shaking her if necessary—Virginia, don't you remember when we took the car trip to Lake George in '27 and I followed the truck down into the sand pit that evening in the rain? or the Sunday afternoons we used to make ice cream and you'd pour in the rock salt and we'd sing, *"There is a tavern in the town, in the town—!"* faster and faster and I'd crank faster and faster along with it until I almost fell over in a dead faint and we'd sit there laughing? Good God, don't you *remember?* Yes, I know, I've changed too, I'm a lot different, too—but can't we get back to the light, solicitous affection we had then, can't we do that somehow?—now, especially, when our only child is swept with misery and loss—?

"Virginia," he said with quiet persistence. "Virginia. She

needs our help, now. This is a terrible time for her, we've got to help her . . ."

"*Help* her," she answered in a wild tone, "—how can we possibly help her now?"

"Many ways. We can—"

"It's beyond help, it was ill-starred from the very beginning—oh! I pleaded with her years ago not to see so much of him, see George Holbrook more, you know, when he was going to Amherst, I begged her not to, I *knew* it was wrong, all wrong . . ." Tearful now, shaking her head blindly, she raced along: "She had no business marrying a man who had been through all that and was going out there again, let herself be—"

"Virginia," he protested, "she *loves* him, she *loved* him—"

"She—*had—no—choice!*" She bent toward him. Her voice, all at once subdued, was thin and rasping, a querulous whisper; her eyes glittered feverishly. "You know as well as I do—all right I'll say it, I held my tongue for months, I believed it was the proper thing to do, I said nothing, not even to you, I didn't think I had to—she *had* to marry him, she had no choice by then! Too late, too late! Oh, the dishonor of it!—the *dishonor* . . ."

Ah. The dishonor. He felt terribly old again, looked away through clouds of cigarette smoke. The dishonor of it: of the good wives and mothers toting up months on fingers, reckoning, murmuring to each other over the bridge tables, eyes sparkling with petty malice. Dishonor . . . But what of the licensed dishonors—what of marriage without love or flattery for advancement or slander or the flaunted pride of heritage? What of these?

No. He would not be overborne by her. Not on this desolate, melancholy evening. Come what may.

"Virginia," he broke in on her, "does that preclude her loving him? Does it? Even if it *were* true—"

"Of *course* it's true!" she cried. She had come over to where he sat and was standing in front of him, pawing at the smoke, her gaunt, lined face glaring down. "Why do you think he came home for *two days*—after he'd had a furlough not two months before? He got an emergency leave, that's why—because that girl was pregnant!—if you didn't want to see it that was your business but it was there to see and that's how it was—"

"All right," he said, raising his voice for the first time, "all right then, and why do you suppose they didn't get married when he *was* home? Because you made your disapproval felt so strongly, among other things. Hasn't it ever occurred to you that might have had something to do with it?"

"*I!*" She put her hand on her breast: a quick, savage gesture. "Sidney, that's outrageous—are you trying to put what they did on *my* head?"

"I didn't say that. I'm talking about what—"

"That's despicable—I will not take the burden of their sin on me, I will not!—"

There was a step at the foot of the stairs; Virginia Lenaine whirled around. Andrea was standing in the doorway with her coat on, the baby in her arms. She had stopped weeping; her face was pale, and set in a dogged expression.

"I'm going over to the Kantaylises' for a while," she said.

Sidney Lenaine got to his feet, filled with a sense of shame and inadequacy. "Do you have to . . . tonight?" he asked softly.

"Yes. I think Danny's mother ought to know. It's up to me to do."

"Can't I run you over?"

"No, I'd like the walk. It's a nice evening. Thanks anyway, Dad."

There was a silence. The two women looked at each other, looked away.

"I'm sorry, Andy," he said. "That you heard all this, if you did. We didn't hear you coming down the stairs . . ."

"It's all right," she said in a spent, level voice. "I don't care. Think anything you like." At the front door she turned and her eyes flashed once at her mother, bright with defiance. "I'll tell you this: Stevie was conceived up at Ned Irish's cabin the night we were married. You can think anything you want to. I don't care any more . . . I'll be back in an hour or so."

Sidney Lenaine let her out at the door, gave her shoulder a slow, affectionate squeeze. She smiled at him wanly and went out, moved briskly along the walk, her fine blond hair floating along her neck and shoulders. Our daughter. He watched her glide away below the street lights. We've lived all this time together, brought her into the world and fed and clothed and educated her and now this disaster has struck her and she turns to her mother-in-law for comfort. Her husband's family. All these years and we—

He leaned against the door jamb weakly, wearily. Their

daughter, their own flesh and blood—and they were of no help to her in her moment of anguish: no help at all. The thought of it surrounded him like a gray, enveloping horror . . . Perhaps, if he weren't so phlegmatic, so afraid of Virginia, so beaten down by her he'd storm out of there, get in the car and drive to Pittsfield, to Topeka or Timbucktoo, leave her for good and for all—even cut his own throat in a transport of blind despair. But such acts took fire and fury, and he hadn't possessed such ingredients as those in years: not in years and years . . .

He pushed himself off the wall and came back into the living room. Virginia was already talking again: a choking, raging exasperation that he found, under the circumstances, absolutely sickening.

"Gone! Gone over to *them*—!"

"Why not?" he demanded. "Why on earth not? What have we done but bicker over what she might or might not have done with the man she loved with all her heart—and at the very moment she's learned he's dead . . . Can't you even see *that?*"

"Are you blaming me again?" She threw open her arms: a wild, theatrical gesture that set his teeth on edge. "Me again? Sidney, that's beyond belief, I swear it! That's despicable! Oh, you've always been against me, both of you, always siding against me ever since—ever since she was four, I saw it happening—"

"Virginia," he protested, "that's not true . . ." She would begin to weep now, he knew; very soon now.

"—you were for this, Sidney, it was you, you always thought the *world* of him, I know—went to all the football games . . ."

"I thought he was a fine boy, yes, and so did a lot of other people, and I still think—"

"You were for this!" she cried hysterically, pointing at the wall. "It was you, not me, I won't be charged with it, you were all for their getting married, the romantic *drama* of it—"

"Virginia," he said, "the point is that Andrea—"

"—and now, see, now see what's happened, with no husband at all and a child to rear and her life ruined—utterly, hopelessly ruined—"

"*Virginia*—"

"—no, you let me finish, I gave in to you then, the way I always give in, and it was the craziest thing I ever did in all my life and you too, if you had the sense to see it! Uniform and medals and all that—a mill hand," she shrilled, "a cheap, common *mill hand!*—and he had his way with her too, seduced her and left her with a child, your grandson, a bastard, and ruined, her whole—"

"All right!" he shouted all at once. "All right. Don't listen. Don't ever." He went to the hall doorway—turned back with a wild, grief-stricken anger such as he hadn't known in years. "Dont' ever try to understand anything about anyone else in the whole, poor world! Not even your own daughter. Just make up your mind that they're all cheap and sinful and totally beyond God's forgiveness—even beyond yours!"

She stared at him, silent, her mouth open. Then wringing her hands more wildly than ever, her face contorted in a shuddering tremor, eyes half closed, she began to weep.

"Oh Sidney," she moaned, "oh, how can you—how can you *talk* to me this way?—when you *know*—"

"No," he said, more calmly. "No, Virginia. No more of that. It's too late for that now. Why don't you try to understand this, Virginia? just try? . . . Look," he cried with soft passion, "the whole world—millions upon millions of human beings no better and no worse than yourself are being burned out of house and home and imprisoned and tortured and executed and God knows what else. Do you honestly believe they all did something to deserve it? Do you honestly?"

She made no reply; shuddered and wept, her face averted. A wave of pure frustration went over him. She was suffering, really suffering. Was she? No. She wasn't: it was something else.

"You just haven't any love, have you," he said. "Any real love: for anybody but yourself. You don't know *what* Andy has borne up under all these months, do you know that?—you don't know what she's gone through because you've never tried, you've never really cared to find out. Because you've shut yourself off from everybody else. Right now you're thinking only about yourself—wallowing in some fancied, concocted grief, some crazy mortification or other while Andy's over there having to tell—"

His voice broke. He swallowed, took a cigarette out of his pocket and held it unlighted in his hand. "If you knew, if you were so sure she was pregnant last November, why were you so set against the marriage? Why, Virginia?" He paused, said in shaking anger, "Because you *wanted* her to be shamed, didn't you?—before all the town. In some queer, crazy, perverted way that would have vindicated your sense of guilt and retribution—even though it would have killed *her* . . . You ought to look down into your heart, Virginia—take a good look at what's going on in there . . ."

He took a step toward her, his hands raised before him—a gauche, suppliant gesture; dropped them to his sides. "Do you think we haven't been bombed and machine-gunned and tortured and deported because we're *good*, because we're better or holier than the French or British or Italians or anyone else? Good God—people are born and grow up and grow old and die, disasters fall upon them from a dozen directions and they bear up under them as best they can, try not to succumb—accept life as it is, try to live with dignity, do what you feel you have to . . . like this boy you despise so, Virginia. Yes—who went back out there a second time for us, fighting for *us*, because he felt he had to—and I doubt if we're worth the sacrifice, any of us—washing machines and bathtubs and movies and all . . . Ah, don't you see, Virginia, life isn't an endless review before some vengeful, celestial parole-board—it's trying to live with other people, taking them as they are, *trying*—at least some of the time—to see the good in them, respect them, love them—try to . . ."

She was not listening: he knew. The lowered lids, the pursed mouth, the unbroken tremor of rampant martyrdom bespoke it. She was shutting him out as he had shut out her wild ranting an hour before. Ah God, what was the hope—? Gazing at this silent, withdrawn figure who was his wife he felt a swift little urge to go out, go down to the tavern or over to Carl Striebel's or the Kantaylises', pour out the accumulated frustration of twenty years. But he knew he never would; he knew he'd go in to the den and finish reading the *Eagle*, would mount the stairs to bed and lie on his side in the dark; sleepless, staring, beset by fierce, tumultuous thoughts of dissolution and despair.

We haven't learned anything, he thought. Not one damned solitary thing. He blew his nose, lighted the cigarette and puffed at it desperately; looked again at his wife. Standing there in the center of the room, shuddering and weeping, drunkenly (yes, drunkenly! he thought: she's on a bender, she who never takes a sinful drop—she's on a spinner far more terrible than any poor old Charlie St. Clair ever went on) obsessed with the spectacle of her own mighty, omnivorous grief, she seemed to epitomize everything about America he knew and feared: the hysterical extremism, the childish irresponsibility and self-enclosure, the endless, blind absorption with things—the inability to conceive of anything that couldn't be fashioned, improvised, turned into something else, preferably something else profitable—the complacent impregnability of attitude; the desperate, desperate want of compassion . . .

And his dereliction had been as great, too—in another way, he saw with a pang. For he had once been brought face to face with disaster, and had allowed himself to grow slothful and forget . . . It wasn't true, he thought despondently, thinking of Danny, remembering the steady gaze, the slow, calm, reassuring smile, it wasn't true that I thought it could never happen again: I just came home and didn't care whether it did or not . . . I should have cared, I should have—oh, I don't know, joined something, maybe worked for international peace back in the days of the League, back when it counted for something, I don't know. Not that it would probably have made any difference, but at least I might not feel quite the way I do this evening . . .

A plane was passing high overhead: a bomber droning south toward Westover Field. For an instant it seemed as ominous as the mutter of implacable, wrath-bearing gods, presaging a nightmare diorama of toppling towers, cities dissolving in a sheet of flame. God help us, he thought in somber dread. God help us when it comes upon us and we sit like that old woman among the shattered rubble of our homes, watching with dazed and hopeless eyes the slow parade of alien soldiery, alien arms . . .

The muttering drone ceased, returned faintly; vanished altogether. Beyond the windows the summer night lay just as before: impossibly inviolate and serene.

10

IT HAD STOPPED raining but the air, though vibrant, was still moisture-laden and heavy, as though it had been transformed into some substance denser and more opaque than real air.

Sunlight glowed on Mount Matenla and clouds hung, edged with silver and billowing, above its summit, streamed off to the northwest in resplendent shades of amber and ruddy gold. To the north guns still rumbled, thumped and bumped in anger; but it was no concern of theirs now. They were relieved for two days: they lay sprawled near their shelterhalves in a little hollow that was like a sea cave, windless and quiet and surrounded by the shaggy mass of banana and ifil trees.

And all sink down together, Newcombe thought; and all sink down together to the bottom of the sea. Around him figures moved in dreamy, languorous attitudes: stretched, lay down, splashed water on themselves from helmet-bowls and stood naked and glistening in the shadows, bathed in the heavy, aqueous light. Sitting in front of the shelterhalf with Kantaylis' pack in his lap he watched through a break in the trees the deep blue of the water beyond the reef. Solace: there was solace in the still, faultless sweep of sea and sky, the saffron-glittering shore—if one were far enough away.

He opened the pack, methodically pulled out a pair of damp, filthy dungaree trousers white with mould, two C-ration cartons, several cans of Japanese beef and crabmeat, some rifle cleaning patches, two green skivvy shirts torn and spattered with mud and dried blood, an extra cleaning tool. The impersonal effects. Danny had stuffed these in here not two days ago, had pulled the straps tight with his strong, broad hands . . .

A pair of clean socks: a patrol cap faded by salt and sun: a little packet of Japanese postcards. Newcombe gazed in mournful abstraction at the printed postage stamp of the first—a shaggy, black samurai mounted and in full armor, wielding a sword; flipped it over revealing columns of delicate rice-grain characters like flowing tears. What was written there? Ah, the timeless, piercing catena of affection, anxiety and solicitude from the women on the wall . . . Why had Danny kept it? Or, beneath that, the brown, blotchy photo of the plump woman and the little child, an embryo replica, both smiling, eyes slitted below the shuttered membrane of the upper lid, their kimonos dark against the feathered willow branches sweeping down . . .? All silent and all slain: she was a widow now, without doubt, the child fatherless. Below it were more postcards, on one of which were traced four Japanese characters and below it the legend: LAND MINES HERE, followed by several laborious copies in pencil. The stamps on all these were—incredibly—a helmet surmounted by a soft white dove with an olive branch in its beak. The minutiae: all the piteous accretions. Beneath them several sheets of notepaper folded twice and smeared with mud; vaguely he opened them, ran his eyes along the wavy, backhanded script:

nineteen pounds, would you believe it? He keeps kicking at me with his left foot, I hold him on my lap standing up and he kicks and kicks and laughs at me. Oh he really looks like you Danny, so much, you'd never guess, your eyes absolutely, your mother saw it right away. She's a darling with him, I took him over there this morning, I've been spending more and more time over there. Things are getting worse and worse with Mother, I've just got to get out of here or blow up at her—which I'm trying not to do on account of Dad who's been wonderful to me all these past months. Besides, your mother's so lonely now with the boys gone. Nick has just been transferred to Arizona, I suppose he's written you. And the whole house is in a whirl over Stella's marriage, of course! I'm awfully happy for her and told her so, Stan will be a wonderful husband for her, she should have married him years ago. I told her that too, when we were alone together once, and she smiled and looked at me with those dark eyes, sometimes she reminds me so much of you it's frightening, and said, "I know it. I was hoping it would be when Danny could be home for good." She's really so sweet.

A beautiful day. You know, clear skies and northwest wind, really the first day of fall in a way, you can feel it in the air. The hot spell is over for good, I think. I ran into Ned going to work yesterday, he's on three-to-eleven tour now with Russ Mallett. He says he likes it better, there's nobody he wants to see in the evening now anyway, with you and Fred away, and he can work in the garden mornings. You should see his tomatoes! I asked him, I don't know why I just said it, if we could have the cabin for a week each year. You know, just go up and laze around, walk in the woods or go sliding, oh how I remember that day! Streaking down the slope in the white whirling powder yelling back and forth and laughing, you know I think of that more than anything else, somehow. Funny the things you find yourself thinking of, going back to over and over, isn't it? Oh Danny, I

*know this must all seem silly to you where you are now,
but it's all there is to write about. I know you'll write
when you can. I'll hold on and be steady, I promise. But
at times I get, well things get too much for me and I let
down, Mother's attitude has been just about enough to
drive me crazy sometimes. Danny I pray and pray you'll
come back safely, I lie in bed at night listening for Stevie
and praying you'll be all right and longing so to have you
here in my arms. Darling, you've no idea how much
everybody here depends on you and wants you home safe
again, your mother and Stella and Maria and Jimmy and
Ned and Carl Striebel and everyone. And me most of all.
Oh I long for you so it makes me tremble all over.
Couldn't you get transferred or something by now?
You've done enough, you know you have, more than
anyone else in the country, practically. Just so you'll be
back here, that war bond tour you could have gone on
when you were back, couldn't you still do that now? And
then get transferred later if you want? Just so you'd be
home for a little while. Oh forgive me darling, it's only
that I can't help it sometimes, I get morbid and worried
in spite of everything I keep telling myself and the radio
going on and on every minute of the day and night, she
never stops listening to it, and not hearing from you in so
long, I suppose the mails are all*

Newcombe gave a sudden, anguished sob that was almost a
sneeze; closed the letter on his thumb. Ah God. He is alive to
her, now: the living object of her love . . . It was true, then:
the war bond tour. He could be a sergeant, could ascend the
steps in immaculate pressed greens, two banks of ribbons,
harangue the assembled artisans over the stutter of rivet-guns.
The evil that men do. Then I, and you, and all of us fell down,
whilst bloody treason—

He raised his eyes in sudden inflamed outrage. Beside him
O'Neill slept, oddly boyish without helmet or beard; a hollow,
restless, twitching sleep. Derekman, naked except for green
skivvy shorts, crouched simian-like in front of a metal disc
and scraped his underchin with a razor. Farther away
Capistron, head propped against a fallen tree, tilted a saki
bottle upward, his throat pulsing in obscene, slow ripples like
a python ingurgitating. Lowering the bottle he belched, wiped
his lips with both hands and sang: *"You had plenny nooky
nineteen forty-three, now you're chasing gookies through the*

shrubber-ee . . .'' Catching Newcombe's eye he winked a slow, cunning wink and called, "Hey, Newcombe! What you doing over there—going into a poetry trance? *Hey!*"

Somberly Newcombe shook his head; pointed to O'Neill and put a finger to his lips.

"Okay, okay, I got you . . ." Capistron nodded in slack disgust. "Don't disturb the dead man. Hey, I got a poem for you, Newcombe. A real—profound—poem." He took a deep breath and intoned: "There'll be no friggin' in the riggin' . . . and no poopin' on the poop-deck—while in this diggin's. Ah?" He belched again and grinned. "Yeah. I made out all right: got my bottle keep me warm . . ." Standing the bottle up on his naked white belly he shouted: "Hey, Helthal, old buddy! Hey come over have a snort. Ah?"

A few feet away Helthal looked up at him dumbly, without interest or even recognition; lowered his eyes to where the stone slipped in quick soundless patterns along the blade of his knife.

"Ah, come on, buddy," Capistron called whiningly. "Don't gimme a bad time. You me we gonna run this squad, now. Run it like it oughta be run, ah?" He chuckled quietly, rocked the bottle back and forth on his swollen paunch. "Yes sir, gonna be no poopin' on the poop-deck unless *I* call the turn . . . Ain't that right, bottle. Ah?"

Newcombe folded the sheets with great care and put them back in the pack; took them out again and put them in his hip pocket. Silence descended over the area, sifted through the foliage like sunlight, in garish patterns: a lace shawl of light and silence . . . The terrible vulnerability of death, that exposes our emotional entrails to public view. By now she has received the wire: or soon, now. Standing on a porch on some quiet street, holding the telegram, unable to open it, unable not to. He lives to her now: living, breathing.

All the loss and bereavement of the day before returned in even greater force; he put his knuckles to his mouth. Oh pardon me, thou bleeding piece of earth. A piece of earth, he was already mouldering in this mucky, oozing soil, penite-sprayed, putrescent; and in the warm sanctity of the sun Capistron lay, a drugged, somnolent bear; and yawned and belched and drank. Out went the candle, and we were left darkling. Pr'ythee, nuncle. Let me kiss that hand. It smells of mortality—

He leaned back and closed his eyes. A darkness crept over him, a melancholy so profound he had the sensation he would be carried away by it, spirited off into some gray, turbulent realm where joy and innocence could never penetrate: a dead, gray universe of grief and loss . . . He lived to her still: the horror of it!—the unbearable fraudulence of circumstances that could dally with a girl's love and hope borne across ten thousand watery miles—

". . . He lives still."

He said the words aloud, with soft implacability, set his jaw. He lives still, and I will write her so: give that filthy yellow telegram the lie. His face fixed in stony, fanatical intensity he took several of the Japanese postcards, pulled the pencil stub from the pocket of his jacket.

Dear Mrs. Kantaylis:

This is no attempt to assuage or minimize your grief. I know better by now than to indulge in such paltry pretensions. Nor is my name important either—we have passed beyond the particularities of identity. And it is likely enough that Danny never mentioned me to you anyway. So let this be simply a few lines from one of the men in his squad, a friend who understood him a little and revered him much, and who would like to give expression to what he

For God's sake come to the point, come to the point: what's the matter with you! He frowned at the last clause, crossed it out. Bent forward again, scowling.

I think he was a very rare man. According to his lights—according to his lights he lived with rare nobility. And how many of us can say that? For Danny didn't live a lot of lies, he didn't float along on half-truths or quarter-truths or no-truths at all, scutter along with them like an old woman collecting faggots in the dark and then condone them with a smile and a shrug, the way most of us do. He had life in him—not just a timid predilection for existence like the rest of us. He knew its infinite value, as we did not; he could accept it completely, calmly, in all its measures. And it was that, I see now, that shone out of his eyes—that steadied us when all the universe flew apart in howls and shrieks. He could gaze at that dread Gorgon's face unafraid—and having looked without fear or duplicity he survived, and was ennobled. He gained back all that we have lost. He is the

*only one of us, God help us all, whom slaying has not
slain. I could tell you of an instance where he*

He paused in agitation; crossed out the uncompleted line.

*Ah, what sense is there in that, when you who love him
(yes, I know you love him as he loved—loves—you) and
know him far better than I ever could, have seen him in
his happiest hours? Why should I enumerate his virtues,
his innate nobility of spirit like items on a stupid shopping list? Let us leave that to the hired mourners, the ones
who never have and never will be torn with bereavement
or inadequacy or awe. What I am groping toward saying
is that his life had—has—meaning for us: he stands for
something in a time gone foul with raging. For he never
lost his compassion. He never lost his sense of humanity.
He walked without faltering through a hell whose terrors
he knew all too glaringly, led us halting and stumbling
through hell fire and saved our lives. And more: he gave
a focus to our disparate concerns, made of us an arm of
righteousness—yes, I mean it, of righteousness—and
when we set free the people on the hill beyond Maidinilla
it was as the sword of the spirit. Without him we are lost
indeed—a race of wrangling, discordant, brutish
pigmies. Fuimus Troies, fuit Ilium: it's that succinct, that
true. Troy is fallen, is fallen—*
*And yet not entirely. For we have his spirit among us,
moving among us, the memory of his soft nobility and
truth. It was not for nothing, is what I want to say.
Though he be dead yet shall he live in our resolve, our un-
deviating obligation to make it a victory not in
arms—where there can be none—but of the spirit. He has
not died, he is not dead! Not while*

He bent forward all at once and covered his face with his
sleeve. Weep no more, kind shepherds, weep no more; for
Lycidas, your sorrow, is not dead, sunk though he be. God.
Help us. Get thee apart and weep. All dark and comfortless—
There was no way. Words were nothing. Words, his
vocation and his passion, melted away in the face of that torn
and bloody form: a puny calligraphy. She would laugh
weeping at their monstrous inadequacy; and go in to her son,
her consolation, and feed him from her breasts. Though he be

dead, yet shall he live in the crowing infant whose left leg kicks and kicks at her thigh . . .

The day swam toward dusk, with faltering shadows. Out of them came Sergeant Hamway who stopped, hands on hips, and said:

"Two men. I want two men."

Capistron tilted his head, regarded Hamway with sleepy guile. "Don't hand me that. Frey said we're in reserve today."

"This is just a work detail. Hauling chow." He looked down at Capistron a moment: a frosty, measuring smile. "Hitting it pretty heavy aren't you, Cappie?"

"Just a nip. No cutting in the cane fields tonight: you know?" Capistron's eyes slipped around the ring of shelter-halves: came to rest on Newcombe. "Hey, poet," he called. "You're up. Wake up your side-kick, there. Give you a little exercise, ah?"

Newcombe stared back at him for a moment without expression.

"They had it last night, Cappie," Woodruff said in a plain-tive drawl. "How about Ensor or Thomas or one of them?"

Capistron turned and squinted coldly at Woodruff. "Who's running this squad, rebel? Me or you? Ah?"

Woodruff shrugged. "Well, sure, you're running it, Cappie, but that's a hell of a way to do, give it to them twice running . . ."

"Well, now you mind your business and I'll mind mine, rebel . . . Do 'em good. Help 'em to put on some weight, they're both getting pretty thin. Put on some weight for you, ah? That right, poet?"

Without reply Newcombe picked up his helmet liner and slipped the postcards in his pack. "Jay," he said, and touched him lightly on the shoulder. "Jay . . ."

O'Neill's eyes rolled in alarm, steadied quickly. "What's up?"

"Our new lord and master has just stuck us with another crud detail."

"So that's how it is."

"That's how it is."

O'Neill sat up and put on his blouse, glanced angrily over at Capistron who was watching them both and grinning.

". . . Hey, is that right, poet? I'm talking to you! . . ."

Newcombe turned and faced the acting sergeant. "Look,

Capistron: I'll do your crud details for you as long as I can. But don't expect me to talk to you too, because I won't.''

"Hey . . . you're plenty salty, buster.''

"I'm just telling you.''

"Take it easy, Al," O'Neill murmured. "Relax, now . . .''

Capistron grinned slowly, held up one fat finger. "Number one. That's you, buster. On my list.''

"It's an honor.''

"Listen to him! An honor! *Listen* to the poet, will ya?'' Capistron roared. "Number one! . . .'' His laughter followed them down the trail: a thick, coughing, derisive bellow.

"Filthy drunken son of a bitch," Newcombe muttered; he was quivering with anger.

"Take it easy, Al," O'Neill repeated softly. "Let him roar.''

"Yeah, but to stick us with—''

"I know. Just hang on. He gets too rough we'll go to Frey. We'll get out from under.''

"—The stupid, swinish bastard!" Newcombe cried savagely. "Do you know what he wants? Do you *know*?''

O'Neill put his arm around Newcombe's shoulders. "Just hang on, Al. Hang on, now.''

11

THERE WAS A leaf. Over a leaf. Sword-blade bobbing punkah leaves like satanic tongues. Between them in the sun-dappled dark an eye: a cold, yellow, unblinking eye—

O'Neill recoiled in terror, saw all at once the lizard, nearly two feet long, lying on the spear-shaped leaf. Deadly and still. Its eye stared coldly, its leathery old man's throat filled and sagged, filled and sagged in the silence.

"Jesus," O'Neill muttered. "Jesus—" He glanced back again, distrusting the image: the lizard had not moved, was still waiting. Waiting for what? His leg was throbbing: blood had soaked through the gauze and caked in a thick mat over which newer, brighter blood was oozing. His own blood flowing out of him without stint, he would bleed to death here by himself in the boondocks and no one would know a thing about it—

Hollow-eyed he gazed around him. Where *was* he? How the hell had he wound up like this, sitting here on the ground? His stomach and kidneys clutched and drained. He put his hand to his forehead, drew it away watery with sweat: he was bathed in water, soaking in water, bobbing in a thick column of water that rippled and wabbled and made him deathly ill. He took several swallows from his canteen, vomited instantly that and more; felt strength drain away from him in a rush. His hands were trembling wildly, beyond his power to control them, and his teeth were chattering.

That bastard Capistron.

Hatred for Capistron gripped him, gave him a fugitive, shuddering strength. That lousy son-of-a-bitching tyrant. If he'd let Al come back with him—Jesus, Al had had enough too, hadn't he?—even if he hadn't stopped anything yet—then he wouldn't be in the fix he was in now. Old Al would have kept him on his feet, kept him going, steered him right . . .

—He was in a room that swept into darkness around him—rooms and hall, everything, on a chill gust of wind. No light at all. He had been sitting at a table, carving the hull of a ship out of a cake of Ivory soap. Now hall, penknife, table no longer existed: everything swam in threatful darkness. Terror such as he had never known convulsed him, nearly stopped his breath. He sat there for what seemed hours but were undoubtedly only seconds swelled to measureless indolence: shivering and rigid. No light from anywhere! Then *candles*, he thought: candles. In the hall cupboard. Matches in the tin holder above the stove, candles in the cupboard. He got to his feet soundlessly, his knees knocking, and crept down the hall nearly too afraid to breathe, the blood thumping in his ears, while the walls, the barrier of darkness pressed in against him evilly; gained the cupboard and wrenched it open, gripped the smooth waxen cylinders and fled back to the kitchen, running heedlessly now, and groped along the wall until his hand encountered the match holder . . . But now, instead of the still, expanding golden solace he remembered, huge, ruffled beings had lurched toward him, surrounded him on all sides: snakes with leopards' heads, or bristling lizardlike porcupines alive with eyes, capering, prancing around him; he put up his hand to ward them off—saw a fleshy condor with the face of

Charlie Tarrasch rear up before him, grinning in delight, laughing soundlessly from a mouth that became all at once a suppurating black hole oozing blood. With a muffled cry he struck out at it, threw an arm across his eyes. The beastlike figures were still there, approached in thickened numbers. A wave of furnace heat went over him. He was dully aware that he was lying on his stomach and retching convulsively. Gasping, his teeth chattering, tormented by the tenacity of the hideous figures he looked helplessly at the wavering, reeling towers of jungle that pressed against him. He was in trouble, bad trouble: not only wounded and bleeding but he had dengué, and had it very, very bad.

He was hit: he knew it beyond a doubt. His calf burned like crossed wires, a twin stab of pain that grew with searing pressure. Someone was shouting wildly. There was the long, rolling roar of a BAR, then two dreamy, faraway cries and silence.

"Corpsman!" he shouted. He raised himself with slow care, pulled up his trouserleg—gazed in fearful fascination at the long, rectangular tear in his flesh where blood welled richly upward, streamed in a violent thick sheen over his calf. His own blood flowing. Stopped one, he thought with fright. All this time. After all this lousy—

"Carry!" he shouted again. *"Carry!"*

". . . Dead," a voice—Helthal's voice—said flatly. "Right through the head."

Al. It was Al. A spasm of cold fear shook him. He lurched to a sitting position and cried, "Who? Who got it?"

"Thomas," a voice said.

"Oh." He sat back, closed his eyes.

"What the hell's the matter with him?" Capistron was saying angrily, from a great distance. "Didn't the stupid bastard know how to take cover?"

"Son of a bitching thing went off in the air. Didn't you see it?"

"Hell, no. I was—"

"Jay. You stop something?"

He opened his eyes. Carrington was bent over him; clean-shaven, his face looked even more tired and wan than it had two days ago. It seemed to swell and diminish by turns, held in a watery, pulsing rhythm . . . He was in tough shape all right: tough shape. His whole body ached with a sudden, monstrous throb that made him groan.

Carrington slit the leg of his trousers, a sharp, tearing rip.

There was a quick cone of pure pain and Carrington said: "Got one of 'em. They'll have to dig the other one out down at Nénetan. See, there."

O'Neill stared at the piece of black metal slick with blood in Carry's fingers. That . . . *that had entered his body.* Where there was still another sliver of iron lying. The thought sickened him all at once, filled him for the first time since D-Day with barren despair. Luck run out, like everyone else. They keep sending you back and sending you back till the odds cut you down. The hell with it: hell with the whole lousy business. Newcombe was crouched beside him, gazing at him with anxious, worn eyes.

"What happened, Jay?"

"I don't know," he muttered. "Damned if I know. He must have thrown it way up in the air when he came out. I don't know . . ."

Newcombe was fading distantly, too: kept receding through black coiling rings laden with nausea and vertigo. Am I going to crap out? he wondered. The hell with it.

"Got a dreamer, Jay." Carrington was bandaging the compress rapidly, expertly. As if he were bandaging a model: a dummy model. "No problem at all. Get plenty sack-time, be out of it for a while."

Out of it. Yeah, but that wasn't the whole of it. It was this other business, which had been reaching over the back of his head all morning, and now had come with a rush. Newcombe's face, suddenly quite clear, looked both anxious and relieved at once.

"It isn't that," he said feebly.

"Isn't what?" Carrington demanded. "You hit someplace else?"

"No. I feel . . . I feel like I been clubbed over the head, Carry. Christ, I can hardly see you."

Carry was looking at his eyelid: his left eyelid. Holding it pressed upward. He couldn't for the life of him stop trembling. Sweat poured into his eyes. He'd been stuck with a needle in one of those mad-scientist time-machines and was growing older by the minute, was soaring into senility fifty-sixty-seventy years an hour while he could only stare aghast at his own withering body. Jesus. He had turned brittle, old and brittle, like those people who left Shangri-La in the movie: his bones, white with age, were crumbling painfully, snapping like twigs—

"Dengué," Carrington said. His mouth was a firm, impassive line. "Welcome to the club. Here: take these."

Dengué fever. With difficulty he swallowed the huge pills, thought glumly, I knew it; I might have known. Fever. He was rotting away with fever now: the world around him swayed and faded and swept in again like ponderous surf. Not enough that he'd stopped half a Goddamned grenade, he had to come down with dengué, too. Luck of the Irish. Maybe they could arrange for malaria, elephantiasis, moo-moo, Bright's disease. Why not? Oh Jesus there were any number to play—

"Just follow the trail."

Capistron had loomed in front of him, mountainous and fat. He was on his feet with no idea of how he had got there: standing on his feet, feeling hollow and strange—a shell through which his old, his former self, had fled, like people from a condemned tenement. Where was he *himself* now? . . . *Stand by!* he told himself crossly.

"Just follow the trail," Capistron was saying. "The way we came. Bring you out at the Kaláhe. Just remember to turn right at the fork, that's all."

"Okay." His voice floated out and away from him, beyond his control. Everything seemed just out of his control. Where the hell were they now? He could *hear* the voices all right, hear the words: but he couldn't catch up with them till later, that was the trouble . . .

"Give us your grenades," Helthal said. "You won't be needing them."

"All right." He reached down to disengage them, was surprised to discover they were already gone: Helthal had them in his hands already. How could he move that fast? Strange . . .

"Let me go back with him." Newcombe was standing in front of Capistron, pointing to him and pleading. "He's in no shape to walk back down there alone, let me go with him . . ."

Capistron shook his head slowly. "Can't see it. We're down fine enough as it is. He's all right—"

"The hell he is, he's got dengué and he's got it bad. He could crap out any time. Let me go back with him, Capistron, please let me . . ."

"You hear me I said no!" Capistron shouted. "Derekman yesterday, him and Thomas today. We need everybody we got. He's on his own . . . You can make it all right, O'Neill." Capistron had turned to him, his flat round face baleful and forbidding. "Can't you?"

He gazed back at them remotely, as if through layers of darkening gauze. They were nobody he knew. His buddies, what was left—his buddies!—nobody he knew . . .

"Sure he can," Capistron was saying. Was pushing him back and forth, hand on his shoulder: great fat gripping hand. What was it all about? Who was conning who? If he only—

"Come on. Let's get going."

"You're a son of a bitch," Newcombe was shouting, his face harassed and white; O'Neill watched them in dull astonishment. "You're a mean son of a bitch, Capistron . . ."

"You want trouble, Newcombe? Is that it?"

"You don't care whether he craps out or not, you want him to—"

"I'm telling you, Newcombe, one more—"

"The hell with you!" Newcombe was screaming. "The hell with you both, you one-way sons of bitches!—"

They were towering in front of Newcombe now: Capistron and Helthal both. Helthal's hand was on the spindly metal haft of the knife. This was bad: real trouble. But he couldn't help Al now: not the way he—

"No, Al," he said heavily, in alarm. "No . . . Take it easy, now. I'm okay."

They were all looking at him. Newcombe had stepped back. The other two had turned away, were already moving off: shambling, ambling, like animals on the prowl.

"Take it easy, Jay. Take care, now . . ."

Old Al, old buddy-ro with hollow, haunted, tragic eyes, mud-smeared: a Barnum and Bailey clown, so soulful! Hand on his arm. A wave of hot remorse went over him; his eyes filled with tears. Ah Christ: after all this time—

"Take it easy," his own furry voice said. "I'll make out."

As they moved off northward they seemed to vanish into a fog-laden marsh, sink immersed like bottles to the bottom of the sea.

The lizard was gone. Had slipped away, left nothing but one cold yellow unblinking eye which vanished too: left him alone and trembling. Or was that before somewhere? There was no leaf above another. No matter where he looked. Jesus: he had to get going: he had to! Using his rifle butt as a staff he got to his feet and started on down the trail again. Leaves swung in at him, clutched him like malicious fingers, animate and terrible. His leg pulsed fire in racing patterns, made him groan softly. Not much farther. It couldn't be much farther, they'd come up here this morning early in half an hour or so . . . But then why did it all look so different? Where were the landmarks? the thirty-seven millimeter cannon lying in the mud, the dead Jap bloated like a blackfish with swollen fingers clutching at heaven, stinking, black with flies, the bicycle tire . . . that brand-new bicycle tire. He'd have seen that, wouldn't he?

The hill rose sheer and inaccessible on his right now, blotted out the sun . . . On his right! There had been no hill on their left this morning, none he could remember. Nor the two towering ifil trees like giant oaks over the stream, which hissed and gurgled softly . . .

The sun, directly overhead, a pitiless burning white ball, gave no sign; the trail was like any other. He was hopelessly lost. There was death here: death and worse all around him in the writhing black pit of jungle. Away! he had to get away—

—He was drunk: hurtling drunk along Standish Street and couldn't for the life of him find his way home, wrong way, had come out at the beach of all places—the beach from Standish!—was stumbling along over the rocks at Brill's Cove, hearing the cold sea-wash, too befuddled to function, hoping to sober up so he could find his way home—

Ah! he was lying in the mud, sprawled in soft, slick mud. His rifle bolt all fouled.

Oh God, help me now.

Lying there he sobbed in shuddering despair. It was too far, all too far and wrong, he couldn't do any more, they'd left him alone in these deadly silent boondocks, abandoned him, sick and wounded as he was, to lie here till he was dead . . .

No. You—will—not.

He mouthed the drill-field command in thick-tongued, drunken implacability. *You—will—not.* Get up. Dragging himself to a sitting position he wiped at his rifle, cleaned it as best he could and worked the operating rod with care. Lorraine's samurai sword hung on him, gouged him in the back and shoulder; he reached for his knife, then stopped. No: he would not part with it. Not for anything at all. The fall—he had tripped over something—seemed to have cleared his head. Still weak, he felt somehow steadier, more capable. Now no more of that, he warned himself with silent ferocity. No more of this panicky elephant crashing. How to get starched. Steady down, now: straighten up and fly right. Easy does it. You're in a tight, boy, he said softly. In a squeeze. And you've got to sweat out of it.

He got up and moved on again, his body bent to the left to favor the wounded leg, hobbling along, all his thought concentrated on steady, resolute progress down that trail, right or wrong. All trails lead somewhere. You're *going* to make it, he told the other, recalcitrant self; you're *going* to make it, *going* to make it—

He heard a voice: another. He checked, weaving slightly, weight on his good leg, and listened.

It was the explosive, high-pitched singsong of Japanese.

Off to the left of the trail was a little clearing with banana trees and silvered, knee-height Kunai grass: another plantation gone to seed. At the far edge of the clearing stood the remains of a rancho, smashed in now and rotted. Between two of the nearer banana trees was a little group of Japanese, crouched over something, talking excitely in low voices.

He glanced to his right, despairing, watched the hill rise steep and dense from the stream. No way. Nothing to do but work by them. No good to wait: if he crapped out he was gone. Nothing else to do. Come on O'Neill, you yellow shanty-Irish bastard, stand fast. You got a chance. You got a good chance. Come on, now . . .

His heart was pounding like doom inside his skull. He had moved along the trail about ten feet or so, swaying and tottering, his body contorted in a crouch, when all at once he heard a thin, sharp cry—a wail of pure agony that sent ripples running over the flesh of his scalp and neck, froze him still again. The cry came once more. One of the Japanese gave a low, muffled exclamation, raised his arm and brought it down violently, and the cry stopped. O'Neill leaned against a tree, raised his head and peered through the mat of leaves and fronds and twisted vines. Another of them threw aside what looked like a piece of cloth, then one of the others moved back a little; and he saw the thin face, the long black hair, the dark, emaciated cylinder of an arm.

Gripping the tree trunk he said silently, You bastards. You filthy swine. She can't be twelve years old: not even twelve. All this crud and you . . . Hatred seethed in him, pumped in his veins like a thick, compressed gas. He ground his teeth back and forth, raging. You rotten, filthy bastards—

There were four of them. Two had rifles slung over their shoulders. Beside one of the others was a Nambu light machine gun, resting delicately on its black, spider-leg bipod. All right, you sons of bitches, he said between his teeth. Never taking his eyes from them he inched around the tree toward the clearing, put his feet down with fragile, wavering care. All right. For this you're going to pay. Pay plenty.

Casually one of the Japanese looked up, turned and stared in his direction. He hung motionless, gripped with fright, holding the rifle steady across his chest, his heart exploding so violently it shook him.

The squatting figure looked down again.

Four of them. With an automatic weapon. He stood there wavering, still panting with fear. Hopeless, it was hopeless, it was suicide—Christ, he could hardly stand up as it was, he had dengué, for God's sake. *Four* of them. He didn't even have any grenades—

You'll get killed, he told himself. You're asking for it. Take off while you've still got a chance, while they're occupied, what the hell do you care—get down to Nénetan or Mágat and crap out, somewhere, you're half off your rocker as it is, Jesus man, you're *seeing things*—

The shrill little cry came again; was choked off. He started to back away: could not. It was as certain to him as anything in all his life that he couldn't let this go. No matter what. He couldn't take off on this.

He got as close as he dared: behind the last good-sized ifil tree a few feet from the edge of the clearing. He raised his rifle, pressed his knuckle against the safety catch. At that moment two of them changed places. One, a fat man with a face round as a moon, laughed once, exposed a vast row of teeth: an infinitely hateful face. He said something to the man holding one of the little girl's legs, and all of them broke into sudden, voluble chatter.

O'Neill lowered the rifle. He was trembling violently, weaving about on his good leg; the sweat was streaming into his eyes, burning, half blinding him. You crazy son of a bitch, you can't even stand up: recoil will knock you silly, you can't hit a barn. Lie prone. No: then you won't even see them in the grass. He thought frantically for a moment, then eased himself down to his knees. The pain in his leg almost made him cry out. He cupped his hand over his mouth, gagged, gagged again, clamped his jaws together with all his might, clutched the tree for support. It passed: he worked a spare clip out of his belt and put it in his breast pocket, leaned his hand against the tree trunk and rested the rifle in the cup between thumb and fingers. Get the one nearest the Nambu first. Him first and then the one who hasn't slung his rifle, then the other two. Left to right. Swing left to right.

The face above the sight was round and yellow: a violent yellow with a heavy stubble of beard and little slitted eyes; big barrel body below. Capistron, he thought with a start. Amazing. An oriental, filthy Capistron, looking on in lustful delight. There was a little round ulcerous place across the upper lip: jungle crud. He hunched his shoulder until he saw the maroon oblong of the cartridge pouch at the belt, held it there and pressed off the safety.

All right, you bastards. All right. Got to get them before they hit the deck. What if you hit the kid? Can't. What if she misfired? The sudden awful memory of the struggle by the tank shot into his mind and frightened him all over again. Well. Then it's all over. No grenades. That *bastard* Helthal! Four rounds in the pistol. It can't. It just can't. The fat body jerked rhythmically above the barrel, swelled and receded, began to grow all at once ominously dark and dulled, shot through with drifting sparks of light. Oh Jesus, he thought, I'm going to crap out. He felt strangely weightless and light as air, tumbling over slowly in a soundless film of ethereal breakers—knew that without his grip on the tree he would have toppled over with a crash. Oh my. God. He clenched his teeth, swaying, breathing through his mouth.

No.

You—will—not.

His vision cleared momentarily. He took a slow, deep lungful of air, held it and squeezed the trigger.

The barrel body jerked upward violently; he squeezed again, swung to the right, the rifle moving on the fulcrum of the tree trunk, hit the next man, moved to the third who was twisting upward and stopped him like a camera action still, swung to the fourth who was diving out of sight, depressed the barrel and went on firing into the grass; heard the tinny *whang!* of the empty clip flying out and away and jammed the fresh one home, conscious of gray smoke hovering about him. The silvered grass stalks waved to the left of where he had fired and there was a succession of cleaverlike chops beside him.

He was flat on the ground with no sure sense of transition: huddled flat beside his rifle, wild with fear. Loused up. He'd loused up now for sure. Oh Jesus. Stand up: you've got to stand up and get him. A grenade went off: the ping-whine of fragments spattered around him on the leaves. Get up. You gutless shanty-Irish bastard *stand up now!* He rose in an agonized lurch, heard something slap the tree trunk above his head like an open hand; fired at the shadow. There was a short, shrill scream and the Jap leaped out of the grass and began running away in a grotesque dance. O'Neill emptied the whole clip at him and he whirled away out of sight.

In the long silence nothing moved. He put a fresh clip in his rifle and leaned against the slick, faintly oily trunk of the ifil, feeling dizzy and weightless again. He realized he hadn't fixed his bayonet, was deeply distressed at the omission and did it fumblingly. The ground began to tilt again—that slow surf-lurch up to the right. He braced his feet and approached warily, in a deep crouch, his eyes riveted on the man who had fired at him, watching for movement. He was dead: the back of his head torn off. The second and third men he came upon he bayoneted rapidly. The fourth, the thin one, the one who had been currently raping the girl, was still conscious and holding his hands to his belly. A thin, lined face, the eyes wide and watery, mouth drawn down imploring. Below his hands the dark, now shrunken member gaped from his open fly.

"No," O'Neill said. He shook his head in slow anger, drove the bayonet down once, wrenched it free; drove down again, panting, turned away.

The little girl—she was appallingly young—had not moved, and for an instant he thought she was dead: eyes wide, glazed with terror, lips pressed tight together, face rigid and gray. They had torn her clothes from her and she lay there naked on the wet grass, her little sticklike legs covered with tropical ulcers, her ribs protruding harshly below the small, un-developed breasts. "Poor kid," he said. On the side of her head was the raw lump of a bruise which was still bleeding, and where several flies clung intently. She was shivering all over, gazing upward, her arms still outstretched in the position in which they'd been held.

"Poor little kid," he said again. He knelt down, reached out to stroke her silky hair, touch her forehead, brush the flies away. In silence she shrank back, her face still frozen with fear.

"No, no," O'Neill said in great distress. "Don't be afraid. MaRInon ameriKAno tsu. AtuNGO mu tsu . . ." She dipped away in a surflike underwater rippling. The oven breath of fever surged over him again; on hands and knees, his head hanging, he breathed slowly and deeply, refused to give in to it. He unscrewed his canteen top and smiled at her, shivering, and said: "MaLAgo hau haHAnum PAra maGImen?" and gently, very gently, made as though to put the canteen to her lips. She flung the back of her hand over her mouth—a swift, mechanical gesture, her eyes still on his face, alive with terror.

"God," he said. "Poor kid . . . The bastards."

He drank from his canteen, vomited almost instantly and sat back gasping. In the reaction from the fire-fight he felt utterly drained of strength or ordered thought, as though not only his body but his mind as well were coming apart in thousands of little pieces. The clearing, the rim of jungle started its ponderous, terrifying slow surf-roll upward, and with the swiftness of light the hundred thousand horrible forms reinvaded his being—bristling forms that, prancing around him, laughed soundlessly and as soundlessly swept away, to be replaced by apparitions still more terrible . . . but what was worse was that they were people he knew, old friends and buddies bewitched, transformed into legions of threatening horrors *turned against him*, it wasn't *right—!*

"No," he shouted at them with the urgency of great anguish, "no! Go away. You're nothing . . . you're—*nothing!"* But they kept gaining power: rising in actuality against him, gaining, tipping the scales against him, he couldn't hold them off for long, they had such *power—*

But worst of all now was his hand. It lay near him, a white writhing hairy excrescence—but it could move: it had a will of its own, a nature apart from his, he knew that, and there was no telling, white filthy palps and all, what it might take it into its evil mind to do—no way to tell! And with this unique and hideous discovery his final defenses gave way, rushed off and left him prone and helpless, quaking, groaning softly, overborne by terrors . . .

—He had been asleep. Was that it? Out for the count. For how long? In dumb panic he raised his head, felt it could not have been long. The sun seemed lower but nothing had changed. The little girl lay transfixed and silent in the grass, the dead Japanese sprawled here and there around them. Nothing had changed. A strange tranquillity possessed him: the teeming horrors were gone. He only felt weak, so weak that the idea of walking frightened him.

A reprieve, though. He'd had a brief reprieve: he would not get another chance like this. He got to his feet, hobbling and groaning aloud, looked down at the little girl. Skin and bones. God, he thought. Not much bigger than Allie. Can't weigh even that much. Slipping the poncho out of the back of his belt he knelt down and spread it out on the ground. Then he turned to her, picked her up and placed her on it carefully. Her whole body winced away from him, rigid and quivering.

"I'm sorry," he said. "Just want to help you. MaLAgo tsu
a TSUda HAgo."

He wrapped the poncho around her; she made no sound.
He bent down and picked her up. She was unbelievably heavy.
Too heavy. If he wasn't so rotten weak! He debated a
moment, then drew his knife and cut the thongs that held the
samurai sword to his pack, let it fall to the ground. Again he
picked the girl up and slung her over his shoulder, supporting
himself with his rifle. The first time he put his weight on his
left foot he let out a muffled cry. The whole leg was stiff now,
informed with a throbbing ache that seemed to lie in the very
bone. Follow the trail, he told himself: follow the trail down.
All trails lead to something. Just pray you don't meet any
more of them. Run on to any more Nips you've had it. Leaves
swept back at him and wetly slapped his clothes, liana vines
caught him in the face. His shoes became heavy, shapeless
lumps of mud.

How far he walked he would never know. He toiled up over
a little rise and down along the edge of a broad, curving valley
in deep shade, where bodies lay in hundreds, bloated and
black and thick with flies: a place of the dead—American or
Japanese, they were indistinguishable now, grappling or
sprawled casually as though they had been dropped from a
tremendous height. Twice he thought he saw faces he
recognized—glanced away in aversion: but they had already
spoken to him, called to him in the eerie, quavering voices of
another kingdom, begging, beseeching him brokenly to
extricate them from their plight. He shut his eyes; the mountainous, fetid stench encircled him, became somehow fused
with the prodigious weight of the girl, his wound, his con-
tinual fear of passing out again. He saw nothing he could
recognize in all he gazed on. But he *would* make it. He
hobbled along through an unending morass of jungle, lashing
himself frankly now, in short, gasping commands: *You WILL
get back, you WILL get back*—while in his fevered ambience
the earth tipped, swirled to the left, to the right, and stabbing
pains came in his belly and back so fierce they made him cry
out drymouthed in pain. Once he slipped in the muck,
sprawled full length and lay sobbing for breath for several
minutes, obsessed with the conviction that his arms and legs
had gone dead, like disconnected electric fixtures, bone and
tendon had been everywhere severed and left him, a
paralyzed, truncated victim, to the elements and the Japanese.
But he was *going to get back*. He dragged himself to his feet

with the hazy, automatic movements of a sleepwalker and
shuffled on again, his head, held back, rolling in exhaustion,
his teeth clenched, eyes half-closed with pain and delirium,
groaning with the preposterous task of finding his way back,
sick and laden as he was, through a jungle that stretched to the
ends of the world . . .

—He was in a clearing: a long one, with two low hills. He
heard all at once the sound of guns. The Nénetan battery for
sure. And an hour or a moment later saw the line of figures,
fanned out, coming toward him. He froze, his heart leaping
dully—recognized the helmets and gave up: sank to his knees
in a spasm of relief.

"He's hit," a voice said. A curious faraway voice with an
accent just like Woodruff's, might be a relation, or a friend,
might ask—

"Hit?"

"Yeah. In the leg."

"What's he doing with the gook kid?"

"Beats me. Found her someplace, maybe."

"Been through the wringer . . ."

They were discussing him, their voices low and sonorous.
As though he weren't there: as though he were dead. Perhaps
this was what it was like, lying in your coffin at your own
wake, hear the Goddamnedest things—

He raised his head, saw a tall man, his face white and oddly
featureless.

"What outfit are you, fella?"

He started to answer but everything had begun to whirl by
at a terrific speed, like looking out at the crowd from a gon-
dola car on the Whip-Wheel at Revere Beach. The ground
beneath him slanted up and away, a madly steepening roof: he
clutched at the tufts of grass with his fingers.

"The kid—" he said finally: but no one seemed to have
heard him. Hands were lifting him up, pulling at him. He
made an effort to find out where the kid was but all at once
something enormously heavy rushed up into his head and
burst like a little bomb; and a roaring, bluish mist enveloped
him, took him down out of his own sight.

The heads of coconut palms swept by high overhead. He
was conscious of a rolling, jarring sensation and that his
helmet was gone. He started to raise himself on his elbows and
a voice said: "Take it easy, mate. Rest easy, now."

Two faces on a drop seat were observing him. He was on a

truck, rolling along on a truck bed: he knew.

"The kid," he said. "Where's the kid?"

One of the men tossed his head, and O'Neill saw her lying on the other drop seat, still covered by his poncho. A series of overbright, narrow apertures through which he could see only snapshots. The calmly observing faces vanished, reappeared; slid away again, as though behind revolving panels.

"Butt?" he asked.

One of the men was extending a pack of cigarettes—a shiny white cellophane pack. Always Buy Chesterfields. Civilization coming ashore, place must be half secured. He took the cigarette, rolled it slowly between thumb and fingers. It fell to his chest. One of the men picked it up, lighted it from his own and passed it down to him. He drew on it slowly, felt his head clear a little; then the wobbling blur swept in at him again, filled with the knifelike pains, made him gasp and grunt. The truck swung to the right, to the left again, slithering in the muck, and stopped with a jolt that jumbled all his bones together in a small, painful heap. He was afloat, air-borne, rocking gently—like Danny, had Danny felt like this coming down from the ravine? ah Jesus, Danny—in air between the two corpsmen: the sky, a deep coppery blue, was swallowed by a dark canopy: the ponchos, they were back on the LST playing pinochle under the ponchos, the old tub rocking up and down and there was Al lying on his sack gazing dreamily into space, gathering wool. Just gathering wool. *Hey, you communing with your muse there, Al?—Sure thing.—Give us a line of great poetry.—Okay. How's this: and the thoughts of you can do better than that.—All right . . . Sunk though he be beneath the watery floor.—Not bad: who's that—Davey Jones?—Davey Jones . . .*

A face so sad and full of lines and furrows it amazed him, leaned down and said: "Name and organization, son."

He gave it quickly, mechanically: or had he? The sad, lined face was still bent over him, expectant; laced with a thousand furrowed lines. He was aware that his mind, now in league with the prancing forms, beguiled by them, had slipped away again, out of reach, was mocking him subtly. It was getting much stronger than he was now. The little girl: that held it back into line. The kid—

He rose feebly on one elbow and said, "The kid, the little kid—she all right?"

The old lined face drifted tiredly away, no wonder, so sad and furrowed. Receded into a dark void where he couldn't follow. It didn't matter: did it? That huge object rushed into the top of his head again, this time with a clang, a series of bell-like *bong-ong-ong* reverberations that filled him with unpleasant confusion. This was bad, real bad. He started to protest, get up, knew he couldn't get up, couldn't do any more, was now finally finished: flat out. The bell-like clanging, the throb, increased, pounded and throbbed still more harshly—and then there was a terrible solid bar of fire searing the inside of his leg, so bright and fierce he remembered all at once the wound, his leg—oh-my-God-*the-leg!*—clenched his teeth and gripped the edge of the table with both hands, his chest arched, straining, his breath singing between his teeth. Then the fire began to burn down, and the throb became dull and slow and released him: and the bell stopped clanging.

"Oh my God," he muttered. "My God . . ."

"That's got it," a voice said cheerily. "Feel better?"

Feel better? Feel better? Feel better? the throbbing echo went: distressing.

"Jeez, I don't know," he said. "Damn if I know . . ."

A slim cold sliver slipped between his teeth, beneath his tongue. Thermometer. Taking my temperature. Way old Doc Seeley used to sit by your bed and pant, wheeze, pant. *Well now* (wheeze) *let's take a look at you, young feller* (wheeze, pant) *see just what the trouble is here* (dry wheeze panting).

The thermometer went away. Another voice, higher and more metallic than the first, said pleasantly: "Fabulous case of dengué all right: one oh four point eight."

"All right. Give him a sack down at the end. I've got to prep this kid from JASCO right away."

One oh four point eight. Was that *him*? Oh my. His eyeballs felt like drops of raw flesh set inside curved blades. Hundred and four point eight. Fabulous. Rough shape, all right. The discordant visions started again, borne on a fierce wave of heat and he said stubbornly, *You will not*, and said aloud:

"The kid. Is the kid all right?"

"What, son?"

He made a great effort and opened his eyes—fought through the foul, dancing shaggy shapes and splotches to the lined, enormously sympathetic face. "Little girl, little Chamorro girl. I brought—she all right?" he demanded through furry leaves of lips. "You take care of her?"

"Yes, yes. You take it easy, son. We just sent her down to Civil Affairs section. She'll be all right."

"Ah, good," he answered. "Good enough . . ."

He was swinging again, stretcher-swinging down the length of the tent like the bottom of the sea. Hands were helping him to a cot, a soft sinking cot whose frame received him like angel arms. Sacked in. It was all over: all over for a while. There wasn't anything more he had to do for a while . . . The hell with it, he said with soft cunning; drew the blanket up to his chin. The hell with what they think. Or anybody else. The bloody hell with the whole roaring blasting whining stupidity, the hell with K-rations and stink and digging and bloated crablike corpses and walking a million million miles, and things rusted and things broken and thrown away and never one solitary thing clean and whole and sacred, never a thing—

The rain came like distant surf on the tent roof high above him and he thought, exulting: By God, it's raining and for once I'm not getting soaked. It was coming down in sheets and he was out of it this time, down in the deep green silence, a clam nestled deep in the sand, two fathoms down . . . The clearing flashed again into his mind's eye, the little knot of Japanese, the big-barrel body jerked up again over the sight; the little girl watched him with her glazed, fearful stare. Had it really happened, all that really happened? Yes. It had happened all right. He heard again the shrill, pitiful, terror-laden cry . . . You crazy bastard, he said. Tears came to his eyes, mildly stinging; grinning foolishly he wagged his head. You crazy Irish bastard: you got out of it; you got away with the whole deal . . . And sick, wounded, weak as water he knew that nothing would stop him now—no wounds or dengué or any other jungle crud was going to carry him off after that long, terrible moment in the clearing. Had their chance, he muttered: Well, that squares it. That squares things. A little. Though what he meant by that he had no clear idea.

The high sea-roar of the rain increased. The most profound lassitude stole over him, flowed into his being from a thousand points of ingress, lapped him entire. He felt one last twinge of apprehension, of regret at the thought of Newcombe still creeping northward toward the sea . . . then sleep took him with a soundless crash.

12

THE MASHED POTATO, pounded flat with the heel of her fork, made a fort at the edge of an island: the wax beans were ships bombarding it. They cruised back and forth, sneaking in close to shell it, as close as they dared.

"Allie," her mother said, "don't play with your food. Food's not to play with."

She blasted holes in the potato with her fork, the ships really, bombarding, and ate that, ate a few of the ships that had sneaked in too close, hit by the shore batteries and sunk. The juice from the meat balls was their oil-slick spreading over the water. It was hard to tell who was going to win. Bobby was imitating her: he always did and then she got blamed for it, for setting him off.

"Eat your food," she whispered to him. "Eat it. Don't play with it." He frowned at her in confusion, milled the beans and potato on his plate, round and round. She glanced at Daddy, but he was reading the paper: he was always reading the paper at meals.

"That's right," he said, while she watched him. His lips drew back from his teeth. "Give them all the planes and tanks to wipe us out with in another five years . . ."

"But they're our allies," Mummy said. "Aren't they?"

Her father raised his eyes over the edge of the paper and stared. He wasn't really angry, though: his eyes were never open that wide when he was. "Allies! What do you know about it. Why, they've got it all rigged. The whole God-damned business."

"Please, Charlie," her mother said.

"Why, for Christ sake we're even *fighting* the wrong people. People we ought to be bombing all to hell are the God-damn Russians."

"Please, I've asked you not to swear in front of the children."

"They're going to hear a lot worse than that before they're through . . . Sure," he went on, nodding. With a sharp crack he snapped the paper inside out, bent it back on itself. "We'll be fighting them in five years . . ."

"Why are we going to fight them?" Allie asked.

"Why?" His face was black and scowling but he wasn't angry. "Because they're reds, that's why."

"Oh. Is that after we beat the Germans and the Japs?"

"That's right. Then the big boys'll realize the damnfool mistake they've made and they'll start beating the drums and all the young chumps will flock to the post offices to enlist all over again. Sure."

The evening breeze whistled softly against the screen, blew the gray curtains in curving streamers, like battle pennants, out over the toaster, the stacks of magazines on the sill. They were fighting in Russia: they were fighting in Europe and Asia and Africa and all over the Pacific where Jay was. Everybody was fighting everywhere and then they were going to fight *against* the Russians instead of *with* the Russians against the Germans.

"Nope," her father said, drumming on the table with his knuckles. "Nope: air power is going to win this war. Don't think it isn't." Again he bent and refolded the paper with a crack like a mainsail filling on a jibe, bent forward studying the lines of names in small print: lines and lines of names. "The chumps," he said. He snorted, wagged his head, and the wide grin came again that showed all his teeth: or almost all of them. "Look at them: stupid ninnies . . ."

"Who—" Allie started, and stopped: her mother had shot her the glance that meant *Be still, I know what you're going to say, don't say it.* She closed her mouth, went on gazing at her mother's face. It was funny: it was so *lined*, much more lined and tired looking than Janice Murray's or Nancy Kresnich's mothers. Mummy was more lovely but her face was older looking in some ways: more *nervous*—

"Finish your supper, Allie." Her mother had looked up again and caught her eye, was looking at her with impatience. She bent over her plate. Finish up that old potato. Did you know what other people were thinking when you were grown up? or did you only know what *children* were thinking?

"Hah," her father said—a startled exclamation, smothered. Leaning forward he smoothed the paper flat on the table with his hairy forearm. "Well, well, well . . ." His eyes behind his glasses dilated: a strange look she'd never seen before. "Well, look who's here." With slow articulation, reading above his moving thumbnail he pronounced: "PFC James—R—O'Neill, USMCR."

Her mother had gasped: her face had gone all white and rigid. Her mouth moved and stopped.

"No," she said. *"No.* It can't be—"

He made as though to thrust the paper toward her. "You want to read it yourself?"

Getting awkwardly to her feet she moved around the table and peered over his shoulder while he read again through narrowed lids: "P—F—C James R. O'Neill . . ."

"R," she said tightly; she was opening and closing one hand. "He's James *A.*, Charlie—you know that just as well as I do. It's someone else. Some other boy—"

"Printer's error, probably. You think they've got time to check every one of these, get them letter-perfect? A list this long? Look at it."

"Providence," she said. Her face was still white: she was very frightened. "It says Providence. If it was Jay it would have said—"

"Now, Grace—come on: how many James R. O'Neills do you think there are in the Marine Corps from Rhode Island? Just how many—"

She closed her eyes, shook her head back and forth. "You haven't any proof," she said. Her voice was louder and trembling. "No proof, Charlie . . . They would have notified me," she said suddenly.

"*Who* would?"

"The government. The War Department. As next of kin. They'd have notified me first, they always do . . ."

He laughed—a short, dry, explosive laugh. "They don't ever make mistakes, I suppose? the government? Come on, now . . ." His eyes rolled up at her. "You think you're Mrs. Skitz of the Ritz? Maybe they don't even know you're the one they're supposed to notify—"

"He put me down. He told me! His allotment and—"

"Maybe he got married down in Carolina, there, picked up some cheap little slut of a—"

"Charlie!"

She glared at him, her hands clenched at her sides; her eyes had filled with tears. "You—oh, I don't see why you have to do this—you don't even know—"

This was bad, now: something very bad about Jay and they were fighting. She had to find out. She had to, no matter what.

She cried out: "What is it? What is it?"

"It's your darling little hero of a cousin," her father said.

"No, it isn't," Mummy broke in, "we have no—there's no proof about it at all—"

"—who's finally turned himself into a hero," her father finished in a loud voice. "A dead one!"

"Dead?" Allie said. "Jay's dead?"

"That's not so," her mother cried, "you have no right to say that, Charlie!"

"Why not? She might as well find out about it now as later . . ."

Jay. They were fighting over whether Jay was dead. "Jay is dead?" she asked softly, filled with fear.

"No! No, he isn't—Charlie, that's rotten to say that when we don't even know—that's rotten!"

"That's what he wanted, isn't it?" her father shouted all at once, banging his hand on the table. "Be a Goddamn hero full of medals? All right he's got it then, good, he got what he went after—"

Beside her Bobby was sniffling, crying silently. She reached under the table and took his hand, murmured, "Hush, Bobby, hush up now," and half-slid from her seat, ready to leave. In a minute Mummy would tell them to leave, go out and play. But not till then.

"Charlie, I've begged and begged you not to talk about Jay, I begged you and you promised—"

"So they won't know, is that it?" His hand swung around the table in a black arc. "So they won't—"

"No, it's not that, it's simply—"

"So they go on, grow up thinking he's a knight in shining armor or some damn thing! Well, they might as well know all about it right now—"

Not yet. But in a minute or two: just a minute now. It was all crackling, crashing apart again, the worst of all—and now Jay, Daddy knew something Mummy didn't, it wasn't fair—!

She kept her eyes riveted on her mother's face, gripped Bobby's hand and said, "It's all right, Bobby, hush now, in a minute—"

"I suppose they shouldn't know any of it," her father was shouting, his face contorted in a snarl, "I suppose they shouldn't know how his delightful clean-living parents wound up, either—"

"Charlie! I've begged you—"

"—how they wound up all smashed up in a car that wasn't theirs—and especially on New Year's Eve. What do you—"

"No, no," she cried, "it was an accident, an accident—"

"*Accident!*" He laughed harshly, and his eyes rolled, all whites. "Accident—when a man's too drunk to know which side of the road—"

"Allie!" her mother said; she was weeping, shaking her head from side to side. "Allie, you and Bobby—"

"Sure! Don't want 'em to hear the truth, do you?"

"That *isn't* the truth!—"

"Sure it is. What do you call it? Go ahead, hide it all the way you always do—"

"Allie: Bobby: go out and play! Leave the table and go out and play! Right now . . ."

Now. Now, if he doesn't. She whispered, "Come on, Bobby"—half-dragged him off his seat and out of the kitchen, pushed the door closed behind her with her free hand. The hall was dim and hot and musty. Mummy was crying now, a broken thin weeping so she couldn't talk, only moaning something and her father was shouting, "Go ahead then, stick their heads in the sand, who cares, who gives a good Goddamn—"

"Come on, Bobby," she said, and led him down the hall to the front door. "We'll go over to the playground. Come on. It's all right."

"Our guns," he said. "We need our guns."

"No, we don't need our *guns*," she began, saw his face screw up again and said quickly, "All right, all right, but hurry up, now. Only if you hurry up. Come on."

In their bedroom they got their guns and she had to wait while Bobby put on his belt and ammunition and his helmet. It was only a helmet liner but it was still much too big for him: his eyes looked out from way back under it like a cat hiding in a cellar.

"Come on, now," she repeated.

He stopped crying by the time they got to Brill's Park but she was still trembling with fear. If Mummy was that upset there must be something wrong. Daddy knew something Mummy didn't: he always did. And now he knew about Jay. Jay had never finished the boat he'd started for them. He had never come to the tree in the playground, he'd written to her he'd had to go back to war again.

"There they are," Bobby said. "Right there!" He crouched down, firing his rifle, made a series of explosive hissing noises with his mouth. "Come on," he cried, "look out!"

She began to cry helplessly, filled with dread. He must be not dead, he must be! People never came back when they were dead. Grandpa Tarrasch never came back: no one did. They went to heaven, Mummy said. Where they could rest. Miss Stickley said they went to heaven if they were good and hell if they were bad. Daddy said they didn't go anywhere at all, just blanked out in nothing. Like standing in the dark for hours and hours, all alone in the dark: terrible, terrible!

Bobby was looking up at her from under the helmet and saying, "What's the matter? What's the matter, Allie?"

She knew what they must do. Without any delay at all.

"We're going to the cave," she said. "Right now."

"Why?" he said.

"Because we're going to pray for Jay not to be dead."

He thrust out his lower lip. "I don't want to go to the cave."

He was going to cry again: make a fuss. She took hold of his arm. "Do you want Jay to come home again ever or not?" she demanded angrily, crying.

He gazed up at her a moment soberly, and nodded.

"All right, then. Come on."

She led the way across the vacant lot by McKelvy's Iron Works, across the tracks and up and down over the rocks until they came to a place where a piece of rock jutted up near them like a sailboat aslant, its mainsail filled and bulging. They stopped and looked around them warily.

"All clear?" she said in a low voice.

"All clear," Bobby said.

With great care she climbed around to the front of the mainsail rock and along a little ledge, lowered herself into a cavelike pocket in the face of the cliff about four feet deep. Putting down her rifle she helped Bobby down from the ledge, grunting with the effort, then picked up a piece of stone and scratched a mark on the roof of the cave next to many others. Squatting they gazed out over the marsh, flooded now at high tide, just the tips of the grasses showing; a feathery porcupine pattern over the still water, gray with evening.

"All right," she said. "Kneel down: the way I am."

He knelt obediently beside her. "Hurts my knees."

"Never mind. Now close your eyes."

"Dear God," she said. "Please bring Jay back home alive." She became conscious of the distance down to the marsh, and with her eyes closed felt dizzy and fearful of falling. She pressed her hands together at her breast, said after a moment: "Please grant this and we'll never pray to You for anything else again in this cave. We vow this, God, Please . . ."

She stopped, trembling, afraid she would never be able to hold to this vow: remembered her mother's anguished, tearful voice at the edge of her bed, several nights ago in the dark. *And some day we'll live in a home on a great big hill with paths and driveways and we'll have a boat and we'll sail all around the world, stop at all the wonderful ports of call and be as free as birds.* Listening, full of dazzling hopes and imaginings she had prayed fervently, Oh yes, please God, let us go some day on a ketch like the Hannons', sail away through the sliding blue water, the three of us and Jay, to Madagascar and Rarotonga and the Tierra del Fuego and away from *him*, from *him*—frightened a little at the passionate depth of her fervor but implacable, desiring it more with every tremulous passage of her mother's voice . . . and aware now that she could never abstain from dreaming that prayer for more than a month, a whole month at most—

Bobby was fidgeting, sniffling one nostril. "My knees—"

"Shut up," she said crossly. "This is for Jay . . .

"I'll never pray that here again, God," she repeated. "Not in this cave. I vow it."

She sighed, opened her eyes: her knees pressing down on the rock and bits of pebble hurt, and her neck. Before her the marsh lay in a reddish gold light, dusty, fading even while she watched it: a heron flapped slowly off toward the sea, flaming in the sun.

"There they come," Bobby said. He was lying down, sighting along the barrel of his rifle, squinting. "Here they come . . . Get down, get down!" he whispered in alarm.

"In a minute," she said. She sighed again; chafed the red indentations that bits of stone had made in her kneecaps. "It's all right. They aren't close enough yet."

13

. . . THE STILLNESS DESCENDED, star-laden and pure; a ghostly, milky light. In the bowl of land a bell sounded once, again, and a gleaming, silver dome rose majestically before him: a star-glittered mystery that brought the tears to his eyes. "What is it?" he whispered. "What is it?" Francisco, kneeling beside him in a white robe, murmured something softly, a devout incantation he couldn't understand but which

contributed overwhelmingly to his sense of awe. *"Ndan-
danowga,"* Francisco said. A figure came toward him out of
the temple, approached him through the moon-laden mist,
swaying: a torn and bloody figure gray with death who
paused, trembling, and with one broken flapping arm
beckoned to him, nodding repeatedly.

NOW HEAR THIS, the stentorian PA voice boomed in the
stillness. NOW HEAR THIS, NEWCOMBE: TOMORROW
WILL BE FAIR AND WARMER: TOMORROW WILL BE
PERFECT FLYING WEATHER. Rising to his feet he saw
that the torn and beckoning figure was Danny Kantaylis—and
he knew then with a swift little heartfelt cry of recognition
where he was going . . .

The shelterhalf was pressed against his face. Beyond it a
long trapezium of night sky alive with stars. He sat up on one
elbow, thrust the flap of the shelterhalf away, his waking
mind still struggling with fragments of images, moonlit domes
and dusty, swirling streets, figures of menace and a PA voice
that blared—what had it blared?

His intestines gave a spastic lurch and release. His belly and
kidneys were aflame. He felt sweat pop out in tiny gouts on
his chest and back, and then a nauseous, palsied weakness
assaulted him in painful waves; drugged with exhaustion and
debility he sank back into a gelatinous fluid, seeing through
the underside of a thick glass plate, darkened, submarine, all
the ages of man, ceaseless misery and recurrent hope, truths
and self-deceptions interlaced like vines.

"Jay," he muttered. "Jay—"

But Jay was gone now, like nearly all the rest, nearly all the
brash, roistering, nervously grinning crew that had dropped
hooting through the hatches that sunny morning so fearfully
long ago. All the good guys . . . Panting, sweating, holding his
sphincter now by sheer force of will, he recalled them one by
one and was filled with an aching sense of loss. One by one
they had gone, claimed by death or wounds or fever or
fatigue, depriving those who remained of far more than their
mere physical presences—ah, far more than that . . .

He rolled out from under his net, rose tottering to his feet.
Gritting his teeth he moved down the slope to the slit
trench—he knew the route by heart now—and eased himself
on to the hard wooden bar, clutching his knees to keep from
falling over backward. For a long time after he had stopped
steaming he sat there, too weak to move; heard the tight, nervous whine of mosquitoes around him, felt their stings on his

thighs and buttocks and did nothing, far too enfeebled to even attempt to drive them away. The dark, reinforced by discordant fragments of dream, loomed large and vaguely overpowering: he had received some stern admonition, some warning, wasn't it?—in a holy place; and somebody had stood in the moonlight beckoning to him urgently . . . He shivered, clamped his hands over his knees. Tomorrow: they said tomorrow would be the last day, they'd reach the sea and put an end to organized resistance; and then they could rest, sink into sleep, sore labor's bath, balm of hurt minds, great nature's second curse . . .

The nausea increased, united subtly with the dysentery until his entire viscera seemed to be upended and crawling, open to the elements. I've got to see Carry, he thought with dull urgency; got to get some more of that stuff. Won't be anything left of me in another few days, won't even be able to carry my own rifle.

He got to his feet and crept with rickety uncertainty through the humming dark, crouched over the end of a shelterhalf and whispered: "Carry . . . *Carry*—"

"Yeah? What's the matter?"

"Carry, I hate to wake you but I got the runs so bad I can hardly stand up. Give me some paregoric, will you?"

Carrington stirred, groped around under his net; he heard the clink of a spoon on glass. "Here you go. For Christ sake, don't spill any of it, now."

A strange mélange of elements: Anise, licorice, camphor, syrup and alcohol. An alchemist's concoction. Newcombe was reminded all at once of a party where as a very young child he had been allowed to sip from a succession of shallow crystal glasses of different densities and hues. He licked the spoon dry and handed it back.

"Mister Paregoric," Carrington said. "One swallow cures all your ills. Glues everything together: like airplane dope. Ever make model planes? When they put you away in Bellevue for dope addiction don't say I never did anything for you, now . . . Hey, wait a minute: you better take a couple of these."

"What's that?"

"Never mind. You got a galloping case of dengué, haven't you?"

"Yes, I guess so."

"Okay. Get these down: they'll put hair on your sagging chest. Maybe feathers. Who knows?"

"Thanks, Carry."

"Anything for the troops. Take it easy, now."

"Take it easy."

The night, hovering toward dawn, was held in a silence of glass. Above him the palm fronds drooped like withered fingers against the sky. The world, rended by agonies, lay quiescent, waiting for the next blinding cataclysm of day.

The land had changed again: a dry, crumbling coral crust that crackled underfoot like some ridiculous peanut brittle. Above the gnarled bushes soared strange trees like eucalyptus, with shaggy bark and rusty, sickle-like leaves that hung lifelessly from their sagging limbs. In the fitful shade of the trees they slowed; their voices, muted, dwindled away altogether. To Newcombe the leaves and tangled branches all seemed to have come alive, to be jiggling as though on little wire springs before his eyes; if he didn't fix his gaze on something trees, vegetation, walking figures swept back and forth in a blurred and dizzying panorama of colors and textures.

"How you making it, old buddy-ro?"

Woodruff was watching him, grinning at him quizzically, blinking in the tenebrous light. A gaunt, yellow-skinned, haggard, scraggle-bearded Woodruff, a Woodruff far older than his years—but still grinning that slow, bemused grin. It was strange. Now, oddly enough, that didn't anger him: Woodruff floated outside his thoughts, in a benign, dispassionate area where nothing mattered too terribly any more—where nothing mattered as much, perhaps, as it should have . . . Was that true? Francisco Allagué, the Chamorran recently attached to them as scout, was proceeding on Newcombe's left with graceful wariness, his face wrinkled like a coconut, precisely like a wrinkled brown coconut husk despite the fact that he was only twenty-four. Capistron, still drinking, still drunk, was glowering about, muttering at them now and then, slack-lipped and sullen, but it didn't matter. His—Newcombe's own—back had tensed with sudden chilling cold, a gripe of pain, but it was of no consequence really, tomorrow would be fair and warmer: tomorrow would be perfect flying weather . . .

Almost instinctively he looked up and saw the sky, a faultless blue in shreds and strips between the treetops. It *was* perfect flying weather; after all the slashing, torrential rains. The dream of the night before still stirred in the pool of his mind, vivid and compelling, more vivid by far than the few ragged lines of poetry it had compelled him to set down that morning in the early light. Curious, this fierce little burst of creative impulsion after so long a drought, and in the midst of all his bodily miseries: he had *had* to get those images down on paper, fashion them a little, clumsily—the nucleus for something good, perhaps; something really meaningful and full of force, he'd have to see. He wasn't much of a judge of things aesthetic these days, truth to tell. Hallowell would doubtless be disappointed in him: disappointed and faintly, mockingly amused. *Do you really find it diverting to let your mind go to pot in this delightful fashion, Newcombe?*

Oddly enough he had never flown: he had traveled by car, by train, by horse and bicycle and boat and amtrack and even once by motorcycle: but he had never flown. Except in fancy . . . Perhaps his spirit, harassed and weary, sensed the end of things—was straining, like a colt in its dark stable, for release: for this was the last day, they said this would be the last, that before dark they would traverse the last three miles to the sea and it would be over; unbelievably, celestially over and they would pierce the deep wood's woven shade and dance upon the level shore, fall upon their knees weeping and cry *Thalatta! Thalatta!* raising paeans of joy and deliverance to the stars—

There was a sudden burst of firing off to their left, the crash and whine of grenades; and scattered cries. He froze, rifle held at high port, staring sightlessly about, gripped again with the immemorial, clutching dread. Francisco, his lower lip thrust out, wrinkled his coconut brow still further and shrugged as if to say, "Not my fault, I have nothing to do with it." Woodruff, perspiring densely, flipped sweat off the end of his nose with a forefinger. The silence grew with their rigidity, their apprehension. Finally, after an interminable wait the word came drifting down to them in slithering sibilants: *Contact—two Nips with grenades—got them both—move out* . . . And they walked forward again.

It became lighter up ahead; it broadened—exploded all at once in a bright, open plateau, slowly rising ground covered with scrub and high grass. To the right were several mounds on which were grouped totemic structures of gray-white stone, intricate and immense, glinting in the sunlight. Newcombe gazed at them for a moment in quiet astonishment.

"Francisco," he murmured. "HAfa enAO?"

Francisco smiled at him and frowned; shrugged softly,

disclaiming any knowledge. "GUman TSUus i na TAOtaomoña . . ."

Houses of praise of the people-of-the-olden-times. Newcombe repeated the Chamorran phrase in an undertone. It meant something: possessed some significance he couldn't fathom. Temples of the ancient people: druidical structures raised to their gods. What kind of gods had they been? Perhaps like Fergus. He had given that poem for declamation once at school, had recited it with glowing, rhapsodic pride, and Mr. Glover had flunked him because it was four lines too short; he had protested violently, attacked the matter of length as any criterion of poetic excellence and had recieved five demerits for that, amid the derisive laughter of the classroom. For Fergus rules the brazen cars . . . What had they believed, those shadowy *naTAOtaomoño*, graceful aborigines who had paddled out to Magellan's listing, rotting galleon bringing taro and SUne and papayas in great bowls?—about whom Francisco knew nothing more than to give his strange, pouting frown, mumur the incantatory phrase . . .

Plodding wearily through the high, silvered grass, favoring the bad foot, he tried to imagine them as they must have been before the Spaniards had come and syphilis had maimed and decimated them: a skipping, elusive montage of beautiful dark bodies at the edge of the reef with arms flung outward, the cast nets floating away in gossamer pink and orange swirls; or seated cross-legged and sedate at ceremonial banquets sipping TUba and Agi from deep ochre gourds, watching the dancing figures move in undulant, martellato rhythms in the rippling light from the fires . . . a life informed with innocence and awe, freed of the starved half-legacies of our own muddled, chaotic, blood-boltered time, the toppling codes and shibboleths we invented by the tens of teeming thousands to obscure and obfuscate our own wretched dissatisfactions, our deplorable barrenness of soul—

Capistron was scowling at him, motioning him to come up in better alignment; turned away again with a few words to Helthal which Newcombe couldn't hear. He quickened his pace a little, favoring the foot, watched out of the corner of his eye Capistron and Helthal walking stride for stride, straining forward, guns at their hips, bulging, bristling with grenades and cartridges and knives, their faces set in the same dulled, deadly intent: Ares' children . . . The war god has a rare impartiality: the slayer is often slain. Was there any truth in that? Only he and Woodruff had survived, along with them: only he and Woodruff. Danny and Freuhof and Lundren mouldered in the wet earth, Klu and Connor and Terrabella and Fellows lay deep in the iron bowels of the *Solace* riding at anchor off Nénetan Point, Ricarno and Harry moaned and writhed under a green tent down at Mágat, and Jay—ah Jay, old friend and brother: what had happened to him? Pray God he'd made it back all right. And Woodruff ambled along yellow-eyed with jaundice and he himself shuffled forward on tortured, fevered limbs . . . while over there, see them, those two stalked in stride, inexorable and pitiless, like Myrmidons, toward the topless, hapless towers of Ilium. Like Myrmidons. The gentle and the noble died in war: the brutish survived and were increased. *There* was the truth of the matter, if truth there was . . .

The temples—the GUman TSUus—were very near now: lordly configurations in stone, terrible and serene. Staring up at them he felt keenly aware of his own earlier paucity of spirit. He'd lacked something very deep, very immense. What had worked in him that fearful emotional withdrawal—had turned him into a baby planet circling coldly round the earth, smiling at the slow parade of human follies, deploring them?

They had been reared incorrectly, perhaps that was it: they had been brought up to believe that life was easy and good, that possessions and vitamins were the unfailing buttress against ill fortune (for ill fortune did not need to happen really, it was somehow or other only the result of carelessness or self-destructive impulses, a consequence of some inherent weakness that good people—really *good people*—never permitted to take root): that they were, in short, Americans—the privileged ones of this earth, endowed with good clothing and good teeth, with destinies sure and sound as the orbit of the moon. The handsome young boy always got the beautiful young girl. The concept of disaster, of an implacable, hostile fate, of a life swept irreparably away from comfort or superiority or even individual identity—such a concept never penetrated their minds: it was not consonant with tile bathooms and tweed jackets and built-in cabinets, all the good things of this world . . .

They had lost that, he saw with sudden burnished clarity: and for this dereliction they had paid—as he himself had—with a terrible estrangement from the rest of the world—an alienation they dimly sensed and which had filled them with a peculiar raging dissatisfaction. And so they had seized on the false trappings, the old economic superiority, had clung to it, flung it riotously in each others' faces, in fevered pride climbed out of bulbous flashing cars and thrown open the doors of extravagant mansions, thrown half-dollars from the rails of liners to dripping divers, chucked the chins of brown-skinned children in picturesque streets, whipped out fantastically expensive cameras and snapped and snapped and snapped—all to veil from themselves their sense of self-repugnance, their guilt, their isolate despair . . .

He walked up the mound and stood among the temples. The bright urgency that had informed the dream came over him again. There was too little time, it seemed, no time at all to waste in this flood of thoughts that swept through him unimpeded, freed of the numbing grip of the twenty-two days before. He put his hand on the rough gray stone shaft carved with fluted bands and strangely devised symbols and thought *Helen* with a vividness that was almost painful—fancied he heard, in the movement of the wind through the grass, the diaphanous ghostly tinkling of the wind-bells on the sunlit porch that faraway afternoon; his perennial image of innocence and beauty. They were all bound up somehow, all one: temples, Helen, wind-bells, Jay, that sweet, agonizing afternoon at the stockade—all were bound in one replete and tender orbit, and at whose center was Helen who had freed him, even while he had thought her inferior, unworthy ᴏf him—who had healed him of his ruthless indifference . .

Yes: it was he who must be worthy of *her*—it was so clear - he would write her when it was over, write all of this in the swift, impelling manner it had come to him, tell her of the GUman TSUus and Fergus and the wind-bells, and again of his joyous, resonant love and his awakening, of the white breast of the dim sea, and all disheveled, wandering stars . . .

He came down the mound on the far side. They walked over a little rise and through a draw he saw the ocean, heaving slowly beyond the reef, glittering, a deep and faultless blue. *Thalatta!* Another mound lay off to the right, thick with shrubs, and he moved toward it, his eyes on the pulsing glitter of the sea.

To his left Helthal had bent down, was pulling at a piece of yellow tarpaulin; he straightened with an exclamation and Newcombe, turning, saw him raise a saki bottle in his fist and call out: "Hey, Cappie! There's a whole cache of the—"

He was down. Lying flat, his whole body ringing and asleep: deprived of breath. A dark, fearful mystery, confounded by the fierce pneumatic slap of a machine gun, far too alien and too loud. From around him, behind him, cries rose faintly, firmer, soaring like the cries of gulls out at Nount's Head, wild drifting cries no longer part of earth or sky—

Hit. He was hit. His vision darkened out of sight, he knew: a boundless void of hollow white stunned emptiness fanned outward from his belly. With great care he turned his head. A slick red claw regarded him, quivering, pulsing blood. A claw that wore his wrist watch as a collar. Amazement held him for a darkening eternity. He was staring trancelike at the earth against his cheek, the minuscule shoots of bright green blades. Corpsman. Now I.

Corpsman, he cried: knew he made no sound. He had no voice for calling. No strength or inclination. Odd. No more. Near him, beyond him he heard the soft roar of the sea. Faneráhan. Helen, if I had. Helen, we could have climbed the slopes of Parnassus, lain soaring in soft dalliance and delight—

No one. Really. Knows. Father forgive us for we. Our Father who ever.

He had crossed a bridge of some kind, a stream that was himself, ebbing away in widening pools beneath him. So did the outward shores be-Lethe selves, without a Charon whirled, for he on honey-dew hath fed, and drunk—

A face materialized above him, peering through the thicket: a face tight and wild and sweating. Japanese. The eyes roved slowly, jaws locked in tension, hand holding a grenade to one ear below the helmet like a child listening entranced to the sea-roar in a shell: *Waaaaaashooooaaawww*. A shame: such fear, such desperation when all that was needed now was that dulcet sea-roar, a sun-washed brilliance of sea and sand and they could step forward in light, smile shyly, tell each other strange, indecipherable, entrancing tales of each other's homeland; there was no need—

Splotches rained down his eyes, huge black coral chains and blotches, a pelting red froth in which he was immersed, drowning, Lethe-borne, sunk though he be: a soft, swift surge of numbed pain extending through all his limbs, now fierce, now numb again—ah Christ, was it all going to run out like this, end like this with the wash of surf (hear it, hear it now, oh hear) a dim recitative beyond him?—in a moon-cold light, one falling body and slowly widening rings of void . . .

But it didn't matter: didn't matter any more, he was

absolved at last, pardoned by the celestial ministrants who did
at last take pity on the desperate and weary. In dreamy
fascination, strangely sundered from all hate and terror, he
watched the frightened, roving eyes that, hollow, apprehensive, rimmed with black, seemed even at this eleventh hour
to hope despairingly too for peace, for an end to the barbarous clangor, for one single radiant instant on the level
shore . . . and why not? Ah Christ, why not?—it was never
too late, one day was as a thousand years in Thy sight, Lord
we were not worthy but speak the word only, speak—

The eyes, darting, passed him by, returned, fell on his own,
dilated in a spasm of hatred. Ah. Too late. Late now. God
please have.

The hand, in a swift, fierce movement, struck the primer
against the helmet: the grenade leaped in the air, a slowly
turning meteor, and came curving down, hissing sparks and
blue-white smoke. With the last, most terrible effort of which
he was capable Newcombe raised his head and cried with all
his might:

"No! . . ."

Night crashed in sheets of livid flame, cascaded him amid
dancing hordes of stars, frosty galaxies through which he
cartwheeled in deep release, freed now, freed from the fury
and the mire, past streaking undulant islands where friends
he'd known turned in incredulity or concern, and the figure of
a woman still as death beat her head in a slow, drunken frenzy
against an implacable iron door: but he had no time now,
soaring as he was with outstretched arms, with flashing eyes
and floating hair, toward Arcturus and the distant Pleiades—

14

THE ELM LEAVES in the Square hung limply, wearily: waiting
for rain. English sparrows shouted their idiot chirping and
someone walked with alacrity along the street below. There
was a pause, the slam of a car door, then the monotonous
wheezing whir of a starter failing to catch: a series of gasping

inhalations, endless and absurd.

Sitting on the chaise longue in her bedroom Charlotte Newcombe pressed her hands in her lap and raised her head, her eyes closed; tilted it farther and farther back until it seemed to hang suspended from her throat. Thoughts darted here and there across the face of her mind, were gone as quickly; departed at last, all of them, leaving her alone. She felt strangely uprooted, insubstantial—almost bodiless, as though she had been deftly scooped out and rendered into a cast figurine of her own self. She shivered—a prolonged nervous shiver that was almost a tremor; remained sitting motionless, rigid, head thrown back, her eyes closed. Outside the sparrows cheeped and chirped and the starter, after a brief hiatus, recommenced its nasal, grinding whir. Time had stopped finally: time had overtaken them all and stopped, had ceased to move . . .

Then with the sudden, soundless flow of a night tide the monstrous import of the telegram covered her consciousness.

"Oh," she said aloud; compressed her lips again. Oh. It has happened. The thing I dreaded most in all the world has happened to me. I must call Amory—

She started to get up, checked herself, remained sitting, feet close together, small fists pressed against each other. He'll never be able to stand this: never. What will I do? What will I do?

I've got to go out, she told herself. I've got to go somewhere, do something, the Lowell—

The telegram lay beside her on the chaise longue. She picked it up and folding it carefully reinserted it in its envelope and put it in her purse. Black suede: her fingers slipped along the soft, gently chafing fabric. Standing before the long mahogany-framed mirror she put on her hat with care.

She moved down the stairs. The walls slid past her in soundless gliding ease, faintly vertiginous: she kept her hold on the banister, held her eyes rigid. Her head ached dully, insistently, and her calves were trembling. She paused a moment at the foot of the stairs and closed her eyes, thinking, forcing herself to think. A little walk: a walk through the Common will help me.

Channing was coming toward her from the kitchen: somber, stiffly solicitous, with saddened eyes.

"Will dinner be as usual, Madam?"

"Yes," she said. "As usual."

"Is there anything at all I can do? Any errand?"

The sad, bleak glance. He knew, then: when he'd handed her the wire he'd known, or guessed. Two youngsters at Girls' Latin. Edna and Carolyn. Very bright, very quiet and studious. No sons. He had no—

I can't speak of it now. I can't. Wait till I've talked with Amory, till I've had time to tell Amory.

"No," she said, and smiled: a smile she knew was bleak and frosty and very pale. "No, I'm afraid not, Channing. Thank you. I'm going for a walk. I'm going over to hear the Lowell Quartet. I'll be back by four, perhaps earlier."

"Oh very good, Madam." He seemed touchingly, inordinately pleased. A pang went through her. Turning, he held the door open for her with courtly, anachronistic grace. "It's fine weather out . . ."

"Yes," she said. "Isn't it."

The door closed behind her with a slow, powerful thump of finality. The nameplate said *Newcombe* in faded spencerian script. *Newcombe*.

She descended the marble steps, walked with care along the sloping sidewalk of worn, polished brick. The air was fine—but warm: warmer than she'd thought. She'd dressed too warmly. At the other end of the square the car starter whirred, stopped, whirred on and on. "Goodness," she murmured irritably, "—can't he get it fixed?" And thought all at once of her flower beds at Marshfield, the distant serene blue of the bay.

Sergeant Callahan was standing at the corner. Portly, solid, competent, his full face informed with wisdom half-cynical, half-naïve, he smiled and tipped his cap.

"Callahan," she said, and nodded.

"Ma'am."

Two sons in the navy. The girl married to a contractor in Belmont. Two sons . . .

She crossed Chestnut Street, walked briskly along Walnut to Beacon and crossed over to the Common. Cries and shouts, muted by the Charles Street traffic, assailed her. Children ran in groups, raced at tag, wrestling, shouting around the recumbent figures of old men sprawled on the worn, grassy slope among newspapers and ragged coats like the remnants of a defeated army: from under crumpled, sweat-stained hatbrims they gazed out at the world in apathy, in timid interest, their shins and forearms like shiny white pipes in the sun. On benches along the paths girls and women talked, rocked baby carriages or sat in patient, placid pregnancy, chattered in-

cessantly with each other. So many babies, they burgeoned
forth in violent profusion now, natural enough of course,
wartime always. *highly irregular and perhaps I have no right
to speak of her under the circumstances; but I've got far
beyond rights and subterfuges and proprieties, for better or
worse. And she loves me, and I love her; and I want to marry
her when it's over, if she'll have me. These are parlous lonely
times—and it strikes me that she might under certain circumstances get in touch with you: and I hope you'll see her,
and like her. She's had none of what we are wont to call the
advantages of birth and breeding (such as they are), but she
possesses something far more valuable, far more rare and
precious: the capacity to love, to feel wholeheartedly and with
commitment. I daresay you're wondering how we came to
know each other so well in so short a time and to that I can
only answer that in times like these, in a world where Zeus is
dethroned*

She was walking too fast, much too fast: she was almost
running. Her heart was pounding fiercely. She slowed her
pace with conscious effort. *The capacity to love . . .* On her
left was the USO building, a weird structure—part bungalow,
part barrack, part manse: this in spite of the civic ordinance
that no building was ever to be erected on Boston Common.
Well: perhaps it was merely one more of the changes, after all
it was for the servicemen, who seemed to be enjoying it
hugely. They leaned on the verandah railing, trooped in and
out in threes and pairs, stood outside chattering with girls who
fluttered around them like the pigeons at their feet. From the
open windows come a blast of jukebox music filled with
thumps and brassy shrieks. War. Wartime. Near her three
sailors stood, the saucy kind with brick-red faces and little
white hats tilted much too far forward over their eyes or
hanging on the back of their heads as if held there by an invisible little hook. "Oh—you like Erskine Hawkins, ah? You
do, ah?" one of them called out brightly, half-mocking, and
the girl nearest him tittered and swayed on slender ankles,
slender heels. Crowds of people moved across the little
plazalike area at Park Street Station, crisscrossed, intersected,
swept away without greeting, without care: like shadows.
Why should they? They all had somewhere to go, some purposeful destiny; time had not stopped around them, their lives
swung around some vortex as yet unshaken . . . Or perhaps
not. In a world at war, in the world of August 26, 1944—

A figure was coming toward her through the crowd from

Tremont Street: a tall, slender young man in a green uniform, moving toward her unerringly in the pale light. She stood rooted in terror, in agony, watched him swing toward her with purpose through the interlacing shadow-figures—saw all at once the violently alien face, thin, hawklike, pale blue eyes. Irish. A sergeant with two banks of ribbons. His eyes swept over her once, blandly, went on.

She felt so weak she thought she would fall. The kiosk: she was standing beside the kiosk. She leaned against it, her hand to her head. Temperature: it told the temperature, all kinds of information . . . Her vision darkened bleakly; she swayed, her hand on the warm iron. Ridiculous. Ridiculous!—what did she think, that a—

"You all right, lady? You all right?"

An accent thick with Dorchester. A young girl stood before her, was looking at her with concern. About seventeen, thin as a rail, the kind of girl he'd never gone out with probably, or perhaps he had, perhaps the girl he'd met in Washington. *Capacity to love.* No way of knowing really. How did you know about anyone? How *could* you?

"You all right, lady?"

"Yes," she said. Her voice had no force: she nodded, to give it emphasis, her lips compressed. Ridiculous. Simply another boy, a marine, home on leave. Had come back from the jungles, from all that—

She turned back, distressed, searching—could no longer see him. He had vanished into air. "Yes," she said again, more firmly. "I'm all right. It's just the heat—"

"Oh." Doubtful, the girl backed away a step, her purse held in front of her in both hands, still regarding her gravely. "It's not so hot out really, today. You sure you're okay, now?"

"Yes. Positive," she replied. "Only temporary. I—thank you."

She watched the girl move uncertainly away, saw her mount the steps to the USO. It struck her that the girl's face had been tremendously tired and hollow. *What we are wont to call the advantages of birth and breeding* . . . We weren't prepared, she thought, held in a rising distress. We weren't prepared for anything like this. The most foolish, the most purposeless waste: what use were all the buildings and bridges, telephones and X-ray machines and radios when *this*—? There was no solace in them . . .

"Lemmings," she said with sudden, helpless inanity, and

clenched her fist. A horde of lemmings: lives without preparation, without direction. Reawakened by the encounter with the sergeant the sense of boundless loss caught her again, full force now—reached her with the slow, overwhelming inundation of sea-borne fog and chilled her to the bone.

The faces on the dials stared back at her stupidly. Antiseptic faces. The temperature was sixty-seven, the wind eighteen miles per hour out of the northwest, the barometer was thirty-one point something: falling. The temperature in Rome, in Bombay, in Damascus, in Helsingfors. He had made maps once, on parchment, and shellacked them: of the Caribbean, the Arafura Sea, the Celebes, adorned with galleons, chests and cutlasses, he used to pore by the hour over that old atlas spread out on the floor in the study down at Marshfield—

Oh.

He doesn't know. Amory. Right now he. What must I do?

She moved away, her lips trembling, walked with short, shaky strides toward Boylston, passed the Boston Massacre tablet. Two little children were staring at it placidly. She drew near; she had never looked at it closely before. Odd: she had walked past it—what?—a thousand times or more, probably; and had never stopped to look. Yes, there he was, Crispus Attucks, fallen, surrounded angrily by others: first to fall. Such a strange name. Smoke billowed from the British rifles. A hand reached out of the bas-relief, bright and shiny in contrast to the sea-green of the rest. The touch of Negroes had done that, she'd heard: Negroes passing by who touched it in reverence, in love; a talismanic ritual. Their martyr in the cause of freedom. First to fall—

She walked on rapidly. The transparent black iron clock atop the *Herald* building said two-twenty. At the corner of Boylston the racked papers shrieked their harsh black cryptograms of heads. PARIS IS FREE! they blared. ALLIES TAKE PARIS. PARIS IS OURS!!! She started toward the papers, swerved away, crossed with the light. Paris. Her mind, now oddly released, seemed to skitter ahead of her like leaves, like chits and scraps of newspaper, dance reflected and vacuous in the chrome gadgets in the drugstore window, swirl in wheeling flocks like pigeons, beyond her grasp; maddened with pain. Please. I've got to. Get my mind off things. A moment's peace. Just a moment's peace and I can face something—

In the little foyer people murmured in polite, measured

voices, turned and nodded to acquaintances approaching. Charlotte Newcombe saw near the ticket window Emily Allerton standing with a group of women—the robust, smiling face, in profile; whirled away in a flash of terror. No. No one today, not now, not anyone I know. I just can't. Never should have got here so early—

Along Tremont Street now, walking quickly, past hashhouses, diners, seedy cigar stores where men in sweated shirts gazed at her with heavy-lidded indifference, where thin young girls hurried on clacking heels, cabbies in frayed jackets crouched over coffee and newspaper in a thick, odorous heat. Two soldiers stood at the corner of Stuart Street, matching coins; one of them, very drunk, kept losing, shook his head at each loss in openmouthed silent laughing bewilderment. Steam burst near her from a sidewalk ventilator, rancid and foul. Hateful, hateful: a world swept by desolation and hideous disfigurement. This is the world he sees no longer, no longer moves in: *this—!*

She squeezed her eyes shut in revulsion; opened them again, saw by a clock in a doughnut shop it was two-twenty-seven, turned and hurried back along Tremont, sightless and panting, bearing repugnance and grief like a hot bar of iron in her vitals; passed the Schubert where she had taken him once long ago to see Walter Hampden in *Cyrano,* one of Hampden's perennial last performances—had watched in the tail of her eye his face turn rapt and glowing . . . Or the sword: in the field behind the house at Marshfield, brandishing it above his head—she would catch glimpses of him occasionally from the kitchen windows—storming and stamping: that old stage sword he'd found in Mr. Stainforth's shop, far in back in a stand with canes and Civil War sabers. Some extra's prop for *Hamlet* or *Lear,* scarred and chipped, the pommel knocked off, he loved it with a passion: it was the possession he had valued most for years. He would call something inaudible—a purposely sotto voce cry—sweep the sword around his head and prance forward, re-enacting Roncesvalles or Crécy or the one he loved most, that last weird battle in the west, the beleaguered Arthur, the twilight kingdom ringed round by death and traitors . . . Or the grenadiers. Standing on the verandah singing it, head on his chest: broken, weary, defeated grenadier. *The song is done: would that I too were dying—but I've a wife and child at home* . . . Then his head up, eyes flashing, hand clenched over the broken sword hilt: *Then armed to the teeth will I arise from the grave—my em-*

peror, my emperor defending—

Can't. Mustn't think this. I can't: can't not. Ah help me—

She walked into the now nearly empty foyer, was shown to her seat as the performers—slim young men carrying their instruments with grace, with purpose—entered the stage. This was important to them. Of course it was. Bowing with restraint to the polite, preliminary applause they seated themselves busily, visited on each other sharp, measuring glances. Programs slithered, chairs creaked, coughs rang out; then a premonitory silence settled over the little hall.

A swift declaration—incisive, unmistakable: then, equally unmistakable, the sweet Mozartian melody under which the cello rose in throaty resonance, paused—and the fiddles leaped in a flurry of bright and intricate counterpoint. Listening, Charlotte Newcombe unclasped her hands and closed her eyes, let her anguished spirit sink into acquiescence. . . . Be at peace, the music said. Be at peace and take the measure of this earth, accede not to despair: there is the world and there is the form man can impose upon it if his vision is great enough, clear enough—now and then, now and then. For beauty lies in laughter, in gentle open-eyed delight at the goodness to be found in the world, here and there, here and there: beauty is truth, truth beauty, in gaily splashing fountains where green-hued nereids incline voluptuous slick bodies to the diamond-dancing water; in the still, vast expanse of northern sea beyond Minot's Light; in willows swaying saffron branches in the spring wind . . . There is somberness, yes, there is sorrow, it intrudes, it leaves its mark—what would you? escape the condition of humanity?—the beast is present in us, true—but it will not have the last word: for man, unwittingly or not, craves order, craves—even when he rails against it—this release of the harmony of form . . .

Tears pressed burgeoning against her closed lids, flooded her eyes. The melody returned, a sylvan thread of a melody; around her the air shimmered with lucidity, with ordered radiance, a delicate arching balance—hear it! oh hear—which bespoke a purity beyond all bereavement and all pain. This was a fact, too—along with the fact of his dying—a fact as implacable as the telegram inside the bag she clutched, as irrefutable—see, here was the proof of it in this crystallized, transcendent beauty achieved and held, which outlasted all loss and desire and dwelt in its own celestial kingdom, inviolate and serene . . . Tears were streaming down her face but it didn't matter, it didn't matter at all. If in a world drunk with ferocity and loss there yet remained one human spirit that declared, "I will impose an order on chaos, I will endow it with eloquence and meaning, offer it in an ordered structure that will delight in its unalterable beauty"—if one man could still say this and others of his kind could still gather to pay homage to it, man could not be destroyed. They cannot kill this, she cried silently, fiercely, choken with weeping, with soft raging denial, this beauty that he too sought to make, they cannot, they cannot—

Applause clattered around her, ran through the hall in pattering waves. It was over: it was done. She rose quickly, hurried up the aisle while the musicians were still taking their first bows (there would be more, she knew, from the rising impetuosity of the applause), moved out into the pale, silvered, overcast sky and stepped into a waiting taxi, was borne up Tremont past the shoe and dress shops, the glittering theater marquees, up Park Street and sped quickly along Beacon, defeating time and despair, sustained by the fierce, resolute aura of the concluding image: We are not beyond redemption; despite our myriad self-inflicted miseries, our criminal defections we are not past salvation while one among us can forge a moment of pure beauty such as that, fling it with defiance in the face of the beast . . . I must get home, she thought urgently. Before it slips away, oozes all away. I must phone Amory. Now.

"By the street lamp," she said to the driver, leaning forward. Amory: who knew as yet nothing of what had rent her heart these past few hours, their loss: he sat with other men around tables and argued, picked up telephones, buzzed for the entrance of young girls in sweaters and incredibly short skirts bearing letters, files, stacks of records and reports. He knew nothing of the bolt she would have to hurl at him. Poor dear fond man! He would sit there—she could see him in his office with the view of the harbor, the Custom House Tower, the old print of the *Flying Cloud* on the wall behind him—he would sit there stunned, his eyes darting, his mouth agape. What shall I do? wait till he comes home? No. Call him now. While I can but don't tell him: only to come home. A little preparation—

She paid the driver, a thin, wizened little man with bad teeth, overtipped him and let herself in, went up the stairs quickly and quietly into Amory's study and sat down at his desk. She was panting and her mouth was dry as chalk. She swallowed, took a deep breath and pressed her hand to her head.

All right now.

As she reached for the phone it started ringing. She stared at it in sudden fright; composed her features as though she were about to enter a roomful of people and picked up the receiver, said in her quiet, even voice: "Hello?"

"Mrs. Newcombe?"

"Yes," she said.

"Mrs. Newcombe, this is Helen Lowry." A young voice: but—"I'm home on vacation and I was up here in Boston doing some shopping and I—I hoped to call you . . ."

"Yes," she said vaguely. "I'm awfully sorry—"

"I know you don't know me, Mrs. Newcombe. It was only that Alan said if I should be—"

Charlotte Newcombe felt a bright flash of dread, of pure panic as though she had been apprehended doing something most shameful. Distraught, she looked around her, passed her eyes over the square, the iron railing, a squat, elderly woman bent over a pekinese. *The girl.* I should have. The girl he loved . . . She doesn't know, she thought with increased agony. She can't know yet: how could she? A limitless sorrow spread through her.

The girl's voice was still going on: a pleasant, soft, deferential voice that wrung her heart: "—till five-thirty, and I thought we might have tea somewhere if you'd like. I haven't heard from Alan in two weeks now and I—well, it's been so lonely down there, not knowing anything, especially now, and I—"

Charlotte Newcombe bent over, weeping all at once, the phone slack in her hand. Too much. Ah, this is too much. This girl—

"Have you heard anything from him, Mrs. Newcombe?"

". . . Yes: I've heard—"

Bent over still farther, sobbing wildly now, unashamedly, bent away from the receiver, this black umbilicus that bound them, the two women who loved him—from the receiver which said:

"Mrs. Newcombe? Mrs. Newcombe?"

"Yes. Come home here, dear," she said, through more anguish then she had ever felt in all her life. "Come here. Can you?"

"Oh yes: are you sure it's all right?—I didn't want to intrude if you have any—"

"No—I'll be here. Come straight home. I'll be expecting you . . . Yes, dear. Goodbye."

She put the receiver back on its cradle; stared blindly out at the square, her mouth trembling, then put her head in her arms and wept in a wild, hopeless rush of abandon. Beyond her heaving shoulders the elms hung in weary resignation against a white, overcast sky.

15

Dear Mrs. Kantaylis,

I know you must be saddened to hear about Danny. I can't know how you feel but realize you must be. Anyway I'm enclosing these three postcards, they are something my buddy was planning to write you about him. I just ran across them. Al was killed just a couple days ago so he didn't get to finish so you'll have to take the will for the deed on that score. He was a poet and went to college and he put it a lot better than any of us ever could, but just about all the rest of us felt the same way about Danny as he did. Maybe it'll hearten you a bit to know how much we thought of him, I don't know, anyway I thought I'd take the chance. I can't begin to put it the way Al did here, but I want you to know Danny was one really wonderful guy and that's straight, and everything Al says here is straight too. Hope you're well and Stevie is fine.

Respectfully,

PFC James A. O'Neill

Andrea Kantaylis set the letter down carefully on the bed beside her. Like the envelope it was wrinkled and smeared with thin terra-cotta streaks, as though it had been scratched by muddy claws. It smelled strangely, too—a thick, musty odor, rancid and penetrating. They always smelled like this, all the letters from there: redolent of rain and filth and exhaustion. The scrawled lines, the blurred pencil strokes bore witness to that.

She picked up the postcards then and read them, followed

the contrasting, tightly convoluted hand; read them with faint confusion, then with a deep, aching comfort—and dismay at where the writing broke off. He'd been killed, the boy who wrote this about Danny. Had he been killed while he was writing it? A sniper's bullet: right at the very instant he'd been writing *He has not died, he is not dead:* he had leaped up with a cry—she pictured him all at once, vividly—dropped the cards, the pencil, sank to the muddy earth: his buddies gathered around him while his eyes fluttered, opened wearily, and he gazed at each of them in turn . . .

From across the room there came a series of fretful, gurgled mutterings. She sighed, rose and crossed to the crib, picked Stevie up and carried him over to the bed where she changed and washed and powdered him, carried him back to her chair by the window. Content, surfeited for a time he watched her, untroubled, amused, laughing soundlessly; in spite of herself she smiled back, pinched his toes, murmured to him—saw his face, as though he had sensed her melancholy mood, turn solemn, the little black eyes piercing and grave: so compelling! Danny's eyes. Her face and Danny's eyes. He would never see his father, how strange not to know your own father—grow up with only the faded, ethereal ligature of snapshots, anecdotes or guarded references. How sad: what kind of a life could that be for him?—as though a stricture had been laid on him, a shadow flung the whole length of his life because of that evening by the lake—

No. She shook her head firmly, frowning down. No more of that: ever. No more sin-and-punishment. She had made a promise, to herself and to him, and she would keep it. When she was through nursing Stevie she'd move in to Pittsfield or go down to Springfield and get a job, do something: get out of this house. It had been wrong, all wrong to come back here. *Here* was where the shadows were, the flapping shadows of cloaked preachers and a wrathful Jehovah avenging the iniquities of those who loved each other and didn't know where to turn, caught floundering in a world berserk with killing and loneliness. Unto the fourth and fifth degenerations, as Dad put it. That sad, sweet, defeated smile: she wouldn't have stayed here this long if it hadn't been for him. Now he'd have to go on with things his way: the best he could. Everybody had to . . .

Stevie was laughing again: an utterly indolent joy. He rocked his round head from side to side, waved his arms, straining to clutch, hold, take in his hands everything in the

sunlit room, even things he could not recognize; and kicked
out with his left foot, over and over . . .

"He will be as fine as Danny," she heard herself saying
with an intensity that amazed her. "He will grow up to be
even finer than Danny, with all his father's sweetness and
strength and nobility—just as that boy said—his beautiful
way of smiling and walking . . . he will be the joy of all of us,
the vindication of all of us," she finished fiercely. "And they
won't have beaten us: they won't have won! . . ."

Turning she picked up the letter, the Japanese postcards
with their strange, hostile stamps and read them through
again. What a strange boy he must have been to write this way
. . . Danny's mother would like to read them, hear what
they'd all felt about him, how he'd kept them all going, saved
their lives: no cold, hideous telegram but letters from two of
the boys in his squad, his friends who loved him, respected
him. In the midst of all the fighting and sickness, only minutes
away from death himself perhaps, he had sat down and written these confused and beautiful lines: and now some girl lay
across her bed in a room in some other town miles away, lay
silently weeping her heart out; weeping and weeping without
pause—

But she herself would not cry any more. She couldn't: she
seemed to have permanently expended her capacity for tears.
Dry-eyed and resolute she got up and dressed, put on a jacket,
picked Stevie up and went out into the hall. Her mother's
door was closed: she was inside lying down, Andrea knew.
Since the night they'd received the wire she had been for the
most part subdued, creeping long-suffering and silent along
the halls, or thrusting the vacuum cleaner through room after
room—a whining, interminable roar; only once had she
lashed out—had turned around brandishing the hoselike
snout of the cleaner, her hair bound up tightly in the ragged
old kerchief, her eyes wild. "Don't think for one minute
anything is solved: not one single thing!"—and had whirled
around again thrusting the snout under the couch legs. Poor,
sad woman: and now she was there inside that door, unasleep,
lying rigid and stark, conjuring up some cosmic vengeance in
which she herself was one of its most mangled victims . . .

Andrea descended the stairs, closed the outside door behind
her with care.

The sky had clouded over: boiling cumulus that trundled
along, billowing, swept the day with waves of harsh sunlight
and blue shade. The wind came in gusts and several early

leaves, the first to fall, drifted lazily to the ground, whirling and spinning; rested limply where they fell. Off to the north the summit of Greylock was obsured in a mildly black broth: she thought suddenly of snow, of the white flank of October Mountain and the keen cold sting of air sweeping down the slope, of herself shrieking, hugging him to her with all her might . . . No, she told herself resolutely, evenly, don't go over it, now. Let it go, that part of it: let it go. That's what he would have said: that was how life was—you went along and if you got a blow in the head you lay low until it healed or until you recovered from it enough, and then you got up quietly and went on again . . .

Tom Price, a bent, gnarled figure in a red shirt, waved to her, one arm resting on the hoe handle, and called: "How's that boy?"

"Fine," she called back, waving, watched beyond his stooped body the silvery clouds trundle along, rolling in the depthless azure of the sky. This was the weather she loved best, with the world swinging toward autumn and the air quivering like the surface of a lake, still yet trembling with some intangible anticipation.

As she turned on to High Street she saw the cars, the commotion of vehicles on the Post Road, felt a momentary twinge of uneasiness; walked on as rapidly as she could, watching still another car come to a halt. A horn blew once, then another in a lower, more blatant key. Shadows raced over her, slipped a slate mantle over the line of cars; and in the swift change of light she saw all at once the thin, gaunt figuure of George Kantaylis bent over the first car, gripping the door handle and gestulating wildly, his white hair blowing back in the wind. Oh dear, she thought, distressed, he's got out again: Stella—

She ran forward now, panting, a bit fearful, burdened with the weight of the baby, ran out into the street to hear him shout hoarsely:

"No more riders! No more riders!"

A woman with a hat like a blue cake-tin, her face violent with anger, was saying from behind the wheel, "I *insist* you let me go, I *insist* you take your hand off my car, do you realize I almost *hit*—"

"No—more—cars!" he shouted, oblivious; wheeled around to confront Sam Flannery who, two cars behind the woman with the cake-tin hat, had got out and was coming up to him.

"Hello, George," Sam Flannery said pleasantly.

"No hope!" George Kantaylis cried. "He's gone! He's gone now!" His voice broke in a wail, resumed hoarsely. "All over! All over now . . . *Go home!*" he roared at the cars, the idling engines, the peering, craning heads. "Return to your homes! Safe—safe conduct will be arranged for those who . . . *go home!*"

He's found out, Andrea thought; he's found out somehow. And the thought distressed her deeply. She touched his sleeve. He turned and recognized her. He took a step back, his hand still on the door handle of the Buick, whose driver kept hissing, "I insist you . . . I insist—" His face, a bony, wasted replica of Danny's, went slack with grief; tears swam in his eyes.

"My dear," he said tentatively. "My dear—"

All at once he whirled around again in a paroxysm. "Send them home!" he shouted. "All of you! Cars will be commandeered—"

"It's all right, George," Sam Flannery was saying in a pleasant, matter-of-fact tone; his glasses flashed as he nodded. "It's all right, old-timer. They're all going, don't you worry about that." He had hold of George Kantaylis' arm now—a gentle, firm pressure. The honking of horns increased, two more cars came up and paused. Blued exhaust swirled around them; turned gray against the massive green umbrella of the Scarborough Oak.

The woman in the cake-tin hat was crying shrilly: "—menace to the highways, a menace, hopelessly drunk I almost *killed* you, if you don't take your hand off my car this instant—"

"Just a minute, madam," Sam Flannery broke in on her in a flat, dry tone. "You just wait a minute. Let's show a little forbearance here—"

He leaned in the car window quickly. The woman's fat red face went blank, then wide-eyed with astonishment; she gazed up wonderingly at George Kantaylis who, turned away, was still haranguing the line of horning, humming cars.

"Oh I *am* sorry, I am, oh the poor man, I had no idea—"

"All right, old-timer, they're going," Sam Flannery said, ignoring her. "It's all okay now. Let's go over and walk on home, okay? Here's Andrea come over with the baby—"

"No!" George Kantaylis recoiled in wild anguish, a hand to his cheek. It was as though he had noticed Stevie for the first time. "Don't bring him any nearer me! They'll get rid of him, too—toss him in the pond. Oh, I know them!'' Shaking off Sam Flannery's arm he glared at the row of curving chrome fangs, the goggling glass bulbs of eyes. "Murderers!'' he roared, and shook his fist. "All of you! You've lost: lost the war, I tell you! Don't *need* cars. Washington—''

"Look, George, why don't we—''

"We need one. To get him, go and get him—''

Sam Flannery gestured amiably. "All right. How about mine, old-timer? Mine all right?''

"Chevrolet.'' George Kantaylis screwed up his eyes in a swift parody of appraisal. "Thirty-eight, isn't it?''

"That's right. Look, let's go over—''

"Too late! My Daniel . . . don't you see? *Don't you see?''* He turned again with that quick, staggering lurch, in faded work-shirt and blue-and-red striped suspenders, his narrow, wasted frame slouching; stared at Andrea a moment in silence, his eyes vast hollows of grief. At the edge of his white hair the great scar darted back along his scalp: a deep, livid lightning bolt.

"Too *late!''* he cried.

Sunlight roared over them, roared away and dark, thunderous shadows swept down again in a rush of wind; and standing there with her hair blowing into her eyes, hugging Stevie, surrounded by a wailing bedlam of horns, Andrea felt the full horror of Danny's death crash in upon her for the first time. It was: it *was* too late, they were all alone and wailing, like his father. All alone now, scattered and lost now, oh Danny, Danny—

Weeping, weeping frantically despite all her intentions, her resolutions, the dry-eyed numbness of the past few days, only half mindful of the rising din of motors, voices, car horns, she came up to him again and took his arm.

"Come home,'' she entreated. "Come home with me. Please come home . . .''

He fell silent; his shoulders sagged, his eyes went suddenly dull and empty, wandered about without focus.

"Won't do any good,'' he muttered. Walking unsurely, stumbling, back across the road with her, all at once docile and withdrawn, he shook his head. "Doesn't matter,'' he repeated wearily. "Too many cars. *They* don't know . . .'' She thought for a moment he was going to fall; but he lurched upright again, stared vacantly at the hurriedly approaching figures of his wife and daughter.

"Well: it's all right,'' he said, as though to comfort her.

"We'll go get him together: all right? Bring him home."

She couldn't answer. Tears kept streaming down her cheeks.

"Even if we've lost it all. Bring Danny home . . ."

16

THE SEA EMBRACED him—a quick, clean envelopment he loved more than anything else in all the world; the familiar shock made him murmur aloud in joy, and bubbles swirled below his eyes. A mystery he never questioned, only basked in—this salt-stinging, dreamy opalescence through which he glided. Above him a figure was treading water uncertainly, splashing: all legs and torso. Woody, braving the deeps. He smiled, doubled himself up in a ball, placed his feet on the bottom and thrust upward, full arm stroke and frog-kick combined, rose swiftly toward the dangling, wavering legs; reached out and pinched a big toe. The legs recoiled violently; surface water boiled above him, swirls of white froth where Woodruff, foreshortened, a peeled and awkward frog, gaped wildly down. Laughing he passed under him and surfaced ten feet away, hearing Woodruff's drawled protest:

"—like to scared me out of three years' growth, you *know* I can't get around too well in this stuff—"

"Lubber, lubber—farmer landlubber," O'Neill chanted gaily. "Sink or swim, sport: sink or swim . . ."

Moving out in the channel he fell into the loose, lazy, arm-lifting crawl that was as natural to him as walking or sleep; conscious for the first time in months of his body, his own naked body as a thing of grace, slipping with miraculous buoyancy and ease through the still water which held him gently, laved him, sluiced him clean. He speeded up the beat, increased his kick to a boiling thrash, pulled with all his might for a dozen strokes or so and then, spent, rolled over on his back, drifting, the sun a bubbling gold light on his lids. Raised his head and looked toward shore.

There it lay—the beach where naked figures stooped and

splashed, the curving, crazy, mophead palms, the swelling ochre waves of hills, the gaunt, dark mountains capped by Matenla: distant now, dark with menace. Giants who had dealt about them death and destruction they brooded balefully now, and gathered strength again. Mount—what had Al used to call it? Mount Procrustes. Yes. Staring up at those harsh escarpments and ravines he had traversed with such fear and weariness and pain he raised all at once a streaming fist and shook it at the mountain.

"You didn't get me," he exulted, angry, half-laughing. "You son of a bitching humpbacked monster—!"

Cascao dust rose in sifting columns from the airstrip of Nénetan Peninsula and from above Púnai where the SeaBees were building a supply depot, the mightiest in the world, they said. On the reef, over to his left, the salt cubes of concrete obstacles stood in irregular rows, like counters in some bizarre, gigantic game. Short weeks ago they had come in there and banged into one of those cubes—had gone leaping and splashing through the shallows where now the hulls of two wrecked amtracks still stood, one with its bow blown into curling waves of steel ribbons, the other turned-turtle, its black curving belly to the sun. Treading water he gazed at them: today, the first full day since his discharge from the field hospital at Mágat, beach and amtracks and reef seemed to bear no immediate relation to him: they were from another time long ago—objects viewed through strange glass . . .

Looking down absently he was startled, ducked his head: he was hovering over what looked like a glowing, enchanted forest. He took a deep breath and dove, descended with increasing delight toward great fans and battlements of coral; palaces of foliate ivory and rose and citrine hues like those Aunt Grace had told him about when he was little. He encountered a giant arch, passed under it, emerged in sunlight again, gliding past its spiculate, crystal fingers that flashed and glittered like heaped hoards of jewels—a spilled treasure-house of Atlantis, riotous and strange: as still as heaven. Out of breath he surfaced, gasping, dove and surfaced and dove again and again until his head was hammering and he could hardly move his arms and legs, and still he dove in secret astonishment, marveling, aware that he had stumbled upon a world so rare and magical no one would believe him if he attempted to describe it—and it was of no consequence if no one did. His dog-tags, now untaped, swirled in front of him like little bronze leaves; tied to them the Christopher medal flashed and twirled . . . She would believe it though, he thought with a quick, pleasurable surge—she would know of this jewel-encrusted forest where fairy queens and water sprites, the benign spirits of the water kingdom sat in state, in a shimmering aqueous light, smiling, waving their wands . . .

His forehead hurt dully; salt water was streaming from his nose. God: sinus. He'd forgotten. He shrugged, gazed in toward land again,—saw Woodruff and several others silhouetted against the sand, bent over in knee-deep water reaching down, their buttocks gleaming like white round globes. Hunting for cat's-eyes. The sight of all those bare buttocks and water-truncated arms and legs set him laughing.

"Cat's-eyes," he murmured, shaking his head. "The chumps! Cat's-eyes . . ."

He swam back slowly, sloppily, following the channel, feeling the old familiar somnolent tiredness overtake him. The wounded leg had begun to ache but he didn't care. Walking out of the water, his hair streaming, his head and eyes smarting with salt, he felt he'd been washed clean of all the savagery and squalor of the weeks before—lithe and restored, replete: once more jubilant and alive.

"Woody," he cried. "Woody-boy! How you doing? Found yourself a pearl necklace yet?"

Woodruff, grinning, raised a hand out of the water, opened the fingers in slow cunning. "How's that?" An oval of pale almond with black rings and center stared vacuously up: a misplaced orb.

"Great one," O'Neill said; he paused. "There's a whole coral forest out there. Where I was swimming. Just like a city, you know? . . . It's really beautiful."

"Whyn't you get yourself some?"

"Didn't want to spoil it."

"Thought for a while there you were going to try to swim back stateside."

"I might do that. One of these days. Get back in shape."

"What'll you do for chow, buddy-ro?"

"Chew seaweed. Algae and sardines: gulp-as-you-go plan." Looking down he saw a crab with a mottled brown shell and flutelike fighting claws scuttle by—pounced on it and pinned it to the bottom; clutching it deftly behind the claws he held it right under the nose of Woodruff, who recoiled in protest.

"*Dayamn!* Don't you come near me with that—!"

"Scared of a crab," O'Neill taunted. "Thought you were

one of America's fighting heroes, there.''

"Not me!" Woodruff went into a long, neighing laugh. "Not no more. I'm going to turn preacher. Get me a Bible and a still and a hot little gal and take off into the hills where they won't find me for a thousand years . . . Hey now, *put* that animal away—!''

"I'm ashamed of you, Woody. Poor little crab wouldn't hurt a fly."

"How'm I going to know who he wouldn't hurt? You can go native if you want: swim around underwater, eat coconuts and crabs. Go ahead . . ."

O'Neill made no reply. Turning away he tossed the crab back, looked south toward Nénetan and the long, dense green mat of Agálap Island. The memory of the evening in the blacked-out building in Pajaña flooded him. Absently he fingered the little gold medal on his breast, saw again Felicia smiling at him: the soft full face, the eyes with little stars dancing at their centers. *No home,* she'd said. *TOdo TSUlang. For you. I want to help you. Come alive through the war, come not killed out of the war.* Her arms had looped around his head, her face close to his: a wan, weary, indomitable smile . . .

He walked out of the water and began to put on his shirt and trousers.

"Hey, buddy-ro! Where you all bound?"

Woodruff, naked, faintly paunchy, was staring at him in mild consternation; his forehead and shoulders were already beginning to burn. O'Neill winked back at him solemnly.

"Going over the hump," he said. "Going native, Woody."

"Dayamn, crazy, cotton-picking O'Neill . . ." Woodruff, grinning, shied a hand at him, bent over again; around him the water pulsed with sliding scales of light.

He walked along the Pajaña-Agálap road, keeping on the water side. A sergeant in a carry-all offered him a ride but he shook his head and flagged him on. He wanted to walk along this stretch where he had lived for days, among shattered trees and vegetation, falled logs, smashed bunkers and ripped and ragged ponchos, their faded, splotchy camouflage brighter now than the withered jungle growth. To the right was the hillock of sand of the first afternoon, and the shattered wall of the mission where they had fought and hung on for so long it had become the yardstick of their woes. Fifty yards below the church, they had said: at the church: above the church . . .

there it stood, its one remaining wall pocked and battered and streaked with cracks, still white and gleaming.

He passed by slowly, went over a shaky temporary bridge thrown across the Atainu, through a gap between the cliffs at Nagián Point where the rock lay out over the water like the head of a camel about to drink; moved on into Pajaña, where all that remained were ghostly shells of white cascao here and there among the shrubbery—yet somewhere, incredibly, he heard a piano, faint as a wind-borne echo. He stopped, his head cocked, listening. Yes: unmistakably a piano. Beating it out, he thought, and chuckled; the idea pleased him strangely. Somebody beating it out. In the heart of downtown Pajaña.

In the Plaza most of the plantings had been crushed or burned, but in one corner he came upon several clumps of flowers and shrubs arranged in a trefoil—a wild coruscation of blooms like scarlet tiger lilies or like foxgloves or rhododendrons only larger and more riotous: they exuded a heady odor that almost dazed him. He wandered about, walked through the blasted, tomblike, ghostly halls of the governor's palace, emerged again in dazzling sunlight and a bustle of activity. It was the old Japanese Commissary, now converted into the distributing center for Civil Affairs. Sea-Bees were shoring up one corner which had been blown away. Groups of Chamorrans and marines were carrying sacks of beans and rice out to six-by-sixes and weapons carriers parked outside, and through the arches of the colonnade within he saw rows of cans, boxes, flamboyant bolts of cloth.

"Land-office business," he said aloud. "Looks like a fire sale." He walked over, hands in his pockets, and looked in through one of the arches, ran his eyes over the chattering, arm-waving figures, the bins of shoes and shirts and dresses—and saw Felicia gazing at him, astonished herself; smiling, her eyes alight. He threw his head back and said, "Well!"

She came toward him quickly; she was dressed in a yellow chinina and turquoise skirt, with a bright red sash tied tightly around her waist. Her hair was held back with two combs and there were little silver earrings like teardrops in her ears. The transformation was so dazzling it shook him: he could hardly believe his eyes.

"Felicia?" he said.

"HÁfa, Oney!" A soft, low voice that stirred him. He was suddenly filled with a pleasurable medley of excitement and calm.

"Wow," he said. "Muy bonito! You look great, kid. With a belt in the back."

She laughed, gestured toward the bins. "Cilifairs. All kin' clothe'."

"And heels!" he cried, pointing in delight.

"Nnnnh—weegies," she explained. "Like saPAtos, a little—like sandals . . ."

"Hey, and the English, you've been learning like crazy. TuMUNGo fino english—"

"Oh yayse. We go moo-veeese nigh' time . . ."

"Of course!—the flicks. UnGUAItsa?"

"Yayse . . . nnnh—GUmas all glaaaaass, cars drive all go like theeese!" Looking past him she arched her neck slightly, gave the overbright, exaggerated smile of the Hollywood ingénue and waved, her full, graceful arm extended, toward the shaggy figure of a papaya tree. "Like tha'!"

He laughed, and nodded. "You got it. You got it, all right . . . Hey, you look wonderful: you know? I mean it. You're a knockout drop."

She shook her head, cried, "TihuTUNGo!"—but she smiled; her eyes were oval and dark, and the little gold points still danced at their centers.

"Oh hey, it's good to see you," he said. "Things been looking up. Since that day . . . I—it's been a long old time between drinks; hasn't it?"

Her face sobered. "TSAtsas hu hau. You so—theeen . . ." She reached toward him—a quick, compassionate gesture that embarrassed him.

"Yeah," he said casually, nodding. "Lost a little weight. I've been in hospital. Mágat. I stopped one. ChetNUdon mu tsu: can you imagine?"

"Ah—" Her face darkened with concern. "MAUlek PAagu hau?"

"Oh, sure. You can't kill an Irishman with anything but a fire axe. Didn't you know that? And then it's got to be laid dead to the pin. See? Baby bakuDANG. Just nicked me over lightly." He felt suddenly hilarious, overjoyed. He raised his trouserleg, showed her the scar—a long purple tear of smooth, strange flesh unlike his own, barely healed; straightened again and tapped the medal under his shirt. "Your boy pulled me through. Mister Christopher."

Her eyes were dark as onyx: deadly grave. "AreNONGa PAra HAgo."

"What?" he said. "TihuTUNGo . . ."

"AreNONGa." She clasped her hands together at her breasts in a swift, pious mimicry of prayer.

"Oh." He felt oddly, deeply moved. "Thank you, Felicia . . ."

"How are friends?" she asked. "Dahnee?"

"MAtai gui."

"Ah." Her face fell: a poignant sorrow. "LAhe MAUlek, atuNGO MAUlek . . . Nnnnh—LAhe hu—" All at once she did a parody of Newcombe's somber, thin face, the hunched shoulders: so deft it startled him.

"No," he said sadly. "HaAni Atrasao PUnu-un. The last day. At the sea. PAra i TAsi."

Saddened, she looked away beyond the shattered, blackened buildings to the water; inside the reef it was a dozen shades of jade and amber and turquoise under the pale hot sky. When she turned back he was surprised to see her eyes were shining again.

"I wai' for you," she said simply, and looked up into his face.

"Yes," he said. "Me too, Felicia. It seems like a thousand years sometimes, doesn't it?" A hundred thousand years of flash-shot night and groping, and here she stood in front of him in the blaring afternoon, right in the heart of downtown Pajaña, her eyes dancing, dressed to the teeth and ankling along on wedgies to boot. A chick! Could you beat it? Could you *beat* it! Marveling at the giddy transformation of things he took her hand and said: "Let's go somewhere. How about it? MAIla SAga suMIsiha GUAhu."

She shook her head. "I can'. Work Cilifairs . . . Tonigh' I see you."

"Work!" he cried. "What are you—an eager beaver? They can't get along without you one afternoon? Everybody's got clothes and chow enough by now, come on . . ."

She laughed—a light, rippling laugh which stirred him to his vitals. "Nnnnh—tonigh'. Tálanai. New village. You know?"

"Sure, but—"

"Okayyy. HAfa te!"

Smiling she turned and went back to the counter—a lithe, vigorous walk: her hips moved with firm undulance beneath her skirt. A chick, he thought in amazement, staring. A *chick*—

"Remember now," he called after her.

"Oh yayse!" She laughed again. Gaily colored forms enveloped her. Calm and excited both—jostled by people sweating, calling, carrying things, he moved away.

He sat dreaming against the trunk of a towering palm and watched the fading sun pour gold over the ranchos, the thatched roofs, the pots and cooking fires. Inside the dwellings figures moved about like dim, entrancing silhouettes. No doors on ranchos, no Chamorro word for door, no locks. There was something to be said for a place without locks or doors. Jesus: imagine Charlie Tarrasch living in a rancho without a lock on it, without a strongbox full of loot or a loose floorboard or some miserly apparatus or other within easy reach: just imagine . . .

Game fowl slipped through the grass near him, clucking; a cock regarded him intently, his red-and-gold comb arrogant and fierce—herded his hens away with martial strides. In a wallow fifty feet away a carabao raised his heavy head, the corrugated swept-back horns and stared at him, masticating endlessly . . . Fancy Charlie-boy in this setting, dependent on the goodwill of neighbors, the toil of his hands, and the compliance of a carabao bull with sweptback horns and wildly rolling eyes . . .

A little boy was standing in front of him as if by magic: an apparition, thin and alert, one bare foot planted on top of the other, hands clasped on his head.

"Hi, there," O'Neill said. "HAfa GAchong."

"HAfa te," the boy replied. "Can-dee, por faVOR? Erseebah?"

O'Neill took a bar of tropical chocolate out of his pocket and extended it toward him—held on to the end of it tightly. "Hey! What do you say?"

"Ersee*BAH!*"

"Oh no. What do you say, now."

"Ah—si TSUus maAsi. Thank-you-okayyy!"

"That's better. HAtsa naANmo?"

"Manuel. Manuel Mendáriz."

"My name's Jay O'Neill." He poked the boy gently in the ribs. "GUAItsa escuEla, Manuel?"

"Nnnnh—faNUi tsu *bayze*ball!" Manuel went into a batter's crouch, swung an imaginary bat with surprising agility and grace, a loose, easy swing, cried, *"Mak!"* and spun back again, laughing.

"You got a hold of it all right. Off the left center-field wall for two bases . . . I got a niece almost your age stateside. Know that?"

"I go' sister hundre' years ol'!" Manuel cried.

"Ah, go on. MAtai gui."

"She dead. My father dead, mother dead." Chewing rhythmically on the chocolate bar he grinned in sheer delight. "ESta MAUlek maKAno, aSUcar."

"DiNANchi hau, Jackson." Kids: they were fabulous. Candy: baseball: dead: good to eat—they shot from one thing to the next like a cue ball with lots of follow. It was terrific the way they bounced back. From anything. Hope of the race—hope of the whole muddled, fouled-up tribe of nature's bipeds—

He was gone: all of a sudden. Was racing away down the path to where a group of children crouched in the dust, scuffling and shouting. Maybe he was one of the kids they'd given chow and clothing to that afternoon up at the stockade: now he was playing baseball and shooting marbles with the other punks, bumming chocolate off every marine he ran across . . . O'Neill leaned back against the tree trunk again, crossed his hands on his knees. The wind, filled with evening, sighed and the palm fronds at the jungle's edge clashed and clattered like wooden swords. The corners of things began to soften perceptibly: smoke spiraled away from cooking fires and the thatching on the roofs deepened to a dull copper, melted into the dying sun. It would all melt away in another few minutes, he knew—huts, jungle, children squatted in the dust playing, all of it would disappear along with the tents and bulldozers and supply dumps and everything else, all would slip away and the only tangible remaining would be the odor: the strange, untraceable odor that hovered just beyond the scan of one's senses . . . What the devil was it, anyway? Not decay: not food or offal or burning either: these were isolate smells, identifiable. This was more like a fermentation, things working in secret, like yeast . . . and an oldness—some immeasurable oldness this entire island was steeped in, so ancient that what it might be no one could ever hope to know . . .

On a sudden impulse he pulled the piece of paper out of a shirt pocket and unfolded it, studied in the dying light the tight, convoluted hand. The first two lines were obliterated in a series of crisscrosses, words deleted, written over, rewritten, indecipherable. Then as though in a sudden flurry of thought, with scarcely any emendations:

trumpets blaring shimmer down the walls
where dancehall shadows spin-step-spin—emerge
weeping from behind the wire: the hand
deals death (another bolt shot home) extends
a butt to frothing lips, evokes a hate
implacable: the slayer often slain.
The P-A thunder booms along the halls,
proclaims: Tomorrow will be fair and warmer:
tomorrow will be perfect flying weather . . .
Lightning races silvered through your eyes,
the chandeliers explode in comet-tails:

Know, stranger, all that you confront is strange—
and your own image

The last poem Al would ever write: the last piece of the last poem. He ought to send it to Helen; or his folks. No—Helen. Pressing his spine against the harsh, fibrous bole of the palm he thought, with a poignancy he knew to be absurd, of Lorraine, of Al and Helen—that last wild, sweet, careening night in D.C., where memory survived for him only in swimming snatches—a beefy, roaring bullet-headed face, a lamp-post, a lavatory floor in blue mosaic close against his eyes—where the devil had *that* been?—and the foolish, lugubrious fragility of the next afternoon. *Know, stranger, all that you confront is strange—and your own image . . .*

It was true: where was there any well-ordered symmetry in the whole hellish, confounding, exhausting business?—any answer at all save in the fierce, unreckoning element in everyone that toted up no odds, considered no consequences, that was its own fanatic justification in the will to survive—that had kept him going all that way, fever-ridden and wounded, with the little girl in his arms; had borne him solely on its incantatory exhortion to resist death and defeat and find his way back. That little girl he'd saved: where was she now, what was she doing? Paralyzed with agony and fear, would she remember any of what he himself could recall only in fitful, pain-dominated flashes? . . . Well, that didn't matter: what did matter was this other thing—this solitary, unwavering point of being that stood like a small black lodestone in the midst of chaos. Yet even then you needed a little help, sometimes. You did what you could, hung in there, went as far as you could go, tried to hope for the best and avert the worst; but even then—

A truck had stopped below at the edge of the clearing: figures jumped down from the tailgate, dispersed with laughter and calls. There was Felicia: she was coming toward him. Swinging undulantly along, one arm raised in greeting, she seemed to grow out of the swiftly falling dusk—take shape from it like a gentle, benign apparition. *She prayed for me.* The thought thrilled him all at once, filled him with a sweet and reckless joy.

"HAfa, baby," he said. Getting to his feet he held out his hands to her: and thought again, She prayed for me . . .

Later in the warm dark they sat on his poncho surrounded by murmuring children and hornyhanded, red-faced SeaBees sucking at cans of green beer and gazed up at the screen where, against a dreamy, unreal background of sparkling skyscrapers and rambling country houses, a shipyard worker, classified 4F, draped himself disconsolately over a succession of plush bars and ate his heart out because he couldn't become a combat infantryman—and was finally inveigled by some GI's into impersonating a returned and decorated hero before a wildly adoring hometown populace, chief among whom seemed to be a scrawny, nervous girl with smoky yellow hair and a thick lower lip distended in a pout of perpetual dissatisfaction at all this chicanery and hysterical rejoicing, with its forebodings of dire things to come.

"Oh my God," O'Neill groaned. "Oh, the stupid, stupid ninnies . . ." Restless and disgusted he murmured; "Let's shove off. This is for the birds. I mean." Felicia said nothing; looking at her he saw her eyes were wide with interest. "Come on," he said. "Let's go, let's go . . ." When he squeezed her arm she glanced around at him in surprise.

"No' finish."

"It's finished, all right. Don't worry about that. It's all through. It never got off the ground. Come on, let's go for a walk. It's a dog: ga-aLAWgo ESte . . ."

"Wha'? TihuTUNGo."

But she got up docilely enough and they slipped away from the massed, staring faces, the distorted wavering rectangle where actors gawped and leered in nonsensical patterns. Holding hands they moved through the soft night. The moon, just risen, floated like a huge, luminous ball above the jungle, splashed light in wild colophon shapes around them. In the distance a night animal called once—a high shrill cry; was still.

"No,' wan' see moo-veeese?" she inquired.

"We saw it," he protested. "We had it. Enough to last us all a lifetime. It's awful. It's terrible."

"TihuTUNGo." She was watching him alertly, fondly, uncomprehending.

"BAba movie. It's a dog: a monster, no kidding. It isn't anything like the way things are: it's phony through and through . . ."

"Bu' finish," she offered timidly.

"Oh—you want to know how it *ends*!" Holding her hand in his, gliding along the trail near the village, he felt the exuberance of the afternoon well up in him again, the old absurd gaiety, bubbling up like a long-dry well replenished. He snorted in delight, swung her arm back and forth. "I can tell you how it *ends*, if that's all that's bothering you. That's easy . . . He tries to get into service again he's so bloody gung-ho about it all, but he still comes up with a 4F classification. So he decides to become a dog so he can join the K9 Corps. He puts in months at the detail—you know, learning to get around on his hands and knees, developing a good chesty bark, all that stuff, lapping up the old Ken-L-Ration . . ." Hunching his shoulders he went off into a high-pitched yelping; a dog somewhere yapped in reply, touched off a wild chorus of howls from the village. "Hear that? I'm a natural. Yeah—this is my life story I'm handing out . . ."

"Oh Oney," she breathed, laughing. "Oh Oney, you so happy!"

"A riot . . . And he makes it. Yeah, the dizzy goof passes the K9 physical. No mean feat either. He completes basic and advance training, he goes ashore on Tarawa, Eniwetok and Bougainville. He's up for two oak-leaf clusters and five how-do-you-dos. And then—trouble: the K9 Commandant—a real sweetheart—finds out he hasn't got a tail to wag. Mare Island and a DD."

"No, no—Oney, you crayyyyyzy . . ."

"As they come. See?—there's nothing to it. Answer all your questions."

"Oney . . ."

"Yeah?—Say, how come you never call me Jay?"

"*Jayyyyy* . . ." she said with distaste, wrinkling up her nose. "No' like *Jayyyy*." She shook her head vehemently, then burst into the liquid, running laugh which was so much like a little girl's and yet not like it at all; a pleasurable tremor rippled over the small of his back. "Like *Oney*!"

"But that's my *last* name."

"You' name."

"Yes, I know—my *last* name. You don't—people like us, you don't call them by their last names."

"Name—like you. Like *you*." She laughed again, her head thrown back. Then turned and said: "Oney . . . sta'-side—faNUi fan tsu CHOogui . . ."

He understood that she was asking him what he did back home, what everyone did, what it was like there. "I used to deliver groceries. For the A&P. Oh, I had a lot of jobs . . . Stateside—oh, it's funny," he mused, staring at the silvered tops of the palms. "There's a lot going on all the time: one thing and another. Well, it's anything you make it, I guess: same as anywhere else. Except for the noise: the Goddamn noise is always with you, you can hardly ever shut it off—you know, jackhammers, traffic, trucks and factories and planes and Christ knows what-all else. It can drive you crazy sometimes, you can't get far enough away—"

He didn't know whether she got any of it or not; but he knew he couldn't for the life of him say it in Chamorro—Christ, they didn't even have the words . . . and maybe that wasn't so bad, either. "It isn't anything like that stupid, simple movie though: I can tell you that . . ."

All at once he turned to her and put his hands on her shoulders. "Felicia, this afternoon I saw a beautiful world: all coral. Do you know it? Out in the channel, below Ngaián; fifteen, twenty feet down. SanHAlum i mamaAti—and quiet! The quietest, dreamiest, most beautiful place in all the world . . . Do you know it? Have you swum out there, bent down there?"

She nodded. She made no reply but it seemed to him, caught up again in the pure joy of the memory, that she knew; had seen that dazzling, silent world. Her eyes, close to his, gleamed like stars.

For a moment they stood in the moonlight motionless, staring at each other; then he drew her to him gently and kissed her full, soft lips.

"Ah, Felicia," he said. "Ah, baby . . ."

She stood perfectly impassive for nearly half a minute; then with a sigh she moved toward him, clung to him and kissed him with a sure, deft passion that nearly took his breath away. Holding her tightly, he was conscious of the sudden insubstantiality of things: the stillness rose around them like the moonlight, pervasive and evanescent. They seemed to be standing on some element that changed its form instant by instant, floating, soaring . . .

"Come," she said simply. "Come . . ."

He followed her down a trail that doubled to the right, doubled back again and emerged at the beach. A light, warm breeze caressed their faces.

"Tálanai," she said. "MANGlo aLUlane NAmun." And he understood that the light wind drove the mosquitoes away.

He spread the poncho out on the ground, aware that he was suddenly unsteady, as though with fever—gazed out at the soft, depthless tropic night; turned to see her standing naked—magically, hauntingly, her hands beneath her breasts which glowed in the moonlight like silvered globes.

"MAIla fan PApa-a, LAhe," she called softly. "MAIla, MAIla GUIni . . ."

Naked himself he embraced her, lay with her on the poncho, conscious of her thick, soft hair, her full breasts rising and falling in deep, panting rhythms. But when he went to move above her she stopped him.

"Ahe," she said.

"What?"

"No' like tha'. Lie—your side. Like theeese: theeese . . ."

She was on her back, her knees drawn up. Tensed and trembling he thought, What the hell—*what the hell* . . . ?—suppressed with an effort his irritation and lay dutifully on his side. With gently pliant hands she held him, guided him toward her; he entered softly, magically, without strain.

"FaNUi HIta ni-i MAIpi CHAlan, FOTgon CHAlan," she said gently.

He felt at first piqued, vaguely frustrated at the absence of contact with her lips and throat; reached out for her breasts, her shoulders. Softly she put his hands aside, softly spoke to him in Chamorro, crooning words he'd never heard—words which recalled all the soothing, early voices he'd ever known or imagined. As she murmured he found he had relaxed deeply; he felt a singing lassitude fuse with the former tension, flow conjoined with it, dominate it—a quiet, subtly balanced delight he would never have believed possible.

"Oh Felicia," he said.

He was aware of a languorous infinity: huge portals like golden bow-doors swung open, revealed vast halls and floodlit terraces where lilies trembled in the reflected light from pools; he was gliding, stroking his way past the jewel-encrusted scintillant coral palaces again, but more effortlessly now, more indolently, held in a steadily expanding bliss that suffused in light, no longer of earth or water, soaring, sweeping in a high, arching radiance—brought to rest at last, gently, at the meeting of their crossed bodies, the nexus of their union.

"Ah, Felicia," he murmured. "Ah, you darling . . ."

The surf beyond the reef pounded with a low roar.

She was asleep; he could tell from her slow, even breathing, the way her fingers faintly twitched against his thigh. Wide awake himself, held in the interlaced complicity of their legs and thighs—neither of them had moved a muscle since they had lain together, nor had they needed to—he turned his head and watched the sky and thought, We don't know everything, that's for certain: we may know a lot but we don't know anything about things like this. Still pervaded by a brimming languor which had nothing to do with depletion or exhaustion he realized he had never made love before in all his young life—that the tensed, feverish grapplings and gaspings he had known were as meaningless, as inadequate as the shell a blind child might hold to his ear in an effort to understand the majesty of the sea . . . Maybe they didn't have floors in their ranchos and didn't wear shoes and couldn't read or write, most of them, and let the carabao bed down in one of the rooms: they knew things we didn't all the same. And who was to say? Maybe those things were the most important, truth to tell . . .

The moon had dipped behind a cloud like beaten silver. Not wanting to wake her he watched her face, scarcely discernible now—the full cheek, the broad straight nose, the hair like a soft dark web of night. Orphans—homeless orphans in a cosmic upheaval not at all of their making—they had yet survived and lay in love, bound in love and dreamed of better days.

A searchlight leaped into the sky—a quick pencil-dart of light: swept a short, ineffectual arc, winked out again. The moon, hidden behind Mount Matenla now, sent a vague iridescent sheen over everything: it was as if they had been immersed in a bowl of murky, glowing fluid instead of air. *All that you confront is strange—and your own image.* Old Newk, he thought, and his eyes for an instant stung with tears. Old Newk . . . They lay in silence, too, not far away, in the thick wet earth above Nénetan and dreamed, too—Newk and Danny and Steve and Jack Freuhof and all the rest: they would lie there forever, would be here when this island returned to a sleepy little emerald-and-turquoise isle, freed from the designs of generals and governments—would still sleep on when the island sank beneath the sea and lay in silent gleaming crystalline majesty forty fathoms down. And Harry and big Klu and Ricarno and Capistron and Chicken lay in silence too, tossed fitfully and dreamed in the tropic night, under the soft roar of the blowers, the dimmed wardroom lights.

There came a muttering rumble, like that of gunfire immensely far away. Instinctively he fell into the old, wary attitude, his head cocked, mouth partly open; heard nothing more. Naval gunfire on Gouméan to the north; or perhaps a patrol had made contact somewhere. No knowing . . . Well. He and Woody and Hethal—that crazy, dulled, cold-blooded Helthal—the three who had survived, would go out on patrol tomorrow or the next day, stalk through the sword grass and boondocks far up in the north end; would watch the island revert to the status of a military post—sleeves rolled down, forbidden areas, troops are forbidden, personnel of this command, it has come to the attention of this command—the never-ending drill and discipline that dogged them wherever they went, that was part of the life they led unless they were up on the line . . .

But there was no hurry: no hurry any more. He could have lain here with this wise, acceptant girl a hundred thousand years—in this magical, new-found somnolent ecstasy, and let it all roar away beyond him. He felt singularly freed from urgency. For he had all the rest of his life now, he knew. He was going to survive, as he had known, ignorantly, fanatically from the very beginning he would: two more, ten more operations, come what may, he was going to survive and return home, and nothing was going to stop him. He was going to be back in the league. He was going to college on this GI Bill, too—why not?—and learn something: have his rights, his rightful place in the scheme of things. A poor shanty-Irish homeless orphan he was nevertheless going home: and they would make way for him. In the name of Newk and Danny and all the others they had Goddamn well better make way for him . . .

One arm cradling his head he lay and watched the stars.

More Bestsellers from Berkley
The books you've been hearing about and want to read